ANGELS OF VENGEANCE

ANGELS OF VENGEANCE

JOHN BIRMINGHAM

BALLANTINE BOOKS

NEW YORK

Copyright © 2011 by John Birmingham

Published in the United States by Del Rey, an imprint of The Random House Publishing Group, a division of Random House, Inc., New York.

DEL REY is a registered trademark and the Del Rey colophon is a trademark of Random House, Inc.

Originally published in Australia by Macmillan, a division of Pan Macmillan Australia Pty Limited, in 2011.

Library of Congress Cataloging-in-Publication Data

Birmingham, John.
Angels of vengeance / John Birmingham.
pages cm
"Originally published in Australia by Macmillan, a division of Pan Macmillan Australia Pty Limited, in 2011"—Title page verso.
ISBN 978-0-345-50293-3 — ISBN 978-0-345-53249-7 (ebook) (print) 1. Political fiction.   1. Title.
PR9619.3.B5136A83 2012
823'.914—dc23
2011048287

Printed in the United States of America on acid-free paper

www.delreybooks.com

2 4 6 8 9 7 5 3 1

First U.S. Edition

Book design by Christopher M. Zucker

For Jane

"Beside every great man . . ."

Well, I'm not that great,
but she is, and she's always there beside me.

Character List

URUGUAY, SOUTH AMERICAN FEDERATION

Staff Sergeant Michelle Royse: squad leader, 160th Special Operations Aviation Battalion, U.S. Army

Caitlin Monroe: Echelon senior field agent

Ramón Lupérico: former prison governor on Guadeloupe, Leeward Islands

SEATTLE, WASHINGTON, AND VANCOUVER, BRITISH COLUMBIA

James Kipper: forty-fourth president of the United States

Jed Culver: White House chief of staff

Barney Tench: Secretary, Department of Reconstruction and Resettlement

Paul McAuley: Secretary, Department of the Treasury

Sarah Humboldt: Secretary, U.S. Immigration and Customs Enforcement

Admiral James Ritchie: National security adviser

Barbara Kipper: America's First Lady

Henry Cesky: CEO, Cesky Enterprises

Wales Larrison: Echelon deputy director and U.S. liaison to Echelon Secretariat

SYDNEY AND DARWIN

Lady Julianne Balwyn: erstwhile smuggler and reluctant fugitive

Rhino A. Ross: part-time fishing boat operator

Narayan Shah: CEO, Shah Security

Piers Downing: lawyer to Mr. Shah

Paras Birendra: operations manager, Shah Security

Nick Pappas: security consultant, former Australian Army SAS operative

Norman Parmenter: contract killer

KANSAS CITY, MISSOURI

Miguel Pieraro: stockyard foreman

Maive Aronson: community college teacher

Sofia Pieraro: high school student, part-time hospital worker

Cindy French: interstate truck driver

Dave Bowman: interstate truck driver

Special Agent Dan Colvin: FBI interagency liaison, Kansas City field office

TEMPLE AND FORT HOOD, TEXAS, ADMINISTRATIVE DIVISION

General Tusk Musso (retd): the U.S. president's special representative in Texas

Master Sergeant Fryderyk Milosz: squad leader, U.S. Army Rangers

Tyrone McCutcheon: aide to Governor Blackstone

Corporal Amy Summers: junior NCO, U.S. Army Rangers

General Jackson Blackstone (retd): Governor of Texas

Bilal Baumer (aka al Banna, the Emir): fugitive terrorist leader

ANGUS AND WILTSHIRE

Bret Melton: gentleman farmer and full-time parent

Francis Dalby: Echelon UK field supervisor

ANGELS OF VENGEANCE

1

FORMER URUGUAYAN–ARGENTINIAN BORDER REGION, SOUTH AMERICAN FEDERATION

Staff Sergeant Michelle Royse of the U.S. Army's much diminished 160th Special Operations Aviation Battalion, scanned the northern banks of the river delta as the Black Hawk pounded up the narrowing channel over dark, choppy waters. Through her night vision goggles, the slightly fuzzy green imagery of heavily wooded banks was blurred even further by the shuddering of the helicopter as it roared along above the wave tops. A solid nor'easter was blowing directly up the mouth of the river, adding an extra thirty knots to their airspeed but demanding extreme levels of concentration from Captain Tim Lindell and his copilot as they guided the chopper through hostile, if poorly guarded, airspace. Far behind them, no one paid their improvised helicopter carrier much mind—a battered and rusty container vessel salvaged from Mexico. Royse didn't like to ponder what would have happened if the vessel had been detected by the South American Federation Navy.

Hell, probably not much to worry about, she consoled herself. *It's just a paper navy at best. Most of their top ships laid up in docks anyhow, just rusting away.*

A bit like the U.S. Navy nowadays, she thought.

Lindell had not spoken for five minutes, which still made him a hell of a lot chattier than their passenger: the spook. Michelle knew the woman had to be a spook because in spite of the faded summer-weight BDUs she wore, the kit they had loaded for her was all high-spec exotic stuff, the sort of gear the military simply couldn't afford nowadays. No way the army or SOCOM was running this operation. They were just providing a bus service for some ghost recon superwoman who'd drifted down from far above the upper reaches of the tier-one food chain.

Michelle snuck a sideways glance at the passenger. The woman wasn't unfriendly, not like some of the ego monsters she'd met while shuttling T1 operators around. But she was entirely self-contained; she spoke only when necessary and had a way of discouraging questions without actually asking you to mind your own business. She stood maybe an inch taller than Michelle, but even in her BDUs, body armor, webbing, and equipment, she seemed . . . well, not slighter—perhaps more wiry. There was a tightly wound intensity about this spook that made being in her presence distinctly uncomfortable. Impossible to guess her age under all that kit, but Michelle thought maybe early to middle thirties. The woman's physique looked totally ripped, but her eyes were old beneath a stray lock of dirty blond hair.

Royse looked away quickly as their mystery passenger shifted position. She was happy enough to attend to her duties while Jane Bond sat in a furious still-life study of cold impacted rage.

For the moment, those duties mostly involved scanning the shoreline north of the river. Nothing appeared to move out there on what once had been the Uruguayan side of the border. Not now, though. Now it was all part of *la Federación.* A few bright emerald pinpricks of light burned in a cluster about ten miles inland, but the shoreline was dark. The Black Hawk banked gently a few degrees to the northeast, taking them over land for the first time. Michelle craned her head to peer over her shoulder into the cabin, which glowed like a child's idea of a fairy cave in her night vision goggles. Far ahead of them, she could make out a faint dome of opalescent light on the horizon, marking the location of the Federation Navy's fleet base.

She would have sneered at the vanity of the pompous title "fleet base" if not for the fact that their own aircraft was held together with hundred-mile-an-hour tape, bailing wire, and promises and that most of the U.S. military bases she'd flown out of in the close to five years since March 2003 had all suffered from the same air of neglect and making do. Salvaged gear left exposed to the elements or in compromised warehouses and storage depots took you only so far.

Yep, two paper tigers staring each other down in a burning barn—that's the world of tomorrow. What a fucking joke.

"Five minutes to insertion."

Captain Lindell's voice barely registered in her earphones over the roar of the engine and the deep thrumming bass note of the chopper blades. It was as though the tension had strangled his voice down to a clenched murmur. Royse held up her hand with all five fingers splayed and nodded at the spook. She was already preparing herself but nodded back, anyway. Michelle had watched the woman take inventory of her load before they lifted off from the container ship, three hundred miles off the coast. She watched her repeat the performance now that they were almost at their destination.

A minute later, obviously having reassured herself that she had not forgotten her passport, wallet, or Gerber Mark 2 fighting knife, the woman closed her eyes and let her head loll back until her helmet touched the bulkhead behind her. It was the first human gesture, the first intimation of weakness, or fear, or exhaustion that Michelle had seen her make, and as quickly as it came, it passed. Her head snapped back up. Her eyes blinked once.

"Two minutes out."

The woman chambered a round in her HK417, a metallic *Kerr-chung* that never failed to lay a cold finger at the base of Royse's spine. The 5.56-mm HK416s she had seen here and there, but the 417 with the heavier 7.62-mm round had been a rumor until tonight. The spook's brand-new Heckler & Koch was another sign that she wasn't your standard issue self-loving spec-ops asshole whispering, "For I am the baddest motherfucker in the valley." No piece-of-shit M16 or M4 for this chick.

Fuck it, she figured. *Another day, another dollar.*

Michelle readied herself at the door, training the electric M134 mini-gun over the treetops, which rippled beneath her feet at 140 knots. Her knees bent to compensate for the sudden twisting, diving flight path as Lindell began to track the nap of the earth, heading for a small clearing marked on their maps as Objective Underwood.

"Thirty seconds."

The Black Hawk pivoted, seeming to turn on a dime, as if Lindell were trying to throw them both out the rear hatch by way of momentum. The woman braced herself against the bulkhead, holding tight to a grab bar over her right shoulder. Royse sank deeper into a squat until her knees were bent almost at right angles. Then the inertia bled away swiftly as they came to hover over a patch of field between two clusters of trees. Michelle checked the ground beneath them and reported that the aircraft was clear. She signaled to the woman to step forward and hook up.

The spook needed no help attaching herself to the fast-rope apparatus. Royse had one second to look into her eyes before she stepped out and dropped away into the night. The woman did not look scared, but there was something haunting her eyes. Something in the back of the deep, clenched lines that made her face appear unusually long and drawn in the low-light amplification of the NVGs.

One brief nod.

A thumbs-up gesture and she was gone, dropping down into the darkness.

Caitlin fast-roped down to the clearing floor, which squelched under the tread of her canvas-sided jungle boots. She scanned the tree line for any hint of enemy presence without expecting to find it. If they were going to be fired on, chances were she would have seen the tracers arcing in while she was dangling, all but defenseless, in midair. Releasing the rope, she signaled to Staff Sergeant Royse that she was clear and hurried off to find cover as the chopper increased power and clawed up into the humid night.

A flick of the wrist revealed the time: 0126 hours.

She had four hours of movement before she would have to lay up for the day. It wouldn't take her all the way to her objective, but she planned to be well within observation range by the time the sun rose.

The Echelon field agent moved quickly away from the drop zone, heading north by northeast, following the track programmed into her mil-grade Navman GPS unit. The brush wrapped itself around her, slowing her down as soon as she'd passed under the first tree canopy. Night vision goggles resolved the environment into a flat, eerily phosphorescent landscape of sinuous roots and vines, of fat nodding leaves and thick snarls of creeper, of rot and genesis. The smell of decay and of new life growing over the top of older worn-out vegetation was strong, almost cloying. Clusters of such flora dotted the grassland steppe behind her during this, the height of the South American summer. It combined the worst of all possible worlds: a main course of humidity with a side platter of wide-open kill zones, topped off with junglelike collections of trees, brush, and other plant life.

Caitlin was familiar with the fecund crush of the jungle. She'd spent a good year and a half tracking two targets through the old-growth forests of Sumatra and Aceh long before the Disappearance while posing as a Peace Corps volunteer helping to build schools. She knew the jungle. They had come to terms.

But the problem now was more than one of terrain—this was a tactical nightmare. She proceeded to the nearest point of cover and pushed farther inside the forest.

Two hundred yards in, she came to a small stream that was a couple of feet across and easily forded. Shallow water gurgled down a slight but noticeable slope, where Caitlin spied a small animal drinking upstream from her, a squat, barrel-shaped grazer of some sort. It sniffed the air cautiously a moment after she'd spotted it but returned to drinking when no obvious threat came charging out of the night. A couple of boulders, huge moss-covered menhirs, formed a natural fort. Caitlin decided to lay up there for a minute.

The stream led most of the distance to her objective, covered by varying degrees of thick vegetation: it was the best bet for a concealed approach in the dark. It was also probably the most obvious . . . She pushed that thought away. Nothing could be done about it. Traipsing through open grassland in full gear was a sure way to get a third eye drilled into her forehead.

Hundreds of bugs scuttled away as she laid her HK417 against the rock. A giant centipede reared up as if to strike. Caitlin swiftly killed the insect with one slash of a spring-loaded wrist blade and then flicked the two halves away with gloved fingers. The last thing she needed was to call in an extraction because of a bug sting.

She let her senses expand out into the surrounding landscape, listening for human speech or footfall, the clink and rattle of poorly secured equipment; she sniffed the air just as the animal had, tasting it for the scent of man, or the last meal he'd eaten, or the soap he had washed with, or not, as might be. When she was certain no immediate danger existed, she relaxed fractionally. Or rather, she redirected her energy to her first lay-up procedure.

Again she inventoried her equipment. Nobody wanted to be the guy who turned up at the beach without his towel, or the state-sponsored killer who forgot her ninja throwing stars . . . *Okay,* she conceded, *I don't have ninja throwing stars. But it would be totally bad-ass if I did.*

Caitlin flipped up the monocular night sight on her PVS-14s to check the digital map Velcroed to her left arm. As was so often the case nowadays, Echelon resources didn't stretch to a live overwatch link. No one had that—not even the Russian SVR had the resources for live overwatch anymore. She was on her own, which was not entirely a bad thing. Nobody was recording her every move for an embarrassing moment with the media farther down the road. Nobody was barking at her through a headset, telling her to do shit that made no sense. She had good data, though, and with that and her experience, there wasn't much else Caitlin needed.

The little stream beside which she'd laid up ran through the center of the dimly illuminated screen. Her position was marked with a blue dot. She hoped to follow the stream upslope for at least three klicks before it began to veer away from her intended destination, one of Roberto's many detention facilities, this one tucked away in an old police station about ten kilometers inland. The best intelligence they had placed her target there. Wales had called it a memory hole: a dark place where the regime stuffed away its mistakes, embarrassments, and occasional secrets. Caitlin wondered if they understood the nature of the secret they had stashed down here in the back forty of the former Uruguayan Republic.

She picked up the 417, resettled her pack a little more comfortably, and took a mouthful of chilled Gatorade from the camelback bladder woven into it. The brush reappeared in eldritch green as she snapped the PVS-14 back down over her dominant eye. The potbellied beast (was it a tapir—was that what they were called?) scuttled back into the undergrowth as she began to move.

You're a long way south, Caitlin thought about the tapir. Maybe it had gotten loose from a zoo or something.

Time to move on herself. Quickly setting the GPS unit to vibrate when she had covered two and a half kilometers, Caitlin carefully stepped down onto the sandy creek bank from the small grassy bend on which she'd been resting.

She was her own point and cover, responsible for her flanks and rear guard. She was alone, her natural state of being. Consciously pushing away thoughts of her husband and baby back at the safe house in Scotland, willfully forgetting the life they had tried to make for themselves on the farm in Wiltshire, Caitlin Monroe, Echelon's senior surviving field agent, let her true nature take over. A predator, she stalked through the primordial heat—claws out, fangs ready, all her senses twitching and straining, searching for prey.

It didn't matter to her that this part of the country, thinly populated before the Disappearance, was even more sparsely peopled now. She had been trained to assume the worst, to prepare for ill chance and disaster as a certainty. There were no large townships within thirty kilometers, and the terrain between here and the objective was undoubtedly deserted. *El colapso* had emptied it, and Roberto Morales's regime kept it that way. But still, she would move forward as though snares blocked her path at every turn.

She advanced in a creeping crouch, her knees bent, her thigh muscles and core strength tested by the weight of her equipment and the unnatural movement. Her body had recovered well from pregnancy and childbirth, however, and from the rigors of hunting and fighting in the huge open mausoleum of New York last spring. Three months back home with Bret and Monique had helped with that—three months in which she regained her strength and bound it tightly with new layers of resolution and a fierce will to lay her hands on the man she blamed for nearly destroying her family.

Bilal Hans Baumer. Al Banna.

Or whatever he was calling himself these days. In Manhattan he had been known as the Emir. Now he was the target. Her target. As he had been for a year before the old world had fallen.

The barrel of Caitlin's 417 swept back and forth in a tight arc as she moved up the creek like a nightmare black arachnid. The burbling splash of the stream covered the sound of her boots. She took care to step where the flow of water would erase any sign of her passage quickly. Mosquitoes hovered around her in a cloud, drawn by the opportunity to feed but thwarted at the last moment by the odorless insect repellent she wore. As the environment adapted to her presence, it also disguised her advance, enfolding her in the shrill, creaking chirrup of a billion insects, the shriek of bats and nocturnal birds of prey, the rustle of larger animals moving through the undergrowth, and once, as she ducked under the limb of a half-fallen tree, the dry hiss of a viper slithering languidly along.

Caitlin dropped a hand to the knife at her hip and with one fluid motion threw it at the snake, spearing it to the branch. While it was fixed in place, she crushed its skull with a swift stroke of the Heckler & Koch's buttstock. Pythons didn't worry her, but vipers were incredibly foul-tempered. Best not to take chances.

After forty minutes the Navman on her forearm began to vibrate ever so slightly, warning her that the stream was about to veer away from her intended heading. She slowed to a stop and took her time absorbing the signs . . . She listened for the slightest fluctuation in the wall of sound thrown up by the insects in her immediate vicinity, the splash of water across the creek bed, which was slightly rockier here. Her eyes took in the noticeable brightening of the world in her goggles under a thinner canopy as a strengthening breeze opened a hole in the silver-gray cloud cover to let moonlight and starlight spill through.

But nothing human.

Still she waited. The slight delay gave her an opportunity to measure her endurance against the task at hand. She ignored the humidity, which lay on the landscape like a wet woolen blanket, making breathing difficult and leaving her with clammy sweat on the backs of her thighs. No one in her right mind would have been out in this, Caitlin realized, but it was a thought that neither eroded her attention to detail nor made her lower her guard even marginally.

Satisfied that she remained alone, the Echelon agent moved off, carefully climbing the northern bank of the stream. Old mineral survey maps had indicated that the soil was thinner here and the vegetation less dense. It was still thick enough to slow her progress. With no natural track to follow, she was forced to push and occasionally hack her way through while trying to keep all noise to a minimum. As much as she could, she traded caution for speed, keen to make as much ground as possible on her objective before the sun climbed over the horizon.

Screaming.

It began sometime before dawn as a feeble, plaintive wailing, a trembling warble of utter hopelessness. Caitlin recognized the exhausted protests of a man who thought he was close to the limit of what he could endure. She knew from personal experience that he was wrong. In the hands of a capable torturer, you could endure far beyond the point where you'd first thought you wanted to die to escape the pain and humiliation.

The humiliation of torture was the surprise for most people. They expected the pain, at least intellectually, although unless they'd been trained for it, the shock was enough to send most over the edge very quickly. The humiliation and shame, however, clung to them for years after the pain had subsided. And that was the jangling note she recognized in the screaming: the shame of someone who'd already broken and given up whatever he had, to no avail. The torture had continued.

It was no concern of hers except from a tactical viewpoint. She didn't want her target, Ramón Lupérico, checking out before she'd had a chance to interrogate him.

She exhaled slowly, took a sip of fluid from her camelback, and peeled the wrapping from a mocha-flavored protein bar. Breakfast of champions.

The detention facility—a grand name for an adobe hut at a straggling, muddy crossing of the two main local roads—was a single-story off-white building fronted by a slumping shaded porch. A high stone wall ran around a compound at the rear. From her position on a small hill two hundred meters back into the woods, overlooking the site, Caitlin couldn't see the prisoners' enclosure, but she'd studied the satellite images closely at the pre-op briefing. A well appeared to provide drinking water, and a beaten-down path marked the circuit the inmates were allowed to walk for exercise each day.

Assuming they were allowed any, of course. She'd half expected to see wooden poles driven into the earth for the traditional blindfold and last cigarette, complete with bloodstains from the coup de grâce, but there were none. The guards most likely executed their victims in the cells and ordered any surviving captives to clean out the mess.

The wailing spiraled up through the old familiar stages.

Horror.

Denial.

Rejection.

Pleading.

Shock.

Then the abject surrender.

All in less than two minutes.

There was no way to know if the screamer was Lupérico. A quick recon of the former police station confirmed the position of two guards outside: only half dressed in uniform, sipping some sort of drink—probably coffee—under the portico. She thought she could even smell the brew.

Hard to get good coffee these days . . . She made a note to snag a bag of beans if the opportunity arose. Black tea with milk and sugar at four in the afternoon with a fistful of cucumber sandwiches just didn't cut it. She was sure the guys on her extraction chopper wouldn't object to a little extra cargo.

So, two men outside, at least four inside. Possibly six. Plus the three prisoners intel said were inside, only one of whom was of interest to her.

All of Caitlin's training, all of her experience, everything, told her to wait this out, to lay up until nightfall, then strike under the cover of darkness. But she had reason to ignore the training and experience. Somewhere down there was Ramón Lupérico, the man who had released Baumer from imprisonment in Guadeloupe. He was a prisoner now himself, and it was a righteous certainty that he could tell her how al Banna had effected that release from his custody, possibly even how he then came to control the pirate gangs and jihadist militia that had infested Manhattan back in April 2007.

She did not fool herself that Lupérico would know how or why Baumer had chosen to reach out and lay his malign touch on her family, but that hardly mattered. She was here because Echelon had tasked her with securing whatever information she could extract from the target. The coincidence of her personal and professional interests created an impetus toward immediate action.

The South American Federation was little better than a mafia state, but it was the only reliable authority south of the Panama Canal Zone. It would no sooner collaborate with Seattle than its self-proclaimed president for life, Roberto Morales, would present himself in The Hague to answer the many charges of crimes against humanity that now stood against his name. In the anarchic, violent world that arose in the wake of the Disappearance, such diplomatic impasses proved less frustrating than they once had been. The states that survived tended to be those which acted to secure their interests directly, expediently, and swiftly. It was a perfectly complete return to Hobbes's state of nature, and Caitlin Monroe, a survivor and a killer, was an instrument of that universe.

She crouched down, motionless and unseen in her hiding spot on the small rise overlooking the crossroads, and resolved to give herself one hour to gather as much intelligence about the situation on the ground here as she could. And then she would act.

2

NORTH KANSAS CITY, MISSOURI

"Drinking coffee? Perhaps the least of your sins, woman! But Elohim punishes all, and you have given him—"

Whatever the man had intended to say was choked off as Miguel Pieraro's fingers closed around his throat. With one thrust of an arm, the former vaquero threw Maive Aronson's tormentor from the stoop. A thin, wiry man with the severe intensity of a fanatic sustained almost entirely by his beliefs, the Mormon witness flew backward at a slight angle—luckily for him. His bony ass landed on the soft turf bordering the hard concrete path that wound from East 23rd Street up to the front door of Maive's small home.

"Oomph!"

The impact punched all the air out of him and rolled him onto the grass in a tangle of muddied elbows and knees. Miguel moved quickly to drive a boot into his guts, intending to kick him a considerable distance back toward the pavement from where he had come to torment the poor widow.

"Miguel, no," she said in a sharp voice. "You'll hurt him."

"Yes, I shall," he replied. But Maive had him by the arm, digging her fingernails into his bicep, pulling him back toward her.

She seemed unsure what to do with the cup of coffee she'd been drinking when the witness had knocked on the front door. Miguel hoped she might throw it over him now, scalding the crazy bastard, but that was not her way. Once the Mexican had made it clear that he was not about to launch himself at this fool, Maive carefully balanced the cup on the wooden rail running around the small decorative porch. She left Miguel on the top step, clenching and unclenching his fists, as she hurried down to help the man to his feet and out of the gate.

The Mormon door knocker shrugged her off, cursing her sinfulness, her muddy lawn, her coffee, and her offer of help. He scowled briefly at Pieraro and looked as though he might like to curse him, too, but the prospect of more rough handling saw him scurrying down the path and out onto the street.

A light rain was starting to fall, beading icily on Miguel's face. The cowboy watched him make his way toward North Kansas City High School, just a block down the road. Once the man had disappeared around the corner, he relaxed a little, although the high school did remind him of another difficult matter, prompting his temper to flare again.

Sofia.

It took another deep breath of cold morning air to douse the fire in his breast.

Maive stood with her back to Miguel, watching the Mormon go. Her shoulders began to hitch, and he could hear her fighting for breath as the tears came. He wanted to place a hand on her shoulder so that she might feel the reassurance of human contact. But it would not be right. Not with both of them still mourning. Instead, he clasped his hands together and stood on the ridiculously small front porch, waiting for her to regain her composure. He felt hemmed in here and awkward, as though he might knock something over at any moment. The lack of space was made worse by a wheelchair ramp that Maive obviously did not need. It probably had been fitted for the benefit of the previous occupants. There was barely room for the two of them to stand in the drizzle and wind. He could see fog condensing on the window behind the screen door, a sign of the warmth awaiting them inside.

The day had dawned bitterly cold, although "dawn" was a poor way to describe the wet, freezing, almost funereal gray shroud that seemed to blanket Kansas City in the morning at this time of year. Dawn here did not feel like the start of something new and vital; it was more a case of the night having simply exhausted its darkness and passed.

Miguel was dressed for the damp chill that pressed against him like a blade. He'd arrived not long before the Mormon caller. It was almost as if the man had been waiting, watching. He was most unlike the Saints he and Sofia had traveled with through Texas. Altogether more . . . what was the word? Biblical—that wasn't right, yet it seemed right.

With his sunken, staring eyes and haggard demeanor, the man looked like some sort of disturbed prophet from the Old Testament. He had been hounding Maive Aronson for the better part of a week now, wearing her down. Miguel had been furious when he'd found out just yesterday and had reacted with intemperate rage at the first opportunity. That is, a minute earlier, when he'd first laid eyes and hands on the *parásito*.

There were more of these Mormons in town every week as they made their way to Kansas City to reclaim lost land and property. Maive told him the community in KC had been second only to that in Salt Lake City for her people. That was a pity, he thought, making sure not to say it aloud. Not all of her fellow worshippers he'd encountered of late seemed to have the good common sense of Cooper and Maive Aronson, Willem D'Age, Ben Randall, and the others. So many were like the fool he had just ejected from her stoop, touched by fervent madness.

Gooseflesh stood out on Maive's unprotected arms while she sobbed and hugged herself in front of the little house the government had let her move into.

"Maive, you should come inside now," Miguel said. "It is too cold to be standing out here. Forget that crazy man. Come inside and have your coffee, warm up."

She hugged herself a little more tightly and bobbed her head up and down a few times before spinning around; her chin was tucked down into her chest so she wouldn't have to look Miguel in the eye as she hurried past him. She forgot the cup she'd perched on the handrail. He retrieved it for her, not surprised that the coffee had lost most of its heat in the brief minute they had been outside. Kansas City was like that, a place of . . . what was the word again? Fickle? Yes, fickle extremes. Like a difficult woman, it was predictable only in the way that you knew things would get worse.

He was certain he hated this city. Surely Seattle had to be a better place, even with the rain, but the resettlement authorities rarely let anyone move there from the frontier lands.

Miguel followed her through the door, careful not to crowd the widow, giving her enough space and time to compose herself. Eight months after losing her husband and most of her friends in that flash flood on the Johnson National Grasslands of northern Texas, she was still subject to unpredictable mood swings and periods of terrible sadness. There were days where she seemed to be healing, but it didn't take much to set her back. Still, he did not judge. His own wounds and losses remained open and raw.

The home provided by the settlement authorities was an old bungalow with dark wooden floors, plaster ceilings, and some fine carpentry that Miguel admired very much. Window seats, book shelving, and a particularly impressive-looking mantelpiece above a fireplace in the living room all spoke of a home that had been built by craftsmen who cared that their work would outlive them by many years, possibly centuries. It was not a large house by American standards—only three bedrooms and two of them quite small, obviously meant for children— but it was very comfortable and well insulated. Miguel did not concern himself with the fate of its previous occupants. They had Disappeared.

He'd wondered initially whether the very simple furnishings and effects such as linen and cutlery had belonged to those unfortunate people, but then he discovered upon being placed in his own residence that such things were drawn from one of the city resource stores scattered throughout the reclaimed areas. All one had to do was present a copy of one's housing assignment and one would be allowed to wander through and select the basics. There were even food vouchers for those who agreed to scour the unclaimed areas for usable materials on behalf of the city, and for a week or so, Miguel and Sofia had worked on that detail until they found better employment. He didn't miss that job at all. It was just one step above shoveling up the remains, sometimes dried, sometimes still thickly gelatinous, of the Disappeared.

People, it turned out, did not like to be surrounded by the leavings of the dead whose homes they had taken. Although, when he thought about it, the clean sheets and towels and simple items of clothing provided by the federales almost certainly had come from dead people as well, even if they were simply the owners of department stores whose stocks had been salvaged.

"Thank you, Miguel," Maive said, so quietly that he had to strain to hear her as he followed her into the kitchen at the rear of the house.

"It is okay," he replied. "It is lucky I had come around, I think."

The kitchen was warm and smelled of wood smoke from an old-fashioned stove. It was too dangerous to operate the gas lines, and the electricity supply could be sporadic. Wood stoves had replaced electric in many homes. If there was one thing Kansas City was blessed with, it was wood. A city in the forest.

Maive had been baking. A tray of muffins sat cooling on a scarred wooden table, resting atop a folded tea towel. She gestured for him to sit down while she splashed some water on her face, drying off with an apron hanging from the handle of the kitchen cupboard. Miguel considered the cup of lukewarm coffee he still held in his hands: the beans were carefully rationed and very expensive, and he didn't like the idea of it going to waste. All the same, he poured out the dregs, rinsed the cup, and set it in the drainer.

"I'm sorry . . . my manners," she said. "Please sit down and let me pour you a hot drink. I could do with one myself."

"So you will not be attending to the advice of your friend about the sinful coffee?"

Maive answered with a sour grimace. "He's no friend of mine. He only turned up here after I registered with the tabernacle. They've had trouble with him, too. Harassing people, new arrivals mostly. I suspect he has a mental illness."

She poured him a mug of coffee and offered cream and sugar, both of which he declined. After retrieving her own cup from the sink, Maive poured herself a full measure, took a sip to taste, and topped it up with another slug, as if to make a point.

"Cooper never was one for superstitions," she said, struggling somewhat. "His faith was . . . practical. My husband just wanted to help people. That was his idea of how to live your life the right way. I'm sorry . . ." Her face suddenly folded into contrary panes of anguish as grief threatened to get the better of her again.

"You have nothing to apologize for, Maive," he said in a gentle voice. "I, on the other hand, should not be so quick with my fists. This is your home. I am sorry if I was too rough with him. Do you mind? These look very good . . ." He indicated the tray of muffins, trying to change the subject.

"Not at all." She sniffed. "I baked them for you and Sofia."

He teased one of the golden-brown treats from the tray. She had topped them with crumble and brown sugar, creating a hard, sweet crust that he very much enjoyed. It was all Miguel could do to resist dunking the muffin top into his coffee. His beloved Mariela used to scold him for such poor manners, and he couldn't imagine Maive Aronson would approve of it, either.

"I am afraid Sofia is not very happy with me at the moment, Maive. The school has suspended her for fighting again, and I have grounded her." He wasn't very happy with her, either. He had been called during his shift at the stockyards in the West Bottoms to deal with it, which meant losing a day's pay while he took the city bus to the high school at Northtown.

Throwing caution to the wind, he broke off a large chunk of crusty muffin top and dunked it quickly into his coffee. The glazed crumble retained its crunch while the cakey center soaked up the warm liquid, becoming gooey and soft. Maive did not approve, but she seemed more concerned about Sofia.

"Oh, I am sorry to hear that, Miguel. I thought she was past the acting-out phase."

He put more food in his mouth and chewed and swallowed mechanically before taking another sip of coffee. All to give himself time to think. It was difficult. He knew how his daughter felt, how much pain she was in every day. But he also knew she could not allow that suffering to take over her life, and she could not take it out on other people. And yet . . .

There was a part of Miguel Pieraro that remained fiercely proud of his daughter and her refusal to bow under the heavy burden fate had laid on her. Witness to the murder of their family in East Texas, survivor of a journey that took the lives of so many others, Cooper Aronson among them, of course. And a fighter, an avenger indeed. One who had saved his life during the gunfight at Crockett, when they'd rescued Maive and her five female companions from the depredations of the road agents. Sofia had grown up beyond her years on the trail. And he could not deny that in many ways, although young, she was now a formidable woman in her own right.

"I do not know what to do, Maive," he admitted finally. "Honestly, some days it seems beyond me without the help of my wife."

Mentioning Mariela aloud was enough to tighten the band of grief that seemed to sit permanently around his chest. He felt his throat closing on a lump that had not been there a few seconds earlier. Another sip of coffee and a deep breath were needed to regain the reins on his feelings. Maive, who had no children of her own but who had mothered and, yes, loved his daughter and the other youngsters on the long exodus from Texas, reached across the table and gave his arm a reassuring squeeze. Unlike him, she seemed to have no compunction about reaching out and touching people.

"You are a good father, Miguel. You would give up your life for her. She knows that. And you will not let her give up on her own. She knows that, too." The Mormon woman smiled, but not happily. "That's why she knows she can test you, and push you, and drive you mad."

He stood up to rinse out his coffee cup, determined to avoid the temptation of another sugary treat. Since they had come off the trail, he had put on a few too many pounds.

"It is hard," he said. "I must punish her because the school requires it. I understand that. I have been a boss of the vaquero—I understand the need to maintain your rule. And yet, I do not think she was wrong. I understand why she was fighting. She was insulted. Our family was insulted. By some dog, some . . . boy at the school. The son of a man who is too important to upset."

A few lonesome flakes of sleet, gray and wet, smeared themselves against the kitchen window over the sink as Miguel washed out the cup. None of the trees retained more than a couple of brown leaves, and their branches resembled the withered hands of dead men reaching up from the grave.

"But does this boy get punished?" he went on. "Oh, no. *I* am the parent who is called in to explain himself. Sofia is the one upon whom correction must fall. While this smirking little *puta* . . ." He paused. "Again, I am sorry."

He found Maive Aronson shaking her head when he turned away from the bleak view out of the window. "That poor child has been through so much, Miguel. I suppose that's what makes her such an attractive target to some. All of that pain, out on display."

"If that is so, they are foolish," Miguel replied. "Great pain she has in abundance, but great strength with it. As this foolish boy discovered while he spit his broken teeth out on the ground."

"Oh, dear," said Maive, although she did not seem particularly disapproving. "So she's at home now, studying, I suppose?"

"Studying, yes," he answered. "Or sulking."

"Well, that is a pity. But it is important that you're seen to do the right thing, even if you disagree with it."

She began clearing the table. Using the tea towel under the cooling muffin tray to brush up the crumbs. Pouring the remains of her drink, more than half the cup again, down the sink after the dregs of Miguel's.

"Will you still want to go to the midweek markets this morning?" she asked.

He nodded. "We will need groceries before the weekend."

It was also true that he looked forward to spending time with Maive, particularly since Trudi Jessup had transferred back to Seattle with her government job. Apart from Maive and Sofia, he knew nobody in Kansas City. Adam, the teenager who had impressed him so much, was now with relatives in Canada. Miguel missed him more than he might have imagined. He had come to regard the boy almost as a son over the long months on the trail. And a friend, if a young one.

He had no friends here, except for Maive, of course. The men he worked with at the railway cattle yards were mostly Indians, and he found them difficult to get on with. They spoke English, true, but sometimes it seemed like they spoke a very different version of the language. Even the Americans had trouble with them from time to time. Mostly he did his job there and came home. It was only a temporary position, at any rate, a place the government had put him so that he'd be available for interviews by investigators, agents, and the small army of men and women who seemed to want to know everything about his time in Texas. Even if they never did anything about what had happened there.

"I should get my bag, then," Maive said. "Shall we walk or drive? The weather isn't that nice, but the radio said it probably wouldn't get much worse, either."

"We shall walk, I think," Miguel decided, mindful of the fact that the federales were cutting back on the paltry gas ration again as well as increasing the price to twenty new dollars a gallon. Maive's salvaged Jeep Wrangler was not the most fuel-efficient vehicle, in any case. "I shall carry your groceries for you," he added gallantly.

"Thank you, Miguel. You're a very good friend."

3

DEARBORN HOUSE, SEATTLE, WASHINGTON

"I don't think you should go to Texas, Mr. President. The precedents aren't good."

James Kipper made a show of furrowing his brow and mashing up his lips. Culver had learned to think of this as his I'm-not-happy face. It was getting an Olympic-standard workout this morning. The White House chief of staff absorbed his boss's displeasure with the unflappable air of a man who knew he was right. Because he was. Jed Culver was always right.

"I think the longer I stay out of Texas, Jed," Kipper protested, "the more it looks like I'm too frightened to show my face down there. He hasn't seceded despite all his Republic of Texas bullshit. We're all still living in the same country. And I really think it's time I went down there. After all, with the election coming up . . ." The president left the statement hanging there, dropping his chin and regarding Culver with an expression that said: *Ha! What d' you think of them apples, fella?*

They were alone, and the chief of staff actually allowed himself a small snicker of amusement. Kip was at his funniest when he was trying to play politics. It just didn't suit the man.

"The last thing we need before the election, Mr. President, is Mad Jack Blackstone kicking your ass from one end of his snaggletooth republic to the other." *That's what I think o' them apples, fella.*

The boss looked even more put out than before, a common occurrence whenever Culver had reason to remind him of his naïveté. That happened less frequently these days, especially after New York. But for a politician, even one press-ganged into high office, Kip could still be maddeningly childlike in the way he viewed the world. Jed felt the need to explain. They still had a few minutes before the cabinet members arrived for the morning meeting.

"Right now, sir, Blackstone is looking for any excuse to paint you as a weak, softhearted fool. And he's very carefully picking his fights to make himself look like the Great White Hope, quite literally. There are so many things we need from him right now that if you fly down to Fort Hood, you'll have no choice but to lay our demands on the table and he'll have no qualms about laughing in your face. He won't even be cruel about it. He'll do it in such a way as to make it obvious that you don't know what you're talking about, you can't possibly be trusted to run the country, you're a lovely man, but soft and weak, and the sooner we get rid of you the better."

Kipper narrowed his eyes and leaned back in his chair, steepling his fingers and frowning at Culver over the top of them. The first real frost of the winter lay hard against the windows of Dearborn House, which had been sheathed in Christmas decorations just that morning. Outside the big picture window that framed Kipper at his desk, dirty gray clouds scudded slowly across the sky, obscuring the upper floors of Seattle's taller buildings. The president seemed to lose himself for a moment, staring at a picture of his daughter, Suzie, in a small silver frame on his desk. He sighed.

"Why am I here, Jed?"

"I'm sorry, Mr. President?"

"No, really. Why am I here? I just wonder some days, that's all. There's so much that needs doing to rebuild this country. We all know what's needed. You, me, Blackstone, Congress, Sarah Palin, Sandra

Harvey—Abe, the guy down at the market who sells me my sausages. We all know what needs to be done. So why the hell can't we just get on and do it? Why can't I do my job? Pass my budget, get my tax law through, the migration bill, the energy bill—any of it? At every single step of the way, I got somebody telling me what I *can't* do. Even though we all agree about what has to be done . . ."

He swiveled his chair around to stare out the window. His mood was as bleak as the weather.

"I'm just wondering what the point is," Kip added resignedly. "That's all."

He'd been like this since the Battle of New York. Or rather, since he'd returned to the Big Apple a couple of weeks after the last of the diehards were killed or run off. It was as though James Kipper had decided to assume responsibility for every death, for every piece of rubble. It didn't matter how many times Jed, Barbara, or anybody else told him that he had done what needed doing, that he had seen off an unexpected but deadly serious threat to the republic and shown the world that an America laid low still would not countenance the designs of any foe on her land or her sovereignty.

Kip had been the most reluctant of warrior kings, and having seen the cost of taking up sword and shield to expel the so-called Emir and his pirate allies from Manhattan, he seemed to have lost the stomach for any kind of fight. He was a tinkerer, a builder, an engineer, not a destroyer. Even his impacted rage at the attacks on settlers in the Texas Federal Mandate had abated as those attacks tapered off. He was a problem solver by nature, and once a problem went away, his interest shifted elsewhere.

Culver, who had been comfortably reclined in a dark leather club chair that had become known as his whenever he was in the Oval Office, put aside the folder of papers he'd been holding and heaved himself up to his feet. A onetime college wrestler, he'd always been a big guy, and he found the constant round of state dinners and cocktail parties in the new national capital ruinous to his waistline. Kipper was a lean and hungry-looking wraith in comparison. Jed grunted as he stood up. He was really going to have to start that walking routine his doctor and Marilyn, his wife, were forever hassling him about.

"You're here because you're here, Kip," he said.

That got his attention. Jed almost never called him by his nickname. The president turned away from the window with its melancholy view of leafless trees and a slate-gray sky.

"Somebody has to do this job," the former Louisiana attorney continued, "and it's better done by a good man like you than an asshole like Blackstone or a feral, crazy eco-Nazi like Sandra fucking Harvey. It's not much fun, but someone's gotta do it. So man up, buddy. You're the guy."

The president smiled as if conceding a pawn in a long game of chess. "Suppose you're right," he admitted. "Nobody held a gun to my head and told me to do this. Although, you know, I think Barbara might have. She really surprised me back then."

She had. Culver well remembered Kipper's shock upon discovering that his wife had been working quietly with the resistance to General Blackstone's martial law regime imposed on the Pacific Northwest in the panic and chaos of spring 2003. She hadn't surprised Culver, however. As soon as he'd met Barbara Kipper, he'd judged her capable of reaching hard conclusions and acting on them in a way that her husband wasn't. Not immediately, anyway. Kip was just too trusting of people. He wanted to think the best of them, and it often stayed his hand when he needed to do his worst.

"Guess we better bring them on in if they're ready," said the president.

He started to straighten up his tie before thinking otherwise and loosening it further. A fire blazed and crackled in the small hearth, adding its warmth to the underfloor heating. As always, Kipper had discarded his jacket as soon as he sat down that morning. He worked with his sleeves rolled up, citing the Kennedy precedent if anyone questioned him. "Anyone" usually meant his wife and occasionally his chief of staff. If they didn't keep a close watch on him, he'd turn up to work in jeans, boots, and one of his old hiking shirts.

Jed buzzed Kipper's secretary, Ronnie, to check whether the cabinet group was ready yet, and when she answered yes, he told her to send them in. Barney Tench was first through the door, still licking his fingers from the small tray of pastries set out for visitors in the anteroom and looking only marginally guilty. Like Barbara, Kip's old pal Tench had thrown in his lot with the resistance, but unlike her, he had suffered for it. Blackstone had issued a warrant for his arrest on charges of sedition. That had been enough to convince Kipper, then a mere city engineer working closely with Blackstone, that the man had to go.

It was tempting to imagine they'd all moved on such a long way from those first horrible days. Barney would seem to be living proof of that, Jed thought. Instead of being arrested and possibly hanged or shot under martial law, Tench was now the chief of Kipper's national reconstruction efforts, a job that brought him into regular contact with Blackstone, who'd gone on to become the governor of Texas. But they hadn't moved on that far, had they? Because Blackstone was still a gigantic pain in the ass, still the most dangerous man in America, at least to Jed's way of thinking. But to a lot of other people he was a hero.

Kipper and Barney greeted each other as old friends and coconspirators, with smiles and handshakes devoid of any pro forma posturing. For one brief moment they really were just a couple of old college buds who didn't get to see each other nearly enough. Not outside the crushing demands of their respective jobs, anyway. Tench was frequently away from Seattle, either supervising some project out in the boonies or overseas wrangling aid and redevelopment funds out of the small coterie of allied nations willing and able to lend a hand.

Behind him entered the treasury secretary, Paul McAuley, followed by the head of Immigration and Customs Enforcement, Sarah Humboldt, and the country's newly minted national security adviser, Admiral James Ritchie. Jed was happy to have the old salt on board. If not for Ritchie, the chances were pretty good that Jed wouldn't be standing here. They'd met in Honolulu during the first hours after the Wave had swept across the continental United States, when Culver had understood the importance of attaching himself to what was left of the nation's power structure. He believed that Ritchie's leadership had been one of the main reasons the remnant population of America hadn't turned on one another in a snarling tangle of fear and madness. He lobbied Kip hard to rescue the man from the backwater he'd been lost in for the last couple of years, securing the military's stock of WMDs; it was important work for sure but not the best use of Ritchie's talents.

"Admiral, good to see you," Culver said. "Pull up a pew and let's get started, shall we. The president's not one for standing on ceremony."

"So I've learned," replied Ritchie, who still insisted on the formalities. A little like Jed, in fact.

As they all distributed themselves around the room, Kipper's secretary wheeled in a trolley bearing coffeepots and plates of cookies.

"Thanks, Ronnie," Kip said.

In a nod to his constant reading of presidential history, Kip referred to the informal working group as his Garage Cabinet, riffing on Andrew Jackson's Kitchen Cabinet. They met in this form once a month. If Kip could have pulled it off, they would have met in greasy Levi's in a garage with a fully stocked beer fridge. His chief of staff, ever the crusher of dreams, had killed that one off but allowed the name to stand. Andrew Jackson might have had Culver shot for such a thing, whereas Kip merely sighed and agreed. A sign of the times.

Full cabinet meetings were scheduled as frequently, but Jed programmed them to run two weeks out from the small meetings. It meant he had to endure constant grumbling from the other cabinet secretaries, who felt themselves locked out of the more important decision-making group, but the bottom line was that this was a much more efficient arrangement. They had everybody at the table, in this case a coffee table, who Jed thought necessary to deal with the most pressing problems and rolling crises.

When they all found their places, settled themselves into chairs, and in most cases poured themselves a coffee and grabbed a cookie—peanut butter and chocolate chip, a specialty of the First Lady—Chief of Staff Culver got the meeting under way.

"Thanks, everyone. It's not much fun traveling through this weather, I know. And I know you're all up to your eyeballs in work. You'll have seen on your agenda papers that we have just a couple of things to get through today, but it'd be good to shake these out before we take them to the cabinet in a fortnight. The president's not looking to lock down a caucus position today. But we've been kicking some of these issues around for a couple of months now, and the time has come to deal with them so we can move on to our next end-of-the-world crisis. Mr. President?"

"Thanks, Jed," said Kipper, examining his fingernails. The presidency had not entirely removed the calluses or the stains of engineering work from his hands. He had a single sheet of paper with the meeting agenda sitting in front of him, held down by a mug of coffee and covered in crumbs from one of his wife's cookies. "What Jed said . . . Miserable weather, and it's only getting worse. Gonna be a snowed-in Christmas, I reckon."

Kipper brushed the crumbs away, folded his arms to hide his hands, and leaned forward over the large teak desk, looking like a student worrying over a term paper.

"So let's get it done. Two items today are related, I think: the budget deficit and Texas. So I think we should deal with the other item first: the prisoners from New York."

Jed could see Paul McAuley consciously subdivide his attention, the treasury man listening closely enough to be able to follow any discussion about the captured enemy aliens in Manhattan while leaving most of his thoughts swirling madly around the Gordian knot of the budget deficit. Sarah Humboldt, naturally, sat forward, putting aside her coffee and fetching a sheaf of documents from the tote bag she had carried into the room with her. The national security adviser nodded slowly, but his expression remained masked.

"Jed tells me we have just under four and a half thousand people in detention on the East Coast," the president continued. "Most of them women and children, relatives of the jihadists who fought for that asshole Baumer."

"I believe his formal title is 'the Emir,'" Barney Tench deadpanned.

"Okay, that asshole the Emir . . . Anyway, we have thousands of displaced people and about three hundred of his former soldiers, or fighters, or whatever you want to call them."

"'Assholes' works for me," said Tench.

Because of Kipper's almost pathological informality, anybody in the room could probably get away with talking like that. But only Barney, his oldest living friend, felt comfortable enough to do so. The president answered his interruption with a lopsided grin before carrying on.

"Question is, as it's always been, what are we going to do with them? I don't want to force repatriation on women and kids when we'd be sending most of them back to a radiated wasteland. Thank you, Israel. On the other hand, having tried to take something by force, these people shouldn't be rewarded by being given what they tried to take. In this case, the right to settle. So, suggestions?"

Jed had one, but it involved putting them all on a garbage scow and towing it out into the mid-Atlantic at the height of hurricane season. Perhaps if he'd been working for Mad Jack Blackstone he would have put it forward, but having tried a few times in this forum, he knew it wouldn't float. So to speak. Instead, he picked a few pieces of lint from the cuffs of his trousers.

The silence in the room ballooned into significance. Sarah Humboldt, as the ICE boss, had responsibility for the matter, but Sarah was a lifelong bureaucrat, more comfortable implementing policy than developing it. Nonetheless, she obviously felt the weight of expectation fall upon her. Clearing her throat, she began to sort through the stack of papers she was carrying. If she was looking for something specific, it remained lost in there, and she grew flustered at her inability to find it. Kip interrupted her embarrassment with a gentle question.

"Sarah, why don't you just tell me what you think? Don't give me options. I don't need to run through every scenario your guys have come up with. You've been working this area your whole life, so just tell me what you think."

Secretary Humboldt looked horrified, but with an observable effort of will, she put aside the briefing notes. "Well, sir . . ."

That was as far as she progressed for a few seconds as she groped wordlessly for the right thing to say.

"Come on, Sarah," Kip urged. "You've been out to the detention camps. You sat in on a lot of interviews. What's your gut feeling?"

Humboldt frowned. All of her training, all of her professional experience, had taught her to divorce her feelings from her judgment.

"Mr. President, most of them are just little people. They've been carried along by events. This is the women and children I'm talking about. Most of them have lost their men in the fighting. They're alone in the world except for each other. If you're asking could they be integrated, I believe the answer is yes."

Culver kept his face neutral, concentrating on taking handwritten notes as Humboldt spoke. Kip had made it clear that he didn't care for his chief of staff intimidating the cabinet secretaries. When Jed spoke, he did so in such a way that Ms. Humboldt could not have known he thought she was a fucking madwoman.

"Madam Secretary, would it be the case that you would differentiate between the women and children and the captured fighters?"

Everyone in the room was interested in the answer. The president waited on her eagerly. Admiral Ritchie bored into her with his unwavering gaze. Even Secretary McAuley gave the impression of concentrating wholly on what she said next, deficits set aside for now. It didn't ease Humboldt's discomfort.

"All of the enemy combatants were initially debriefed by the military. I don't have access to the raw transcripts or interview recordings, just executive summaries. Some of the prisoners, the surviving leadership cadre, as I understand it, have been separated out and remain under military control. The lower ranks—if that's an appropriate description—can probably be roughly sorted into two groups: true believers and, well, soldiers of fortune, I suppose. Opportunists. Like the pirate bands they were fighting with but nominally motivated by religious conviction. Most of the second group, I believe, were less interested in Baumer's jihad than they were in securing land and life for themselves and their families. They're not true believers. If we were serious about taking them up into the broader migration program"— she said that very carefully, watching to see if Culver would react—"I would recommend that only this latter cohort, the opportunists if you will, those without strong ideological attachment to Baumer, be accepted, and then with certain caveats."

Thank God for that at least, Jed thought. Caveats he could work with. Especially big, ass-kicking caveats that effectively guaranteed most of these punks a trip back to sea on his garbage scow.

"What sort of restrictions would we be looking at?" he asked.

A deep crease formed in the middle of Humboldt's brow. "I don't believe it would be good policy to maintain the integrity of the original cohort," she said, lapsing into bureaucratese.

When she failed to explain any further, Kipper prompted, "So, what, you're talking about breaking them up?"

She nodded. "Yes, sir. Not family groups, of course. But I think we would find that integrating them into existing communities would be a smoother process if they weren't allowed to cluster."

This time a querying frown from the president caused her to hurry on with an explanation. "They're less likely to cause trouble, much more likely to settle in, if we bed them down well away from any bad influences. And from each other. They're not ideologues. For the most part, they're young widows with quite young children, often three or four of them, to look after. And no men, of course, to provide for them. I think they could be settled if we placed them within compatible communities."

"Such as?" Jed asked, his skepticism leaking through.

At that, Humboldt shrugged briefly. "Many of the Indian nationals we've taken in to work on the railway programs came from that country's Muslim community. After the war with Pakistan, they weren't entirely welcome in their homeland anymore. But they've had no trouble fitting in here. Most are observant in their faith but not politicized by it. There are enough of them now that we could salt most of our East Coast detainees through their population without ghettoizing them."

"And the fighters?" Kipper quizzed, saving Jed the effort. "The men?"

Culver was certain he saw Humboldt flick her eyes quickly over at Admiral Ritchie.

"It's not within the purview of my department, Mr. President. But we have been turning this matter over for a while now, both in this working group and in the wider cabinet, and there have been a couple of position papers drawn up that might be of help."

The Immigration and Customs Enforcement head started rifling through the thick wad of papers she'd extracted from her tote bag. She kept her head down, studiously avoiding eye contact with Culver, who knew nothing of any so-called position papers. Retrieving what she wanted, she passed copies around the room. Ritchie, he noted, didn't need to scan the document even for a moment. He gave the impression of being familiar with it.

"The fighters are a more difficult question," Humboldt said. "Especially if we accept the settlement of the noncombatants. Many of the fighters, nearly two-thirds of them, have relatives among the women and children we are holding. We cannot separate them, in law or in conscience."

The hell we can't, Jed thought.

Kipper was nodding slowly, feeding himself small chunks of cookie that he broke off the mother lode like a kid trying to make a treat last a little longer. Jed could not be sure he was nodding in agreement with Ms. Humboldt; he simply might have been acknowledging her. The president liked people to know he was listening to them. The chief of staff, in contrast, was having trouble restraining himself. He didn't like where this was going, and he felt blindsided by whatever arrangement Humboldt and Ritchie had come to before the meeting. Jed was going to have to reassess his reading of the national security adviser. It appeared that Ritchie was more practiced at the dark arts of politics than he had imagined when lobbying Kipper on the admiral's behalf.

"ICE sought input from all the major stakeholders on this question . . ."

But not from me, thought Culver.

". . . and as you would imagine, their responses varied considerably. Defense and the NIA argued strongly in favor of continued detention. Treasury"—she spared a glance for McAuley at that point—"has been updating its forward estimates for funding a number of scenarios. And we at ICE, of course, are in constant contact with Reconstruction about their needs for various skill sets that remain undersubscribed."

Barney Tench appeared to be nonplussed by the inclusion of his department in Sarah's magic circle. But as Jed examined his shorthand notes of what she'd just said, he suppressed a sour grin of admiration. Humboldt had drawn the other players in the room into whatever gambit she was about to make simply by stating the fucking obvious. Of course Reconstruction and Treasury were in constant contact with Immigration and Customs Enforcement about labor shortfalls and funding requirements; that didn't mean they were on board for every program Humboldt wanted to push. As tempted as he was to interrupt, the chief of staff thought it best to let her play her hand.

"It would be possible," she continued, "to include most of the problematic cohort, the fighters with family ties to our noncombatant detainees, as part of the general intake into this year's frontier militia forces."

At that, Jed had reached the limit of his forbearance.

"Seriously? You seriously want to integrate these nutjobs into our *military forces?*"

"The frontier militias aren't part of the regular military," James Ritchie corrected.

The unexpected intervention drew Culver up short, and he cursed himself for making such an undergraduate mistake. "Sorry," he said. "But you're splitting hairs. No, the frontier militias are not part of the armed forces. You know that, I know that, but such fine gradations of meaning are well beyond most people. And it's most people who'll go apeshit at the mere suggestion of letting these guys out of their cage, handing them a gun, and sending them off into the wilderness."

"He has a point," Kip said.

The president wasn't nearly as worked up as Jed, but one could see he was puzzled by the suggestion. That was a relief. To Culver's dismay, though, Ritchie took up the role of explaining Humboldt's idea, confirming any suspicions about his prior knowledge of it.

"The frontier militias' chain of command runs up through Reconstruction, not Defense. They're an armed force but an irregular one. The duties can vary from securing the boundaries of small settlements, just like a garrison force, to riding shotgun on reclamation crews in the big cities or scouting wilderness in the Declared Zones. It's dangerous work. Very dangerous. And a lot of it is done in small teams thousands of miles away from civilization. If we were to take in a small number of these fighters, break them up, and scatter them through the militia, making sure they were posted well out into the badlands, and impose, say, a ten-year probationary period, we could sell it as both punishment and redemption. Their families would become, well . . . our hostages, to be brutally frank. If their men gave us any trouble, we'd just toss them all on Jed's garbage scow and wave them off at the dock. For lesser infringements, we'd cancel home leave, maybe transfer the women and children to some more godforsaken hole—that sort of thing."

The sleet slapping against the window behind the presidential desk had thickened into a serious dump of snow. Gusting contrary winds whipped fractal patterns through the white haze and rattled the old wooden window in its frame. Kipper frowned and searched in his desk drawer for some notepaper. As he ripped out a piece, folded it, and folded it again a few times, he turned his back on them to jam the makeshift wedge into the window and muffle the rattling, talking while he did so.

"Is there any reason any of these guys would agree to this?" he asked. "I imagine you'd be planning to break them up completely so that you only had one of Baumer's fighters attached to any particular unit. But really, how's it going to work in practice? Ten years? That's a hell of a long time. A hell of an incentive to cut and run the first chance you had."

Having fixed the window, Kipper returned to his desk and a cup of coffee that had gone cold. He grimaced when he tried it.

Ritchie continued. "The majority of our existing frontier militia, the lower ranks, anyway, are made up of migrants, Mr. President. It's a fast track into the settlement programs and citizenship for most of them. They're willing to take the risks—and they are very real risks—for the payoff. Now, returning to the situation at hand. If, say, for the sake of argument, we accepted only those fighters who had family connections among the civilian detainees, it would be a matter of little or no trouble to hold over them the fact that we control their access to their loved ones. Maybe ten years *is* too long. Five might be better. The point is, we control them and we control access to what they want: their families. It's just a matter of striking the right balance between punishment and reward. Maybe they get to come back for a week every six months, maybe two weeks every twelve. The proof of the pudding will be in the eating, to some extent. To all intents and purposes, they'd still be our captives. But their jail would be the frontier."

Silence, pregnant with possibilities, not all of them good, seemed to press down on the Oval Office. Barney Tench looked every bit as shocked as Jed had felt a few minutes earlier. McAuley was frowning furiously.

Finding himself in the unusual position of not knowing exactly what to think, Jed Culver settled for trying to read Kipper's reaction. He knew the president's natural inclination would be forgiving rather than punitive, at least toward the spear-carriers and foot soldiers. The altogether less liberal approach of effectively exiling them into the wilderness for a decade and allowing only tightly controlled access to their wives and children probably didn't appeal to him as much. But Kip had been initially skeptical of Sarah Humboldt's plan. Or Humboldt and Ritchie's plan, he supposed, given how well they'd gamed the proposal.

The president took his time mulling it all over. Nobody spoke while he was deep in thought. Jed used the brief interlude to examine the idea from all the worst possible angles. His main concern was not that a handful of nutjobs would run wild in an empty city. They'd been smashed flat in New York City when they were part of a much larger, well-organized fighting force. No, as individuals rattling around the interior of a nearly empty continent, there just wasn't much mischief they could get up to, and his reading of human nature led him to believe that Humboldt was probably right—most of those former grunts for hire could be reformed and even assimilated, given enough time. As for the true believers, Baumer's hard-core jihadi, they had no future here. And Jedediah Armstrong Culver of the Louisiana bar would not rest until they were gone or dead. After all, war crimes trials were in the offing for a number of them. Even the more moderate elements of President Kipper's Garage Cabinet were agreed on this point, thankfully.

The main threat, however, as always, was Jackson Blackstone. It made one's head spin to think about the merry hell he would play with something like this. It was almost a certainty he'd have his lapdog state house pass a law banning the presence of any former enemy combatants within the borders of Texas and its protectorate territories. Having done that, the sneaky little fuck probably would want to make sure a couple of them actually wandered over the state line just so he could be seen to hunt 'em down and string 'em up.

In contrast, a merciful peacemaking gesture would play very well here in the Northwest, especially with Sandra Harvey's Greens. They weren't running a candidate in the presidential election. Sandra was smart enough to know she could only ever play the role of a spoiler for Kip's chances. And for all of her many, many issues with his administration, she regarded the possibility of a Blackstone-led government with visceral horror. He was just running the math in his head on whether a Green endorsement would bring in more votes than it burned off when Kipper broke the silence.

"The women and the children should be allowed to stay, with certain . . . provisos," he began. Everybody seemed to lean forward just a little bit. "It's reasonable, I think, that we require of them everything we require of any other settler, and more. English-language proficiency. Civic education. Training in whatever base-level skills we deem necessary. All the usual. And because of the circumstances under which they came here, we need to ask—no, we need to *demand*—more of them."

"I think loyalty pledges went out with *Catch-22,* sir," said Jed, barely restraining the sarcastic tone he wanted to use. Kip, as was his style, shrugged it off as the chief of staff went on. "The last time such measures were tried out was back during the time of Lincoln with former Confederates. It didn't work all that well back then, and it probably wouldn't work well in the here and now."

Aside from the notion that it would do no good, in Culver's estimation, this was just the sort of thing the Seattle press would sink its teeth into and not let go of. He figured it was best to steer Kipper away from that path.

"You know that's not what I'm talking about, Jed," the president replied. "Let me make myself understood: I'm not in favor of sending thousands of women and children who themselves have done nothing wrong back into the wastelands they used to call home." Kip held up his hand like a traffic cop to head off any further interruption. "And before anybody says anything, I am well aware that some of these people originally set out from Europe, not the Middle East—I do actually read your briefing papers, you know. In those cases, I am open to the argument that they should be repatriated." He smiled now. "I doubt Chancellor Merkel or President Sarkozy will want them back, but you'll be pleased to know, Jed, I don't much care."

Culver took the ribbing in good faith as Ronnie ghosted in through the door to see if anybody needed a refill on the coffee. He lifted his cup and waggled it at her while Kip spoke again.

"Bottom line, anyone who can prove refugee status by demonstrating they came from one of the countries nuked by Israel—and my understanding is that quite a few of them did—well, in those cases I am open to the possibility of our accepting them in the spirit of forgiveness and reconciliation."

For Jed, the urge to groan was almost too strong to stifle. He could already imagine how Blackstone was going to play this, and though Admiral Ritchie may have been on board, Culver suspected that many of the rank and file in the military were not going to be pleased. The lack of pay, poor treatment in Seattle, and the winding back of benefits were loaded onto a platter already overloaded with heavy losses in New York City. Those who remained in the much-reduced U.S. armed forces would not require many more incentives to head to Texas.

"But I am not a soft touch," Kipper continued. "I like the idea of some of these characters being made to earn our trust out on the frontier. And I think ten years is a heavy enough sentence to levy on them for the crime of serving in Pharaoh's army. Admiral, I'm happy to take your advice on how we might structure that program, including how we tweak it in such a way that, for them, getting back into the settled areas to see their family is incentive enough to stay on the straight and narrow. For the noncombatants, the women and children—well, the women, I guess—we really need some way to use them productively, to make them understand that they could have a future here. But that it's *our* future, the one we envision, not some medieval theocracy they might've signed up for a year or two back. I'm not even going to pretend I know how to go about doing that, but then, I don't have to. That's your job, Sarah. And yours, Jed."

"What?"

Culver nearly snorted fresh hot coffee out through his nose. Humbolt looked just as surprised.

Kipper regarded him with a grin that was positively malign. "I can see they caught you with your pants down on this, buddy," he said. "And I know without even looking at you that you think the idea sucks dog's balls. Excuse my French, Sarah."

"That's okay, Mr. President," she shot back. Ms. Humboldt was still unsettled by the revelation that she'd be working with Jed Culver.

"I know you're already being tortured by nightmares about Mad Jack using this against us," Kipper resumed. "That's why I want you to oversee the program for me. I have no doubt, Jed, you'll come up with some way of making it look as though allowing these prisoners to stay is a punishment for them and a boon for us. I dunno, maybe you could find a genuine turncoat in there. Somebody who thought they had permission to wander into New York and take it over. And having been led astray by the devious Emir, he now burns with holy fire to wreak his vengeance and prove his loyalty to the country that gave him a chance and took him in, yada yada yada. You'll work it out, I'm sure."

"But *why*, Kip?" he said, perplexed that they would put themselves to so much trouble for no observable benefit. "Why help these bastards get what they wanted in the first place? And after we spilled so much blood to deny them . . ."

Now the president favored him with an almost indulgent smile.

"I'm not going to patronize you by telling you it's the right thing to do, Jed. By many folks' way of figuring these things, it's not. But I believe it is, not for the sake of those women and children but for us. We have *fallen,* Jed. We have fallen far and hard, and we are hurting. It would be tempting—even more than tempting, it would be a terrible *pleasure*—to try to soften that hurt by laying it off on someone else. Particularly someone as deserving as a man who was trying to kill us not so long ago. But that way lies desolation, my friend. The madness of revenge seeking is seductive, but it's still madness. We can only think of ourselves as better than them if we really *are* better than them."

"I'm not a child. I know a lot of those women hate us with a passion. Even before we took their men from them, they hated us. Or at least the *idea* of us. What they'd been raised to think of us and, if truth be known, what they're raising their children to think of us in the very camps where we hold them captive at the moment. But we can change that. Because we are better than their low opinion of us."

Kipper's words gave the impression of him becoming more intense as he spoke, but in fact he seemed to relax and grow almost abstracted. It was as if he were examining an engineering challenge because it interested him rather than because some vital outcome rested upon his solving it.

"Revenge is the pleasure of a small and feeble mind—I read that somewhere back in college. It rang true then, and even more now. Nothing good ever comes of it. How many of the true believers, the real holy warriors, who came here and died did so to revenge themselves on an America that doesn't even exist anymore? Where are they now? Are they an example worth following, do you think? No, let's take these people in, the ones we have some hope of saving. And let's have our revenge on them by turning them into something they once hated. Into us. Because we are better than them."

Jed Culver found himself in an unusual position. He was at a loss for words.

4

FORMER URUGUAYAN–ARGENTINIAN BORDER REGION, SOUTH AMERICAN FEDERATION

She had logged four guards now. Her two indolent drinkers still lounged under the thick portico of the former police station. They had switched from caffeine to cigarillos and appeared to be engaged in an argument about soccer. Every few minutes one of them would stand and laboriously work through a pantomime of some disputed passage of play while the other theatrically dismissed his efforts with glorious excess, smacking hands over eyes, throwing arms into the air, and calling out *"¡No no no!"* so loudly that she had no trouble hearing it. Two other guards wandered out at random intervals, the first to bum smokes and the second to watch the theatrics and add a few dismissive words of his own. None of them looked like A-listers, but she worried about the unseen men.

Her briefing notes were clear. This was a small detention facility run by the local Federation militia. It was more of a way station where prisoners often were held before transfer to the fleet base for interrogation by the Oficina Seguridad, Roberto's personal Gestapo.

The jail was staffed by a militia commander, a deputy, and four other men. Given the air of neglect, the sloppiness, and the general dereliction of duty that seemed to characterize "Facility 183," Caitlin did not imagine the commander to be a bright and shining star of the regime. It was unlikely he'd have adequate security in place, relying instead on the fearsome reputation of Roberto's security apparatus to dissuade anyone from interfering with his little fiefdom. As a militia enforcer, he was probably a former gang member who'd thrown in his lot with Morales as the dictator grew ever stronger during the post-Wave chaos. *El colapso,* as it was now known across most of South America.

Chances were, the CO was the one wielding the blowtorch, tire iron, or whatever it was that had reduced the screaming man to such a pitiable state. Caitlin tried to swallow on a dry mouth as memories of her imprisonment and torture in Noisy-le-Sec tried to break out of a small black box at the back of her mind. She attended to her craft, as she always did when needing to put aside unpleasant realities.

The Echelon agent reached into her small khaki backpack and checked her notes on when the guards had appeared from inside the crumbling stucco building. No patterns. She scanned the entire compound again, using her binoculars, searching for entry and egress points and logging at least three. She plotted her approach, mentally rehearsing the stealthy advance down the hill under the cover of the forest canopy, her emergence from the brush, the possible scenarios that might play out as she engaged the guards. She was particularly concerned about the thick stone pillars holding up the red-tiled roof of the portico that shaded the front of the building. They would provide good cover to anyone firing at her. She spent some time pondering how to turn that tactical disadvantage to her favor.

She had no schematic of the building's interior but based her best guesstimate of the layout on what she could see of the rough L-shaped block. The door through which the two wandering guards, the smoker, and the soccer expert sometimes appeared undoubtedly led into the facility's reception area. Caitlin couldn't make out any details through the windows at that end of the building, but the fact that the windows were glass and unsecured told her there were no cells behind them. There might be an open-plan office, perhaps, like a detectives' bullpen. There might be a warren of rooms. But the cells where she would find Lupérico were undoubtedly at the other end of the structure. There, small, mean windows—just holes in the adobe no larger than a man's head, all of them barred by iron grilles—looked out over a motor pool. Two of the vehicles there were civilian, but Caitlin noted an ancient-looking police car from the building's previous life. The rust-streaked sedan had sunk down on deflated tires and a thick bed of weeds. It obviously hadn't moved in years.

As she took another sip of water, a new player appeared. His uniform was neat, and he moved with purpose and some grace. A thin man with a widow's peak on a high forehead, he barked a few commands at the two guards on the front veranda. They scrambled from their chairs, one almost falling over as he lost his balance. Caitlin focused on the officer through her binoculars.

He was in an altogether different class from the men he was busy bossing around. She recognized the bearing of somebody used to giving orders and being obeyed, even feared. He lashed at his underlings with his voice but never raised a hand in their direction. This guy was no former gangbanger; he was a militia officer.

Ex-cop? Ex-military, maybe?

She wondered if he was the facility's commander or deputy. Or possibly an outsider come in to supervise the questioning of Ramón Lupérico.

She warned herself off personalizing his backstory. Just because Lupérico was important to her, it didn't necessarily make him important to the regime out in this part of the world. The fact that he'd ended up in this backwater rather than being tortured by professionals down south at Puerto Belgrano implied that the Oficina Seguridad had not been clued in to his potential value.

Steam was rising from the undergrowth as the sun climbed higher with the morning's passing. Caitlin was sweating inside her brush camouflage. She wished she was closer—take down this officer and the two unfortunates flinching under his harsh commands and she'd almost certainly draw a couple more guards out the door, scratching their heads and squeezing their dicks, wondering what the hell was going on. With her brand-new HK417 providing kick-ass moral support, she'd wipe out most of the opposition and force an entry in just a few seconds. She pondered the odds.

The Heckler & Koch had been selected as Echelon's long arm for nonurban fieldwork just five months earlier. Bearing some similarities to the old M4 carbine on which it was based, it had been reengineered by the old German gunsmithing firm primarily for use by special forces. A proprietary short-stroke, piston-driven system kept the weapon's interior free of combustion gases, making it much more reliable than the impingement systems used in the M16 and the M4.

Dozens of other tweaks, some major and some minor, had gone into the design of the 417 to craft an exemplary killing implement. Added to which, Echelon had provided an unusually hefty flash and sound suppressor, courtesy of the agency's engineering shop in the London Cage. It fitted snuggly onto a bespoke barrel for those occasions when operators such as Caitlin Monroe needed to send a withering bullet storm downrange into the body mass of some ne'er-do-well. Discreetly, in a quiet, voiceless reproach.

But her observation post now was too far removed for such precipitate action. She watched, chagrined, as all three men returned to the dark, unknown interior of Facility 183.

Two hours later, with the noonday sun burning through the canopy, she lay on her stomach, concealed by a thicket of brightly colored foliage, all waxy green leaves and startling pink and red flowers that formed giant cups in which rainwater collected so deeply that dozens of tiny frogs had colonized the self-contained ecosphere. The former police station was directly across the road from her new position.

The screaming had stopped abruptly an hour earlier, giving her a few moments of concern that these clowns had killed Lupérico, if indeed that was who the torture victim was, before she could "debrief" him herself. But nothing else indicated anything untoward. No bodies appeared, being manhandled by the disheveled guards, and the few glimpses of movement she had inside the front windows spoke of no urgency. Quite the opposite. The militia troops moved about with languorous sloth. She saw cigarettes glowing and once or twice heard raucous laughter. She wondered when they might eat lunch and whether any of them would sneak away into a quiet corner afterward for a siesta. That fucking ramrod-straight *funcionario* didn't look the type for napping on *el presidente*'s dollar, but the hapless slobs under his jackboot surely did.

At half past twelve, smoke drifted up from a small chimney pipe she'd previously observed at the rear of the facility. She couldn't see it now, lying in this shallow, overgrown depression by the side of the road, but she knew there was only one such stovepipe, protruding from the roof of a small annex at the administrative end of the building, well away from the cells. It carried scents of wood smoke and meat. Caitlin had last had a hot meal nearly twenty-four hours earlier, and her mouth watered at the rich smells. She spit quietly into the brush mulch on which she lay.

She had just resolved to give the guards another hour, when the portico's heavy wooden door creaked open and two of them emerged, smoking and laughing. She recognized both characters from earlier on: the latte sippers. The pair walked around to the motor pool and took one of the muddy pickups parked there before driving away to the south. They certainly didn't look like men with an important mission hanging over them. More like errand boys sent out to fetch tobacco and *cerveza*.

The front door remained open. Caitlin withdrew into the forest, fading back into the gloom until she was sure she could move without being seen. She then shifted position to the south before creeping forward again. With a better view through the open door, she could make out more details.

The reception area did indeed appear to give onto an open-plan office, leading back to the annex where she had noted the chimney, a kitchen of sorts. With the two men just gone, she was able to mark three other militiamen: two of the guards and what looked like an older, fatter man in an officer's uniform, though he was not nearly as well turned out as his deputy. Caitlin was sure now that the more impressive-looking *funcionario* was actually Facility 183's second in command. Only a boss hog could get away with such a slovenly 'tude around a martinet like that.

After a few minutes she withdrew into the brush again, the germ of a plan having formed as she observed them. She would need luck. If the coffee-and-cigarillo twins had driven away at the end of their shift or gone off to fetch more personnel, it wouldn't work. Not if they returned in a number of vehicles. If, however, they'd simply fucked off to the small village about twelve miles down the road for more supplies, as the Echelon agent suspected, she had a good chance.

Caitlin took a moment to study the digital map in the Navman unit on her forearm. The road curved gently for a mile before climbing into a series of switchbacks as it approached the small hilltop community. There wasn't much to the place: a cluster of mud-brick huts, a cantina, a chapel, a couple of stands where the local farmers sold produce in the mornings. Her briefing set hadn't included any more data. The village was tiny and poor, but this undoubtedly had protected it as *el colapso* took down one South American government after another. It was so small and isolated, the murderous anarchy unleashed in the wake of the Disappearance had largely passed it by. The daily lives of the inhabitants there were probably little different as the loyal subjects of Roberto Morales, *el presidente por vida,* from what they'd been as loyal subjects of the long line of Latin brutocrats stretching back centuries before him.

The electronic map, together with some quick and dirty math, indicated she had about half an hour to get into position at the base of the climb to catch the two guards on their return journey. Caitlin could run the mile there in much less than that if she took the road, but that would be ill advised. She could be seen anywhere along that long, gentle curve. There was nothing for it but to cut a path as fast as she could through the thinner scrub at the road's edge.

She made slow but steady progress, sometimes being able to dash forward through shaded patches of trees and brush. Only once did a vehicle pass by—an old Chevy with what looked like close to a thousand goats crammed in the back. It didn't slow down.

Caitlin made it to her ambush point with a notional five minutes to spare. The terrain rose steeply from the river basin there, climbing nearly three hundred yards up to the plateau where the village lay. She made a brief study of the area before deciding to lay up inside a curving U shape formed by the thick root system of an ancient hardwood tree. It gave her a clear line of fire into the second-to-last switchback before the road leveled out. The ground fell away steeply into tangles of liana on the open side, and a small creek gave her an escape route if needed.

She prepared her main weapon, the HK417, before pulling out the hand-tooled flash suppressor from her pack. She screwed the black foot-long tube tightly into place on the barrel. The suppressor wouldn't completely eliminate the sound of gunfire, but it would muffle things considerably. The forest would do the rest. She checked her mags, lined up a spare, and pulled the charging handle, racking a round into the chamber.

She then settled her cheek against the cool plastic stock of the German-made assault rifle. With the grip seated firmly in the palm of her hand, she thumbed the selector switch from safe to auto. She waited over iron sights. No need for fancy optics this time.

Birdsong, the buzz of insects, the gurgling of the stream behind her, all seemed to grow louder as she ignored the torrid humidity. Caitlin listened for the sound of an approaching engine. She thought she heard one, but the droning, somewhere far off in the distance, faded away. Her webbing and equipment weighed her down and chafed wherever they rubbed against her skin. Sweat trickled down her legs inside the trousers she had bloused into her boots to prevent stingers from crawling inside. She took a sip from the camelback water bladder just as the unmistakable sound of a vehicle grinding through its gears reached her. Whoever was coming was having trouble negotiating the steep descent.

Good. She hoped they'd be traveling with care, moving slowly and attending to the road.

She wiped a slick of perspiration from her face, not wanting to be inconvenienced by the sting of sweat in her eyes at the wrong moment.

The engine strained and misfired just once as the truck—it sounded like a truck—negotiated the twisting road above. All the while, she didn't flinch or take her focus off the hairpin bend she had chosen. About a minute later the old pickup inched its way around the turn. Caitlin took a half-second sight picture of the driver and passenger, laying the gun's front sight post on the driver first. Having confirmed them as her guys, she settled into a slightly more comfortable shooting stance, bending her knees fractionally, breathing out, bracing her core muscles to accept the recoil.

As the truck turned toward her, giving the assassin a clear view of the cabin, she squeezed the trigger once, twice, a third time. One, two, three bursts downrange.

The driver slumped forward. His passenger reached for the wheel as Caitlin shifted just a notch, laying the sights on his right temple.

Repeat. One, two, three more bursts of automatic fire.

Nine rounds from the twenty-round mag. A mix of armor-piercing and hollow-point and a tracer for every third shot. The bullets exited the small black hole in the business end of the suppressor in a fraction under one second, with a rapid thrumming noise. Their impact was less than discreet, shattering the windscreen of the aged Ford and tearing into the occupants like the threshing claws of a terrible unseen carnivore. The men were dead before the vehicle veered slowly off the road and crashed down the hillside into the safety net of a dense strand of thorny vines. The engine coughed and stalled.

Caitlin swapped her magazine for a new clip. This time it was a fifty-round drum mag in the same arrangement she had just used. Before turning back toward the old police station, she shouldered the 417, unholstered her pistol, and half slid, half jumped down the wide path cut through the brush by the uncontrolled passage of the vehicle. She knew both men had taken at least one round to the head, but she was nothing if not thorough.

Reaching the cabin of the trashed utility, she swung into an awkward shooter's stance on the steep incline, pointing the Kimber Custom pistol in at her targets. The windshield had deflected her rounds a bit, but no coup de grâce was necessary.

Caitlin knew of men and a few women in her profession who marked every kill with ceremony. Some were religious, others merely cruel. A couple were borderline psychotic. It wasn't a need she had ever felt.

She didn't pause to consider the life paths that had led these men to their deaths at her hand nor that they may have had full, even worthy lives outside the hours each day when they wore the uniforms in which they'd died.

She merely killed them and moved on.

5

CENTRAL SYDNEY, NEW SOUTH WALES

Jules scoped the hitter well before he made his move. She caught him watching her in the mirror behind the bar of the small neighborhood dive. At first she thought he was just an old perv, eyeballing her in her fabulous new silk shirt. She had tied her hair, recently dyed black, into a ponytail, and he wasn't the only man whose attention she'd caught. His was definitely unwanted, however.

She'd been drinking here at the Idler Bar for the past three weeks and had come to know most of the regulars, at least on a nodding basis. It was a local haunt, the clientele drawn from the warren of streets and back alleys of The Rocks, all within a five-minute walk: Australians, younger Brits, and other travelers who'd overstayed their visas after the Wave had hit in March 2003 and who'd lucked in when the government granted an amnesty a few weeks later.

And there were Americans, of course. Everywhere she went here, always Americans. Enough of them that Sydney was now the third largest American city in the world. Bigger even than Darwin. That was why her Romanian hit man stood out. She recognized the fierce guttural accent when he demanded that the waitress bring him a glass of Palinca, cursing the poor girl when she didn't have a clue what he was talking about.

Displaced Europeans were not uncommon in Sydney, but they tended to come from the older EU countries, bearing professional qualifications and bags of money. She knew of a small Russian enclave out at Bondi Beach—an unusual mix of businessmen, academic refugees, and gangsters—but apart from them and the city's original, thoroughly assimilated postwar Slavic migrants, refugees from Eastern Europe were thin on the ground. Especially those from collapsing shitholes like Romania. The Australian government may have thrown open the floodgates to certain types of migrants and refugees after the Disappearance, but to others the way to the great southern sanctuary was irrevocably closed. The best illegals could hope for if they were caught was a couple of years on a government prison farm before being deported.

Not her problem. As a subject of Her Majesty, Lady Julianne Balwyn was free to come and go as she pleased from the antipodes, and for the moment it pleased her to stay exactly where she was, in a quiet bar where nobody knew her real name. The Idler was a small, cozy, almost domestic space; it looked very much as though somebody had thrown open the downstairs rooms of her home to passing drinkers. Because she had. The proprietors had converted the bottom floor of what had been a private residence into a bar, completing the circle of life for this 160-year-old building, which had been built as a pub in the former slum district back when some of the older residents could still boast of having arrived in the colony in the holds of convict transports.

Jules liked the Idler because it felt like some of the old drinking holes she remembered from her college days, right down to the Home County accents. Fitting in here was not a problem for her. The Romanian, by contrast, stood out like tits on a bull. A cheap leatherette jacket two sizes too big and way too heavy for the humid summer evening, a bright Hawaiian shirt, shiny pants, and slip-on shoes—the only reason he got past the bouncers was that the Idler didn't have any. It was a cool place that relied on its patrons' good manners.

The Romanian caught her eye when she was halfway through her second gin and tonic and deep in conversation with a young American couple who'd lit out of Acapulco a day before she had. She'd actually been enjoying herself here. Relaxing for the first time in weeks. Spending some of her stash. The Americans, Donna and Jeff, were on their second bottle of Chardonnay, and Jules had fallen so easily into chatting with them that she'd finished her first drink before she picked up on the warm but unmistakably sexual vibe coming off the woman. Jules smiled, a little flattered that they were trying to pick her up and . . . Well, what the hell. It'd been a long time. The hot night, some very chilled tunes, the mellow warmth of candlelight flickering on the bare sandstone walls of the bar . . . it all put her in a generous, open frame of mind.

That is, until she caught a glimpse of the man in the heavy imitation-leather jacket regarding her with the cold, flat stare of a snake sizing up a newly hatched chick. His eyes flicked away as soon as she made him. He shifted in his seat, pretending not to have noticed her. The nasty, ill-fitting jacket grabbed under his armpit, outlining something there. A gun, she was certain.

A chain-mail fist clenched just under her heart, and all the warm, mellow feeling she had been enjoying sluiced out of her in an icy rush.

"Are you all right?" Donna asked, reaching over and lightly running her fingertips down Jules's forearm. A few minutes earlier it might have elicited a tingle of sexual response. Now she felt nothing.

"Sorry. I have to go."

"Hey," said Donna's boyfriend, "is everything okay? Did we . . . ?"

The Englishwoman regarded him kindly but with detachment. She could have told them that there was a man in the bar who might have been paid to kill her. But Jeff probably would get himself hurt or worse by confronting the guy. And if she left with them now, they'd either get in the way of what she had to do or get themselves killed. There was nothing for it. She had to shut them down.

"Sorry," she repeated. "Gotta go."

Julianne pushed away the unfinished drink, picked up her bag, and left without another word. Estimating there might only be a few moments before the Romanian followed her—and assuming she wasn't being a paranoid head case, of course—she hurried away from the small bespoke tavern.

The streets were still busy. The Rocks, which had once been one of the most densely populated slums in Sydney, was crowded again, with long terraces of old stone houses playing host to the latest wave of migrants who were adding to the city's human alloy. It was common to find a dozen or more of them bedding down under one roof, hot bunking in many cases—one mattress shared between somebody working the night shift and another who worked days. Sometimes even couples or whole families took turns like that. It was a curious ghetto, however, given the money the displaced had brought with them. Poor refugees could not afford to stay in the city. Most lived in the outer suburbs, where jobs could be found at the industrial parks, or on the work farms beyond the mountains. Closer to the harbor, life was still pressured but more pleasant, as it always had been.

Small knots of drinkers stood about on the footpath in front of microbars like the Idler. Others weaved along the pavement, singing and laughing as they moved between venues. She could hear the distant sibilant roar of the crowd down at the nearby Circular Quay, but instead of heading toward it, Julianne set her course for the shadowed, less populated streets on the far side of the rocky headland. There were many paths down to the wharf district, but Ferry Lane, a paper cut through the massive sandstone ridge overlooking Walsh Bay, was the one she needed.

On her first night in Sydney, an old sea dog propping up the bar at the Hero of Waterloo had told her that Ferry Lane was the site of a bubonic plague outbreak back in 1901. He had said the first victim had been a drinker at the Hero and was one of the few who contracted the disease and survived. "Thanks to his medicine," the old coot had added with a grin, hoisting up a pint of dark bitter. Not really caring whether the story was true or just a tale to entertain a pretty girl, Jules had wandered down there the next day and noted that the cottages lining the ancient passage were all empty, undergoing renovation by the department of housing. It was one of the few streets in the center of Sydney that wasn't seething with life. That made it perfect for her purposes now.

The revelry faded quickly as she hurried on. From the unseen docks up ahead, the sound of shipping containers impacting on steel decks boomed up through the winding, narrow streetscape. She was pretty sure she had a follower.

At the next turn Jules increased her pace, giving her some distance but, as she'd intended, not enough to shake the tail. Another turn, a burst of speed, a few more meters between them, and she was into Ferry Lane, thankful she had worn her Doc Martens instead of the Fendi FMBs she'd considered earlier. The heels would have been murder on the cobblestone surface. Instead, sure of her footing, she raced now, counting her steps before taking cover behind a huge metal crate full of trash from the building site. From her shoulder bag she retrieved an M26 mil-grade taser and crouched down out of sight, gathering a handful of pebbles while she waited.

He was not long in coming. She heard his footsteps crunching toward her as he hurried to catch up, undoubtedly surprised that she'd slipped ahead of him. He faltered momentarily at the alley's entrance before continuing.

Julianne counted his footsteps, compensating for the longer strides she had taken when running. When she judged him to be in range, she tossed the pebbles off to her left, where they plinked against a broken window. Not waiting to see if the distraction had worked, she committed herself to action: standing, leveling the weapon, and triggering it as soon as she recognized the squat outline of the man in the leather jacket.

For a half second she panicked, worried that his poxy pretend-leather coat might shed the prongs. But she needn't have been concerned. The charge from the M26 could arc through two inches of clothing, and anyway, he was reaching for the pistol in his shoulder holster, exposing most of his center mass. The darts struck him in the chest and channeled a solid hit of high-voltage ass kicking directly into his body.

The effect was . . . well, electric.

The Romanian grunted and dropped to the road surface, falling heavily onto broken bricks and rusted steel pickets. Jules had paid nearly five hundred bucks to have the M26 modified, removing the five-second limit on the charge. She let him have a good long taste of the juice until she was certain she'd crippled him, at least temporarily. His gun had clattered to the ground and lay somewhere underneath him, a small problem she solved by hitting him again with brief bursts from the taser interspersed with solid kicks into the back of his head. It was enough, after a few seconds, to move his body clear of the weapon. Jules stunned him once more as she darted in to retrieve it.

Holding the gun on her would-be assailant, the Englishwoman suffered just a second's doubt. What if she had just zapped a completely innocent man?

"Bullshit," she muttered, hefting the pistol for reassurance. "Who sent you?"

Another taste of the taser, a quick one.

"Was it Cesky? Did Henry Cesky send you?"

Zap.

The only answer she received was more grunting and panting as the voltage slammed into him. She took a length of heavy steel rebar from the skip, checked up and down the empty alley, and broke his kneecap with one vicious swing. He would have screamed if she had not cut him off with another burst of crippling taser fire.

"Did someone send you after me?"

She backed away a few feet, still holding both weapons. The man had soiled himself. The stench was foul. His whole body was shuddering involuntarily. As he recovered slowly and marginally, he began to moan.

"I'm really not interested in your sob stories," Julianne said. "Unless you want me to break your other knee and hit you in the back of the neck, you need to give up the information now. Were you being paid to get me?"

"Yes." His voice was so weak and broken, she almost missed the answer.

"What's that? Yes? Did you say yes? So who sent you?"

She let him have another two seconds of voltage.

"My boss, my boss," he replied, sounding as though he was pleading. "My boss take contract. I do job."

A surge of anger boiled up inside Julianne, and she smashed the bar down on the middle of his thigh. He screamed until she cut him off with the 26.

"And who do you work for, eh? Who sent you out to ruin a perfectly good evening? I could've had fun tonight. I could've got *laid*. Instead I'm stuck here having a shitty time with you and . . . and . . . Oh, fuck, you've got blood all over my new shirt!"

Jules could no longer control herself. She was so sick of running and hiding and running again. It was all she had done since escaping from New York with the Rhino. A red mist of rage clouded her vision as she let loose with both the taser and the rebar. She could feel the jolt of the power surge every time she hit him, but she couldn't stop. Her fury, her fear, her sick satisfaction at finally being able to lash out when previously she had felt only impotence and frustration—they all combined to doom this Romanian who had been sent after her.

When she was done, when she finally had regained some control over herself, he was long dead. A ship's horn wailed nearby as she collapsed against the edge of the crate, dropping the iron bar to the road. It was filthy with matted hair, bone fragments, and clumps of gray matter. Julianne vomited.

She heard voices close by and almost fled, but her father's memory, speaking calmly to her across the years, stayed her reaction. "Better to be found at the scene than fleeing it," the late Lord Balwyn always said. "One always looks so bloody guilty when fleeing."

She gulped in a couple of long, halting breaths, gathered her disordered wits, and checked her surroundings again. Nobody. Not even voices or footfalls this time.

The body was heavy, a dead weight, but Julianne was strong from years of shipboard life and months on the run with Rhino across the American frontier. She detached the taser darts from the corpse and dragged it over to a builder's garbage crate that was only half full.

"Bugger me," she grunted, heaving him over the side of the industrial bin. "Weighed down by your sins, I'll bet."

Her would-be killer thumped down on top of a mound of plastic wrapping and cardboard. She took a few moments to cover him with rubbish she gathered from another bin, and thought about washing away the blood. But what was the point? In her experience the streets around here were caked with blood and vomit every morning. She did take the iron bar and the taser with her, however. She would have to dispose of them properly.

It would have been foolish to walk back up the hill toward the pub. If she ran into Donna and Jeff, there would be no way to explain what had happened. And even if she didn't, she looked a frightful mess, covered in hot blood and brain flecks. Best she keep heading down to the docklands, where the bottom-feeding whores plied their trade. There at least she could toss the rebar into the harbor.

She was going to have to get out of Sydney, though. The cops were hardly likely to break a sweat over a dead Romanian hit man, but they weren't the problem. Cesky was. He had found her again.

Julianne started walking. She didn't spend much time wondering where she might go next, because there was only one choice, really, the only place in this country she had any real friends.

6

DEARBORN HOUSE, SEATTLE, WASHINGTON

They took a break late in the morning. The discussion about what to do with the prisoners in the East continued for at least an hour after Kip had made it clear he wanted to take Sarah Humboldt's settlement plan to the cabinet. Having been told it was his responsibility to make sure any plan was workable and salable, Jed Culver applied himself in spite of his misgivings. He still thought the best solution was to pack them on a raft made out of beer barrels and wave them off at the docks during hurricane season. But he understood the president's reasoning and was grateful that he himself would have some control over the outcome. It might even be possible, according to Ritchie, to turn some of the fighters completely around and send them back against . . .

Against whom?

Bilal Baumer's movement seemed to have topped out with him. As best they could tell, he had been killed in Manhattan. It was unfortunate they hadn't been able to lay hands on a body or even a scrap of

DNA. This wasn't going to turn out like bin Laden, with a couple of goat farmers wandering into town with his severed head on a stick and their hands held out for the reward money. But there was very good intelligence placing Baumer in the ruins of Rockefeller Center, surrounded by U.S. ground forces, an hour before 2nd Bomb Wing's B-52s had atomized the complex and everybody in it. As far as anyone knew, none of the leadership cadre had survived. The U.S. Army had captured only small-unit commanders away from the site of Baumer's last stand, all of them now held out at the Fort Leavenworth federal penitentiary north of Kansas City. None of those bastards knew of any higher authority than their so-called Emir. The pirate bands that had been captured, especially the Serbs and Russians, who had surrendered en masse once they'd seen the hammer come down on Baumer, were likewise convinced that he was the mastermind. And deader than disco.

In the darkest corners of his heart, Jed remained unconvinced, and he knew that Kipper, even though he wanted to put the episode behind them, couldn't do so until he was certain the men responsible for New York had all been captured or killed. The president might ignore the pawns, but he wanted to know for sure the king had been taken from the board.

"Sorry about the ambush."

James Ritchie had caught him unaware, woolgathering by a window looking out past the Christmas tinsel and over the grounds of Dearborn House. A good couple of inches of snow had fallen, blanketing the ground and capping the hedges and garden furniture. Culver abandoned his thoughts to the cold.

"You didn't need to sandbag me like that," he said, cutting to the point. "I pushed the president pretty hard to get you in here. I was impressed with the way you held it all together out in Hawaii. If you thought Sarah's plan was a good one, you could've just told me. I might not have agreed, but I would have taken your opinion seriously."

Ritchie had the good grace to look embarrassed.. "Yes, I can see it was a mistake now. But Ms. Humboldt sought me out in confidence and asked if I would keep her proposal to myself. It didn't seem an unreasonable request. I've spent my life inside a chain of command that operates on a need-to-know basis. Needless to say, I'm still finding my feet here."

He moved his shoulders around inside his off-the-rack navy blue suit. It was obvious to Jed that the national security adviser needed a tailor who could do more than sew patches onto jackets.

"To be frank," Ritchie continued, "I miss the certainties of wearing a uniform."

Just then, Kipper's secretary waved to them from the far end of the hallway, calling them back to the meeting. Culver clapped a hand on the admiral's shoulder, taking note of the cheap fabric. He decided not to ruin the peace gesture by saying as much. Instead, he made a mental note to see about getting this guy to a tailor.

"If keeping someone's secret is the worst thing you do in politics, you can consider yourself lucky, Admiral."

"Politics?" Ritchie looked surprised. "I don't think of this as politics, Jed. More like public service."

"That's the spirit," Culver said, brightening considerably. "Dissembling with the best of us."

They walked down the hallway, observed by portraits of presidents past, and reentered Kip's office via the anteroom, the door being held open for them by a Secret Service officer. The current U.S. president was finishing off a sandwich, gazing out the window at the snowfall. He waved them back to their seats as he returned to his own place behind the generously proportioned desk that dominated one side of the room.

"Now, Paul's going to take us through the budgetary position, using small words and big numbers so that I can understand," he said with a warning tone that wasn't to be taken entirely as a joke. Secretary McAuley, who seemed not to have moved at all during the break, preferring to remain in his chair reviewing his papers, thanked the president.

"Did you read that book I gave you on the Federalist Era, Mr. President?" Culver asked. "I'm not joking—you'll find this treasury stuff a whole lot easier to digest if you have a sense of history."

Kip looked pained. "I'm trying, Jed. I'm trying. I'm more of a biography man."

"I gave you a copy of Miller's biography of Alexander Hamilton as well," the chief of staff pointed out.

Kipper rubbed his head at that. "Well, the Federalist book is easier, but not by much. Paul, break it down for us laymen, if you would."

"Certainly, Mr. President. The situation remains dire," he began, "although there are some positives. The call for supplementary spending for the armed forces has abated considerably as the last federal units rotate out of New York. Governor Schimmel's state militia have resumed control of Manhattan and the surrounding boroughs, augmented by private security forces funded from salvage concessions in the interior rather than directly out of consolidated revenue."

"If I may, Mr. Secretary?" Ritchie raised his hand. "Some of those savings should come by leaving heavy equipment stored in New York for future use either by the state or by federal authorities in the future. Am I correct?"

"That is correct," McAuley replied, nodding his head. "We only have to bear the cost of transporting troops who are still on active duty or wish to return to their original duty stations for discharge. Some troops will be discharged directly into New York's state militias or into the civilian workforce, which will serve to reduce expenditures even further."

"So we're not doing too badly, then," Culver interjected. "If there's a safe place on the eastern seaboard today, it has to be New York. Next to KC and the Hood, it's the most heavily armed and populated outpost in CONUS." He felt pretty good about that. Maybe in another year the joint naval base of Norfolk would join that list if the Brits got a move on.

"This is significant," Paul McAuley agreed. "Even after the end of major combat in the city, we were still hemorrhaging funds there. That difficult period is now behind us."

The secretary of the treasury shifted in his seat, crossing his legs as though settling in for the long haul. Jed decided to avail himself of the sandwich plate. In many respects, McAuley was potentially the most powerful man in the room, relegating Chief of Staff Culver to second place. Fortunately, although McAuley had Alexander Hamilton's grasp of economics combined with a modern-day understanding of the imploded global economy, the egomania wasn't included in the package, for which Culver was eternally grateful.

"The line of credit negotiated with our Vancouver Alliance partners was activated at midnight last Friday," the treasury chief continued, "guaranteeing our recurrent funding needs for the next twelve months. Once we agreed to pay our surviving creditors at face value with regular interest payments, our ability to regain credit was somewhat restored."

"So let me get this straight, Paul . . ." It was Kipper now who held his hand up. "We're just going to make the minimum payment. We're not going to try to pay all of the debt off?"

"We couldn't if we wanted to, sir. Everyone knows that. It was not possible to pay off our debt prior to the Wave, either. However, if we maintain our interest payments to the top six surviving creditors—aside from China, which is no longer a unitary state creditor—then we can restore a minimum level of faith, enough to grant us credit for funds to sustain us through the short term."

"I'll never quite get over this notion that debt can be a good thing," Kip said sighing. "You pay your bills; that's what I was taught."

Culver could not resist. "Spoken like a true Republican, Mr. President."

Kipper glowered at him.

The approval of the Vancouver treaty nations wasn't news to anybody in the room, but Jed was aware of a palpable sense of relief. So wretched had the government's finances become at one point shortly after the Battle of New York that the treasury had been forced to issue IOUs to employees and creditors. There naturally had been rampant speculation on those IOUs. Many people had sold theirs off in exchange for more viable currency or food and resources. Some hoped to keep the value of the IOUs down, whereas others hoped for a profit if and when the government decided to honor those promissory notes at face value.

The chief of staff still woke up some nights with a pain in his chest, worrying about the speculative bubble. Marilyn had forced him to see a doctor in the end, so frequent had those episodes become. Apparently the federal budget deficit had been giving him killer indigestion. After the amount of vomiting he did from the acid reflux, Jed marveled at the need to let out his trousers farther and farther.

"Negotiations to roll over the line of credit at the end of its period will commence in Auckland next week," McAuley was saying. "Both the vice president and I will be in attendance." He glanced up at Kipper, as if confirming his permission to attend. Kip nodded. "Of course, our capacity to repay these loans by drawing on liquid assets is severely limited. We have been able to service some of the loans through barter, exchanging military surplus to our top six lenders. However, their capacity and need for such surplus is reaching an end, as is our ability to provide anything more they could want or feasibly integrate into their own militaries."

"I take it no one wants to buy another carrier?" Culver asked.

"The Brits have the one Nimitz-class they want," Ritchie noted. "Frankly, it's the only one they can afford."

"Continue, Paul," the president said, dragging them back on topic.

"I will cover the accounts receivable first. We should start to see royalty flows from the mining leases taken up by BHP Billiton, West Rand, and JCI within a six- to eight-month window, but it will still be three to four years before those companies ramp up to full production."

Jed nodded. The United States, contrary to popular belief, still possessed vast mineral resources, especially in the form of coal. The mining corporations were required by law to hire at least 40 percent of their workforce from the local civilian population. It was dangerous, dirty work, but it paid relatively well compared with what else was available in the post-Disappearance economy.

McAuley went on. "The exchange of old U.S. bonds and currency for the new treasury bonds continues, with several major corporations and private investors buying in. They are able to exchange pre-Wave bonds for a variable face value that's tied to their interest-rate payments. Currency exchange with overseas asset holders continues at 20 percent of face value, although there is a deadline for final exchanges set for this time next year."

Jed suppressed a grin at the glaze he could see frosting over Kip's eyes. He, however, found this shit fascinating. A lot of folks were getting rich off the new bonds, deepening their credit or using the paper to levy purchases of vacant land in the Wave-affected territories. Cesky

Enterprises immediately came to mind as one of the major players in that brand of rampant land speculation. The U.S. government would accept bonds as payment at face value for land, whereas the best a bondholder could get on the open market was less than 30 percent of face value.

It was simple enough: buy the land on the cheap, dumping the bonds on someone else in the process, and hope that the value of the land would rise, generating a profit. Several other corporations, such as Boeing, Microsoft, and Starbucks, had opened land offices with a similar objective in mind. The only problem was the same one that had faced the Confederation Congress before the Constitutional Convention of 1787. Back then, they'd also tried to sell land in order to pay the bills, without much success. The territory, the much-contested Ohio River Valley, was difficult to secure against the British and the Native Americans. This instability ensured that the land, though valuable on the surface, sold for far less than it was worth until the central government gained true control over the valley.

Funny how history could loop back and bite you on the ass like that. Spheres of control were ringed by looser rings of what might be called influence. The land in those areas did yield decent gains. However, outside those areas? Selling that land was a lot like eating rat poison: it would fill your belly with blood while you slowly starved to death.

"The profits from the bond and overseas currency exchange should be enough to restore short-term faith in the solvency of the government," Paul McAuley continued. "We will still be in debt, to be certain. However, the United States of America has rarely been without a national debt."

"The history books tell me as much, Paul," Kipper said. "Still, the blue-collar engineer in me would like to make that debt a bit more manageable."

"We are fortunate in the cold fact that many who received government entitlements were . . ." McAuley struggled for a moment to find the right words.

"We get it," Culver said. "The Republicans got their wish with social security. It went away."

Behind the desk, his boss sighed. "Enough, Jed. Let him continue. Go on, Paul."

"Eliminating government agencies and departments which are not needed by our much-reduced population will allow us to write off a great deal of the interagency governmental debt. This should allow us to stop the worst of the fiscal hemorrhaging and focus on servicing the foreign debt." Secretary McAuley shook his head as he moved on to the next point. "In the meantime, we remain at an impasse with Fort Hood over the issue of state taxes levied on the oil industry down in Texas and the related issue of Governor Blackstone signing extractive leases with foreign corporations but without reference to us. Under the Federal–State Revenues Act of 2005, the Blackstone administration is supposed to remit—"

"Yeah, yeah, we know," Kipper complained. "Believe me, Paul, we know all about it. Bottom line—how much is Blackstone stealing?"

He wasn't looking at the treasury secretary as he asked the question. He was hunched over the desk, rubbing his eyeballs, as though trying to massage away a gathering headache. Or possibly a stroke.

"Twelve billion New American Dollars in the last three quarters, Mr. President."

It was Kip's turn to shake his head. "Son of a bitch. You know, we wouldn't need a line of credit, or at least not one as big as we have, if that asshole would just play by the rules we both agreed to."

Jed put aside the remains of the crab and avocado sandwich he'd been eating. In some ways, he thought, and not for the first time, their troubles were not that much different from the ones that had faced the country when Washington became president back in 1789. They had a huge debt, a wide-open frontier, and no shortage of foreign powers hoping for their failure. And they didn't lack for internal strife or factionalism, either.

Blackstone, Culver realized, was the difference. Even if George Washington were available to advise Kipper, he probably would counsel caution. It was one thing to send an army to put down an uprising of farmers during the Whiskey Rebellion of the 1790s, quite another thing entirely to send a broken military up against a well-armed, -funded, and -motivated separatist.

Secretary McAuley, reluctant as always to comment on a purely political matter, remained silent. Ritchie and Sarah Humboldt both looked to the chief of staff as though expecting him to say something.

Jed felt like rubbing his eyes, so tired and exasperated was he with the never-ending perdition of having to deal with Jackson Blackstone. Or rather, of having to deal with him while the president insisted on tying one hand behind his back. The best solution would be for Blackstone to fall out of his executive helicopter while touring the ruins of Dallas–Fort Worth, he thought. Newton could take care of the details.

He took a deep breath. They couldn't get that lucky.

"This is one of those issues we were talking about, Mr. President," he said. "One of the reasons you need to go to Texas and the very reason you cannot. There is a small dark corner of my heart wherein I believe Governor Blackstone is doing this not simply to starve us of funds and destabilize this administration but also to draw you into a political confrontation you can't hope to win. He would love to see you down there, on your knees, begging for a handout. Or even better, on your feet, demanding he hold to the letter of the agreement. It would make him look so much stronger when he says no."

Kipper lifted his head, but only enough to peer through the gate he'd made of his fingers. His eyes looked bloodshot and watery. The storm howled outside, raking at the brickwork of Dearborn House with claws of ice and snow. The makeshift jamb still held the window firmly in its frame. But Jed was certain he could feel freezing tendrils of subzero air creeping in through the less than perfect seal. He felt a sudden need to throw a few more logs into the small fireplace.

The president pulled them back on topic. "Admiral, you're new to all this. Perhaps you have a fresh perspective you could share." He said it in an uncertain voice, as though picking his way through the sentence with great care. The national security adviser frowned as if he'd been presented with a lump of questionable street meat wrapped in a soggy hot dog bun.

"The man should pay his bills," Ritchie replied flatly.

The bald statement fell into silence, punctuated a few seconds later by Kipper's bark of laughter.

"Yes, yes, he really should! But short of driving a tank into his office and demanding the money at gunpoint, I don't see it happening."

"You could always haul him off to the courts, I suppose," Ritchie suggested, causing Paul McAuley to lean forward with avid interest.

"Oh, believe me, we've thought about it," Kip said. "Even tried once or twice on some minor fed–state issues. But Jed here won't let me use the full-court press, so to speak."

The chief of staff found every eye in the room turned on him. "We'll have the same problem that Andrew Jackson's Supreme Court faced," he explained. "Yes, the courts would find in our favor. Legally our case is sound. Enforcing the decision, on the other hand, is another matter."

Culver rose from his warm chair and wandered over to the window. The world outside had turned completely white. It was difficult to pick out any details from the garden through the blizzard. A native of Louisiana, he wondered if Seattle had suffered from this sort of weather before the Wave or, more accurately, before the pollution storms that raged when the continent burned and fucked up the weather.

He turned and faced the Garage Cabinet.

"We have to stop thinking of Blackstone as a reasonable man. Outwardly he appears to be reasonable, but rest assured, he is not. He's a power-seeking loon who probably would have talked his way straight into a quiet retirement if not for the Disappearance. He will overreach himself. The trick is for us not to be caught off balance at the same time."

Jed took a wander around the Oval Office. Barbara Kipper had placed about the room framed photos and other relics from her husband's college days: pictures from mountain walks, a few knickknacks picked up while scuba diving. The Secret Service would not let him anywhere near an open body of water with scuba gear on his back. The best they'd grant him was some time in a pool ringed with agents. Kip understandably thought it wasn't worth the trouble.

"The last thing we need to do, Mr. President, is give this asshole the opportunity to say, 'I'm laughing in the face of the Supreme Court.' I can already see him hee-hawing through a performance on fucking Fox, slandering each of the justices as some pissant backwoods lawyer who tripped over his dick to fall onto the bench. Again, apologies, Sarah."

Secretary Humboldt smiled. "Quite all right, Mr. Culver."

"Fucking Fox," Kipper muttered. "Three hundred million people turned into jelly by the Wave, and Rupert Murdoch wasn't one of them. There is no God."

McAuley lifted his briefing note. "If I might, Mr. President?"

"Sure, Paul, knock yourself out."

McAuley began quoting from reams of figures contained in a table that summarized federal government income and outlays for the next six months. Culver was all too familiar with the math. Even with the reduced need for federal spending, the fact was that they weren't generating enough revenue to meet that reduced need and service the debt at the same time. The line of credit would mask the shortfall in their receipts, but although they'd be able to meet their obligations in the short term, the underlying deficit would continue to grow. A population of 20 million simply could not handle the tab left by 300 million. Land sales, speculation, trading away this for that, had only slowed the slide.

It simply wasn't sustainable. Nor was it James Kipper's fault, nor Paul McAuley's. The secretary of the Treasury was obliged to prepare the government's financials according to law. But as long as Blackstone willfully ignored the law as it required him to remit monies to Seattle, there would always be a black hole in the middle of the accounts, sucking everything into it like the fucking maelstrom in that Edgar Allan Poe story.

As McAuley droned on through his delivery, Jed turned his thoughts to the crux of the problem. He couldn't advise military force. That simply wasn't an option. Down that road was the ruin of both Seattle and Texas. But Mad Jack Blackstone had to go, one way or another.

He snuck a peek at his president. A decent man who almost certainly would demur when faced with the necessity for hard and questionable action. Culver made a note to himself that he would have to talk to Sarah Humboldt after the meeting.

7

NORTH KANSAS CITY, MISSOURI

Maive and Miguel settled into their seats on the crowded city bus. They had strolled down Armor Road, past the storefronts, some still abandoned and some recently reopened, in an effort to see if there was anything worthwhile. As they walked, they passed a single-screen movie theater showing the latest Aussie blockbuster, *On the Other Side,* starring Russell Crowe and Cate Blanchett.

Some people thought that just like in the movie, the Disappeared were still alive somewhere, perhaps in some alternative universe. Young Adam Coupland probably could have explained it, but to Miguel Pieraro it all seemed to be wishful thinking. He pushed the idea out of his mind as the bus coughed and stuttered down Swift toward the Missouri River. The warmth of the heaters allowed him to drop away from reality and into his own thoughts for a few precious moments.

Miguel still wore the jacket in which he had set out from home a lifetime ago. He could have replaced it easily enough. They had passed through a number of small towns on the way north and even skated around the edges of a couple of larger cities. At any point along the trail he could have ditched this filthy, often sodden lamb's-wool-lined coat for something new, something that didn't remind him of loss and grief. But he found it impossible to let go.

He still had the Winchester rifle with which he'd killed three of the men who had murdered his family and with which he had killed more as he rode north, taking Sofia to safety. These days, the Winchester was secured within the gun cabinet he had erected back at the apartment he shared with his daughter. Kansas City might have become a frontier settlement now, but it was not the frontier. You couldn't walk the streets here bearing arms; there were police officers to stop you if you tried. They drove cruisers, wore blue uniforms, and made every effort to act as though the Wave had never happened. If they didn't stop you, the local militia would, one way or the other.

For some months after they had arrived here, the lack of a weapon to hand had left the Mexican journeyman feeling insecure, feeling like he was unable to protect his daughter. But he had recognized this as a form of madness. She was much better off living in a place where people did not carry firearms routinely. Particularly given the number of Indians and Pakistanis working in the city, he thought. He had lost count of the number of fights he'd broken up at the railway yards, just as the Heartland resettlement authorities had long since given up trying to intermingle the two populations. The Indians tended to live down in the dilapidated buildings in the West Bottoms, spreading across the Kansas River to another part of the city. The Pakistanis ended up near the River Market, where Sofia was sulking right now.

In any case, over the weeks and months, he got used to sleeping in a bed each night, to not riding a horse every day, to not worrying about road agents, bandits, or crazed wanderers stealing into camp to slit his throat and make away with the women. He did not want to get used to the idea of being without his family, however. For some reason he felt that keeping the jacket he had worn around his home, lately in Texas and before that in Mexico, might help maintain some link with the past. For that reason, too, he repaired his boots rather than picking up a pair from an empty store. There was the picture of Mariela and the children also, which he carried with him, the one he had taken from the silver frame in the bedroom the day he'd been forced to spirit Sofia away. He felt around inside the soft woolen interior of the jacket until he found his wallet, where he knew the photo was safe. It gave him no ease, though.

The bus rolled onto Burlington Avenue and accelerated southbound past the warehouses and storefronts. A loud, angry whine filled his ears as another military transport took off from the local airport. For a time, the planes were flying nonstop, bringing new settlers and equipment into the city while flying out valuable goods needed elsewhere in the country. When he'd first arrived in KC, the jets and the rumbling of the trains had conspired to keep him awake at night. The trains still kept him up, but the planes now came every other day, always in waves, never alone.

Looking ahead, Miguel could see the ice floes on the Missouri River float beneath the Heart of America Bridge. The bus was the only vehicle not powered by muscle that was crossing at the moment. Everyone else walked, rode a bicycle, or used a draft animal of one type or another. The smell of droppings reassured him in an odd way. It was as familiar to the former vaquero as his coat.

The skyscrapers, in contrast, were not. As cities went, Kansas City did not boast a large skyline, yet perched on a high rise above the river, they still dominated the landscape for miles around. They were a mix of modern glass and steel buildings with a leavening of concrete structures that Miguel thought might have been built in the 1930s. They looked like the sort of thing one saw in old black-and-white movies. The tallest of them, a more recent glass and steel monstrosity, still featured a large gash in the side near the top third of the structure where a plane had buried itself on Wave Day.

The only one he could readily identify by name was the Federal Courthouse, a barrel-like design with a large bank of windows that faced north, toward the direction from which they had traveled. Many of the endless interviews with the federales had taken place deep within the heavy stone walls of that building. At first, Miguel had viewed it as a symbol of stability, of order and hope. Now as he looked on the sand-colored structure, the courthouse seemed to be the very embodiment of crushing futility.

He did not have long to gaze at the skyline. The bus turned off toward the River Market, passing the old warehouses, now loft apartment buildings, in one of which Sofia probably was nursing a cold rage at that very moment. The vehicle came to a stop a block or two short of the midweek market and unloaded its passengers.

As he walked beside Maive Aronson, deep crevices of worry creased his already rumpled features. He found himself thinking often of Maive lately and finding succor in those thoughts. Uncomfortable with where that might lead, he shook his head, forcing himself back to practical matters.

"Have you spoken recently to the investigators?" he asked her.

"Which ones, Miguel? There've been so many of them since we got here. They all ask the same questions over and over again. I wonder some days why they can't just compare notes."

He had no answer for that because he'd been thinking the very same thing almost from the moment they had presented themselves and their story to the first federal authorities they came across. The venue had been a humble sentry hut guarding the entrance to a militia training ground, formerly an airfield, near the ghost town of Grandview, south of Kansas City. Miguel soon lost track of the number of people he had talked to since then about the attack on his family, the actions of the road agents he had witnessed in Texas, and the trials they had borne to escape the clutches of Governor Blackstone. That was how he described it: "the clutches of Blackstone."

The agents and investigators didn't always want to hear the truths he had to tell them, but it was not his concern that the truth as he knew it was ugly and inconvenient for them. He knew that Maive was giving them the same accounts and so was Sofia. Adam had taken many dozens of photographs with which to corroborate their tales of bloody murder and perdition down in the Republic of Texas. In addition, Trudi Jessup, a government employee, one of their own people, had verified everything. Yet they still didn't seem to accept, or want to accept, the truth of what had happened. They were "isolated incidents," the investigators told him. Unfortunate events. The frontier was a dangerous place everywhere, they said.

Miguel shook his head in frustration. He wished Trudi were with them now. For a government woman, she was akin to an angel. She had been such a good friend to them, not just on the trail but after they'd finally made it to Kansas City, too.

He cast his mind back to early August, to the morning he arrived at the café in the River Market for their weekly breakfast meeting. They were falling into the routine of city life by that time. Sofia had settled uneasily into the notion of becoming a Northtown Hornet at the high school. He was working. They had the pleasure of routine, meeting Trudi and Maive every week to catch up, as the women called it. That particular day, the barista greeted Miguel with a sad look and handed him a note: Trudi was gone. He knew it before he opened the slip of paper. She had been transferred back to Seattle with immediate effect, with no time even to say her good-byes.

"Penny for your thoughts?" Maive asked, bringing him back to the cold reality of this stark winter morning.

"They are worth less than that."

"They're worth something to me," she said gently.

They reached a corner and waited as a small convoy of military trucks, gears grinding, rumbled by. The troops in the back looked wet and miserable, as though they had been out in the weather all night.

"You know," Maive said, speaking up to be heard over the engine noise, "there were times when I wanted to tear my hair out talking to those migration people. Honestly, Miguel, it was like they were investigating *you,* not the road agents. But don't worry. I told them I would go straight to the press, to the Huffington Post, if I thought for a moment they were trying to cause trouble for you or Sofia. I know that Trudi said the same thing. I think that drew them up short—the idea that they might have to account for the fact that they'd let a bunch of rapists and murderers run wild in their precious mandate. I think it might even explain why they transferred her so quickly."

They set off again as the trucks rumbled away down the street, belching dark smoke from their exhausts.

"You might be right. But thank you," Miguel said. "It must have helped. When we first arrived, I thought they might send us back to Mexico. Or what is left of her."

The chill seeped in through his clothes as they walked. He thrust his hands deep into his pockets, but it did not warm them much. Icy gusts of wind picked up wet leaf litter that slapped against his legs, sticking to his jeans and boots. He took in the trees that lined the streets. As in many other places, nature had surged into the void left by the disappearance of humanity. He marveled at the vibrant blue-green specks of moss that grew on the bark.

As they drew closer to the markets, there were more people in the streets, often carrying bags or backpacks and sometimes pushing wheeled trolleys, all obviously intending to load up with groceries for a few days or more. There were very few cars, however. Vehicles were readily available and, with the right sort of effort, could be made to run again. But even a healthy car would never get far without gasoline, which only the government seemed to have enough of these days. Although many businesses received a weekly ration, it was never really enough.

No, for people like Miguel and Maive, ordinary people, it was the bus, walking, or horseback. He and Sofia still had the horses on which they'd fled the homestead. But most days his mount, Flossie, grazed in a field across the road from the apartment the government had given them. For the last few weeks, the horses had been stabled because of the poor weather.

He could smell the markets now. Not just livestock but the tang of fresh herbs and greens, which were expensive at this time of year because they'd come out of local greenhouses. One trailer by the entrance offered halal meat roasted on spits for the Pakistanis and anyone else who was interested. The salty-sweet tang of kettle corn churned in the cold air with roasting nuts, coffee, and mulled wine. As always, a small crowd had gathered around the entrance to the River Market. Another makeshift trailer was set up there with two giant steel pots steaming and slowly bubbling away, tended by a Canadian family, nomad Québécois whose mulled wine was a favorite with the locals.

"I wonder if I might tempt you with just one cup this week," Miguel suggested, his eyes twinkling with mischief. They both knew the answer already.

"It doesn't matter that the alcohol has been cooked off, Miguel. I still cannot drink it. It's against the rules."

"So is drinking coffee, according to that crazy man this morning."

"That's a different rule," said Maive. "A silly one, best ignored."

Still, they waited in line while Miguel bought a paper cup full of hot spiced wine for himself. He wasn't entirely sure where the wine for the pots came from. Perhaps they made their own locally. Or maybe it was salvage—always salvage in this country. The gringos were living off their own dead. Looking around in the chill air, he couldn't imagine that the area was good for grapes, though. Trudi Jessup probably could have explained it. She had led him into wine drinking on the journey up from Texas, although he imagined she would be horrified to find him drinking something like this. Trudi took her wine, as well as her food, very seriously.

"After this we can see about a cup of hot cocoa, perhaps."

She smiled. "Yes, why not?"

The actual marketplace was a series of outer brick buildings formed into a loose square. In the middle of that square stood three long shelters fitted with garage doors that were kept shut in the winter months. Merchants willing to pay a little extra for heated stall space were set up within the shelters, but the frugal or the unlucky toughed it out in the elements.

Miguel found it to be just a little warmer inside the gates than wandering the streets outside. The scent of barbecue in the air warmed him up a notch more as well. Winslow's Barbecue was at one end of the square, serving meat rubbed with a curry-inspired spice that Miguel had come to like. It was hotter than the usual American fare. Under the awning of the barbecue joint sat a jazz band playing a tune he did not recognize.

"Louis Armstrong," Maive noted.

"I'm afraid I wouldn't know," the Mexican admitted. However, as he listened to more of it, he thought it might grow on him.

They walked up a gentle slope toward a line of buildings strung out along the western end of the market. Maive seemed to know where she was going. Miguel followed her lead, taking in the sights. It still struck him as odd after all this time to see so many different types of people in one place, some of whom were darker-skinned than he was. One group was missing or at least harder to spot.

There were not many Latinos like himself at the River Market. Recent woes with the South American Federation had fueled a latent prejudice against his kind that seemed to infect those *yanquis* who had survived the Disappearance.

Maive approached a Chinese woman of indeterminate age and began to haggle over the price of some vegetables. Looking around, Miguel had to admit that he regretted having had to ground Sofia. She loved coming out to the River Market, shopping for groceries and planning their meals for the next couple of days. More often than not, she'd run into somebody she knew, one of her friends from school or someone from the local militia. She had her own money, just a little bit from a part-time job at the hospital, where she helped look after many of the soldiers who had returned from New York so terribly wounded. Miguel thought it good for her to be able to experience a place like this—somewhere with so much life and color, where people were happy—after she spent so long in school or studying at home or working in the rather grim environment of the hospital. Not for the first time, he found himself confused by the way parenthood forced him to do things he really did not want to do.

The haggling concluded, and Miguel drew his head back from the clouds.

"Do you think I could borrow your strong arms, *señor*?" Maive asked him. She was holding up two bags: Idaho and sweet potatoes. "I thought I would cook up dinner for all of us tomorrow evening. I'm sure if you read the fine print, you'll find Sofia is allowed to come around for a meal as long as she remains firmly under your thumb."

It was almost as if she had read his thoughts, or maybe just his feelings, and knew exactly what to say.

"I suppose having dinner with two old people will be sufficient punishment for a teenage girl," he mused. "Especially if we sit around talking about how things used to be. Before the Wave."

"Totes," Maive said with a grin. "That's what all the cool kids say, by the way. Totes. So I say it, too, just to bug the hell out of them."

"You would make an excellent parent," he replied, taking the thick paper bags of potatoes from her before quickly regretting having said it.

He knew the Aronsons had never had children, but he was not sure why. In his village, a woman like Maive, strong and winsome, would be married off and surrounded by a brood of *niños* in her early twenties. He did not know her exact age. It seemed impolite to ask, and many people had aged an extra decade in just a few years since the Disappearance. But he didn't think she could be much older than forty, maybe three or four years older than Mariela would have been by now. His wife had suffered greatly during childbirth. Manuel's arrival had nearly killed her. It was possible, he supposed, that Maive Aronson was afflicted with a problem not unlike that of his poor wife, or worse, and because of that never had been blessed with children.

All those thoughts raced through his mind in half a second after he had ventured his careless remark about her potential parenting skills. But whereas he once might have blurted out an apology—and then stumbled over an apology for making the apology—a few months in the company of the manbivalent Ms. Jessup had taught him that American womenfolk could be strangely inured to his oafishness. Trudi had even seemed to find it amusing, and much to his relief, Maive Aronson appeared to take no offense at his suggestion that she might have walked well down the path of motherhood.

"I thought a joint of beef might be good," she said, apparently not even noticing his remark. "A rib roast, slow cooked, with all of the trimmings. I could probably live off the leftovers for three or four days. Would mean I didn't have to cook when I got home in the evenings."

He knew she often worked late at Northtown Community College, where she taught English to the migrant workers and, sadly, to native speakers who needed improvement. It would be a temptation for somebody living on her own to eat most of her meals out of a can. He suspected that was exactly what he would do if it were not for Sofia.

"Then because it would help you, we shall have this meal," Miguel said, with mock generosity. "Sofia should be free from her shift at the hospital in time for dinner."

Maive nodded. "How does she like it there?"

He shrugged in reply. "She wanted to join the local militia, but I said no. Not until she finished school. I'm hoping by then she'll lose interest."

"Miguel . . ." Maive sighed. "I hope you're right about that. She's seen enough fighting for one lifetime, I think."

Over the next half hour, they went about gathering the rest of the ingredients as well as two bags of groceries for the Pieraro household. Once or twice Miguel lost sight of Maive in the heavy crowds of shoppers and was able to find her only by scanning the sea of heads on tiptoe. The light, intermittent falls of sleet had thickened into snow flurries by the time they exited past the Québécois clan, who were still tending their mulled wine. The line in front of their trailer seemed to be twice as long now.

Miguel's appreciation of the mundane beauty of the scene was broken by a quartet of local militiamen milling through the crowd with rifles on their shoulders. He did not enjoy the idea of his precious, beautiful daughter one day joining their ranks.

Miguel carried most of the load: a large box filled with the fruit and vegetables, along with a couple of string bags swinging from his forearms that were stuffed with rolls, cheese, and a few jars of preserves. The weather closing in could not depress his mood, which had lightened considerably after the unpleasantness earlier in the morning outside Maive's home. She, too, walked with a lighter step, having thrown off her own lowness of spirit. They briefly discussed catching the bus back lest they be caught out in worsening weather, but the next one was not due for an hour and both were enjoying their walk. The simple experience of plunging themselves into a happy crowd of people at the markets, of gathering the elements of a fine meal to be enjoyed the next day, and also of allowing themselves to enjoy each other's company had greatly improved their humor.

Miguel did his best to amuse her with a few carefully chosen stories about his voyage on the big yacht belonging to the famous and Disappeared golfer Mr. Greg Norman. The former vaquero very carefully avoided making mention of his family, and Maive very carefully avoided asking him about any of them. But he knew she had always been greatly amused at tales of his friend the Rhinoceros and poor Miss Fifi, who had always been very kind—for somebody who seemed happier the larger the gun she was carrying. And, of course, of Miss Jules, who had not really wanted to take any of them on the boat but who had relented because, in Miguel's opinion, she was a good person despite all her protests to the contrary.

"I have come across people like her," Maive said as they left behind the hubbub of the market crowds. She blew snowflakes from the tip of her nose as they walked along. "Cooper used to know a few people like that—I suppose I should add, through his academic work studying gangs. They weren't very common, but every now and then he would meet somebody he said was doomed to do the right thing for all the wrong reasons."

Stepping carefully down off the footpath into a leaf-choked gutter, having to peer around the edge of the large cardboard box full of groceries while doing so, Miguel thought he understood what she was saying. Miss Julianne was indeed someone who had ended up helping others while maintaining that she was really only looking after herself.

"Yes, but sadly, it is more common to meet the other kind of person," he replied. "Somebody who does the wrong thing for the wrong reasons. I have met many of them."

"I think we've both met our fair share of those bastards," Maive said in a quiet voice.

She surprised him. It was almost unheard of for her to curse. Miguel hurried on, not wanting her to return to thoughts of Texas and the road agents.

"True," he agreed. "But they are not worth thinking of. I have known two famous people in my life, did you know?" He could tell by Maive's smile that she was more than a little curious.

"Really?"

"Well, I suppose I did not *know* Mr. Norman when we took his boat. But not many people can say they have sailed on the yacht of such a famous person, can they?"

"No, they can't, Miguel," she conceded with good humor. "And the other famous person?"

He paused for dramatic effect. "Roberto," he said. "That's President Morales of the South American Federation to you, worthless gringo lady!"

She'd been about to blow another snowflake from the tip of her nose but laughed instead. "I don't know that that's something I'd be bragging about if I was you, Mr. Pieraro. How on earth did you meet such a creature?"

"In Acapulco. In the very first days of *el colapso,* I was caught up there, just before I met Miss Julianne and Miss Fifi. I was running a small security crew for one of the hotels—well, more like a bunch of thugs than a crew. But the hotel employed them to keep the other thugs away from the guests, and they employed me to keep them in line. Roberto was one of those thugs, my second in command. He was a terrible man even then."

They picked up their pace by unspoken agreement as the snow fell more heavily, pushed along by a sharp southerly wind. Miguel was glad he had worn his hat. It stopped most of the snowflakes that would have fallen onto his face. Maive had to keep wiping her eyes clear with her upper arm because of the two bags she was carrying.

"What happened?" She sounded like a child being told an exciting bedtime story.

"Between Roberto and I? Not much. We did not like each other, and I suppose, had I not left him to it, there would have been blood between us in the end."

"Maybe it would've been better for a lot of people if there had been, Miguel," she replied. "Have you ever considered how many people's lives you might have saved if you had, I don't know . . . *dealt with him* back then?"

"I had never thought of it like that," he said, meaning it. "You may be right. For some people, that would almost certainly be true. Hugo Chávez might still be with us."

"Ah. Snap."

He wasn't quite sure what Maive meant by that, but she seemed to be conceding the point that speculating about what might have been was foolish.

"If it had not been Roberto, it would have been someone else," Miguel continued. "Some general, some gangster, somebody was always going to take over down there when it fell apart. I was very surprised when I found out it was him, and yet, not at all. He has a political background. Maybe even military. He had the stink of the death squads about him. But yes, for a few days I stood on a barricade with *el presidente,* protecting the clothes and jewelry of wealthy holiday makers without the sense to realize they were not wealthy anymore and they really should have got out of Acapulco."

"That is a very good story, Miguel," she said. "And now I have bragging rights because I know someone who knew someone who became a real-life dictator."

They were just two blocks from Maive's home and crossing at an intersection when Miguel saw him: the thin streak of misery and madness, the unhinged Mormon witness he had thrown from Maive Aronson's front porch that morning. Visibility had become very bad, and the man was dressed in a light gray hooded jacket that served to camouflage him inside the flurries and swirls of snow, but Miguel had laid hands on the *loco* and recognized him immediately. The strange angular way he held his body, the tension in his neck and back, the way he focused intently when he saw the two of them.

The vaquero burned with righteous anger. He struggled to maintain a tight grip on the hot gust of rage that welled up inside his breast. Maive appeared not to have noticed her tormentor even though she was closer to the man. He looked to be talking on a cell phone, which surprised Miguel. He had not thought that a crazy man—and the witness was most assuredly crazy—would have access to such technology or know how to use it.

Did Kansas City even have a cell phone service? This madman was the first person he'd seen using a cellular phone in a long time. Only government people seemed to use them now.

Miguel let Maive chatter on while he skewered her stalker with a malevolent glare. No matter how disconnected from reality this maniac might have been, there could be no mistaking the malignant intent with which the Mexican was fixing him. Miguel wished he could hear what the man was saying on the phone. Almost certainly gibberish, but if he was talking about Maive, that might be important to know to gauge the depth of his obsession. Unfortunately, the thickness of the snowfall was deadening all sound, even with her voice just an arm's length away.

Miguel shook his head and scolded himself. *This fool is no threat. He probably believes he is talking directly to God himself.*

If he had been somewhere else, out on the range, say, picking his way through a forest, breaking trail on horseback, he might have recognized the ambush a few seconds earlier. Perhaps he would have been able to do something about it.

But Miguel Pieraro, father, widower, a vaquero's vaquero, was not a man of city streets and built-up places. He was most at home in the saddle. Not shuffling along a footpath, his arms loaded down with groceries carried for a woman who was making him feel more and more every day that he might move beyond the horror and loss he had sustained down in East Texas.

The car that hit Miguel and Maive as they crossed the intersection while his attention was focused entirely on the tall, rake-thin fanatic was traveling at over sixty miles an hour. A dangerous speed on pot-holed streets under the best of conditions. Calculated insanity during a heavy snowstorm.

It was a quiet car, chosen for that very reason. Solid iron bull bars recently affixed to the front of the vehicle absorbed most of the damage when it struck them. Investigators examining the burned-out hulk of the vehicle—the murder weapon—after it was found not long afterward would make a note about that detail. It implied a good deal of planning and preparation.

The police officers who would come to visit Sofia Pieraro on that terrible Thursday to tell her of her father's death were not investigators. They were just beat cops. They couldn't do much for her. The only solace they had to offer was the assurance that her papa had died instantly and that his friend Mrs. Aronson had not suffered. She was in a coma when the paramedics arrived.

8

FORMER URUGUAYAN–ARGENTINIAN BORDER REGION, SOUTH AMERICAN FEDERATION

The rough path she'd earlier cut through the forest sped her return to the crossroads. Caitlin took up a position where she could fire on the entrance to the building without easily being fired on. She placed herself so that the heavy mud-brick columns supporting the roof of the portico blocked any line of sight to her from inside.

Then she waited.

They wouldn't come charging through the door, guns out, the minute their colleagues were overdue. Facility 183 did not impress her as a model of the world's best practice for secret detention and torture camps. Unless the tobacco or pornography supply had run out, it probably would be thirty or forty minutes before anyone even noticed the men she'd killed hadn't returned.

Caitlin sought a meditative frame of mind she had learned in Japan during her eleven months of intensive aikido training on the Senshusei course at the Yoshinkan Honbu Dojo. It had been an unusual time in her early career, strangely restful yet grueling. Every day of that short year she had spent in pain of one form or another. Not only from combat training, in which broken bones, concussions, and voluminous bloodshed were a common occurrence, but also from the insanely repetitive and punishing minutiae of dojo life. The agonies of *suwariwaza,* for instance—kneeling techniques in which she spent hours of her first weeks dizzy with suffering as the skin peeled from her knees, followed by the thin mantle of flesh over her kneecaps. Those wounds would scab over at night, only to crack open with exquisite pain the next morning as she bent to the tatami mat again.

The dojo was life itself. Unyielding, unforgiving, and inescapable.

Lying prone in decaying leaf matter with insects crawling all over her and slick with sweat, Caitlin reached now for the lesson of Yoshinkan Honbu. It was something she'd learned only at the very end of her training, when her technique, her *jutsu,* or art, had been honed to a cutting edge as dangerous as a Sengo Muramasa blade, a weapon forged by the infamous Muromachi period swordsmith and reputedly imbued with his violent madness. It was said that the steel of a Muramasa katana was "hungry."

After eleven months of shit kicking, shit eating, and having the shit kicked out of her by remote and often witlessly vindictive *sensei* and *uki,* Caitlin Monroe, too, was hungry. Chosen to fight in a closed tournament, to test herself against some of the instructors before an audience of invited masters from other schools, she stepped onto the tatami where she had spilled so much blood and sweat and, yes, even tears. She felt herself to be the most dangerous woman in the world.

I am become death, she thought.

Her first opponent, a potbellied man with only half his teeth and toe-curling halitosis, took her apart as perfectly as a fugu chef removing the poisonous liver from a puffer fish. Before she could initiate her opening attack, she had been punched in the face and taken two shuddering elbow strikes in her rib cage. As the injury exploded through her nervous system with white-hot shock, her opponent swept her leading leg out from underneath her and drove a kick into her sternum when she dropped to the mat.

The young woman regained her feet and took up a fighting stance again, suddenly aware of just how many old masters were watching and judging her. Every time she advanced, the gap-toothed, potbellied fiend was just outside her line of attack. Every defense she threw up, he swarmed over. Within two minutes she was breathing hard, laboring for air. At the end of that first session of *kumite,* she felt herself entirely defeated. With another nine fights ahead of her.

She fought on.

Every opponent bested her. She failed to land a single blow or kick. Her arms turned black with bruises as poorly focused blocks warded off strike after strike. But still she fought on. Not because she knew this would end but because as the other fighters came on, she came to understand this would never end. This was life.

It. Would. Never. End. Not until life itself ended.

When they were done with her, the crisp white *gi* she had specially laundered for the day was heavy with sweat and pink with her blood. And only her blood. Her stiff black belt, the obi of a newly minted *shodan,* was limp and foul. She hurt everywhere. In her joints, her meat, deep down in her bones. But the pain was a distant, illusory thing.

She could hardly stand to bow off the mat, yet she could not leave without doing so. Every man she had fought lined up and bowed deeply to her, the young American whom they had bested. Inside, she felt empty. But happy in a way she had never known before. She had lost herself in battle, her actual self.

An arrogant, self-conscious, and pitiably vain student had stepped onto the tatami just a short time ago. A warrior limped off.

Nine years afterward, she found that same unspoiled clarity of mind as she breathed out and let go of vanity, of desire, of worldly attachments—including the attachment to life itself. She became death, and she waited.

Forty minutes later, Caitlin Monroe attacked.

The heavy wooden door swung open on creaky hinges just as the day was reaching its hottest hour. Perhaps if the two errand boys had returned by now, Facility 183 already would have been dozing through an afternoon siesta. But they would never return, and when enough time had passed, the two most junior militiamen were sent out to investigate. This they accomplished by slowly stepping off the veranda and squinting into the sun, shading their eyes with their hands.

Concealed within the thick brush growth not much more than a long stone's throw from them, Caitlin flicked off the safety on her HK417, laid the iron sights on the center mass of the larger, closer man, and breathed out.

Three rounds sped downrange with methodical, calm, singular squeezes of the trigger. As before, it was a mix of armor-piercing and hollow-point, with Caitlin channeling the recoil into a short, efficient movement that swept the muzzle of the suppressor from the first target onto the second. The men died instantly. A bloody squall of viscera and shattered bone chips sprayed the dirty white stucco behind them. Instantly, she shifted her aim to the front door, where, as she had hoped, the facility's corpulent, hapless commander soon ducked his head around.

A single pull put a round of 7.62-mm through the officer's forehead, spraying hair, bone, and brain back into the building. Another brace of shots destroyed the junction box, where a single phone line ran into the building.

She rolled to the right, retreating a few steps into the heavy undergrowth. The assassin moved swiftly along the same path as before, emerging at speed at a point by the side of the road where she could approach the building at a run without being directly seen from inside. Not that Caitlin expected the altogether more impressive deputy commander, the only surviving militiaman in there now, to show himself.

Sprinting across the road, she leaped high onto the old hitching rail, using it to boost herself into a second leap skyward. She grasped the broken clay halfpipe of the building's guttering and used her momentum to swing up onto the roof in one fluid movement. Caitlin crossed to the rear, where she quickly darted her head over the roofline to recon what lay below. It seemed to correspond with the fuzzy satellite image in her data set. Pressing on with her attack from a completely different direction now, she swung down from the roof and landed with feline grace and very little noise next to a blank section of the rear wall.

Crouching to keep her head below the line of a window, the Echelon agent moved quickly to enter the building through the small cook-house. She adjusted the stock of the HK for close-quarters work. A small hand mirror on a telescoping extension allowed her to survey the interior before swinging in. Two pots stood bubbling on the wood-fired stove next to an old coffeepot. The kitchen was longer than it was wide, leaving no room for a table. An internal doorway gave out onto the small open-plan office she had spied earlier from the brush. There was no sign of the second militia officer.

She took care now. Unlike his boss and the men under him, this one was no fool. He knew the layout of the building and would use it to good effect. Caitlin eeled around the corner, gun up, safety off, ready to fire and roll.

Nothing. Only the cries of the prisoners in the cell block. They were mostly incoherent, although one did babble, calling for help from his *"compadre."* Caitlin ignored them. They were not yet relevant.

Covering the small area of the barracks she could see through the kitchen doorway, she moved forward cautiously again, taking up a se-cure position just before the entrance to the office area. Once more, she used the mirror to scope out the room before entering, crouching down at first to take a view from about knee level before slowly sliding back up and holding the mirror high so that she could look down on the space, hoping to catch the man if he'd hidden himself behind a desk.

Few things were more nerve-racking than trying single-handedly to clear a building of an enemy who knew you were coming and who knew the ground on which you would have to fight. As important as it was not to just charge in and get your head blown off, Caitlin was aware that it could be fatal to hesitate. Having initiated the attack, she could very easily defeat herself now by giving in to uncertainty. "Di-vided energies," they had called it back at Yoshinkan Hombu, a fatal tipping point between fight and flight where the unprepared so often died.

She mapped out the room in her head. To her front, a cluster of desks. On her right, the grimy windows overlooking the dirt road that ran in front of the building. The heavy wooden doors hanging open, with the reception counter just inside of them. Behind that counter lay a closed door, undoubtedly leading to the cells.

Like a chess master running through every possible combination of moves before committing her piece to a new square on the board, Caitlin studied the line of attack from her opponent's point of view. Which items of furniture would provide him with the best cover, which firing angles the greatest chance of taking her down? To all of the possibilities she assigned a rough probability.

And then she moved, sweeping into the larger open space, terribly exposed to an attack that might or might not come.

Using the heavy wooden desks as cover, Caitlin advanced across the killing ground with her senses opened to the flood of stimuli pouring in: a fan turning slowly from a ceiling mount, the protests of the prisoners, the buzzing of flies around a plate of beans and sausages abandoned on a desk . . . But no sign of Facility 183's deputy commander.

The Echelon agent took a few moments to make sure she hadn't missed him. But the very fact that she was still breathing, that nobody had fired on her, told Caitlin he wasn't in this part of the building.

The door to the prison cells stood firmly closed and mute just in front of her. In her peripheral vision she could see the legs of a man she had shot down in the road out front. The stench of his death, an animal stink of voided bowels, was much stronger over here by the main entrance.

Caitlin did not have time to weigh all the imponderables; there were too many of them. She detached a couple of flash-bangs from her webbing and advanced on the door leading to the cells. There was no way to tell what lay immediately on the other side. A constricted passageway or more open space? Perhaps even another office. The *funcionario* could have been waiting for her behind a sandbagged machine gun for all she knew. There was nothing for it but to press on.

She noted from the lack of hinges that the door opened inward, making her next move slightly easier. Filling her lungs with air, she pulled the pins on the two stun grenades, then timed a powerful side kick to crash through the obstacle a second before the grenades were primed to detonate.

As the door smashed inward, she lobbed them down a short dark stairway, diving to her right, still out in the reception area, while a short burst of gunfire exploded up out of the shadows. Partway through her flight, Caitlin grunted with shock and pain as a bullet struck her body armor a glancing blow, turning her as though she'd been roundhouse kicked. She went with the movement, spinning out of the doorway before the grenades went off, the detonations following one after the other so quickly that they rolled into a single clap of thunder and a flash of strobed lightning.

There was no time to pay heed to her injuries or the fact that she was winded so badly that she couldn't breathe in. Caitlin threw herself back into the dimly lit stairwell area and down the short set of steps, her senses questing for the last man she had to kill. She knew he had to be within reach as soon as her boots hit level ground.

There was no light down there, and thick acrid smoke from the flash-bangs burned her eyes. She could not risk firing her weapon yet for fear of hitting Lupérico, but she had to clear a path ahead. All her nerve endings sang with the knowledge that even though she couldn't see him, the deputy was staggering around, disoriented by the stun grenades, not more than a few feet away.

Caitlin twisted her torso and swept her left leg up in a powerful crescent kick that swished through the air directly in front of her but connected with nothing. She heard the man cough and gag—so close now—and poured more energy into the momentum she had generated with the first kick, turning and spinning as she lashed out with the other foot. This time, connection was made: soft tissue at about head height.

A male voice screamed, and a single shot crashed out in the semi-darkness, ricocheting dangerously around in the closed stone room. Then Caitlin heard the unmistakable sound of a human body dropping to a hard surface. A sick, crunching thud.

She sank to the floor, too. Although by her count she had now taken care of all the militiamen, there was no guarantee more guards weren't stationed down there. The intelligence data sets were never perfect, and there was always a chance she had missed someone in her surveillance. She heard movement and a slight groan to her left, where she had dropped the deputy.

Caitlin rolled, drawing her Gerber combat knife as she went, mounting the man's chest and slitting his throat in one efficient movement. The groan became a wet gurgling sound that persisted for a few seconds as he struggled desperately for air. When all the life had run out of his body, she relaxed fractionally.

"Are there any more guards down here?" she called out in Spanish.

The confusion of voices that came back at her was practically impossible to decipher. They begged for release, for mercy, for the indulgence of their gods.

Rolling off the dead man, she asked again, more loudly this time: "Are there any more militia down here?"

"*¿Señora?*" A slight hesitation, disbelief, as they realized that this killer was a woman.

"No, no more guards," replied one cracked and faltering voice. "He was the only one. He hid down here when the shooting started."

Caitlin's eyes were beginning to adjust to the low-light environment, but she took a moment to fit her NVGs and power them up. The scene resolved itself into opalescent green fogged by the residual smoke from the stun grenades. The body of the deputy commander, lying next to a World War I–vintage rifle, was bleeding out on the flagstone floor. A line of four cells ran away from her down one side of a long rectangular room; a bare wall faced them. Material she took to be heavy black plastic had been taped up over the high window openings she'd noted during her surveillance that morning. All the better to disorient the prisoners, of course, to create the impression that time had no meaning down there. She would have bet good money that the officer she had just killed was responsible for this innovation. It was almost sophisticated.

The man in the cell directly in front of her was not Ramón Lupérico. He looked about twenty years too old and fifty pounds too heavy. He was a jabbering mess and had wet himself.

The prisoner in the next cell down was older still, a thin, hatchet-faced character. Caitlin could see him straining to make her out in the gloom. He'd pinned himself up against the bars as if he might push himself through them by sheer force of will. As she moved farther down the long room, he listened intently, hoping to fix her position. Once she was within arm's reach, he lashed out with one hand, hoping to grab her. Almost absentmindedly, she slashed off two of his fingers with her combat knife before moving past his cage while he shrieked in shock and outrage.

Lupérico was in the third cell. He, too, was standing near the bars, attempting to pick her out in the gloom. But unlike the man she had just cut, her target remained out of reach, about a foot back behind the safety of the dark iron bars.

"Stand back, Lupérico," she said in French. "I am here to get you out."

She saw him jump with surprise.

"You are French, then? But why . . . why would you come here for me?"

"To get you out. Now stand back," she repeated, again in French rather than in her native language. All the better to muddy any trail by convincing Lupérico's cell mates he'd been released by the agency of some meddling European power.

The former jailer did as he was told, carefully shuffling backward to the rear of his cell. Caitlin had a quick look around on the floor and on the walls for any keys but found nothing. She molded a small lump of plastic explosive to the lock and retreated to the end of the hallway, warning Lupérico to shield himself.

The tiny blast made her ears ring in the constricted space and caused the prisoners to cry out in distress. Well, most of them, anyway. The guy whose fingers she'd just hacked off had other things to worry about.

Her man was disoriented and greatly unsettled, but he responded as best he could when she ordered him, still in French, out of the cell and up the stairs. They had to get away now as quickly as possible.

"What about us?" cried one of the other prisoners.

She did not answer him.

9

DEARBORN HOUSE, SEATTLE, WASHINGTON

The color did not leach entirely from Sarah Humboldt's face when Jed sidled up to her in Kip's office at the end of the Garage Cabinet meeting to take her gently by the elbow and ask for a few minutes of her time. But she did lose a few shades of color. She had blindsided him on the detainee question, after all, and he'd spent quite some time polishing his reputation as a man one did not fuck with.

"Mr. Culver," she said, making an effort to keep her voice neutral, "can I help you?"

"Relax, Sarah," Jed told her. "Because as a matter of fact you can. I could've brought it up during the meeting, except it wasn't strictly an agenda item. Even though I think it is related to some of the problems we were discussing."

Humboldt managed to look both intrigued and relieved at the same time. She smiled at James Ritchie as he slowed down to pass by, reassuring him that she didn't seem to be in trouble with the chief of staff. From the open doorway of the Oval Office, Ritchie and McAuley said their good-byes and left to see whether their drivers were able to get them back to their offices across town.

The snowstorm had evolved very quickly into a reasonably intense blizzard. The president had no immediate responsibility for organizing Seattle's defenses in such circumstances, but Jed could see the former city engineer's mind already turning back to small-scale crisis management: clearing roads, keeping the power on, making sure all the kids who'd been dropped off at the city's schools in the cold, if comparatively mild, weather that morning were going to be okay. It wasn't the man's job anymore, but for once Culver was happy to leave him to the distraction as, across the room from them, he picked up the phone to check on the snowplows.

"Everything all right, Jed?" he asked, standing up at his desk.

He had picked up on the interchange between the two, but his attention was focused on the storm. He just wanted to get on with sticking his nose in where it wasn't really needed. President James Kipper could be quite the micromanager where Seattle was concerned. The city authorities resented the interference but happily accepted the federal government resources it delivered to them.

"We're fine, Mr. President," Jed said. "There's a few things I need to discuss with Sarah about this new job you've given us."

"Sarah, is that okay?" Kipper asked.

"I'm sure I'll be fine, sir," Humboldt replied. "I don't think he's going to throw me down an elevator shaft, and we do have a lot to talk about."

Reassured that he wasn't about to lose one of his top civil servants to Jed Culver's legendary reputation for payback, Kip was nodding and dialing out before she'd finished speaking.

While the president's private secretary fussed around them, clearing up the debris from the meeting—china cups, sandwich plates, and some leftover cookies—Jed shepherded the Immigration and Customs Enforcement boss out through the anteroom, snatching a couple of Barbara Kipper's choc-chip and peanut butter heart stoppers as he went. Ronnie gave him the stink eye as he scavenged.

"In case we get completely snowed in," he told her. "Emergency supplies."

"You're worse than Barney. Get out," Ronnie said. "And don't get crumbs all through your office, either. You'll be cleaning them up yourself."

He took his dressing-down with good grace. Besides Kip, Ronnie Freeman was probably the only person on staff at Dearborn House who could put him in his place. Bad things tended to happen to those who crossed her. For one, one might not get fed, which in Jed's world was pretty bad. Or the food might be cold, or one's coffee ration would magically disappear. Ronnie was on good terms with the army chefs who kept the kitchen running there. She also had a finely honed reputation as someone one just didn't fuck with. With a bulk that matched Culver's, she was likely to tackle a person in a dark closet for what her father used to call "some wall-to-wall counseling."

No, Jed thought, *best not to upset Ronnie.*

His office was only a few doors down from the president's, and because of the antique layout of the old mansion, there was no separate room for his assistant, Ms. Devers. She worked in the pool down the hall. He led Sarah Humboldt into his domain, a surprisingly small room for a man who often was thought of as the real power in the Kipper administration. A large wooden desk carved from dark oak and topped with some sort of light brown leather stretched two-thirds of the way across the width of the space. Bookshelves ran from ceiling to floor, crammed along their length with bound volumes of congressional proceedings, government reports, and distressed, dog-eared buff-colored folders fat with more paper. There were dozens of works of nonfiction, with a sizable helping of biographies and history, including Bernard Bailyn's work on the American Revolution and Forrest McDonald's *Novus Ordo Seclorum.* As busy as he was, Culver did his best to get in at least an hour of reading a day. The latest book on the stack was going to require a lot of those single hours. He was just a hundred pages into a massive tome, Eric Foner's *Reconstruction.*

Brushing the Foner with one thumb as he flicked on the lights, Culver contemplated the book and wondered if it was worth his time. At least with it on his shelves no one could accuse him of taking the Dunning School too seriously. The room was dark and smelled slightly musty, for which he apologized. A large window behind his desk afforded a view into the gardens, but there was little to see at the moment, thanks to the snow plastered to the outside of the glass.

"Sit down, Sarah," he said. "And relax. Please. I'm not going to go upside your head for that tag-team effort you and Ritchie laid on me back there. In a way, it was kind of admirable. The sort of thing I would do, since Kip was never going to go with my suggestion to just push them all off the end of a dock and tell 'em to keep swimming until they reach France. With that said, this settlement scheme you've got can probably be turned to our advantage, as long as I can sell the harsher, more punitive aspects of it."

"I'm sure that's where you'll shine," she replied, accepting his offer of a chair, one of two single-seater Chesterfields standing sentry in front of his desk.

He closed the door and maneuvered around the end of the long table into his own chair. It took some doing in the tight space.

"The program will be fine," Jed said. "It's just a matter of how we frame it. If we could choose a few diehards to expel from the country, or even better, to execute for crimes against humanity, it would show everyone we're not a soft touch."

Humboldt shifted uncomfortably in her seat. "Well, I don't know that I—"

"Of course you wouldn't put it like that, Sarah. You're a nice person. Unlike me. You just want the best for everyone. I don't. I want the best for this administration, because I think, most things being equal, that means getting the best for the country as well. Sometimes that's going to mean hurting somebody's feelings, possibly breaking a few heads—or even shooting a few guys in the back of the head. Guys who desperately need it, I'd add. But that's not what I wanted to talk to you about today."

"Good," she said with real relief. She had not been at all comfortable with the direction of his thoughts.

Jed figured Ms. Humboldt to be the type who lived in liberal Blogistan and faithfully followed its constant bloviating about the conditions for detainees at Fort Leavenworth. *Heaven forbid that we waterboard anyone or use their holy book for cigarette papers. We couldn't possibly sink to the same level as those guys, who saw off heads and put them up in streaming video feeds on the Internet.*

Frankly, such people reminded him entirely too much of his grade-school teachers and their endless preaching about how violence never solved anything. It was a funny thing; they never seemed to mention the hundred or so historical examples he could think of right now in which violence really had solved problems.

He could have sighed. Sometimes it was a drag being the smartest guy in the room.

Humboldt straightened herself in the armchair, gathering the courage to speak her mind. 'Jed, I must say I find the way you characterize these things to be very unpleasant and often unnecessary.'

"Unpleasant I'll give you. *Unnecessary* is a moot point. But since we are on the topic, I wanted to talk about the unpleasantness down in Texas. Specifically about the attacks on some of our settler families in the Federal Mandate."

He could see he'd taken her by surprise. The incidence of settler families being run off their properties and in some cases even murdered wasn't really high enough to have registered with the public, the efforts of the Blogistan irregulars notwithstanding. Not when so many people had died in the Battle of New York. Not when a few thousand free-booters and pirates still roamed the dead cities of the eastern seaboard despite the efforts of the military and militias to drive them off. A family missing here, a homesteader there—it wasn't much when laid against the butcher's bill in Manhattan. Bloodshed was the one thing they had an ample surplus of, and it saturated the media, numbing the much-reduced masses to anything but the most insensate savagery.

"Do you propose to do something about the security arrangements?" asked Humboldt. "My office has been arguing in favor of a mandate militia for nearly two years."

Jed smiled grimly. Technically, they did have federal troops in Texas, elements of the regular army and air force. Their ability to act, however, was limited strictly to territorial defense; they were not a police force or a militia. The responsibility for internal security lay squarely on the shoulders of Governor Jackson Blackstone, who simply claimed to be doing the best he could with what he had.

"I totally agree with you, Sarah. If we had our own troops down there instead of having to rely on the Texas Defense Force, I think you'd see these attacks drop away completely. There'd still be a few raids and even killings in some of the more remote locations, because a lot of genuine bandits come up north through Mexico. But make no mistake, I believe some of the bandits, particularly these road-agent gangs, are indulged by Fort Hood even if they're not directed by them. I know things aren't as bad as they were last year, but these gangs still make life difficult for our people. They create a lot of fear and uncertainty in the mandate, and that makes them a good thing in Blackstone's book. It doesn't take much effort to do nothing, after all, and that's what he's been doing on this issue. Sweet fuck-all."

He waited to see how she would react to such a bald-faced accusation of villainy. The secretary for ICE nodded quietly, her lips pressed together.

"That's my understanding," she said. "It's certainly the belief of those settlers we've already sent down there, and you're right, it makes it very difficult to place suitable candidates into the settlement program for the Mandate. But I ask again, what are you going to do about it? A dedicated frontier militia would solve most of the problems overnight."

A sour expression creased the chief of staff's features. "Agreed. But our memorandum of understanding with Fort Hood does not allow us to deploy militia into the mandate. Blackstone only agreed to waive administrative control of that land when we agreed to leave policing the interior and securing the boundaries to the TDF."

"Oh, my God, Culver," she replied, clearly exasperated. "We just spent the better part of two hours complaining about him not keeping to the letter of that agreement. Or the spirit of it. Or anything. If he doesn't play by the rules, why should we?"

He smiled like a mischievous child. It was amazing how someone like Sarah Humboldt would get upset about his way of describing things, demand that they do the right thing in a legal manner, and then advocate chucking the rule book out the window when it suited her. A moralizing, self-righteous liberal hypocrite, Jed decided. At least they were far easier to manipulate into action than others.

"Feel the power of the dark side, Sarah. I am with you one hundred percent. But the president is a firm believer in best practices, and that does not include reneging on our agreements while we bitch and moan about other people not holding to theirs."

The wind shrieked louder for a second, smashing a tree branch into the highest pane of his window with such force that he thought it might break. It knocked free a large clump of snow, which fell to the ground outside with a muffled thump. Secretary Humbolt jumped a little in her chair. Opposite her, Jed pushed himself back from the desk so he could open one of the drawers and retrieve a folder. He dropped it on the desk and pushed it a little way toward her. He explained as she opened it.

"I've been keeping tabs on the settler situation down in Texas. Just informally. I'm sure you have much better records. Statements of interview with survivors, crime-scene photographs, that sort of thing. I have a little bit of that, but mostly press reports. They're pretty thin, as you can see. The frontier really is the great unknown again. We're not quite back to the Pony Express, but it can still take a few days for news to get from the outlying homesteads back to one of our settlement centers. And, of course, very few media organizations have the resources to send their people that far out into the badlands. Not for an unremarkable story."

A deep crease appeared between Sarah Humboldt's eyebrows. "I don't know that I would call it 'unremarkable,' Mr. Culver," she countered. "Our people are being run off their land, and some of them are being killed. And I don't know whether or not Fort Hood is conniving at this—that would be an extraordinary allegation—but they're certainly not moving heaven and earth to stop it happening."

Culver dismissed her sense of outrage. "I'm afraid it is the very definition of an unremarkable story, Sarah. Not just compared to a bloodbath like New York but to life anywhere else on the frontier. We have trouble securing the homesteads a hundred miles out from Kansas City—hell, we've even had raiders down in the Willamette Valley. You don't get very far beyond the edge of Seattle or KC without stumbling into brute creation. This is a huge country, and it's mostly open for the taking. There's still thousands of pirate raiders on the East Coast, thousands more up in Canada drifting down over the border as it suits them, and hordes of real bandits coming up from the south and the Caribbean. A couple of raids here and there in Texas might mean something to *us,* but it's just a droplet in a fast-flowing fucking river of blood that's running all over this country."

Frowning as she leafed through the folder he had given her, Humboldt calmed herself a little. "You didn't invite me in here to complain about the world. What's on your mind, Mr. Culver?"

He gave it a moment, as though thinking over what he might say next. But Jed had made up his mind long ago.

"I need information, Sarah. And please stop calling me 'Mr. Culver.' You make me feel like I've done something wrong."

She smiled, and he continued.

"I need your files. Or copies of your files, at least. Everything you have on all of the attacks on our people down in the mandate."

The confusion on her face was evident. "Well, those files are confidential," she began. "But if the president's office requested them, I'm sure there'd be no problem making them available . . . Although I must admit, I'm confused as to why they'd be of interest now. The attacks have tapered off. Not entirely, but they're not nearly as bad as in '06 or early this year."

"I need them now because I have need of them now, Sarah. Simple as that," said Culver. "And the president's office won't be requesting them. Ever. *I* am requesting them. I need them, and I need to be sure that nobody ever knows I have had access to them. This is not an official request. Quite the opposite."

An old ship's chronometer took up some of the space on the bookshelf to Jed's right. Even with the sound of the storm, its solid tick-tock timekeeping seemed loud.

"I see," said Humboldt.

"No, you don't, Sarah. You never will. But if you want to secure the future of your settlements down in the Texas Mandate and ensure that those responsible for attacking them in the past meet with some form of justice, this is what it will take."

"Might I ask why?"

"It is best if you do not know," Jed Culver replied. "Trust me."

10

NORTH KANSAS CITY, MISSOURI

She worried about the horses. The snow had been falling for hours and now lay in a thick white shroud over the park. Sofia pressed her nose up against the enormous plate-glass window that formed one entire wall of their loft apartment, offering a view of the park across the road, where they kept the horses. One of her neighbors, a creepy-looking man with a long shaggy beard, coaxed his animals out of the herd with something in his hand. He hitched them to a wagon that had been made from tubes and steel mesh welded together over a pair of axles fitted with bicycle tires. As the combination pulled away, Sofia was surprised that the horses hadn't flipped the contraption. It had to be impossibly light.

She never had actually counted the horses, but from many hours of standing at the window and gazing out over the parkland, she esti-mated that there might be two or three dozen roaming around down there. The city was happy for its citizens to keep their horses in this way. For many people, they had become as important as cars once had been. And as important as horses had been before that, she thought.

So the city authorities—or maybe it was the government out in Seattle; she wasn't sure—let people graze their horses and other animals in the public parks, which otherwise were used as market gardens. A good deal of Kansas City's food supply normally lay out there in the warmer months. Today, having to peer through the snow, she could make out a few hardy goats and dairy cattle. There was only the most basic stabling for the animals when the weather turned bad, though, and Sofia worried that their horses, Flossie and Marvin, would suffer in the cold. She had named both, of course, much to her father's dismay.

Maybe later she would run some apples out to them. Papa wouldn't get too upset about that. Being trapped inside was giving her a severe case of the crazies, in any case, and if he got upset, so what.

Truth be told, she didn't care a damn about what her father thought at the moment. He was off enjoying himself at the markets with Maive. Sofia felt a stab of jealousy at that without being able to pin down exactly who she felt jealous of and why. All the fifteen-year-old knew for sure was that she was stuck here in the loft, concerned about the horses and bored out of her brains.

She sighed, and her breath fogged the glass directly in front of her face. She rubbed it clean with the arm of her sweater, wiping away a few marks she hadn't known were there. They looked like ghostly impressions of her face, probably left over from the last time she'd stood pressed to the window while being held prisoner in the apartment.

The glass vibrated against her forehead. Living one floor above them was a rail-thin, long-haired meth head who cranked his stereo up during the day to sleep off the previous night's drug binge. His favorite pastime of late was to stand in his window, waving his genitals to passersby while shouting, "I'M OKAY!!! I'M ALL RIGHT!!!" Complaints to the landlord and the local authorities achieved nothing. There weren't enough cops to respond or medical personnel to treat him, and they didn't have room in the jails or psych wards, anyway. She knew that from her part-time job, her three afternoon and evening shifts a week at North Kansas City General. The man was a public nuisance, but no one could quite bring himself to throw him out on his own. He was a veteran, anyway, and so virtually untouchable. Her father had threatened him more than once, which a sane man would have taken to heart. But their neighbor was not sane. He was a crazy fucking loser. Papa eventually had given up trying to do anything about him, just as he had given up on so much else.

The meth head was just one of many in the neighborhood. On the rare occasions when she watched the news, Sofia saw a fantasy version of what life was like here in Kansas City. Safe streets patrolled by friendly cops and militia working side by side with wholesome smiling families—they always seemed to be gringo families, to use her father's embarrassing term—rebuilding America.

Above her, the volume went up as her neighbor started dancing, rattling the plates in her kitchen cabinet. She considered going upstairs and punching the genital helicopter square in the face but thought better of it. One assault a week was enough.

Her knuckles still hurt from that last one, a foolish situation that she cursed herself for now. She never should have hit that asshole at school the way she had. No, she should have whacked him with a hammer fist, breaking his jaw with the hard, callused edge of her hand, like someone pounding his fist on a table to make a point, the way her father and Trudi Jessup had taught her to punch when they'd all been running from the road agents.

It was a terrible thing, but in some ways she missed those days. Not the madness of it or the raw anguish of having lost everyone in her family except for Papa. Mama, Grandma Ana. Little Maya, and her brothers. Her uncles and aunts. She gladly would have cut her arm off to avoid having to live through that. In fact, she knew she would have given her own life to spare them—the trail had taught her that. God had given her life, had given all of his children life, to be lived, and if necessary to be spent, for others. But standing here, witless with tedium, feeling as though she had been imprisoned within these walls, Sofia missed the hard freedom of that horrific time.

It was the same in school. Within a minute or two of sitting down at her desk at Northtown High, she would find her mind wandering. She had killed people. Shot them down as they raged and ran about during the gunfight at the Hy Top Club in Crockett. She had watched as her father gutted two men, and she'd felt nothing bad about it. So it was too much to ask to expect her to sit indoors with a classroom full of drones and assholes, listening to the same old shit day after day. And so much of it about a world that was gone. *Gone.* When were people going to get over it?

The glass fogged up again. Her breath had come hot and fast as she'd grown agitated, thinking about the kid who was responsible for her being locked up like this.

Scotty Morrison. A jerk. He had been on her case for days.

Morrison was like that. He'd decide to get on someone's case and then simply wouldn't give up. He just rode them and rode them into the ground. And everyone had to put up with it, of course, because his father was on the North Kansas City Council and an even bigger asshole than little Scott. From what Sofia had heard, if you got on the wrong side of Councillor Morrison, you'd find yourself kicked out of your cozy government-approved apartment or house. Your easy eight-to-six job in an office somewhere could just disappear overnight. And then you were suddenly living in one of the emergency shelters or migrant camps, shoveling dead-people goo out of whatever suburb the city had decided to reclaim next.

His father was powerful enough to buy the latest imported clothes, shipped direct from Seattle. No salvaged rags from Abercrombie & Fitch or American Eagle for his son. Only the best for little Scotty. It was Daddy Morrison's way of waving his dick in everyone's face and telling them to suck it up.

So people took the kid's bullshit and smiled and said thank you very much. But not Sofia.

She'd pretty much let it slide the first time Scotty had confronted her. She hadn't been at all intimidated when she'd taken her head out of her locker during morning recess to find herself surrounded by Morrison and his posse. Four more pathetic whitey bitch boys who stood sneering as he loomed over her and said he'd heard she was a good ride.

All that time in the saddle. You know.

He was a great rider, too. You know.

He tried to stop her as she moved to push past him, and she made a pointed fist, the trail-hardened knuckle forming a blunt spearhead, which she then drove up into his armpit with the speed of a striking rattler. He yelped as his arm spasmed and white-hot chain lightning ran down into his fingers.

Trudi had taught her that one, too.

The next day, though, she'd known it was serious. One didn't enrage a little boy like Scotty Morrison, and one really didn't enrage and embarrass him in front of his posse. It meant he had to come back at you. The gossip mills were rolling hard with word of Scotty's humiliation. It was much worse than the time Amy Place had giggled at the size of his so-called ride. As Sofia moved down the purple and gray hallways toward the school cafeteria, everyone gave her a wide berth. Guilt by association could be a very real problem where the Morrisons were concerned. Nothing happened, though. She spent the day on edge for no good reason.

The bus ride home was equally uneventful. Perhaps he was going to let it slide.

When she found him and his crew waiting on the steps outside the apartment block, Sofia realized she'd underestimated him. Scotty sneered as she approached. He was trying to look like the scariest motherfucker in the world in his Hugo Boss jeans and Lacoste windbreaker, and of course his well-dressed boyfriends were backing him up. But he was nothing. The lamest trail bandit she'd ever crossed could have frightened Scott Morrison into wetting his pants just by saying "Boo!" His eyes flicked nervously away from her steady gaze, and she could have sworn his curled lip quivered just a little when she didn't even break stride. This would have to be settled today, she knew, one way or another.

Sofia didn't even let him get a word in. She saw him physically gather up his resolve as he pushed himself off the steps. As soon as he got in her face, she swung on the asshole, a short-arm roundhouse punch to the jaw. Put all of her body into the pivot and snapped her hips in there, too. Felt the jawbone go under the impact, heard it crunch. But in the rush of the moment, she'd hit him the old-fashioned way. With her fist bunched up, leading with the knuckles.

Sofia knew it was a mistake less than half a heartbeat after she'd felt his jaw shatter as pain suddenly lanced up through her wrist. It didn't stop her from swinging a boot into his face as he went down and then again into his stomach when he'd hit the ground. And she still put her fists up when she spun around to face the others, when she could actually see she'd done something stupid. Her knuckles were badly damaged; one of them had been sort of pushed back up her hand. It was enough to make her a little sick, just looking at the thing.

But it was one of Scotty's bitches who threw up when he saw it. And then Morrison Lite puked, too. The posse all ran off then, leaving their leader choking on his own vomit at her feet.

Sofia sighed now and left the arctic vista of the picture window. She clenched and unclenched that fist. It still hurt.

She pushed the thermostat up a couple of degrees. The day was getting so cold, they might need to draw the heavy curtains across the large, exposed windows of the former warehouse space to keep in the heat. Rubbing at her swollen right hand again, she had to acknowledge that Papa was right: he had to be seen to punish her or the boy's father would become involved. Not that Morrison Senior wasn't straining like a pit bull at the end of his leash, anyway. Oh, Lord, had there been trouble over Scotty's broken face . . .

Her heart beat a little faster thinking about how she'd endangered their position here by beating up the city councillor's boy. Papa was right. If it wasn't for the government in Seattle looking after them—or, to be more accurate, having an interest in them because of their road-agent stories—Scotty's old man would have had them out of the loft and probably barred from bunking down with the Indians over at the railway camp. They'd have been on the road again, run out of town.

Her father and the principal of Northtown High School had decided that she should serve a three-day suspension. And there would also be the supplementary grounding to contend with, of course.

Sofia pulled up the chair where she'd been sitting earlier at the big table in the open space by the kitchen. They ate their meals there. There was no dining room, no separate living areas in the house. Just their bedrooms, the combined bathroom-laundry, and the communal room here. She found it annoying sometimes to have nowhere she could be alone save for her room. But such thoughts were always followed by a flush of shame that the only reason she could truly be alone these days was that apart from Papa, her whole family was gone.

She sat down in front of the textbooks she was supposed to be studying and tried to settle herself into a more academic frame of mind. The snow was falling so heavily now, whipped into twisting curlicues and sheets of white, that the park was almost entirely obscured. She shook her head and pulled the thickest textbook, which wasn't very thick at all, over to her.

She opened it at the chapter relevant to her assignment. The history of the Great Depression. Like anyone cared.

Sofia tried to read a short passage, an interview in which a man described how he'd worked seven hours to earn the money to buy a bottle of baby formula for his kid and how he'd run three miles to the drugstore for it only to find that the place was closed. As much as she could see that the situation sucked big-time, his story still didn't compare with what she'd been through.

Hey, try running to the store chased by half a dozen of Blackstone's road agents, she thought.

Sofia flinched away from remembering the day the gang had attacked their hacienda while she and her father had been out checking the back pastures. She could only ever recall those awful moments in her nightmares. Trying to think about them while conscious was impossible, like stabbing herself slowly in the eye. But she had no trouble remembering other times, some of them just as bad.

An observer watching Sofia Pieraro over the next few minutes would have been astounded by the change that came over the teenager. Psychologists would have called it a fugue state. For Sofia, it was akin to time travel. It was what happened when she found herself zoning out at school. She wasn't simply recalling events. Her mind, her whole consciousness, was back there.

The moaning wind that bent the leafless branches of the trees in the park—she heard it no more. She did not see the great white rectangle of the picture window or the complete whiteout brought on by a blizzard for the ages. The Great Depression had never happened. The poor man with the hungry child vanished altogether from history.

She was back in the scrub in Crockett, Texas. Deep night, and she deep within it, having stolen away from the relative safety of the women's camp against Papa's strict instructions. She had heard the phrase "heart in mouth" before, but until this moment she had never experienced anything remotely like it. But as she watched her father perform a drunken pantomime as he approached the two road-agent sentries, her heart beat so powerfully and rapidly and her stomach seemed to contract with such force that she felt as though she might vomit all of her insides out through her teeth at any moment.

She found it all but impossible to watch the small life-and-death drama unfold through the hunting telescope on her rifle, at least until she swung the sight off Papa and concentrated instead on the two men he was trying to silence. When she first caught one of them between the crosshairs of her Remington—a fat, ugly pig's ass of a man, to borrow a phrase she had learned in the refugee camp outside Sydney—it was all she could do not to squeeze the trigger and put a round through his head.

Only the sure knowledge that to do so would alert the other gang members at the clubhouse nearby stayed her hand. She was aware of the ugly scowl that settled over her face as she observed this pair of thieves and killers. The very ugliness of thought and deed that she could see etched into the repulsive features of the man in her scope contorted her face into a rictus of congealing rage as she watched him. Only when her father plunged his bowie knife into the first of them did her expression change.

She smiled.

She smiled under the cover of night in Crockett, Texas, as the ice and frozen soil underneath her thawed from her body heat, soaking her clothes and chilling her to the bone.

And she smiled at the table of the comfortable renovated loft she shared with her father a thousand miles away, safe in Kansas City. Her eyes, unfocused and unseeing in the present, gazing nine months back to the same night when she'd not just watched men die but had taken their lives with her own hands. Not up close, as she would have wished if given the chance—to see the red spark of existence snuffed out of their eyes. But close enough. More than close enough.

She'd almost lost her meager dinner when the enormous Mormon they called Big Ben had brought a sledgehammer down on his first victim's skull in the opening seconds of the attack on the Hy Top Club. Choking down her nausea, she brought out the Remington and waited for a target to present itself. In the excitement, she nearly opened fire on the first thing that resolved in her telescope, bracketed against the fire and torchlight of the camp. That would have meant shooting Orin, one of her own group, not to mention giving herself away. Sneakiness was the watchword of the evening, she reminded herself, sneakiness and not shooting the wrong people. She forced herself to wait.

When the first camp whore screamed, she tracked the muzzle onto her, but a sledgehammer blow silenced the woman before Sofia could fire. The whore's boyfriend struggled to rise off the couch, where he'd crashed, drunken and sated, on the grass just in front of the tumble-down clubhouse. She recalled him as if he were standing right in front of her in the loft in Kansas City. A bearded, shaggy, potbellied maggot with a red bandana tied over his head.

Sofia brought the crosshairs of her Remington up to Bandana Boy's unibrow, took a deep breath, and let it out. As she exhaled, she kept the muzzle on target until her finger had completed the trigger pull. Bucking in her arms, the rifle put a single round through the road agent's forehead, disintegrating the top half of his skull in a spectacular shower of bloody gruel and dropping the corpse back onto the couch. She felt a surge of anger and . . . something else.

A feeling she did not recognize, but it was powerful. No, it was power itself.

She felt her power over the man she had shot, whose life she had taken. It was a good feeling.

Sofia forced herself to work the bolt mechanically, spitting out the spent .30–06 casing and sliding a fresh round into the chamber. The Mormon men, having traded the sledgehammers for M16s, took cover uselessly behind the couch and exchanged fire with those attempting to run back inside the Hy Top.

She tracked two more road agents sprinting for the door, dispatching the first with a clean torso shot that spun her target off his feet and into the dry wall façade with a crash that shook the entire front of the building. The other man she drilled in the ass, slowing him down long enough for the Mormons to pour a stream of tracer fire into his back. So intense was the fire, it disassembled him from the hip up to shoulder height.

She'd expected this to be hard, yet she felt nothing beyond a deep sense of satisfaction as she scanned the windows of the Hy Top for more targets. Rifle fire popped around her, but she paid it no mind. The adrenaline flow gave her a rush that was far more intense than anything she'd experienced when out deer hunting.

The same rush, attenuated by time and distance but strong enough to leave her dizzy and gasping for breath, stole over her as she sat at the table in the loft at Northtown and vanished into the past. Her cheeks burned bright red and her eyes were lost, staring far beyond the walls of the apartment.

She heard the *tok-tok-tok* of semiautomatic weapon fire again. Recognized it as a Chinese assault rifle, cycling through a magazine.

Then she recognized it as something quite different. It was knocking, loud and insistent knocking, on the door of the apartment . . . Torn out of her pleasant reverie, she pushed her chair back, almost upending it as she hurried to answer the door.

She had no idea whom it could be. Papa had his keys; he was wearing them on the ring he always carried at his hip. Besides, he would have been calling her name. Sofia put her eye to the peephole. Her heart stopped beating. It actually stopped, dead in her chest, she was sure.

Two uniformed police officers were standing in the hallway outside her apartment.

Her first thought was for her father.

Papa?

II

FORMER URUGUAYAN–ARGENTINIAN BORDER REGION, SOUTH AMERICAN FEDERATION

Ramón Lupérico was much weakened by his ordeal. The former administrator of the small French detention center in Guadeloupe, a state-run facility that appeared nowhere in the public records of the French state, he did his best to match the pace of his liberator as they hurried through the thick forest. He was desperately glad to be free, of course, but not at all comfortable about being dragged through the primordial wilds by this woman. His lungs burned and his muscles quivered, and he'd been stung more times than he could count by fiendish insects of all sorts: ants, flies, mosquitoes, even a wasp on one occasion, he was sure. The woman had sprayed some sort of aerosol in his face when he complained, but otherwise she seemed entirely unsympathetic. At least the spray had kept the insects at bay.

He had thought her French when she'd spoken back at Facility 183, although now he was not so sure. She hadn't talked much since pushing him out the door of the old police station, past the bodies of his former jailers, but when she did speak, he was sure he detected a slightly guttural North American tone in her accent. Canadian, perhaps—a Québécois?

But he doubted it. The Canadians had always been a civilized people. And even now, with the world turned inside out and savagery the first refuge of scoundrels and good men alike, it seemed improbable that any government in Vancouver would have dispatched somebody like this she-devil into the wilds of the South American Federation purely for his benefit. Indeed, it seemed unlikely to Lupérico that she had been dispatched for his benefit at all.

His armed escort prodded him deeper into the brush, sparing no thought for the injuries he had sustained under torture, or for the fact that he hadn't eaten properly in days, and ignoring his protests to stop just for a moment to let him gather what little strength he had left. The farther into the forest they penetrated, the more conflicted he felt. It was good to put some distance between themselves and the prison, to get as far away as possible from any chance of being recaptured, yet his anxiety continued to grow. The trees seemed enormous, like vast and ancient cathedral pillars, soaring far overhead. The vines and thorny creepers through which they fought seemed utterly impenetrable to him, but the woman hacked and slashed a way through by using her long, black-bladed machete. Occasionally he would catch a glint of dappled sunlight on its sharpened edge and worry about what might become of him while in this killer's company. Nobody but she knew he was here now. Nobody even knew he was alive.

Whenever it seemed as though he might flag, she urged him forward with monosyllabic orders and once with the toe of a boot applied with some force to his posterior. A posterior that had been whipped with electrical cords just two days earlier. Not to extract information from him, it should be noted. What could he possibly have told those militia brutes that they would have found interesting? No, they had whipped him and humiliated him purely for the fun of it.

As a man who had supervised the hostile debriefing of any number of the French Republic's enemies himself, Lupérico found the oafish, horribly unprofessional behavior of his former captors almost as upsetting as the torture itself. He realized that this might have seemed like a ridiculous point of distinction. After all, nobody *likes* being tortured, and the attitude of one's tormentor should hardly make a difference when the battery clamps go on. Except that it did. Especially for somebody like him, who knew that professionals would stop when they had what they wanted.

There were times in his cell when Lupérico lost all hope, because he had no idea what those animals were after beyond the momentary pleasure of causing him pain and inestimable grief. He felt not a shred of sympathy for them regardless of the way in which they'd lost their lives. He would have spit on the corpse of the deputy commander had he been able to raise sufficient moisture in his mouth to do so.

"Continuez," Caitlin ordered as he slowed down about halfway up a small hill.

She forced him along the rudimentary trail she had cut earlier, but it was not an easy passage. The undergrowth grabbed at his already tattered clothing. He stumbled and tripped every few meters on tree roots and sharp rocks, crying out as they lacerated his bare feet, while the canopy grew so thick overhead that it seemed twilight was upon them. At times Lupérico had trouble discerning where she wanted him to go. He would stop and turn on her with a wounded look, seeking direction, flinching from an expected rebuke.

"I do speak English, you know," he told her now. "Your façade is not necessary."

"Save your breath. You'll need it."

She pushed him on relentlessly, allowing him to stop and rest only while she checked for any sign of pursuit. Once at the edge of a small clearing covered in a bright, startling blanket of red flowers. Another time in a deep V-shaped hollow formed by the roots of some monster tree. He was never unobserved during those brief interludes. But caution and field craft demanded that Caitlin take a few moments to direct her attention back along the trail they'd just covered. Lupérico gave no impression of planning an escape or an assault. He was an administrator, not a killer. Not like her.

The worst heat of the day was upon them, ramified into a terrible crushing humidity under the tree canopy. They avoided the occasional open areas covered with nothing but grass, skirting around them whenever they reached a clearing. All the while sweat poured out of Caitlin's companion in great torrents, and she made sure that he was keeping well hydrated. He sipped from a spare canteen she passed to him, containing not water but a flavored nutrient drink. It tasted salty and a little sweet at the same time. Probably better, though, than the food bar she'd made him sit down and eat about half an hour after they'd set out. That motherfucker looked like chocolate but tasted of cardboard. He wolfed it down nevertheless, ravenous and pathetically grateful.

Presently they reached another small clearing, in this case more a crude hollowing out of the undergrowth where she earlier had cut away at thick vines and dense masses of ferns with her machete. Some of the cuts and slashes were still raw, dripping with sap.

Caitlin gestured for him to sit on a small log, and he lowered himself gratefully and carefully to the ground. The day was passing, and she noted a change in the clamor and tenor of bird and animals noises around them. The world was quieter now as those creatures that hunted and fed during the day repaired to their burrows and nests to take refuge from the night stalkers. The long, pencil-thin shafts of light that penetrated the canopy had shifted from bright white to a softer golden hue.

After close to three hours of rigorous trekking through the forest, Lupérico was exhausted and close to emotional collapse. She could tell that the idea he might actually escape the nightmare of the Federation's wretched sinkhole was finally becoming real to him. He might live. He might escape, get far away from here, and survive to such an age that the terrors of the last few years, especially the last six months, receded into the dark numbness of the long ago.

As long as he could give this woman what she wanted.

She could read all this in his face because she had seen that stupid, futile hope in the faces of so many other men that she had lost count.

He silently watched her interrogate the data pad strapped to her forearm. She busied herself with that for a minute, fixing their location, while he sipped again from the canteen. His limbs were shaking, whether from extreme fatigue or shock she could not say and didn't much care. But he tried not to let his weakness seem so obvious. His eyes told her he was already turning his thoughts to what she might ask of him next.

What possible interest could she have had in him?

Caitlin was content to let him stew.

She knew that the years of *el colapso* had not been kind to Ramón Lupérico. He had lost his position in Guadeloupe in October 2003, a few months after the civil war in France. "The intifada," they called it, but he probably knew better. Even living in virtual exile thousands of miles from metropolitan France, taking care of the republic's dirty laundry in the quiet, grim, but well-maintained little detention center that had been his fiefdom, Lupérico still would have had enough contacts among the more significant *bureaux* back in Paris to have understood that the street fighting and urban warfare was not merely a more violent reprise of 1968. No, the state had been at war with itself.

She knew Lupérico was not a stupid man. He would have understood that, in such times, it was the tiny little cogs in the wheels of politics that were most likely to be stripped and crushed. As the collapse accelerated, according to her briefing set, Lupérico had very wisely looked to his own interests.

For the life of him, Ramón Lupérico could not see how his interests intersected with those of this American woman. At least he could take some satisfaction, some small sense of control, from having earlier recognized the broad American accent of her natural voice even as she spoke in French and Spanish. But he could not place her within that much-reduced nation. She had neither the drawn-out cowboy twang of a Southerner nor the nasal drone of a couple of Americans he'd met from that region once known as New England. If anything, her voice sounded as though it had been scrubbed of any identifying inflections, as if she'd been taught to speak anew at some time. It was possible, he supposed, that she wasn't American at all.

Whatever her origin, Lupérico had a very bad feeling about her. He didn't fool himself for even a moment that he might get the better of her merely because she was a woman. A lifelong jailer, a professional custodian of the criminal classes and later of the political enemies of the state, he had encountered more than enough cruel and psychopathic females to disabuse himself of such a notion.

No, this woman was a hazard to life and limb. There was a terrible machinelike quality to her movements. As they forced a passage through the forest and her arm raised and fell, blurring the arc of the machete, he could see not the slightest waste of effort. Where he had flagged simply trying to keep up with her, she appeared to have ocean-deep reserves of energy on which she could call. And he'd seen the carnage she had left in her wake back at the prison. Just one woman. It did not bear thinking about. The best he could hope for was to give her whatever she sought. Unlike his former captors, she was very obviously a professional, a state actor, and as long as he remained of use to her, he was certain she would do her best to preserve him.

But what use could he be?

She surely had not fought her way into the Federation, murdering all of his guards and the Sweet Virgin only knew who else, merely to question him about the invoices he had padded out for the prison kitchen—back when he'd paid a handful of suppliers grossly inflated prices for foodstuffs they never delivered, preparatory to splitting the profit with them, of course. Nor did he imagine that she was here to carry out an audit of his former workplace because of the unusually high turnover in expensive computer equipment. All nefarious deeds, yes, but hardly worthy of state-sanctioned murder. Not even by the Americans. Racking his memory for the details of every tawdry little scam he had run back then, he could come up with nothing to explain her presence.

The woman appeared satisfied with whatever information she had exchanged with the little computer attached to her arm. She took a drink from her own supply before unwrapping two more of the unpleasant-tasting chocolate bars. Lupérico thought she might share one with him, but she ate both.

She took a few seconds to chew through the small meal, regarding him without apparent affect as she did so. Then something crashed through the undergrowth nearby, causing her to cock one ear in that direction and even to sniff the air like an animal, but she detected nothing to alarm her. Another drink, a quick check of their surroundings, and she seemed ready to deal with him. It did not leave him feeling confident.

"You ran a detention facility, an undeclared asset, for the French government in Guadeloupe."

It was a statement, not a question. Lupérico nodded warily. He'd been sure this would be about that period. He'd lived hand to mouth, stitching together one arrangement after another, since losing his position in the colony. Although he'd involved himself in any number of questionable activities during that time—some of which had finally brought him undone when he trespassed on the prerogatives of Roberto Morales's mafia state—none suggested themselves as likely to elicit the very precise form of violence this woman, this *opératif,* had visited upon the militia. His mind began to race all over again, desperately searching for some memory that might explain her arrival. In the meantime, there was little point in lying to her. Indeed, it probably would prove to be dangerous.

"I was the administrator there, yes," he answered.

"You remember a prisoner, a German national of Turkish background, by the name of Bilal Baumer? You would have received him via extraordinary rendition sometime after the Paris intifada."

Lupérico tried to keep his face neutral, but he feared that the woman could read his underlying anxiety. He now knew this was political, and political intrigues were always the most problematic, no matter that his own involvement might be tangential. Again, he saw no point in lying to her. She obviously knew that the prisoner had been through his facility.

"Well, we had a large number of renditions after September 11," he replied, watching her carefully for any sign of a reaction while he tried to reach back through the years. She gave none, which he found even more unsettling. He did not want to displease her. A German national? Of Turkish background.

Think, he told himself. *Think.*

"I didn't say September 11," she corrected him. "I said you would have received the prisoner after the intifada."

"But of course," he said, desperately searching his memory and finally coming up with a face to put to the name she had given him. *Baumer.* It had been so long ago, and that had been a different life. He nodded vigorously, wanting her to know he could help. He was useful. "Yes, we had more after the intifada. I think I recall your German now. He was young and very much assimilated into Western culture. Not like most of the crazies we took in around then."

"Do you recall the circumstances of his release?"

Lupérico could not help himself. This could be dangerous ground. He averted his gaze, staring instead into the brush, as though his memories might lie in there.

"Well, as I said, we had a number, a large number, of renditions pass through in those days. I am afraid I do not recall the details attending each of them. They were not really my responsibility. I was a processor, not an . . . *end user*—is that the term? And also, I'm afraid that part of my life . . . it was a long time ago. Much has happened, and I am no longer working in the service of the French state. As you can see, I have been abandoned."

If he had hoped for a flicker of sympathy, he was disappointed. The woman's eyes seemed as cold and fathomless as a frozen lake.

"Think hard, Lupérico. You may not survive the wrong answer. Was Baumer's release authorized by the Ministry of Foreign Affairs in Paris, or did you release him on your own authority?"

Lupérico had been thirsty before, but he now found that his mouth was unnaturally dry. There could be no doubt that he was in great peril. His tongue rasped against the back of his teeth, sticking there. His heartbeat, previously thready and uncertain, seemed to have slowed down considerably, as though every contraction were struggling hard to pump double the normal volume of blood.

"Understand me," said the woman. "I do not care what scams or shakedown rackets you had going in Guadeloupe at the end. I know how things fell apart. They fell apart everywhere. I don't need contrition or evasion from you; I need information. Why did you release Bilal Baumer?"

She did nothing as crude or obvious as turning her gun on him, but everything about the American and her lethal demeanor spoke to Lupérico of the gravest consequences if he didn't tell her what she wanted to hear. He shook his head involuntarily, as if arguing with himself.

"You are right, of course. Everything was falling apart. Once the intifada began, the *guerre civile,* the colonies were very quickly cut off. We had no—"

"I'm not interested in a history lesson on the manifest inadequacies of the French state," she interrupted. "You are obviously getting to Baumer. Just take the direct route and save us some time."

Lupérico couldn't believe it. It was impossible that something so simple should rebound on him so many years later. My God, the terrible things he had done in the last days at Guadeloupe . . . He shook his head again. He had thought for a moment he might have had to answer for prostituting his female prisoners or, in the final extremes of *el colapso,* for organ harvesting some of his charges for a Chinese billionaire who flew into the facility on his own plane. But no.

The man sat on the brush floor with moisture seeping in through the seat of his pants, marveling at how a simple payoff could have brought him undone.

He slapped at a flying bloodsucker attempting to make a meal of his earlobe. The high-pitched buzz was distressing in and of itself. The sun still had enough power to make the terrible press of heat and humidity utterly unpleasant, but the small clearing in the forest remained heavily shaded by the thick intersecting layers of overhead canopy. Lupérico reached for any recall of the smaller details of those days, for something that might just reduce the pitiless stare with which his liberator/captor regarded him.

He remembered that when it became obvious that Paris had forgotten them, that the whole world was falling apart, he had moved quickly to secure his immediate future.

And yes, that did mean he released a few of the prisoners before their time. He remembered the young German well now. The memories came rushing back, as if a dam wall had collapsed. This Baumer stood out for two reasons. When the man arrived in Guadeloupe, his file was sealed. Lupérico was given no idea of the prisoner's background or of what had led him into expedient detention—a form of incarceration in which the individual was held without acknowledgment, *"au plaisir du Président."*

"Baumer, yes, I did release him," he admitted finally. "But you must understand, our situation was quite desperate. We—"

"Not interested. Why did you release him? It wasn't from the kindness of your heart."

Lupérico had difficulty maintaining eye contact with her. Her gaze, although almost inhumanly cold, still seemed to weigh him in judgment. Was it his imagination, or did the forest seem unnaturally quiet now?

"Well, I was paid, of course. A bribe, if you must. We are both adults, señorita . . ."

He waited, hoping she might give him something, but the woman's demeanor did not change. She didn't speak. She simply stared at him, waiting for him to continue.

"Look," he went on, gesturing helplessly, "it was obvious to me he was one of the bearded crazies. Even though he was clean-shaven. I have dealt with enough of them to recognize the type. Fanatics, all of them . . . But you would know that, after 9/11," he added, hoping to create a common link. "This German was no different. A fanatic with more sense than most, but still a death-obsessed medieval god botherer, no? But what did it matter? Their great Satan was gone. There could be no return to France for him. Not when Sarkozy prevailed in the war. So what did it matter, letting one more savage out into the wild?"

The log on which he sat was rotten, and it crumbled underneath him as he shifted his weight. Lupérico's backside cracked the thin husk of the hollow fallen tree trunk with a loud crunch, and he dropped a couple of inches before emitting a little shriek when he realized he was covered in stinging red ants. He leaped to his feet and tried to brush them from his pants. The woman was on him before his heart could beat again. He had no idea what she did to him, but he felt his legs suddenly swept out from under him as his shoulders were driven down into the ground—into the giant ants' nest he had just disturbed. He would have shrieked aloud and for much longer, but the fierceness of the expression on her face, now less than a foot from his, unmanned him. She looked predatory, carnivorous.

"Tell me exactly how he was released."

He tried to speak, but she was choking him. He could feel his eyes bulging and his face turning red as he spluttered and slapped ineffectually at her stranglehold. She regained control of herself just as he felt himself about to pass out, but he remained unable to answer her with any alacrity. Instead he rolled away from the ants, coughing and gagging for air.

"It was another Turk," he said with great difficulty, fighting the urge to vomit. "A businessman. He described himself as Baumer's uncle, but that was almost . . . almost certainly a lie. But he was a businessman. He was in shipping. One of his ships was in port, and he offered to take Baumer away. What did I care? It was one less prisoner to feed, one less crazy to worry about. The world was at an end. It did not matter."

His tone was almost pleading. The woman had withdrawn to the other side of the clearing and gave a very strong impression of having to restrain herself. Why did she care about all this? What was it to her? Like him, she was just a functionary.

"The name of the Turk," she demanded. "The one who came and took your prisoner, the one who bribed you. What was his name?"

Lupérico noticed the tips of her fingers moving rhythmically, tapping the black holster in which she wore her sidearm. Panic sluiced through the former jailer. If she intended to frighten the information out of him, she was doing herself no favors. How was he supposed to think with the prospect of execution hanging over him?

"I-I do not remember."

"You need to remember, believe me."

He felt ants crawling around under his clothes, biting him and tearing small pieces of flesh from the open wounds inflicted by his torturers. He was terrified and in agony.

"It is too hard . . ." he protested. "Those days, they were the end of days. The end of the world. How can you expect me to remember the name of one fat Turk?"

She seemed to understand that she was distressing him. The woman folded her arms and made an obvious effort to collect whatever feelings were threatening to run away with her.

"So you were bribed by a Turk. A businessman with shipping interests. Do you remember the name of the ship you said was in port?"

"*Sweet mother of God, why would I remember that?* I don't remember his name. I never saw his ship. I had no reason to! Do you know what sort of traffic we had coming through in those days?"

The woman took in a deep breath, composing herself again. He watched her, wary of what she might do next.

She seemed to resolve a debate within herself. He flinched as she reached inside her combat vest, but rather than producing a weapon, she pulled out a resealable plastic bag. She unfastened the Ziploc and removed five or six pieces of paper. Photographs.

She dropped them on the ground in front of him before stepping back, paying him the compliment, he supposed, of at least pretending he was a threat to her. Lupérico didn't need to be told to pick them up. Brushing ants off himself, resisting the urge to shake his legs like a wet dog to throw more off, he bent down to retrieve the images.

There were six of them, all men, two of whom were white; the remainder were Arabs or maybe Persians. For one brief, shining instant, his spirits actually lifted—he recognized one of them.

"This is him! He's the Turk who offered me the bribe, without a doubt."

The woman nodded as though she had known all along. Satisfied at last.

For the first time since he'd been picked up by the Oficina Seguridad, perhaps for the first time since he had fled Guadeloupe on one of the last flights out of the airport, Ramón Lupérico felt as though circumstances had finally broken his way. For close to five years he had grifted and scavenged a path through the anarchy of *el colapso* and the brutal consolidation of Roberto's Federation until his luck had run out.

But perhaps this might be his chance to escape. He had helped this woman with something that was obviously very important to her and the people who had sent her. And it was such a small thing. So many of the jihadists passed through that Baumer would surely not have been his responsibility for much longer, anyway. He had done a small wrong in this instance, no more. The woman had said she was not at all interested in those instances. And she was American, which was good. The Americans were looking to rebuild the empty land. A man of his talents, they would surely . . .

A loud metallic click interrupted his happy thoughts of redemption. He looked up from his reveries. Confused. The woman was pointing something at him. He was looking right at it.

He did not finish the thought.

12

NORTH KANSAS CITY, MISSOURI

"You can't do this to us, mister. We ain't done nothin' worth a hangin'."

In her dream, the three men, the three surviving road agents from the gunfight at Crockett, were already dead. And yet they lived. They sat astride their horses on legs broken so badly that the feet of the youngest one were turned completely around in the stirrups. His accomplices, the old one and the fat one, were no better. Shattered femurs poked through torn jeans, and flies crawled in the old gringo's gnarled and mangled mess of bloody kneecaps, destroyed by a shotgun blast from the look of them. The unholy dead paid it no heed.

Instead they complained of the injustice of being hanged for raping whores and driving off banditos. The "whores" stood in front of them, a clutch of pale-faced trembling Mormon women. One of the so-called bandits, her father, slipped a noose over the ruined skull of the morbidly obese road agent sitting on the horse in the center.

In her dream, even the horses looked as though they had ridden from the gates of hell. Their eyes were burning coals, and when they snorted and threw their heads back in protest at the burdens they were forced to carry, they spit long fiery tendrils of magma that burst into dirty blossoms of oily black and orange flame upon hitting the ground.

Sofia was angry. Not with the road agents. Not these ones, anyway. They would soon be on their way to punishment. Her anger was directed at her father, and she was angry in the way that only a teenager could be with an adult. She had saved his life last night, at considerable risk to her own, and for this she was rewarded with a whipping the likes of which she could not recall from her childhood.

Didn't he understand that she was capable of protecting herself? What if she'd had her Remington with her the day the family had been attacked? She could have picked off the agents from the hilltop. Maybe she could have shot down the men who assaulted Mama. She just wanted to be somewhere safe, with all of her family still alive and untouched by the evils of the road agents. Not standing under a tree in the middle of a wasteland, surrounded by wailing women who had not been strong enough to defend themselves. She wanted everything back as it had been.

Part of her hoped that this retribution might draw a line under it all.

Among the three dead men they had captured and strung up for execution, for some reason she took a particular dislike to the fat one in the middle. There was just something gross and upsetting about even looking at him, something deeper than the surface details of the maggots seething in his wounds, of a giant worm nosing blindly around in the bloody crater on the side of his head. It was something deeper and more elemental than that: a sense of his complete evil. Maybe it had something to do with knowing what he had done to the captured women. They had not spoken about it in detail, of course, but in her dream—a very distant and rational but disconnected part of her understood that it was a dream—Sofia had a very good idea of the indignities visited on the Mormon women.

Although none of the ghouls her father prepared for execution had been at their homestead, they were of the same type—they were monsters. And according to Papa, they all worked for the same end and the same man, anyway. This devil in Fort Hood called Blackstone. It was he who should have been bound and trussed up on one of those satanic mounts with a noose of rusted razor wire around his neck, but she kept those thoughts to herself. She knew the Mormon women were uncomfortable around her, finding her hunger for vengeance unseemly and disturbing. But Sofia did not care. She put it down to their being Mormons. She was a Catholic, and in its heart the one true church believed in the redemptive value of blood sacrifice. Also, it quietly regarded all outsiders as marked for purgatory at the very best.

The agents, however, were going straight to hell. And as awful as she expected it to be, she wanted to watch them go. How annoying, then, that she should miss the drop of the gross one in the middle because she had rushed—or floated, really, this being a dream—to the side of the girl called Sally Gray, who had fainted under the taunts of the youngest of the condemned.

"You even told me you liked it; you said you wanted it that way," he called out from the back of his horse, causing a blush to discolor her wan features before her eyes fluttered and she dropped to the ground with a small, barely perceptible groan.

Sofia did not pause for a moment's thought. She hurried over to Sally to see if she might help. Indeed, in the dream, she flew quite literally to her side, as an angel might. But no sooner had she taken her eyes off the road agents than she heard a few harsh words and a horse whinnying just before a sharp, collective gasp from the small gathering and the sudden snap and thrumming of the hanging chain being jerked tight. She was aware somehow that the razor wire her father had wrapped around their necks had morphed into thick, rusted chains, each link cruelly barbed with fangs of sharpened bones taken from the bodies of the innocents these men had killed. She turned her head quickly to see the giant troll's body swinging dramatically and his legs kicking and jerking while her father looked on.

The oldest of the road agents appeared as a desiccated husk, a puppet of dry bones and wolf hide. He laughed at Papa, a sound like thousands of rats scurrying through a darkened basement. And the more he laughed, the stronger he seemed to grow and the weaker and more translucent her father became. Fading away, fading away until a terror took her by the throat, a fear that he might be laughed out of existence altogether.

It was all too much to understand, and Sofia didn't know why they hadn't simply shot the men down like rabid dogs when they first had the chance. She had even offered to do the work herself if the others didn't have the stomach for it. What was the problem?

If they had just shot them down, if they had just shown these agents the same lack of mercy they had shown the victims. If only she had been stronger. Her father would not be fading away. Papa would not be . . .

In the dream she screamed, but no sound came from her throat. All she could hear was the laughter of the dead man.

In her hospital bed, she screamed, and a nurse came running.

Her second awakening, late on Friday night, came easier. She emerged from a dreamless darkness into a soft, drugged consciousness. She remembered, in great detail but with no feeling, having woken earlier. Screaming, howling, and clawing at her bedclothes, swinging her damaged fist at a male nurse who tried to calm her down. She remembered the sting of a hypodermic and a sense of panic as darkness rushed up to meet her. But she was not panicking now.

She knew Papa was dead. The police officers who had come to the loft had told her that. She knew it, yet between her and that knowing stretched a great gulf over which she could only barely glimpse the oceans of sadness that waited to claim her. But she no sooner could swim over to that grief, through the thick numbness of whatever drug they had given her, than she could have her father back. Sorrow enclosed her, but it was a loose fit. Like a dark heavy coat, a man's coat, worn by a child playing dress-up.

Her room was empty aside from herself. The North Kansas City Federal Medical Center had a surplus of rooms to go around. She could smell steamed vegetables and chicken, a thin, almost metallic aroma. Like iron filings at the back of her throat. A television suspended from the ceiling was tuned to one of the three channels provided by the Armed Forces Heartland Network. It appeared to be the music video hour. She thought she recognized the band, some wave punk thing from Germany. Apart from the hall light, the flickering images on the TV screen provided the only illumination in the room. Full dark had fallen outside, and a high wind moaned as it rushed around the hospital buildings, rattling her window in its frame.

Papa was dead, and Maive was gone with him.

The only people she had left in the world, or at least in this part of it. She thought of Trudi Jessup, who had been so kind to her on the trail, and Adam, whom she liked very much. But they were both gone now, Trudi back in Seattle and Adam living somewhere in Canada with relatives.

Her head felt as though it had been packed in cotton wool soaked in sleeping gas or anesthetic or something. She was not groggy so much as numb. She stared out the window overlooking the darkened hospital grounds. Through the blowing snow she could just make out the lights of the Cerner Corporation Campus, where the Heartland Territorial Government had set up. After their initial arrival in Kansas City, they had spent a week on the former office campus going through a series of health checks, interviews, and screenings not all that different from the ones they had gone through for the homestead program in Texas. They stayed in a hotel room at the casino down the road, a musty, depressing room still marked by the stains of the departed.

She was transfixed for a moment by the reflection of the TV screen, which seemed to hang in the air outside her room. It floated in the darkness, seemingly as disconnected from consequence and meaning as she was.

Given the view, not to mention her familiarity with the hospital, she realized she was probably five or six floors up, facing the east. On a good day one could see the restored power plant from up there.

Sofia tested her freedom of movement. She wasn't hooked up to any drips or restrained in any way. A chunky plastic remote sitting on the bedside table looked like something she could use to call the nurses' station. But she didn't. Without being sure why, she carefully swung her legs out over the side of the bed and tried to balance her weight as she stood up. She was a little faint, and dizzy with it, but a few deep breaths saw her regain her equilibrium.

Her thoughts moved slowly. Her father's death seemed like a great dark mountain, with her standing at the foot of it, looking up and wondering how she could ever scale such a thing or even move around it. As slow and stupid as the drugs made her feel, she was glad of them.

Papa.

He was gone, and she knew his loss would soon hurt much worse. Worse than the loss of an arm or even a leg. Her heart had been ripped from her chest. But for now she remained deadened to the pain. That was good. She knew it gave her a chance to get moving, to act before she was paralyzed by the weight of it all. That was one of the things she had learned as they crept and sometimes fought their way free in Blackstone's Texas. Sometimes, no matter how grave the injury or outrage, you just had to move. To stand still was to die. You'd be overwhelmed, plowed under. Like everyone who had died in that flood on the Johnson National Grasslands. They hadn't moved, or they hadn't moved quickly enough.

Sofia moved. She quickly stripped off her loose cotton hospital gown and began changing back into the clothes she had been wearing. They were folded neatly on an armchair in the corner of the room, a pair of relatively new Levi's, a long-sleeved T-shirt, and a black hoodie. She was almost undone by the thought that Papa should have been sitting there waiting for her when she woke up. That was what fathers did. They watched over you. They were there for you when you woke up.

But that way lay madness, she knew. Even with the numbing cushion of the drugs to protect her, Sofia knew not to poke at that wound. It would pain her soon enough. As she climbed into her jeans and boots, listening for any sound of movement outside the room, she began to gather her wits. The fog was clearing from her thoughts, if not her feelings.

Maive.

Sofia had thought her dead. But no, she was not—not yet, anyway. She had survived the attack, the two police officers had said. As muzzy and clouded as the teenager's thoughts might have been, she was clearheaded on that issue. Her father and Maive had been attacked, not simply run down in some random accident. And Maive had survived.

She would be here somewhere. Sofia remembered that now: Maive was still alive but very badly injured. Was she in a coma? Was she undergoing surgery? Sofia was sure she'd known the answer to that once, but like a poor student, she had forgotten. It would be frustrating if she were not inoculated against feeling anything.

She tucked the white T-shirt into her jeans and put on the thick, fleecy hoodie. As she concentrated on dressing herself, she remembered. Maive was in intensive care. The nurses had told her that when the paramedics had brought her in, after she'd collapsed back at the apartment. Maive was alive, but she was in intensive care. That was why Sofia couldn't see her. She recalled asking them if Mrs. Aronson would be all right but couldn't remember what they had told her. Perhaps the nurses had avoided the question. It didn't matter. What mattered was that Sofia would not be able to see her. Not if she hoped to get away from here.

And for now that was all she wanted to do. To get away from this hospital, away from this city and back to Texas, where her family had been murdered. And where she could find the man her father blamed for the deaths.

The tyrant Blackstone.

Sofia Pieraro would return to Texas, as her father had promised to, and there she would settle with the man who had taken everything from her. She was done playing stupid games with the federales. They had done nothing in all the time she and Papa had been here in Kansas City. Nothing but talk. She was the last Pieraro. She had no choice—she would act.

13

DEARBORN HOUSE, SEATTLE, WASHINGTON

A fixer's work was never done. And a fixer he most surely was—not an aide, not a staff member, not even the chief of staff, despite what it said on his office door. Jed Culver was a fixer of small things, such as disputes between cabinet secretaries about who got the corner office, and big things, such as existential threats to the republic. And that was what he was certain he was looking at here: the death of the American Republic.

It was a hell of a thing when you thought about it. The Disappearance hadn't destroyed the United States, even though it had killed pretty much everyone on the continent save for a few lucky survivors in the Pacific Northwest and up into Alaska. Those survivors were doing the best they could to bind up the massive wound inflicted on the nation, but they were going to fail. America was going to die, and it was all because of one self-obsessed asshole. General Jackson Blackstone.

Or Governor Jackson Blackstone as he was these days. And hadn't winning the territorial elections back in 2005 earned him the title fair and square?

Culver grimaced. Mad Jack simply demonstrated that the power of the people could be a very sharp, double-edged sword. After all, how could any right-thinking American resist a staunch defender of the nation who fought the good fight against the granola- and tofu-chewing hippies of Seattle? Because, of course, your granola-chewing tofu types could never be real Americans, could they?

If only it were that simple, Jed thought.

He leaned back in his office chair, needing a little extra room to cross his legs, as he contemplated the photograph of Blackstone he was holding. It was a typical press shot of the former U.S. Army Ranger in his green dress uniform, bedecked in ribbons and stars, smiling at the camera with the pre-Wave flag of the United States draped artfully behind his right shoulder. He came across as a country grandpa of sorts, eager to get out of the army-issue suit and tie for some fishing by the river. When Blackstone wasn't angry, he could even sound like your granddaddy, calmly telling you the facts of life with the same patience that one might use in teaching a child how to thread a worm onto a fishing hook. Or throw a roomful of duly elected civilian representatives into confinement for arguing over Oreo cookies.

There was a bit of the Roman in him, too, perhaps, something that to Jed's eye brought to mind the old busts of Pompey and Vespasian. The great leonine head, the long nose and imperial bearing that seemed to fill out his uniform with extra awesomeness. You could understand why people might turn to him during the End Times. The motherfucker had a glint in his eye that whispered of your salvation or, to Jed's practiced and cynical eye, of Blackstone's messiah complex.

He tossed the color photo onto a pile of more recent matte black-and-white photographs that was threatening to spill over the edge of his desk. In the later shots, Blackstone had offset his bald pate with a grandfatherly beard that was slowly going white with age. The Santa Claus look, Kipper called it.

Culver's special project took up all the available space in his rather cramped office. The desk wasn't a mess by any means. Jed Culver's mind was too organized to countenance sloppiness of thought or deed, but it was a mind possessed of an unnatural ability to take in and process vast amounts of information. It was why he had been such a successful attorney once upon a time. Having learned something, he retained that knowledge. But more important, he understood it within the context of everything else he had learned. That was the mistake people made, Jed thought: they confused information with meaning. It was all very well to have a so-called photographic memory—he didn't; he simply had a very well-organized and partitioned memory—but unless you could synthesize all the random bits of information, the data points, the seemingly disconnected instances and episodes and reams of evidence and counterevidence into a coherent narrative that was firmly grounded in reality, not what you wanted reality to be, you were fucked.

A subzero gale rattled his office window in its frame, as if applauding this grim, Darwinian opinion. Jed grunted in irritation. He'd jammed a folded wedge of paper in there a couple of hours earlier, Kipper style, to stop the damned thing from annoying him. He wondered if they'd had these same problems of working in an old, antiquated building back in the original White House.

He dropped down on one knee to search for the missing wedge. For all his justly famed powers of concentration, rattling windows drove him nuts and left him unable to think. He found the makeshift wadding behind the floor-length curtain and jammed it back in between the sash and the frame, restoring blessed quiet to his office.

His desk looked as though children had made a game of constructing a city out of manila folders crammed thick with paper. Small towers of the buff-colored folders rose up from the leather desktop in a strict grid formation, giving the impression in the soft lamplight of a city skyline built for play. But games he didn't need. Culver was tired.

He glanced across at the old brass wind-up chronometer on his bookshelf. It was coming up on six in the evening. The ticking of the clock and the green-shaded desk lamps throwing their mellow light down on the miniature city blocks of paper files but leaving the upper reaches of his high-ceilinged office in relative gloom created the impression of an archaic museum exhibit. The office of a university don preserved from the late 1800s. But he preferred it that way. Clockwork timepieces did not fail when the power went down or their batteries ran out, and the necessity of winding them up at regular intervals imposed an exemplary discipline on the mind. The paper files, too, might give the impression of bygone inefficiency, but in his experience, the efficiency with which electronic files could be copied and rapidly disseminated to a virtually infinite audience made working with hard copy a no-brainer. The security issue he dealt with by having two marines on guard at his door whenever he had to break out the files. These folders, for instance, would remain stacked on his desk overnight just in case he was able to sneak away from the president's fund-raiser in a couple of hours to squeeze in a little bit more Machiavellian plotting.

For now, unfortunately, duty called him back to human contact. He had a short amount of time to freshen up and change before dinner and drinks with a roomful of potential donors. He already knew from past experience that Kipper would be absolutely hopeless when it came to putting the bite on people, so that was another unpleasant necessity that would fall to him.

He stood with arms folded, his chin resting on his broad chest, and sighed. Somewhere in that mini-Manhattan of paper was an answer. He had towers of documents detailing Blackstone's official efforts to resist and undermine the settlement programs down in the Federal Mandate and two solid blocks of binders containing classified files, among them investigators' reports about Fort Hood's suspected complicity in the "unofficial" resistance to Seattle's settlement program.

Thank you, Sarah Humboldt. Thank you, FBI.

He had treasury reports going into fine, granular detail about Blackstone's abrogation of federal–state cost- and revenue-sharing agreements and more Treasury reports, from the Secret Service this time, particularizing his administration's many and complex contractual arrangements with foreign governments and corporations, all of them of contested legality, all of them designed to siphon off income that should have been going into the federal budget. Salvage agreements, mining and pastoral leases, technology transfer, even military sales. Blackstone was effectively running a shadow state. It didn't matter how many times they dragged him off to the Supreme Court; his state law officers simply played to delay or reformatted any commercial agreements to negate the case against them. Or sometimes, Jed thought with a great deal of chagrin, Blackstone just did as he damned well pleased and flipped off any court ruling he found inconvenient. As Kipper and he had discussed to the point of collapse, a law that could not be enforced was not a law. It was a fatal weakness and a provocation to calumny.

He collected his jacket from the hanger on the back of his door, accepting that he would be back here later in the evening, probably working until the early hours. Because somewhere in that mountain range of files, he knew there had to be some point of weakness where he could apply pressure and break the administration of General Jackson Blackstone like a dry twig.

As he left the office, the two marines standing guard outside, both of them armed, snapped to attention.

"Thanks, fellas," he said. "I'm sorry you got this shit job, but I'm very grateful that you're doing it. When's your changeover?"

"We will be relieved at 2100 hours, Mr. Culver," replied the marine nearest him. "It could be worse, sir. We could be standing sentry out in the cold."

"I suppose you could," he conceded. "And at least you'll get to see some pretty secretaries walk by when they all go home in half an hour."

"Sir, yes sir!" the men replied in unison, bringing a smile to Culver's face.

"Okay, same drill as always, then. Nobody goes in there but me. Also, the damn window is rattling around. I've got it locked, but I really don't want to trust the security of the nation to a Depression-era thumb latch. So maybe if you just put your head in there occasionally and chase off any cat burglars who might come by, that'd be cool, too."

"I'm a dog person, sir. It would be my pleasure," said the first marine.

"Good to hear. There's hope for this country yet."

He gave them a friendly wink and left to find his driver.

Jed had his family ensconced in a large four-bedroom house over in Madison Park. Back in 2003 it had been leased by Arthur Andersen on behalf of one of his executives who was working in-house with Boeing.

The place itself had been owned by a two-dollar shelf company, the ownership of which had receded in clarity through a series of property trusts, holding companies, and increasingly obscure corporate entities. The executive, and Arthur Andersen for that matter, had Disappeared. For all intents and purposes, then, the house had no owner. Under the Real Property Act of 2005, it had become an asset of the state and from there the family home of the chief of staff of the president of the United States. It wasn't a sweetheart deal. He was paying full market price for the lease.

Marilyn and the kids loved the house. Unfortunately, for Culver's purposes, it was just too far away. There were weeks when he virtually lived in his office, and to save time he had taken a small one-bedroom apartment two minutes away from Dearborn House. His wife, his third wife, actually, who loved, loved, *loved* to socialize, was waiting for him in her underwear when he rushed up from the town car. Sadly, Marilyn had no high jinks in mind. She was simply suffering from option paralysis, unable to decide what to wear to the fund-raiser.

"Jedi Master!" she squealed when he hurried in through the door.

Marilyn Culver was not going to be bothering the selection committee at Mensa anytime soon, but Jed had not married her for her brains. He had been attracted by her smokin'-hot bod and well-preserved looks, unashamedly so. She was one of those women other women hate, the sort who looked better as they got older. Because he had been drawn to his previous wives by their looks, however, that had not been enough to put a ring on her finger. In Marilyn, Jed found an innocent soul possessed of a naive faith in humanity that was entirely uplifting after having to spend his working day dealing with the worst aspects of his fellow man. Some of which aspects, he had to confess, he himself possessed in full measure.

He knew, as soon as he saw her standing all but naked in front of the full-length mirror at the end of the hallway, holding three formal dresses under her chin, what had been going on. She had been trying to choose an outfit for hours. The bed would be piled high with them. Even though this was just their bolt hole in the city, Marilyn maintained a full wardrobe here. Some men would have lost patience, but he felt his spirits lifting and his eyes crinkling with a delighted smile.

"There will be a great disturbance in the Force if you do not wear the glittery silver one that shows off your boobs, sweetheart," he called out down the hall.

She brought it to the forefront and tipped her head to one side, considering his advice. "You think so?"

"If you don't wear that dress, Marilyn, the terrorists have won."

"Can't have that, then," she said, sounding convinced.

He gave her a peck on the cheek and a playful pat on the rump as he hurried past to have a quick shower and climb into his monkey suit. "Don't be long now," he told her. "We have to be at Kip and Barb's place by seven."

"Just making myself beautiful," Marilyn said, pouting.

"Too late," he shot back. "You already maxed out on that. Now, get into that sexy, sexy dress and get ready to distract some rich morons while I shake them down for filthy lucre."

Unlike the choice of formal wear, which really could go on for hours—days if you counted the phone hookups and girlfriend conferencing that went into compiling a short list—Marilyn Culver was something of a Picasso with a makeup case. A few minimal brushstrokes here and there and she could create a masterpiece.

Jed found himself stirring with arousal as he emerged from the bedroom doing up the buttons of his dress shirt. She really was stunning, and unlike the trolls he had married by accident, her beauty went deep. It was a pity to waste it on some of the assholes she'd be entrancing tonight.

"Come on," he said. "Let's take you out to dinner and a show."

"And I'm the show?" She beamed.

"No, you are *on show*. The entertainment tonight will probably be provided by Henry Cesky, about fifteen minutes after he hits the open bar."

"Oh, him . . ." She frowned now. "He's not very nice, is he."

"Well, you'll just have to make up for any shortfall on his account, won't you?"

14

CENTRAL SYDNEY, NEW SOUTH WALES

In her go bag, Julianne had fifteen hundred dollars in local currency, two changes of clothes, a first-aid kit, and three plastic cards, two of them credit cards and one an international driver's license establishing her identity as Julia Black, a British woman, a resident of Florida when the Wave had removed all human life from that part of the North American continent. Julia had been spared being turned into apocalyptic blood pudding by virtue of being on holiday in Spain with her husband. (In fact, Julia Black's earthly remains were almost certainly staining the couch, carpet, toilet, or whatever of her Miami home.) The sudden disappearance of more than 300 million Americans like Mrs. Black was a boon to the likes of Lady Julianne Balwyn, that is, to those individuals who, through misadventure and a certain moral flexibility, often found themselves in need of a spare identity and disinclined to let good manners prevent them from stealing one from the mysteriously departed. It wasn't like the Disappeared were using them anymore, and of course the great majority of people lived their lives as unknowns, anyway, dying in the same useful state.

Jules swung the small backpack over her shoulder as she stepped up into the Greyhound, departing the bus terminal at the city end of Oxford Street for Brisbane, a thousand miles to the north. She wished she had a gun in the bag. She wished she had more money. She really wished she wasn't climbing on board a fucking Greyhound and riding the pooch for the next twenty-four hours in the company of fifty or so fucking lumpen proles smelling of fast food and existential failure. But she couldn't afford a plane ticket all the way to Darwin, and at any rate security at the airports and train stations was much tougher than on the bus routes. A series of Jemaah Islamiyah suicide bombings a couple of years back had seen to that. She didn't imagine that the local wallopers would break a sweat investigating the death of a small-time crim, but she was developing a healthy paranoia about Cesky's ability to hunt her down.

She checked her ticket—seat 20A—and was relieved to find herself sitting next to a young woman who smiled nervously at her approach before putting her head back inside a fantasy novel the size of a house brick. Jules nodded brusquely, establishing the precedent of not talking to anyone. She stowed her bag in the luggage rack over the seat in front of her, where she could keep an eye on it, and tried not to regret the six months' rent she had paid in advance on her bed-sit in The Rocks. The rental market was so tight with the city full of refugees that if she hadn't been able to stump up the cash, she'd have had no chance of securing her digs. That deposit had siphoned off a good deal of her liquid funds. And now she'd had to abandon the place, to get out of the city where she'd been tracked, and run north to the only people she could trust in this country or possibly the whole bloody world.

"Come on, honey, it'll be a great adventure."

"No, it won't. This sucks. This whole country sucks. I just want to go home."

American voices. There was no escaping them. Maybe a third of the passengers traveling north were displaced Americans. The unlucky ones, those who arrived without capital or connections. They probably were heading north for the fruit-picking season, although they probably would be a month too late to score the best jobs. That was why they were on this bus, like Julianne. Because they were losers.

The father and daughter, the angry princess who just wanted to go home, wrestled their heavy backpacks past her on their way to the rear of the bus. The bags looked way too heavy for carry-on luggage, leading Jules to suspect they probably contained most of the worldly goods of this woebegone pair. She'd seen it so often the last couple of years: people moving around with everything they owned strapped to their backs. There was nothing unusual about that, of course. People had been living like that for thousands of years. But not white, middle-class Americans.

She was in no position to look down on them. Not fleeing the city with her little go bag and her fake ID.

The big metal doors of the Greyhound's luggage compartment slammed closed outside as the last of the passengers shuffled in and claimed their seats. She sent a silent prayer of thanks up to the god she didn't believe in that the morbidly obese man with the apocalyptic body odor who got on last was not her seat buddy. Stealing a quick glance at the Tolkien fan next to her, she smiled. The young woman obviously had had exactly the same thought at just that moment. They shared a conspiratorial smile.

Jules wished she had thought to pack a novel in her getaway bag, but entertainment hadn't seemed like a high priority when she'd put it together. She was just going to have to sleep through most of the trip. Luckily, they were driving through the night.

"Good evening, ladies and gentlemen; my name is Tim Blair, and I'll be your coach captain for the run up to Lismore."

Oh, God. Shoot me now, Jules thought. *A fucking coach captain. Where do they find these drop-kicks?*

Blair started in on his predeparture spiel, explaining the "features" of their state-of-the-art vehicle. Julianne stared out of the window and tried to ignore him. A baby started crying somewhere a few seats behind her. The emo zombie across the aisle turned his MP3 player up to an eardrum-shredding volume.

". . . and we'll be stopping for dinner just after midnight in the town of Hexham," said Coach Captain Blair, "which in the opinion of this professional long-haul transport systems operator does the finest chicken-n-chips in the southern hemisphere."

For the first time since she had slotted the Romanian, Lady Julianne Balwyn wondered whether she might be better off staying in Sydney and taking her chances with whatever contract killer Henry Cesky sent after her next.

Too keyed up to sleep properly—not that it was really an option on a bus, anyway—she spent the first four-hour leg of the trip, a frustrating, drawn-out, stop-and-start crawl through the gridlock of the central business district and the semipermanent traffic jam of the northern suburbs, throwing a little pity party for herself. Julianne knew she had much to be grateful for. Unlike Pete and Fifi, she was at least drawing breath. She hadn't taken a bullet during a pirate raid, and she'd dodged any number of bullets since. In spite of Cesky's best efforts to get at her. And in the larger scheme of things, of course, she knew she should be grateful that they hadn't pushed their yacht a little harder back in 2003 to make the rendezvous with the *Pong Su,* a North Korean freighter carrying $4 million worth of perfectly counterfeited U.S. currency that they would take in exchange for the $1 million worth of genuine greenbacks, somewhat soiled by their connection to a series of drug transactions, stashed in the hold of the MV *Diamantina.*

If Pete had been a more diligent smuggler, they'd have been about ten nautical miles inside the Wave when it swept over the *Pong Su.* Thankfully, Pete was a doofus. A great mate, to be sure, and she missed him terribly, but a doofus.

A thin blanket served to ward off the chill of the air-conditioning as they pulled onto the freeway and accelerated away from Sydney. Unable to do more than nap fitfully, Julianne found herself replaying the last few years, wondering which particular ill-chosen life path had put her on this shitty bus in the middle of the night at the ass end of the civilized world. As always, she came back to her father. She had loved her old man, rogue that he was, and the old devil had done his best to provide for her in his own way, salting away some of his ill-gotten gains through a series of bank accounts tucked away in remote jurisdictions with famously lax attitudes toward regulatory oversight. But it hadn't been enough. Not nearly enough. Julianne wondered whether she might have been happier living an alternative life with a normal father who hadn't raised her to live well outside the norms that most decent people accepted as the price one paid for civilization.

However, she was, arguably, better prepared to have survived the last couple of years. She flicked a glance up at her backpack and shifted position in her seat to take her weight off the wallet in her back pocket, where Julia Black's driver's license, credit cards, and refugee papers sat. Would she have thought to lay in such preparations if a scoundrel had not raised her? Would she even be alive today? Probably not, she thought as the bus rolled through a striking series of canyons cut deep into the thick layer of sandstone that lay under the Sydney Basin. Powerful uplighting illuminated the soaring rock walls, throwing them into beautiful relief.

"Do you have anyone waiting for you up north?"

"What?"

The Tolkien fan had taken her by surprise, laying down her book and asking a question. Julianne had no desire to get into a conversation with anyone and kept herself closed off.

"You look a little bit lost is all," said the girl. "Like you have nothing to look forward to. Are you going up to Queensland to work or to meet someone?"

"Oh," said Julianne, searching for an answer. As much as she wanted to just keep to herself, she had always been taught that good manners cost nothing and often could serve as useful camouflage for one's true nature. "I have a friend who's sick," she said. "I'm going up to visit him. To help out a bit."

"That's nice," said the girl. "You seem like a nice person. I hope it works out for you." And with that she went back to Middle Earth.

The girl left the bus in Coffs Harbour, a pleasant enough seaside town where they stopped for breakfast the next morning. Julianne's luck ran out at that point, when the seat next to her was taken by an unwashed young man whose body mass was 50 percent composed of stainless steel piercings. He played loud, terrible music through his disgracefully cheap headphones and farted with joyous abandon all the way to Brisbane.

She couldn't really afford a good hotel room, but Julia Black could, and so Jules booked a night at the Sheraton as soon as she arrived in the northern capital. She had no intention of staying for long. She felt the urgency of her need to get to Darwin as a physical discomfort. Soaking in her bath at the hotel, washing away the unpleasantness of the road trip with a bottle of champagne from the minibar, Julianne called down to the concierge desk.

"I need to get in contact with someone in Darwin," she said. "A Mr. Narayan Shah. He runs a security consultancy up there, but I'm afraid I'm not quite sure of the name of his company. I wonder if you might be a dear and see if you could track it down for me. That's Narayan Shah. He's a former Ghurkha, if that helps . . . okay. Thank you."

The phone next to her bed rang ten minutes later while she was tying up the thick white bathrobe and contemplating a room service binge. If she was going to burn Julia Black's ID and credit rating, she might as well torch it in high style.

"Ms. Black, it is Arthur at the front desk. I have Mr. Shah on the line for you."

She heard a click and a beep, and then Shah's voice was in her ear.

"Ms. Black? This is Narayan Shah. How can I help you?"

"You can stop calling me Ms. Black for a start. It's Jules, Shah. From the *Aussie Rules.* How are you?"

He was, it seemed, surprised and delighted to hear from her.

"Miss Julianne, this is a pleasure. I had heard you were back in Australia and was hoping you would call."

She smiled at the rough, familiar tone of the old sergeant's voice.

"Hello, Shah," she said. "It's lovely to talk to you. And yes, I'm sorry I haven't been in contact, but you know, trying to keep a low profile and all."

She sat down on the bed and snugged the dressing gown closer around her.

"I understand," said Shah. "The authorities, they did not make it easy for you with Mr. Norman's boat and some of your passengers."

He meant the Pieraro family. Her wealthy American refugees had walked down the gangplank and into the warm embrace of the locals. Not so much the penniless Mexican family.

"Is there something I can do for you, Miss Julianne?" Shah asked. "I still regard myself as being in your debt."

"Oh, don't be silly. It's me who owes you. We would not have made it without you and your men. And I'm afraid I have to call on your grace and favor again. I'm in a spot of bother, Shah, and it might be something that affects you eventually. And maybe the Rhino, too. Did he make it up to Darwin? I know he was headed there and wondered if you might have been in contact."

There was a slight pause before the former Gurkha answered.

"The Rhino, yes, he is up here. I have seen him once or twice. But he is a proud man, Miss Julianne, and he keeps his problems to himself. I would very much like to help him, and you if you are in need. But I cannot say that Mr. Ross will want our help."

Julianne gazed for a moment out of the hotel window. Julia Black had booked a room on the executive level for the added security rather than for the extra luxury. The elevation afforded her sweeping views across the city and out toward the coast.

"Well, he's going to need our help," she said. "And I'm going to need yours, Shah. Someone's trying to kill me."

"Fascinating," said the soldier turned businessman. "Somebody is trying to kill me as well."

There was silence between them for two heartbeats.

"Oh, I'm sorry, Shah. I fear I may have dragged you into something awful."

His laughter was unexpected but reassuring.

"Miss Julianne, nobody drags me anywhere. Except my wife down to the shops during the sales. I cannot stay long on the phone to discuss this with you now. I really do have some pressing matters to attend to here. But I wonder how quickly you might get to Darwin."

"Not quickly at all, unfortunately," she admitted. "My resources aren't what they were."

She hated having to talk with Shah like this, as if he were a mark. It spoke well of the man that he recognized what she was doing but did not hold it against her.

"Nonsense," he said. "I shall organize a ticket for you on the next available flight. You are in Brisbane, yes? And traveling incognito? As Ms. Julianne Black?"

"Julia. For now," she said. "I'll probably need another ID in a couple of days. It's Cesky, if you remember him, from Acapulco. The guy we didn't let on the boat. The vengeful prick just won't give up. He's had a couple of goes at both the Rhino and me back Stateside. And I think he's found us over here now, too."

"I see," said Shah, sounding preoccupied. "It is settled, then," he said. "I shall organize you transport as soon as possible."

"I need to get to the Rhino as quickly as possible, too," she said. "He's probably in danger. And you said you have had some trouble?"

"Some, yes. I do not wish to be rude, Miss Julianne, but I would like to address these problems with dispatch. If you remain at your hotel, I will send through details of your flights when they are booked."

"And the Rhino?"

"He is working with one of the trawler companies up here. He may be out on the water; I do not know," Shah said. "But I shall have my men check for him, and when I send through your travel details, I will also include some contacts for him. Places you might look when you get into town. I assume you'll want to start straight away."

"I will," Julianne said. "I've had enough of this shit."

15

DEARBORN HOUSE, SEATTLE, WASHINGTON

James Kipper was grumpy. As soon as he and Marilyn were admitted to the president's private quarters, Jed could see he was grumpy simply because he was in the process of getting dressed. He had just his dinner jacket and black bow tie, known by presidential decree as "the Asphyxiator," to go. He would have started complaining as soon as he pulled his pants on and stepped it up while trying to get the cummerbund to sit properly around his nonexistent waist. The performance would soon be reaching a crescendo of mumbling and grumbling about "these stupid monkey clothes" while Barb attempted to do up the Asphyxiator. The president of the United States was nothing if not consistent. As was his wife. She sported the same furiously furrowed brow that Culver recognized from any number of these occasions over the last couple of years.

"He was trying to get away with wearing a clip-on. Can you imagine that, Jed?"

"All too easily," he snorted. "I wouldn't have been surprised if he'd tried turning up in a Hawaiian shirt or with a motorized bow tie that could spin like a propeller."

"Hey, I am the president, you know, fella," Kip protested. "And that sounds mighty like sedition talk to me. Don't make me call the Secret Service."

"Just shut up and let me finish this," his wife scolded as she fussed some more with the Asphyxiator. "I can't do this while you're flapping your gums around."

"I love what you've done with your hair, Babs," said Marilyn. It was an artful attempt to push the conversation away from Kipper's deep-seated aversion to dressing like a grown-up and onto a topic with which Jed's wife was familiar, one in which she was frighteningly over-qualified, in fact.

"Oh, this?" The First Lady blew a freshly cut fringe of hair back out of her eyes. "It was getting too long. I had to do something."

She finished with her husband's bow tie and banished him to the walk-in closet for his jacket. The two women fell into conversation as Culver joined his boss.

"I know you hate these things, Kip," he said, as always, getting his attention immediately with the informal manner of address. "But it's as much a part of your job as dealing with budgets, railroads, and re-construction and more a part of your job than worrying about snow-blowers and power lines around the city like you were this afternoon."

"Jesus, Jed, did Barbara word you up before you got here? Because I've been getting slammed by her for the same thing all evening."

The chief of staff helped Kipper get his arms into the dinner jacket and even tugged at the lapels a couple of times to make it sit properly on his shoulders.

"That's because she's right," he said. "You're not the city engineer anymore. You're the president. City engineers worry about snow-storms. Presidents worry about reelection."

Kipper frowned. "I thought I was supposed to worry about a lot more than that."

"It's all moot if you don't get reelected. And that's not going to hap-pen unless you campaign properly. And you cannot campaign properly without money. So that's what tonight is about—raising money to get you back into office so you can do your job, clearing roads, rebuilding railways, and pissing off the Greens by opening up a nasty new power plant somewhere. It's all good. But none of it is going to happen if you don't get the votes."

Kipper coughed out a short, humorless laugh. "I think all those things will happen whether I get reelected or not, Jed. Some things aren't political. They just have to happen."

"Really? Seriously? You actually live inside that gingerbread house?" Culver asked in a gentle voice. "You think Sandra Harvey would let the French build that shiny new pebble bed reactor you're so keen on? You think Blackstone would run your settlement program completely blind to race, color, or creed? You happy with the way he's virtually outlawed labor unions down there in Texas?"

He had him, of course, which didn't improve Kip's mood. He hated being pushed into a corner. But at least when you got him there, he had the good grace to stay put.

"I suppose so," he sighed. "Well, are we going to get this done?"

They exited the large closet and rejoined their wives, who had moved on from complimenting each other's outfits to discussing the children. Marilyn had never had any of her own, but she had been stepmother to Melanie and Roger for long enough to have earned her spurs. Jed pursed his lips at the incongruity of it all, the banality of everyday life within the insanely pressurized environment of supreme executive power. Even if that power was a dim shadow of its former greatness.

A soft knock at the door, and the protocol chief, Allan Horbach, admitted himself after a greeting from Barbara.

"Time for cocktails," he announced.

"Well, at least there's that," Kipper said in a funereal tone. But in fact, there wasn't, not for him.

The four of them walked the short distance to the reception room, where the buzz of conversation grew noticeably louder with their arrival. Jed nodded in satisfaction. All the big checkbooks were there: Microsoft, Boeing, Amazon, Costco, Cesky Enterprises, T-Mobile, the biotechs. All maneuvering for access to the president, who would need to keep his head straight while he talked to them. After being an-nounced to the room by Horbach, both Jed and Kip were handed champagne flutes by the White House head of protocol. On Culver's instructions, both contained sparkling apple juice.

"But I don't even like champagne," Kipper muttered out of the side of his mouth.

"Then you'll be fine," his chief of staff replied without sympathy. "Because you're not getting any." He could have murdered for a whis-key sour himself, but he had learned as a baby lawyer that drinking was best done after work, not during, and this was definitely work.

"Mr. President!"

Really. Hard. Work.

Henry Cesky, all bulk and bravado, had elbowed his way through the crowd to claim pole position in the race for Kipper's attention. His shoulders moved around under the expensive fabric of his dinner jacket like barrels loose on the deck of a schooner.

"Hey, Henry," Kip said, pleasantly enough while Culver went into a full-throttle, double-grip handshake, with shoulder punching and a bit of locker-room roughhousing thrown in. He could pull it off, having been a college wrestler. Kip couldn't. And Cesky was one of those guys who didn't just like to cultivate a rough-handed, working-stiff-made-good image. He was the real thing. Even if he hadn't always done good to make good and even if that roughness of character sometimes made him a risky choice at events like this. He was entirely capable of getting liquored up and throwing a punch at someone, perhaps a business rival or somebody who looked askance at his wife. Even the secretary of the treasury if Cesky was in a bad mood after filing his taxes. Rough, un-kempt black hair and a twice-broken nose added to the impression that Henry had spent decades in a boxing ring, never knowing when to give up.

It was a wonder Kipper and he didn't get along better. After all, it was Cesky putting a couple of hundred of his workmen onto the street, armed with sledgehammers and crowbars, that had added enough muscle to the popular uprising against Blackstone to see the fascist lit-tle prick tipped off his throne back in April 2003. But Kip, like Mari-lyn, just didn't like the man. He hid it well enough, though. And that was all Jed could ask. Henry Cesky was a fucking cash cow.

The reception room at Dearborn House wasn't so crowded that people were being jostled, unless they'd been in Cesky's way when he moved across the room to see Kipper. But it was crowded enough that people were beginning to raise their voices to be heard over one another. A string quartet borrowed from the city's symphony orchestra kept it light with a bit of Vivaldi while waiters circulated with more food than drinks. For now.

"How's business, Henry?" the president asked. "I was in KC a couple of weeks ago with Barney. He said the power grid over there was working almost perfectly now, thanks to your guys and the work they did at the plant."

Brooklyn-based before the Wave and Polish-born long before that, Cesky was a short but powerfully built man. You could see him levitating an inch or two with the compliment.

"That's good to hear, Mr. President," he roared back altogether too loudly.

Kip's Secret Service detail momentarily switched their attention from scanning the room to focus in on the loudmouth. As soon as they saw it was Cesky, however, their interest evaporated.

"Anything my guys can do to help, we're there," the construction tsar added, raising his glass in salute.

"And I'm sure anything the government can do to help one of our biggest employers and taxpayers," said Jed, "well, I'm sure we'll be there, too."

Cesky snagged a beer from a passing waiter, causing the president's face to crumple in naked envy. He sipped at his sparkling apple juice with no pleasure at all.

"Well, on that, I gotta tell you, Mr. President—Kip—I'm looking forward to this tax review you got going on. And I'm hoping your people are going to listen to my idea about one simple flat rate that everyone pays. No deductions. No paperwork. No fucking around with any of that stuff. We just hand over, say, 20 percent. And the government gets off our backs. What do you say?"

"I'd say it sounds like the sort of idea I would've come up with when I had an honest job," Kipper replied, giving Cesky cause to float another inch off the carpet. "But like all my best ideas, Henry, I bet yours would hit the brick wall of the bureaucracy and splatter like an egg."

Culver had to hand it to Kip. He really knew how to tell a guy what he wanted to hear while letting him down at the same time. Of course, it was always possible that he agreed with Cesky's crazy flat-tax idea, in which case it was probably a good thing he assumed it would splatter when tossed against the proverbial wall. Oh, if only funding a crippled government at the end of the world was as simple as passing the hat around, Jed thought. Intending to move his boss through the room, he was already scanning the crowd looking for the next donor when Cesky surprised him.

"You know, Kip," the big man said, feeling perfectly comfortable addressing the president as though he were speaking to some beer buddy, "if you'd just make that bastard down in Texas pay his way, you could probably afford a decent tax package. Okay, maybe not *my* idea. I know people are always gonna be suspicious of a guy with too much money saying he should pay less tax, but as long as that asshole is holding out on the rest of the country, you can't get nothing done. That's why I don't push back too hard when my invoices don't get paid right away by the Treasury. Because I know that rat fuck is holding out on you!"

The Secret Service was watching again, but Kip had switched from polite interest to genuine engagement with the construction magnate. Cesky had found one of the president's hot-button issues. He took a gulp from the champagne flute full of apple juice as if he'd forgotten it wasn't a real drink.

"I fucking tell you, Henry, I wish I had a few more guys like you working for me," Kipper said. "This is exactly what I've been saying for over a year. Do you know how many of my problems would go away if that guy would just pay his bills?"

And just like that, the energy between them shifted and they suddenly looked like old beer buddies after all, intent on saving the world with a couple of six-packs and a bunch of f-bombs. But Jed Culver didn't like the way this was going. He could almost see Kip agreeing to road-trip down to Texas in Cesky's pickup with a keg on the seat between them and an ass kicking for Governor Blackstone in the offing. Not that the idea didn't appeal on a deeply undergraduate level, but a large part of his job involved protecting Kip from his often naive enthusiasm.

Jed was just about to step in and break up the bromance when the First Lady appeared with Marilyn and insisted that the president come over and meet a real-live Hollywood star, Sigourney Weaver. Ms. Weaver had been spared the fate of so many of her colleagues by happening to be overseas promoting some long-forgotten kid film with Jon Voight and Shia LaBeouf when Brad and Clint and Arnie and Angelina were all reduced to pink mud.

"Really?" Cesky said, instantly losing interest in tax policy and federal–state relations. "I loved those *Alien* films. And I heard she was going to be in the new one, with those predators they had in that old Schwarzenegger movie. How cool would that be? Although, you know, it's the Brits making it. So it'll probably be shit."

"You liked those films? I *loved* those fucking films, man!" Kipper enthused, forgetting himself in his surprise that he'd found more common ground with the construction magnate. "Especially the second one, with the marines. It was the only one where you felt like the good guys actually had a chance. You know, right up until they got eaten."

Here was a conversation James Kipper could really get lost in. But the ladies did Jed's job for him, Marilyn in particular. The third Mrs. Culver let the businessman have a couple of thousand watts of eyes, tits, and teeth before skillfully prizing the president away and hurrying him off through the crowd to safety in a fashion that would have done his Secret Service detail proud.

"I'll tell Sigourney you're a big fan, Henry," Marilyn said. "Come and meet her later. But I have to introduce Kip first or that dreadful protocol Nazi will have kittens. Come on, Mr. President."

Culver and Cesky were left on their own.

"Jeez, women, eh?" sighed Cesky, still a little dazed by Marilyn's performance.

"Henry, I don't know how we've managed to keep them in their place for six thousand years."

Cesky rewarded that crack with a raucous laugh. He threw down the rest of his beer just in time to swap his glass for another, which came floating past on a tray.

"Yeah, women—can't live with 'em, can't live without 'em, unless you wanna go gay or something! But all joking aside, Jed," he said, "I'm fucking serious about this Blackstone. The day is coming when you're gonna have to crack him upside the head. Knock him down so hard he doesn't get back up again. Did you know that bastard has me blacklisted down there? All of that construction and salvage and clearance work he's got going on, and I can't get a taste of it. He's a vengeful cocksucker, I tell you."

Seeing his chance, the chief of staff closed in, putting his arm around the other man's shoulder, creating a small conspiratorial air between them in the middle of the roaring reception.

"Oh, I hear you, Henry. I hear you . . . Which brings me to the happy topic of what you can do to help us give the worthless cocksucker a kick in the ass. Because if he ever moves his operation from Texas up here to Seattle, my friend, you can kiss good-bye any government work *anywhere* in this country."

Cesky's expression was grim enough that Culver knew he'd hit home.

"Yeah. You're fucking right about that. I'll write you a check before I go tonight."

16

NORTH KANSAS CITY, MISSOURI

She could not return home. They would look for her there. It pained her not to be able to go back to the loft to collect any personal items, but she realized it was a small sacrifice to make. In spite of all that had taken place in her life and all she had done since that black spring day in East Texas, Sofia Pieraro was still considered a child. The police officers hadn't come around to the apartment simply to tell her that Papa was dead; they had also meant to take her into protective custody. Without her having any relatives or friends to stay with in Kansas City, she knew the authorities would move quickly to place her in foster care. Or even worse, if she tried to leave and failed, they'd probably put her into some sort of juvenile detention program. Like a common criminal. So no, she could not return home. She had to get out of this city and back down to Texas before anybody thought to look for her.

The federales would do nothing about that tyrant Blackstone. Sofia had watched her father's resolve wither away over the last few months as he'd come to understand his own powerlessness. But he hadn't been lying when he vowed to lay the family's vengeance upon the man he blamed for their deaths; she knew that. Miguel Pieraro had proved himself to be utterly without mercy when dealing with the governor's agents both at the homestead and later during their escape from Texas. But here, in the altogether more civilized surroundings of Kansas City, he had found himself drained of that resolve by the demands of the same authorities who promised to protect him—or, rather, his daughter, she thought with some shame—and levy a harsh punishment on anyone they could prove was responsible for the slaughter of the Pieraro clan.

But what have they done? Sofia asked herself again as she pulled the hood of her sweatshirt up over her head and jammed her hands deep into the pockets against the cold of the night. She worried about how much colder it would be outside and wondered whether she might be wise to find a heavy jacket somewhere. Perhaps steal one from a room. But momentum pushed her forward, and caution. It wouldn't do to be caught stealing when all she wanted was to get away.

Midnight had come and gone some twenty minutes earlier, and she knew from her work here that a new shift would just be settling in. She kept her head down as she made her way down the dimly lit corridor, hoping nobody would recognize her. She knew a few people working the graveyard shift this week, but apart from a television running a news channel feed from Seattle and the rattle of a cleaner's metal bucket somewhere nearby, this part of the hospital was quiet. Papa's death and her arrival as a patient no doubt had been noted by the staff and passed around as an item of gossip or concern. It didn't matter which to Sofia. What mattered was getting away without being seen.

The main reception desk was not staffed right now. A few desolate individuals scattered here and there on the rows of cheap plastic chairs that occupied about half the foyer gave her no more than a passing glance as she hurried through. It would be busier in emergency, she knew. There were always doctors on duty in the ER at the far north end of the building, and always plenty of patients for them to see. Drunken militiamen busted up in a bar fight. Farm and construction laborers injured at work. Auto accident victims—a lot of them in this weather. At the southern entrance, however, near the remains of a never-completed parking garage, she was able to pass through unobserved.

Sofia patted the back pocket of her jeans, checking for her wallet. She had thirteen newbies in there, the only money she had in the world now. It would be enough for her immediate requirements; she'd just have to scavenge what she needed along the way. She hurried down the steps toward the taxi rank, where a couple of cabs sat idling to power their heaters, generating thick white clouds of exhaust. Sofia swore and shivered in the cold as she increased her pace to a light jog. It felt as though frozen fingers were clenching inside her body.

She scrabbled at the handle of the door to the nearest taxi. The grip was so cold that it frost burned her shaking hand. As she quickly climbed in and closed the door behind her, the contrasting warm air was almost unbearable at first. Her eyes watered, and the exposed skin on her face and hands felt like it had been scalded. She was going to need warmer clothing fast.

The cab driver was Indian. Most of them were. She'd learned from the Indian kids at school that many of the refugees working in the railway yards took second jobs at night, driving cabs mainly or cleaning or doing whatever they could to scratch together a few newbies.

"Good evening, miss," said the driver.

"I need to get out to the truck stop, the Flying J on Corrington," she said through chattering teeth. "Out by the power plant."

The driver, a middle-aged man in a pale blue turban, looked like he was about to ask why a girl her age would be heading out to Hawthorne at this time of night.

"Can we get going?" Sofia asked as she tried to rub some warmth back into her arms. "I'm late for my shift in the kitchen. They'll dock me half a night's pay if I'm even five minutes late." A complete lie but explanation enough for a man most likely working his second job, a man who'd probably also had more than his fair share of unreasonable bosses.

He put the battered yellow cab into gear, and they pulled away from the curb.

"Were you visiting somebody in the hospital, miss?"

A conversation was the last thing she wanted. But she had enough of her wits about her to know she shouldn't draw attention to herself by snapping back unreasonably at his question.

"Yes, I was sitting with a friend. She broke her arm, and they're putting a metal plate in it tomorrow."

Again, she was surprised at how easily the lie came. Sofia closed her eyes and folded her arms, leaning her head back as though she wanted to sleep. She was still shivering. The driver took the hint and bothered her no more.

They moved onto Clay Edwards Drive, counterclockwise around the loop that would take them in front of the ER. She pulled the hoodie down over her head as they passed. No one ran out to stop the taxi. Surrendering to inertia as the car completed the long, slow turn, Sofia let her head roll over and loll on one shoulder, allowing her to peer out of the window into the dark, bleak winter landscape. Snow no longer was falling, but it lay heavily on the ground, creating an eerie atmosphere similar to some accursed realm from a children's fairy tale in which evil spirits had eaten all the light and warmth of the world.

She was still numbed by the drugs the nurses had given her. Not physically. As soon as she'd started moving around, in fact, she had recovered her equilibrium quickly, and tonight's brutal wind chill sort of helped, too. The Siberian Express, having sharpened itself on the frozen wastes of the Missouri River Valley, had sliced through her when she left the building, electrifying her senses.

Sofia's psyche, however, was numb, allowing her to reflect on her father's death as well as the idea of poor Maive Aronson plugged via a tangle of tubes into the life-support machines in intensive care. She wished she'd been able to say good-bye to Maive. But she could afford no regrets.

Sofia Pieraro was not a stupid girl. She realized that something far worse than regret lay ahead for her. She knew that howling grief and loss and a feeling of tumbling end over end into a pitch-black chasm all awaited her soon enough.

At fifteen, she was not the simple farm girl she surely would have grown up to be had the Wave not arrived to sweep destruction across the globe. She would cope with whatever came, because she always had. She remembered very little else in her life. Sofia Pieraro had escaped the first moments of *el colapso* when Acapulco fell into madness. She had sailed halfway around the world, battling pirates. She had worked on the refugee farms in Australia and gone to school there with children whose stories were every bit as fantastic as her own. She had helped make the family farm in Texas, the one the federales had told them would be theirs forever one day, into a great success. She had seen that promise snatched away by Blackstone's road agents. She had seen her family murdered. She had trekked over a thousand miles with her father and Maive and her people. She had survived more banditry on the way and the great flood, constant deprivation, and once even an attack from a giant pack of wolves on the outskirts of Tulsa. Sofia Pieraro might have appeared to be nothing more than a young girl to somebody like this taxi driver, but she had lived and learned enough for four or five lifetimes in the last four or five years alone.

She would survive her grief. But Jackson Blackstone would not survive her determination to settle with him.

The cab struggled down Highway 210, going west toward Interstate 435. The driver took his own sweet time, saying he was fearful that the snow-clotted roads would pitch him into the median, where they could run out of gas and freeze to death. Sofia shrugged. She'd heard that freezing to death was not a bad way to go if you had to go.

Once they were on the I-435 MO–KS Missouri River Bridge, the young girl in the dark hoodie sat up, tensing her body, willing the car not to slide off into the river. The driver's knuckles were tight on the steering wheel; his was the only vehicle in the southbound lanes at that time of night. A lone Humvee crawled along northbound in the direction of one of the casinos the government had converted to dormitories. Covered over in plastic canvas, the poor souls in that vehicle would be frozen to the bone.

Once they had cleared the bridge, Sofia slipped into a brief, fitful slumber, losing just a few minutes. She woke when the taxi bounced through a deep pothole in the tarmac, opening her eyes to the sight of the all-night diner at the Flying J truck plaza. Fairy lights and yellow neon bathed the interior of the cab, casting a sick, malarial pallor over her skin and disorienting her for a moment. Startled awake, she had the unpleasant sensation of not knowing where she was and then recalling the events of the previous evening anew—*Papa, no!*—before scolding herself for dozing off when she was so vulnerable. For one brief moment she was about to cry, but she managed to stuff her feelings back into the tight little container she stowed them in.

The truck stop was busy with all manner of vehicles military and civilian. Most of the truck drivers were probably wary about pushing out into the ink-black night, where petty criminals waited to pick them off if they didn't go with their assigned military escort. Here and there, small knots of men and women stood outside in the brutal cold, smoking and clapping their hands together.

"Here we are," her driver said. "I hope you do not get in trouble for being late. I drove as fast as I could."

"S'okay," said Sofia.

He pulled up directly in front of the door to the recently built diner, for which she was grateful. Although they had taken a good twenty minutes, the distance traveled was not great and the fare was only $6.50. Newbies did go a long way. She didn't tip, and the driver seemed to think nothing of it. Now that everybody was scratching to survive on the minimum federal wage, no one had anything to spare. She'd just spent half of all the money she possessed.

Sofia thanked him and hopped out, hurrying toward the humid, greasy heat of fried food behind the sliding doors. In the short time she was exposed to the cold, she felt like the skin was being flayed from her body with dull iron knives. The oily, metallic stench of diesel in the air propelled her to the warmth inside. She had no idea how the smokers did it. They were banished so far from the gas stop, they must have been exposed to the full, bitter fury of the weather.

Addiction, she thought. *A killing weakness.*

Once she walked through the doors, the smell was all fat, fried meat, salt, and sugar. Gringo music, stupid with drums and crunching guitars, crackled out of speakers fixed high on the wall above the counter. Heads turned in her direction as she entered, a few of the men not bothering to look away or even have the decency to be embarrassed when she caught them staring at her lecherously. It was wrong. As a good Catholic, she marveled at their lack of shame. A small part of her, the lost little girl she once had been, wanted to turn around and run away. But inside her mind, she found that little girl and quietly, methodically shoved her into a small dark box for the duration. There would be no time for weakness and sorrow on this trip. She had nothing to run to and nobody to protect her. She had to push through with this.

Sofia was not hungry, which was just as well. The food looked awful. Premade hamburgers bundled up in wax paper sat inside glass hot boxes, leaking grease through their wrapping. She was about to buy a bottle of water when she noticed an old aluminum tray near the cash register that was piled high with glasses and a water jug. After pouring one for herself, she took a seat in the corner, where she could keep an eye on the other patrons. She knew she couldn't stay here without ordering something but was reluctant to spend what little money she had.

A waitress came over, an older woman who looked like everything from the chest up had slumped southward in some terrible landslide of collapsing body mass a couple of years ago. She frowned at the youngster's glass of water.

"What can I get for you, darlin'?"

"A plate of fries, thank you," said Sofia. "No cheese."

They were the last thing she wanted, and her stomach turned at the thought of having to eat them. But fries were one of the cheapest things on the menu, and she could always string out the time by eating them one by one. It was the sort of thing the staff here would expect a teenager to do. The carbs would provide energy, too. Another lesson from those months on the trail: store energy whenever you can.

With her order placed, Sofia went back to surveying the room. It didn't look too promising. The majority of the truckers were older men, enormously fat for the most part, probably as a result of sitting on their asses all day eating crap like this. There were a couple of younger drivers, but she didn't like the look of them. The lines on their faces were drawn too long and too deeply. There was a crude ugliness of character that seemed to ooze out of their pores under the harsh, flat lights of the diner. Methamphetamine. The telltale signs were all there.

Unlike the fat pigs, the two meth heads were razor-thin with sunken cheeks. Their teeth were worn nubs, consumed by the constant need for sugar. You could turn a pretty good trade in Kansas City if you started cooking up crystal meth in an abandoned home or disused McDonald's. Workers trying to get through grueling shifts or long drives frequently resorted to it, trading short-term alertness for long-term health problems.

Their eyes stared out at her now from darkened pits. One man caught her looking at him and smiled back with real malevolence. Not that one, she decided.

She wished she had something to read, something to hold in front of her face and hide behind, but no way was she going to waste money buying a copy of the local newspaper. It would just be filled with the usual garbage from the resettlement authorities, proclaiming Kansas City to be a paradise found. Not a word about the meth epidemic, of course, or the shootings, stabbings, and other crimes that were a regular occurrence in the lives of most people here. Or at least the people she knew. Sofia took to staring out of the window at the big rigs as they grunted and rumbled around on the tarmac. Occasionally one of her fellow diners would finish his meal, get up, and leave, but most of them seemed content to sit for a while. She wasn't sure what they were waiting for. The weather wasn't likely to improve any, and it wouldn't be light for many hours. Perhaps they were all worried about bandits.

Sofia picked at her fries when they arrived, hating the oily taste. But the more she ate, the hungrier she seemed to grow. After half an hour, she had finished the lot.

She became aware that the two youngest drivers, the speed freaks, were staring openly at her. They appeared to be talking about her, pointing, greatly amused by something or other. It made her wish she'd been able to stop by the apartment. Papa kept three guns there in a cabinet: his saddle gun—a sort of sawed-off shotgun he'd always carried with him on horseback—his Winchester repeater, and the .357 Colt he had been teaching her to use. She would have been grateful to have that handgun with her now, tucked inside the waist of her Levi's or hidden under the weight of her hoodie top.

Thoughts of the loft at Northtown, and her father, seemed to uncap a deep wellspring of sorrow, which bubbled up inside her so quickly that she was almost overwhelmed. She took a deep breath and threw down the rest of the water. The drugs must have been wearing off, she realized. All she wanted to do was go home, crawl into her bed, and wake up in the morning to discover that it had all been a horrible, cruel dream. To find her father there making breakfast for them both and teasing her about how grumpy she was in the morning. If she could do that, she would promise Jesus and Mary never to disrespect Papa again. To always do as she was asked. And forever after to appreciate what she had.

Sofia pressed her lips together lest the merest whimper escape from them. She bit down and swallowed her grief. She would allow herself to grieve properly later on, in private. For now, she had other priorities. Actions changed the world for the better, not feelings. Papa had taught her that.

She looked over again at the meth-head pair and returned their stare, hoping to infuse it with enough hostility to forestall any interest on their part. So intently was she glaring at them that she completely missed the threat approaching her from the side.

"Seems like you might be in a lot of trouble, miss."

17

DEARBORN HOUSE, SEATTLE, WASHINGTON

Hours later, back in his office upstairs and nursing a Gentleman Jack, Jed Culver had reason to ponder the role of serendipity. He was not somebody who believed in chance. Victory went to those who prepared, stayed focused, and did not relent no matter how much damage they were taking. And yet, sometimes the merest happenstance could change everything.

It was something Henry Cesky had said while he was bitching about Blackstone locking him out of government work down in Texas. Jed had no doubts that the businessman had been blacklisted for his role in toppling Mad Jack's military junta a month or so after the Wave and then for publicly and volubly aligning himself with Kipper during the election that eventually followed. Blackstone was indeed a vengeful cocksucker. Bill Gates wasn't welcome down in Fort Hood, either.

But he was a sloppy, arrogant, overreaching cocksucker, too.

Culver sipped at his bourbon and enjoyed a warm, satisfied smile as he flipped through the folder he'd just received by safe-hand courier from Vancouver. Some things were worth sitting up late for.

He had seen this file before. Or rather, he had been briefed on its contents a few weeks earlier. The briefing had not covered the sort of information most people would have thought relevant to the files in front of him, amid his cityscape of stacked folders and binders crammed with information about the government of Texas. But Jed Culver, alone in all the land, now knew there was a link. The safe-hand courier had traveled down from Echelon HQ in Vancouver because a short while after Cesky had complained of being locked out of salvage operations in Texas, the vast archive of information stored inside Jed's gray matter had begun to reformat itself around a potential link between two apparently disconnected data points.

He held in his hand an after-action report, written up, he was gratified to see, by Special Agent Caitlin Monroe. He well remembered talking to this woman shortly before she parachuted into New York in a last desperate attempt to lay hands on the Emir. Baumer was his real name, of course. But back in the old world, with its old wars and blood hatreds, he also had been known as al Banna, and he had been a medium-level functionary of al-Qaeda's globally franchised jihad. The task of infiltrating and disrupting his particular cell of that hydra-headed monster had been the responsibility of one Special Agent Caitlin Monroe. Not surprising, then, that she'd been the one to tag him as the provocateur behind New York.

Jed flipped slowly through the Echelon file.

"Oh, Agent Monroe," he said softly to himself. "You are going to be my new best friend."

He read and reread the relevant paragraph:

The Subject Lupérico stated that extraction of Subject Baumer was effected by Subject Ozal using the assets of the Hejaz Shipping Line, a wholly owned subsidiary of Subject Ozal's Hazm Unternehmen (Corporation).

"My new best friend forever," he added with a smile.

Culver now turned his attention to the file balanced on his lap: a report from the secretary of the treasury's office concerning contracts signed by the government of Texas, ultra vires—in layman's terms, "beyond the powers" of that government. On page 25 of Annex B, he had what he wanted: a listing for a salvage contract worth 25 million New American Dollars signed between the Blackstone administration and Hazm Unternehmen. The contracts were notarized and exchanged one week before the Hejaz Shipping Line was confirmed by Echelon London to have sent three large vessels carrying somewhere between four hundred and five hundred combatants from the Libyan port of Tobruk into American waters, where they eventually made landfall on the East Coast. At New York.

"Gotcha . . ."

18

KANSAS CITY, MISSOURI

"Cindy French is my name. I haul that big-ass classic Kenworth out there, the one with the sky-blue cab? Rocky Mountain double? Got me a load of Maersk containers heading down to Corpus Christi."

Sofia hadn't said a word, hadn't invited her to sit down, but that was what Cindy was doing, sliding herself into the booth, juggling a plate piled high with fried chicken and mashed potatoes and two huge paper cups filled with Coke. When she had herself comfortably settled into the booth, she pushed one of the drinks across and smiled. The smile reached into Cindy's clear blue eyes, drawing to Sofia's mind memories of her grandmother.

"Here, hon," she offered. "The Coke isn't half bad here. And take some of these taters off of my hands. They're probably instant, but beggars can't be choosers. I loaded myself down with a dozen-piece chicken meal, so if you want a drumstick, I'd be willing to spare one.

But the *gravy*—oh, that is first-rate sausage gravy right there, straight out of the pan. You can't go wrong with that."

Sofia checked across the room. The two men who'd been creeping her out had lost interest.

"Don't you worry about them, hon," said the woman. "They won't bother you while I'm here. I once gave those boys an ass whoopin' with my favorite tire iron. Taught them some manners. I won't abide poor manners in a man."

She picked up a chicken breast and bit into it with evident relish, rolling her blue eyes as she chewed. Sofia watched the woman, who was shorter than she was by a good few inches, work her way through the plate of food. It was hard to tell her age. There was a strange child-like quality to her, especially in the giddy way she ate. Behind that veneer, however, there lurked something else. Sofia wasn't sure what it was, but at the end of a long and terrible day she found she wanted to trust this woman very much.

After swallowing her mouthful of food, Cindy spoke again, not looking at Sofia but still concentrating on her plate.

"You know, I'm not going to be here for long."

She finally looked up. The smile was still there.

Sofia didn't know what to say. For a split second just now, she thought she'd been tracked down by the police. Instead she seemed to have attracted the attention of a crazy person. Kindly but possibly crazy. Who went up to complete strangers at a truck stop, sat themselves down, and started insisting they share their food, all the while telling them they were in trouble? No one she had encountered. Everyone wanted something; that was the rule Sofia Pieraro had learned.

Still, she could turn this to her advantage. She had come to the diner looking for someone like Cindy French. Not so much a crazy woman but somebody she might be able to trust to move her a little bit farther down the road.

"I am not in trouble," she said quietly. "I'm just looking for a ride."

French laughed. Indeed, she laughed so much that she had to stop eating.

"If you came here looking for a ride, believe me, you *are* in trouble young lady!" She took a long pull on her Coke, indicating that Sofia should do the same. "You look like you need a little pick-me-up. And you don't look old enough to drink coffee. Go on, you got about half a gallon of Coke Vault in there, enough to keep you buzzing until sunup. Take a drink."

She did need something to wake her up, it was true. Her nap in the taxi had been entirely too short, and she was finding it difficult to keep her eyes open here, even under the harsh fluorescents, with the music cranked up loud and the other diners roaring at one another. She was wrung out, all but destroyed by one of the worst days of her life. And she'd had some bad ones.

"You said you needed a ride, hon. Where you headed?"

The girl found herself momentarily unable to answer. She had come looking for a lift down to Fort Hood in central Texas or at least in that direction. But she'd intended to seek out the transport herself by approaching someone she thought looked trustworthy. She may well have approached this chicken-eating Cindy French had she seen her first.

"I am going to Texas," she said in the end, deciding to run with a version of the truth.

"Really? Going down to the Federal Mandate, are we?" The truck driver pulled a drumstick out and tossed it onto the spare plate. "Go on. Eat up."

She was almost tempted to lie and say yes, she was headed for the mandate, but she caught herself at the last moment. Anybody with a legitimate reason for traveling down to the Texas Federal Mandate would have had any number of legitimate means of getting there. The government did not expect settlers to make their own way through the badlands. Most people would know that, and somebody like French, who probably drove those routes all the time, definitely would know.

"No," Sofia replied. "I need to get to Fort Hood." There, she had done it.

Cindy continued with her meal but raised one eyebrow as if Sofia had played a particularly interesting hand in a game of cards. She steered a ball of mashed potato onto the end of the fork and used it to mop up some gravy. The mouthful of food prevented her from speaking, but it was obvious she was giving some thought to what she would say next.

Sofia took the opportunity to look around the diner once more. A quartet of soldiers came in from the cold, snapping their hats against their thighs before heading off to the counter. As they passed her, she waited to see if they were army or local militia. One of the younger ones smiled at her, shaking his head before moving on to get a drink.

She was becoming worried that this was taking too long, that a police cruiser would pull up in the next minute or so and the officers who had come to collect her at the apartment would find her here, obviously preparing to run away. If they found her, they'd make certain that she didn't get another opportunity for a long time. Oh, they'd say they were doing it in her interests, but they didn't truly know what her interests were.

"Fort Hood? That's an unusual place for a young lady to be lighting out to on a night like this," said French. "Especially a young lady like you."

She gave Sofia a look that contained a long unspoken reproach for her foolishness. "You're Mexican, aren't you? I mean, originally. I can tell from your accent you moved around a little bit. I guess we all have the last couple of years. My dad was part Mexican himself, served in the army. He's dead now."

"The Wave?"

Cindy shook her head. "No, he died long before that. My mother broke his heart. She could be a real bitch. Now the Wave, it *did* get her. Surprised it didn't spit the old dragon right back out. Anyway, come summertime, I park the rig on the beach for a week and pick up some sun. I get dark pretty quick, like you. That's thanks to the old man. Or rather, his mama."

Sofia nodded and took another piece of chicken. She was much happier talking about their past than providing details of her plans for the future. She even relaxed for the first time as she took up her own greasy fork to scoop up some of the mashed.

"I was young when we left Mexico," Sofia said. "My father . . ." Her voice caught for a second before she forced herself to move on. "Papa got us onto a boat leaving Acapulco. Just before all the really bad riots and the killing started. The boat took us to Australia, and we worked on the big farms there. For the government. It was not so bad. The work was no harder than we had known at home, and the camp where we lived was very good. Nuns came to teach us. We came to America to settle."

She was unwilling to go into greater detail. If French found out what had happened to her family down in Mexico or even what had happened to her father more recently, she would call the police immediately. There could be no good reason why somebody like Sofia would want to return to a place that was the source of so much misery. Best to let the woman's imagination fill in the gaps for her.

"That would explain your accent," she said. "I've heard some mighty strange ones the last couple of years, pushing eighteen wheels all over the country. Yours sounds like you don't really come from anywhere. Or maybe that you come from everywhere."

It seemed a rather rude thing to say, but Sofia refused to bristle in response. Perhaps Cindy was simply teasing her, trying to get on her nerves to see how she would react. It was quite obvious she was intrigued, possibly even suspicious.

"My voice sounds normal to me," Sofia replied with a shrug. "But what is normal? You are right; we hear many voices these days. In my class at school, there are people from twenty-six different countries. We have all of our flags pinned up on the wall."

"So, you're at school here, then?"

Madre de dios . . . She cursed herself for having given away such a crucial piece of information. Schoolchildren no longer lived the sheltered lives they had in the past. A typical school day ran until lunch, and then they all went off to their respective jobs, such as hers at the hospital. They were all expected to work in the gardens, in the salvage efforts, in any position that needed filling, even if it happened to be shoveling the remains out of the reclamation zones. And as she had found out down in the mandate, even to risk their lives on the frontier.

But there was no good reason why a schoolgirl would be in the Corrington Road truckers' diner looking for a ride down to Texas, particularly not a schoolgirl like her. A Mexican. She might well have had a job washing dishes here until two o'clock in the morning, of course, but there was no way she should have been this far south, sticking her thumb out by the highway. She tried to cover total ignorance of what to say next by filling her mouth with more potato.

The clink of knives and forks around them seemed much louder than it had just a minute earlier. Cindy's cutlery was crossed perfectly on her plate. The woman said nothing more, apparently content to wait on an answer. When the silence became difficult to endure, Sofia spoke up again.

"I said I went to school here," she muttered, unable to keep a petulant tone out of her voice.

"That you did. That you did." Cindy smiled again and pushed the plate away. She'd finished the meal and was leaning back now, enjoying what was left of her drink. "But you didn't say why you were traveling to Texas. And that's what makes me think you're in trouble."

If Sofia had a guardian angel, he whispered into her ear at this point.

"I'm not in trouble," she said in a flash of improvisation. "My sister is in trouble."

She received a nod in acknowledgment of that. "I see, and just what sort of trouble is your sister in down in Texas?"

"Meth," she replied. "To begin with, anyway. Then she had to pay for the drugs."

French regarded her with a blank face, as though she had yet to make up her mind about the story. "And how is she paying for it? A Mexican girl down in Texas."

Sofia wasn't sure just how far to push the story. She hesitated to say anything. The woman seemed to take her reticence as a form of distress. Her face softened, becoming almost motherly.

"Is she working in one of the government brothels down there, hon?"

Sofia hadn't thought of that. Her imagination didn't run to such things, but it sounded like a good story. She nodded uncertainly, her eyes darting around the dining room as if she were concerned someone might overhear.

"And so, do you mind me asking, young lady . . . I don't even know your name, by the way."

"My name is Sofia," she answered, instantly regretting it. She should have used a false name. If the police put out a bulletin, it could be picked up by the radio stations, and then everybody would be looking for the little runaway Mexican girl called Sofia.

Damn. The mistakes just kept piling up.

"Thank you, Sofia. Now, if you don't mind me asking, why are you looking for your sister? You said you came here with your family. Surely it doesn't fall to you to bring her home."

She really did have to lie this time. But as she was learning, it was always easier to wrap a lie around a kernel of truth. "I am all she has left," she said. "Our father . . . died recently."

She felt awful. It surely must have been a mortal sin to invoke her father's name in such a fashion. And yet she was doing this to avenge him and all of the family. So no, she thought, rallying silently, she was not doing the wrong thing by using Papa's memory in such a fashion. She was doing what needed to be done.

It was upsetting, however, and Cindy seemed to be attuned to her distress. The truck-driving lady suddenly looked older under the harsh, flat light inside the diner. She even reached across and squeezed Sofia's hand. It was the sort of thing that usually would have caused the teenager to jerk away. She didn't like people touching her. Yet oddly enough, she sat there, transfixed by Cindy's warm blue eyes.

"Sorry, hon," she said. "I can be a pushy old hippie sometimes. I didn't mean to pry. You are obviously carrying a world of hurt. I could see that as soon as I came in. I can also see those assholes Jasper and T Dawg sizing you up. It wouldn't be the first time. Fuckers . . . Pardon my French."

She finished the last of her Coke, sucking up a few final drops with a loud slurping sound before wiping her mouth with a napkin.

"Tell you what, Sofia, I'm really not happy with the idea of you trying to haul ass all the way down to Texas on your own. You can ride with me if you want. I can see, sitting here across from you, that there's going to be no telling you otherwise. You won't be talked out of this, will you?"

Sofia Pieraro shook her head.

Cindy smiled. "Too much like me. I can also see you got a few miles on you, kid, but you got some hard road ahead of you, too. And God knows what you intend to do when you get down there. I can't imagine some fat government pimp in Fort Hood is going to stand for you waltzing into his bordello and carrying off your sister. Is she of age?"

Sofia's face must have communicated her confusion.

"I mean, is she over eighteen years old?"

"Oh, no," she said. "She is only fourteen."

That seemed to satisfy Cindy French. She nodded once.

"Okay, then. What you need to do when you get there is keep your head down and get your ass in to see the padre at the 58th Street chapel. You tell him your sister is underage and where she's working. Father Michael will take care of it." She paused as if remembering something important. "You are Catholic, aren't you? I'm sorry if I jumped to conclusions."

Sofia sketched a tired smile and fluttered one hand at Cindy. "I am. We all are. Or were, anyway. I will talk to the priest. Thank you. I . . . I wasn't sure how I was going to be able to do this. I spoke to the government here, but they didn't seem to care."

That information, as false as it was, didn't seem to surprise the truck driver. "Well, there's a news flash," she replied. "I'm sorry you had to waste your time barking up that tree. But I know from having to haul freight from Corpus Christi to Seattle that Blackstone and Kipper's people don't get along. The number of times I had to fill out one form for Texas and then exactly the same form for Seattle a ways down the road . . . I tell you. If they're not going to help, then I don't see why the government can't just get out of the way of people and let them get on with rebuilding their lives."

It didn't seem to be the sort of statement that required an answer, so Sofia kept her mouth shut. She had told so many lies in the last few minutes, she feared she'd begin to trip over them if she said anything more. Cindy picked up the check that the waitress had left and squinted at it suspiciously before pulling a couple of newbies out of her pocket and weighing them down on top of the bill with a salt shaker.

"Come on," she said. "There's a few of us meeting up. We're going to convoy down past Tulsa on I-35. It's always safer when you can ride along with someone."

Throwing a filthy look in the direction of Jasper and T Dawg as she followed Cindy out of the diner, Sofia could only agree.

19

KANSAS CITY, MISSOURI

Cindy French's semitrailer was pulled up a short walk away from the diner in the parking bay of the Flying J truck stop. The rig was enormous and blue, matching her eyes. Indeed, Cindy was a study in blues: denim jeans, a blue hoodie under her Eddie Bauer blue winter coat, and a royal blue knitted scarf. Her outfit was topped off by a strange animal-like white hat with cartoon eyes and tails that dropped down to her collar. Sofia couldn't decide if the hat was a rat, a cat, or some sort of bunny rabbit. In a crowd of fat male truckers, Cindy French stood out. Short as she was, just the way she carried herself gave off a strong impression that it would be unwise to cross her. The .45 on her hip reinforced that for anyone fool enough to base rash judgments on her size and gender alone.

She was smirking as she took in Sofia's reaction to her striking fashion statement. Especially the hat. A cartoon puppy hat, Sofia decided.

"Yeah, I get a lot of looks," Cindy admitted as her breath jetted out in thick white clouds.

The contrast with the overly warm, almost cloying, greasy interior of the diner was stunning. Subzero wind chill knifed into Sofia with lethal intent. The hooded sweatshirt was in no way adequate against the elements, and she was soon shivering, then shuddering with deep body tremors.

"I think maybe you're taking the whole 'travel light' thing a little too far," opined Cindy. "Get into the cab before you catch your death."

She couldn't answer because her teeth were chattering. The older woman hurried over to the cab of *Mary Lou,* the big blue truck, and Sofia climbed in as soon as it was unlocked.

"There's a blanket on the passenger seat," Cindy called up from outside. "Wrap yourself up, I'll turn over the engine, get the heat going, and then we'll see about finding you some warmer gear."

Rooting around in the cab, Sofia pulled out a SpongeBob SquarePants comforter. She wrapped herself deep in the folds, catching the scent of fabric softener, laundry detergent, and perhaps a hint of perfume. It took a minute for the vehicle's heating system to dull the pain of the icy fangs gnawing away at her bones. Cindy was dressed warmly, but even so, Sofia couldn't understand how she could bear to be outside for more than a minute at a time.

The trucker insisted on joining three other drivers, who were warming their hands around a burning oil barrel on the far side of the road. Perhaps they were the ones she meant to travel in convoy with when they departed. Like many of the truck drivers, their clothes looked like they'd been salvaged from quality camping stores some time ago but a few years on the road had roughed them up some. Sofia wondered why they didn't just replace the aging jackets and winter gear.

The men appeared to be in good spirits despite the weather. One was drinking a steaming beverage from a thermos flask. The other two were smoking, which explained why they'd had to remove themselves from the truck plaza. Even the diner had been aggressively plastered with no-smoking signs. Cindy pointed back toward her truck, and Sofia nodded at the men as their gaze followed the gesture. They seemed harmless enough. Middle-aged, running to fat, probably family men.

She shut down that line of thought immediately lest it lead her to dwell on her own family. There was nothing to be gained from that at the moment.

One of the male truckers disappeared, hurrying away into the darkness, before returning a minute later with a heavy fleece-lined coat. Cindy appeared to thank him. They all checked their watches and said their good-byes before the thermos man tossed away the dregs of his drink, and without further ceremony they were on the move.

Cindy hurried over to her rig, taking care not to slip on the compacted ice.

"Here you go, darlin'," she said as she climbed back into the cabin. "I knew Dave had this old thing stashed away in his bunk. He's been using it as a pillow, but it's okay. He doesn't have cooties. It'll keep you a lot warmer than those thin scraps of cotton you're wearing. At any rate, it'll do until we can stop somewhere and kit you out properly."

"Thank you," said Sofia, feeling guilty at relying on the charity of people she was lying to.

For the Burton ski jacket, however, with its thick inner lining—real lamb's wool unless she was mistaken—the teenage runaway could only feel desperately thankful. As soon as she slipped her arms through the sleeves, she could tell that it would go a long way toward protecting her from the viciousness of the weather outside. Sofia wrapped the coat around herself and sank back into the soft, warm embrace of the bucket seat. With the heater blowing and Dave's jacket, she hardly needed the SpongeBob blanket.

"We're going to rendezvous down 35 a ways," Cindy informed her, "and push on down to Ottawa, Kansas. That's the first town outside KC's security zone; Emporia's the next one. But they're both close enough to the federal settlement that the scavengers haven't really picked 'em over. There's still a fair chance of getting picked off by the cavalry if they do. We can take a toilet break down at Emporia, which we're gonna need after those Cokes, girl. See if we can get you a road pack there, too."

She applied a little shoe leather to the pedals and crunched through a complicated ballet with the gears, and the mighty Kenworth lurched forward.

Sofia frowned. "But wouldn't *we* be scavenging?" she asked. "If there was a cavalry patrol down there, why wouldn't they arrest us, or even shoot us, for looting?" The last thing she wanted was to fall back into the clutches of the authorities now that she was so close to escaping from them.

Cindy smiled. "Well, legally, we would be scavenging, yes. And if the cav swooped down in one of their helicopters or rode by in a Hummer and shot the hell out of us, legally—officially—we wouldn't have a lot to complain about. But *unofficially,* the cavalry is well aware that the trucking lines use the two towns as supply depots. They're well beyond the city limits, and the cav don't much care. Anything that greases the axles, you know. Besides, we're regulars. They come to us for news on the road, and it wouldn't do to get on our bad side."

The truckie didn't seem too concerned at the prospect of helicopter gunships hammering down on them while they picked through a camping-goods store. She bounced in the seat as they pulled out of the Flying J travel plaza and turned westbound down Front Street, passing under Interstate 435.

"Hauling road freight can be a dangerous business, Sofia," Cindy explained. "Seattle needs that freight hauled, especially with all the trouble they've been having on the railway lines. So any informal arrangements that smooth the process, well, the people in the field tend to look the other way. I suppose there'll come a day when this is all less of a frontier . . ." She waved at the darkness outside the truck windows as she spoke. "But for now, frontier rules apply."

Sofia turned sideways in her seat, leaning against the padded headrest behind her. "And what are the frontier rules?" she asked.

"Whatever it takes, hon. Whatever it takes."

"I am familiar with that rule," Sofia said in a quiet voice.

The driver appeared to measure her with a long calculating look, long enough that Sofia began to worry that Cindy wasn't paying attention to the road. But she seemed to know where she was on the highway even though it was covered in snow. Warehouses flanked both sides of Front Street, many of them still dark, deserted. Every so often, an island of lights would appear in the inky, snowy night where someone had established a business of one type or another in the ruins of the old civilization.

"Yes, I imagine you are familiar with it, Sofia," she replied before turning away to check her rearview mirrors. By leaning forward a few inches, Sofia was able to find the other trucks in a small convoy strung out behind them.

They passed—bounced perhaps was more accurate—across the Chouteau Trafficway intersection. Kansas City Power and Light maintained a large facility of spare parts at the northwest corner of the intersection. Rows of repair trucks idled in the yard, waiting for the stressed power grid to fail under the weight of the blizzard. Down the road, it was just possible to make out the gray skyline of Kansas City's skyscrapers. Most of the roads had long been cleared of debris and wrecks.

Trains powered through the yards on the south side of Front Street, bearing the logos of Kansas City Southern and Union Pacific. Sofia remembered how her father would take her down to the railroad tracks along the Missouri River, back when they'd first arrived here, to watch the trains rumble by. It bored her witless, but Papa seemed to find the sight reassuring. "They are stitching the wounds of this land together," he would say.

There was very little traffic on Front Street, mostly large trucks like Cindy's, some of them pulling two trailer beds, reminding her of the massive articulated road trains she'd seen down in Australia. That was what they called them—"road trains." An evocative phrase but accurate, too. As best she could tell, none of the trucks in her convoy were pulling more than one trailer.

Her eyelids grew heavy and began to droop as *Mary Lou* ate up the miles. She had imagined Cindy would want to talk, but the trucker seemed content to concentrate on the drive, as if she understood that her passenger needed to rest. With a belly full of warm, heavy food and snug in the fleecy cocoon of her new coat, Sofia wanted nothing more than to slip into a deep slumber. Yet she found it impossible to get any rest. Every time she closed her eyes, Cindy's rig would slam into yet another pothole, bouncing her head against the side window. Pothole repair was near the bottom of the city's list of priorities. The post-Wave firestorms may have spared KC, but at times it seemed as though it might fall apart anyway.

"Sorry, hon," Cindy said. "The roads are shit in this town. Always have been, even before the troubles. It'll be better once we hit 35. Sometimes I wonder why they don't just knock it all down and start from scratch."

Once they'd pulled onto the Downtown Loop, the ride smoothed out. The dark shadows of the snow shrouded the world outside as they made their way around the loop until arriving on the I-35 southbound. They were rolling through parts of Kansas City she had never seen, past the West Side, where the city's original Latino population lived. Now it was crammed with the latest generation of migrants: Indians and some Chinese mixed in with arrivals from a dozen other countries. Some of her friends at school lived down here, in the West Bottoms.

Friends. Did she really have friends? She wouldn't miss anyone from Kansas City; that much was certain.

She was vaguely aware of Cindy flicking off the citizens band radio to allow her to get some rest just before her eyes closed for the last time in Kansas City.

20

DEARBORN HOUSE, SEATTLE, WASHINGTON

"Don't patronize me, Jed," Kip warned. "Whenever you tell me I'm doing something admirable, I get a lecture about how I'm also being stupid and need to accept changed realities, or the situation on the ground, or some crap like that. Not this time."

James Kipper folded his arms, creating a barrier between them. "I agree you're on to something," he went on. "But the way we do this is by the book. You turn it over to the FBI—"

"Oh, please, not the feebs."

"Yes. The FBI. And you let them run the investigation. If they agree there is enough to go on."

Kip bit off a mouthful of cheese cruller, his breakfast of choice when Barb wasn't around, and washed it down with a slug of hot chocolate, another indulgence. He, too, had a hangover after slamming down a six-pack with Barney Tench at the end of last night. It wasn't improving his mood or his judgment this morning.

A small field of documents lay between them, the bare minimum Jed needed to make his case that Blackstone might have been involved, even if unwittingly or at some remove, with Baumer's New York jihad. Kipper was impressed by Jed's prosecution of the matter but remained entirely skeptical about the chief of staff's preferred option for dealing with it.

"Agent Monroe may well be the world expert on this guy," he conceded, spilling a few cruller flakes onto the blotter. "But you know as well as I do that she is a grossly inappropriate choice to take this any further. Putting aside the fact that she's personally compromised because of the attack on her family, she's Echelon, Jed. She can't blow her nose within the borders of the United States without breaking half a dozen laws."

Culver didn't think much of that objection, and it showed. His eyes burned with sleeplessness, and fatigue cramped the muscles in the backs of his legs. He could feel his calves jumping and twitching as early-morning traffic appeared on the streets outside Kipper's office window.

"If you turn this over to the bureau, sir, they will do their usual thorough job, which will take about eighteen years. During which time Blackstone will get wind of what's happening, giving him plenty of opportunity to build a large, roaring bonfire of incriminating evidence that could heat this city for Christmas and beyond. Monroe has the skill set, the background, and the motivation to close the file in weeks, if not days."

Kipper's hand cut through the air in front of him like a heavy blade. "Enough! Agent Monroe, who now works for Echelon UK, as far as I remember, Jed, is not a criminal investigator. She's an *assassin,* for God's sake! I can't imagine a worse person to send down to Fort Hood under our imprimatur."

Culver stood up to stretch the painful knots out of his legs but also because his frustration was mounting to the point where he had to walk it off. He stalked over to the fireplace.

"She is not just a trigger puller, Mr. President. She's a lot more than that. Fact is, she had two years' training at Quantico, pre-Wave. An accelerated investigator's course. She can play an undercover cop if it helps to think of her in that fashion."

"No, Jed," Kipper said. "It doesn't." The president pushed away the better part of his breakfast, uneaten, before continuing. "I don't much like what Agent Monroe does in the name of this country, what she represents about us, or at least the way we used to do things. I can accept that she herself is a dedicated servant of the people, and I'm happy to acknowledge the sacrifices she's made and the dangers she has faced in that service. What she did in New York, or tried to do, was outstanding. But she is the wrong person for this job. The wrong tool."

Culver's spirits flagged a bit at that. When Kip got going on the engineering metaphors, it usually meant he'd made up his mind or was very close to getting there. His tone grew ever more sarcastic as he spoke.

"I mean, where is this Lupérico she talks about in her report? This guy running Sarkozy's secret dungeon. Oh, that's right—she blew his brains out in the jungle. No chance for anybody to verify his information, not to mention the illegality, the basic . . . *wrongness* of an extrajudicial execution. And make no mistake, that's what happened. She flew into a sovereign country, committed an act of war, kidnapped a man, tortured him for all we know, and then executed him. What part of that process are you comfortable with, Jed? Because it sickens me from start to finish, and if I'd had any say in the matter, it simply wouldn't have happened. I'm furious that it did, even if responsibility for the murder can't be laid directly back on us. Calling it an Echelon operation and saying it had nothing to do with us, it's just . . . it's weasel words, that's what it is. And we won't be doing it again."

His face had become flushed with anger, and when he finished speaking, he smacked his desk with an open hand to emphasize the point. Jed struggled manfully to restrain his own rising anger. He knew that getting into a fight with Kipper would serve no purpose.

"Mr. President," he said wearily, "I'm not suggesting we send her down there to whack him. But I am suggesting that unusual circumstances demand unusual responses. Having the FBI roll up on Blackstone's front door to ask him to come down to the office to answer a few questions isn't going to work. I don't see why the justice system should be preferenced when dealing with what is essentially a black operation. New York was a black op. For Baumer. And possibly for Blackstone. Two different operations, maybe, I'll concede. And maybe Blackstone's went horribly wrong. There will come a time when we have to address the legal consequences of what happened. But right now, I would argue very strongly that we are still in the operational moment. And that moment demands a Caitlin Monroe, not a district attorney."

Kip shook his head. He had his anger under control, but he had not changed his mind. "No, Jed," he said. "If our system is not strong enough to do things the right way, it is not worth the effort we put into maintaining it. We either do things lawfully or we're as bad as Baumer and Mad Jack. Now I want you to get on the phone to the FBI and have them send over a team to take charge of the case you've built up. I want that to happen today. Are we clear?"

"Yes, Mr. President."

Jed checked his watch. Dawn had arrived, but the world outside Kipper's window looked even darker.

21

EMPORIA, KANSAS

She dreamed again. Not of Texas this time but Oklahoma. In the strange attenuated temporal landscape of dreams, they had only just escaped the flood. Their clothes hung in rags from them. The horses had all been swept away, drowned and torn apart when the raging waters dashed them against rocky outcrops in the accursed valley.

Papa was with her, supporting her on his strong right arm as he helped Adam and Maive escape the pull of the roaring river that had boiled up around them. As terrified as she was, Sofia's heart swelled with joy at the touch of her father. She felt safe just being with him, knowing that he would let nothing bad happen to her.

And then the river was gone. Not receded, not fallen away—simply gone. They stood on the outskirts of Tulsa, which looked as though an Old Testament God had rained down fire and damnation upon it, smashing it flat, burning the ruins, before smashing a fist down on it again. It was as if they were standing on the verge of a city ruined in antiquity rather than just a few years earlier. They had come to Tulsa seeking supplies, needing to replace all they had lost in the flood, but instead found themselves staring at a wasteland of ash and desolation.

The others spoke in her dream, but she could not understand them. Fear began to fill up the empty places inside her as the four of them advanced cautiously through the charred remains of the city under a lowering sky of poisonous clouds turned the color of bad blood and meat sickness. She clutched Papa's hand tightly as dark shapes flitted at the edge of her vision.

The dead and the Disappeared. They had all come back from wherever the damned go when the world is done with them.

She was a little girl again, tugging on her father's arm to gain his attention. But he seemed not to notice, as if he didn't know she was there. No matter how hard she tried to pull him away, he just led them deeper and deeper into the dead city. And then she lost her grip on him. It didn't slip or falter; he was just gone.

No . . . he was up ahead but holding hands with Maive and leading Adam into the ruins of a 7-Eleven that somehow had escaped the worst of the conflagration. It was as if he had forgotten her. Had left her behind.

She was suddenly paralyzed with terror. There were wolves stalking them, along with the specters of the dead and the Disappeared that lay in wait inside the shell of that building. Why was he going in there? Why had he left her?

Increasingly she was able to make out the features of the ghouls and shadows circling them at a distance, drawing in more tightly with each pass, like sharks intending to feed. She saw the shape of Cooper Aronson, his neck bent at an impossible angle, his eyes just dark ragged holes. Insensate fury twisted the rotting remains of his face into a rictus of ill-favored rage as the animated corpse contemplated the vision of his wife walking hand in hand with Miguel Pieraro.

Sofia tried to call out to her father, but then Aronson was gone, and she shuddered as she felt the cold claws of a dead man brush her shoulder. Turning, somehow as swiftly as the flight of an arrow but as slowly as specks of frozen dust floating through the vacuum of space, she turned and turned . . . and her mouth fell open in a silent scream when she saw Orin, the young Mormon boy they'd found ten miles down-stream from where the flood had overtaken them, his body suspended in a tree as if crucified. He reached out to her, his black bloated hands closing around her throat.

"Sofia!"

She came awake, gasping and trembling. Cindy had one hand on her shoulder, shaking her lightly.

"Sofia, are you all right?"

For a few seconds her waking panic was every bit as deep-seated and animalistic as her terror in the dream. She had no idea where she was or what she was doing. It was daylight—morning. Why was she not in bed? Where was her father? This wasn't their apartment . . .

And then she remembered and wished she could have fallen back into confusion and ignorance. A pitiable moan escaped her throat until she clamped her mouth shut, forcing herself to accept what she could not hope to change.

"I'm sorry," she said, as much to stop herself from moaning again as anything. "A bad dream. Memories."

"That's all right; you're safe now. Just take a moment and get your soul back," said Cindy French.

A ragged breath escaped her. She realized her bladder was painfully full and was relieved that at least she hadn't wet herself in her terror. She must have slept through the convoy's earlier stop at Ottawa.

The truck's powerful motor propelled them through the dull glare of morning. The road ahead was deserted, but their path was framed between ramparts of twisted metal: the disintegrating bodies of crashed automobiles bulldozed off the highway by army engineers. The government hadn't bothered removing the wreckage this far out from Kansas City. Eventually it would all decompose into the earth. Sofia had seen the same thing many times when coming up from Texas. Clearing the nation's highways often meant simply sweeping the debris to one side.

"I'm okay," she told Cindy in a voice that was still shaky. "I just get nightmares."

The truck driver mulled that over for a while. The only sound in the cabin was the steady growl of the engine and the hum of the eighteen wheels on the highway.

"I think we all do," Cindy admitted. "Anybody who remembers, anyway."

She turned to face Sofia again in the same disconcerting way as before, taking her eyes off the road. At some point in the last few hours, Cindy had removed her own coat and hoodie, leaving a pink T-shirt with a frustrated-looking cartoon mouse diligently working at a school desk. Underneath the cartoon was a single line of text: NO ANIMAL TESTING.

"Aren't you cold?" Sofia asked.

Cindy shook her head. "Nah, I'm hot, in truth. But it isn't menopause."

Sofia pulled her jacket in tighter around her. "If you say so."

"Anyway, I know the younger kids are okay with it all—you know, if you were young enough when the Wave came, the world just is what it is now. But I guess you're old enough to remember it pretty well, eh?"

She replied with a brief nod as Cindy's gaze turned back to the monotonous passage of Interstate 35.

"I was up in Alaska when it happened, driving tankers for Exxon. I hated that work, but it saved my life. For what it was worth." Her voice took on a mournful tone. "My family was all down here. Granted, it was no great loss, losing my husband. Part of why I had to go to Alaska in the first place was to pay off the income taxes he never filed. The Wave gave me the divorce I always wanted. But I'd take it all back to see my kids and grandbabies again."

For the first time in their journey together, Sofia thought Cindy's jolly exterior might fail. Her features squeezed in on her blue eyes, the tears welling up and falling freely. She wiped her eyes and took a deep breath. With one hand, she waved at her face until the tears faded.

"Oh, Lord, it never gets any easier." She cleared her throat and sniffed. "I still have two sons in the corps. They were in Iraq. But everyone else, well . . . I'd always driven short-haul routes before then. My worthless husband saved my life with his laziness."

Everybody she met had one of these stories, Sofia thought. All the Americans, anyway. You could sort them by type. There were those who hated the Wave for everything it had taken away. There were others who were grateful for the Wave because it gave them a clean slate to start over again. And you had your fence-sitters like Cindy, who saw it as a mixed blessing but mainly bad.

Most of them seemed to think that Sofia's own history—when she was telling it straight—sounded exciting and adventurous. Right up to the point where they learned about what had happened to her family. But apart from telling the trucker that her father had died recently, she hadn't shared much of a personal nature since they'd met.

"I'm sorry about your family, Cindy," Sofia said. "You must miss them very much."

"Every day," she replied, wiping at one eye with the back of her hand. "And I get the nightmares with it, just like you."

Probably not just like me, Sofia thought. But she kept that to herself.

Cindy cleared her throat before powering up the radio and calling up the other trucks. "Hey, fellas, we're about ten minutes out. Y' all up for a pit stop?"

A speaker box crackled somewhere above their heads, and a man's voice answered.

"Sure enough. How's your passenger doing?"

"She's fine, Dave. Slept like a baby inside your old coat."

"Good to hear. Signing off. See you in ten."

There was nothing about the approach to Emporia, Kansas, that marked it as being any different from a thousand other haunted towns other than the banks of tangled vehicle wreckage by the side of the road that told of an obvious effort to clear a path. As Sofia knew only too well, so many places remained exactly as they'd been left when human life departed from them on March 14, 2003.

Or rather, as the towns and cities had become in the hours, days, and weeks afterward. She still marveled at the biblical scale of destruction she had witnessed when walking and riding up from Texas. It was not sinful to compare the perdition that had come upon America with the Old Testament tales that the nuns had scared her with as a child. The cities of the plain had nothing on the Midwestern ruins she'd seen.

As they entered the outskirts of Emporia, the roadside wreckage began to thin out.

"What happened to all the old cars?" Sofia asked.

Cindy French nodded, apparently pleased that she'd noticed. "We did a lot of it ourselves," she replied, which Sofia took to mean the trucking companies, not her three friends in the rigs behind them. "Had to clear a path through for the trucks, of course. But all that crap had to be moved because of ambushes as well. You get a convoy coming into a place like this, especially if they're fully loaded, all those big trucks slowing down—well, it makes a tempting target for raiders. And big piles of crap by the side of the road; that's a pretty handy ambush spot, right? So over time we did our best to clear it out. And here's the thing—you remember before when I told you about the feds turning a blind eye out this way? That wasn't entirely true. They sent the army engineers down here to check on our clearance work and even assigned a company of soldiers and a couple of dozers to bring it up to spec!" She smacked the steering wheel with her open palm, as if the story had amazed even her.

Sofia nodded and tried to look sympathetic, but she found the prospect of ambush out in the wastelands unsettling. She'd had her fill of those, from both sides.

"So there's nobody here in Emporia?" she asked. "No soldiers or militia or anything?"

Cindy ground down through the gears as they entered the center of town. "No, it's too far out from KC to be worth securing. But like I said, it's still a little too close to the city for any bandits or freebooters to feel completely comfortable setting up shop around here. Sometimes the army or the militia will make a temporary camp out this way for deeper patrols into Kansas and Oklahoma, but for the most part it's a ghost town."

Sofia's concern must have been obvious, because Cindy reached over and patted her on the arm. Again, the teenager didn't flinch. Something about this older woman disarmed her, and that alone made her a bit nervous. Sofia Pieraro wasn't a touchy-feely type of person.

"Don't you worry yourself about it, girl. There was another group of drivers came through here yesterday evening. We spoke to them on the radio before I got to the diner. The town's empty. And safe."

With the toxic effect of the nightmare still coursing through her nervous system, Sofia found the reassurance difficult to accept. But she had no choice. She was beholden to Cindy and the others in the convoy for her transport south. There was no point arguing about the details.

They drove through a ground mist almost thick enough to obscure the road surface. Even at this hour of the morning, it seemed to lie all over the town, and the bright halogen lamps of Cindy's Kenworth were at just the right height to illuminate the fog bank without actually piercing it. The effect on the deserted town was creepy enough to have her shivering again. After her dream, she could very easily imagine the doors of all those haunted homes creaking open as the soulless, reembodied corpses of the Disappeared shambled out into the night. Gooseflesh convulsed up and down her arms and across her shoulders.

"Spooky, isn't it?" Cindy grinned. "I hate coming through here by myself. Almost never do it, in fact. But we should take a break, and you really need to hit the stores. This is the last secure stop we'll be able to make before we get to the federal depot down in Wellington."

Sofia hugged herself against the cold she could no longer feel.

She wondered if it was possible to get a gun here.

22

DARWIN, NORTHERN TERRITORY

The recently retired smuggler and zone runner was drunk but not ruinously so. You needed terrifying quantities of alcohol to drop three hundred pounds of dense, hard-muscled pachyderm meat. But as he shouldered his way through a dozen or so sailors who were heading into the pub, he had reason to believe that six bottles of the Duckpond Tavern's proprietary lager might have left him a couple of sheets to the wind.

The sailors, decked out in civvies, were from the amphibious assault carrier USS *Bataan,* back in Darwin after two months out with the Combined Fleet. He tried to greet them as they passed. It was always good to bump into another exile. But Darwin's humidity and the gargantuan size of the beer bottles they called stubbies in this part of the world—all six or seven (or, shit, maybe even *eight*) of which he'd sucked down on an empty stomach—conspired to unman him. And so it was that Rhino A. Ross, formerly of the U.S. Coast Guard, suddenly found his head spinning, his feet entangled, and his balance absent without leave.

One of the sailors caught him before Newton's laws took hold. "Whoa there, big guy!"

The sailors were pretty good about it, but nothing would distract them from their appointed rounds. The Rhino was passed and pushed through their group until he staggered out onto the curb, here made up of old railway timbers, where more drinkers stood around the huge open-sided shed that was the Duckpond Tavern, laughing, cursing, and roaring. A steady trade in empties and newly filled glasses continued through the vast openings, where slatted wooden bifold shutters had been lashed back to allow a tepid breeze some chance of flushing out the crowded beer hall.

A couple of the brown-shirted local cops meandered past, showing zero interest in enforcing the city ordinances against drinking in the street. They'd have been more zealous in the old town, but the tavern sat squarely in the middle of twenty blocks of warehouses, factories, cheap boardinghouses, brothels, and bars that had filled up a couple of acres of waste ground behind the old Darwin Duckpond marina. Even now the Rhino thought he could hear the grumble of earthmoving equipment and the dull concussion of explosive excavation work a short distance south, at the site of the abandoned convention center. A giant wharf was going in there to service the Combined Fleet of the newly formed Pacific Alliance.

The Rhino decided to head in exactly the opposite direction from the cops. Turning awkwardly, he fought the head spins that threatened to send him spiraling into the old railway sleepers—a Wild West design touch that extended only as far as the corners of the tavern. If he fell, drunk, to the ground beyond that, he'd face-plant in the mud and the brown shirts probably wouldn't ignore him. Besides, he had a powerful need to get something other than Duckpond Lager into his belly, and there was a take-out rib joint around the next corner that did a Rhino-size newspaper cone filled to the brim with buffalo wings in hot sauce. His stomach started rumbling a split second before he'd even made a conscious decision to drop his last ten bucks on a feed there.

Raising himself up to his considerable height, he sucked in a deep breath and laid a course for Blue Smoke Ribs and Barbecue.

New Town, Shah told her, was even more crowded than usual because of the fleet's arrival in port. Thousands of U.S. personnel and as many allied sailors and marines thronged the streets: hanging out of the windows of pubs, lining up at the government-licensed bordellos, and crowding the tattoo parlors, betting shops, and burger joints. Tupac and Snoop Dogg mingled with Garth Brooks and George Strait in a sonic train wreck that threatened to bring on a brain embolism if Jules had to listen to much more of it. She checked the list of bars and greasy spoons where Shah said Rhino hung out. It would be tempting to head straight to his boat to wait for him, but he might not go back there for hours, possibly even a day or two if he was on a bender. So an old-fashioned snipe hunt it was.

Music mingled with the scent of fried meat, which was strong enough to overpower the rank odor of thousands of men and women all rubbing up hard against one another in the hot, dank air. Not all of the city was the same, she knew. There was old money here in Darwin and new money that didn't care for the sour stench of the gutter. They would have their own enclaves. But New Town was all gutter. It was where the city's considerable population of the transient and the displaced gathered to feel as if they still had some purchase on the world. Every port town she'd ever passed through was the same. Class mattered in these sorts of places. Her father would have understood that as soon as he drew in the first breath of fetid air. He'd have stayed in one of the old colonial neighborhoods somehow, but he'd have done his best work down here, in the worst part of town.

As Julianne weaved through the heaving crowds, she heard American voices everywhere. Enlisted men and women. The proles of the service. Unless they were sending their money home, the officers most likely would take their leisure in Darwin's older, more exclusive quarter, spending six months of accumulated pay on electronics and clothing and finer brands of firewater than the lesser ranks were inclined to shell out for. Attachment to the Combined Fleet was a much-sought-after billet. It was one of the few postings in the present-day U.S. military where you were guaranteed that your pay would arrive. Granted, payday had taken a step backward, away from electronic accounts. Post-Wave, it consisted of a petty officer or sergeant, accompanied by a pair of armed guards, counting out currency to sailors, marines, and anyone else waiting in line. But nobody here was complaining.

These idiots were just as happy to spend Australian dollars, Korean won, and Japanese yen, all of which were changing hands around her, as American newbies. A couple of happy sailors who looked too young to be wearing the uniform slipped past her with a much-prized PlayStation 3. The stupid toy probably had cost those sailors their combined pay for the last six months, and now they'd have to start saving for the games. Whatever happened to blowing your money on hookers and tattoos? She shook her head as she threaded through a curbside shiatsu parlor: three massage tables, all occupied, dropped into the crush of foot traffic like stones in a river.

Jules stopped outside a noodle house to reorient herself, needing to make sure she was still headed toward the cigar stand Shah said the Rhino used. She'd had no luck at the marina earlier and now was working her way through a list of his haunts. She remembered, on their long run out of New York, that the old chief had talked about signing up for another hitch himself. At age fifty-two, he was still relatively young, and twenty years in the coast guard would count in his favor with the navy. But of course, even if he did make it in, he might well end up on some old tub, trawling up and down the Atlantic coast running antipiracy patrols instead of serving on board something like the *Bataan*. There'd be retraining, and he'd have to serve the needs of the U.S. Navy, not the other way around. He wouldn't even get his former coast guard rank back—be lucky to get petty officer third-class, in fact. All that rubbish plus zero desire on his part to find himself back on the East Coast anytime soon had swiftly put an end to thoughts of reenlistment. Like her, the Rhino's main desire after the clusterfuck in Manhattan was a quiet life.

He'd broken the news at the bar of the Idler shortly after they'd sailed "the lake" yet again, leaving the United States for good, landing in Sydney, hoping that Cesky had no pull so far away from Seattle.

"Best bet for this particular megafaunal rarity is to stay hunkered the fuck down, as low as my massive horn will permit, Miss Jules. And I hunker best on my lonesome."

Thus, while she'd tried to blend into the cashed-up refugee scene in Sydney, paying her way with a few salvaged trinkets, he'd fetched up in Darwin, the northernmost city of Australia, at the ass end of the world, a weird frontier boomtown that had doubled in size, then doubled again, and doubled *again* in the years since 2003. Military and civilian alike, tens of thousands of the Rhino's fellow Americans had come here, drifting down—or sometimes running headlong—from the chaos that had swept through Asia after the Disappearance.

Darwin hosted former CEOs of merchant banks and vice presidents of software companies who now worked as debt collectors, truck drivers in uranium mines, or laborers on the huge government farms out on the Ord River. Like a lot of frontier towns, Darwin was a rude, bruising crossroads settlement, full of chancers, thieves, and strong-arm men. It was a good place to get lost, and that, he'd told her, was fine by him. There was nothing back home for Rhino A. Ross, just burned bridges and enemies. Or one enemy in particular, at least, one worth the effort of losing himself down here with all the other losers.

Jules squinted into the fierce sun as she left behind the cover of a wide veranda awning that shaded the front of an Irish-themed pub, with the thematic verisimilitude provided by a couple of drunken Paddies beating each other to death with bar stools just inside the swinging doors. Above, a pair of marine Harriers off the *Bataan* flew over and drowned out all background noise momentarily with the howl of their engines. She searched her shirt pockets for the pair of faux Gucci sunglasses she'd picked up that morning but seemed to have lost them. She was worried about the Rhino, and not just because of what had happened to her back in Sydney. When they'd gone their separate ways, he'd seemed bleak and beaten down, which was not at all his natural state of being. She had been in Darwin only a few hours, but already she knew it to be the sort of place people went to when they thought they'd run out of options.

Six lanes of traffic pulsed and crawled along Perrett Street, although calling the arrangement lanes implied more order than was really the case. In effect, two thick, snaking streams of vehicles, each about three cars across, ground past one another, sometimes mingling, even crunching together as horns blared and drivers hurled abuse into the hot gray sky in a couple of dozen languages. Again she heard American voices everywhere, shouting down or trying to shout down the flat, nasal Strine of the locals or the chittering tonal curses of Chinese, Tagalog, and Javanese motorists. A siren wailed somewhere but never seemed to move, and heat shimmered off the bodies of the cars, rolling over her as though she'd stepped in front of an open furnace door.

She used her elbows and shoulders to force a path through the crowds that spilled out into the fringes of the traffic jam, leading to more near misses and abuse. Part of the problem was the lack of any real division between road and curb, but also there were just too many people attempting to force their way through too small a space.

"Another perfect day," Julianne muttered as she fought through the heaving masses of sour, sweating bodies on a sidewalk that had reverted to rammed earth. The city still hadn't gotten around to paving the New Town development, and water trucks rolled through every couple of hours, spraying to settle the dust down until the monsoon arrived in late afternoon to turn it to mud. If the monsoon arrived. Mostly it did, but even now the weather remained unpredictable.

He felt a little better being mobile again and heading toward a meal. With any sort of luck, he'd get paid this afternoon when Hughie came back from the seafood markets with their cut from the week's haul. With a wad of the folding stuff in his pocket, a decent feed, and maybe a nap to sleep off the worst of the daytime drink, he might even turn his mind to the depressing topic of what next.

The Rhino had been in Darwin for three months and in that time had done no more than establish the flimsiest toehold. The free port was one of the busiest, most kinetic places he'd been to since the Disappearance. Vast flows of money and people passed through it, and the power structure of the city was constantly shifting, protean, moving in time with the erratic tidal changes that the fall of America had sent washing around the globe. As much as the presence of thousands of

U.S. servicemen and women created the impression that Seattle was the big dog around here, the Rhino knew differently.

We're just the dumb muscle, he figured, *like a boxer who's taken too many hits to the head. They'll keep us around until they don't need the help, and then we'll get flushed like a used condom.*

The real power here took the form of Indian money changers and the former Chinese Communist Party bosses, legions of them, who'd survived the civil war and transformed themselves into princes of the Middle Kingdom's coastal megacities. The old CCP chiefs rarely appeared on the streets of Darwin, but the city seemed to clench in on itself whenever they arrived in numbers. They flew in and choppered straight out to the rooftop landing pad of the new Mirvac Mirage Hotel in the old city, there to contend for the mountains of coal, iron ore, gold, and uranium being raked out of the earth's oldest continent. And, perhaps even more crucially, to bid for the crops of one of the few reliable large-scale food exporters left in the world.

The Rhino rubbed a massive paw over his face, flicking droplets of salty sweat onto the dirt in front of him. Traffic crawled along the gravel road, raising a miasma of red dust that slightly dulled the fierce sunburst glinting off chrome and tinted windshields. He grinned at the plight of two black stretch Hummer limos trapped in the slow-moving snarl. Small flags hung limp from their aerials: the new red and gold ensign of the South American Federation. Newcomers in town and utterly clueless about it. He wondered what had brought them all the way here. It wasn't as though Roberto's operation lacked resources. Sprawled across the territories of half a dozen former states, the Federation was ridiculously wealthy, at least in potential. It remained a prison camp, however, with the Colombian gangster turned dictator still smashing his fist down wherever he thought he detected the slightest opposition.

Although he knew it was foolish, even a little conceited, the Rhino faded away from the gutter and back into the crush of the crowd, not wanting to be seen by the occupants of the diplomatic convoy. They were probably just in town to negotiate with a few of the local mining companies, offering a generous cut of the profits if the Australians, or increasingly the South African companies that were moving here, would assist in restarting production at any one of the *Federación*'s hundreds of projects that had imploded during the general collapse. It was also possible that they were here to see about joining the Alliance, but he didn't think the current member states would be game for that. Seattle still had enough clout, just barely, to block any membership bid.

The Rhino had witnessed part of the collapse firsthand when Acapulco, the Mexican port on the southern fringe of the Wave, fell apart. And almost certainly alone among the masses of people swarming through Darwin, he'd played a small role in the rise of *el presidente por vida*, Roberto Morales. In those days—an age ago in less than five years—Roberto had been nothing but a small-time local hood fortunate enough to score a sweet deal providing muscle to a couple of the more expensive resorts, such as the Fairmont. Fortunate because he had lucked into a crew run by one Miguel Pieraro, a man who had, in the Rhino's opinion, probably shot dogs with more highly developed codes of honor than Morales.

The Rhino had no idea where Pieraro was now, of course, but he wished him and his family well. He knew they'd spent some time in the refugee camps outside Sydney when they'd gotten off Miss Julianne's boat and that they'd applied to move to America as part of President Kipper's resettlement program. Roberto meanwhile was ensconced in his newly constructed presidential palace in Caracas.

The traffic snarl edged forward, gradually taking the two Hummers away as the Rhino rounded the corner into Perrett Street, a wide, sprawling boulevard that had been a boggy salt marsh five years earlier. Or maybe the town dump. He'd heard that a couple of blocks of New Town lay over the city's former garbage dump, which was rumored to be the last resting place of a dozen or so Javanese gangsters who'd tried to take over the waterfront markets in the fearful confusion that had followed the Disappearance. Probably bullshit. In his experience, frontier towns loved their own creation mythology so much that they tended to its growth like a pot-addled hippie with a bumper crop of hand-raised weed. There was no shortage of that here, either, if a Rhino were so inclined. As it stood, though, he'd never acquired a taste for the stuff, preferring his cigars. And those, sadly, were hard to come by these days, at least ones of appreciable quality.

The smell of wood smoke in the air, mingled with the meat of the nearby barbecue pits, drew him on. He was glad the rib joint was only a few steps away now. Farther up Perrett, where the three official casinos had spun off a dense cluster of parasite businesses such as the Korean and Thai brothels, the crowds were neutron-star-dense. If the hookers didn't flick your Bic or if you'd already had it flicked, you could try the slots, some blackjack, or maybe poker at the unlicensed gaming houses. When you got hungry, you had your choice of corn dogs, pretzels, yaki mandu, and gaegogi from the food carts. Streetwalkers and black-market dopers draped themselves around canvas stalls selling cheap Nike and Reebok knockoffs. The path through was nearly impassable to most but merely a nuisance for a determined Rhino.

For now, only a dozen or so hungry fans were pressed up against Blue Smoke's small serving window, including a few sailors trying to get a taste of a home that no longer existed. Later, when the dry-rubbed baby back pork and Texas-style beef ribs came out of the barbecue pit, the curbside here would be gridlocked with his fellow countrymen bidding up the price of everything 400 or 500 percent. Including the cone full of buffalo wings he was about to buy with a fistful of local currency.

Much as it pained him, he accepted payment in anything except the newbie these days. He still kept a stash of noobs, though, in the hope that maybe someday they just might be worth something. If things ever got really tight, he could sell some to the speculators, who were forever trying to keep the street price down or praying for a rapid rise. But things weren't that tight for the Rhino, not just yet.

He could only shake his head at the business smarts of the two smokehouse assholes who'd come up with the idea of auctioning off their wares during peak hour. A couple of guys from Houston who'd moved Down Under long before the Wave swept away their hometown, they'd run a successful barbecue joint in Sydney and expanded in a big way when the first American refugees poured into the camps there back in 2003. Assholes didn't even work the grill anymore. They'd franchised and retired about a year after coming up with the idea of swapping set menu prices for a bidding war during the busiest hour of service—just after they opened up the pits for lunch. The

Rhino didn't know whether he resented them for making their baby back pork ribs so prohibitively fucking expensive that he could never afford to eat them or because he hadn't thought of some similarly cunning idea to enrich himself out in the end of the world.

All he'd managed was to get his ass nearly shot off in New York on a wild fucking goose hunt for some asshole who didn't even exist except as a lure for some other asshole who wanted him dead simply because he'd helped Miss Jules get out of Acapulco alive.

The cast-iron doors of the smoker swung open, and an employee reached in with tongs to pull the ribs out. He held a batch of pork ribs up for all to see while the initial price went up on a chalkboard. Hands full of currency were in the air as the shouting began. Casting a sideways glance at the sailors, the Rhino saw their crestfallen faces as the price soon soared out of their reach.

He'd moved to the head of the line—rather, the front of the crush—while he'd been contemplating his sorry lot. Well, at least he was still drawing breath. He hadn't Disappeared, leaving behind a puddle of meaty gruel and stained clothes. He hadn't gone down screaming in the great die-off that followed. He hadn't been turned into radioactive glass in the Middle East.

Or been stomped to death in a food riot. Or gone into a mass grave in China.

He hadn't been gunned down during the Paris intifada, either. Even pirates and great storms in the Southern Ocean hadn't come close to seeing off Rhino A. Ross.

He was still here. And by God, he was going to enjoy his goddamn buffalo wings. If he could just get his hands on some.

"The tangled fucking webs we weave . . ." Rhino muttered, approaching a second window, this one devoted to poultry. A stocky Korean leaned out to take his order.

"A dozen hot wings?"

"Fifteen dollars," the Korean said in impeccable English.

"Ten?" Rhino asked hopefully.

"No, no, American. Fifteen or nothing."

"Fuck, what happened to haggling? How about twelve?" He knew he had some change in his pockets.

The Korean grinned. "Thirteen fifty. Final price."

"Fucking rapists," the Rhino grumbled, holding out the greasy dollars and mining his pockets for change. He found a couple of local two-dollar coins. They looked like tiny gold doubloons. "*Kamsamnida,* compadre."

The shopkeeper blinked. "*Cheonmaneyo,* American."

The Korean had been generous, adding a couple of extra wings to the Rhino's order. He was still licking the thick, tangy sauce from his fingers when he arrived back at his boat at the Gonzales Road Marina. Like so much of the city, the marina was a recent addition, a temporary floating dock, not much more sophisticated than the jerry-rigged Mulberry harbors they'd used after the D-Day landings. Except that this one had lasted three years rather than just a few weeks in spite of Darwin's spectacular tropical storms. It had grown, unregulated and unplanned, over the mouth of a wide inlet that ran north from Frances Bay toward an older, more established canal development.

An almost incoherent system of locks supposedly allowed boat owners farther up the river to negotiate passage out into Darwin Harbor, but the arrangements were so arbitrary that most of those with the money had long ago berthed their vessels elsewhere and those without it had simply given up. Rhino had never seen the locks open, and a couple of supposedly mobile stalls that had set up shop on one of them, selling dry goods and small marine supplies to the boats tied up at Gonzales Road, had taken on a very permanent appearance. As he squinted into the glare, he noticed for the first time that a dredge had pulled up on the marsh flats across Frances Bay, on the edge of the small national park over there. Perhaps the mooted extension of the crowded marina across and into the park was going to happen, after all.

The floating walkways undulated beneath his deck shoes as he stumbled home, the latter being a small cabin cruiser he'd liberated from the ghost town of Winchester Bay, a couple of hours south of Seattle. He and Jules had salvaged the boat as soon as they hit the West Coast after a two month cross-country hell drive. Piloted it across the Pacific with no intention of ever making the return voyage. Not after New York.

He nodded to a couple of his neighbors, other Americans mostly, although there was also a small community of displaced Mexicans at Gonzales Road, refugees resourceful enough to have bought, fought, or simply sailed their way out of the post-Wave collapse and into the safe haven of Sydney. His immediate neighbors, the Gueros, had owned a sizable fishing company in Mexico before the Disappearance and had come north after escaping to Sydney, hoping to break into the industry here. The fact that they were his neighbors spoke poorly of their success.

He was still groggy from the beer, although the buffalo wings had helped steady his spinning head. The pontoons bobbed around enough, however, to make him careful of his step. Although he knew he'd pay for it with a headache later, the Rhino figured on getting some shut-eye before chasing down Hughie for his pay. If they'd scored well at the fish markets, he might even have enough to buy into an honest poker game he knew of back in New Town.

Perhaps that was all he needed. One good break, a decent score, and he could set himself up with something a little more substantial than casual deckhand work. Maybe even enough to buy a shrimping subli-cense from one of the Chinese combines or to lease a fast boat to make a few undeclared runs out to the fishing grounds off Papua. Their patrols were a lot less trouble to avoid than the Aussie navy and customs guys.

The Gueros were at home, cooking fish on a grill made from a collection of fifty-five-gallon drums. He made his way down the last turn into his row, at the farthest reach of the floating dock, sizing up his chances. The scent of sizzling garlic and lemon set his stomach to grumbling again in spite of the food he'd picked up at Blue Smoke. Although, to be fair, even the much-reinforced cone of chicken wings was grossly inadequate fare when it came to feeding a hungry Rhino.

He didn't much fancy getting caught chewing the fat with Carlos Guero, and Lord knew there was no such thing as a quick chat with the man. That said, Carlos was a generous soul, as generous with his grill as he was with his conversation, and the Rhino did feel as though just a little more eatin' might set him up well for his afternoon siesta. All the better to sharpen mind and body for an evening out in New Town.

"*Buenos tardes, Señor Carlos, Señora Juanita,*" he called out, very much aware of how tipsy he felt and thinking he must look like a staggering drunk as he veered back and forth with the rocking of the pontoons. "Permission to come aboard?"

"Ah, Mr. Ross. Come, come, we have barramundi fish—a large one. Come, and I shall make you a fish sandwich."

"Mighty kind of you, neighbor," he called back. Saliva squirted into his mouth as a sluggish breeze off the bay carried the smell of Guero's grill to him.

Juanita Guero produced a round of flat bread from within a foil packet at her feet and passed it to her husband. Unlike him, she rarely spoke to anyone outside the family. They had three teenagers who were lucky enough to have places in one of the open-air schools run by the Catholic Church. The kids would not be around until much later in the day. As payment for their tuition, they worked for two hours every afternoon in the church market gardens. The Rhino wondered why Carlos wasn't over at the seafood markets like Hughie, but he knew better than to ask. Everyone in Darwin knew better than to ask about one another's affairs. You just took people as they came.

"*Muchas gracias,*" Rhino said, accepting the warm flatbread from Guero. He had stuffed it generously with the char-grilled meaty flesh of the barramundi and a few scraps of salad.

"There was a lady looking for you this morning," Carlos said as he squeezed some lemon juice over a fish roll for his wife.

The Rhino was instantly on guard. "Official, was it? Migration or customs? Brown shirts, maybe?"

"Oh, no, I do not think so. She was an English lady, pretty, but not at all official. She would not tell me what she wanted you for. Would not leave a name. She was very evading of my questions. She wished to know which boat was yours, but I am afraid I would not tell her. I hope that was the right thing."

The Rhino chewed slowly and nodded. *An English lady?* He didn't ask; the less said, the better. "Anybody else?" he wondered aloud.

Both of the Gueros shook their heads. "We have not been here all day," Carlos explained. "I was delayed this morning awaiting a call from the fisheries people. My license, Mr. Rhino, it is to be approved this week."

Guero was beaming as he spoke, and his wife nodded and smiled as though a burden had been lifted off her chest.

"It is only a small operator's license," he continued. "Two shrimp trawlers, when once I had a fleet of factory ships, yes? But I did not start with a fleet, my friend. Not then and not now. This is good news, and so we have come home to celebrate. I shall open a bottle of wine tonight and . . ." He glanced across at his wife and smiled fondly. "And I was wondering if we might prevail upon you, my friend. The children—I wonder if they might visit with you this evening, just for a few hours? I would normally ask the Carascalaos to mind them, but they are working late at the cathedral tonight. Helping the father with the new arrivals."

Most of what Carlos had said passed right through the Rhino's skull without lodging, but when he realized the Mexican was after a favor, he pulled himself out of his reverie.

"Oh, sure thing, Carlos . . . Sorry. I was pondering pretty English ladies come to visit. But sure—hell yes, send your kids over. I have somewhere to be later in the evening, but not until way later."

"Excellent. I shall send them with a bottle of beer and my thanks. And some dinner, of course. More fish—if you have the appetite for it?"

"That'd be fine, Carlos. I'll look forward it, and congrats on your news. That's excellent, buddy. But if you don't mind me dining and dashing, I'd best get back to my berth. I'd like to make a few calls, find out who this pretty lady was. There are not so many pretty ladies in my life that I can afford to let them get away these days."

The other man nodded. "Of course. We will talk later. Perhaps I might have something more to offer than beer and fish after tonight."

Carlos waved him away. Juanita smiled a little bashfully, then busied herself with preparing the next piece of fish for the grill. They seemed to have a cooler brimming with fillets.

The Rhino folded the rest of the sandwich into his mouth as he walked down the end of the row to his boat. The pretty English lady was almost certainly Miss Julianne, although her calling on him could not be good news. They'd agreed after escaping from the States and Henry Cesky's vengeful reach that it would be better if they parted ways. The last he'd seen of her, she'd been walking away from him up

George Street in Sydney. They hadn't parted on bad terms despite the epic fuckup in New York, but if Cesky had men looking for them, Jules and he were much more likely to stand out traveling in a pair than they were on their own.

He frowned murderously whenever he thought of Cesky. The man's power seemed to grow every day. His wealth was approaching the levels of Boeing and Microsoft, two lucky corporate survivors of the Disappearance by reason of their being headquartered just outside the fall of the Wave and having products that were still in demand. *Starbucks, too, unfortunately,* Rhino thought. It was a sign of how far the pre-Wave corporations had fallen and how fast Cesky's rise had been.

Why here? Rhino pondered that one. He couldn't imagine why Julianne would be in Darwin or how she'd even found him. That alone was reason to worry.

He scoped out his boat as he approached the end of the floating walkway. The *Redneck Princessa* was a thirty-two-foot motor yacht. She looked battered and careworn after the run across the pond from Winchester Bay and three months tied up as a houseboat here at Gonzales Road. The trim had faded. Her chrome surfaces were dull and speckled with spots of rust. Blobs of guano marred the deck and flying bridge. Perhaps it was the midday beers or the humidity, but he felt slightly nauseous contemplating the decay and air of abandonment. He never would have allowed any of his crew to get away with such slackness back in the coast guard, and he had no excuse for it now. This was worse than having his old charter shot up back in Acapulco. This was his own fault.

Feeling ashamed of himself, the Rhino climbed aboard awkwardly, looking for any sign that someone had been there while he'd been out on the shrimp boat for the previous two days. Rainwater had pooled here and there, dumped by the monsoon falls. The fish scraps left for the stray cat he'd taken to feeding were mostly gone; the bowl now was full of water and probably mosquito larvae. He bent down to pick it up too quickly . . . The rush of blood out of his head, the sulfurous humidity, the beers, the greasy food, all combined to send his stomach pitching and rolling. He half lunged, half fell toward the gunwale to hurl over the side, but the safety rail struck him below his center of gravity and he felt the world tip away.

"Rhino!"

The voice was familiar but far away. An English accent. Educated, privileged.

He recognized Miss Julianne's voice a split second before tumbling over the edge. And then the boat disintegrated in a violent explosion that flung him feetfirst far across the water, turning and burning, torn by pain and rage and a bone-deep sense of violation that passed only as darkness welled up and claimed him.

23

DARWIN, NORTHERN TERRITORY

Nearly eight months since she'd escaped from New York, and her nerves were still scraped raw. She flinched and ducked when the motor yacht exploded, dropping to the rough nonslip pontoon deck, closing her eyes, and breathing out as the blast wave ripped over them.

Rhino, no!

Julianne was too late. She retained a shutter-speed flicker of memory, an image of the Rhino consumed in the explosion, of a woman sitting nearby, filleting fish, beheaded by a chunk of bright steel shrapnel. But no more. Nothing that might give her any hope that her friend had survived.

She'd come such a long way to warn him just to fail in the last moments. The thunder rolled on through the hot, muggy early afternoon, and small pieces of fiberglass and twisted chrome rained down on the deck around her. A large cinder fell on her neck and burned the exposed skin. She yelped and swiped it away, the sudden pain jerking her back into the moment after shock had threatened to numb and dull her responses.

"Quick, we must hurry, Miss Julianne."

She heard Shah's rough voice as though muffled by many layers of cotton wool. His grip on her upper arm was firm enough to be uncomfortable as he dragged Jules to her feet and back to reality. Acrid smoke stung in her eyes, and she could taste diesel fumes at the back of her throat. Hundreds of birds screeched and swooped overhead. She coughed as she tried to take a deep breath. Her head swam, and she was afraid she might lose her balance and tumble into the oily water.

The Nepalese soldier urged her forward, pushing her past the grotesque scene of a man hugging a headless female corpse and wailing as if to call her back from the dead. Boats burned, and the heat rolling off the inferno seemed to shrink the skin on Jules's face. She squinted and raised a hand to her eyes. A useless gesture. She staggered on anyway, but Shah had left her behind; he was running into the conflagration now, leaping onto the deck of a blazing cruiser, bounding across, and diving into the water. She heard the splash but nothing else as a secondary explosion drove her back.

Voices. Some shouting. Others screaming in pain or horror.

She stumbled over the leg of the crying man. He had spooned himself into the back of the dead woman, and they were lying as if in bed. He was moaning in a way she'd never heard before. It looked as though he was trying to bore his head into her back.

She apologized for tripping over him, immediately struck by the banality of her mumbled "Sorry" when measured against the bloody ruin of the crater where the woman's head had been separated from her body.

"Oh, God . . ."

She vomited, reaching for a handhold as the contractions doubled her over. Finding nothing to grab, Julianne hugged herself and set her feet to steady her balance while she grunted and heaved. She heard boots pounding toward her and men cursing. An outboard engine coughed and spluttered into life somewhere between her and the marina office, a small shed at the end of Gonzales Road. When she was certain she'd finished retching, she searched for the source of the noise.

A small unpainted motorboat—"tinnies" they called them here—

shot out into the bay with two would-be rescuers on board. One steered while the other pointed ahead. They were moving quickly enough to lift the front of the boat well clear of a small bow wave.

Men and women appeared on the dock in small groups, most of them from within the cabins of their boats. There were a lot of Americans, she noted. A small refugee commune. Some ran off immediately, heading for shore. Others tried to prevent the fires from spreading, producing small handheld extinguishers and battling the flames with whooshing plumes of white foam. A siren warbled very far away, then faded. Jules gathered her wits and moved back from the terrible scene of the man and his dead woman.

An empty berth allowed her an unobstructed view of the bay, where she saw the two men in the runabout helping Mr. Shah wrestle the Rhino's body into the boat. The former sergeant of the Gurkhas was a strong man, but the channel was deep and the Rhino was no midget. The tinnie rocked so far one way and then the other, she thought it might be swamped, but they managed to drag him on board after a struggle.

Jules wondered about crocodiles—or were they alligators? She'd heard they were all over Darwin's waterways. She peered into the mangroves on the far shore, imagining giant carnivores launching themselves into the murky water and speeding toward Shah.

An invisible fist squeezed her heart as the old coast guard chief raised his hand to grip the forearm of one of his rescuers. He was alive . . . Bloodied and burned and probably broken in parts, but alive for now.

Julianne turned and ran for the marina office, dodging and elbowing past the gathering crowd. Some of them had mobile phones, and she could hear the calls for emergency crews going out, but she had to do something herself. Perhaps irrationally, she figured that a call from the marina management might get fire crews and ambulances dispatched more quickly.

The small shed was empty, with the door open and the last of the cool air pouring out into the sultry afternoon. There wasn't much to the setup: a counter, a chair, a very old computer, and three metal filing cabinets. A map of Darwin Harbor covered one wall, and pictures cut from fishing and hunting magazines had been taped up to most of the other surfaces. An old landline phone was off the hook and beeping on the counter. Jules hung it up and dialed emergency, having to think for a second of the number they used here. She half expected to hit an engaged signal, but the call went through to the dispatcher.

"What service, please?"

"Fire. And ambulance!"

"Location?"

"Oh . . ." For an infuriating second her mind went blank. "The marina. Gonzales Road Ma—"

"Units are en route," came the clipped reply. "Please clear the line."

The call cut off, leaving her with a dial tone.

She heard choppers a few moments before any sirens, and shading her eyes against the glare, she picked them out, flying up from the south. They were gray and looked very much like the helicopter that had lifted them out of New York.

Military, then, she thought. Probably off that huge carrier in the port, although it was possible that one of the private military companies was responding. She knew they had contracts for emergency response as well as border and city security. The fierce glare made it difficult to pick out details, though, until one of the helicopters flew across the sun and she spotted the U.S. markings on the other.

Fire trucks and a small fleet of ambulances arrived, horns blaring to clear a path down Gonzales Road. Behind them, she saw police cruisers and a couple of black SUVs she recognized as belonging to Sandline Security. The first responders shook themselves out, with the ambulances and fire engines pulling into two distinct laagers. Brown-shirted police officers in wide-brimmed cowboy hats threw open the doors of their vehicles as an amplified voice blared out of roof-mounted loudspeakers. Hundreds of spectators were now pouring in from New Town to watch the show, many of them holding drinks and food, taking shots with phone cameras.

"Clear the area. Clear the area immediately. Go on—get out! This area is dangerous."

Firefighters in yellow coveralls and heavy flame-retardant gear leaped from their bright red trucks and hurried to unload equipment with fast, practiced movements. Jules ran to the nearest ambulance and collared the two men who emerged. One of them carried an old-fashioned stretcher. His name tag read DWYER.

"This way. Follow me!" the Englishwoman ordered, inflecting her voice with the same command imperative her father would use for running off debt collectors. "There are casualties down this way. I was just there."

"Go on, then, love. We'll follow," said Dwyer.

The brown shirts and Sandliners were coordinating their efforts to clear the dock of gawking onlookers. The Sandline mercs, who stood out in their urban-gray camouflage coveralls, were no rougher than the cops, but Jules could see people moving out of their way with a far greater sense of urgency. She ignored them. She was safely associated with the paramedics now. For a moment she worried that she might not be able to find the small motorboat that had gone out to get the Rhino, but as the crowds parted and began to move off the floating docks, she saw Sergeant Shah carefully manhandling the Rhino up on the decking. The American's clothes were bloody and burned and one arm was badly singed. Half of his hair seemed to be missing, but he was conscious and seemed to be trying to help his rescuers.

She bade the stretcher bearers to follow her and led them down, ignoring the cries of any of the other injured. They weren't her concern.

"He got blown right off the boat that exploded," she said as the paramedics moved swiftly to take over, thanking the civilians who'd pulled him out but letting them know their work was done.

Shah was soaked with both oil and water. He used a shirtsleeve to mop his face clean before positioning himself just behind the ambulance men to help keep the dock clear. "Back, back," he ordered in a parade-ground voice, pushing the small crowd that had re-formed away from the stretcher. More stretcher bearers ran by, heading toward the weeping man who still clung to that headless corpse. Two Sandline troopers fought through the crush and began using batons to push the onlookers back toward dry land.

"Miss Jules," the Rhino croaked. "This is a pleasant surprise."

"I'm so sorry, Rhino," she said. "I should have stayed this morning until I'd warned you. But . . ."

He reached out one trembling hand to still her as the paramedics settled him onto the stretcher.

"S'okay. A coupla scratches. Horn's still attached. I'll live."

"Move!" Dwyer shouted before taking a grip on the stretcher handles and nodding to his colleague. "One, two, three—lift."

They hoisted their giant patient with audible grunts. Shah moved quickly to take some of the weight, and Jules took an awkward grip on the opposite side.

"Cesky?" the Rhino asked, looking into Jules's eyes.

"Who else?" she answered. But he already had passed out.

She thought he'd be taken to Royal Darwin Hospital, which had developed an unenviable expertise in trauma surgery over the last few years. Hundreds of victims of the Bali bombing in October 2002 had been treated there, and later tens of thousands of evacuees from the fighting in Indonesia had fled to the city, many of them needing emergency care. The Rhino would have been well looked after up at Royal Darwin. Instead he was loaded onto one of the U.S. Navy helicopters and lifted away.

"They'll take him out to the *Bataan,*" Dwyer told her. "Got a great trauma center on board. He'll be fine. We send cases to the Yanks all the time."

"He *is* a Yank," she said, feeling useless.

"There you go, then. He'll be right at home."

But it wasn't his treatment she was worried about. Both Jules and the Rhino had had reason for putting thousands of miles between themselves and the United States after getting out of New York. She watched the chopper haul itself into the sky and turn south, heading for the Combined Fleet anchorage. She assumed the ship's doctors had gained a lot of unwanted experience at treating burns and blast injuries over the last few years. But the Rhino wouldn't want to linger in the sick bay.

"Miss Julianne."

She was surprised to find Shah beside her again. He had a knack for appearing and disappearing at will.

"Perhaps we should leave," he said in a low voice. "Before the police secure the docks and begin to search for witnesses. It would not be convenient."

"No," she agreed. "Best not to get caught up with the wallopers."

They allowed themselves to be swept along in the tide of people being pushed away from the docks, where some boats still burned. A small third explosion boomed behind them, possibly a gas canister, panicking the onlookers, who started to push and move with greater urgency. Jules and Shah cut across the flow, emerging onto clear ground, or at least less crowded, on the road that ran around the bay.

The buildings there were all new and very spare in their simplicity. Fiber cement siding and external metal joists, giant roller doors, and huge rumbling air-con plants. The area was zoned for light industry, and unsurprisingly, it had been colonized by marine engineering firms and suppliers servicing the trawler and naval fleets. A few weed-choked lots still stood empty, but even they had been marked off for development, and Jules could see earthmoving equipment in some.

Shah's vehicle, a Land Rover of battered but rugged appearance, stood in front of one such lot, partially blocking a sign that announced that development approval had been granted to erect a battery-manufacturing plant on the site. A young, fit-looking Nepalese man, another Gurkha, stood holding the rear door open for them. Jules wondered if Shah might want to change to avoid getting oil and sea sludge all over the seats, but he waved her in and followed without delay.

Their driver—Shah introduced him as Ganesh—moved quickly and gracefully around the vehicle and into the driver's seat. They pulled away before she was able to secure her belt.

"If this was Cesky, it is best we not linger," Shah said. "He will have men watching the dock. They will not move openly with so many witnesses, but they will note our presence and Mr. Ross's survival. They will regroup and try again."

She didn't need telling. After blundering into the ambush Henry Cesky had set for them in Manhattan, they'd narrowly avoided another in Galveston, Texas, where they'd holed up to count their losses and plot the next move. Jules had hoped Cesky's influence would be marginal in Texas, what with him being such a butt boy of the Kipper administration. But she'd been wrong. He didn't need influence. He just needed reach.

"I have a compound out near the airport," Shah said. "It is secure. We should go there. Ganesh, call ahead to Birendra. Have him send men to meet us as soon as possible."

The driver acknowledged the direction with a very military "Yes, sir" and fitted a hands-free earpiece to his mobile phone.

"Birendra is still with you?" Jules asked. "The same Birendra?"

He nodded. "Yes. He is my second here. A good man. Now, do you have any idea who Cesky is using? Does he have his own men or just contractors?"

"Cutouts, I'm sure," she replied as they swept onto the ring road that encircled New Town. The crowd on the edge of the red-light district was heaving now, spilling out onto the road. "The guys who tried to take us in New York were hired out of Mexico. Or, you know, what was left of Mexico. That freakish Commando Barbie chick who saved our arses said they were hitters from one of the old cartels. In Galveston it was a couple of cashiered army guys, and the chap who tried to shiv me in Sydney last week was a Romanian. A nobody, really. Just some hard man providing muscle for the Russian maf down there."

"Not so hard now, however?"

"No. Not so much. Dumb and dead mostly. What about the guys who tried to hit you, Mr. Shah? Any luck tracing them?"

He frowned. "I am afraid the men who planted the bomb at my home did not survive their incompetence. One died on the spot, the other in hospital. Not by my hand, I assure you. I wished very much to talk with them, but they were under guard. I assumed a business rival hired them, perhaps even a private military company—Sandline or one of Blackwater's franchise operators. They have been pressuring smaller security firms like myself to fold our business into theirs. There has been violence, but nothing on this scale. I do not think the police would stand for it, even as powerful as the private contractors are. Until you contacted me, Miss Julianne, I would never have considered this Cesky character. To be truthful. I had forgotten him. After all, he did not make the voyage with us from Acapulco."

"And that's his issue," said Jules. "Hard to believe a bloke who's done so well out of the last few years would screw around like this just to settle an old score. But that's his nature as I understand it and . . ." She paused, wondering how best to put this.

"Yes?"

The Land Rover grunted as Ganesh took them onto the Stuart Highway, heading north, and picked up speed as they passed the headquarters of the Free Port Development Authority, the real power in the city. A huge, soaring structure of blue and gold glass that was somehow narrower at the base than up on its top floors, it reminded Jules of a rolled-up newspaper.

"He lost a daughter," Jules began. "She didn't make it to Seattle."

"I see," said Shah, his face unreadable. "Did she die in Acapulco, in the collapse?"

"No. They were on a refugee boat with about a hundred or so other Americans. It wasn't much of a boat. Not like the *Aussie Rules,* I'm afraid. It foundered off the coast south of Washington State. A lot of people drowned, apparently. Cesky was lucky to get most of his family ashore, but his smallest girl didn't make it."

"I see," Shah said again.

"Oh, God, Shah," she blurted suddenly. "You remember what it was like. We *couldn't* have taken Cesky. He would have led a mutiny within a few days. That's what—"

The former NCO held up one huge brown hand.

"You are not to blame for the death of the child, Miss Julianne. I remember discussing this Cesky with Mr. Pieraro after we had escaped Acapulco. He told me he faced down Cesky because he knew the man would have brought us all to grief."

"Yeah, Miguel." Jules sighed. "He was a good bloke . . . Oh, for fuck's sake. I've been so fucking selfish. Cesky will have Miguel at the top of his list. Unless he's saving him until last. Shah, I have to warn him."

"Do you know where he is?"

"I have absolutely no idea. I know he and his family were here for a while, in Australia. They were working on one of the government farms down south. I heard he'd applied to go back to the U.S. as a settler. Well, not *back,* you know, but . . ."

Shah grunted and lifted his shoulders as a signal that she should move on.

"They've been in the U.S. for a few years now. Homesteaders. Running cattle, of course. I wouldn't know how to begin looking for him. It's not like the old days. You can't just open a phone book. It's more like the really old days of the bloody Wild West. He's probably on some ranch in the middle of an awful fucking cowboy movie somewhere. Contactable only by smoke signal and Pony Express."

As she began to babble, Shah patted the air in front of him, making a shushing gesture. A couple of police cars screamed past, their blue lights and sirens going.

"I have contacts in both Seattle and Fort Hood," he said, "They are both customers, although I must admit, Governor Blackstone is the more reliable. He pays in cash, whereas in Seattle they often try to haggle concessions on salvage as payment. It is most difficult. But I do have contacts. If Mr. Pieraro is registered as a settler, I am sure I can find him and you can get a message to him."

"Thank you, Shah," she said, feeling some measure of relief for the first time that day.

The traffic thickened but flowed more swiftly as they headed out toward the airport, leaving behind the stop-and-start driving of the city proper. For a while there was very little sign of the great changes that had remade the face of Darwin in the few years it had been operating as a tax-free entrepot and more recently as a home port for the Combined Fleet. The suburbs were older, more settled, with less evidence of rapid redevelopment. Out near Darwin International Airport, a long stretch of the highway was bounded on the southern side by light manufacturing and wholesaling businesses. A huge pornography supermarket painted bright yellow and pink nestled in next to rival pool-pump vendors and a piping supplier. Out of her window, on the northern side, Jules could see an enormously fat military plane parked on the tarmac at the airport. Light armored cars bounced down a rear ramp, and in the background giant bulldozers scraped away at the red earth to build the new, third runway.

"It's a pity about those morons blowing themselves up at your place, Shah," she said. "Not that I'd have wanted them to succeed, of course,

but it would've been useful to have had a chat. Three times these buggers have had a go at me, and I've never yet been able to confirm they
were Cesky's hires. Except for one idiot in New York who gave it away
before Barbie slotted him."

"How so?" Shah asked as they pulled up at an intersection. Two
more Land Rovers pulled in and flanked them. Shah nodded to the
drivers, his drivers, and Jules tried to spot Birendra, but he didn't appear to be in the small convoy.

"How'd she slot him? . . . No, sorry. Silly question. You mean how
did he give it away? The cartel guys opened up on us as we were heading to a prearranged address where our entirely fictional client had
promised there was fortune and glory awaiting us if we could retrieve
some documents from a safe in his apartment. Well, not *his* apartment.
He was a lawyer supposedly representing a man called Rubin. Said
Rubin had papers giving him drilling rights over some part of the Sonoma field off the U.S. West Coast."

"Did you investigate the claim?"

Jules smiled bitterly. "Our investigation consisted of sneaking into
New York and getting our arses shot off. Look, I'll admit, my due diligence wasn't the best. But it was a plausible story. Establishing exactly
who owns what in America right now is a nightmare. Anyway, long
story short, we were duped into a free-fire zone by this Rubin character, or his pretend lawyer at least, and there was a team waiting for us
near the apartment we were supposed to clean out. Neat, really. I mean,
who's going to notice two more dead bodies in New York? They
could've dropped anvils tied to elephants on us from the top of the
bloody Chrysler Building and nobody would've batted an eye. But anyway. They thought they had us, and one of these losers called out, 'Mr.
Cesky sends his regards!' Would have been all over, Red Rover, if
Commando Barbie hadn't stuck her psychotic, perky little nose in at
that point."

The car grunted forward again, and they turned off the main strip
into a warren of dusty streets crowded with light trucks and four-
wheel-drives. It was a busy part of town, if not the most salubrious lo-
cale.

"You mention this commando named Barbie, again," said Shah,

looking intrigued. "Surely Barbie had a name tag if she was a soldier. A unit patch? Did Mr. Rhino not take note of his rescuer?"

Jules smiled, but she was tired and distressed, and the gesture faded before reaching her eyes. "Again, sorry, Shah. We've been picking it over for months now. 'Commando Barbie' is just a nickname I gave her. I have no idea who she was, but I'd bet the family silver—if my family still had any—that she was no garden-variety squaddie. She was too good, for one thing, and she was operating alone, deep in the badlands. She went through our would-be executioners like a dose of salts, and for a while I thought she might very well neck us, too, just for the sake of convenience. No name tags. No unit patches. Just urban-combat battle dress and enough artillery to kit out the Brigade of Gurkhas, with a few whiz-bangs left over for shits and giggles. She never gave us a name, but in the helicopter I thought I heard one bloke call her Cate, or Katie, or something like that."

The trio of Land Rovers rolled past the Winnellie Hotel-Motel, which seemed to be enjoying full occupancy to judge by the car park full of pickups and utility vehicles, and then turned right into a dogleg corner. A high steel fence topped by razor wire protected the compound into which they drove. A pair of armed guards, both of them looking like ex-Gurkhas as well, waved them in. The men wore kukri daggers at the hip, although the submachine guns both carried impressed Jules more.

"The ruse of sending you to New York is interesting," said Shah. "Quite an elaborate cutout scheme. If Cesky is behind this, he will be standing well behind. He has much to lose now, being such a prominent figure. I wonder who is acting as his agent, assuming a now-respectable businessman would not hold meetings in his office with potential contract killers."

Jules shrugged. "Couldn't tell you. Maybe the same guy who fronted us on behalf of Rubin. Who knows? But Cesky's not that respectable. He's in construction, for God's sake. My father dealt with a few of them, said they were all crooks. The unions, the bosses, the companies—all of them. And Cesky wasn't shy about putting muscle on the street in Seattle when Kipper led his little people's uprising back after the Wave. He made quite a show of it, I heard. Having dealt with him just briefly, Cesky didn't strike me as being squeamish about using the strong-arm to get his way."

The three heavy vehicles pulled into parking bays on a dirty concrete slab outside a remarkable office that had been constructed from shipping crates. Jules had heard of apartments in Europe fashioned the same way before the Disappearance, but they were high-end architectural experiments. This looked like frontier engineering. Shah's headquarters was literally pieced together from metal shipping containers like a giant's LEGO set. He'd had doors and windows cut out; one container had been dropped on top of another, which had been joined end on end with a third. The old Gurkha saw her examining the unusual arrangement and smiled.

"We took over this lot when building materials were in very short supply in Darwin," he explained. "This was cheap and very easily run up. It works well, although the air-conditioning is a heavy power drain."

"I can imagine," she replied as they stepped out of the chilled interior of the vehicle. The oppressive damp heat of the tropical afternoon slammed down and wrapped itself around her in a heavy shroud. The compound covered a few hundred square yards, and three newer buildings, all sheds, were of more conventional appearance. She had half expected to find a small regiment of armored cars, even tanks, in there, but instead she saw only more off-road vehicles, Land Rovers, a few anonymous sedans, and flatbed pickup trucks loaded with crates and strongboxes. At least half of the personnel were Nepalese, like Shah, but the rest, maybe a dozen or so that she could see, were a mix of locals and imports.

"Come through," Shah said, leading her toward the sliding glass door that gave entry into the reception area of his security firm. "We shall have some tea and get properly reacquainted. We have had no chance to do so yet with the rush of the day. And then we shall set ourselves to determining whether this Cesky creature truly is behind the attempts on our lives and what we might do about it."

Jules followed him inside, where he immediately was besieged by members of his staff, all with urgent demands on his time. At least in here the air was noticeably cooler and drier.

"Okay. I could murder a cup of tea," she said, more to herself than to anyone else.

But beyond that she had no idea of how to proceed. Henry Cesky might be a crazed revenger, but he was smart, rich, and increasingly powerful. He was also a major and very public supporter of the president of the United States.

24

VANCOUVER, BRITISH COLUMBIA

Jed Culver was surprised to find himself nervous. Not wetting-his-pants nervous but more anxious about attending a meeting than he had been in a long while. He was not the sort of man who was prone to unproductive worry and doubt. When he found himself without information, he sought it out. In a situation in which he lacked control, he would fight and scheme and work away until he had it. That was why James Kipper valued him as a sword and shield. He did not blanch from the hard necessities, yet as he hurried down the hallway, flanked by his aides, a feeling not unlike indigestion gnawed at him. He recognized it for what it was: anxiety.

He told no one, of course, allowed no sign to show on his face or interrupt his stride along the corridors of Echelon's headquarters in Vancouver. The office was unremarkable, resembling any other civil-service facility. The accents were mainly Canadian and American, although leavened by occasional British and Australian voices and once the unmistakable strangled vowels of a New Zealander.

He was satisfied to see that some standards were maintained there, at least. Like him, everyone was dressed in proper business attire, the men in suits and ties and the women in a wider selection of smart office wear. Kip's well-known preference for casual clothing hadn't made much of an impact here, apparently, even though Vancouver and Seattle had grown so close as to become one in many other ways.

"Mr. Culver."

Jed looked up from the briefing paper he'd been skimming. One of the reasons Echelon ran such a tight ship was standing in front of him, waiting outside a conference room: Wales Larrison, the deputy director of special clearances and research.

"Ah, Director Larrison."

"Glad you could make it, sir," said Larrison. "We don't get many visitors from so far up the food chain dropping in on us."

"I hardly need to," Culver replied. "Unlike so many of my other charges, you don't cause me problems. You solve them."

"We try." The director shrugged. "If you'll follow me, we're in here today. No staffers, of course."

Jed felt rather than saw the way his two aides bristled at the dismissal. Even hailing from a much-reduced White House, the young men and women who fetched and carried for him were little different from their forebears. Their own importance loomed very large in their consideration.

"Of course," Culver said, defusing any issue with a wave of his hand. "Mike, I'll need the president's revised schedule for his APEC trip by this afternoon, if you think you can shake that out of the trees over at State. Sally, you go, too. It might need both of you yelling at them to wake someone up over there."

The aides nodded and hurried away to tend to the very important business of making phone calls and establishing just how much more important they were than the people they were talking to.

"That'll keep 'em happy for hours," he said.

Larrison murmured something to his own aide, a young Welsh woman, to judge by her lilting tone. She made a few notes in a folder before gliding away to attend to whatever villainy her boss had just set in train. When the two men were alone, the Echelon spy chief used a magnetic key to open the solid-looking double doors to the conference room.

Jed set his features to disguise the acid burn in his stomach and stepped through to take his meeting with a killer. That wasn't the reason for his anxiety. Rather, he knew that by being here he was disobeying a direct order from the president of the United States. He'd done as Kip had asked by bringing the FBI in on the link between Ozal's shipping company and Blackstone, but he hadn't pressed the issue with them, hadn't made it a priority. The bureau didn't have the resources to assign strike teams of special agents on the whims of a political operator like himself, and he trusted them to take their time, working slowly and methodically away at the documents he had provided.

In the meantime, the chief of staff would do what he'd always done. He would take control of events, even at risk to himself. He knew there was only one person he trusted to strike hard and fast at Blackstone's newly exposed weak point, and she was the only person in the room when he and Director Larrison entered.

A young woman, maybe thirty—Jed was increasingly thinking of people in their thirties as young. Her features struck him as handsome rather than pretty. She wasn't masculine, but all the lines and planes of her face seemed very cut and angular, like an athlete who had stripped her body fat back to a single-figure percentage. He was aware of his own very generous belly pulling at the buttons of his waistcoat. He hated himself for doing it, but before he could stop himself, he tried to suck in his stomach.

"Ms. Monroe," he said, nodding as she looked up from the table where she'd been reading through a sheaf of papers. Most normal people, he imagined, would have been drawn to the view outside the floor-to-ceiling windows. Downtown Vancouver stretched away to the river, and the North Shore Mountains in the distance sparkled under a fierce winter sun. Monroe appeared to have drawn a curtain specifically to block the vista or, more likely, to block any view from the outside, even though she must have known the glass had been treated with a film that turned it into a mirror when viewed from the street.

Special Agent Monroe stood up but waited for Culver to move toward her and extend his hand. Her grip was strong, but it was the rough, callused texture of her palm that he noticed. It felt like he was shaking hands with a violinist whose second job was bricklaying.

"Mr. Culver," she said. Her voice put him right back inside the conversation she'd had with Kip as she flew into the Battle of New York, looking for Baumer. She'd been dressed in black combat coveralls and shouting over the roar of a C-130. She had been angry, too, he recalled. Dangerously angry. In person, her voice was quite soft and she spoke with a distant, ironic tone that made him feel as though he'd already been judged.

"How's your family, Ms. Monroe? Bret and . . . Monique, isn't it?"

"Do you care?" she asked flatly.

"Caitlin . . ." Wales Larrison growled.

The assassin gave a lopsided grin that went nowhere near softening her features.

"I was just wondering."

"I'm sorry, Mr. Culver," Larrison said, frowning at his senior student. "Agent Monroe can be unusually and unjustifiably difficult at times."

Jed blew them both off. His smile was genuine: the "you got me" grin of an old-time grifter caught out by his mark.

"No. It's fair enough, Larrison. Like I give a fuck about her family. We all know I read the briefing sheet before coming over here to give me some personal stake to play when we met. I care about Ms. Monroe's personal affairs as much as she cares about mine, no doubt: minimally and only so much as it impacts on our business. So, Ms. Monroe, how *is* your family? Are they safe?"

She unpacked a smile and handed it back to him, but with a touch less frost than before. "They are safe, as you'd know, sir. The Brits have them tucked away on a farm up in Scotland. They have good people looking after them and more taking care of our farm while we're away. They're not a distraction. They're a motivation. Is that what you wanted to hear, Mr. Culver?"

Jed nodded, just a slight bobbing of the head. "It's good that you're motivated," he told her, "because I have something to ask of you."

"You do?" she shot back. "Or the president does?"

Larrison looked like he was preparing to get all stern and old school again, but Culver shook his head as if to say *Don't bother.*

"I'll tell you straight, Ms. Monroe. Caitlin. You mind if I call you Caitlin?"

"The list of things I care about is very short."

He took a seat in the nearest swivel chair and motioned for the others to do the same as he gazed out over the city. Before the Wave had swept away most of Canada's population, Vancouver had been a small city. About half a million people, as he recalled. It had twice that number now, swollen with Canadians and Americans returned from abroad, where they had avoided the fate of their compatriots. Crowded, too, with migrants, another quarter million of them from China and the Punjab mostly, although a few neighborhoods were solidly Vietnamese and, surprisingly, Japanese. For the capital of such an empty, haunted country, Vancouver was crowded. Evidence of new, unregulated building was everywhere. Office towers had been given over to residential use without much planning, and new developments were spreading out on the city's edge. Jed crinkled his eyes against the glare of the winter sun before turning away from the view.

"The president knows nothing of this meeting and never will," he said, "unless I'm called to testify in my own criminal trial at some point in the future."

Agent Monroe did not react. She simply waited for him to continue. He admired that. Jed Culver had never been one for hysterics and drama queens.

"Frankly, I'd have been happy if any arrangement you and I might come to could've been settled without the involvement of your boss here. I see no need to involve Mr. Larrison."

"Well, I can see plenty, Mr. Culver," said the director. "Starting with the fact that my agents do not act without my say-so. I've reviewed your case, and I agree there is a role for us to play—if Special Agent Monroe is willing. Operationally, she remains on secondment to the London Cage. But your concerns about Texas appear to overlap with unfinished business of ours. Perhaps they don't, but the possibility that they do invites us to speculate and study the matter further. Agent Monroe is our in-house counsel on Baumer, to borrow a phrase from your former career. I also understand why the president needs to be kept out of it. From our perspective, sir, that is a matter of little import. Echelon is not an American agency. We answer to the Alliance Secretariat. But nor are we your Praetorian Guard, sir, nor Ms. Monroe your personal emissary or executioner. If she runs with this, she does so on my dime."

Jed conceded the point with a tilt of his head. "You've read the brief, ma'am?" he asked.

"Yep," said Monroe. "I've been back here for a week. Reading and writing reports and briefing notes is all I've done."

"And?"

"What can I say? We're already in motion. The French didn't release Baumer. Ahmet Ozal got him out, and Ozal had a connection to Fort Hood through that salvage contract for Hazm. Contract's not even registered in Texas, as I understand it. Treasury got the information from Hamburg. Lupérico says—"

"Wait a minute—Lupérico *says*? I thought he was dead," said Culver, suddenly concerned that perhaps Echelon had stashed him somewhere.

"Sorry. Poor phrasing," Monroe replied. "Lupérico *is* dead."

"Okay. Because I understood it was only you and him at the end."

"That's right. He told me what we needed, and then I settled our personal account."

"Is that something you're in the habit of doing, Ms. Monroe . . . Caitlin?" asked Culver. "Settling personal business on company time?" He was still a little put out.

She shrugged. "Business and pleasure. It can be hard to tell them apart some days. If you don't like it, get someone else. I've got diapers to change."

She wasn't smiling as she said it. Jed felt the need to test her further.

"It didn't occur to you that there was more we could've learned by debriefing him out of the field?"

"My mission parameters covered a hostile in-field debrief," she said without emotion, as if that concluded the matter. "The subject was terminated at the end of the debrief. I infiltrated the AO and followed my trail of crumbs home."

Culver regarded her with the same caution he'd give a coiled rattler.

Monroe was both an anachronism and a harbinger of the changed world. Fashioned as a weapon long before the Disappearance, she had proved she could adapt to altered realities more swiftly and with less apparent disinclination than most of the people he worked with. In his or her own way, everybody seemed to be trying to hold on to how things had once been even as that history cracked apart and broke up like a giant ice shelf.

He exhaled slowly. It was her world, not his. There would soon be more like her rather than fewer. Jed pressed at his stomach and tried to control the boiling underneath his right-hand bottom rib. Quite honestly, he preferred Lupérico dead. The fewer loose threads to unravel, the better.

"So you've read the brief, Agent. You know what we need."

"I read the summary. I only got it when I arrived. Ten minutes before you." There was no hint of accusation in her tone. Merely a statement of fact.

"Well, read it all before you agree to anything," he said. "Because in spite of what will undoubtedly be sterling efforts on your behalf from Mr. Larrison here, you'll have zero ass cover if this goes wrong. And it could go wrong about ten ways from Sunday."

"In my experience, Mr. Culver, life can and does go wrong more often than not."

He leaned forward, not getting into her personal space but approaching as near as he dared. "You're a realist, Ms. Monroe. That's good. Because here's the reality: this country is dying. The Wave ripped our heart out, and we're just staggering forward, carried along by our own momentum. We could be at war with Roberto's little pirate kingdom within six months, and we could lose if it doesn't go nuclear. If we're not at war with him, we might just turn on ourselves. Mad Jack's got his Heart of Darkness routine polished to an obsidian fucking sheen down there in Texas, and it's getting to a point where even my boss, the sainted and peace-loving James Kipper, might just have to stand to his guns in response. You were in Manhattan, Ms. Monroe. You know what that fight took out of us. We cannot win against Morales. And we probably can't win against Blackstone, either. Not that anyone ever really wins a civil war in any case."

As the White House chief of staff spoke, his earlier anxiety at meeting this woman fell away, replaced by the fears that really underlay his nervous agitation. They were the fears of negation, total collapse, and the return of a dark age that would envelop the whole world.

"I need you in Texas, Ms. Monroe," he went on. "In the belly of the beast. You are not going to find Bilal Baumer there. Frankly, I don't think you're ever going to find him. In my admittedly amateurish opinion, Mr. Baumer was pulverized into pink rat giblets by the U.S. Air Force when they knocked flat about ten blocks of New York around the old Rock Center last April. But the reason Baumer was there, the reason he nearly bled us out—and, incidentally, the reason your husband and daughter were nearly killed, too—*that* I believe you will find in Texas. That's why Director Larrison has agreed to assign you a special clearance to operate within CONUS. That's why I'm willing to go against the wishes of my boss and risk a good thirty years in the pen if it all goes wrong. That's why I want you down in Tusk Musso's office ASAP, by way of KC, where you can start doing some primary research on Governor Blackstone's policies. Kansas City is our main forward base, and my people there know more about the dark corners of Blackstone's evil empire than most would care to. A day spent with them will help you adjust your perceptions."

Both Monroe and Larrison were silent and still as Jed spoke with more passion and genuine fear than he had for a long time.

"When you've done your homework there," Culver said in conclusion, "you get down to General Musso's and find out how and why Blackstone entered into an arrangement with a company owned by Ahmet Ozal one week before Ozal took ship for the New World, there to make an enormous and fatal pain in the ass of himself."

"It sounds like I'm going to have to get right up next to Blackstone," she said. "Why would he let me do that?"

Jed dismissed the question with a snort.

"Mad Jack's jumping around with a red-hot poker up his ass at the moment," he said. "Has been for months. The poker got jammed up there thanks to Roberto Morales."

He could see he'd surprised her for the first time.

"Yeah, I know. I don't really understand it either, but Blackstone is convinced Roberto looks toward his little patch of heaven down Texas way with covetous eyes. He's been trying to convince the president to pull forces out of the Pacific and put them in the Caribbean. That's your way in. You're going down as my personal envoy to give the governor a chance to make his case. Off the record. We keep everything informal. That's how I do my best work, and Blackstone knows it. He'll give you an audience. Access. You use that as you see fit."

"What about Musso?" Monroe asked. "He was the guy at Guantánamo, wasn't he? Is he in the loop on this?"

Wales Larrison answered the question. "He is. It's not my preference, but Mr. Culver has his reasons and I can live with them."

"Tusk Musso's a patriot," said Jed. "And he worked a goddamn *miracle* down at Gitmo. But the corps, they dropped him like a turd at a tea party because he ran up the white flag. I got him that job in Temple, running the Federal Center there, because it's not all that different from what he had to do in Cuba, dealing with a hostile power hunkered down just outside his fence line. The president didn't need much convincing, I might add. He thought Musso did a great job, too. Bottom line—you can trust Musso; he knows the score. But only him, okay? He won't be your overwatch authority, but you can go to him if you need to."

"And you're cool with this, Wales?" Agent Monroe asked. The familiarity between them wasn't lost on Jed. He was very much the outsider here. That made him vulnerable. He could use these people, but he couldn't trust them.

The deputy director didn't look happy, but he shrugged.

"We don't have the luxury of time with this, Caitlin," he said. "You spent years building your case file on Baumer, but—"

"But we don't have years," Jed put in. "We don't have months or even weeks. Every day that Mad Jack sits down there getting stronger is an affront to the republic and a hazard to its future. I think he fucked us in New York. And I intend to fuck him back, severely and without consent. With your help, Agent Monroe."

"It will be my pleasure." Caitlin smiled. It was a thin smile that only hardened her face.

She should have fangs, he thought.

"Your pleasure will be finding shit out and doing nothing about it," Culver emphasized. "Do you understand? You will bring any evidence you discover to me. And I will ensure that Mad Jack Blackstone pays with his life for this treason. But *you* won't be taking that life. It is owed to the American people. Is that clear?"

Caitlin Monroe nodded. Slowly. Once.

Jed leaned back. Spent. He had rolled the dice on the largest bet he'd ever made in his life. Indeed, he might well have just bet his life on the outcome.

25

ARDMORE, OKLAHOMA

Traffic on Interstate 35 picked up as they approached the Oklahoma–Texas border, their small convoy augmented by another three trucks they'd picked up in Wellington. The snow thinned out, too, revealing a layer of gray-brown weeds beneath the icy slush. Sofia had long ago lost interest in gawking at the vehicle wrecks strung along the side of the highway and the charred ruins of towns that had burned down to war-torn streetscapes. She focused her thoughts instead on Fort Hood.

Snuggled up in the SpongeBob blanket, warm inside the surprisingly comfortable steel cocoon of *Mary Lou*'s cabin, she dozed on and off, roused only by the grinding of gears or a particularly nasty bump. The convoy wasn't able to risk going much faster than thirty-five miles an hour on some stretches because of ice, snow, and giant potholes.

Cindy French had passed the early leg of the journey talking about her family in a bit more detail. The interior of the cab was plastered with pictures of her "grandbabies." Dozens of images following the lives of five little tykes from baby blankets to sleep-outs in the backyard. And then, of course, the pictoral history stopped. From time to time, Sofia caught the trucker looking at one of them, tearing up before wiping her eyes and waving her hands to drive the sadness away. The teenager wondered if she herself might one day feel something other than a cold background rage.

Cindy had the truck's shortwave tuned to a station playing endless loops of old comedy, all from comedians who, like her family, had not survived the Wave. It was a uniquely American type of humor that often lay well beyond Sofia's comprehension. Jokes about bodily functions, jokes about private sexual things, and so many jokes about the insecurities of the comedians themselves. Some were funny, but most were just embarrassing. She shuddered to think what the nuns would have thought of them.

She asked Cindy once, as they drove past the wreckage of a downed passenger jet, whether they could pick up any news stations.

"We've got the real world all around us right now, kid," the truckie replied, chewing on a drinking straw. "Whenever I listen to the news, all I hear is 'Blah, blah, blah.' Ever watch *Charlie Brown,* the cartoon?"

"Yes," said Sofia. She'd seen a video of the cartoon dog Snoopy in the refugee camp in Sydney. It was funnier than the comedians she was forced to listen to in Cindy's truck, that was for sure.

"And ever noticed how all the adults sound muffled, like 'Wah-wah-wah'? Well, that's what the news is like for me. Can't stand it. Wah-wah-wah."

Okay. No news, Sofia thought. A pity. She was hoping to start building up her knowledge of life in Texas under Blackstone, especially within the limits of Fort Hood. She knew from listening to the news in Kansas City that you couldn't always trust the radio to tell you the truth about things. Or about the details, anyway, and the meaning behind those details. But even the broad outlines could be useful to know.

She craned her neck to followed the flight path of a pair of gunships that hammered overhead as afternoon settled across the bleak Oklahoma landscape. They surprised her, completely unexpected. Cindy hit her horn three times, snapped off the shortwave, and turned on her CB. "Ardmore coming up. We stopping?"

"Reckon so," Dave said. *"Time to stretch the legs, get a late lunch, and the like."*

They didn't go into Ardmore proper, though, the ruins of which Sofia could see as Cindy pulled into yet another Flying J truck stop, this one on Cooper Drive, just off the highway. Unlike so much of the Midwest, Ardmore appeared to be marked for resettlement and redevelopment. Sofia had passed through there on the way north late in the spring, and the town had been deserted then. They hadn't even stopped for salvage, preferring to move quickly after having encountered signs of bandits on the trail the previous day. If those ne'er-do-wells had made their camp in Ardmore, as her father suspected, they obviously had been driven off in the months since Sofia had last been here. But by whom? Her heart beat a little heavier inside her rib cage as she wondered whether she might be about to encounter the TDF for the first time. They used the same equipment as the U.S. Army, of course, so there was no way of telling if those helicopters had belonged to Blackstone or President Kipper.

"Is this a Blackstone settlement?" she asked, trying to keep her voice steady.

Cindy smiled. "No. We ain't quite in the belly of the beast yet, my friend. Seattle runs this here burg. Those were air force birds that flew over us before. You can unpucker for now—nobody's gonna press you into a work gang here, Sof."

The Kenworth rolled slowly into a parking bay, crunching and hissing down through the gears before jolting ever so slightly to a complete stop.

"Come on, hon. Let's go get us some supplies."

"Cindy . . . I only have a few dollars," Sofia confessed, feeling unexpected shame. She had taken so much from this kind woman, and all under false pretenses.

"Ppfft!" The trucker blew off her worries. "Look, there's a federal salvage depot across the road from the J. Anything you need, you can pick it up there. Is there something you need?"

A shrug.

"I would like a map of Fort Hood and of this place Temple, where the federales are," she said. "And a small radio, if I could. I should've thought to get one earlier, in Wellington, when we stopped and met those other lady drivers."

"Well, come on, then. We'll get fed and head on to the depot before we light out. See what we can do. I don't know about the radio, but they'll have maps for sure."

Sofia followed the blue-clad truck driver's lead and hopped out of the cab with her spirits lifted slightly, glad to be able to stretch her legs and empty her bladder. Her breath fogged up again, but the cold was nowhere near as unpleasant as it had been in Kansas City. The borrowed jacket was more than enough to ward off the chill.

A tall, thin man approached from the rear of Cindy's rig. She'd met Dave Bowman back at Emporia. He was a little strange, she thought, and unlike so many of the middle-aged drivers here, he didn't have a potbelly. Dave seemed to glide across the cement surface.

"Coat still warm enough for you, young lady?" he asked.

Sofia nodded. "Yes, thank you."

"No problemo," Dave said.

Cindy circled around from the driver's side, chatting with another female trucker, who also wore a furry creature hat. A rabbit of some sort, Sofia thought. Perhaps Bugs Bunny.

"Mel, where's Brian?" Cindy asked the other woman.

"Feeding the bunnies," Mel said. She was about the same height as Cindy French and seemed too refined to be a trucker. With her unusually straight posture and precision of movement, Sofia wondered if she might be a veteran. They all moved the same way, she thought.

"You keep the rabbits for food?" Sofia asked. "I had my share of them. I could cook a pot for you if you'd like."

Mel actually took a step back as a wash of pale horror fell across her features.

"*Pets,* hon," Cindy said quickly, taking the teenager by the shoulder. "Melissa keeps bunnies as pets in her rig. They're kinda cute . . . Hey, Mel, is Brian gonna come too, then?"

"No," the woman in the bunny hat replied, recovering herself but smiling a little awkwardly at Sofia. "I'll take him something. Let's go eat."

Inside the Flying J's government-run canteen, it smelled of fresh paint, disinfectant, and greasy food. As she joined the line of diners, Sofia kept one eye on the television suspended from the ceiling in a corner of the dining area, but it seemed to be playing only reruns of some pre-Wave show hosted by a man called Jerry in which fat people attacked one another in a TV studio. Sometimes they wore costumes that made them look like perverts. It was incomprehensible, and eventually she gave up.

Soldiers and civilians moved down the queue, each clutching a metal tray. Occasionally they'd glance over at the TV screen, too, but mostly they busied themselves scooping up piles of the usual bland but plentiful government food. Stiff, dry potato bake, frankfurters, bacon-like jerky, fatty ham, and the always popular shit on a shingle. In front of her in the line, thin Dave Bowman shook his head at it all, deeply unimpressed.

"Give me an apple and a whole wheat roll," he said.

"Don't want much, do ya?" the man serving behind the counter replied. He tossed a sad-looking yellow apple over. "Bread's over at the bench, dude."

Dave noticed Sofia focusing again on the television and elbowed her gently. "Sure you want to go to Fort Hood?" he asked. "They're all like that down there, you know."

"My sister's there," Sofia lied yet again. "I have to help her. What do you know about the place, Mr. Bowman? Anything you can tell me would be useful. I've heard it will be difficult for me because I'm from Mexico. Although that seems unfair. I don't remember anything of life before the boat journey to Australia. I am from nowhere now."

Bowman gazed off into the distance for a moment, apparently able to see through the clouded windows of the canteen as Sofia filled a bowl with beans and bacon chunks. He worked at slicing his mushy apple up into manageable components before they took a seat at the table with the others. But not Cindy yet; she was still in line, picking over the sad gray franks.

"Fort Hood's not what Seattle says it is," Dave said. "On the other hand, not everything Seattle says is wrong, either. It isn't the old unreconstructed South, for instance."

"I'm sorry, what?" Sofia asked, confused.

"I mean, it isn't a bunch of rich white folks owning everything, including other people. A lot of army vets live down there. The other services, too, but mainly army. Drawn down there by money, benefits, and the kind of jobs Seattle can't or won't provide."

"What about Mexicans?" she asked. "My sort of people." She wondered if Dave wasn't someone who agreed with Blackstone, perhaps even supported the tyrant.

"I've seen them down there as well," he said. "Normally, if they aren't in the military, they're stuck doing the menial jobs in town, in Killeen, or laboring on the big farms. That isn't all that different from before the Wave, is it? Or Down Under, where you were, from what I've heard tell."

"No," Sofia admitted. "Although, the farm my family worked on in New South Wales was not a prison, either. And the homestead killings—are they truly as people say, the work of Blackstone's agents?"

Bowman regarded her warily now. "Well, there's some that say that, of course. But I wouldn't be so free with my opinions when I reached Fort Hood if I was you, young lady."

"Well, it's a hell of a thing when a young woman can't feel free with her opinions, don't you think?" Cindy interrupted, having arrived from the chow line hauling a tray loaded with cheesy taters and franks. Almost as large a stack as she'd had of chicken when Sofia first had met her.

"No politics at the table," Melissa called over, adopting a warning tone.

Thin Dave Bowman's face had been clouding over, but that seemed to pass now like a single cloud on a clear day.

Cindy hooked a plastic chair with one foot before sitting down next to Sofia. "Old Dave here is quite the fan of Governor Blackstone," she said, smirking.

"Now, you know that's not true, Cindy," he protested. "I have issues with the man, too. Serious issues. But I don't think he's as bad as everyone makes out back in cloud-cuckoo-land."

"Where?" Sofia chimed in, looking to her friend for a translation.

"He means Seattle, hon." The trucker turned back to Bowman. "Now then, Dave, Sofia here is heading down to Fort Hood to rescue her sister from a brothel—as you well know, because I explained it to you, chapter and verse, back in KC. A government brothel, Dave. Of the sort that is utterly illegal back in cloud-cuckoo-land. So you can see why she might have *issues* with a Blackstone policy here and there."

He had the decency to look mildly embarrassed, going so far as to take off his baseball cap and sweep it in front of him while performing a half bow. "You're right. I was being an ass," he said by way of apology.

"It's all right," Sofia replied, even though it was not.

Dave leaned forward slightly. "Was there something specific you needed to know about Fort Hood? Out of all these reprobates," he added, indicating his fellow drivers, "I've probably hauled more loads into and out of the Hood than anyone."

Sofia swallowed a mouthful of beans and tried to forgive the man opposite her for not thinking ill of Jackson Blackstone. If this Dave Bowman could be of help, she would take his help, just as she'd taken his jacket.

"I will need to find this bordello where they are holding my sister," she said. "How will I do that, and how will I get there from Temple without getting into trouble myself?"

Bowman grinned. "Well, I'm not at all familiar with the brothels of Fort Hood," he said to the scoffing laughter of some of the other truckers, "but if I were you, I wouldn't be going there alone. I think you'll be fine getting around town without someone holding your hand, but a girl of your age really doesn't want to be heading into the red-light district on her own."

She nodded appreciatively. She had no interest at all in the red-light districts of Fort Hood but a great deal of interest in how much attention she might draw to herself while wandering the streets of the town on her own. Back in Kansas City, people had made it sound as though Fort Hood was completely segregated. Sofia Pieraro resolved to put aside any resentment she felt at finding out that Dave was a Blackstone supporter. Instead, she was determined to pick him clean for every useful detail on Fort Hood that he might provide.

26

NORTH DARWIN, NORTHERN TERRITORY

NORTH DARWIN, NORTHERN TERRITORY

Narayan Shah had done well for himself, much better than Julianne, since they'd last met. It was obvious he was pivotal to the everyday running of his private security firm; that was clear from the second they had walked in there, with the appearance of four of his underlings bearing news they thought he must hear or documents he must see. More impressive from her point of view was the man's enduring grace and calm under pressure. Shah dismissed them all courteously but firmly, instructing that tea be served upstairs for his English guest and himself.

The old soldier had partitioned at least half of one shipping container as his private office. This particular giant metal crate sat atop the L-shaped arrangement of identical faded-orange containers that formed the entrance to his compound. A quiet young Nepalese woman was performing the duties he'd requested, filling two coarse-looking stone mugs with piping-hot green tea. She was dressed in Western clothes but carried herself with the demure reserve Jules thought characteristic of many Asian societies. Shah smiled at her while she poured.

"Thank you, my dear," he said as the young Nepali withdrew.

"You are welcome, Father," she replied, answering a question Julianne had kept to herself.

"It is a rough environment for a young lady, I will admit," Shah said, once the two of them were alone. "I hire the best men I can find, and I insist on civility in the workplace. But this business attracts a very particular type, and I worry sometimes about exposing my daughters to that."

Julianne leaned forward and carefully picked up the tea. The simple pottery mug had no handle, forcing her to hold it carefully around the rim lest she burn her fingers.

"But you would rather have your girls close by," she ventured. "It's nice, Shah, and understandable, especially now. My father did something similar, although his motives were less admirable." She smiled ruefully. "He often dressed me up to distract the chaps from whom he was intent on milking funds."

Shah grinned so widely at this that his head, which had always reminded her of a giant inverted brown pot, seemed to split right open.

"Ah, Miss Jules, I do recall with fondness the many stories you told of your father on our voyage to Australia. Hard times they were, but very simple in some ways. Sail the boat, fight the pirates, do not die. Now . . ." He waved his hands around the room, encompassing the unseen compound and perhaps the whole city beyond it. "Now complications are all I have."

Jules took a cautious sip of her drink. She didn't much fancy green tea, given a choice, but this blend was sweeter and less smoky than usual. She would have preferred a pot of Taylors Scottish Breakfast Tea with milk and sugar but found herself taking longer drafts of Shah's brew as it cooled. It settled her nerves.

The space in which they sat was fiercely utilitarian, with very few flourishes of decoration: a calendar with photographs of interesting golf courses on the wall behind Shah, a sheathed kukri dagger in a glass-front box hanging beside it. Nothing else. Not even a few family photos.

"How long have you been here?" she asked. "In Darwin, with your business, I mean."

"Nearly two years now," Shah replied. "The city was perhaps half its current size when I arrived. Even then, it had grown significantly. I remember it from the Timor mission in '99, when it was much smaller. Many of the Americans who were caught in this region after the Disappearance found their way here. A large number remain, although more were just passing through on their way to the southern cities, and I suppose, like our friend Miguel, many have returned home now. But Darwin was growing when I arrived, Miss Jules, one of the few places that was. The granting of free-port status amplified the rush of money and people seeking haven here after the Wave. It seemed a good choice to locate my business. There was much demand for security contractors then. There still is."

He emptied the last few drops from his cup before refilling it. The absence of a handle did not seem to bother him, Jules noted. He held the scalding hot vessel in his thick brown fingers with no discernible discomfort.

"I must thank you again, Miss Julianne, for the opportunity you offered us back in Acapulco. My comrades and I did well to cross your path, and great honor accrued to you for ensuring our contract was fulfilled even after the authorities in Sydney seized the *Rules* and those assets you had set aside for our payment. It allowed me to fund the beginnings of this business, and the money we make is very important to our people back home. Your name is well regarded in our villages."

She waved off the compliment. "Daddy would have disowned me if I hadn't learned at a very young age how to hide a few baubles and trinkets from the fuzz. Anyway, you and your chaps earned it, Mr. Shah. We wouldn't have made it to Sydney without you. Not all of us did, of course," she added with residual sadness.

"To absent friends," he said, raising his cup.

Jules returned the toast and then set the empty cup aside. "So this is your main place of business now?" she asked. "It's not an idle question. You said you'd had dealings with both Seattle and Fort Hood. Do you do much work in the U.S.? Do you have a profile there? I'm just wondering how it was that Cesky drew a bead on you all the way down here in Darwin."

Shah was not a demonstrative man. An almost imperceptible down-turn of the mouth, the faintest shrug—they were his only reactions.

"I have a small office in Seattle, yes," he said. "We have contracts to provide security for some of the reclamation crews working the West Coast cities. We do recruit in the U.S., mostly ex-military people, espe-cially if they are familiar with the territory in which we are operating. But as far as possible, I try to use men from the regiment. The income they remit home is important, as I said."

"And in Fort Hood?"

Shah gestured as though he were swatting away a fly. "A two-man operation. Or rather, one man and his wife, working as his secretary. I have no other personnel permanently stationed in Texas. The adminis-tration there controls access and movement very closely. Blackstone's people are very businesslike, very easy to make a deal with in many ways. But the men I send there fly in, do the job, and fly out again. Fort Hood is open for business but not always . . . welcoming. Perhaps if I hired more men from the local military population . . ."

"Whitey, you mean?"

He nodded slowly. "So you noticed."

"The Rhino and I were down there for a few weeks after New York. It was like taking a little holiday in GI Joe World at Disneyland in, like, 1953."

"Mr. Ross was with you when you were attacked by Cesky's men in Texas?"

Julianne's eyes crinkled with delight. "God, I so rarely hear the Rhino referred to by his real name. I doubt even his parents used it."

She noticed then that her hands were shaking—delayed shock, she assumed. Well, it wasn't the first time something had blown up in her face.

"Do you mind?" she said, standing up and heading to the window. "I need to move around. Bit of nervous tension to burn off. And I'm very worried about him."

"Of course. His injuries were severe."

She remembered this about Mr. Shah. He didn't sugarcoat things.

She paced the room for a few seconds before leaning up against the window that had been cut into the side of the insulated shipping container. Shah's office looked down over the concrete slab where they had left the car and afforded him a view into two of the large sheds in which some of his heavier vehicles were undergoing maintenance. The glass was cool to the touch thanks to the air-conditioning, but she could feel the fierce Darwin heat beating against it on the outside. She was up high enough to see over the rooftops of buildings in the surrounding streets. A heat haze shimmered over all the corrugated-iron and aluminum sheeting. There was very little greenery in this older industrial subdivision.

"The guys who came after us at Galveston were even more hapless than those losers in New York," Jules continued, still taking in the vista. "We were on our guard, as you'd imagine. Even though we weren't really expecting anything to happen down there. Seattle and Texas are different worlds, and Cesky is very much a Kipper man.

"Anyway, these blaggers, ex-military both of them, fronted us in a bar. We were just playing pool, and they came in and laid down some coins, reserving the table. The Rhino got talking to them, as he does, the friendly fucking pachyderm." She smiled again, as if thinking well of him might speed his mending. "Then, after a few minutes, one of them insists on buying him a drink on the basis that his old man had been in the coast guard, just like Rhino, and he makes a point of buying a round for every old salt he meets. Problem was, though, this bloke'd already had a few himself, as had his skeevy mate, and neither the Rhino nor I had ever mentioned anything about him being in the coast guard."

Jules turned away from the window now, propping herself up against the sill and folding her arms to steady her hands.

"We couldn't get rid of them. 'Farts in a telephone booth' doesn't even begin to describe their stickiness. The bar closed, and they insisted on coming with us, their new best friends and all, for one more drink. They knew a place, naturally. We thought fuck that for a game of tiddlywinks and invited them back to where we were staying. It was isolated, well away from the militia's usual patrol routes. God, Shah, it makes me sick just remembering it—we knew these cheeky fuckers were going to try it, probably as soon as we were out of public view. But better on our ground than theirs."

He nodded to indicate that she should keep going. "I assume you did not give them the chance to try it on, then."

"Once upon a time, maybe. I can remember the days when I didn't assume every stranger I met was trying to slot me. But no, we didn't give them a chance. I walked into the apartment first, gave them a bit of ass wiggle to think about. The Rhino mustered them in from behind. The door wasn't even closed before he kicked out the knee of the bloke just in front of him. Smashed him in the head with a bourbon bottle as he went down. His mate was reaching for a gun, but not quickly enough. I head tapped him twice with the .22 I had ready in my purse. Two in the noggin."

"And you are certain they were contract killers?"

"We searched them before dumping the bodies. They had heavy coats. They were both carrying duct tape, gags, and pistols with suppressors. The one I shot had a little video camera, too. Fucking freak. But then Cesky probably needed some proof before paying out on the contract. We didn't go looking for a vehicle, but if we had, I'm sure we'd have found heavy plastic bags and cutting tools in the back. They were hitters for certain. Drunken, incompetent hitters."

"But with nothing about their persons to tie them to Cesky."

"I think we're a little beyond the realm of reasonable doubt. No, they weren't carrying notarized contracts for our execution or a line of credit from Henry's personal banker. But the duct tape and the silencers were good enough for me."

They were good enough for Mr. Shah, too, she could tell. One brusque nod was the extent of his comment on the matter. Jules found that her hands had stopped shaking while she was telling the story. Perhaps it had taken her mind off recent unpleasant events, although her stomach remained a hot, roiling mess at the memory of her friend disappearing inside the explosion that had destroyed his boat. She had just resumed her seat when they were interrupted by three soft knocks on the door.

"Yes," Shah barked. He had left instructions not to be interrupted.

The door opened, and Jules beamed at the sight of another face from the past. She'd not yet had a chance to say hello to the man she had known as Corporal Birendra, once of Her Majesty's Royal Gurkha Regiment.

"Miss Julianne," he said, returning the smile.

She was out of her chair before Shah could reprimand him. "Oh, my God, Birendra, it feels like years! Well, it *has* been years, but it feels even longer. Jesus, how are you? I'm so glad to see you. Nowadays I'm glad to see any familiar face, let alone a friendly one."

Shah cleared his throat loudly behind her as Birendra shuffled into the room. Jules rushed over to give the man a hug. He disentangled himself with apologies before addressing his boss.

"I did not wish to interrupt you, but it is the police, sir. They are on the phone again, insisting on another interview."

"Do they have further information about the bombing at my house?" Shah asked him.

Birendra looked chagrined. "I do not think so, sir. They are insisting you attend an interview with them this afternoon. At the Bagot Road station."

"And they have given no indication of what they wish to discuss?"

"I am sorry, no. They would not say any more."

Shah frowned and began moving pieces of paper and pens around his desk, obviously unhappy. "This cannot be a coincidence, Miss Julianne," he said. "I have heard nothing from these detectives in four days. And now, an hour after the attempt on Mr. Ross's life, they insist on my attendance. I find myself in a quandary."

He picked up an expensive-looking fountain pen from the blotter in front of him and began drumming it rapidly on the desk.

"I cannot help but feel it is connected to this Cesky business. We have not had time to consider all of the intricacies involved, yet I think it might serve us well were you to accompany me in some guise or capacity. You have been dealing with this matter for some months now—"

"I wouldn't say I've been *dealing* with it, Shah," Jules corrected. "More like running away from it."

"Nevertheless," Shah responded, "I have only just begun to grapple with the implications of having this man as a possible enemy. Whereas you and Mr. Ross have been contemplating the matter since you left New York City."

He gave the blotter one loud and final drum stroke with the pen. A decision made.

"Birendra, tell the police officers we shall meet them at four o'clock. Have my lawyer attend as well. And make sure he knows that my other lawyer will be coming with us."

"Your other lawyer, sir?"

Shah smiled like a gray nurse shark. "Miss Julianne has a classical education, Birendra. A shower, some clean clothes, and an empty brief-case, and I'm sure no one will question her presence at this interview."

"What about your actual lawyer?" Jules asked, not at all sure this was a good idea.

"He will probably bill me for your time," the old Gurkha replied with another wide grin. "And of course I will pay him. He is most un-derstanding when his bills are paid promptly."

Shah stood up and rubbed his hands like a man contemplating a long-awaited lunch. He looked over at his faithful number two. "Birendra, summon my daughter. She can show Miss Julianne through to the ladies' wash facilities and provide her with some clean clothes. They are about the same size, and I know Ashmi keeps outfits hidden from me so that she might sneak out with her friends when she thinks my attention is elsewhere."

Julianne found herself hustled out of the office in Birendra's wake. She wanted to object but was swept along by the two men. And in spite of her misgivings, she admitted it was possible that Shah was right. They had not had time to compare notes in the few hours since she'd first contacted him this morning. She was unknown to the authorities in Darwin. She might well pass unnoticed in the meeting, and if the police did wish to discuss either of the bomb attacks with Shah, she might well pick up on something that meant nothing to him.

"And Birendra," said Shah, "find Mr. Pappas if he is in the city. We may need to consult him as well."

"Yes, sir."

Jules tried to imagine herself in the role of Narayan Shah's lawyer. She had considered studying law once. Her father had encouraged her with all his might and main. For a man who had never worked hard at anything but cards and calumny, Lord Balwyn's enthusiasm for plac-ing one of his own deep within the corpus of the justice system was unsettling. In fact, it was all the warning she needed. After a brief flirtation with the idea of donning lawyer's robes, Jules had decided to study the classics instead. When she went up to Trinity, she took honors in drinking, with a double major in shopping and fucking.

The Bagot Road police station, like the suburb it serviced, was painfully new. That wasn't just a metaphor. The lowering sun blazed down with restrained ferocity in the late afternoon, throwing intense sunbursts off the steel and glass façade of the building. Jules caught a flash in one eye and flinched. The afterimage burned a streak across her retina, and for a moment she feared a migraine might be coming on. She'd only ever had one, and that had been caused by an inopportune flash of light off a chrome benchtop.

She fumbled in the pockets of the military-cut green silk shirt she had borrowed from Shah's daughter before remembering that her sunglasses were perched on top of her head. With the imitation D&G shades in place—another item on loan from Ashmi—Jules no longer had to squint into the harsh glare.

The station was just west of the airport, only a few minutes' drive from the compound. A hunched, brutalist structure, it squatted on the busy road opposite a small golf course, a nine-hole eccentricity owned and operated by the Royal Australian Air Force. The airport runway ended in a concrete apron maybe half a mile or so away, over an empty field on the far side of the golf links. A fat-bellied military transport plane roared in to land directly over her head. The shadow flitted across the golf course like a giant awkward bird of prey. Julianne assumed that the unusual arrangement was a leftover from the city's pre-Wave frontier history. There wasn't much else left over from that time in this small area of northern Darwin.

"This was all a waste ground when I arrived," Shah remarked, sweeping his hand in a graceful arc. "You cannot see it now, but the ocean is only a few minutes' walk away."

Jules tried to catch a glimpse of the striking jade-green waters she'd flown in over, but the suburb across the road from the RAAF's beautifully maintained lawns had been developed so densely, it presented as a solid wall of concrete, fibrous cement, tinted glass, steel, and aluminum. Small commercial setups and government enterprises, among them the police station and an office of the Free Port Development Authority, faced onto Bagot Road. Shah had told her that the streets tucked in behind those buildings had been built up with expensive town houses right down to the water's edge. One of them was his family home, which explained why the Bagot Road detectives had taken charge of investigating the attempted bombing of his house.

"It is mostly new people around here," said Shah. "Businesspeople like me, who have set up in the last few years. A few Americans, but mostly from the region. Many Indonesians, many, many Chinese. The FPDA controls the building regulations, not the city council . . . so there are no regulations."

He stopped and laughed at his own joke, a rich stentorian laugh that teased a smile from Jules in return. Still, she wondered why the hell Shah was giving her the tour-guide spiel while they stood around roasting in the tropical heat.

"But it is very expensive to buy in here," he went on, seemingly oblivious. "That is what regulates development. Not law. My own home was built in less than four months. The laborers worked night and day. It is a lovely space, Miss Julianne, but it was very, very expensive to build. You must come around to dinner tonight. The rest of my family will want to meet you. They call you the Deliverer, you know."

"That's lovely," replied Jules, who had felt her skin starting to burn after just a minute in this sun. "But—"

"Ah, he is here."

A white Bentley pulled into the car park of the police station and maneuvered into the slot next to Shah's Land Rover. A tall, thin gray-haired man stepped out, wearing a lightweight cream-colored linen suit. He retrieved a briefcase and a Panama hat from the rear seat before locking up and greeting his client.

Shah's lawyer had arrived.

"Hello, hello, everyone. You must be Ms. Balwyn. I understand you will be acting as my junior today. Sitting in on the conference. Very good, very good. You can take notes. I imagine I'll do all the talking, but if there is something you desperately need to ask of our city's finest, feel free to whisper in my shell-like and we'll see what we can shake loose from John Law."

"Oh, okay, then," said Jules.

"Excellent. Home Counties girl, I judge, by your lovely accent. Better and better. Piers Downing, by the way." He launched a hand across to seal the deal. "Wouldn't do to have our little charade come a cropper because you didn't know me from Arthur or Martha, would it? And *hello*, Mr. Shah. Hello, hello. Dreadful business, all this. I can only hope Law has some news for us about these villains who blew themselves up on your lawn, but probably not. Your man Birendra brought me up to speed on this morning's shenanigans. I understand they touched on your interests somewhat tangentially. Doubtless that's why we are all here sweltering in this wretched bloody heat. Shall we away?"

"So you're not from around here, then, Mr. Downing?" Jules asked, stating the obvious, as they made their way up the concrete steps of the station.

The entrance was sheltered by massive sails of shade cloth artfully arranged to provide maximum cover during the hottest part of the day. Julianne felt the temperature ease off just a few degrees as they passed underneath them. The heat was still pulsing, however. At least until they pushed through a revolving door, and the ubiquitous, superchilled air-con washed over her in a merciful release.

"No, not from these parts, no," said Downing on the other side. "Falkland Islands, actually, if you can believe it. Long way from home and all, but everyone is these days. Especially in this benighted city. Took my degree back in Old Blighty and practiced in the City for twelve years. I was out here for a holiday in '03—well, a working holiday, tax write-offs and all that. Didn't fancy heading back home after everything turned to custard, either to the Falklands or to London, as you can imagine. Prospects in both places a bit too bleak for me, thank you. And you, Ms. Balwyn—made it back home at all?"

"No," Jules replied, deciding she didn't trust the lawyer very much. His hail-fellow-well-met routine reminded her an awful lot of her father just before he cheated people out of a drink, a meal, or their retirement savings. Shah, she noted, had said nothing since Downing's arrival and was sporting one of his enigmatic smiles as the three of them approached the reception desk.

"Piers Downing!" the dapper Brit bellowed to the brown-shirted duty officer, startling Jules in the process. "Of Downing, Street and

Kemp. Here with my client Mr. Shah to see Detectives Palmer and Dennis."

Julianne gave Shah a curious sidelong glance at the name of the law firm, but his smile remained in place. The man behind the desk, a sergeant whose shirt was straining at the buttons from a few too many years off the beat, stifled a groan as he pulled out an appointment book.

"Always a pleasure, Mr. Downing," he grunted in a way intended to ensure that everyone understood it was not. "I'll just call up and see if the detectives are in."

"They'd want to be," the lawyer replied. "They're the ones who insisted Mr. Shah attend this afternoon. We'll just head up now, shall we?"

Downing made as if to pass behind the counter, but the old cop slammed down a swing-top section, cutting him off. Otherwise, the sergeant ignored the three visitors. He reached somebody on the phone, inquired as to whether he or she was available, and then hung up.

"You can take a seat over there. Detective Palmer will be through in a moment," he said before pointedly turning away to busy himself at a computer and switching on a small radio at his desk. Johnny Cash jumped down into a burnin' ring of fire as Downing led the group over to the small waiting area.

The layout took Jules by surprise: a three-piece lounge setting arranged around a glass-top coffee table scattered with fresh magazines and today's newspaper. The mags held her interest—local versions of now-defunct American titles such as *Rolling Stone* and *People*—whereas the paper obviously had been published some hours before the bomb blast down at the marina. Its front page trumpeted the arrival of the Combined Fleet and the money it would pour into the coffers of the city's traders.

She sank into one of the leather lounge chairs. This was all a bit luxe compared with the police stations she'd visited so often as a young lady to bail out her father. But she supposed they didn't let any old riffraff swan about here in the foyer at Bagot Road. The villains most probably were bundled into cells via some sort of receiving dock around the back. And if this station serviced an enclave of rich émigré business exiles, as her Nepalese friend had implied, perhaps they felt the need to put their best face forward.

"It's all a bit swish, isn't it?" Jules spoke the words in a stage whisper.

Shah said nothing, content to gaze around the reception area as if it were his first time there. Downing leaned forward and rubbed the tips of his fingers together.

"Baksheesh," he explained, rolling the word around in his mouth like a particularly fine sweet. Without bothering to lower his voice, he went on. "I happen to know this lounge setting was a gift from one of the local notables, a furniture importer from China who had a spot of bother with customs a while back. Some eager young thing holding up consignments of stock by insisting on searching for contraband in the containers. Outrageous imposition on the free flow of commerce. All sorted out now, of course, thanks to some backdoor lobbying by inter-ested parties not a million miles removed from this fine police station. Our boys in brown think if they put these things out on public display, it's like declaring their pecuniary interests. Take a look at some of the top-shelf gear they've got behind closed doors . . . You strike me as a woman of refined tastes, Ms. Balwyn. I'd be interested to see what you make of it all."

Julianne crossed her legs and tried to admire the cut of the black dress pants she had borrowed. They flared slightly at the cuffs in a style she'd always liked, matching the medium-heeled boots she had worn when leaving her hotel this morning. One of Shah's assistants had pol-ished them to a high military sheen while she'd showered and changed back at the compound. She was hoping the lawyer might tone it down if she didn't respond, but he carried on regardless in his best courtroom voice. Shah seemed happy to ignore his tales of official malfeasance, but they made Jules increasingly uncomfortable. Daddy had always taught her to keep her mouth shut around the authorities.

When Downing finally paused to draw breath, she leaned toward him, shaking her head. "But I don't see how any of this can be so," she said. "The police aren't allowed to accept gifts, are they? This isn't South America."

He smiled as though she'd walked into a trap. "Ah. But it is not their place to say yea or nay to largesse. Not in this form, anyway. Mr. Shah probably told you on the way over that this station is a recent addition to our good city. As is the very pleasant little community over which it stands watch. And I can make that judgment without fear of contradiction because many of my clients hail from the Palms. A delightful community, one that pays its bills promptly."

He fanned himself with his Panama hat even though Jules was beginning to shiver in the chill of the arctic air-conditioning.

"This station," he continued, waving the hat around, "indeed, all of the new police stations built in Darwin since it was given free-port status by the federal government—seven of them in total—they were all built and funded, and *remain* funded, by the FPDA. The Free Port Development Authority. The lawful chain of command runs back to the minister in Parliament, but the FPDA controls the purse strings, and with them the parameters within which the officers in this station must operate. The Free Port Development Authority, of course, although established by an act of Parliament, is a self-funded corporatized entity. That funding is levied from the commercial sector of the city."

And with that he fell silent, staring at Jules, his features lit with the merest trace of a smile that would have done credit to Shah for its ambivalence. As for the Gurkha veteran, he leaned forward and spoke for the first time since they'd entered the police station. His voice was much softer than Downing's.

"Things in this city are not always as they should be or even as they appear," he said.

Downing leaned forward, too, thus forming a quiet conclave over the expensive glass coffee table. Jules began to wonder just how expensive.

"I need you to understand, Ms. Balwyn, that power in this city is a fickle beast. The men we will talk to are agents of the state. But the state is not a unitary concept here. The Wave, everything that has come after it, smashed all that, washed it away. Given the nature of your recent tribulations, you must always bear this in mind. Power is not settled here. It is restless and seething and often wont to turn back on itself."

The lawyer's voice was so soft now that Jules found herself drawn forward until his face seemed mere inches from hers. They were close enough that she could see where he had missed a spot while shaving that morning.

"This is the new world," said Downing. "Born of chaos and madness. Remember that, if nothing else."

Before she could reply, a door opened to her left, next to the reception counter, and a large, immaculately dressed man in a business suit stood looking at her.

"Detective Palmer!" Piers Downing boomed. "Always a pleasure."

27

NORTH KANSAS CITY, MISSOURI

For the purposes of her first special-clearance mission within the borders of the United States, Caitlin Monroe became Colonel Katherine Murdoch, USAF (Reserve), special adviser to the White House chief of staff on military liaison with the Texas Defense Force. The TDF was what happened when perfectly good national guardsmen fell under the control of a disgraced former general with a Caesar complex and robust levels of popular support—or *populist* support, Caitlin corrected herself—among a significant minority of a traumatized, deeply riven survivor population.

The TDF was part genuine kick-ass military force, part state militia, and part Praetorian Guard for the emperor of Fort Hood. Disgruntled veterans from the federal forces, many of them forcibly demobilized and slated for resettlement in Alaska before the Wave lifted in March 2004, had rallied to Blackstone's standard. It wouldn't have been Caitlin's first choice in that situation, but then, she had options that these soldiers did not. If you had a family to feed and no money or food to put on the table, a spot in the Texas Defense Force was certainly an improvement over nothing but crumbs and cold, empty promises in the Alaskan wastes.

Patronage. It worked for the Romans, and Blackstone was making it work for him.

At least he hasn't gone the full Caligula on us yet, Caitlin thought as she sat up on the bed. Colonel Murdoch took a room here at the former Harrah's Casino Hotel, fresh in from Vancouver before heading out to the Cerner Corporation Campus for an intense afternoon and early evening of presentations from Mr. Culver's "people." Now, just on nine o'clock, Caitlin had retired to the solitude of her hotel room to review her briefing package before flying out to Texas tomorrow.

She hadn't much bothered with domestic politics before the Disappearance. The endless pig circus had been largely irrelevant to her concerns, and it had felt even more pointless in the years since, especially once she'd settled into life on the farm with Bret and Monique. To be honest, there had been times when she'd imagined herself never setting foot in America again. Caitlin used to simply tune it out. Care factor zero, she said. Until now.

Bret, in contrast, couldn't give up his old habits as a former combat journalist. He'd been a good one. Indeed, many of the reports on the TDF in her mission brief were freelance articles filed by none other than Bret Melton. He kept pretty close tabs on the plight of the demobilized veterans, particularly since some of them were peeps he'd met over in the desert. At night he would sit up with Monique in his arms, holding a bottle, listening to the BBC reports.

She ate her dinner—chicken salad without dressing washed down with spring water—while committing the TDF's order of battle to memory.

The Texas Defense Force drew upon the infrastructure left over from two active-duty army divisions and a national guard division. All three of those divisions were "legacy forces" designed to fight a conventional combined-arms war against a conventional enemy. In many cases, their Abrams tanks and Bradley Fighting Vehicles would have required a fair amount of refit before returning to service. No doubt that was what new inductees spent a lot of their time doing.

Blackstone had re-formed those forces into brigade combat teams with a full strength of close to three thousand effectives per team. On paper, Mad Jack could draw on six brigades with armor, infantry, and artillery battalions. They were supported by two aviation brigades equipped with the latest Apache gunships. As impressive as the full combat teams sounded, however, they were rarely concentrated at brigade strength. Many of his units were scattered about as battalion-size task forces.

A good 60 percent of that combat power was oriented along the northern approaches to Texas, ostensibly on internal security patrols for criminal elements and the like. No one in Seattle believed that story, and neither did Caitlin. The remaining 40 percent was divided evenly between the so-called Panamanian Expeditionary Force and the Gulf coastline, backed up by a small collection of patrol boats and a pair of destroyers, which combined to form the naval component.

Once you tossed in a number of squadrons drawn from air force F-16s and navy F/A-18 Hornets, she concluded, what you had was a first-order military power within U.S. territory. And she hadn't even reached the reserve structure table of organization yet. In theory, every citizen in Texas could be mobilized for active duty. With one-quarter of the current U.S. population living in the Lone Star State, that number could top out at 3 to 4 million.

She shook her head. Blackstone would never need that many. The campaign in New York had left most of the remaining federal ground forces a complete wreck. It would take years, perhaps decades, for them to recover. The only elements receiving full funding were the naval and marine forces attached to the Combined Fleet. Everything else was falling apart from a lack of financial resources.

As accustomed as she'd become to the changed world, Caitlin Monroe still struggled to accept the idea of a rival power establishing itself on the North American continent. Because that was what Blackstone's regime was starting to look like. Putting aside her own privileged access to information, there was simply no avoiding the conclusion that he was preparing for a confrontation with Seattle either to break them or to break with them. That was hardly white-hot raw intelligence. The old media and the new filled up miles of on-screen real estate yammering about it every day.

As always with politics, Caitlin just didn't care. It might have been something more than sound and fury, signifying nothing, but to her, for now, the deepening cold war within the United States was just an operational parameter. She still drew a pay check from Echelon, but that was a multinational concern now. The old order, in which the United States had been first among equals—she couldn't help but smile at that polite fantasy—had been swept away. Seattle was just a spear-carrier these days. The America she once had defended was gone.

When she was done with Blackstone and had confirmed to the best of her abilities that al Banna was dead, she would be gone, too. Gone from this open-air mausoleum, gone from the continent of the dead, gone from Echelon, gone from the world of her past. Gone to her future.

At the thought of her husband and child, Caitlin checked her watch again. Another three minutes until she would be able to make a secure connection. She put aside the various briefing papers now to finish her dinner. She didn't want to be shoving food in her mouth while talking to Bret and Monique.

Taking the salad bowl with her, she walked over to the window, where she had drawn the curtains against the cold darkness as evening closed in. Dropping the room lights so that not even a fragment of her silhouette would show, she indulged herself in a moment of sightseeing, peeking through a gap in the drapes.

For the most part, it was pitch-black. Her window looked to the southeast, over the Missouri River. She thought she could make out the lights of the recently restored Hawthorne Power Plant in the distance. Somewhere near that location was a truck stop and travel plaza where convoys and buses readied for their journey across a landscape deserted by all but the most desperate or antisocial types. Caitlin closed the curtains before the void out there sucked all the joy from her soul.

She had never been to Kansas City before, but she'd learned from her briefings as Colonel Murdoch that it hadn't changed much since being reclaimed as the U.S. government's principal settlement center in the Midwest. Her first few hours in the city, however, had confirmed what she'd been told about the great demographic changes resettlement had wrought there. The city's population was still only half of its pre-Wave size, and just over 50 percent of the current residents were migrants, many of them from India, working on the railroads, along with many from China laboring on the government's huge collective farms. It wasn't yet public knowledge, but Kansas City was slated to take the lion's share of the displaced aliens currently being detained on the East Coast.

She scoffed at that. Such a move surely would drive more people to Blackstone's standard. On the rare instances when she allowed herself to ponder such things, she wondered what was in the water in Seattle. There had to be something, or perhaps it was the coffee. Again, not her problem.

The displaced aliens were the women and children of the jihadis she'd fought in New York. Chief of Staff Culver had thought she should understand what Seattle had planned for them before she committed to the job in Texas. Not that she gave a shit if Kipper wanted to reward his enemies by handing them the very thing they'd tried to take by force. She was just gonna kill whoever needed killing, and then she was outta there.

Peeping through the curtains again, Caitlin could see that large areas of the city remained in darkness, yet to be reclaimed. Some of them, she knew, had not even been cleared of the remains of the dead. When she'd first arrived in this hotel room, she'd spent an unpleasant minute or two looking for the telltale stains of the Disappeared. Only once she'd noticed the fresh paint throughout and new carpet did she relax just a bit. The lingering presence of the Disappeared was something she found . . . unacceptable, even uncomfortable, and that surprised her.

Most of her adult life had been spent in an intimate correspondence with death. She had thought herself inured to it, yet she could not deny a sort of spiritual nausea at the idea of being surrounded by hundreds of millions of vanished souls. She had experienced it first in New York, and the longer she remained on this continent, the stronger the feeling grew. As soon as she could walk away from death, she would.

Not being able to account for the fate of Bilal Baumer was frustrating, even worrying to the part of her that had been trained at a cellular level to confirm a kill. But Caitlin was also aware that sometimes you just didn't know. In her world, the only real certainty was your own eventual negation. Culver was almost certainly right. The air force probably had killed him when it demolished Rockefeller Center. Still . . .

Her laptop chimed. She abandoned thoughts of the haunted city and crossed the room in five long strides to sit at the large curvilinear executive workstation. Glorified civil servant she may have been, but at least she wasn't traveling cattle class. Seattle had leased the hotel to what remained of the Starwood chain but had reserved suites on the top floor for its own use. Hers was more like an apartment than a hotel room, and Caitlin wished that Bret could have been there to enjoy a bit of luxury with her. Then again, she could think of about a thousand places she would rather have taken him than Kansas fucking City. Perhaps that was what they would do when this was all over: just disappear for six months with Monique. Cash out some of her black funds and visit a few places where they could kick back and not worry about having to outrun a bullet.

After checking the cable connection on the laptop, she plugged the one-time digital key into a USB port and entered her code. A small window appeared on screen, a progress bar. It moved painfully slowly as her machine reached out through a dedicated fibre-optic link to the National Intelligence Agency server at Cerner, from where her comms protocols were forwarded as flash traffic across the Vancouver Alliance military satellite network on a stand-alone channel dedicated to Echelon data.

Thousands of miles away, on a scarred kitchen table that had entered its second century the year Queen Victoria had ascended the throne, another laptop encased in its own formidable digital armor shook hands with hers. A second later her husband winked into existence on the screen in front of her. He was holding the baby, asleep, against his shoulder. Caitlin's heart lurched when she saw how much Monique had grown. She was a baby no longer.

"Oh, honey, *oh, my God!* Look how *big* she is! Is she walking yet?"

Her question was accented with a faintly distressed note. The child was living another life, growing up in a world far removed from the one in which she moved. Caitlin was not an automaton, but though familiar with fear, she had learned to control it. Fear was a variable, something to be used. But now she felt fear as a runaway horse. Her daughter was growing up without her, not knowing her. Caitlin's stomach clenched. What the hell was she even doing here, playing charades and dress-up for Jed Culver? She should have been at home.

"Not walking, no," answered Bret, who hadn't picked up on her sudden spiral into maternal shame and panic. "But it won't be long before she's crawling, I reckon. I've already moved everything up off the bottom shelves."

And what had Caitlin done while Dad had been readying the family home for the day their daughter was able to crawl off her play mat for the first time? Killed half a dozen men down in South America, that was what. Some of them undoubtedly fathers like Bret.

And now she had assumed yet another identity, preparing to infiltrate a potentially hostile regime on the soil, the scorched earth, of her homeland. Or was it her *former* homeland? She couldn't be sure of anything now other than the pain she felt just under her ribs when looking at her husband and child.

"And how are you, honey?" Bret asked. He knew better than to ask her any specifics about where she might be, what she was doing, or even when she might be home. The reassuring banalities of everyday life, the cushion of normality on which the relationships of real people rested. But not Caitlin Monroe's. He had no idea he was talking to Colonel Katherine Murdoch, for instance. He had no need to know.

"I'm a little tired," she said. "Been moving around a bit with work."

Or: *I blew a man's brains out the other day, darling. He was indirectly responsible for the attack on you and Monique. So I hunted him down and put a bullet between his eyes after he'd told me what I needed to hear. Oh, and the sort of ammunition I used created a vacuum wave inside his collapsing skull. Turned his brain to hot mush and sucked it out behind the bullet as it left the back of his skull. Hey, did I mention the ejecta—that's what we call the shit that comes out of an exit wound at high speed—did I mention that it was black with crawling ants before it had stopped steaming? No? Oh, that's right—I don't talk about my work.*

She tried to make out some details of the kitchen behind Bret. She wondered what he'd had for dinner, whether he fed Monique from a bottle or spooned out baby food for her. She obviously wasn't sleeping through yet. It was even later in Scotland—about two in the morning, she thought shamefacedly—and the little webcam he was using wasn't good enough to display much in the gloom behind him. She was just able to pick out some lonely-looking Christmas decorations, which made her feel even worse, as he spoke to her from shrouded darkness.

"I'm not doing anything exciting at the moment," she reassured him. "Just lots of reading and talking to people."

I've just been reviewing a case about a Mexican man named Miguel Pieraro. He and his teenage daughter escaped from Texas last spring after witnessing the massacre of their loved ones. It's hell down there, my love. A madman has taken dominion. These poor people saw their whole family cut down. They believe the madman was ultimately responsible. And so do I.

"Well, we saw the Loch Ness Monster the other day, didn't we?" said Bret, patting their daughter gently on her back. "Daddy and some of the men from Mommy's work went for a long drive. We visited the special farms where they make the firewater around these parts. And we went to the lake where they have the monster. But all we got was this . . ."

He held up a cuddly stuffed toy, which he obviously had meant for Monique to show her before she'd fallen asleep. Caitlin had to force herself not to upbraid him for giving away operational security. He shouldn't have been discussing his movements or mentioning a security detail even on a scrambled link.

Fuck, Caitlin thought, rebuking herself instead. *What the fuck am I thinking? They just had a nice day out for a change. A tour of some fucking distilleries. It's not like they're trying to avoid a Stasi wetwork squad, for fuck's sake.*

"Have you had any word from the farm?" she asked. Her brain wanted to seize up from having to talk in these dull and meaningless generalities at the same time that she longed to be able to live a life with Bret in which she could be bored by the little things.

"Spoke to someone from the Ministry of Resources," he replied. "Another two families moved on last week. Took places on the *Nimitz,*

I think, going back to the U.S. Good luck to them. I hope it works out. Otherwise, same old same old. Apparently the GM crops are doing well."

And I spoke to someone today, husband. A very senior someone. The president's sword and shield. He wants me to infiltrate the camp of this madman. To go into that heart of darkness, earn their trust, and, of course, betray them. I'll do it, too, sweetheart. Because that's what I am. An infiltrator. A betrayer. A killer.

A peacekeeper also, she tried to reassure herself. But she was just so damned tired of keeping the peace.

"That's good news," she said. "I'm really looking forward to coming home, Bret. I *miss* you guys, every day."

"We miss you too, honey. And we both love you and want you with us as soon as you're finished over there."

He carefully moved one hand from where he was supporting the baby to blow a kiss, then took Monique's hand gently between two fingers and made her wave in her sleep.

"I love you, too," Caitlin said as she felt the tears coming.

And I would miss you every moment of every day, except I can't. There are times I can't even think of you. Because if I'm not totally invested in what I'm doing here, I will die. And we will never see each other again. And that's why I'm crying. Not because I miss you but because I don't. Because I can't.

She felt herself adrift. She and Bret spun out the final few seconds of their time together repeating the same phrases. Miss you. Love you. Good-bye. Good-bye. And then he was gone. The brief window she had secured on Echelon's dedicated channel closed.

Caitlin shut down the laptop and sat for a minute, staring at the drifts of paper on her king-size bed. She still had so much work to review. More briefings on the TDF for her cover story. Backgrounders from Treasury explaining the fraught relations between Seattle and Fort Hood in terms of the fascinating history of post-Disappearance federal–state fiscal arrangements. There were "Top-Secret Absolute" (read/erase) one-time files on the NIA server she had to take in before the morning. And case notes from Resettlement on fifty-four incidents in the Federal Mandate, ranging from forced repatriation of homesteader families to wholesale murder.

Too much. It was all too much. She needed to shake off her feelings of being buffeted by events, of reacting to the agendas of others. She had to refocus. Establish autonomy.

She changed into her gym gear and left the suite after keying the security system. The top floor of the hotel was secured, but Caitlin's room was flagged for special containment. Before she had even made the elevators at the end of the corridor, a security man appeared, nodded to her, and moved to take up station.

"Colonel Murdoch," he said.

She half acknowledged him as she swept past. He fell in behind her as she made her way to the elevators. There was a large fitness facility in one of the former convention rooms, just off from the pool and hot-tub area. It was tempting to default to the hot tub and simply soak her worries away. But Caitlin knew from experience that she would find no peace of mind or body without earning it. Besides, if she hit the tub alone, she'd have to fend off any number of interested parties. No, the gym was the only answer.

She didn't like to exercise so soon after eating, but the chicken salad had been small and light. Lean protein and leafy carbs made a good fuel. And if she started with some weight training after a moderate warm-up, she could burn it off before throwing herself into any high-intensity cardio. She knew she wouldn't be able to concentrate on the documents upstairs until she'd cleared herself of the emotional blockage that had built up during her conversation with Bret.

Her nose wrinkled when she hit the lobby. It always smelled of old socks and stale cigarettes even though it was a no-smoking facility and the other guests presumably used the laundry facilities. In the distance, she could make out the crunching noise of some raunchy dance tune, the clinking of glasses and silverware, the forced merriment of so many people trying to relieve themselves of the burden of living in a necropolis. She had no desire to explore whatever level of desperation waited in that direction.

Moving through the vaulted lobby, past the gift shop to her left and the pool to her right, she took a quick turn down the corridor leading to the hotel's gym. It wasn't crowded at this time of the night, but she did not have it to herself. Two women were chatting while using the elliptical trainers, barely raising a sweat. In Caitlin's opinion, if you had the breath to flap your gums, you weren't training hard enough. A couple of guys were pounding through the miles on the treadmills. She would have picked them for military because of their haircuts and physique even if they hadn't been wearing PT shorts with the USAF emblem printed on them. She was glad her own gym clothing was civilian. She didn't fancy having to play the Murdoch role with those two. The other users down there she lumped into two broad groups: government and business travelers. All of them huffing and puffing in a desultory fashion, grinding through the same exercises they'd probably been doing for the last ten years. No doubt they'd train at half intensity for about a third of the time they actually needed to before rewarding themselves with a pig-out at the hotel buffet.

Still frowning and feeling bleak, Caitlin started her routine under the black cloud that had settled in over her. She began with a quarter hour of dynamic stretching before taking the last of the cross trainers and blocking out the inane chatter of the women beside her. It would have been easier if she'd had a music player and some headphones, but she didn't like the way it was possible to zone out when wearing those things. Zoning out was the enemy of situational awareness.

After half an hour she was sufficiently limber to attack the weight stations, which she did with a vengeance for the next hour and a half, mixing up weight training with bursts of high-intensity cardio intervals. One of the air force types did his best to attract her attention, but she froze him out. She wished she could have worn her wedding ring to warn these creeps off, but for a field agent, that telltale golden band screamed: *Weakness.* A pressure point. A chink in the armor.

Isolation was her armor, and Caitlin's was restored by the time she'd finished and was heading back up in the elevator, just after ten. Again, it would have been nice to have indulged in something as unremarkable as a hot tub, but she had no desire to have to shut down anybody foolish enough to talk to her. And she still had hours of work to get through before she could even think about sleep.

The same security man was standing outside her room, with his feet planted on the carpet like a statue personifying iron steadfastness. She'd have preferred it if he'd been moving around a bit rather than perfecting his North Korean border-guard stoicism. Less chance of boredom and vaguing out. But she thanked him, anyway, and said good night once he'd supervised her entering the access code and voice-print.

After a session in the room's glass and marble shower unit, she was soon propped up in bed in her dressing gown, ready to start work again. The first file she picked up was from the inspector general of the Department of Reconstruction and Resettlement, bearing a title in bold red print: *Case Note: Baker Lake/Madison/Pieraro/TDF-Bravo 2/14, ivet/13CC.*

She sighed. Those poor bastards again.

This was exactly the sort of thing Caitlin had not wanted to deal with in her agitated state earlier in the evening. Jed Culver had red-flagged four files like this, in which homesteaders had not simply been forced off their farms but also murdered. Like the other three she had lined up to read, the Pieraro case was interesting because witnesses had survived. In all four instances, they spoke of attacks by "road agents," who reminded Caitlin of the irregular forces used by third-rate villains such as Slobodan Milošević when they wanted to bring terror to bear, but with a convenient degree of separation from themselves. The road agents, unlike the Serbian militia she had encountered a couple of times, did not present as an irregular arm of state policy. Blackstone condemned them and occasionally even caught a few and executed them. But, she noted, those executions were always carried out sum-marily, in the field, far from independent verification. No road agent had ever faced trial in Texas, which amounted to a significant absence from the public record of Fort Hood's often repeated insistence that it took the matter of banditry within the Federal Mandate seriously.

Caitlin sipped at her cool water. The Pieraro file was thick. Investi-gators had pored over everything except the site of the atrocity, which had since been allocated to another family. They'd also conducted in-terviews with Miguel Pieraro, his daughter Sofia, and, interestingly, four other subjects who'd arrived in Kansas City with the Pieraros: a woman, Maive Aronson, and a teenage boy named Adam Coupland, both survivors of a Mormon party that had been driving a herd of cattle to market when set upon by a gang of road agents; Trudi Jessup, a civil servant in the federal government's food security program; and a Marsha Gross, described in the case note as a "camp follower" of the gang that had attacked Aronson's party.

"And thereby hangs a tale, I'll bet," Caitlin said to herself.

Even though she was doing this research only as an exercise in due diligence, to better inform herself about the administration she had been tasked to infiltrate, Caitlin found herself drawn into the story of homesteaders being forced off their land and into flight. She couldn't help but sympathize with Pieraro's anguish, his need to choose between avenging himself on the agents and getting his sole surviving child to safety. She thought him a man crushed between the weight of two worlds.

Before she became too deeply enmeshed with the narrative, the Echelon agent called room service and ordered up a pot of coffee and an omelet.

"Miles to go before I sleep," she said to the empty room. But it wasn't all bad. She had forgotten about Bret and Monique again.

28

NORTH DARWIN, NORTHERN TERRITORY

"I understand you went for a swim this morning, Mr. Shah."

"The weather, Detective; it is very hot this time of year."

Julianne, keen to stay in character as the dutiful junior lawyer, held her pen poised over an old-fashioned legal pad even though Downing was recording the whole interview on a microcassette. Shah had answered the policeman's loaded question happily enough but did not offer to elaborate. It seemed unlike him to act the fool with the law. Not for the first time, Jules wondered what the hell was going on here.

Detective Palmer, a powerfully built, thirtysomething man wearing what looked like a bespoke suit, leaned back in his gas lift chair and regarded the old Gurkha as if he were an interesting crossword puzzle.

Alerted by Downing, Jules had spied the chairs, six of them in total, as soon as they'd entered the interview room. She recognized the model as a Herman Miller Aeron, a couple of thousand dollars' worth of sit-down technology. They were positioned around a long hardwood table. A large mirror threw back their reflections from one wall at the end of the room. Undoubtedly, an observation area stood behind it, but otherwise the interview room in no way resembled the grim concrete boxes in which suspects usually found themselves. She had no doubt that somewhere in this building such a space existed, probably three or four of them. Shah and his legal team were enjoying gentle, kid-gloves treatment, it seemed. Nevertheless, Palmer still wanted to know what he'd been doing down at the Gonzales Road Marina when the Rhino's boat had blown up.

Jules just hoped nobody would recognize her from the scene. That would have taken some explaining, since she was supposed to be Piers Downing's assistant.

"Did you know any of the victims, Mr. Shah?" Palmer asked. "Did you have some reason for being down there?"

"The man who was injured, the one I helped pull back to shore, his name is Rhino Ross. He is a friend of mine."

Jules felt a pulse beating slowly and powerfully in her temple. If he explained too much about his connection to the Rhino, her role in bringing them together might be exposed. Still, the detective seemed satisfied that Shah had admitted to being at the marina and knowing the victim. She had to admire her Nepalese friend for having the sense to play it straight. Her natural inclination when dealing with the authorities was to bury them in bullshit. But Palmer undoubtedly would have been making inquiries over the last couple of hours.

"Do you believe there might be some connection between the attempted bombing at my house and the attack on Mr. Ross today?" Shah asked.

Palmer pressed his lips together as though forcing himself to remain quiet. "Investigations continue. But if you know of anything that might explain why two refugees should be targeted like this, I'm all ears."

"I object to the term 'refugee'," Downing interjected. "Mr. Shah is a respected and highly valued member of this community."

"We respect all the members of our community, Mr. Downing," Palmer said. "Whether they're black fellas who've been here for ten thousand years or reffos who blew in last week, we treat them all the same."

Jules wasn't entirely sure what he meant by that. Was it sarcasm or sincerity? He had an excellent poker face.

"My point exactly," the lawyer countered, choosing to bet on sarcasm. "Is there some reason you dragged my client and myself down here? I'm not sure why we couldn't have had this conversation by telephone."

"Bringing people together, Mr. Downing, that's what I'm all about." Palmer leaned back again and crossed his legs. He looked like he might be settling in for the duration. "And what brought you and Mr. Ross together, Mr. Shah? Did you have some reason for visiting him at lunchtime, just before he was blown up? Or was it more of a pop-in visit, a friendly call? You know, just before the fucking bomb exploded."

Julianne was doing her best to paraphrase the questions in note form, but she'd never learned shorthand and most of her note taking at college had consisted of jotting down phone numbers and the addresses of parties. Part of her, the last remnants of childhood's trusting naïveté she supposed, wanted to be done with the façade and tell Palmer all about New York, the attack in Texas, the Romanian who tried to knife her in Sydney, about Cesky, and Acapulco, and how the two bomb blasts that had gone off in this city over the last week probably were tied in with them. But Shah, who knew all this, revealed nothing to the police officer, and Jules trusted him far more than she did Detective Palmer in his beautiful hand stitched suit. So she scratched out her notes and kept her mouth shut.

"I would have liked Mr. Ross to work for me," said Shah. "He is a good man, and in my business they can be hard to find. But the Rhino, he is very much an individual. An old-fashioned American. He prefers to set his own course. There is no telling with this kind of man."

It was obvious that Palmer was dissatisfied with the answer. He regarded his interviewee with a stony face for at least two seconds.

"You must surely have some idea of why somebody wants you dead," he said eventually. "*Both* of you dead." His voice took on a harder, embittered edge with every word. "Because that's what we're talking about here, mate. Somebody has your number. Both you and Mr. Ross. And it defies belief that you don't have any idea who that might be. Come on, give it up. We're not in *court*. There's no fucking *rules of evidence* to worry about today." The detective threw a hostile glare at Downing before continuing. "What I do have to worry about is some dickhead running around town blowing up fucking reffos. I'm not having it, Shah. Not on my fucking manor. I don't know who or what you think you're protecting, but it's certainly not your family. If that bomb had gone off at your place the way it was supposed to, your wife and your two daughters would be dead now."

Jules expected Shah to stiffen at the taunt, and she did see Downing move as if to placate his client. But the old warrior didn't react at all. Rather than having to calm him down or restrain him, Downing picked up a pen and scratched a meaningless doodle onto the yellow legal pad in front of him, covering his own precipitate reaction.

"Can we safely assume, then, Detective Palmer," he said without looking up from the pad, "that you haven't the foggiest idea of why somebody attacked my client? At his home. Would it be the case, Detective, that you don't even have a lead to be getting on with, since the surviving bomber died without talking? So, is it the case you thought you might have Mr. Shah in here this afternoon to see if he could do your job for you?"

Unlike Shah, Palmer did not hide his irritation. Two distinct spots of color rose to his cheeks, which were fairly burning with resentment, as he glared at the lawyer.

"If your client could answer a perfectly simple and reasonable question, it might give me a lead, Mr. Downing. But for some reason he seems to have not a single thought on the matter of what connection there might be between the attempted bombing four days ago and the actual bombing of a known associate of his today. A bombing in which a woman was killed. A good woman, a wife and a mother who will be very much missed by her family."

The policeman's face was suffused with angry blotches now. Jules had to take a deep breath to still a swirl of dizziness as an unwanted memory, vivid and gruesome, arose before her eyes: a man cradling the headless body of a woman, his wife, in a foul slick of blood at the marina . . . She shook herself ever so slightly in an effort to clear the image from her head.

"Or, might it be the case, Mr. Shah," Palmer continued, oblivious to her reaction, "that bombs explode and people die around you so fucking frequently, it's barely worth remarking on? I wonder if we shouldn't be looking at the issue of your security license. It might be that the background checks weren't nearly thorough enough and we've missed some unsavory connections somewhere. The sort of connections we don't need in this city."

Julianne felt Downing tap her foot twice with his shoe: *Pay attention.*

"That sounds remarkably like a ham-fisted attempt at intimidation, Detective," he said, making a great play of looking at the microcassette recorder rather than the police officer. "You do understand that my client is a member in good standing of the Chamber of Commerce, the city's Business Roundtable, and the Free Port Development Authority's Commercial Consultancy Board?" He emphasized the last point by cocking an eyebrow at Palmer, a gesture that would go unrecorded on the audiotape, of course.

"Mr. Shah is not some barefoot coolie just off the boat, Detective Palmer. And unlike some other contractors I could mention, his business is run in an exemplary fashion. I know that because I have oversight of the administrative requirements. Shah Security has never been cited for unauthorized lethality, collateral injury, or property damage. You will find all his documentation is in order, including the quarterly reviews by the FPDA's audit and risk management bureau. The Free Port Development Authority has no reason to find fault with Mr. Shah or his operations, and his licensing fees are fully paid up. In advance, I might add."

Rather than reminding the cop of who paid his salary, it only served to enrage him further.

"What *I* know, Mr. Downing, is that this city is overrun with security contractors and bottom-feeding mercenaries, and suspending the license of one for refusing to cooperate with the police isn't going to make a blind bloody bit of difference to anybody. Except Mr. Shah, of course."

As hard as it was to keep up with and write down the exchanges flying across the hardwood table, Jules persevered. She took a moment to glance up at Shah, however, to see how he was doing. The soldier turned businessman remained impassive. Palmer was making a concerted effort to break him down, but Downing was spoiling all of his attacks.

"When last I checked, Detective, the licensing of military-grade security contractors in the Northern Territory was not the responsibility of the local police. Final authority rests with the federal government, and they act on advice from the Free Port Development Authority. I will stand corrected, of course, but I don't think the development authority is even required to consult with you on such matters."

Surely Downing had pushed it too far. Palmer looked as angry as Julianne had ever seen a man look without reaching for a weapon. A vein throbbed dark and purple on the side of his neck, and he jutted his chin at the Falklander like a gun turret. Shah preempted him before he could fire back a reply.

"Is there any news of my friend, Detective?"

Palmer stared at him, uncomprehending, for a heartbeat.

"Mr. Ross . . . Rhino," Shah added. "We have had no word of him since the explosion. I understand he was evacuated to one of the American ships in port. I wonder if you might have any information about that or his condition."

The big policeman gave his head a quick shake not to answer the question in the negative but to hide his surprise at it. He patted his jacket pocket as if searching for something. "Sorry, I ah . . . Just give me a second, would you?"

Palmer pushed himself back from the table and stood up to leave, exiting via a door next to the one-way mirror.

"What the fu—" Jules began.

Downing tapped the back of her hand with two fingers and shook his head almost imperceptibly. He rolled his eyes around the room. They were, of course, still being observed.

Jules nodded and did her best to tidy up the appalling mess of notes she'd scribbled all over her legal pad. She circled a few questions she had written down for herself. Who had informed Palmer that Shah had been down at the marina? Was it significant that the cop didn't seem to know who she was? Why had they been dragged to the station to answer a couple of questions that, as Downing had pointed out, could just as easily have been dealt with over the phone? The obvious threat to Shah's business—was it credible? Did anyone stand behind it, or was Palmer overreaching?

"I'm dreadfully sorry about all this, Mr. Shah," Downing said, breaking the silence. "There really is no reason for you to have to put up with it. This is the lowest form of harassment and quite unacceptable. Give me the word and I will make a formal complaint."

To Julianne, the lawyer seemed to be saying exactly what anyone watching and recording them would have expected him to say. Role playing, and he was good at it. Shah replied with a shrug just as Palmer returned with a colleague.

"Detective Constable Bill Dennis," the new man said, introducing himself. "My apologies, folks. I meant to be here earlier, but I got caught up in traffic getting back from the navy base. Went out to see your mate, Ross. He's still with us but a bit banged up."

Jules had to exert a tremendous effort of will to keep herself quiet. Downing seemed to understand her frustration. She was quite desperate for news of the Rhino and found herself feeling guilty that she hadn't done more to find out how he was. If he had never met her, he wouldn't be lying in a hospital bed right now.

"How badly was Mr. Ross injured, Detective Constable?" the lawyer asked affably. "He's a friend of my client, and we've had no word. If possible, I'm sure Mr. Shah would like to visit him. But we don't even know where he is being treated."

One wouldn't have known from the agreeable tone of Piers Downing's voice that he had locked horns so seriously with Dennis's partner just a few minutes earlier. Jules couldn't help thinking that if her father had had this chap in his corner when it all went wrong, he might not have retired to the billiards room with his service revolver.

Both cops sat down, Palmer pushing back from the table a fraction, as Dennis pulled up a chair and opened a manila folder, from which he began to extract details.

"Mr. Ross has second-degree burns to 30 percent of his body. A broken shoulder blade. Four broken ribs. And possible internal injuries. Sorry, I don't have details on that yet. They're still operating. He's being treated on the American ship USS *Bataan*. When they have him stable, they'll transfer him to Royal Darwin. No word on when that might be, though."

Like Palmer, Bill Dennis was a tall, athletic-looking man somewhere in his thirties. He was also very well dressed for a detective. The stitching and material of his suit spoke of the care and attention of an expert tailor: no sign of uneven weave or missing threads. There was no way this guy was wearing some glue-seamed piece of shit. As Detective Dennis hunched forward over the table to read from the file, the suit seemed to flow around him rather than bunching and wrinkling. When he moved back, it returned to its smooth and pristine state. It had been a while since Julianne had bothered with such things, but she would have wagered that between them, Detectives Dennis and Palmer were strutting about in eight or nine grand's worth of tailoring. If not for the imposing mirror filling that far wall, the impression created would have been that of two senior executives at the boardroom table of a wealthy mining company. Downing had been right. Everything about the Bagot Road police station suggested an almost limitless source of funds.

"Thank you for those details, Detective," Shah said. "It helps to have some information."

"Sure," Dennis replied, favoring both Downing and Shah with a sympathetic smile. "It does. And you know, if there was anything, even the smallest thing, that came to mind about why anybody would want to hurt Mr. Ross and you, Mr. Shah, that'd be very useful information for us to have."

The Australian sounded so reasonable, so friendly and eager to help out, that it was a moment before Jules realized that he and Palmer were running a good cop–bad cop routine. She almost blinked in disbelief. One, that they would even try, and two, that she hadn't spotted it as soon as the amiable Detective Dennis had wandered in sporting such a disarming expression on his handsome face.

Downing returned the smile as though he were a kindly and benevolent uncle.

"I am sure my client will give the matter due consideration," he said. "Of course, it defies belief that two men with a common history—friends, indeed—should be targeted in such a fashion in what for them, remember, remains a foreign city, even if they have chosen to make it their new home. I assure you, Detectives, that if Mr. Shah is able to make such a connection, you will find out about it. But as you would appreciate, he works in an industry which, while crucial to maintaining the security and even the good governance of the city and the territory, is nonetheless plagued by any number of unscrupulous operators, many of whom would not hesitate to step well beyond the boundaries of decency and law to achieve an advantage for themselves."

Jules wrote down on the notepad: "Shah targeted by rivals??" She circled the question three times. She didn't believe for a second that that was the case, but the Nepali himself had folded his massive arms and nodded once, grunting in approval. When she'd sought him out after arriving in Darwin, Shah's assumption about the bombing was that rival security operators, most likely one of the big mercenary companies such as Sandline, had lost patience with his refusal to accept their buyout offers. But she knew he didn't think that now. He agreed with her that the most likely attacker was Henry Cesky. The construction magnate had means, motive, and form.

"Have you received any threats?" Palmer asked. "From business rivals, I mean." He seemed highly skeptical.

"These are not people who are foolish enough to make threats," Shah replied, before his legal mouthpiece could answer. "They decide. They act."

Neither of the detectives was comfortable with the idea of a turf war breaking out between rival military companies in their city. For one thing, the police would be completely overmatched in any such scenario. Shah Security was relatively small, but some of the bigger operators, which provided border control and interdiction services, ran to some serious heavy metal in their inventories. Helicopter gunships, light armored vehicles, even jet fighters operating out of private airfields in Papua New Guinea and on a couple of islands throughout the Indonesian archipelago, where they usually protected giant mining operations. The mercs weren't allowed to deploy anything like that here. And even if they were, they would have been completely outclassed by the huge military presence in and around Darwin.

Nevertheless, the large PMCs still had thousands of personnel stationed throughout the city and the Northern Territory, almost all of them ex-military with combat experience. Their declared role in Australia was to provide "aid to the civil power," a conveniently ambiguous mission statement. Those duties encompassed everything from running the giant government farms down on the Ord River—prison farms, really, for hundreds of thousands of refugees from countries such as Vietnam and the Philippines but not, curiously enough, the United States—to antipiracy patrols and even search-and-destroy missions throughout the remnants of the Indonesian state. The long chain of thousands of Indonesian islands fanning out north and northwest of Australia had fallen into anarchy and an impossible confusion of internecine revolt.

Shah's lawyer lazily tapped at a sheaf of notepaper with an expensive-looking fountain pen. Jules was almost certain it was a Montblanc. "So perhaps," he said, "you officers might consider focusing your initial investigative efforts on some of the PMCs that have made it quite clear to my client that they seek a hostile takeover of his operation should he not be disposed to entertaining thoughts of a more amenable arrangement."

"Amenable to Sandline and Blackwater," Shah added.

It was difficult to tell whether Palmer was uncomfortable, disgusted, or utterly pissed off. Jules put her money on all three.

"You stated before that you had no idea who might be involved in this," he said through gritted teeth. "And I don't see how the attack at the marina fits into this bullshit idea that one of the merc operators is responsible. What the fuck would they get out of blowing up an old drunk on a boat?"

Jules bristled at the insult to her friend but managed to control her reaction with a breathing exercise. Shah was not the only one who could swallow his rage.

"Nothing," the former Gurkha replied with a shrug. "This is why I do not speculate for you, Detective. Until the attack on Mr. Ross, I had my reasons for believing that my rivals may have made the attempt on my family. I even believed the bombing at my house was bungled as a warning—that shoddy operators were used, and possibly even sacrificed, simply to send a message. You cannot deny there is much maneuvering and ill feeling in my industry at the moment. There has been blood, and there will be more. So it is natural for me to suspect a rival in my own case. For Mr. Ross, however, I have no explanation. That is why I do not answer your question, Detective Palmer. I truly have no idea."

It seemed that everyone in the room was acting out a role of some sort. Jules knew Shah was lying but not why. Although Cesky may have been able to hire men to do his bidding all the way down here, she didn't imagine he had any real influence in this city. His power base was in Seattle. There may have been a huge American presence in Darwin because of the local expatriate population and the recent porting of the Combined Fleet, but American power was not what it used to be. She'd been here only a day, but already she could tell that Darwin was one of those cities fated by history to be a place in which rising empires and falling giants contended for dominance. Cesky might operate here, from a distance, but he was not important to the city or the powers that had gathered here. There would be a good reason, Jules was sure, that Shah and his lawyer hadn't thrown his name on the table during this interview.

"Well, I think that probably concludes our business, Detectives," Downing announced, calmly returning the lid to his expensive pen. "And really, I can't reiterate it enough: my client has an obvious personal interest in seeing this matter resolved. But this is not the way to go about it. This is merely wasting everybody's time. We are more than happy to make ourselves available for interviews whenever necessary, for good reason. But next time, perhaps a phone call might suffice. Now, if that's all?"

Detective Dennis began shaking hands and saying farewells before Palmer could further poison the atmosphere.

"Mr. Downing . . . Mr. Shah . . . and Ms. . . . ?"

"Julianne," she answered with what she hoped was a pleasant, distracting smile. "Jules, if you like."

"Jules, then," Dennis said before turning back to the other two. "I'm sorry if this is all a bit difficult, gentlemen. But it's important we chase down every possibility. I'm sure you understand."

"Of course," Downing gushed. "But do feel free to simply call next time."

Palmer grunted something and excused himself from the room as Mr. Shah and his legal team prepared to leave.

"You're English," said Dennis while Jules was gathering up her notes. "Been in town very long?"

"No." She shook her head.

"Julianne is our newest associate," Downing interjected in something of a rush. "She's very new in town."

"Oh, okay, then. Maybe I'll see you around again, Jules."

Was he trying to pick her up? Jules retreated into character.

"Well, I'm just filling in on this case. Short-handed at the office, you know." She threw her supposed boss a look that cried, *Help me!*

"Shorthanded indeed," Downing agreed. "But I'm afraid it's back to conveyancing and land titles for you, young lady, when you've typed up these notes. This job can't all be about bloody murder and intrigue now, can it, eh?"

"We live in hope," said Jules.

29

She set her alarm to wake her after two sleep cycles. Three hours. It wasn't ideal, going into the first day of an infiltration already fatigued after a two-day crunch of briefings, presentations, liaising, and general immersion in all things Blackstone.

"Life is pain, Princess. Suck it up," she groaned after forcing herself out of bed as the clock radio came on.

The room's previous occupant had tuned the radio to the Armed Forces Heartland Network, on which a newsreader was now ticking off the overnight items. The U.S. Navy was continuing to scale back its antipiracy patrols along the East Coast. A severe blizzard that had shut down the West Coast was heading inland and was expected to be over Kansas City by nightfall, a point that left Caitlin feeling satisfied with her decision to fly out that morning. Local police were still appealing for witnesses to a hit-and-run accident near the River Market. And tickets for three Avril Lavigne concerts at Kemper Arena in February next year had sold out yesterday within an hour of being made available online.

Caitlin changed into her clothes for the day: jeans, a red Kansas City Chiefs sweatshirt she'd bought from the gift shop in the hotel lobby, and a leather jacket. There would be time enough to get into uniform as Colonel Katherine Murdoch once she arrived in Fort Hood. She inhaled an oatmeal cookie and an apple for breakfast, brushed her teeth, and tossed the toiletries bag into her suitcase. She was done with Kansas City. All the files and briefing notes she had reviewed were sitting in the room's safe. She always packed her bags the night before departure, and so she had nothing to do now besides organizing a ride to the airport and confirming the handover of the room to the security detachment. She was just reaching for the phone when it rang.

"Colonel Murdoch? This is Special Agent Dan Colvin. We met briefly yesterday afternoon, you might recall. There's something I need to discuss with you if it's not too inconvenient."

Caitlin was still groggy and not ready to face anything more challenging than a cup of shitty hotel coffee. The voice on the other end of the line sounded oddly upbeat and cheerful. It was a little too early in the morning to be dealing with . . . well, with morning people.

She remembered this Colvin guy, though. He was with the FBI's field office here in Kansas City, handling interagency liaison. He'd been one of her first contact points when she arrived as the emissary of Chief of Staff Culver. He had taken her to a couple of agencies and briefings. Built like a runner, with a face chiseled out of hard, unforgiving brown basalt, Special Agent Colvin was the type of man who left an impression.

"Hang on, would you, Agent?"

Caitlin tossed the phone on the bed without giving him a chance to reply. She went through to the bathroom, splashed water on her face, and toweled off, which woke her up some. She took three seconds to force herself into the role of Colonel Katherine Murdoch. It was the mental equivalent of pulling on somebody else's skin.

"Sorry," she said upon returning to the line. "I didn't get much sleep last night. Is there something I can help you with?"

"I doubt it, ma'am, but there may be something I can help you with.

I have a file note, a request from Mr. Culver in fact, to contact you in case of developments in a couple of our investigations. It concerns one of our mandate settlers, a Mr. Miguel Pieraro."

"Er, yeah . . . I know of him," she replied. "I was just reviewing his file last night. What's up?"

"I'm afraid Mr. Pieraro has been killed. A hit-and-run incident three days ago."

That woke her up, stunning her into consciousness more effectively than the ice-cold water she'd splashed on her face. Caitlin noticed that Colvin didn't say "accident." She looked at her bags, which were packed and standing by the door, ready to go. "I'm sorry to hear that, Agent Colvin," she told him, sincere even through the fogginess still clouding her head. She had really felt for the man who had lost everything save for one daughter. She felt these things more deeply now, having her own child, no matter how hard she tried to shut down her feelings when she was out in the field. "That guy deserved a break. But I'm a little pressed for time here, unfortunately. Is there some reason you contacted me beyond professional courtesy?"

It was a rather discourteous thing to ask, but there had to be some reason Colvin had called. And she really was pressed for time.

"Maybe," he said. "The traffic cops called in their colleagues from homicide pretty quickly on this one. And homicide called us when they saw that Pieraro's name was flagged with a link to the federal databases. I figured Mr. Culver would want you to know."

Caitlin could hear the curiosity in back of Colvin's words. Why would the White House chief of staff want a military adviser from his office to know about this sort of stuff? She was glad he didn't press the matter.

She sat down on the bed, accepting the delay. "Homicide?"

"Yeah," said the FBI man. "All of the evidence adds up to Pieraro and the woman he was with, a Maive Aronson, being deliberately run down."

"I see . . ." Her mind was racing ahead now. Was this important enough to delay her departure? "Agent Colvin, I'm very grateful that you called me, and I apologize if I seemed a little brusque. I was just heading out the door for the airport."

"Ah, that's cool," he replied. He seemed to have decided to dispense with interagency formalities, after all. "Look, if you'd like, I could swing by and pick you up. Our office is just a couple of minutes away from the old Harrah's, and you'd be welcome to go through the evidence they've put together so far. If you think you need to brief Mr. Culver on it."

Again, he spoke with a slightly rising inflection as his professional curiosity kicked in.

Caitlin frowned, unsure which way to jump. Culver had made it clear that he was interested in anything to do with Blackstone's complicity in the attacks on those homesteaders down in the mandate. But he'd also stated that anything besides tying Blackstone to Ahmet Ozal was of secondary importance.

"I suppose it couldn't hurt," she said, opting to cover both bases. "Mr. Culver is *very* interested in the security situation down in the mandate. As you'd know. I can't say if this plays into that in any way, but if he wanted you to reach out to me, I guess I need to take a look at what you have. I'll be down in the foyer in a minute or two."

"Oh, that's fine. I'm on my way out the door now. See you in five."

He broke the connection. Caitlin forced herself to make one last check of the room before putting a call in to the security detail to let them know she was leaving. Two uniformed protective service officers appeared at her door less than a minute later. Their ready room was just down the hallway. She handed over her pass and confirmed the presence of the files in the safe before she left.

The same two air force men—officers, as it turned out—she'd seen in the gym the previous night were waiting at the elevator when she arrived.

"Think we'll get to fly this month?" one asked the other.

His friend shook his head. "Nope. Shot our wad over New York. I reckon that was the last flight of the Buffs for a while."

Caitlin took the information in without comment as they all stepped into the elevator. Probably pilots from Whiteman on a pass. She turned up the frost on her stone face to its most glacial. The ride down to the lobby was excruciating.

"Dyke," one of them muttered as she strode out through the sliding doors.

Almost certainly the guy who had tried to catch her attention over by the treadmills. An egomaniacal man-child. It was a pity she had no compelling reason to engage them in character as Colonel Murdoch. Could have been useful practice, tearing this jerk a new one.

She turned into the marble lobby. At least it looked like marble; it could just as well have been some sort of veneer; she wasn't sure. The whole place had been completely refitted during reclamation. As she wheeled her luggage over to the counter, Caitlin passed a dark spot scoured onto the otherwise smooth, creamy surface. She wondered if she'd just passed over the final resting place of one of the Disappeared. Screens above the desk ran news feeds, the local weather radar, and flight information for Charles B. Wheeler Downtown Airport. She considered buying a trinket from the gift shop to take home to Monique before thinking better of it.

Best to cut that shit off now, sister.

She dropped her key card off at the desk and made her way over to the entrance to wait for Dan Colvin. She wasn't sure what, if any, meaning she should look for in the killing of the homesteader. There was no obvious connection to her primary interest, namely, Baumer, Ozal, and the undeclared salvage contract the latter's company, Hazm Unternehmen, had obtained down in Texas. And it wasn't as though settlers didn't have it tough on the frontier, anyway. There were more than enough real pirates and banditos out there.

Just as she was shaking her head at the muddy, opaque nature of it all, she recognized Special Agent Colvin coming toward her through the revolving doors. A black GSA 2002 Chevy Suburban sat idling outside for them.

"Colonel Murdoch," he said, offering her a smile. Dressed in jeans and an anonymous sports coat, he looked like any other government contractor. Apparently there was not much call for the suit-and-tie look of the Hoover era these days.

"Thanks for the lift," she said.

"De nada." He took her suitcase without preamble and wheeled it out toward the car. "Where are you flying off to?"

"Just the next stop on my never-ending End of the World Tour," Caitlin replied.

If Special Agent Colvin was sufficiently alert to have noticed that she hadn't answered him, he was also good-mannered enough to make nothing of it. He took care when hoisting her luggage into the back of the Suburban. Although there was nothing breakable in there, Caitlin appreciated the thought. She couldn't help noticing a number of foreign-language books piled up in a plastic bin in the trunk, among them *The Complete Idiot's Guide to French* and a similar Spanish title. A third book looked like a text from the now defunct Defense Language Institute.

She indicated the collection with a tilt of her head. "How many languages do you speak?"

He didn't seem the type to puff up his chest and brag about himself. "Oh, three if you count Arabic. How about you?"

"None," she lied. "I have a hard enough time with English."

She picked up a manila folder from the passenger seat, Miguel Pieraro's name handwritten on its cover in thick black ink. "Do you mind?" she asked as they strapped themselves in.

"Sure, knock yourself out, ma'am."

He put the Suburban into gear before navigating his way around the potholes, following a route that took them east toward the Chouteau Trafficway. There was no light to wait for at any of the intersections. He simply stopped long enough to avoid a pair of Hummers leaving the militia substation at the Chouteau Bridge before proceeding north to the ramp for Highway 210.

Traffic was pretty thin on 210, with a few people on horseback as they turned westbound. On her right the Cerner Campus was a hub of activity, with soldiers running their morning PT and vehicles moving out into the city. Towering over the campus, a short way from the road, was the rechristened North Kansas City Federal Medical Center. An army Black Hawk emblazoned with the Red Cross logo lifted off from a helipad beyond her line of sight to travel to points unknown.

As they moved closer to North Kansas City proper, the already light vehicular traffic began to thin out further. KC didn't really have a peak hour anymore. Most people seemed to get about by bus, the service for which was regular enough that there were always one or two commuter shuttles in view. The remainder of the traffic consisted of government and military vehicles and a hefty spread of civilian ones featuring the logo of Cesky Enterprises, the biggest reconstruction contractor in town.

"Now, what you've got there," said Colvin, nodding toward the folder in her hands, "is basically everything the accident investigators and homicide guys have so far."

"This Aronson woman," she asked, turning over a page, "what shape is she in?"

"She's seen better days, poor woman. She's in a coma up at the hospital. Doctors can't say yet whether she'll come out of it. So she's not going to be much help."

Caitlin grunted, already distracted by the details in the file. The accident investigation squad had concluded very quickly that the hit-and-run was no accident. The assailant's vehicle, a blue Toyota pickup, had accelerated quickly from a standing start, driven in an almost perfectly straight line, until a few meters out from where it had struck the victims; at that point, it had swerved to line them up with the center of its bull bars. Pieraro had been struck first, and his body had flown into Aronson, protecting her from the worst of the impact. The Toyota had stopped in a controlled fashion a little farther down the road, the report went on. There it picked up a passenger, a large male, judging by the boot prints he'd left preserved in the snow. The investigators had been able to track the vehicle for a short distance because of the same snowfall that had provided them with such a rich haul of evidence at the site of the incident.

Caitlin looked up to collect her thoughts as they passed by an old burned-out McDonald's on the right-hand side of the road. The familiar feel of suburban sprawl with a slight edge of the End Times. She couldn't help thinking, given his effectiveness when steering his charges to safety amid the road-agent gangs of Texas, that Miguel Pieraro somehow would have sensed a vehicle approaching in this environment.

"I seem to recall hearing that Thursday was blown out by a blizzard," she said eventually.

"It was, later on," Colvin explained. "But we got lucky with the weather. There was a light fall on Thursday morning. And then an hour-and-a-half hiatus during which the temperature really fell away but before the big dump came on. One of the first people onto the scene was a city road worker. He'd cleaned up after a few accidents in the past and knew to preserve the scene at this one. Accident investigators got there inside of ten minutes when he called it in. Sometimes the stars align."

"Not for Pieraro."

"No," Colvin said quietly. "I suppose not."

"Any sign of the vehicle?"

"Yeah, you'll find something about three-quarters of the way through." He waved a hand, indicating the file again. "Doused with gasoline and burned down to its axles about thirty miles outside of town."

"Oh, that's not suspicious."

"Nope. Happens all the time."

She fell silent again, hurrying to absorb all the information before they reached her destination. She was hoping for something about the identity of the driver and the man—they were all assuming it was a man—who had gotten into the vehicle farther down the road. The Chevrolet passed under I-35 as Highway 210 transformed itself into a four-lane thoroughfare. Not too far down the highway, she could make out a nine-story red-brick building. It dominated the local landscape. The perfect place for a sniper if you had good intel ahead of time . . . *A spotter, maybe?*

"How's cell phone coverage in KC, Colvin?" she asked suddenly. "Like, for normal folk."

He shook his close-cropped, rather boxy head as the tall brick building swept by. "If you don't have access to the federal network, you're pretty much fucked. Capacity is very limited. But having said that, demand is low. Most people do hard physical work from sunup to sundown, usually on the government dollar. Sitting on your butt all day, surfing around on the Net, or calling a friend to meet up for coffee at Starbucks just isn't that common anymore. Why d' you ask?"

Caitlin held up a couple of crime-scene photographs. "Somebody's probably thought of this already," she offered up front, "but the second man looks like a spotter to me. You know, like a second pair of eyes for a sniper. Or a forward air controller."

"I do," Colvin said, glancing over. "What makes you think that?"

"The angles. If I had time, I'd drive over there and take a look for myself, but from these photographs it seems to me like the guy on the street had a good angle to watch Pieraro and Aronson as they approached. The driver of the vehicle didn't. But the tire marks, the almost perfect timing, even the way he veered just a little bit at the end to line them up with his hood ornament—it all looks like somebody was *guiding* him in. Like a forward air controller will talk close air support in on top of a target. You pull the cell phone records for that area at that time and you'll probably get the call. Especially if you check for sat phones. Might've been made on a burner, of course. Did they find any melted cell phone components inside the burned-out wreck?"

The FBI man shook his head uncertainly. "I'm not sure I have to confess, I'm not fully up to speed on this one. I just picked this up because it was flagged as being of interest to Jed Culver's office. But if there's no note there about cell phones, I'm sure I could get the local guys to look into it. Or I could probably pull the logs myself if you want. Is there some way I can contact you when you leave KC?"

She could see that Colvin was intrigued. She had to admire the guy. He was an investigator; it must have been driving him batshit. Particularly why she'd been interested in the homesteader *before* he was killed. You had your mysteries, wrapped in your enigmas, dropped into a bottomless black hole, and he wasn't allowed even to strike a match and chuck it in there. She could imagine the bumper crop of rumors that would spring up after she'd left. Probably all swirling around the possibility of an armed federal intervention down in the mandate.

"Thank you, Agent Colvin," she said as graciously as she could manage on three hours' sleep. "I'm in transit for the next few days, but I'll have Mr. Culver's office get in contact with you. They can handle anything you turn up about those phone logs. I really do appreciate your help on this."

"I'm a people person." He gave a shrug, accompanying the movement with a goofy grin. "I live to help out."

She closed the file and reached around to drop it on the backseat. There wasn't much else in there for her, but what she'd seen was worthy of note. Caitlin turned to gaze out the window once more, looking for some perspective.

Northtown was a faithful copy of Norman Rockwell's small-town America. The road had compressed down to two lanes here, with angled parking spots on both sides, most of which were empty of any vehicles. Wrought-iron benches that no one had time to sit in anymore poked through the snow every block or so. One shopfront featured a marquee advertising the latest Bond film, with the new guy.

Clusters of early-morning commuters trudged down the sidewalks toward a bus station in front of an old drugstore with their hard hats and safety vests in hand. Probably on their way to scoop up the Disappeared. Bundled up against the cold as they were, Caitlin noticed that most of them were white, with a sprinkling of African Americans and Hispanics thrown in. No sign of the many Indians she knew to be resident here. Kansas City was dividing itself into camps, or ghettos.

After they'd turned onto Burlington, Colvin accelerated southbound. "Got more twists and turns than a pretzel factory out here," he said. "At least you don't have to go out to the international airport. In this weather, we'd be looking at an hour-long drive."

Caitlin nodded, still lost in her thoughts. A pair of F-16s with wing tanks howled into the air on the other side of the railway tracks, en route to patrol the southern approaches to Kansas City.

She was certain that Pieraro's death had no connection to Ozal and through him to Baumer, so in that sense she had no dog in this fight. But she'd agreed to take on the job in Texas because there was at least a prima facie case linking Ozal—however indirectly—to Blackstone. And for Caitlin, that was motivation enough to maintain a watching brief on the matter of Miguel Pieraro. It was a loose thread that was worth pulling.

After the long series of twisting streets and hairpin bends through a part of Northtown that Colvin called Harlem, they arrived at Charles B. Wheeler Downtown Airport. Such as it was. The main terminal building dated back to the 1930s and resembled a cross between a Quonset hut and a postmodern ecohome. A trio of C-130s sat on the flight line near the brown-brick building of the former TWA headquarters. Someone had told her on the ride into Harrah's that Howard Hughes's ghost haunted the place. As far as Caitlin was concerned, this whole country was haunted. The sooner she got on the plane and got this done, the better.

The flight was a regular military shuttle, but there were no other passengers. Still, she didn't like to keep people waiting. When Colvin pulled into the drop-off zone, the Echelon agent turned down his offer to wait with her, but in as polite and friendly a manner as possible.

"I'll chase those phone logs up for you," he said over his shoulder while extracting her suitcase from its place beside his container full of books.

"If you could, that would be great," she replied. "Mr. Pieraro had a daughter. She will want to see somebody punished for this."

Colonel Katherine Murdoch waved good-bye and walked into the departure lounge.

30

Julianne changed motel rooms after the interview at the police station, a precaution and an easy one. She was traveling light. She arrived outside Shah's house in the Palms as the sun was dropping low over a wide bay in which a few dozen sailboats and larger yachts lay at anchor. The burned orange light of sunset had already colored the green waters to a sparkling copper sheet.

Looking up from the street at the modern pole-and-beam home, Jules couldn't help thinking that a spectacular view awaited her on the open-plan area that defined the upper story, where a few people were enjoying drinks and chatting in small groups. She'd been expecting a quiet family dinner with perhaps Birendra or even Downing in attendance, but it seemed that a cocktail party was under way.

She guessed that the interior of the house opened up onto a vast shaded platform with clear views across an undeveloped strip of coastal scrub. From down here at street level, however, she couldn't tell where the inside became the outside. But there was no mistaking the scar left behind on the footpath by the attempted bombing. A patch of grass roughly six or seven feet across had been charred down to burned red earth on the verge in front of the postbox. Or what had been the postbox. The blast had torn huge chunks out of the sandstone plinth that had served as one.

The killing heat of the afternoon no longer hammered down out of a hot gray sky. But stepping out of her air-conditioned taxi onto the dark scab of scorched earth where Shah's would-be assailants had fumbled their package and destroyed themselves, Jules still felt the crush of hot, moist tropical air. Her light silk shirt, the one she had borrowed from Ashmi, was sticking to her back by the time she'd walked up the driveway to the front door. Shrapnel from the explosion, stone chips, and small pieces of metal still pitted the dark wooden double doors. She was reaching for an antique iron knocker when the door opened and Shah greeted her, smiling effusively.

"Come in, come in, Miss Julianne. The others are already here, having a drink upstairs. It is not a very large gathering, just some friends, people we can trust. And there's somebody I want you to meet. He may be able to help."

Unsettled for a moment—she hadn't expected to have to socialize—Jules apologized for not bringing anything with her. "Oh, Shah, if you'd said something, I would've picked up some wine."

The host dismissed her concerns. "Pah! I shall not have you placing me further in your debt, Miss Julianne, when I already owe you so much," he said. "Come through, please. As I recall from our time on the golfer's boat, you were always fond of bubble drink, and I have some very good French champagnes in my cellar downstairs. I always wanted a cellar, and now I have one. Let me send one of the girls down to fetch you something. Do I remember correctly that Pol Roger was your favorite? . . . Ah, here is my wife, Pasang. Please, say hello."

She had been about to say that only French bubbles could be called champagne and that yes, she shared a love of Pol Roger with Winston Churchill. But before she could throw the switch to small talk, a diminutive Nepalese woman exquisitely dressed in European clothes—

French, too, if Jules's eye for fashion did not mislead her—appeared at Shah's elbow bearing champagne flutes.

"Miss Julianne Balwyn," she said with the tone of someone reading from a script. "Please excuse my English. Unlike husband, I am not longed with speaking it. But I practice and learn every day so that once I may thank you for taking him home to me and our daughters. And for the . . . the honoring of arrangements you make. You always in a special place for our family's heart."

Pasang passed her a drink and performed a small bow. Jules found herself strangely touched, which wasn't like her at all. Shah had already thanked her for sticking to their original deal, as difficult as that had been after the *Aussie Rules* was impounded. She'd known that he and the other Gurkhas still had a long and dangerous, perhaps even impossible, trek in front of them to make it home to Nepal. After everything that had happened, making sure they got paid as agreed just seemed the decent thing to do.

So no, not at all like her.

"Thank you," she replied, faltering briefly over the woman's name, ". . . Pasang."

"Thank you, thank you. You are the Deliverer, Miss Julianne." The Nepali's pretty, jewel-like eyes sparkled with delight.

Shah gave his wife a peck on the cheek before taking Jules gently by the elbow and steering her into a large reception room, with Pasang following closely behind. Dark slate tiles had soaked up the chill from a silent, invisible air-conditioning system. After the uncomfortable humidity of the street, it was blissful to walk into a space that seemed to breathe a gentle, almost wintry gift of frost onto her exposed, sunburned skin. She sipped her champagne, struggling with the urge to throw down the whole glass in one go.

The antechamber was quite beautiful. A few pieces of modern art hung on the white walls, offsetting a couple of artifacts that obviously had traveled all the way from their home village in Nepal. Julianne had to admire the restrained taste. She never would have thought it of someone like Shah, a rough-handed soldier and a former noncom, not even an officer.

But with that unworthy thought came immediate embarrassment.

Who was she to be judging others on their aesthetics? She had spent the last five or six years mostly unwashed and dressed in stinking rags. First as a smuggler with Pete and Fifi, then as a pirate, a glorified looter in New York, and of late as a fugitive, scurrying from one bolt-hole to the next. Shah was a fine man. Someone who had taken whatever talents he had been given and done his best with them to secure a good life for his family and, from what Jules could see at the compound, for anyone who worked for him.

"This is a lovely home, Pasang," she said quietly. "Sha . . . um, Narayan tells me you built it yourself."

Pasang took Jules by the arm and patted her like a child.

"No, no. We did not build this. We paid the men to build it. You are hungry? I have made food."

"That would be lovely," Jules answered.

A brief whispered conversation followed between the former Gurkha and his wife as the three of them passed out of the greeting hall and into what looked like an open lounge or family room. They proceeded up a brushed-glass staircase that took them through another entrance guarded by heavy mahogany doors and into the small crowd that had gathered out on the . . . gallery? The balcony? It was hard to say. White cotton drapery hung from the ceiling, swaying in a warm breeze and seeming to define a point at which the room flowed outside.

"I must see to the guests," said Pasang. "And to something to eat for you."

With that, she disappeared into the crowd, halting briefly to say hello to some of the people she passed.

Jules saw Birendra and thought she recognized one of the men he was talking to. It looked like Thapa, who also had been with them on the massive superyacht. Birendra waved when he saw her, and the other man turned around. It was indeed Thapa. Shah had brought another of her old crewmates with him to Darwin. It gave Jules pause. She had lost so many friends over the last few years. Fifi had had quite a crush on Thapa.

"Over here is the man I wish you to meet, Miss Julianne," said Shah.

He guided her toward the buffet table. There she spotted Piers Downing picking at a pile of sticky blackened chicken wings and talking to a thickset middle-aged man with iron-gray hair and the build of a rugby pro whose championship days were behind him but not too far behind.

"Ah, my junior has arrived," Downing quipped.

The lawyer was looking much less buttoned down than before, having discarded his suit for a pair of cream-colored moleskin pants and a white cotton shirt that was more poolside bar than Old Bailey. More guests arrived as Shah introduced her to Downing's companion.

"Miss Julianne, this is Mr. Pappas."

"Nick Pappas," the man added as he held out his hand.

Jules returned his strong grip. Years of boat work and more recently of hauling herself and bags of loot and weapons through some of the worst places in the world had given her a stronger grip than many men. Nick Pappas, however, was possessed of giant bear paws, one of which probably could enfold both of her hands and crush them to bone splinters. She could feel a lot of restrained power idling at low throttle within his massive frame, but Pappas appeared to be one of those big men who had spent his life learning to be gentle.

"Nick knows about our complications," said Shah. "In the past he has helped me out with similar problems. Business problems, not personal. But similar."

Julianne thought she understood what he meant. She wondered about the people standing around out there, talking amiably, laughing and drinking Shah's excellent wine and grazing on the food his wife and maybe his daughters had prepared. Were they all somehow connected to his business?

"So how do you two know each other, if that's not a little awkward?" she asked.

Both men grinned. "Timor," they answered in unison before Shah deferred to the Australian.

"I was in the army in those days," Pappas began.

"SAS," Shah prompted.

Pappas gave him a look that said he was quite capable of doing his own bragging to the pretty girl, thank you very much. He continued. "We ran into each other outside a militia shithole called Los Palos. Gurkhas had long-range patrols encircling the place, as did we. The

Indonesian battalion based there was raised locally. Timorese traitors. Not a good look for them once the Indonesians pulled out. Or for the pro-Jakarta gangs that were always hanging around like scabby dogs. We had the devil's own job stopping them from killing every peasant within twenty miles. Still"—He dropped one meaty hand on the shoulder of his old comrade—"we did good. I looked up my little mate here as soon as I knew he was in Darwin. He tried to offer me a job, the cheeky bugger!"

The two ex-soldiers shared some private joke at that.

"So you're a security contractor, too, Nick?" Jules asked.

"No, not really. I do risk management now. A lot of assessment for the mining companies, the big migration agents, some work for the government along with some risk mitigation. Removing the sources of risk," he added, pausing to let her understand the import of the euphemism. "From what I hear, you could do with some help."

Guests continued to arrive through the heavy wooden doors. A pleasant draft of chilled air wafted over her every time a newcomer entered the Shah family's huge entertainment space. Jules estimated that maybe twenty-five or thirty people were there now, half of them locals, judging by their accents, and most of the others neighborhood people or possibly business contacts. Shah had told her that the majority of his neighbors were Chinese and Javanese exiles, and she'd already spotted more than a few of them in attendance. The Javanese made her uneasy. She had never been back to Indonesia after a crooked general had run them off a few months before the Wave.

"It's quite noisy up here," said Downing, who had been hovering at the edge of the conversation without saying anything. "Perhaps you could show us this wine cellar you're so proud of, old boy. I'd be very interested to see it. I've had some diabolical difficulties convincing the local yokels that serving pinot noir at room temperature doesn't mean serving it up like a goblet of hot blood."

"But of course," Shah replied. "You must come also, Nick. Perhaps we can teach you to drink something more than beer now that you are a sophisticated businessman who no longer sleeps in his boots."

"Doubt it," he scoffed. "But do your worst."

As instructed by their host, Jules abandoned her champagne flute at the buffet table, which was so heavily laden with food that she had trouble finding a spot for the glass. She was hungry, starving actually, and grabbed a couple of little fish cakes before their small group made to leave. They tasted beautiful, still warm and springy and spiced in a way she'd never come across before. Jules didn't imagine that fish cakes featured heavily in the national cuisine of mountainous Nepal, but perhaps Pasang Shah had picked up the recipe while they'd been stationed somewhere such as Singapore.

Their home was decorated throughout with objets d'art, photographs, and mementos from all over the world. Shah seemed to have traveled even more extensively than she had, although the Englishwoman was sure that if she asked, she'd find that every piece told the story of a posting with the Royal Gurkha Regiment. Even the construction of the house looked like it had been undertaken as an exercise in storing memories within architecture. They passed an internal garden she recognized as a common feature of many Arabic dwellings, and the formal dining space reminded her of tribal long rooms she had seen in Borneo. Nothing so gauche as crossed spears or shields hung from the walls here. It appeared to Julianne that the Shahs had spent a lot of time discussing the significant moments of their shared life with a very expensive architect. A life that had been spent in the service of a regiment that had dispatched them from one end of the world to the other.

Julianne had grown up around money or, in her family's case, the memory and the carefully contrived appearance of money, and she recognized the real thing when she rubbed up against it. Shah had done very well for himself. She was happy for him.

The wine cellar was indeed a cellar rather than merely a temperature- and atmosphere-controlled room crammed into a downstairs or underground living area as an afterthought. The four of them—Jules, the two old army pals, and Shah's lawyer, the displaced pantomime Englishman—proceeded in single file down a narrow staircase that doglegged back on itself before reaching a heavy steel door. This Shah opened by tapping a code into a wall-mounted keypad.

"You must have some exceptionally good wine stored down here, my friend," Downing said.

"I do," Shah replied. "To be truthful, I do not care for it myself. But then, I am the only man in the house, and I'm sure Miss Julianne will tell you that the ladies do enjoy a nice glass of wine."

"In a climate like this," Jules chimed in, "I can imagine I'd have a glass permanently in hand. Need to drink it fast, though. It would lose its chill very quickly."

Hidden bolts clunked somewhere inside the heavy steel door before it whispered open at a touch. Soft lighting flickered on inside the cellar, dimly at first, before warming and brightening. As they trooped in, she saw immediately that Shah had built not just a wine cellar but a safe room. Climate-controlled refrigeration units lined both main walls, with red wines marching away to the left and white wines to the right. In the center of the room, a solid steel counter presented a formidable barrier to any intruders trying to rush into this subterranean haven, just as it offered excellent cover for people who might be sheltering here. Especially if those people armed themselves from the gun rack positioned against the rear wall. Julianne was impressed.

"Nice setup," Pappas agreed.

"A panic room?" Downing asked. "With a well-stocked bar. Commendable combination."

"I prefer to think of it as a stronghold," Shah said. "It has secure and dedicated communication links, separate to the lines for the rest of the house. It is defended. Although, without prior warning, it would have been of no use last week in the bomb blast."

"So, down to business," said Pappas. "Do you have any beer down here?"

Shah chuckled and shuffled down to a door at the very end of the line of fridges that held his white wine collection. "I have Bintang," he called back. "From one of the last shipments out of Jakarta before the insurgents burned down the brewery. Savages. Mr. Downing, Miss Jules, would you prefer beer or something more feminine?"

The lawyer smirked. "I had been thinking of asking for a nice bottle of Sancerre, as I know Mrs. Shah is partial to a drop. But I feel I've been rather snookered now. So a Bintang it is. Ms. Balwyn?"

"I'd love a beer."

Shah brought out four small brown bottles and opened them on the massive slab atop the steel structure in the middle of the cellar space. It turned out the counter was not a solid chunk of metal, after all. He'd had storage and more refrigeration built into the far side. Possibly more weapons lockers, too, if Julianne knew him well.

"My apologies for all that up there," Shah said to her. "I had originally intended that we might host you to a small family dinner tonight. But after discussing the matter with Nick and Mr. Downing, we thought it better to hide in plain sight."

She wasn't sure she followed him. The confusion must have shown.

"The best place to hide a pebble is in a quarry," Shah explained. "These small parties are quite common among the exiled people here. For those who can afford them, anyway. I do not feel it myself, but many of those upstairs very much feel themselves to be in Darwin under sufferance. They worry that their sanctuary may be denied them on the whim of a politician in the south. The free-port status has brought great wealth to this country in a time when so much wealth has been destroyed. But of course it has brought a tide of people with it, many of them not the sort of people who would have easily gained entry to Australia in the past."

Jules took a long pull from her beer, appreciating the cold bite and the lack of fizz. She'd always rated Bintang as a great hot-weather beer, especially in humid climes.

"The boat people, the real boat people, you mean," she said. "The poor ones."

"Yes. Certainly not the Americans or displaced English folk like Mr. Downing here. They have always been welcome. But peasants and coolies arriving in hordes, not as much."

"Well, I hardly think that describes many of your guests upstairs. If they're refugees, they look like they flew here first-class hauling baggage trains of money behind them."

Nick Pappas stepped in at that point. "They did, Julianne."

"As did I," Shah conceded. "The business migration scheme which allowed me to come here with my family was very generous. It gets even more generous, depending on the amount of business you bring with you."

"Fascinating," said Jules. "But why is it relevant, Shah?"

"Oh, it's not, I suppose. Not immediately. But it is important that you understand where you are now, Miss Julianne, and how the city works. You and I have a problem not because of assassins and bomb makers, no matter how clumsy they are, but because of *power*. Henry Cesky is a long way from here, but he is a powerful man; thus he can reach out and touch us. His power insulates him from any attempt we might make to reach out in return. Even to accuse Cesky is fraught. He is a hero of the second American Revolution, a confidant of power because he is a prominent supporter of the president. You are a smuggler, a thief, a killer. I am a mercenary. Our word counts for nothing against his. And as you saw at the police station this afternoon, my position here, while not untenable, could be made precarious. By the application of power."

Downing hoisted himself up onto the brushed-metal surface of the counter. It seemed unusual, completely out of character for him, Jules thought. But he looked comfortable enough sitting up there sipping his beer. She had a sudden vision of him as an undergraduate student in cheap digs in London, propped up on the kitchen counter, talking and drinking into the wee hours.

"Mr. Shah is right, Julianne," the Englishman said, using her first name for a change. "You need to understand that we must be careful. Very careful. This isn't a problem that's amenable to being tackled in the same way you'd see off a bunch of pirates. That's why I suggested the little soiree upstairs. As Mr. Shah says, they're quite common among the émigré population. People like to gather together for support. And it makes it a little less remarkable that I should be here, or Mr. Pappas. We both have clients upstairs, and, of course, Nick is a friend of the family."

It was Pappas's turn to take up the chore of explanation. He'd already downed his beer and seemed perfectly relaxed, grabbing another one from the fridge at the back of the room, talking as he went.

"I'm happy to help out, Julianne. A place like Darwin, you have to look out for your mates. I still have a lot of contacts inside the Australian government, not just the army. It helps that I do a lot of work for them still. But because I do that work, like Shah, I have to tread lightly. If you're right and this Cesky prick has your names on a list, that's bad fucking news. I made a few quick calls today after Piers brought me in on this. I couldn't get much because of the time difference. Everyone was asleep in the U.S. But from what little I could gather today, Cesky has burrowed himself right in under the skin of the Kipper administration. I don't know how close he is to the president himself. But he's a big donor, a public defender of the government who'll take on all comers. And, of course, he put his own blokes on the street back in '03, when the Yanks had their little uprising and threw out that mad fucking general who tried to take over. Cesky's a thug, basically. But a very well connected thug."

The champagne and beer were going to Jules's head. She hadn't eaten since breakfast save for the couple of fish cakes she'd inhaled just now. It had been a bitch of a day after a shitty week back in Sydney. And she was worried about the Rhino.

"But you're not telling me anything I don't already know about this bastard," she said, speaking to all three. "I knew he was a thug as soon as I met him back in Acapulco. That's why we didn't let them on the boat. Jesus Christ, you remember that scene in the bar when we were looking for passengers, Shah, before Miguel beat him down . . . The guy wasn't even on board and he was already trying to take over! And hey, I know he's got connections. They've been trying to bloody kill me for months. And now they're after you." She tipped the neck of her beer bottle Shah's way before going on.

"What I still don't know is what we can do about it. Killing his hired help doesn't seem to discourage him. And I don't think we have the option of wandering into Seattle to deal with him directly. We are not at sea anymore, nor is this New York. So yeah, you're right, I can't just stick a shotgun up his ass and let him have a couple of barrels of change-your-fucking-mind-Princess. I mean, Jesus, if he's hanging around with government types, you'd probably get popped by the Secret Service for even looking sideways at him. They're a lot more trigger-happy than they used to be."

Shah and his lawyer looked to Pappas for an answer. The big Aussie folded his arms, creating the impression of a human bulwark of even greater mass and solidity than the steel bench around which they were gathered.

"First thing is, we need to lay our hands on the blokes they're using locally. Those two no-hopers they sent around to have a crack at you, Shah, are gone. But whoever went after your mate Rhino, Julianne, will still be hanging around. The guys'll have to go back at Rhino if he lives. But as long as he's on that American ship, he's probably fine. When they move him back on shore into a civilian facility, then they'll have another go. In the meantime, they've got two other options—assuming they picked up the contract on you and Shah. And even if they didn't, someone has."

He finished his beer and placed it down in front of him.

"Shah's got a couple of dozen heavily armed ruffians looking after him and his family. We lay down some defence in depth around him, and getting at him will be as difficult as you trying to walk into Cesky's office."

All three men were now looking at her.

"But you're a different matter, Julianne. As far as they know, you've only got two friends in this town, and they've already taken down one of them. If we can put a little distance between you and Shah, put you out on the range, so to speak, they will come after you. And as long as you refrain from blowing their heads off, we should be able to tackle one of these cheeky fuckers and have a quiet word. Then, if we can start to trace the connection back to Cesky, we'll be in a much better position to turn it back on him. But we're going to need to grab whoever he sends after you."

Jules cocked one eyebrow at him. "Presumably before he puts a bullet in the back of my neck."

Pappas smiled. "Well, yeah, that goes without saying."

31

TEMPLE, TEXAS, ADMINISTRATIVE DIVISION

"I'm sorry; I can't get you any closer to the Federal Center," said Cindy French. "But it's not too far up thataway."

They were both standing beside *Mary Lou,* underneath the chrome Aphrodite hood ornament, stamping their feet and moving around to maintain some body warmth. Cindy pointed down an avenue running east. Dawn was probably three-quarters of an hour away, but already the sky in that direction was noticeably lighter. In a few minutes, Sofia knew, she would be able to make out a band of pale pink behind the skyline of the dead city. It was still cold outside, but merely a notch or two above freezing as opposed to the Siberian misery they'd left behind to the north. The snow petered out altogether a few hours after they'd crossed the Texas–Oklahoma border, and the convoy finally split back in Waco, with the drivers saying their good-byes and wishing Sofia the best before peeling off toward their respective destinations.

"I have my street map," she said, patting the folded-up sheet of paper in her back pocket. "I won't get lost."

"You hurry straight on down there," Cindy told her, "and you'll be fine. You don't need to worry about bandits or lowlife of any kind in Temple. There's only a couple of hundred people living here, if that, and they're all feds. Army maintains a small force down here—the real army, by the way, not those TDF misanthropes. They keep the place well policed. Matter of fact, you'll probably run into one of their patrols on your way over to Main Street. Just tell them you're waiting for the shuttle bus to the Hood and that you're going over to see Father Michael at the chapel. Tell them you have family business but don't tarry over there any longer than you have to. And don't wander around on your own more than is absolutely necessary. Got it, hon?"

Sofia nodded and hoisted her small backpack to settle it more comfortably on one shoulder. "Thank you, Cindy," she said, smiling with real warmth.

The trucker reached out and hugged her. Sofia allowed herself to relax into the hug, returning it in kind. She knew she wouldn't have made it this far without the help of this kindly woman. It was a shame she'd had to mislead her the whole way, but having done so made it easier to soften their passing with one last lie.

"I shall write to you in Seattle when I have my sister back home," she said.

And then, not wanting to prolong the farewell any further, she thanked her again before turning her back on the study in blue that · was Cindy French, tossing a wave back over her shoulder and striding away in the direction of the federal government outpost. She didn't look back even though it seemed like a long time before the Kenworth went into gear and pulled away, gradually building up speed as it disappeared down I-35. The deep growl of the massive eighteen-wheel semitrailer was audible for another minute or so afterward.

Temple was not a ghost town, but apart from the federales stationed there because of the mandate, there was no activity to be seen. The avenue down which she walked was clear of the sort of wreckage or debris that inevitably choked the streets of any settlement larger than a hamlet or a small village. But Sofia could see that many of the side streets were still impassable, with great piles of burned-out automobiles and in one instance a twin-bladed military helicopter. Here and there she passed the shells of buildings that had gone up in flames after the Disappearance. Sometimes whole blocks lay in ruins. But for some reason, Temple had been spared the heavy-handed destruction that had fallen on so many larger towns and cities. She had no idea why and did not much care. She supposed that the authorities in Seattle had chosen this place for the outpost because its center needed relatively little cleaning up before they could move the people in and because Temple was convenient to Blackstone's headquarters but far enough away from him that it didn't feel as though his boot was on your neck.

Wary of being spotted by one of the patrols Cindy had mentioned, Sofia ducked into the next side street she passed. It appeared as though an old school bus had collided with a refrigerated truck when the drivers and all the children had Disappeared. She felt sad about the kids and hoped they'd been unaware of the horror that fell upon them. Not like her brother and sisters. The intersection was blocked completely by the wreckage, which snaked away down the street in a concertina of mangled steel and rusted flame-ravaged car bodies. Weeds and thigh-high grass, coarse and wiry, choked the pavement and covered most of the road surface. The ruins of small commercial buildings she'd passed near the junction with the highway now gave way to a more suburban setting. The small houses and bungalows, many of them with broken windows and slumping roofs, looked as though no human being had set foot in them for many years.

Her flesh crawled as she carefully picked her way through the thick carpet of vegetation. The ghosts did not bother her as they had her father, but there would be snakes and possibly packs of feral animals. The army patrols probably shot any they came across and laid bait for the others, but still, with no way of defending herself, the teenager felt terribly vulnerable. That was why she had to push on. She stopped when she reached a bare concrete patch of driveway in front of a large church. The area was big enough that it hadn't been colonized by the vegetation as had happened elsewhere.

Checking the old pre-Wave street map of Temple she had picked up in Ardmore, Sofia located herself near the intersection of Avenue L and South 49th Street. She frowned, not really sure of her bearings. It was always like this in the ghost towns—so easy to get turned around and lose your sense of direction. At least it wasn't dark now.

Sofia planted her feet as though she meant to take root in the concrete. She held the map in both hands, angling it to catch the faint gray light leaking into the day. After a short while looking from the map, to the crossroads, to the steeply pitched roof of the Heights Baptist Church, she was reasonably sure she needed to backtrack two or three blocks to the west and south. She really could have used a machete and resolved to get one as soon as possible. There had been a rack full of them in the federal depot at Ardmore, but she'd had no plausible story to explain why a fifteen-year-old girl might need one in Fort Hood.

At least this car park beside the church was relatively open ground. She jogged across it, but her progress slowed as she hit the next avenue and another catastrophic confusion of decaying wreckage. The vehicles were piled up so badly here that she wondered whether the federales had used this particular road as a dumping ground. The obstruction forced her another block south, where she got lost for a couple of minutes before backtracking along George Drive and up into West Avenue North. There she found what she was looking for: the storefront of JM Firearms.

It was obvious this had been a small, single-operator gunsmithing business, not the sort of big-box artillery warehouse that would attract the attention of looters or the authorities. Papa had taught her to seek these places out while they'd been running north to escape from the road agents. At establishments like this, inventories often remained completely intact and weapons and ammunition were almost always stored properly. And she was more likely to find the singular sort of item she needed in a small, bespoke gunsmithing house than at some haunted Walmart store.

The .357 Magnum was identical to the handgun she'd trained with back in Kansas City save for the burnished redwood inlay of the pistol grip. Sofia had spent so many hours on the government firing range with that weapon that to hold one again felt as though she'd just rediscovered a part of herself that had gone missing. She would have been so much more comfortable on the drive down from Kansas City if she'd had her own pistol. Like all the truckers, Cindy French kept a shotgun in the cabin of her rig, and it had been reassuring to look up and see the weapon there as they rolled through the American wastelands. But it was not the same as having one's own piece. On the trail north, she had never been more than a step away from a firearm, even when bathing with the other women.

She took her time, sitting at the kitchen table of this downtown apartment on South Main Street, radio on softly in the background, while she stripped the protective coating from the revolver, which was fresh from its packaging. One of the great benefits of a revolver was that it was a relatively easy weapon to maintain. She found the familiar movement and rhythm soothing. Concentrating on this task, which felt as natural to her as breathing, she could lose herself, forgetting for a short time all that had happened to those she loved.

The apartment was a few blocks away from the Federal Center, but even with the windows closed against the chill of the morning, she could hear some light traffic noise drifting across the rooftops. The streets immediately below her were gridlocked with car wrecks, so there was no chance of a patrol driving by. Even so, she wouldn't be staying here long. When night fell, she would move again. Somewhere a little farther away from what few inhabitants there were here. She'd heard voices and the crunch of boots on broken glass at one point, sending her flying off into the bedroom, there to keep a silent vigil in the gloom until they had passed.

It had been a nerve-racking experience getting here after the gunsmith's, but she certainly hadn't wanted to stay in that part of town. It was very close to the interstate but removed enough from the Federal Center that she'd worried about falling outside the protective envelope offered by their presence. Even in Kansas City, people clustered around the heart of the city and the relatively crowded resettlement areas; it was not unknown for small raiding parties to prey on homesteads farther out. All of Sofia's previous experience in Texas led her to imagine that it would be much worse this time, seeing as she couldn't even trust the authorities to look after her. The federales would return her to a foster home or possibly some form of "protective" detention if they found her.

And if she ran into troopers from Blackstone's TDF—what then?

She swore under her breath as she cleaned out the barrel of the handgun.

A song that she liked came on, and she turned up the volume on her little transistor radio just a notch. A risk, but worth it. It was an English band. She wasn't sure of the name, but the tune was very danceable, and it had been all over the pop stations right before she'd left home.

The table blurred in front of her eyes, and the Magnum became a silvery waterfall as tears filled her eyes. She carefully rested the pistol on the white cotton pillowcase on which she'd been cleaning it and pushed her chair away from the table. The apartment was small and the bedroom only a few steps away, but she found she was hurrying to throw herself onto the mattress.

Her grief had been coming like this, rolling over her in unexpected waves, ever since she'd parted company with Cindy. There was no mystery to it. Sofia had been forced to maintain an iron grip on her feelings while in the company of the other woman. Cindy's maternal instincts obviously had been aroused by her plight no matter how fictional it might have been, and Sofia hadn't wanted her deciding that she was too much of a basket case to be left on her own. But now that she was on her own, she was free to give vent to the agonies of her soul.

The bedclothes were disheveled and the pillow still wet from the floods of tears she had poured into it less than an hour ago. As wretched and powerless as she felt, however, as tormented by her lot as she may have been, there remained a cold, disconnected part of her mind that all but told her to get on with the business of grieving for her lost father, to get it out of the way so that it would not interfere with what she had to do to avenge him. The callous tenor of that voice at the back of her mind did nothing to attenuate the torrent of grief pouring out of the girl. She was forced into smothering herself, so fiercely did she jam her face into the pillow to prevent the sound of her moaning cries from escaping the apartment.

Alone.

She was alone in the world. Everybody she had ever loved had been taken from her. Not by the cosmic dice roll of something like the Disappearance, which would have been bad enough. No, she had lost everyone and everything to the evil of one man's ambitions. She'd watched her beloved father hollowed out by his impotence, by his complete inability to do anything about what had happened to their family. It was almost as though, having delivered her to Kansas City, he had suffered a moral collapse and could find within himself none of the resources needed to turn around and do what he'd promised to do on the day those road agents had attacked the homestead. Instead, he had tried to content himself with the idea that the federales could be trusted to bring the killers to justice and that his responsibilities had contracted to the altogether more humble end of seeing that she, Sofia, made it to school every day, passed her exams, and didn't get into any sort of trouble so trifling it was barely worthy of the word.

Oh, Papa . . .

Her feelings about her father roared and rushed around her like the swift and deadly waters of the flash flood that had destroyed their party and the Mormons' cattle in northern Texas. She felt torn one way and then the other, as likely to be dashed on the submerged rocks of her anger at him as she was to be lifted up and thrown free of danger by all that he had done for her.

She wasn't sure how long she lay on the bed, curled into a fetal ball, racked by violent sorrow. She checked her watch and found it was well after one o'clock when this particular episode of unrestrained anguish finally abated. Fifteen minutes may have passed, perhaps as much as an hour. Undeniably, though, she felt much better for having allowed it to run its course. Almost rested, in fact.

Sofia dried her eyes and rubbed her face with the sleeve of her hooded sweatshirt. She took in a deep breath and held it before letting it go slowly, like an athlete recovering from a hard race. She shivered once, and then it was all over. She was able to return to cleaning her pistol. She methodically worked through the remainder of the process with the Magnum before putting it aside to study the other weapons she had taken from JM Firearms.

The machete was not primarily a weapon. She had grabbed it to cut a path through the thickets of scrub and wild grass that strangled most of the city. But in a pinch the honed edge could be useful against man or beast. She gave the blade a polish but nothing more. She was not an obsessive. For Sofia, guns and knives were simply tools. Having grown up on a farm, she'd been taught to think of them that way, and nothing had changed her opinion in the intervening years. Not even the hard necessity of having had to kill men with a firearm. They remained tools, implements for taking life.

Because she wasn't obsessed with guns, there was much about the other weapon in front of her that she didn't know—its name, for instance. She was sure that something as particular as this would have had a special name. She recognized the gun, an assault rifle, as a variation of the kind she had seen some road agents and individual bandits carry at various times. AK-47s, they were known as, although this one looked like a much nastier and improved version of the old wood-and-stamped-metal machine gun preferred by peasant armies the world over. It may have come from China or somewhere in Eastern Europe, perhaps even Pakistan before the recent war there. She neither knew nor cared. What had drawn her to this weapon the moment she saw it was its reputation for reliable lethality.

During the long trek north in the spring, she had often listened to the men discussing their firearms. Adam, too, had been an invaluable teacher in that regard. Like many teenage boys, he was fascinated by guns and had studied them in much greater detail than she would ever have bothered to. Something he used to say that seemed to amuse him greatly had impressed itself upon her memory:

"AK-47. When you absolutely, positively got to kill every mother-fucker in the room . . ."

32

KILLEEN, TEXAS, ADMINISTRATIVE DIVISION

By the time she got to Texas, she was entirely someone else: Colonel Katherine Murdoch, U.S. Air Force, Kate to her friends, of whom she had none in Fort Hood. Colvin had almost caught her off guard at the hotel in Kansas City, exhausted as she was, but the flight south allowed Caitlin to assume the role and persona of her cover properly. The travel requisition that got her on the C-130 flight from Kansas City to Robert Gray Army Airfield, southwest of Fort Hood, put her on the passenger manifest in her jacket. To the flight crew, she was a USAF officer seconded to the White House chief of staff in an advisory role. As she was to the feds and Texas state authorities. As she had been to Colvin and everyone she met in Kansas City. There was only one man down here who knew she wasn't some sort of military liaison officer for Jed Culver, and he surprised her by turning up personally to collect her from the airport.

General Tusk Musso, U.S. Marine Corps (retired), the president's "special representative" in Texas, was Seattle's ambassador in all but name. He was waiting for Caitlin at baggage collection, which for federal officers in the Hood meant a large unventilated tin shed at the northern end of the airfield. The day was cool and overcast, but she couldn't help wondering what this place would be like in high summer. Unbearable, probably.

"They know how to make you feel special from the get-go down here, don't they, sir?" she said as Musso shook her hand.

He smiled. Shaven-headed, slab-shouldered, clad in Hugo Boss khakis and a windbreaker, he managed to maintain a military bearing even in civilian garb. "Colonel Monroe, nice to meet you," he replied. "And yes, Southern hospitality is not what it used to be."

The general took her large suitcase and wheeled it out of the shed.

"Did you ever see that old British movie *Khartoum*?" he asked as they walked out to his forest-green camouflaged soft-top Hummer. "That was a damn fine movie. But some days I feel like Charlton Heston, waiting for the barbarians to swarm through the gates and stick a spear in my ass."

Caitlin vaguely remembered the film. It had been a favorite of her dad's, an air force man himself, which was one of the reasons she'd chosen the Murdoch jacket as her cover. She had grown up on USAF bases, and the culture was as familiar to her as family. She also vaguely knew of Musso even before reading his bio in the mission brief. The former Marine Corps lawyer had gained some notoriety as the senior officer at Guantánamo Bay back on Wave Day, which, with the disappearance of everyone north of where he stood, made him the senior man in all of Northern Command. He'd quickly struck up an alliance of convenience with a Cuban military officer, who was later eaten by the Wave when he strayed too close, but not before the two of them had sent back some of the first close-up images and reports on conditions at the event horizon.

Musso had a second shot at fame a few weeks later, when he led the defense of Guantánamo and of a few thousand refugees who'd fled there against an opportunistic attack by the then president of Venezuela, Hugo Chávez. His bio claimed the corps "let him go" during the great downsizing of the next few years, but Culver had taken her aside in Seattle to explain otherwise. Musso had been ass fucked after "losing" Guantánamo. He owed his role here to Culver's patronage.

The general, who towered over her and retained a fighter's physique, tossed Caitlin's bags in the back of his Humvee as if they were empty. She hopped into the passenger seat with a thud, its gray-green seat pad being almost nonexistent. Musso joined her up front and immediately flipped the starter switch, waiting for the dashboard light to go out. Once it had, he pulled the switch over, firing up the vehicle. With the drop of the parking brake, the man universally known as Tusk put the automatic into drive and rolled out.

"Not too shabby for a ride that sat in the open for two years. Hope you don't mind a detour," he said. "There's checkpoints all through Killeen and Fort Hood. Looking for infiltrators." He rolled his eyes. "But mostly, I think, looking to piss me off. I get stopped and searched at every single one. I ask you, Colonel, do I *look* like one of Roberto's scrawny-ass little spies?"

"No, sir," she replied with a grin, feeling better about this part of the mission already. "No, you do not."

"So we'll skirt around Killeen if you don't mind, swing south of the lake, and head back to the expressway just before we hit Salado. It hasn't been cleared yet. Nor has most of Temple, where I'm holed up, but it'll do."

The names brought up a flickering montage of imagery from Caitlin's briefing set. Musso had just described the southern limits of her so-called area of operation.

The day remained cool and gray as they motored away from the airfield but mild compared with the deep freeze of the Midwest she recently had left behind. She was glad of the leather jacket, though. It prevented the chill of the cab from getting through to her. Hummers weren't the most comfortable of chariots.

"I'd run the heater, but it isn't working," Musso said. "Probably never will work again. I can't seem to get parts even though Blackstone is sitting on a mountain of them."

"Should I take that as an indication of your working relationship with the governor, sir?" she asked. The fact that the general here was headquartered a fair way east at Temple, not in Fort Hood itself, made the question redundant, but it was worth getting his take.

"Governor Blackstone has an open-door policy," Musso explained, having to speak loudly because of the engine's roar. "When he needs something from us, his door is wide open. When he's got what he wants, the door is still open—but only so's he can slam it on my ass as I leave."

The former marine seemed inexplicably amused by what had to be a fairly fraught situation. But then, given his record in Gitmo, Tusk Musso probably was entitled to regard his latest posting as a milk run.

"What's he going to want out of me? Or, rather, out of Colonel Murdoch?" Caitlin asked as they sped away down the well-maintained blacktop of Clear Creek Road.

Regimented lines of shake 'n' bake housing slipped by on Musso's left, but the terrain outside her zipper-shut plastic window was wilder, more unkempt. All scrubby thornbush, trees, and what looked like waist-high grass broken up here and there by patches of sand and dirt. If it weren't for the difference in temperature, this part of east-central Texas easily could have been mistaken for some of the wasteland around Kansas City. The orderly presentation of dormitory suburbs spoke well of the effort that had gone into reclamation down here. There was certainly no way of telling that Killeen had lain empty for so long—until midway through 2005, when the newly elected Governor Blackstone turned his energies toward reconstruction. But the bleak wastes on the right-hand side of the road emphasized what a small, insignificant impact the return of humankind had had on this part of Texas.

"What will he want? From you, Colonel Murdoch?" said Musso. A purely rhetorical question. "He'll want what he's been after for months now: a reassurance the president won't leave him with his nuts swinging in the breeze if and when Roberto decides to come against him with full power instead of sniping at the margins. He's worked himself into quite the fucking tizz over this. It's why he's agreed to see you, as Jed Culver's advance man. Or woman, sorry."

Caitlin smiled. "Well, as you know, I'm not really a military genius," she admitted. "But Kipper would hardly be likely to let that happen, would he? Letting Roberto roll in here, I mean."

Musso gave the impression of studying her question seriously as they turned southbound onto SH-195, a four-lane state highway that cut through long stretches of countryside gone back to brute creation. The road itself was clear, yet cracks could be seen in the tarmac through which native grass and other plant life conspired to undo what humanity had wrought. Tusk worked the wheel around a scattering of potholes large enough to swallow the front tires.

"One of my drivers got caught in one of those last week and cracked the front axle," he said of the obstacle. "I had the truck towed back for spare parts, since I'll probably never get it fixed."

"No working heater in that one, either?"

"Nope," the general replied. "That was missing before we got our hands on it, along with the roof and the doors."

She saw more evidence of the Disappearance as they moved away from Governor Blackstone's administrative heartland. The blackened hulks of car wrecks that had been pushed off the blacktop and left to rust among the weeds just off from the hard shoulder or shoved into the brush-clotted median. A tangled pile of metal she recognized as a downed plane, blocking a side road about a hundred yards in from the intersection. Dense stands of scrub and trees growing right down to the roadside in some places, obscuring all but the rooflines of a few isolated buildings left to rot and collapse. She could barely see a northbound HEMMT as the eight-wheeler sped by on the opposite side of the highway.

"Now, as for the South American Federation," said Musso, getting back on topic, "I don't know what the president will do. You were in New York; you saw how hard-pressed we were up there. Blackstone could've made it much easier for us if he'd just released a couple of TDF battalions into the fight. But he didn't. Said he was already overcommitted—securing the Panama Canal, dealing with his own pirate issues down in the Caribbean, the bandits on the frontier, and the southern flank against the Federation. All the best legal advice says the federal–state accords back him up. He wasn't obliged to release one grunt to the battle in New York. But it left a sour taste in the mouth when he didn't, whether all those other things were true or not, don't you think?"

Caitlin didn't answer immediately. Fact was, if she hadn't had a personal investment in what had occurred in New York City, she never would have gone there. It would have been hypocritical, therefore, for her to judge Blackstone for having stayed out of it.

Or would it? she wondered. Her choices were personal. His were political. And arguably he had a responsibility that went well beyond his individual inclinations. A quarter of the post-Wave population of the United States was clustered around Mad Jack's holdings in the Texas Administrative Division. One could argue that he had a duty first and foremost to see that they were protected.

Caitlin was glad of this opportunity to be free of the need to maintain her cover. It spoke well of Musso, she thought, that he'd given up his Sunday afternoon to come out and collect her. He could have sent a driver or just left her to make her own way. In Caitlin's experience, a lot of ambassadors—and that was what he was in all but name—didn't much care to have undeclared agents spooking about on their turf, yet he seemed not at all concerned. He drove south for about ten klicks before turning off at the 2484 junction, where the ruins of Red's BBQ were returning to the dust. The land out here seemed used up, leached of any real fecundity, and overrun by noxious weeds and creepers. Caitlin doubted whether she could have penetrated more than a few feet into the growth without a machete, and even then she'd have been hacking and slashing away with all her might to advance very slowly through the thornbushes and wait-a-while vines. In places, the road was almost completely overgrown, and it was only her driver's familiarity with the track that kept them on the crumbling tarmac. The Hummer jumped around as it fought for traction, clambering over giant tree roots and the occasional monster vine that had snuck out over the road.

"Was this trip really necessary?" she asked, only half joking.

"As inconvenient as it might be, Colonel, this route's still better than waiting at a roadblock for an hour while they check my credentials, believe me."

"Seriously? It's that bad?" Caitlin noticed that her voice was warbling with the violence of their passage.

"Depends on whether he's sending a message on any given day," Musso said, as he steered them off the old road surface and around a fallen tree.

Scorch marks blackened the blasted stump where it had been felled by lightning; the vegetation around it had been burned to a cinder for about fifty yards. On the far side, however, the path opened up again.

"If I manage to get on Mad Jack's grade A shit list or if Seattle does something that aggravates his indigestion, he's not above placing checkpoints at every intersection between Fort Hood and Temple. He's really been on our asses of late. I think it's his idea of turning up the heat on Seattle because they won't take him seriously about Morales. It can turn a half hour's drive into a daylong adventure."

"Must play hell with his own people, no?" she suggested.

"The spot checks are random," Tusk Musso replied. "But they always seem to randomly select vehicles with federal plates and tags. So I send a couple of HEMMTs through here every few days just to bash down the scrub and keep a way open. It's a rat run, a long way out of my way, but it means we have an alternative route to the airfield."

The windshield began to spot with drizzle as they finally swung off the southern heading and began to track gradually back to the north, taking them past an old sand-mining operation. A petrol tanker had left the road and driven straight into a tailings dam, presumably on the morning of the Disappearance. Caitlin could tell at a glance that Blackstone had made no effort to restart the operation of the mine. She wondered what would happen to Musso's rat run when he did. Would there be checkpoints every couple of hundred yards along here as well?

"You're not rocking my world, sir. I need to gain the trust of these people, but it doesn't sound like they're going to let me get to first base."

Musso flicked on the wipers as the rain thickened. Past the old sand mine, the forest on either side of the road grew so dense again that she couldn't see more than a few yards into it. Every now and then, however, Caitlin spotted the remnants of driveways, completely overgrown but not as thickly as the scrub around them, or glimpsed slumping buildings otherwise hidden by vegetation.

"Oh, I think you'll be okay," the general assured her. "After all, I'm just Seattle's step-'n'-fetch-it bitch. You, though, have something Blackstone actually needs. Or he thinks you do."

"You mean the report I'm supposed to be putting together for Jed Culver on the military threat from the Federation?"

"Supposed to be, yes. Don't worry—I've already written it for you. You won't have to do any real work while you're going through people's garbage cans and reading their mail when they're not looking."

"And is there a military threat?" she asked. "A credible one?"

"Depends what you mean by a threat. Could Morales make life down here distinctly unpleasant? Of course he could. He already is. He doesn't have the force projection capabilities to take and hold significant ground, but that hasn't stopped him from making a damn nuisance of himself at the edges. It's no coincidence that we get an upturn in banditry and insurgent activity down in Panama every time he sends his ambassador up to demand we turn over control of the canal to the Federation. Most of the piracy in the Caribbean is almost certainly his fault. Plus, when he started stitching his little bandit kingdom together, Roberto didn't make the mistake of trying to maintain all the capabilities he'd inherited—he just cherry-picked the best bits and concentrated on maintaining them."

"There's a lot of talk in Vancouver about the *São Paulo*," Caitlin said, referring to the South American Federation's aircraft carrier.

"Talk's all it is," Musso replied. "One deployment to the Gulf with two frigates is not enough to cause me to lose any sleep at night. He's demobilized most of his obsolete combat aircraft, sticking with the F-16s he inherited. Bad news for Morales is that we're sitting on most of the spare parts for that plane. He's got a pretty large navy on paper, once you add up all the frigates, subs, and Peru's old big-gun cruiser, but most of those tubs spend their time in port for want of funds to operate them. Much like ours do, I might add."

"So he shouldn't be taken too seriously?"

The big old marine shrugged. "I know there's some pro forma concern up in Seattle about his capability and intent. And down here, concern turns to howling paranoia, let me tell you. But for now, most of his attention is directed toward internal control. He's built up his army, but it's not an expeditionary force. Five, ten years from now, that might be different. But five years from now, hopefully, our own situation should be much improved, too."

He slowed down as the rain reduced visibility to some hundred and fifty yards.

"As long as Seattle and Fort Hood don't decide to get into Civil War reenactment in a big way," said Caitlin.

"Yeah," he agreed in a flat voice. Musso was concentrating fiercely on the road now, what little he could see of it. He didn't look directly at her as he spoke, but he spoke very carefully. "That's why I worry about your investigation, Agent Monroe." It was the first time he'd used her real name. "I had to fly back to Seattle to receive a personal briefing about your mission from Jed Culver. He gave me to understand that knowledge of what you're doing goes no higher up the command chain than his office. The president knows nothing of this."

Caitlin nodded. "You would also know, sir, there's nothing unusual about that. Presidents don't know everything. It's often better that they don't."

Judging by his stern facial expression, Tusk wasn't much impressed with that line of argument. "You can serve me up that horseshit on the finest bone china, Ms. Monroe," he shot back, "but I'm still not going to eat it."

"And yet you agreed to allow the mission to go ahead with the support of your office, General."

"No," he corrected her, "with *my* support. My personal support. That's not the same thing. Mr. Culver, Deputy Director Larrison, yourself, you're all running a black operation with no plausible deniability, in complete contravention of a law that prohibits Echelon operations on U.S. soil. My office cannot support that. That's why I'm the only person here who's been fully briefed. But you need to understand, as I have given Deputy Director Larrison and Mr. Culver to understand, that if this goes wrong, I will not be covering up for you."

They had slowed almost to a crawl as Musso picked his way through a section of road where the tarmac had been partially washed away.

"If this goes wrong," said Caitlin, "I doubt congressional inquiries and criminal charges will be the worst of it. Getting out alive will be the first challenge. And as for the prohibition on operating within the boundaries of CONUS, that applies to start-up and stand-alone missions. But I didn't start working on Baumer when I got off that plane just now. I've been on his case since well before the Disappearance. He may be dead, and his network may no longer constitute a clear and present danger, but the investigation of that network and how it effected its operation in New York—which killed a couple of thousand American personnel, you may recall—is ongoing. That's why I'm here, sir. I have no doubts about the legality of this mission or the justness of this cause."

Musso smiled slowly as they cleared the ruined stretch of road. "From what I know of you, Agent Monroe, you very rarely have doubts about anything."

"Then you don't know me at all," she said quietly but not unkindly. "So why? Why did you agree to this? If you had your doubts, and you obviously do, why not just take them up the command chain? All the way if need be."

They'd reached a major intersection with I-35. Musso took the northern entrance and accelerated as soon as he'd left the difficult conditions of the market road behind them. The highway obviously had been cleared properly and was well maintained. The weather wasn't much improved, though.

"I still have my doubts," he replied. "But probably not of the sort you'd imagine. Frankly, I find the idea of anybody cozying up with the likes of Ozal or Baumer to be anathema. Let's just get that out in the open. If Blackstone thought to gain some advantage by creating a tactical difficulty for us in New York—and by 'us' I mean the United States of America—then he should swing by his neck for the crime of treason. Even if treason was not his intent. Even if he had some other agenda of which we are not aware. I agreed to support your mission here because I believe we need to ventilate this whole septic mess. Sunlight is the best disinfectant. If you can break open the seal and let some light in on this, it'll burn him alive. And it needs to."

For the first time since turning off the main road from the airfield, Caitlin could see traffic. Mostly heavy haulers and not very many of them, but it was still reassuring to find they weren't the only people rattling around on the vast plains of Texas.

"And your doubts?" she prompted.

"My doubts are about the consequences. What happens when you find out exactly what the arrangement with Ozal was? If there was indeed an arrangement. What happens then?"

"That's up to Culver and Larrison," she said without inflection.

If it was up to her, if Caitlin Monroe found out that Blackstone was in any way responsible, even indirectly, for freeing Bilal Baumer, her first inclination would be to put a bullet in his brain. But she had reasons for sticking to the playbook for now. Two of them were hiding out in Aviemore, Scotland.

"There is another reason why I agreed," Musso said as they came up on a truck stop that was open for business.

"Don't leave a lady guessing, sir."

"I was in NORTHCOM when everything turned to shit back in 2003," he began.

"You weren't just *in* NORTHCOM," she corrected him, "you *were* NORTHCOM."

"Very flattering, Agent Monroe." He laughed a little bitterly. "But I gave up smoking a long time ago, so I'll thank you not to blow any up my ass."

"Okay."

"I was Johnny on the spot at Gitmo," Musso said, as if that explained everything. He cocked an eyebrow at her as they passed the truckers' diner. "This isn't the first time I've encountered you, Agent Monroe. That's why you're here now. When everything was turning to shit-flavored custard in Gitmo, and France, and Britain, and pretty much everywhere else, the surviving Joint Chiefs, of which I was an acting member, received word from an asset in France about the real reason behind the intifada there and the roll-up of Echelon's network. It was an impressive job of work, from a lone operator, to survive that piece of villainy and turn out the bad guys. It might even have changed the outcome of that attempted coup. You were that operator, I believe."

Caitlin remained silent for just a second too long. "You can believe what you want, General Musso," she replied. "It's a free country. For now."

He smiled. "And you're discreet. I like that in a secret agent."

33

NORTH DARWIN, NORTHERN TERRITORY

Julianne left Shah's soiree just before midnight in a taxi driven by one of his men. She didn't ask why Shah owned a taxi license. She didn't need to. The driver was an Australian who introduced himself as Granger. She wondered how realistic it was having such a fit- and competent-looking white man driving a cab in a city like Darwin, where all the worst jobs were performed by refugees. Then again, did it matter? The cab was the cover, not the driver, and truth be known, she felt much better riding next to him. Better still because of the pistol she could see bulging under his lightweight cotton jacket and the sawed-off shotgun he'd handed her when they got under way.

"Boss man says you're staying in a motel over by Doctors Gully," he said. "Must be pretty noisy, eh, with all the construction down at the new wharves."

Jules had been exhausted when she'd arrived in Darwin. Now she found herself wrung out from the shock and high emotions of that lunch down at the marina, worn down by the intrigues of the afternoon and evening. Whenever she thought of the Rhino, her stomach churned with an acid mix of worry and guilt, and when she found herself not having thought about him in a while, the guilt came rushing back with twice as much force. She didn't much feel like talking, but she'd been brought up to value good manners. For her father, they had been an excellent disguise.

"I'm so bloody tired, I suspect nothing will wake me once I get to sleep tonight," she said. "Assuming I can sleep at all, of course, given all the current hullabaloo."

"You'll be all right, Ms. Balwyn," Shah's man assured her. "I'll make sure you get back safely. And we've got a couple of other blokes watching out for you. Put your head down, get some rack time. Nobody's gonna be sneaking into your room tonight. Not unless they want to have a very nasty accident."

"Thanks," she said. Her eyes were watering, but that was from exhaustion.

She tried to take in as much of the city as she could while they drove south. If she was going to be here for a while, she would need to understand it. The Palms, the shake 'n' bake upscale émigré ghetto where Shah had built his house, was easy enough to come to grips with. It was no different from any other expensive gated community. She hadn't been back to the United Kingdom in years, but she understood there were hundreds of them over there now, with plenty in Europe also. Almost as though the rich were returning to a feudal arrangement by which they walled themselves off from the dangerous masses and hired men like Granger to patrol the walls. Even Shah and Pappas were just glorified gatekeepers, captains of the gate, perhaps, but little more.

Julianne yawned. She had run away, hooked up with Pete and Fifi, to get out from behind the walls of expectation and inherited duty that had fallen to her as the daughter of a landed family. Now it seemed as if the walls had expanded to enclose the whole world, and they were topped with razor wire and policed by the murderous hirelings of some low-rent bully—someone from the fucking *building trade,* of all things! A man with ideas above his station and more money and clout than was seemly even in a world as mad as this one had become of late.

The driver took her along the highway, back in toward the city. A hot, pulsing dome of light marked the location of New Town, where neon lights and Jumbotrons kept the darkness at bay. There was no missing it. Some Chinese tycoon had covered two whole city blocks with an immense and gaudy spectacle in the form of a towering casino constructed to mirror the look of the Athenian Parthenon. Laser packs and spotlights swept ceaselessly over the black marble façade, although Jules was certain that on closer inspection it would turn out not to be marble but polished concrete painted to a high-gloss noir. Great dark columns held aloft a massive portico, and volcanic geysers of fire snaked and roared their length from gas vents built into the base of each plinth. The traffic stream thickened and slowed considerably outside this awesome grotesquerie. Granger cursed under his breath as he muscled the car through the worst of the congestion.

"Sorry, miss," he said, "but as bad as this looks, it's heaps worse round the back, on the waterfront. Once the sun goes down, it's a fuckin' bloodhouse out there. That place where your mate got in a bit of strife today, the old marina, they throw up these massive bloody iron barricades of an evening. Lock themselves down behind them. Be an unusual morning when the sun didn't come up on half a dozen or so corpses around the edge of Newie. So, sorry, but we're better going through here."

"It's okay," Jules replied. "I need to get my bearings, anyway. So this place goes back what, four or five blocks to the inner harbor?"

Granger leaned on the horn, mounted the median strip, and forced a passage past a couple of maxi-taxis spilling drunken sailors directly onto the tarmac of the highway.

"Fuckwits," he muttered. "Yeah, five blocks along the southern edge. Maybe eight or nine along the waterfront down by the marina and three or four out of the arse end of Hong Kong Charlie's here. The whole thing's a fucking mess. Shaped like a heart. A blackened, hateful heart." He grinned, pleased with his literary allusion.

"Probably best you don't head in there," the Australian continued as they bounced down off the median strip. "There's three main roads run through the place, but soon as you get off them, you're fucked. The Authority laid them down when the whole place was nothing more than a bit of waste ground with a few surveyors' pegs on it. Pretty much everything else in there, every cross-street, every alley, every little fucking cut-through—and there's dozens of them, maybe hundreds—they all just sorta sprang up along the natural lay of the land between bits of ground grabbed up by whoever built on it. Sometimes a place will burn down, or maybe it gets burned down, you know, and the next morning there's a new cross street. Probably with a handful of food carts, hookers, and pickpockets already claiming it as their turf. Until someone bigger comes along, kicks them off, and runs up something like a fried chicken joint where you can get a bit of crystal meth and a dodgy tattoo with your bucket of spicy wings."

A fight broke out on the footpath just beside her window, a brawling knot of civilians by the look of them. Maybe construction workers, Jules thought, judging by the high-visibility vests a couple of them wore and the muddy steel-capped boots they were using to kick the shit out of a small Asian man they'd surrounded. Before she could see how that turned out—poorly, she would have guessed—Granger found a gap in the traffic and accelerated away.

She had no trouble picking out the new developments that had climbed skyward over the quaint-looking older quarters of the city. The three blocks ahead of them, on the driver's side of the car, had been buried under the footing of a gargantuan resort hotel: the Mirvac Mirage, forty-one stories topping out in a private helipad facility, with its own control tower, which could land four big commercial choppers at the same time. Jules leaned forward and craned her head upward, peering up into the night. She thought she could see the pulse of landing lights on the roof, but it was hard to tell in the dazzling artificial daylight down at street level.

In spite of the late hour, hundreds of people streamed in and out of the foyer of the Mirage. Unlike the mob scene just a few blocks away in front of the Grecian-themed casino, the crowds were all dressed in business attire, resort wear, or, in a couple of cases, black tie and formal gowns. Limousines and town cars idled bumper to bumper, the drivers undoubtedly running the air-conditioning against the sweltering evening. It appeared that taxis weren't allowed in the forecourt of the hotel, but there was a rank full of them on the opposite side of the road.

The police presence was much heavier now, although it didn't seem to be needed. She had seen none of the Northern Territory's brown-shirted cops anywhere near where the construction workers had been kicking the life out of that little Chinese man. Here, though, she counted four horse-mounted patrols clip-clopping through the large well-behaved crowds.

"Have a look at these dickheads, would you," Granger said. He pointed down a street on the less developed side of the road.

At first Jules wasn't quite sure what he was pointing at, but then she picked them out of the gloom, maybe a hundred meters or so back. Two armored cars painted in black and gray urban camouflage were surrounded by a dozen troopers in similarly patterned uniforms.

"Sandline," he explained before she could ask. "What they call their Public Safety Response Team. Fuckin' beat-down artists mostly. Trun-cheons, tasers, capsicum spray, rubber bullets, and real ones, too, in case somebody who really knows what they're doing decides to have a go."

He was driving quickly enough that she'd caught only a glimpse of them. "They didn't seem to be doing much," she ventured.

Granger took a right-hand turn two blocks beyond the Mirvac Mirage Hotel. Jules found herself disoriented by how quickly the streetscape changed. They were now back on a quiet suburban lane, tree-lined, with family homes buttoned up and only porch lights and occasionally little solar-powered garden lights burning in the night. There was no foot traffic, and the street was lined with cars, each one obviously parked outside its owner's home at the end of the working day.

Her driver returned to the topic of the Sandline security squad they'd passed. "Not much for them to do since they kicked out the black fellas, and after them some of the refugee gangs that fetched up here back in the early days after the Wave. Proper reffos, I mean—boat people. Indonesians mostly, but lots of Malays, too. Jesus Christ, there were some willing fuckin' brawls in those days, mate. That's how those Sandline bastards got a look in. Cops couldn't handle it, so the Authority contracted in their own security. It worked so fucking well, they outsourced everything they could in the end. As long as they don't crack the wrong head open, the private forces pretty much have a free hand."

They'd driven another block, and Jules could see the lights of the harbor through the trees. In fact, it looked as though one of the giant warships of the Combined Fleet, sporting a South Korean flag, had parked itself at the bottom of the street. Of course, that was merely an illusion. It probably had dropped anchor half a mile out.

"Forgive my impertinence," she said with a smile. "But aren't *you* working for a private security force?"

"Yeah, but we're more of an old-fashioned outfit. We don't do much work in Darwin or even the territory. This is just a base for us. Most of our business is up in New Guinea, securing the mines and keeping loggers out of the forests along the border. Old-school stuff. Not this cryptofascist bullshit." He waved his hand back in the direction they'd come. "Anyway, here we go. Just give me a second . . ."

Granger pulled a small handheld radio from a pocket inside his jacket.

"I'm in the golf buggy," he said. "On approach. Can I play through?"

A heavily distorted voice replied through a rush of static: *"You are clear. Come on through."*

"What on earth?" Jules asked, bewildered by Granger's outgoing message.

"A little in-joke," he admitted. "Reference to your stealing Greg Norman's yacht."

She shook her head as he accelerated smoothly toward the lit-up sign of the Banyan View Lodge, the motel she'd checked into after arriving in Darwin the previous night. It had begun life as a low-budget travelers' rest, but there weren't many low-budget travelers in Darwin these days. Most of the guests seemed to be miners transiting to and from the ore fields hundreds of miles south or deep out in the western deserts. She'd seen a shuttle bus running a large group of them out to the airport when she'd arrived.

As planned, two men were waiting for them in the car park. Neither was wielding an obvious weapon like the cut-down shotgun Granger had handed her, but she imagined that like him, they probably were carrying concealed sidearms. It made her feel a lot better. Her mood improved even more when she recognized one of them as Birendra.

"Miss Julianne," said the young Ghurkha. "I am sorry I did not get to talk with you at Mr. Shah's party. I had to leave early to supervise your arrangements here. We have swapped your room again, and myself and the other men will be keeping watch overnight. Mr. Cooley has equipped you, I see?"

She found herself at a loss for a moment until she realized he was talking about Granger, the cab driver. And the shotgun he'd given her.

"Oh, yes," she replied. "All good."

Birendra handed her a set of room keys and walked her over to a stairwell. She waved good-bye and thanks to Granger, even though, apparently, he would be hanging around. "No worries," he called back.

"We've put you up on the second floor," said Birendra. "Fewer lines of attack than the ground-floor apartment you were in. I hope that is okay."

She laid her hand on his shoulder and squeezed. "It's perfect, thank you."

The wharves still rumbled with the noise of heavy construction work. It would continue through the night, but her eyes were drooping, filled with sand, and Jules didn't think she'd even notice. She promised herself that come morning, she would find some way of making contact with the Rhino. For now, she could barely walk in a straight line.

It did not occur to her to ask Birendra how he'd gained access to her room to move her bags into the new lodgings. Perhaps a bribe to the manager. Perhaps a spot of coercion. She didn't care. When she was alone again, after he had done a final sweep of the new room and left her to rest, Jules forced herself to have a shower, washing away the grime and sweat of a long and terrible day. By the time she crawled into a T-shirt and then into bed—having carefully placed the shottie, pointing away from her, on the bedside table—she was struggling to remain conscious. She fell into a deep sleep within seconds of laying her head down.

34

TEMPLE, TEXAS, ADMINISTRATIVE DIVISION

Unlike the prim dormitory suburbs of Killeen, the ruination of Temple announced itself from a great distance. They approached from the southwest, sweeping up along Interstate 35, the wheels of the Humvee throwing up small fantails of water from the puddles that had gathered on the tarmac. Caitlin could tell from a few minutes out that large parts of the town had burned back in 2003. The southern suburbs seemed to grin at her through the rain like shattered teeth in a skull. Thick stands of trees grew up through the foundations of houses that were now no more than blackened stumps and stagnant pools of runoff, festering in former cellars. The site reminded her of ruins she had seen in the jungles of South America and Asia.

"Looks a little shabby," she said. "You couldn't have tidied up before I got here?"

"We really are a pretty minor operation here," Tusk Musso replied. "It's just my eighty-seven staff, two platoons of army rangers to provide security, and a floating population of about a dozen or so, who might be here at any time on temporary assignment."

"Rangers? That's a little excessive for garrison duty."

"You'd think so, but a lot of my people are out in the field, and they need class A security out there. Standard procedure is to send a stick of rangers out to scout ahead while another one rides shotgun over the resettlement teams."

"What's your problem? Bandits? Road agents?"

"Mostly both, yeah," said Musso. "But we've had to stand down the occasional TDF unit as well. Turf disputes. Misunderstandings about exactly how much autonomy federal officers have, even outside the mandate. Some of these guys forgot that Texas is still part of the U.S."

They rolled through the remains of a former commercial precinct, or perhaps a light industrial neighborhood, on the very edge of town. Weeds and saplings grew thick within the ruins.

"So how much of the place burned?" she asked, looking ahead out the windshield.

"A lot of the suburbs in the north and maybe about a third here on the southern edge," he said. "The center of town, where we are, isn't as bad. There was some fire damage back on the day, but a lot of the commercial buildings were protected by their automated systems. There's been some flash flooding in the intervening years, however. That messed up the road network worse than all the crashes on Wave Day."

Some major ground-zero effects could be seen at the intersection of I-35 and a multilane loop road—the Dodgen Loop, if she recalled from the briefing notes. It looked like a couple of acres had been bulldozed. Musso saw her frowning at the devastation.

"A total clusterfuck, Agent Monroe. Army engineers came through, demolished everything. It wasn't just the usual automotive cataclysm. A tanker that had been circling to land over at the fort on Wave Day decided to come down here instead when it lost its crew. It's lucky the whole city didn't go up, but the freeway acted as a firebreak and a line of storms passed through the same day to damp everything down."

Again Caitlin had that weird, almost extrasensory impression of thousands of ghosts pressing in on her. And hundreds of millions beyond them. Outside of New York, Seattle, and most recently Kansas City, she hadn't traveled at all in the United States since returning for the Battle of New York in April. Like everyone, she'd read a few articles about the ecological catastrophe that followed the Disappearance, and she and Bret had watched the David Attenborough documentary series on the BBC, *Life after the Americans,* about the natural world recolonizing the continent. Or at least they'd watched the first two episodes. She'd found it fascinating, but Bret was too upset to watch any more than that.

She craned her head around as the Humvee rumbled through the rebuilt intersection. She felt that for the first time she really had some idea of the magnitude of what had happened here in 2003. It wasn't just the people who'd gone missing. The very land had violently and almost instantly begun to rearrange itself.

"I've seen worse," Musso said, reading her thoughts. "Sometimes whole cities just gone, like photographs of Hiroshima after the bomb, but worse. You look at those old photos, and they only ever show the city. I remember flying across the country when we were doing the first surveys, after I got back from Gitmo and they didn't know what to do with me. I tell you, Caitlin, the things I saw. Scorched earth for hundreds of miles beyond the edges of some cities. Reminded me a bit of Iraq after Saddam lit off the oil wells that first time. Except much, much worse. Out in the desert, there was nothing to die under those clouds. Here it was different."

The general's face had a faraway look to it, and she wondered whether he was even aware he'd just called her by her first name. They continued up I-35 for a couple of minutes until he took an off-ramp at Lengfeld Drive, the primary route into the heart of Temple by virtue of it being the only one that had been completely cleared. The gateway to the city consisted of a couple of rubble-strewn blocks that looked as though the Army Corps of Engineers had done as thorough a job on them as it had a little farther back up the highway. Small mountains of concrete, twisted I beams, bricks, car bodies, and the shattered frames of a couple of dozen small buildings had all been piled up like an offering to an angel of destruction.

"Is that all left over from when you opened the place up?" she asked him.

Musso threw off his distracted air. "Yeah. It was a real mess in there.

And when we settled on Temple for the Federal Center, this road we're on offered the best access for the smallest investment. Engineers just smashed a way through, built a big pile of crap at the nearest convenient dumping ground." The general waved a hand toward his window. "Most of the city hasn't been cleared. The roads are still blocked with auto wreckage, and in the burned-out sections there's whole forests grown up and over the street grid."

She could see railway yards on the right as they approached the center of town. A big diesel engine was chugging through at a walking pace.

"So it's all about the railway line?"

"No, it's partly about the railway line. Partly about the highway. Mostly about the Hood. If they weren't here, we'd have left this place to the coyotes and the vermin. But the road and rail links are important, and God knows, if we ever sort out the politics, Temple will probably revert to its first life as a transport hub."

As they entered the fringe of the old central business district, General Musso slowed down and waved to a foot patrol trudging through the drizzle. A small wedge of the city center between Lengfeld and the Amtrak station had been cleared but not reclaimed. The buildings looked woebegone. Many of the windows were broken, and here and there where a façade had collapsed, the debris had merely been pushed back off the footpath. Caitlin wondered whether the sticky black puddles of grease that marked the last resting place of the Disappeared had been cleaned out of them or whether the buildings functioned as mausoleums. She thought the latter more likely. Even back in Kansas City, large swaths of the city had not been cleared of the dead.

"Looks a little gloomy, I know," Musso said dryly. "But in her defense, you did catch us on a wet Sunday afternoon. You wait till you see rush hour tomorrow morning. There can be upward of half a dozen cars between the hotel and the municipal building. It can take the better part of a minute to drive between them."

She allowed herself a smile. "I'll make sure to set my alarm."

"Don't make it too early," warned the former marine as he turned onto Main Street and took them past the elegant old pile of the municipal building, which now housed the federal government in central Texas. "We're having drinks tonight. I've set up a meeting with Blackstone's right-hand man, Ty McCutcheon. Worked as Mad Jack's aide when he was up at Fort Lewis. He's Blackstone's Jed Culver down here, you might say. A charming devil—emphasis on 'devil.' Did Culver tell you much about him?"

"Made it clear he didn't like him much," Caitlin replied. "Told me not to trust him, but I filed that under 'Well, duh.'"

Musso laughed at that. "Yeah. They got some history, those two. Butted heads back in Seattle during week one of the Disappearance. McCutcheon was Blackstone's knife hand back then. Still is. He did a lot of the dirty work on the resistance in Seattle. Undercover stuff, black bag jobs. Kinda nasty, if truth be known. Lot of people got snatched out of their homes and beds because of Ty McCutcheon. He tried to bludgeon Jed Culver into submission, too. Didn't work out so well for him."

"I can imagine," Caitlin said, with a thin, bleak facsimile of a smile. Culver might have looked like Mr. Stay Puft, but the evil one from *Ghostbusters*.

They pulled up in front of the Kyle Hotel. Built decades ago but recently refurbished, it retained the stolid, immovable appearance of much of the city's older architecture.

"He'll meet us here, your new home," Musso told her. "We rebuilt the old bar downstairs. Fitted it out with some of the best salvage we could pick up around town. It's not a bad spot, even if I say so myself. Always wanted to run my own bar."

"And McCutcheon was happy to come over?"

He cranked on the hand brake and turned off the engine.

"Yes. For two reasons. As I explained earlier, you have something they want. And as I explained to McCutcheon, Colonel Kate Murdoch is very easy on the eye. Sorry about that. He asked."

Caitlin rubbed at her finger where her wedding ring should have been. "Great," she said wearily. "The mortal enemy of Mr. Stay Puft is a ladies' man."

The listening devices in her hotel room were of Israeli design but at least five years old. That told Special Agent Monroe she wasn't dealing with Mossad. Or the NIA. Or even with some embarrassing effort by Tusk Musso's security team to monitor her presence in their midst. No, the Verint Systems bugs she found in the landline phone, the alarm clock, and the dead television set were the sort of cast-offs Tel Aviv would be happy to hand over to Blackstone's security services as an unacknowledged part of the wider technology-transfer agreement he had with the Israeli government. It took her less than ten minutes to sweep the room and locate them all.

No biggie, she thought.

She left the devices in place. No point tipping off anybody at Fort Hood. Colonel Murdoch wouldn't have thought to look for such things. Not here in Temple, anyway. She reexamined and discarded the idea that Musso might have planted them. The tech wasn't standard issue for the feds, and the chances of him acting so stupidly were as close to zero as made no difference. He was aware of her capabilities, at least in a basic sense. The only question she had was whether to inform him that his own security had been compromised.

Again, a no-brainer. She'd keep the information to herself.

A few hours stretched out ahead for Colonel Murdoch before McCutcheon was due to arrive. She had her own traps and snares to put in place before the evening, in preparation for which she would need the help of Musso and at least one of his staff in the bar downstairs. That took all of ten minutes to organize, by which time the rain had eased off, allowing her to explore the streets around the Federal Center and familiarize herself with what she thought of as her lay-up point.

There wasn't much to see. The Army Corps of Engineers had done an excellent job of clearing the debris of apocalypse, large and small, from the neighborhood. If it weren't for the damaged shop fronts, the occasional burned-out building shell, and the large numbers of broken windows on the upper floors along Main Street, it could have been any small city on a wet public holiday: no traffic, very few people walking around, nothing open.

The Texas Administrative Division's Federal Center was housed in the old town hall, a fine-looking building a few minutes' walk down the street from the Kyle Hotel, where she and everyone else in Temple were staying. She had an office inside the Federal Center, where she would be expected to compile her report on the military capabilities and intentions of the South American Federation and what, if any, additional U.S. military forces might be necessary to counter any threat from them. She was grateful to Musso for having seen to that already. It was a pain when you had to work as hard at the cover story as you did on the mission behind it.

It was telling, though, she thought, that Blackstone took Roberto seriously enough to have approached Seattle on the matter. After spending the last couple of years making life as difficult as possible for the feds, it had to be significant that the governor had turned around and begged them to commit more forces to the southern flank, as he insisted on calling it. Having so recently been in the Federation herself, Caitlin had no illusions about the malignant nature of Roberto Morales's regime, but she did not see it as a credible threat. Assuming he even survived—*el presidente por vida* or not—Morales would need another five to ten years to consolidate his rule, after which there'd be an unknown amount of time before he was able to project power very far beyond the borders of his empire. If he did manage to pull all that off, it would be quite the strategic challenge for the next generation of American leaders to deal with a hostile superstate stretching from the Panama Canal to the southern tip of Chile. But that was a long way off in the future, and chances were that it would never happen. If she had to put money on the barrelhead, Caitlin Monroe would bet heavily against any sort of unitary state surviving down there. It was only the chaos of *el colapso* that had enabled the Colombian gang boss to gather so much power to himself so quickly. Once the imperative of survival passed, Morales, like all dictators, would soon build up a complex of grinding fault lines and fractures within the structure of his regime, what the old Soviets used to call inherent contradictions. She had seen it time and again, before and after the Wave: the more oppressive the dictatorship, the more stable it appeared to be, right up to the moment it collapsed. And they all collapsed in the end. Closed, authoritarian systems simply could not regulate themselves. The complexities eventually undid them.

Did that mean that Blackstone was paranoid to be obsessing about the Federation? Had he transferred his irrational resentments and fears from James Kipper to Morales? Was that something she'd have to factor into her mission? Playing to the man's neuroses could be a fast track into his trusted circle. Or it could make her look like she was patronizing him.

After covering a couple of blocks around the old city office building and memorizing the terrain, Caitlin turned around and headed back to the hotel. There were a few people out walking the streets now that the weather had cleared up slightly. There was hardly a wealth of things to do in Temple, Texas, and she imagined that one could quickly go nuts cooped up in the Kyle. She wondered if the junior members of the mission were subjected to the same level of harassment Mussu had described. If so, it would certainly discourage them from heading over to Fort Hood during their downtime even though the recreational facilities out that way had to be so much better.

As she reached the corner of the block on which the hotel stood, she caught the eye of a man out walking by himself. He was thin, with a heavy black mustache, and seemed tightly wrapped up in himself. He was dressed in plainclothes but with a soldier's bearing and appearance and something more with it.

"Hello. Excuse me," she said as they drew level. "I just got into town. I was wondering if there was anywhere to eat besides the hotel."

The man smiled and nodded, a strangely formal gesture. When he spoke, it was with a thick Polish accent.

"I am afraid, madam, no, there is not. It is a pity and inexplicable to me, Fryderyk Milosz, once of Polish GROM, now of U.S. Army Rangers. When I accepted transfer here to be closer to brother's family, who come to farm in the Federal Mandate, I did so on promise of posting where nothing happens and only danger I, Milosz, would face would be risk of growing dangerously fat on excellent barbecue foods."

Caitlin opened her mouth, but he forged on. Apparently Fryderyk Milosz, once of Polish GROM, now of U.S. Army Rangers, had a lot to get off his chest.

"I fought with the pirate asswits in New York, madam, and despite their best efforts, I survive, thanks to excellent GROM training and intervention of two crooked smugglers who save Milosz from asswits but not from disappointment, which is another story, unrelated to immediate disappointment of barbecue. A quiet posting and too much barbecue, is that too much to ask? I fight for this country; now all I wish is pulled pork roll. Yes. Apparently it is too much. And so now I am deranged with hunger and disappointment. So much that I have neglected my manners. I am Master Sergeant Fryderyk Milosz, once of Polish GROM. And you are?"

She actually giggled, charmed by this old-world eccentric. "I am Colonel Kate Murdoch, Sergeant Milosz. U.S. Air Force."

"Ah," said the ranger, bowing formally again. "You are to be investigating this bandit fool Morales, yes? We have heard about you. Temple is very small town. Smaller even than my home in Poland. No. I will not speak of it. You will mispronounce name if I try to tell you. It translates roughly as 'little hamlet of hovels at the foot of the big hill, smelling of sulfur, where it rained all the time and nobody had enough to eat.'"

"So you must feel at home here, then, Master Sergeant."

Milosz grinned appreciatively. "An air force colonel with wit! This is exceptional improvement to fortunes of Milosz. Do you read, Madam Colonel? I have explored ruins of local library. There are many well-preserved books to be found there. So few of my comrades here read or wish to discuss ideas if ideas prove unrelated to strange football games with body armor or the salvaging of old cars for purpose of racing in circles."

Caitlin put up her hands. "Master Sergeant, take a breath. I am indeed a reader. When I get the opportunity. But I'm afraid on this trip all of my reading will be for work."

She took a step to signal her intention to keep moving.

"I wonder, though, Master Sergeant," she said, "whether you've ever tried your luck over in Killeen or Fort Hood? There's a lot more people over there. I'm sure they could find both pulled pork and a good book."

A shadow darkened the ranger's face. "I am afraid Milosz is not welcome in the kingdom of Blackstone," he replied. "At first I thought his stupid TDF troopers were prejudiced against Poles because of our superior intellect and handsome looks and winning ways with the ladies. But then I realize pretend soldiers of TDF simply prejudiced against everyone. So like everyone, I stay away from Fort Hood."

"I'm sorry to hear that, Master Sergeant," she told him, aware that she'd better head back and change for the meeting with McCutcheon. "Tell you what, though. I have a meeting with Mr. Blackstone's aide later this evening. You can rest assured that I'll see to it you can move freely around Fort Hood."

The diminutive senior noncom appeared to stand a foot taller as he smiled. It was an almost cartoonish grin that lifted Caitlin's spirits for no reason she could identify. "That would be most excellent, Madam Colonel," he said. "I shall continue my walk and hope to see you again."

They bade each other good-bye without military formality, and Caitlin resumed her journey back to the hotel. She was intrigued by Milosz's mention of the two smugglers in New York. Could they be connected to the pair of clowns she'd encountered when looking for Baumer's command post on the Upper East Side? Or was it even those two themselves—the shifty Sloane Ranger and her idiot Viking side-kick, that slob with the busted-ass novelty cow-horn helmet? Jesus, what a fucking pair of retards.

She made a mental note to contact Vancouver to request an en-crypted burst of Master Sergeant Milosz's service record. If she had even an indirect connection to him via those looters, she'd need to be careful about maintaining her cover here.

The refurbished lobby of the Kyle Hotel was alive with activity, at least for Temple on a wet weekend afternoon. Ten or more people were enjoying a drink in the bar that Musso told her they'd built from salvage collected around the city. It was a comfortable but eclectic space, unsurprisingly, with no theme to tie the disparate elements to-gether. Was it a sports bar, a ladies' reading lounge, a Victorian-era gentlemen's club, or a military mess? Depending on where one looked, it could have been any of those things. It worked as a social space, how-ever. Food, drink, company. All one had to do was ask.

Caitlin drew a few looks as she hurried through the lobby. A new face always would in an environment like this. She took the elevator to her room on the fourth floor and ran a hot shower. She'd read McCutcheon's profile in the briefing package back in Kansas City: air force major; forty-two years old; unmarried at the time of the Wave; no children; working on secondment as Blackstone's aide at Fort Lewis;

resigned his commission the same day as the general and followed him down to Texas, where he ran Mad Jack's successful campaign for governor in 2005. A fixer in the style of Jed Culver if she wasn't mistaken.

And a ladies' man.

Would have been easier if he was gay, she thought as she stepped under the hot water. It felt scalding on the parts of her body that had been exposed out in the cold air: her fingers, face, and neck. After a few seconds she grew used to it, appreciating the way the heat worked out some of the cramps she'd picked up on the flight down here.

After toweling off, she debated what to wear to the meeting, eventually going with casual drill pants, a black T-shirt, and her leather jacket. After all, it was just a getting-to-know-you drink on a slow Sunday afternoon. She didn't want McCutcheon thinking that Colonel Murdoch had gone to any special trouble for him.

At 1800 hours sharp—Katherine Murdoch was nothing if not punctual—she stepped out of the elevator into the lobby and made her way to the bar. She saw Musso right away, sitting with an athletic-looking middle-aged man, who seemed a couple of years older than forty-two because of his iron-gray hair. Major Tyrone McCutcheon.

The two men stood as she approached while being observed by everybody in the bar. The crowd seem to have swelled to two or three times the number she'd noted earlier.

"Colonel Katherine Murdoch," said Tusk Musso, "I'd like you to meet Governor Blackstone's senior aide, Ty McCutcheon . . . Mr. McCutcheon, Colonel Murdoch has joined us from Dearborn House to have a look at the situation with Roberto. I'm hoping you'll be able to work well together."

"So am I," McCutcheon replied, smiling.

She took his hand.

"That depends on whether or not you're going to try to shake me down with all the chickenshit security theater you've been using to make everyone's life a fucking misery around here," she spit out before sitting herself down and signaling to the waitress that she was ready for a drink.

She was the only person moving or making any noise in the room.

35

DARWIN, NORTHERN TERRITORY

Shah's men were good. Julianne slept through the night, and when she awoke—well after dawn, to judge by the brightness of the morning light streaming in around the edges of the curtains—she realized with a slight start that they'd been in her room. In just a few hours her fusty, crushed, stinking clothes seemed to have been quietly spirited out of her small backpack, laundered, and returned, crisp, dry, and folded. A small selection of other items of clothing, all of them more suited to summer in the tropics than her rags were, hung from the door handle or lay draped across the back of the room's only chair.

She put aside her surprise, however, and any natural disquiet. Birendra was supervising them, after all, and these men had gathered around her in a protective shield at the behest of Narayan Shah. At any rate, her concern was marginal. After years of shipboard life, she had a high tolerance for people messing around in her personal space. Sometimes it was necessary. No point being precious.

Jules swung her feet out of bed and padded over to the windows to edge the curtain open a few inches, just enough to brighten the room so she could move around without tripping. While she was mixing and matching outfits from the pieces scattered around, she noticed a couple of significant accessories: a mobile phone and a handgun. The phone was a Nokia, one of the new models with a large color screen and Internet access. Sitting next to it on the dressing table was a SIG Sauer pistol with three spare clips of ammunition. The shotgun Granger had given her was gone. Fair enough, she thought. Darwin was a frontier town, entirely feral in parts, but she doubted the local wallopers would stand for her walking around with a sawed-off elephant gun.

In the bathroom, she found additional evidence of unusual thoughtfulness on the part of Shah's men. Or perhaps the beautiful Ashmi had been in their ears. The cheap no-name toiletries supplied by the motel had been replaced by body gel, shampoo, and conditioner from Crabtree & Evelyn. Jules nearly swooned.

She toweled off her damp hair after a long shower, turning her mind to the practicalities of having burned her fallback ID, the increasingly compromised Julia Black. She had just over a thousand dollars in cash, which wouldn't last long in Darwin. However, she had three credit cards in the name of Ms. Black. Three cards she could no longer use because they'd automatically give away her location to any interested parties. Shah undoubtedly would support her, but she'd need to be able to look after herself.

The answer, at least a temporary one, slipped under the door as she was getting dressed: a large white envelope with her name inked on the front. Jules finished buttoning up the sky-blue linen shirt she'd thrown on over a pair of khaki shorts before retrieving the envelope.

Inside she found two thousand Australian dollars in "pineapples"— the bright yellow plastic fifty-quid notes they used down here. There was also a note from Nick Pappas and a printout of a Microsoft Where 2.0 map downloaded from the Web. The map showed her the route to a waterfront café where she should meet Pappas in half an hour.

She fitted a holster for the pistol to the thick, soft, brown leather belt Shah had supplied. The gun sat comfortably in the small of her back, covered by the long tail of the shirt. She found the placement awkward, having carried her weapons openly for the last few years. But then, for the last few years, she mostly had been traveling well beyond the edge of the civilized world.

She finished lacing up a pair of sturdy comfortable walking boots and divided the cash into three lots, adding some to the thousand dollars in her wallet and securing the rest in two pockets she could zip closed. Her complexion had tanned to a deep caramel over the years of shipboard exposure, but she took the time to apply a layer of moisturizer with a high UV rating anyway. In her opinion, Australian women had old rhino hide for skin, and Julianne did not intend to emulate them for want of five minutes' basic skin care.

That thought led naturally to worrying about the Rhino and wondering how she might be able to contact him. Those two cops up at Bagot Road obviously hadn't come through with anything for Piers Downing. Reminding herself to ask Pappas, Jules left the room.

Her bodyguards were nowhere to be seen outside. The note from the former SAS man told her they would be around, but she couldn't see them at all.

She joined Pappas at a table tucked into a back corner of a dining room that enjoyed views over the ocean. The Sirocco Café, according to the Australian, was a real-world example of how the power structure of this city had been wrenched free of its moorings by the Wave. Change had come quickly, and it had run deep.

"The army used to own all this land," he said, waving his fork back in the direction of the long, low-lying headland along which she had just walked.

It was not yet nine o'clock, but already the heat was stifling. Jules was frosted with drying sweat as she fanned herself with the menu and leaned back to allow chilled air to spill over her from the air-conditioning vent directly above their table. Bifold doors retracted to open the Sirocco up to a vista that stretched from the million-dollar yachts anchored in Cullen Bay around to the open waters outside Darwin Harbor. The water changed from the striking, almost opalescent green of the shallows close inshore to a deep cerulean blue a few hundred meters out.

"I spent a lot of time here at the end of the '90s," he added. "At the barracks down at the start of Allen Avenue."

"The old brick buildings I walked through, the shops."

He grinned as he carved up a thick rasher of bacon. "Yeah, the frock shops and wine bars and little trinket places. Pretty, weren't they?"

They were indeed very pretty and looked hideously expensive, too. Not that the Sirocco was a greasy spoon with its dark bentwood chairs, fresh white linen, and a minimalist layout that suggested that an architect had been paid a lot of money to do nothing. However, the patrons and trophy wives sunning themselves and enjoying breakfast out on the terrace, though looking well fed and content, didn't seem to be in the same league as the new money she'd seen flaunting itself down on Allen Avenue. Even so, many of them were probably the well-insulated, well-off types who never let the cares of the world affect them.

"This whole headland used to be mostly open ground," said Pappas, his big rugby player's frame expanding as two arms stretched out to provide some idea of the size of the area being discussed. "It was the barracks, some pretty dreary housing, and a lot of brown grass keeping the dust down."

That didn't describe the neighborhood she had just walked through. It looked to have been extruded, fully formed, within the last twenty-four hours from the wet dreams of a property developer with an Ayn Rand fetish. Condo complexes, pukka low-rise residential villages, stand-alone mansions of steel and glass that implied astronomical power bills to keep them cool, satellite dishes, in-ground pools, and long tidy avenues shaded by old-growth trees. The sorts of trees you could transplant, but only at massive expense.

"Seems a short time for such a complete makeover, though, right?" Jules asked. "New money, I suppose."

"Like you would not believe. Hundreds of billions of dollars poured in here, looking for a safe haven. It was like a tsunami, a blast wave. It swept everything away. There's an army base about thirty klicks outside the city, replaced the barracks here. There are two infantry divisions out there, one armored regiment, and a marine expeditionary unit that the Yanks kicked in to give the Combined Fleet an amphibious assault capability. *And,* of course, because they couldn't afford to run a marine expeditionary unit themselves anymore; now the Pacific Alliance picks up the tab. Anyway, all of the infrastructure, all of the matériel, every bloody cubic meter of concrete, every nail, everything—it was all paid for by the development authority."

"Just like Old Bill's nick yesterday," Jules ventured, nodding slowly. "All on account with the FPDA."

"Too right. Except we call 'em brown shirts here," he added with a grin. "And all just so they could get the military out of the city and the developers onto the headland. That's how much money they have, and that's how much power it brings."

He began forking his bacon onto a piece of toast, which he dunked in the yolk of a fried egg. "Still," he said with a shrug, "I suppose it makes sense. If anybody ever decided to lob a couple of cruise missiles at that base, at least our cafés and resort-style executive residences would be spared."

She had the distinct impression that Nick Pappas did not approve. She scooped up the last of her yogurt and muesli and washed it down with a sip of English breakfast tea. They were alone in their darkened corner of the Sirocco. The whole terrace was well shaded and comparatively cool despite lying beyond the chilled-air curtain protecting the interior of the café. Most of the other customers preferred to take their leisure out there, and Pappas seemed to know the proprietor well enough that he and his guest enjoyed an exclusion zone around their table. He had taken a seat in the corner, affording him both a clear tactical overview of the room and an exit through the door to the kitchen, which was just a few feet away.

"So what now?" Jules asked.

"A couple of things. For you, unfortunately, a nervous few days, or hours, or who knows, maybe even minutes while we wait for these pricks to have another go at you."

"Hmm. I can't honestly say that the sit-around-and-wait-to-get-slotted plan is filling me with confidence, Nick."

Pappas finished his breakfast and began patting down his pockets as though looking for something before stopping, frustrated. "Bugger," he muttered. "I keep forgetting I'm supposed to be giving up the smokes . . . No, look, Julianne, it doesn't really appeal to me, either, so I think we need to get on the right foot. Shah's given me a pretty good backgrounder on this bloke Cesky and your past with him. But what would really help is sitting down with you now and working our way through everything you know. Not just about him, which I'm assuming isn't much more than I already know, but also about everybody you had on that yacht who you reckon he might have it in for. If this bloke is working through a revenge fantasy, it'd help me to know who he's likely to hit and where I might find them. Or what's left of them."

Jules adjusted her chair so that she wasn't looking directly into the fierce glint of the sun coming off the water. "Do you have a pen and paper?" she asked.

He produced a notepad and a small digital recorder, and she told him everything she could remember about the week they had spent in Acapulco at the end of March 2003.

Cesky hadn't even figured that much in her calculations at the time. He'd wanted to get his wife and four daughters to Seattle, she recalled. Some crap about big business opportunities there, with that shimmering death haze on its doorstep. Proved himself to be an instant pain in the ass—well, a bigger one than most of the passengers she eventually took on, which was saying something—and Miguel Pieraro had done her a solid favor by beating him down when he did. She knew Cesky was hanging around the Fairmont on the day Shah came in to evacuate the paying passengers and Miguel's extended family. She smiled fondly at that—*extended* family; he couldn't have extended the numbers much further—although she'd been furious at the time. Apart from that moment, neither Shah nor the Mexican had had to deal directly with him. Miguel had given old Henry a pretty good scare, not to mention a public humiliation. The vindictive little prick had then blasted out text messages all over the city saying that people who needed to be evacuated could rely on Julianne Balwyn to get them out on her boat. Thousands turned up.

Being honest about it, Jules could see why Cesky would imagine he owed them some payback. Any normal person would feel the same, especially if he'd been abandoned in a dangerous shithole teetering on the edge of collapse. But normal people wouldn't take it any further than that.

And normal people, she had to admit, probably wouldn't have gotten themselves and their families out of Acapulco. They'd have died there. Cesky had shown himself to have the balls to cope with being kicked off her boat and to leverage himself and his family onto another one. A pity it sank and one of his kids drowned. Perhaps if that hadn't happened, she wouldn't be sitting here talking to Pappas. Perhaps he could have just let it go and been content to have escaped.

"So the other passengers you took on," Nick asked when she'd finished, "these rich reffos and wetbacks—what about them? Who were they, and where are they now?"

Julianne shook her head. "Not all of them made it across. We lost a few when we ran into the *Viarsa,* a big pirate ship, in the South Pacific. And I'm afraid that once we made Sydney, I didn't exactly bother getting forwarding addresses for my Christmas card list."

Pappas, who was scribbling away even though his recorder was picking it all up, gave a little shake of the head. "Doesn't matter," he said. "If they're kicking around somewhere, I'll find them. Especially if Cesky has already had a go. You said that before this mate of yours, the Mexican bloke, gave him a bit of a touch-up, Cesky had had a fight with some Internet porn guy?"

She laughed loudly enough to attract the attention of a couple of diners sitting outside.

"Oh, God, Larry Zood! I still have to take a shower when I think about him! It's like having somebody's unwashed underpants inside your head."

A smile flickered at the corner of the former commando's mouth as he kept taking notes.

"I have no idea where he is now," she continued, "but he was one of those turds who would always float to the top of the bathtub. He shouldn't be too hard to find, because he'll be standing on top of a building somewhere, holding his little willie and shouting his name out as loudly as he possibly can."

"In that case, he's probably dead already," Pappas said. "If he made it onto Cesky's list, that is."

"I suppose you're right." Still, she couldn't find it within herself to feel any sympathy for the odious little bastard. Zood almost hadn't made it onto the boat, either. It was only a sports bag full of fake Fabergé eggs encrusted with real jewels and the solemn promise to stay in his cabin with two of his porn pixies for the duration of the trip that had allowed him on board. Well, that and the fact that Jules didn't see him as a troublemaker in the same league as Henry Cesky. Larry Zood the porn king was not likely to lead a mutiny.

"What about other crew members?" Pappas asked. "And are you sure our friend Shah didn't come into contact with Cesky at any other time?"

Jules chose a tile on the spotless white floor and stared hard in concentration. "God, it's been a few years now, and you'd have to ask him yourself, I guess. But no, I can't imagine any other occasion where their paths might've crossed, let alone any direct confrontation. Although Shah was responsible for security on the day of the evacuation, of course. It was his job to make sure we didn't have trouble from Cesky. Or any of the thousands of drunken college kids who turned up looking for a free ride after he sent those texts."

A waitress arrived to clear away their plates and asked whether either of them wanted anything else. Pappas ordered an espresso. Jules thought about having her teapot refilled but settled on a glass of water instead. Her warm cheeks told her that she needed to hydrate. The heat and humidity were going to be murderous.

"What about the Rhino, then?" Pappas asked. "He wasn't on shore with you when you were selecting passengers, was he? He stayed out on the boat, as I recall."

Jules had to work hard to dredge up all the details. As she cast her mind back again to that frenetic week they'd all spent in the Mexican resort city, a warship hoved into view around East Point, a wedge-shaped promontory on the far side of the bay over which the Sirocco enjoyed such a fine outlook. It looked fast and sleek, and as it steamed west for the harbor, Jules could make out a French ensign at the stern. But the warship was dwarfed by one of the largest yachts the English-woman had ever seen: painted in dark blue and white, with its own helicopter deck and runabouts, this superyacht made the 240-foot *Aus-*

sie Rules seem like a bloody canoe. *Le Grand Bleu* and her Russian owner were the talk of the town.

She turned her attention back to the table. "I'm pretty sure Fifi and I hired the Rhino down at the marina, where we'd tied up the big sport fisher off the *Aussie Rules*. We had a hut down there that we were using as a base. You know, for gathering stores before we transferred them out to the yacht and for taking on crew but not passengers. As far as I recall, we took him on pretty much as soon as we saw him. He had that coast guard background. Made him an easy pick. So he would've gone straight out to the *Rules* and never even laid eyes on Cesky, surely. Miguel merely beat Cesky down. Rhino probably would've killed him."

"Too bad he didn't."

"Yeah. Too bad."

Pappas frowned. "So why send somebody all the way to Darwin to chop him?"

Jules shook her head before replying as she watched the French frigate slicing through a gentle swell. "I guess he did his research. Cesky, I mean. When the police seized the *Aussie Rules* after we got to Sydney, the crew pretty much went their separate ways. Shah, Birendra, and their lads headed for home. The bloody Aussies tossed poor Mr. Lee in jail—called him an illegal immigrant and deported him to Indonesia about a week later. I haven't heard from him since. The rest of the crew were fine, probably because they were all Europeans." She shook her head again, in disgust now. "And the Yanks, of course, the refugees, they were double-plus good because they were all rich and white, right? I think Canberra was taking in as many Americans as it could at that point, probably hoping to gather enough of them down here that they'd have first call on what was left of the U.S. military if the shit hit the fan."

A small lift of his massive shoulders signaled Pappas's agreement. Old news.

"So within a couple of days, everyone had scattered. Except for the Rhino and myself. After the cops seized the yacht and pretty much everything on it apart from a few trinkets and baubles I managed to stash away to pay off the Gurkhas, I was broke. The Rhino was no better off, so we talked it over and agreed to go into the . . . er, salvage business."

Pappas grinned at the euphemism.

"We'd got lucky with Greg Norman's yacht," she continued, "and figured there might be some more easy pickings like that out there. Had to have been a couple of thousand vessels affected by the Wave, just drifting on the ocean."

"And how'd that work out for you?"

"Not nearly as well as I had imagined," she admitted. "It took us a couple of weeks to organize passage back across the Pacific, and by the time we'd done that, it was too late. The place was swarming with pirates who'd come up from the south. Anyway, to cut a long and dreary story short, after the Wave lifted, we decided to try our luck back on shore. That ended with us in New York, having our arses pulled out of the fire by a couple of U.S. Army Rangers and Commando Barbie . . . Well, actually, we got the rangers' cocks off the chopping block, and they paid us back with a helicopter ride. For a slice of our profits, which turned out to be one-tenth of one percent of fuck-all."

Now Pappas regarded her with a quizzical look; he might have been questioning her judgment, or even her sanity, for having gone to New York in the first place. Or maybe it was in reaction to her and Rhino having welched on a deal with a couple of heavily armed special operators. She shrugged.

"The rangers were cool. We ran into them about a week later. Told them what had happened. They were somewhat pissed, but then they would've been dead if we hadn't stuck our noses in their business in the first place. We called it even."

Shaking his head as though he were having trouble keeping it all straight, Nick Pappas checked his digital recorder to make sure he still had disk space.

"So anyway," said Jules, "the Rhino and I had been working together for quite a while by the time Cesky made his first attempt on us, back last April or whenever it was. I guess he decided on a two-for-one deal. As somebody who's not unfamiliar with the odd scam, I do have to give him credit for how he put it together. He played us like a pair of fools, led us by the nose all the way into New York, and put us exactly where he wanted us—right in the middle of a bloody war, where he could have us slotted and nobody would even notice. Unfortunately for him, he should've hired a better class of goon. But then, even if he had, I don't know that they'd have been much chop against the Bond girl fantasy we ran into. Seriously, Nick, I don't know that 007 himself would have stood much of a chance against her."

The waitress returned with a single shot of coffee in a small stainless-steel cup. Pappas nodded before downing it in one swallow and turning back toward Julianne.

"Yeah, Shah told me a little about this woman. All secondhand from you, of course. She sounds interesting."

"Interesting?" She laughed. "I suppose so."

"She wasn't special forces," said Pappas, sounding very sure of himself. "She must've been NIA. Or possibly Echelon. They've got some scary fuckers working for them, let me tell you. And they're all grumpy as hell since the Vancouver treaty dragged them into the light of day. Yeah, it's interesting . . . I wonder what she was doing there. They almost never operate in-house."

He seemed so intrigued by the woman who had saved their lives in Manhattan and so surprisingly confident about her possible backstory that it gave Jules pause to wonder whether Nick Pappas's own background might have involved a tad more skullduggery and spooking about the place than was seemly. Even for an old boy of the Special Air Service.

"I'd very much like to visit Rhino if I could," she told him. "Do you think that might be possible? I've been sick with worry."

He thumbed off the power switch on his digital recorder and relaxed just a little, reclining back in his chair and spinning the tiny stainless-steel espresso cup on its stainless-steel saucer. A terrible affectation, in Julianne's opinion. The stainless steel, that was. Coffee should be served in a proper cup.

"I've got a few things to chase up here," Pappas said, tapping the recorder with one finger. "If it turns out Cesky's knocked off half a dozen people, it might be possible to handle this straight up. Just turn it over to the authorities and let them sort it out. After all, he'd have a hell of a time explaining the coincidence."

She didn't much fancy that idea. Jules's father had inculcated in her a deep-body distrust of the authorities because of how difficult they made it for him to separate gullible characters from their hard-earned quids without legal consequence. On general principle, she did everything she could to avoid dealing with agents of the state. In this case, however, she could discern a clear and present danger in Henry Cesky. As she'd been reminded down in Shah's wine cellar the night before, he was a bum chum of the U.S. president; she was a smuggler, a thief, a killer in her own right. And, never to be forgotten in this part of the world, Jules was the woman who had hosed the sticky remains of Greg Norman off the poop deck of his yacht before sailing away on her without so much as a by-your-leave.

Pappas picked up on her discomfort immediately. "I know you have issues, and I'm not saying we're about to pop into the local wallopers and file a formal complaint."

"Oh, Jesus, no," said Jules, remembering the trip to Bagot Road with Shah and Downing. "I wouldn't trust those slick bastards as far as I could throw them."

"All I'm saying, Julianne, is you have to accept that this guy, if he is responsible, may well be beyond your power."

"What power?"

"Exactly. But this is real, not a trashy movie. Guys like James Kipper, they don't want shit like this blowing back on them. If Cesky is your guy, they'll cut him loose. It's just a question of how we get that information to them."

"I'm open to suggestions," she replied with more than a little bit of sarcasm in her tone.

He smiled. "You leave that to me. You have other things to worry about. If you want to go see your mate, it'd be best if you didn't just roll in with a six-pack and a get-well-soon card. Somebody tried to blow him up, and a couple of other punters died because of that. Wherever they've got Rhino now, the police will be keeping an eye on him and everybody who comes to visit. If you're going to go calling on Mr. Ross, you might want to give Piers a call. He can send you along on official business, so to speak. Let him set it up and just present yourself as one of his junior lawyers when you get there."

She nodded. It would mean having to pick up some office clothes, but that wouldn't take more than an hour or so in the city.

"And my other little problem?"

"The bloke over here now who wants to kill you, you mean?" Pappas grinned. "I'm afraid that unless I can make some headway," he added, holding up his notes, "we're going to have to go with our original plan. Put you out there. Let them try. And hope we can reach out and grab them before they put a bullet in the back of your neck or a bomb under your arse. How's that sound?"

"Spiffing."

36

TEMPLE, TEXAS, ADMINISTRATIVE DIVISION

To the aide's credit, his cheesy grin didn't freeze in place and shatter when Colonel Murdoch went upside his head. Tusk Musso looked as though he was about to have a litter of kittens, but if anything, McCutcheon's smile was even wider and sunnier than before.

"Ma'am," he said, "I'm sure you're exaggerating. We do take security very seriously over at Fort Hood. I had to stop at two checkpoints myself coming here. That's why we invited you down—we have a real security problem."

The two men lowered themselves into their armchairs as one of the off-duty enlisted arrived to take Caitlin's drink order. In many ways, it was a very informal bar based on the honor system. A large pickle jar full of newbies watched by what she assumed was an off-duty sergeant ensured that it would remain honorable. Soldiers and civilians could and did walk behind the bar to get what they were looking for, holding it up for the noncom's approval before dropping their coins into the jar. The drinks were free, government salvage, but the tips went to the staff.

"I think I saw a bottle of Highland Park back there. If I could get one of those with a single ice cube, that'd be great," she told their waitress. "And in a decent glass, please, the crystal. If you're gonna drink well, you should treat your drink well."

Musso and McCutcheon both called for resupply on the beers, and the female soldier disappeared to fill the order. At the far end of the room was a massive media wall. A pair of rangers sat on recliner lounges with game controllers in their hands, firing at some sort of alien on the sixty-inch plasma. Thank Christ they wore earphones. Two other men worked around the room, picking up the empties and polishing the tables.

"Is this on the duty roster?" she asked.

"Yep," said Musso. "Probably the most popular duty we have. I've always been surprised that it's worked as well as it has."

Caitlin returned her attention to the fixer in chief of the Blackstone administration, fixing him with a gamma ray stare.

"I'll make a judgment about that security situation of yours in the next couple of days, Mr. McCutcheon. But I've already made a judgment about the unnecessary harassment and intimidation of federal officers within the administrative area of Fort Hood and Killeen. Before I lift a finger on this project, you will take measures to ensure this harassment ends. Immediately."

The ambient noise level in the hotel bar fell away completely. Again. Caitlin was aware of everybody trying, without actually staring, to follow what was happening within the little tableau presented by the three of them. Musso looked deeply uncomfortable but willing to let her play it out in character. McCutcheon seemed amused. He held up his hands in mock surrender.

"Damn, working with you is going to be fun, Colonel."

"Not if I don't get my way," she said without a trace of humor.

McCutcheon's blue eyes were twinkling, and two small creases had formed at one side of his mouth as he suppressed a smirk.

"Okay, you got me. We do like to have our fun down here, and I will admit sometimes we might take a joke a bit too far. But I wasn't joking before, ma'am." He allowed the boyish grin to fade as he rearranged his features to telegraph Deep Concern. It was quite an act. "I know that all the way up there in the Northwest, y'all don't think much of Roberto as a threat. But he is pushing us every opportunity he gets. Before we brought down the hammer, we had his people all over the state. They were openly sizing us up for a smack-down. If it feels like a bit of an armed camp here, in contrast with friendly old hippieville up in Washington State, it's because we *are* an armed camp. I hope you'll come to see the necessity of that over the next couple of days. Governor feels we need a lot more assets in the Caribbean, on the canal, and all the way down through Mexico into Central America. Only the federal government can do that. You have the reach; the TDF does not."

The drinks arrived, changing the atmosphere.

"Thank you, darlin'," McCutcheon purred, winking at the soldier. Caitlin almost expected him to slap her on the ass as she walked away. But what little remained of his military bearing, coupled with years of enforced sensitivity training, seemed to have stayed his wandering hand. For the moment, at any rate.

She had the distinct impression he was just playing dumb. For one thing, y'all, he wasn't a good old boy. Tyrone McCutcheon, she knew from his bio in her briefing set, had been born and raised in Alaska. He hadn't picked up his Southern drawl in Juneau. All he was missing was a pair of shitkickers, a Stetson, and a belt buckle the size of a hubcap to complete the impression that he was a down-and-out bull rider whose eight seconds of fame had come and gone.

"You can make a sales pitch tomorrow," said Caitlin, beginning to enjoy herself in the role of hard-assed Colonel Murdoch. "But only after I've received a guarantee from you that the imposition of unreasonable restrictions on Federal Center personnel will end. It is ridiculous that these people have to drive thirty or forty miles out of their way just to get to the goddamn airport."

Having gotten nowhere with his naughty schoolboy routine, the governor's right-hand man opted for remorse and sincerity. Or at least a reasonable imitation.

"Okay, okay, I get it," he replied. "You had to take the detour to get here today. Okay. I apologize for that. And I tell you what, as soon as I'm done here, I will personally call the relevant people and make it right by you. My promise."

Colonel Murdoch cocked one eyebrow at him. "I'd have thought *you* were the relevant people, but I'll take you on trust. For now."

McCutcheon nodded slowly, as if he'd just been dealt a hand of cards he didn't much like but knew he could play.

"Well, that wasn't at all uncomfortable," Musso rumbled, feeling like a third wheel.

Caitlin softened her features and allowed some of the tension to run out of her posture. She had made her point.

"Oh, Mr. McCutcheon is a big boy, General. I'm sure a bit of rough play won't put him off his game." She favored McCutcheon with a smile of such beatific innocence that after the performance of the previous few minutes he could have doubted her sanity.

"Why don't you call me Ty," he suggested. "And you, Colonel, were you born with that rank?" He managed to inflect his voice with an acknowledgment that he was pushing the boundaries, but he was still playing.

"I'm sometimes known as Kate," she conceded. "When I'm off duty and around friends like General Musso here."

"Welcome to Texas, then, Kate."

"Thank you, Ty. It's nice to be here," she replied, finally giving him something.

Musso blew out his cheeks. "Lucky thing we make everyone check their personal weapons at the front desk," he said. "Now, Mr. McCutcheon . . ."

"You, too, General," he said, teasing. "We're all new best friends now. How about you call me Ty, and I freshen up these drinks?"

The president's official representative in Texas didn't look wary so much as calculating. "I'm always happy to be friendly over a couple of beers . . . Ty. But Colonel Murdoch does have a point. It's a lot easier to be friends with someone when they're not trying to ass-fuck you on a daily basis."

Tusk's voice sounded reasonable enough, friendly even, but there was no mistaking the steel underlying his tone. It seemed to have no effect on McCutcheon. He caught the female soldier's attention with a backward tilt of his head and signaled for another round before answering the general.

"Look," he said, showing them his open, honest palms. "We got us a face-facts moment here. I can't pretend relations between my boss and yours have been good. I can't even pretend I've done anything to make that better until now. The two men have their history, and there's probably no forgetting it. Hell, I was with General Blackstone in Seattle, and I've been with him ever since. I can guarantee you there's no forgetting what happened up there for him. And to be honest? There's no forgiving, either."

Caitlin accepted the second drink when it arrived, but she put it aside. The background buzz in the room had come up again, but she was aware that their group was still the center of attention. McCutcheon seemed to be aware of it, too. She was certain he was playing to the audience, in fact.

"But this isn't 2003. Those days are gone, thank God, and we recognize there's a whole new set of problems down here. Problems that are a hell of a lot bigger than any personal disagreements between the president and the governor of Texas. We are willing to put all of that behind us, to admit we made mistakes. More than our fair share of them. And to move on with making up for those mistakes."

Caitlin said nothing. She agreed with Musso that Morales simply wasn't a major threat. However, that didn't mean Blackstone didn't see him as one. He might be a raging ego monster, but in some ways Mad Jack was also a very delicate soul. Ego monsters were often like that: hard but brittle. If she wanted to gain the former ranger's trust, appealing to his fears and indulging his delusions might just pay off. Across from her, however, leaning back deep into the embrace of a black leather club chair, with one foot propped up on the coffee table, General Tusk Musso appeared to be less inclined to let bygones be bygones. Perhaps he'd been inspired by Colonel Murdoch, the castrating bitch from central casting. Or perhaps he just felt like getting his own back for all the hours he'd spent trapped at McCutcheon's roadblocks.

"I would hope, Ty," he said, carefully enunciating each word, "that if you're not just feeding us a line, if your boss is serious about a rapprochement, then it would extend to a lot more than simply coordinating deployments between your militia and the real military."

If the old Marine Corps lawyer was trying to be elaborately offensive, McCutcheon wasn't rising to the bait. He absorbed any insult and waited for Musso to continue.

"Because, Ty, I don't think I need to list my grievances with your administration. You would be well aware of them. Even disregarding the way you run things in the Hood, there is the matter of the security situation within the mandate, which we very foolishly handed over to you. There's the matter of the federal–state accords, the revenue-sharing deals, the contracts and treaties you've been signing ultra vires with foreign corporations and powers, and . . . Well, I'm sorry—I said I wasn't going to list my grievances, but there, I went and did it anyway. Because they are *grievances,* Ty. Real and legitimate grievances. And I'm disinclined to trade favors over them just because Blackstone has his pantaloons in a twist over Roberto."

McCutcheon made an effort to interject but Musso waved him off.

"The president takes the security of the nation very seriously. If he thinks there's a threat from Morales, he will crush him like a bug. I guarantee that. But security doesn't come from guns alone. The only thing that comes from the barrel of a gun is a fucking bullet, not security. If this country is ever to be secure again, it won't be because of a president tossing a couple of regiments here and there or moving the *Lincoln* out of the Pacific and into the Caribbean and the Atlantic. It will be because we all decide to work together to make ourselves strong again. Do you think we can do that, Ty? Do you think we can get past everything that happened in the last few years and work together?"

Caitlin took a sip from her single malt and regarded McCutcheon with a neutral expression. There was a reason Blackstone had sent him into the enemy camp. He didn't disappoint.

"Can we kiss and make up? Fuck, yes! We might have differences of opinion, but our interests are the same at heart. We just want the best for the country. Honest Injun now—if you can take just a couple of steps toward us, I know Jackson Blackstone will meet you halfway, sir."

The moment hung suspended while everybody waited on Tusk Musso's response. Caitlin could feel the sense of relief through her pores when he nodded and growled, "Okay, then. Let's try."

Maintaining her cover, Echelon's senior field agent displayed no reaction beyond taking another drink and watching McCutcheon like a hunter in a blind. Her stone face covered her feelings of uncertainty. Had Musso planned to go off like that? Or had he been inspired by McCutcheon's response to the uncompromising Colonel Murdoch? Even more intriguing, why had Tusk spoken in anodyne euphemisms about the security situation in the Federal Mandate? The question was at the forefront of her mind, she realized, thanks to the recent murder of Miguel Pieraro.

Lower-level bureaucratic harassment was one thing, amateur-hour genocide quite another. And from her reading of the Blackstone administration, they had some hard questions to answer about what had been happening to people like the Pieraro clan. She doubted that Blackstone possessed the means or even the base-level competence to have reached out and touched Pieraro in Missouri. But she had no doubt that the road agents had been able to run wild in Texas through an act of omission, if not commission, on his part.

She placed McCutcheon's new-best-friend routine firmly within the context of the listening devices she'd turned over in her room. To have planted them successfully, Blackstone must have turned at least one member of Musso's staff or somehow planted an agent here. Either operation would require a significant commitment of intelligence resources to the task of subverting Musso's command. Tyrone and his boss were overreaching, but that just made them more dangerous.

Special Agent Monroe resolved then that although she would maintain her mission focus on establishing the meaning of the link between Blackstone and Ozal, and through him to Bilal Baumer, she would not lose sight of any opportunity to nail the motherfucker for the fate of anybody in the mandate who might have lost his or her life on his say-so.

"I think this calls for a real drink," she said to McCutcheon. "Are you a bourbon man, Ty?"

37

Sunday night was pork chop night. The president of the United States of America said so. On Sunday nights, there were to be no formal state dinners, no working suppers shared with staff, no late-night pizzas, no Chinese takeout scarfed down at the desk. Because Sunday night was pork chop night. President James Kipper was working the grill, because on pork chop night he got to be a regular guy again. The staff was excused. Suzie was packed off to bed with a book for lights out at 1930 hours, and the First Lady was banished to a hot deep tub with a glass of wine while Kip worked his barbecue magic.

Manning the grill in the wintertime normally didn't faze Seattle's former chief engineer in the least. He actually enjoyed standing in the cold with a brew in one hand and tongs in the other. The smoky flavor of brats, burgers, and every so often strip steak seemed that much more intense in the brisk cold air. Unfortunately, this evening the blizzard conditions outside meant he was restricted to using a little hibachi unit on the kitchen counter rather than being able to work the tongs on the big, honking eight-burner beast that sat, forlorn and neglected now, under a huge loaf of snow.

Not to worry. His thick boneless pork chops had been marinated to within an inch of their life in a generous measure of Arthur Bryant's special KC barbecue rub. During his last visit to Kansas City, he'd managed to slip away long enough to visit the site of that famous restaurant at 1727 Brooklyn Avenue, near the city's old Jazz District. The meat in the pit had long since turned to dust, yet the smell—that delicious greasy smell of well-prepared pork, burned rinds, ham, and turkey—was still there.

Although it was getting harder and harder to find these days, the wonder rub had survived the years of neglect well enough. The sauce, that special vinegary creation that old Arthur himself used to mix up in five-gallon glass bottles, not so well. A small clique that included expatriate Kansas City folk and other barbecue aficionados from the South and the Midwest had been trying to reformulate the sauce. The president had a bottle of their concoction in the cabinet, but it never tasted quite right. Still, it didn't taste like curry, either, and for that he was grateful.

Someone's gonna get that sauce right someday, he thought. *Maybe after I get out of this job, it'll be me.*

Barbara once had accused him of resettling Kansas City simply so he could get production restarted on this old favorite, which he'd first discovered during an engineering convention back in the pre-Wave years. Not that she didn't have her own personal indulgences, such as raiding the stocks of Williams-Sonoma and the Pottery Barn to refurbish Dearborn House.

Looking around the well-equipped, painfully clean and modern kitchen, Kip marveled at the tongs in his hands. They cost enough to buy a whole set of utensils from Walmart back in his college days. He was still getting used to the amount of space here, since he used the kitchen only on Sundays. It smelled of coffee, baked sweet potato, and now slow-cooking pork.

He was halfway through his first growler of the local Elliott Bay

Demolition Ale, although, it had to be said, the main reason he drank the stuff was that no one could reproduce a decent Boulevard Pale Ale, another of Kansas City's former delicacies. A fridge dedicated to his favorite beers stood in the kitchen's small anteroom, not that he ever had enough time to sample them. Tonight was different, though. Tonight the president of the United States would make time for beer. It was an executive decision.

The country was not at war, he had a late start tomorrow, and he was gonna get absolutely shit-faced tonight. Perhaps, if Barb had another glass of pinot noir, he might be getting lucky, too. And if not, he was going to attack the beer fridge and soak in the tub while reading a growing backlog of L.L. Bean catalogues. He had a postpresidential canoe trip to plan, after all.

It was at that very moment, as the first chop began to sizzle and smoke and fill up the kitchen with its heady smell of porktastic goodness, that Jed Culver appeared at the kitchen door to put the zap on his mellow.

"If I could, Mr. President—just a minute before I head out home?"

Oh, fuck this for a joke . . .

"Really, Jed? Working late on a Sunday? You sure you wouldn't like to forget about it and have a beer instead? I just tapped a new keg."

The chief of staff looked as though he was tempted, although it could have been the smell of the pork chops, of course. Culver was a fool for the barbecue arts and definitely more of a Texas man than Kipper. In fact, they'd had many debates over the relative merits of Kansas City barbecue versus Texas or Memphis style. Seattle had a barbecue culture of its own, but Kip didn't take it very seriously. General Murphy, a reluctant Missourian himself, had remarked at his retirement ceremony the previous month: "My boots should stick to the grease on the floors of a good barbecue joint. I never get that feeling here in Eeyore-land; it feels too squeaky clean, like eating in a surgical suite."

Jed cocked his head one way, looking at the beer keg, then another as he checked his watch. Satisfied, he bobbed his head in a nod. He seemed grim, more so than usual. It had been days since he'd even mentioned the looming election campaign. Kip wondered what was bugging him so that he could make a note to do it more often. He loved not thinking about electoral bullshit.

"Well, maybe just one beer," Jed muttered. "But I'll still need a minute of your time."

"Pork chop night, Jed," said Kipper, as if that might save him.

Culver fetched a glass from the draining rack over the sink and poured himself an ale with a practiced hand. Kip remembered him saying once that he had tended bar while at college. It seemed there was very little that the Louisianan didn't have some working knowledge of.

"I'd offer you dinner, Jed," he said. "But Barbara only picked up enough for two. And I'm not good at sharing."

Culver set his glass down on the galaxy-black granite countertop and held up both hands. "I wouldn't want to interrupt pork chop night, Mr. President."

Kipper resisted the temptation to start turning the meat. In his humble opinion, too-frequent turning made the meat tough and dry and was a crime against humanity. There should probably be a law against it. He'd have to look into that. After another beer.

"So, what was it you wanted to bug me about? Your minute starts now."

"Just an update, Mr. President. Secretary Humboldt just sent over a briefing note from her department on how we might handle dispersing the women and children out of the camps in the east. I've read the executive summary, and I'll try to digest the whole thing later tonight. But from a practical point of view, it looks okay. We're going to keep the families together but break up the tribal groups and scatter them like chaff. Most will be going out to the frontier to work on government farms, so they'll be under supervision. And working plenty hard with it."

Kip found that he could work the spatula under the chops without having to push too hard, a sure sign they were ready to flip. He was about to call Barb down when she appeared at the door in her dressing gown and slippers, looking rested and even a little flushed from the hot water and the alcohol.

"Hi, Jed," she said. "You staying for dinner?"

"No," both men answered at the same time. Culver found a weary smile somewhere and added, "I'm picking up Marilyn at the apartment, and we're going out to dinner. Although I have to say my mouth is watering right now and I could be talked out of it—except that your husband and my wife wouldn't approve."

He emptied his beer in two long pulls before rinsing out the glass and replacing it on the draining rack. "And anyway, I really was just dropping in on my way through. We can discuss how we handle Sarah's plan tomorrow," he added, turning back to his boss. "And I'll need to have a word with you about Texas as well."

"Okay, then," Kip replied. "Right now I have perfectly cooked pork, cold beer, and a smoking-hot wife. I'm afraid I don't intend to be distracted from that by affairs of state."

"I'm sorry, sir. But I did speak to the bureau, as you instructed, about the Texas matter. They're going to do what they can, but it will take time. I just—"

Kipper held up his free hand like a nightclub doorman. "Nope, Jed. Not tonight. There's nothing I can do about it tonight. And even if there was, I wouldn't. Because it's pork chop night. You want me to ring Director Naoum first thing in the morning and lean on him, that's fine. But it's not happening tonight."

He expected a fight and was preparing himself for one, getting a rein on his temper before it got away from him, but the chief of staff merely sighed and shook his head, almost as if he were trying to shake off a wearisome thought or mood.

"No, sir. That won't be necessary. You said you wanted the FBI on this. They're on it in their own methodical, dilatory fashion. I'm sure they'll do a thorough job. But I just want you to know it will take *time*. And there are alternatives that I could set in play before I have my first martini tonight."

"Only if you really want to go to jail, Jed," the president said, half in jest but with a tone to his voice that, he hoped, implied he was serious, also.

"Fair enough," Culver replied, finally seeming to accept that he'd lost. "Tomorrow morning, then. Barb." He dipped his head to say good-bye and left to locate his driver.

"Not a happy customer," Barb said once he had gone. "Can I help there?"

"Sweet potato bake and trees are in the oven. They'll be good to go by now," Kipper told her, trying to recover his good mood from earlier. He was relieved that Jed hadn't pressed the point about Blackstone and, he presumed, that damned Echelon woman, but he was still pissed off he'd even had to think about it this evening. That was the problem with living where you worked: there was no escaping the office.

Barbara busied herself with removing the two porcelain baking trays from the oven, one heavily burdened with a large sweet potato done au gratin and the smaller one holding the obligatory greens: broccoli baked with lemon wedges. "Trees," as Kip still called them. A term from his childhood. Broccoli he wouldn't eat, but trees he would. Just like their daughter now. There were times it drove Barbara batshit, right up there with the fart jokes when Barney Tench was around.

He lifted down two square, white dinner plates from the crockery cupboard and wondered why they had to be square. What was wrong with round, normal-looking plates, for chrissakes? American dinner plates. *Fucking Seattle; sometimes they just push things too far here.* He definitely needed more beer.

Once he'd drained his beer and handed the glass to Barbara, he found that he was too hungry to give a damn but that his mood had improved. The beer, of course. And the prospect of another one. Barb returned with a refill, giving him a kiss.

"Thanks," he said. "Good to know the president still has some supporters."

He pulled down a tray, loaded the plates on top, and followed his wife into the media room, a techie's wet dream of entertainment equipment, most of it Korean or Japanese these days. A sixty-inch Samsung LCD came to life as Barb settled down on the leather couch that dominated the center of the room.

She smiled. "Snuggle time, Mr. President."

James Kipper had never been much of a TV-dinner guy before falling ass backward into the presidential rumble seat. But he found nowadays that once he was free of the office, all he wanted to do at night was smash down a beer or two, have a nice dinner, and put his feet up in front of the tube. It was a pity there was never anything on but reruns and imports, especially from Britain. Local Seattle television had started to offer a sitcom called *Forever Wild* that Barbara seemed drawn to. It followed a bunch of "econauts" around various protests and coffee shops while they made lame jokes about the military-industrial complex. *Econuts, more likely,* Kip thought. He preferred his comedy delivered stand-up and low-brow. Frankly, he missed Jeff Foxworthy.

And he really missed wall-to-wall sports broadcasting on ESPN, ESPN2, and ESPN Classic. Granted, he had never had time to watch much, but it had been nice to have the choice in theory. Now, with the economy only just grinding its way out of the subsistence years, there simply wasn't the money for professional sports the way there had been before. The reconstituted National Football League and Major League Baseball were filled with wannabes and a few broken-down retirees who coulda been outplayed by any decent high school team. Paul McAuley assured him it would come back. Even New Zealand, with a population still many times smaller than America's, managed to support a service-driven, consumption-based economy. But then, they hadn't had to rebuild themselves from the ruins of the Wave.

"Damn, I forgot to kiss Suzie good night," Kipper said just after sitting down. "Is she still awake, reading?"

"Worst. Father. Ever," Barb said. "She's been down for about half an hour. Fell asleep reading Harry Potter."

Neither of them wanted to watch the news or the woeful Christmas specials. Kipper couldn't handle yet another dose of Jane Austen on PBS's *Masterpiece Theater,* either. English costume dramas just didn't do it for him. And the First Lady had banned any consideration of repeats of pre-Disappearance sports highlights shows. They couldn't understand the accents on the Australian soap operas. It was too early for any of the cooking shows, so they settled on *Grand Designs,* an English program that followed couples—for some reason it was always couples—as they built or renovated their dream homes. Every week it was the same thing: the couples always underestimated the budget; their dreams always ran ahead of their resources and the available time; and it was as if nobody had ever heard of employing a project manager. Barb enjoyed the aesthetics of some of the old houses being brought back to life, and Kip, who'd had to be ordered to keep his nose out of the Dearborn House restoration efforts, enjoyed shaking his head and muttering "assholes" under his breath as those idiots made the same basic engineering errors and project management mistakes week after week.

At least it made him feel better about his own manifest inadequacies. He was the type who loved to crack wise about Dubya before the Wave. Now he imagined a pantheon of departed American presidents looking down on him, smacking their foreheads in constant aggravation and cursing, "What a fucking moron!"

The commercial breaks also had changed greatly since 2003. Many of the spots were taken by the Advertising Council. A particularly entertaining one tonight featured an African-American male doing pull-ups for the camera and stating that he didn't need to take his heart medication because he was just fine. As he hoisted up into the camera for the last time, he could be seen twitching before dropping off the bars and out of view with a loud thud. It ended with a reminder to go see your doctor and take care of your heart.

The ads for private businesses tended to be hyperlocal. One shaky camcorder spot featured a large man in bib overalls rocking back and forth on his feet, trying to convince folks that they needed his lawn-tending services. Kip's favorite place in Pike Place Market, Frellman's Brats and Sausage Hut, was a little slicker. Home of the Thrown Brats, it gave you a fishing net to snare the bangers out of the air.

He was surprised to see a lengthy, much more professional-looking ad for Cesky Enterprises' new prestige apartment project in the renovated Smith Tower. It reminded him of the days when television advertising wasn't a cottage industry.

"What did Jed want to talk about, honey?" Barbara asked when they had finished eating.

"Oh, I've had him and Sarah working on what we might do with all those people in the camps back east," Kipper declared around licking his fingers. He knew he couldn't tell her the real reason Culver had called in: to try to bully him into sending Agent Monroe to Fort Hood.

"They're mostly women and children, aren't they?" his wife asked.

"Mostly. There's a couple of old geezers in there. And we've got another camp full of fighters who survived New York. They're more of a problem. But most of them have ties to the women and children."

Barb finished her wine and thought about pouring another one before deciding against it. She placed the empty glass carefully on the coffee table, next to her plate.

"Can't send them home, then?"

"Not all of them, no." Kip sighed. "A lot of places in Europe, if that's where they hailed from, won't have them back. And a lot of their original homelands still glow in the dark."

The show was returning from another ad break, but Barb used the remote to mute it. "And I'll bet Jed is worried about how you sell the idea of letting them stay," she ventured.

"Hell, I'm worried about that myself. Honestly, they don't deserve to stay. If he had his way, he'd stick them on a garbage barge, tow them out past the twelve-mile line, and sink them if they tried to come back."

"Most people would."

"I know. And I totally get that. But these guys were just servants, followers. After every war we've ever fought, we've eventually forgiven the enemy. It's what makes us better than them. Stronger, I believe, in the end."

He wondered if there could ever be forgiveness between Blackstone and himself. Probably not if the FBI turned the case Jed Culver had made into a real indictment. Hell, it could even lead to the mad bastard trying to secede. But Kipper didn't see that he had any choice. If there was some link between the governor of Texas and the Emir's forces in Manhattan, the president had to maintain as much distance from the investigation as possible. When they finally went public, there could be no suggestion of political interference. Jed, however, wanted to handle the whole thing in as Machiavellian a fashion as possible.

"Why?" Barb asked. She turned around to face him on the couch.

"Huh?" She'd surprised him. Was she talking about Jed—about Monroe even? Had he mumbled something in a beer haze? "Er, why what, Barb?"

"Why does it make us stronger than them?" she said, dragging him back on topic.

Kip's heart sank. He really didn't want to get into this, not on pork chop night. Still, at least he hadn't inadvertently blown the Blackstone investigation.

"A couple of things," he began. "The strong forgive because they can and because holding on to their hatred makes no sense past a certain point. You beat your enemy, and then you move on. If you can't do that, you become as obsessed with your never-ending war as he probably was to begin with. You start to see everything as part of the war. In the end, you'll lose your life to it as surely as you would by getting killed on the battlefield."

He finished his drink but, unlike his wife, decided to have another one. He stood up to go to the kitchen, picking up her glass, too, as he did so. Barb shook her head.

"I thought we might go to bed early," she said. "We could snuggle a bit."

"I'm all for snuggling," he replied, heading for the door while at the same time finding he was warming to his little dissertation. "But you know, the other thing is, we can *use* these people. We can use everyone who's willing to put up their hands and declare for us at the moment. Those fighters, if they want to live here, if they want to see their families again, they can damn well earn the privilege fighting for *us*. I'm more than happy to watch them get chewed up seeing off pirates on the East Coast. Plus, the intelligence guys tell me we can turn them and send them out pretty much anytime we want. As long as they've made the commitment to us. They become our weapons."

"And Texas?"

"I have no idea," Kip said, unconvincingly. "Jed's forever scheming against Blackstone. He leaves me out of it, thank God. In some ways they're made for each other. But I'm not sure exactly what he's up to at the moment. Guess I'll find out tomorrow. Gotta say, though, my gut feeling is that I should just go down there and have it out with Mad Jack myself."

His wife looked skeptical. "Kip, he's such an asshole."

"Yeah, but maybe he's a well-intentioned asshole. I really think he only wants what's best for the country. It's just that, you know, he's an asshole about it."

"Well, I'm sure if you fly down and tell him that man to man," she said, cocking one eyebrow at him, "he'll totally come around to your way of seeing things."

He could tell that she'd be just as hard to convince as his chief of staff. The more he thought about what Jed had told him, however, the more likely it seemed that he was going to have to go down and confront Blackstone, even if it was all behind closed doors. Because if the FBI did confirm a link to Baumer and New York, there was no way Mad Jack would go quietly. He'd scream and kick and fight this thing every inch of the way.

It made the option of sending somebody like Special Agent Caitlin Monroe down there even more tempting. Not to whack the guy but perhaps to ease him out of power quietly, informally. Kipper was adamant, however: Monroe was going nowhere near Fort Hood.

38

TEMPLE, TEXAS, ADMINISTRATIVE DIVISION

Forget about coming up with a plan to sneak into Blackstone's lair at Fort Hood. She might not live that long. There were five dogs in the pack. Not wolves or coyotes but vicious and hungry-looking ferals with none of the light or kindness of man's best friend in their eyes. They had been born to the wild and had the rank stench of it about them. They circled in front of her, growling. She was almost backed up against the brick wall in an alley behind the supermarket. The pack could not get behind her to rush in and snap at her heels, but she didn't have anywhere to fall back to.

Sofia tracked the largest of the beasts with her handgun. She could shoot it down and drive away the other dogs, but to do so would bring the soldiers running. There were two patrols out on the streets of Temple that she knew of this evening. They were proper American soldiers, and as much as she held no fears that harm would come her way from them, the Mexican teenager had no intention of being taken into custody, protective or otherwise. Shooting the dogs, though not out of the question, would not be ideal. She hefted the machete in her other hand, waiting for the right moment to make that choice.

She knew it was coming. The growls were getting lower and more intense, turning into short, aggressive barks. Her flesh crawled, an ancient reflex she was powerless to control. She had learned this when she was last in Texas. A brave woman was not fearless. She simply refused to become a prisoner of her fears, to let them rule her. The feelings that coursed through her body, the racing heartbeat, tensed muscles, the way all her senses seemed to open wide and let the world flood in, were all symptomatic of the fear that wanted to cripple and kill her. But she'd survived on the trail because she had learned from her father, from Maive and Trudi and the others, that the very same feelings could be channeled into a killing rage.

And so she waited.

The pack snarled and skinned their lips back from long yellow fangs. She fancied she could smell the foul odor of their breath, and even in the darkness there was light enough from the moon and stars that their eyes shone like silver dollars laid on the orbs of a dead man. She knew the attack was moments away when two of the animals moved, attempting to flank her on both sides. Ears pinned back, they lowered themselves onto their haunches, where massive knots of muscle and meat quivered and twitched with anticipation of the kill. The sound of their growling slowed like a powerful engine winding down.

Sophia took a long, deep breath.

The pack leader lunged forward, ripping out a fusillade of barks, snapping its jaw like a threshing machine as its pack mates launched themselves in from the side. They came flying at the girl as though hurled from catapults. But she already had moved, leaping toward the dog to her left as she swung the machete in a vicious blur of sharpened steel that connected with the animal just below its ear. The sickening crunch of blade on bone and gristle was simultaneous with the horrified, outraged howl of the beast and the crack of the pack leader's skull as it impacted the brick wall where she'd been standing. A fraction of a second later, she heard the dull thud of the third animal colliding with the top dog as she used the momentum of her first strike to draw the blade down and out while she pivoted around for an upward stroke that sliced off the snout of the nearest dog, halfway along its jawline.

The attack collapsed in a hideous discord of animal shrieks and yelps. She was drenched in hot blood and urine: the dogs' and her own. But the threat had dissolved in a heartbeat as those that could flee did so. The beast she had all but decapitated spasmed at her feet. She brought one booted foot down on its head in a hammer kick, telling herself she was putting the mutt out of its misery as her father had always taught her. But she knew that in a darker place she was punishing the thing for having attacked her, taking vengeance on a dangerous but defeated enemy.

And then it really was over.

The protests of the vanquished pack drifted farther away until she could hear them no more. Adrenaline backwashed through her nervous system, bringing with it nausea and tremors. She had to lean against the wall and take a minute to breathe deeply and slowly. For the first time since Sofia had realized she was being hunted, she heard the twittering song of night birds again. She listened hard for any sound of a footfall or human voices but heard nothing. The short, savage caterwauling din of a dogfight was not unusual in Temple, as she had learned.

Time to move.

The grocery market lay next to a railway line that ran through the eastern side of town. On the far side of the tracks, a wasteland of charred ruins stretched away to the horizon. A few houses stood undamaged, but the farther away from the train tracks she looked, the more the scene recalled the devastation of a city beset by war. Sofia did not dwell on the reason the firestorm that had burned so many acres of housing had died out before leaping to this side of the tracks. Fire, she had learned, was as arbitrary as a tornado, sometimes wiping out half of a street while leaving the other half untouched. Having survived the dog pack, she did not care to spend a second longer than necessary contemplating the ruins of Temple. She moved off, uncomfortable and a little disgusted in her blood- and piss-stained clothes.

The market had been built right up to the edge of the road surface, and a large tarmac remained largely free of vegetation. A few hardy weeds poked through cracks in the concrete here and there, but unlike in so much of this ghost town, she did not have to wade through waist-high grass in which any number of dangers might lie.

The doors of the market were jammed open. They had attempted to close on a shopping cart on the morning of the Disappearance. No moonlight penetrated the interior. Sofia pushed the cart out of the way, forcing it over the pile of clothes that lay just behind it. After holstering her Magnum and flicking on a small flashlight, she could see the remains of the Disappeared everywhere. The authorities had not been through here to clean them up, and there had been no attempt at salvage. That made sense. Unlike her, the federales could rely on being properly fed and watered, and by now, Sofia knew, most of the contents of this store would be unusable. The fresh food had all rotted away or been eaten by vermin years ago, along with most of the packaged food. But her needs were simple.

Crossing herself and murmuring a prayer for the dead, she stepped deeper into the gloom. Her senses were still amplified after the fight for her life. She could hear rats scurrying deep inside the market building but nothing larger than that.

The first of her provisions she found in the third aisle: five-gallon plastic bottles of water. The contents would taste foul after all this time, but water did not go bad as long as the seal on the bottles remained unbroken. With no running water in the motel she'd chosen to lay up in tonight, she had no choice but to seek out potable supplies. Food was more of a challenge. On the journey to Kansas City, they had hunted and trapped wherever possible, but occasionally they had come across stores of food preserved well enough to use. Sofia knew what to look for, thanks to Trudi Jessup, who had schooled all of them in the shelf life of canned and dried groceries.

Into her backpack went half a dozen cans of corn, a tin of peaches, two packets of vacuum-sealed lentils, and, the Lord Jesus be praised, one large canned Christmas cake. A real score. She checked the tins for dents and swelling and the packets of dried food for any sign of insect infestation. She would do a more thorough check back in her room, but as an experienced scavenger, she was confident she'd just secured enough food and water for three days.

Once upon a time she would have thought nothing of walking the ten or twelve blocks back to her new hideout, a trip of fifteen or twenty minutes. But returning from the market this night, she was heavily weighed down as she negotiated a treacherous passage through more streets overgrown with vegetation and blocked by wreckage and fallen trees. Advancing in short bursts of movement, scurrying from cover to cover, always watching and listening to avoid being discovered, Sofia took over two hours to return to the Economy Inn, a two-story motel of brown bricks and weather-faded trim on the southern edge of Temple's town center. It was close enough for her to feel as though she was in some sort of contact with the federales but far enough removed from their comings and goings that she didn't have to remain in hiding every hour of the day.

Despite the chill of the night, she was sweating by the time she got home.

Home.

How sad that she should think of the Economy Inn as her home.

Although a young teen in years, Sofia Pieraro was experienced in the dictates of survival. She did not hurry into the motel; she remained in cover where she could observe from a safe distance. Having killed bandits who had returned to their campsites without taking the precaution of checking for ambushes laid in their absence, she knew to wait and watch for at least an hour. Even though, in this instance, she was certain long before then that it was safe to enter, Sofia cleaved to the lessons of the past. Only when a full hour had passed with no sign of anybody lying in wait for her did she complete the last, short leg of her return trip.

Even then she was not done with caution. Leaving her supplies at the front desk, she retrieved the AK-47 from where she had stashed it, behind a fire hose in a closet on the ground floor. Without night vision equipment, she had to fix the little flashlight to the barrel with a couple of thick rubber bands she carried for that purpose. Safety off, finger on the trigger, selector to full auto, she performed the last rite of her careful passage back into hiding, effecting an entry into her motel room as though she knew it to be occupied by an intruder.

It wasn't, and after a quick sweep of the few places where somebody could be hiding, she collected her food and water and shut herself in.

First priority was to clean herself up and dispose of her soiled clothing. She wouldn't waste water on laundry, not when clothes could be scavenged so easily right here in the motel. She stripped and then washed herself with a cup of water and a hand towel and soap from the bathroom. Changed into a clean pair of jeans and a dark blue flannel shirt. Bundled up her dirty clothing and tossed it into the room next door. Working by moonlight, she fed herself from the dwindling supplies she had brought with her, leaving it until morning to examine the cans and packages she'd taken from the market. Dinner consisted of two muesli bars, a sachet of protein gel, and two cups of water.

She was exhausted but wired, still coming down from the shock of fighting off the pack of wild dogs. Part of her, the weak, unworthy part, longed to crawl into bed and dream of happier days. But there could be no happiness for her, not while there was breath in the body of the man she blamed for the death of her family, perhaps even for that of her father. The tyrant Blackstone might not have driven the car that had run him down, but he certainly had driven Miguel Pieraro to Kansas City, where he had perished.

Wrapping herself around the small, dark furnace of her loathing for Jackson Blackstone, Sofia crawled into bed with the small transistor radio, which was tuned to one of the two talk stations broadcasting from Killeen. Other local stations played music, and she might well have been able to calm down and sleep while listening to one of them, but she found the talk stations an excellent way of learning about Fort Hood and Killeen. Not so much about the Hood's interminable feuds with Seattle or its worries about Roberto Morales, Caribbean pirates, migrants, and West Coast liberals, all of which seemed to exercise the imaginations of the people phoning in. Rather, she was interested in the calls that gave her insight into how things actually worked here.

She knew, for instance, that all the rumors back in Kansas City about only white people being able to walk the streets were wrong. There were many African-American families, Asians, and even some Latinos living in Blackstone's capital. But they were all military people who had joined the Texas Defense Force. Among the settler families that had come here, fewer hailed from all over the world compared with Kansas City. There were no Indians and Pakistanis working on the railways in Killeen. No Arab doctors in the hospitals. No Mexican farmers tending to their own associates. But there were hundreds of them working on government farms that sounded similar in some ways to those her family had worked on as refugees in Australia. But they were very, very different in some ways. On the government farm outside Sydney, they had been free to come and go when not working, whereas here, workers seemed to move only between the fields and the barracks that housed them. Sofia knew that because of callers like Estelle, who right then was complaining to the host of the midnight shift about the number of beaners she had seen walking around, as free as birds, when she'd done her shopping that morning.

"What I want to know is where were their bosses and foremen, Ray? Where were they? I didn't see 'em. I didn't see 'em anywhere. Do we let these people run around like this nowadays? Is that how things are now? Just like Seattle, where anything goes? Because you can see what happens when anything goes, Ray. It goes to hell in a handbasket."

Sofia had heard this complaint a few times. The good people of Killeen and Fort Hood seemed most put out that they should be inconvenienced by frequent traffic stops and checkpoints while beaners and servants seemed to have the run of the town.

Ray assured Estelle that he was certain Governor Blackstone would not condone a situation in which anything went. Governor Blackstone would make sure that Estelle had nothing to worry about. Ray, Sofia had learned, spent a good deal of his time on air assuring Estelle and her ilk of Governor Blackstone's best intentions.

Estelle seemed unconvinced, but Sofia was satisfied. This was the fourth caller she had heard complaining about unescorted servants being allowed to wander around the town unsupervised. That was interesting she thought. She added it to a growing list of interesting facts she had learned from the radio or gleaned from her conversations with Dave Bowman.

Most interesting of all was the fact that Blackstone lived "among his people." In a simple house on the base.

Yes, that was very, very interesting.

39

TEMPLE, TEXAS, ADMINISTRATIVE DIVISION

The alarm woke Caitlin Monroe at six the next morning, relatively late for her. Tusk Musso had been right in telling her not to set it too early. After a tense start to the evening, the three of them had drunk well into the night. At one point McCutcheon had even suggested they pile into a couple of pickups—the table had attracted at least a dozen rowdy hangers-on by that point—and all drive over to the Hood for some real eatin' and drinkin'. That plan went nowhere.

Nobody was sober enough to drive except for Caitlin, and only she knew that. She'd secretly swapped out her whiskey to iced tea after the second drink. She was tired enough to act drunk, which, in character as the punishing Kate Murdoch, simply meant becoming more taciturn and red-eyed as the night went on. Ty McCutcheon was a natural performer and everybody's new best friend, encouraging them all to drink up and filling the bar with raucous good vibes and the promise of more to come. Naturally, he made a pass at "Katie" about halfway through the night, but then, he made a pass at every woman in the room. Hell, he might even have scored.

When Caitlin excused herself and tottered unsteadily away—a very convincing if quiet drunk—McCutcheon had two administrative assistants in his lap pouring him tequila laybacks. The Echelon operator caught Musso's eye as she was leaving, long enough for him to share a look that told her he thought this might be all for the good. It was a chance for his people to blow off some steam and maybe create a little goodwill at the top of the food chain over in Fort Hood. He, too, had switched drinking tactics early in the night but had resorted to light beer rather than the complete fake-out she'd pulled. Unless, of course, he'd had ginger ale in those beer cans.

The Polish sergeant, Milosz, who was one of the first to gate crash the table, had hauled out a stash of Cuban cigars as his calling card. One of the worst hangovers Caitlin could ever recall, from her college years—and she could recall it only dimly—had involved whiskey and cigars. It had been her first and last two-day hangover, an experience she was more than happy to avoid repeating by bailing early and taking a shower to wash the smell of alcohol and smoke out of her skin and hair. Tired not just from work and travel but from the constant strain of maintaining cover, she fell asleep soon after pulling up the covers and before her thoughts could turn to home.

Outside now, she could hear a platoon of rangers going through their morning physical training, shouting the cadence without the usual level of enthusiasm. A glance out the window revealed more than a few of last night's revelers struggling to go through the routine of side-straddle hops, squat thrusts, and the hello Dolly exercise, punctuated by frequent commands to drop into the front leaning rest for another round of push-ups.

"So glad I didn't choose the army for my cover," she said aloud. It was just the type of pointless dumb-ass physical training she hated. They'd probably follow it up with a ten-mile run to sober up all the alcoholics. No doubt, out at Fort Hood at this very instant, the same ritual was taking place. Or maybe not. As Musso said, it wasn't the regular army anymore.

She'd woken up feeling refreshed but hungry. There had been a promise of dinner with Musso and McCutcheon, she remembered, but after a few drinks that promise had turned into an untidy pile of corn chips and peanuts, an orgy of trashy carbs and additives she'd decided to skip.

After changing into exercise clothes and hitting the gym, she logged a long session of high-intensity cardio intervals, strength training, and the Tensho and Saifa *kata* of the Gyokushin *ryu* before searching for breakfast. Returning to the hotel bar, she found that the whole area had been thoroughly cleared of the debris de partay before the caterers set up the morning buffet. She wasn't surprised to see a lot of fried meat on offer, most of it the fruit of the pig. Caitlin indulged herself in one half rasher of bacon but stuck to her usual breakfast of oatmeal with berries, two eggs on a piece of wholemeal toast, and a cup of black coffee. She would have liked some citrus, but there was none to be found.

"Impressive effort, Colonel. I wouldn't have imagined any human being could face poached eggs the morning after besting a bottle of single malt in close-quarter combat."

Looming over her table, Tusk Musso was holding a plate of sausages and scrambled eggs and waiting for an invitation to sit down. He caught her with a mouthful of food, necessitating some awkward hand gestures as she juggled a knife and fork and her cup of coffee. Musso took the seat opposite.

"Saw you in the gym this morning as I shuffled past." he said chuckling. "I'm afraid I don't practice the combat arts as much as I used to. I'm getting a bit old and brittle for it. Most dangerous cripple in America, that's me."

"You don't look like you're about to fall over," Caitlin replied, smiling. "Unlike some this morning."

The general grinned with the appreciative malevolence of somebody who hadn't drunk too much. "I don't imagine Ty McCutcheon will be putting his head in there or here anytime soon," he said. "Last I saw of him, he was being dragged off to his room by a couple of rangers."

So he didn't score. Useful to know . . . Even gossip could be useful to know.

"Well, you know the air force, sir," she joked. "The hardest drinkingest service of all. Although I'll give you your due. For a leath-erneck, you didn't do too badly last night."

Musso started in on his scrambled eggs, bulldozing them up with a piece of beef sausage. "Do you think it helped?" he asked, ignoring the troll bait.

It was the sort of question he would ask of his military liaison officer, but of course they both knew she was nothing of the sort. Caitlin won-dered whether he was genuinely curious about her reading of the night or just playing to her cover.

"Depends," she said, "on how straight he was with us. On how much influence he has with Blackstone. Maybe even on whether he wakes up with sailor's nuts and gets pissed off he didn't get to have his end away with those two cuties he was bouncing on his knee last night."

A look appeared on Musso's face that was a little confused but mostly inquisitive.

"Have his end away? You sound like you spent some time in En-gland, Colonel Murdoch."

Caitlin mopped up some runny yolk with a piece of toast on the end of her fork. The eggs looked to be free range from the rich, bright orange of the yolk. She wondered where they sourced them. They reminded her of the farm in Wiltshire.

"That's how I missed the Wave," she said, dropping into the back-ground story of her mission jacket. "I was on a posting with the RAF. Only supposed to be there six months. Ended up staying nearly three years in all the confusion. Never developed a taste for warm beer, but I did get some schooling in how to drink whiskey during a stint up in Scotland at RAF Leuchars."

A few people were beginning to drift into the repurposed bar for their breakfast, but nobody she recognized from last night.

"That's good," Musso replied. "Because you'll need your wits about you today even if McCutcheon doesn't have his. We have a meeting with Governor Blackstone at 0900 hours."

"We?"

"Indeed. We, including my new buddy Tyrone."

"Somebody had better go wake him up, then. Bags not me."

"You have been over the pond awhile, haven't you? Don't worry about McCutcheon. I've already put Sergeant Milosz onto that hazardous duty."

She cocked her head a little. "You know, General, Milosz didn't look like he was going to be much better off this morning, last time I saw him."

Musso shrugged. "I think they gave Sergeant Milosz potato vodka instead of baby formula at whatever collectivized communist child-care facility he was raised in. He was probably up before you with the rest of the rangers, giving them a metric ton of shit for their unmanly inability to hold their liquor. Probably worked Melville into his cadence, too. His guys love him, but they hate it when he tries to improve them."

Caitlin washed down the last of the toast with black coffee, ready to face the day.

"I ran into him yesterday," she said. "Seemed a good guy. He was partly why I went in so hard at the start of last night. I wanted to knock McCutcheon off balance, get a concession from him before we even got things under way. I hope you're okay with that. You looked a little taken aback."

The former marine shook his head, dismissing her concerns. "You did take me by surprise, but McCutcheon was a lot more surprised. And it worked. Or it seemed to, anyway. I guess we'll see about that today. I'm going to send a few people over to pick up some basic supplies at the PX. We'll see whether or not the chickenshit is persistent."

He finished his breakfast, placed his knife and fork next to each other on the plate, and leaned back, giving Caitlin a calculating once-over.

"Is it your intention to go in against Blackstone the same way, Colonel?" he asked. "Because I don't know if the same tactics would be as successful with him. He is a prickly character."

She could see a number of stress lines working away under the surface with Musso. It was real now. She was in play. But of course she was running more than one play, and although Kipper's man in Texas had pledged to support her, he was also aware that his people would bear the consequences of any miscalculation by Colonel Katherine Murdoch. Even if Caitlin's real mission was a washout, Katherine could still have great influence over the next couple of days, for good or ill, and Tusk Musso was alone in knowing that she was largely unqualified to do what everybody else was expecting of her, namely, to create a bridge between contending powers.

Musso knew, as did she, that creation was not her forte. Caitlin Monroe's special gift was for destruction.

"I'll deal with the man on his merits," she assured him. "But I won't be dissuaded from doing what I have to."

A small convoy of Humvees followed by a solitary M35 cargo truck proceeded from Temple to Fort Hood, led by a very seedy-looking Ty McCutcheon, who undoubtedly was still too drunk to drive his Jeep Wrangler but who insisted on doing so anyway. Nobody was going to be pulling Governor Blackstone's right-hand man over to the roadside for a breath test, and he wanted to take point to make sure there was no problem when they started hitting the ubiquitous checkpoints.

Caitlin thought about taking the passenger seat in his car, but climbing into a vehicle with someone who was still obviously over the limit was not something Colonel Murdoch would do. Instead, she sat in the back of a four-passenger Hummer with Musso, driven by the redoubtable Milosz, who seemed unaffected by the ravages of whiskey and cigars. Maybe he really had been suckled on potato vodka as a child.

The direct route between the federal outpost and Blackstone's seat of power was much shorter than the long and winding detour Musso had taken from the airfield. The transition to the area controlled by the state government could not be missed. The devastation of the Wave and the entropy that had run wild as soon as humankind's hand had been lifted from the world disappeared when they crossed an invisible line southwest of Belton, a small satellite town nestled at the junction of I-35 and Route 190, which ran west to Killeen and the Hood. No rusting car hulks or broken-down machinery marred the landscape here. Out in the fields, hundreds of workers moved along freshly plowed fields, hand weeding winter crops. Caitlin wished she had a pair of binoculars. She was certain they all looked like guest workers from well south of this region. Officially, there were no migrants from south of the Rio Grande in Texas.

She settled back into her soft brown leather seat, which had been scavenged from a luxury SUV of some type. The ride was much smoother today, no doubt to the eternal relief of the private rubbing his forehead in the passenger seat up front, who looked like a bullet for breakfast would not have been a bad idea. Each time the radio beeped with traffic, the young man grunted, picked up the hand mike, and groaned out a response. Sergeant Milosz ignored him.

Unable to talk openly, Caitlin and Musso were content to listen to the Polish NCO as he gave them chapter and verse on the adventures of his brother's family on a farm in the Federal Mandate.

"Is supposed to be cattle farm," Milosz explained. "But niece has rescued baby lamb and raised it as a puppy because my brother will not have dog in the house. And yet, he allows the sheep, which now goes by the name of Vince, to wander around wherever it pleases. It sits on the couch. Sleeps on children's bed. And sneaks behind the lounge for purpose of stealthy farting, just like a dog. But with misadvantages of not being trained properly to be in house and leaving little round pebbles of sheep shit everywhere. Including in my room when I visit. I say to brother and wife they should get rid of this Vince. But they tell me the children love him. I would love him, too, with mint sauce and baked potatoes. But does anybody listen to Milosz? No, nobody ever listens to Milosz."

"We're listening," Caitlin said from the backseat as they rolled through well-tended fields. The overcast weather of the previous day had cleared, and although it was still cold, the sun shone down hard and bright.

"Has your family had any problems with the state government?" she asked as they passed a collection of residences called Cimarron Park. They didn't appear to be occupied, but a lot of work had gone into keeping down the vegetation and preserving the buildings, giving the impression of a newly built housing estate.

"Not problems for my brother Radoslaw, no," Milosz called back over his shoulder. "Resettlement people put them into new strategic village as soon as they arrive, and when I visit, I have helped them to improve defenses. They have seen no road agents. But other families who have been longer tell Radoslaw that agents are fewer now. Have been much smaller pain in ass for maybe three months. Maybe four."

Musso leaned forward to be heard over the engine noise.

"Whereabouts is your family based, Sergeant?"

"They are with six families in strategic village built in old town called Richards. Is north of Houston. Many bandits in there. Radoslaw tells me it was almost as bad as New York for a while. Until the TDF kicked them out."

"And the TDF; your brother is happy with the security they provide?"

"Oh, yes, sir. For a bunch of ignorant bigots and rednecks who scrape all the skin of their knuckles as they walk along, the TDF are okay in the judgment of Radoslaw. Of course, Radoslaw allows Vince the sheep to do stealthy farts behind couch, so perhaps his judgment is not to be relied upon."

They were deep into the suburbs now, with no sign of any security checkpoints or roadblocks. Local traffic had appeared, a smattering of merchants were opening their businesses, and increasing numbers of people were walking the streets, some holding cups of coffee and others carrying bread and milk. It seemed to Caitlin that the Hummer could have been touring a massive open-air art installation. Life before the Disappearance.

She sat forward now to quiz their Polish raconteur. "Do you mind if I ask, Sergeant? The other families in the settlement with your brother—do you know where they come from?"

"Two from Poland, good people," Milosz replied. "Two more came from refugee camps in England, the working farms. And the others I am not sure. From Seattle, maybe."

She said nothing in response, preferring to mull it over in private. The families that had arrived from England probably had come off a farm not unlike hers and Bret's. The other Poles would have been people like Milosz's family, descended from hardy peasant stock and selected for the resettlement program because of their familiarity with agricultural work. They might have gained extra points toward selection if they had a relative, like Fryderyk Milosz, who had volunteered for federal service. The final two, from Seattle, she could not guess at.

"One more question," she said. "These families down in Richards, are they all white?"

"Oh, yes," the ranger said, without a trace of discomfort. "No nig nogs or sand bandits in my brother's village."

It took them thirty minutes to cover the distance from Temple to the gates of Fort Hood. As Milosz moved on to other topics, Caitlin pondered Jackson Blackstone.

It made sense, she supposed, for Blackstone to have set himself up in the former headquarters of Fort Hood. The base itself was more easily secured than the civilian town center, to its east. He had recruited actively among former members of the military for his own migration and resettlement program. The base's infrastructure had survived well, and with thousands of disgruntled, footloose former U.S. military personnel to draw on, ramping the place back up to becoming a functioning facility would have been a lot easier than the task Musso faced over in Temple. An additional argument could be made that the Hood was simply too valuable to leave unattended, given that it was the largest existing U.S. Army installation in North America. Roberto didn't have power projection capability yet, but he would have everything he needed if he could get to Fort Hood.

Still, it said a lot about Mad Jack that his first thought was to go for the guns. There was plenty of evidence, if one wanted to look, that Texas under Blackstone was a militarized society, and nowhere more so than here at the heart of his administration. TDF armed squads patrolled the streets in armored Humvees, and although McCutcheon kept to his word and their convoy wasn't stopped, Caitlin noted the telltale signs of semipermanent checkpoints at least six times before reaching the base perimeter. She had no doubt that random roadblocks could be thrown up almost anywhere within the greater city of Killeen at a few minutes' notice.

The residents she saw on the drive through Killeen into Fort Hood seemed to care not at all. They had none of the beaten-down furtive air that usually hung around the subjects of a tyrant. Sparkling under the morning sun, still wet with yesterday's rain, the new capital of the Texas Administrative Division presented as an advertisement for Arcadia. A white, heavily armed, middle-class Arcadia.

Milosz stuck close to McCutcheon's Jeep, tailing him through the enormous military facility, a city within a city. The other vehicles in the small procession had peeled off earlier to seek out some basic supplies, fresh fruit being one item much needed back in Temple. McCutcheon had mentioned that the post exchange had a good supply, but he'd never said where it came from. Caitlin was hoping they might score some oranges or tangerines.

Like the air force bases her father had served at, a lot of Fort Hood could have passed for any patch of American suburbia, with a smattering of warehouses and industrial centers dropped into the mix. Brick barracks that looked more like college dorms were faced by large multibay garages where TDF personnel and civilians went about the task of salvaging and maintaining the massive fleet of military hardware. A cluster of soldiers took a break at one motor pool, gathering around a light tan food truck to purchase sandwiches, sodas, and other products from the fried, fat, salt, grease, and sugar food groups.

Any thoughts that the Hood was simply an office park in uniform were dispelled, however, by the sight of an Abrams tank at an intersection close to the 1st Cavalry Division Museum on Headquarters Avenue. The modern tank stood in stark contrast to the collection of mostly olive-drab vehicles from the U.S. Army's past. The crew waved at McCutcheon, receiving a hand wave in return.

"The tanks are a bit excessive, aren't they?" Caitlin asked.

"Probably there for your benefit," Musso said. "This checkpoint is normally manned with Hummers. It's just Mad Jack putting on the ritz."

The III Corps headquarters came into view across a browned-out, wide-open parade field. Caitlin half expected to see troops marching back and forth, but apparently they had better things to do. A single soldier made his or her way across the field, destination unknown. Headquarters itself could well have been any building in any industrial park throughout North America, although the silver-gray structure was certainly distinctive enough with its three-wing design. A banner hanging across the façade under the III Corps name proclaimed the following: WELCOME TO FORT HOOD. PROVISIONAL CAPITAL OF THE STATE OF TEXAS.

They pulled up behind McCutcheon as he swung down from the Jeep, a pair of Ray-Bans in place to protect his bloodshot eyes from the glare of the morning sun.

"Sergeant," he said, addressing Milosz, "we'll probably be a couple of hours. If you and the private here are feeling peckish, you can get yourselves fixed up on base, or if you'd be more comfortable in town—and as long as your boss is fine with that, of course—I can recommend the breakfast burger at Graybeard's back in Willow Springs. That was the last little shopping village we rolled through before hitting the base. But if General Musso wants you to stay close, there's also the Burger King down the road, although it doesn't quite serve the old-fashioned Whopper we all remember and love."

"Is not to be worrying," Milosz replied. "I have seagull's breakfast today. A drink of water and a look around."

"Go get yourself a coffee and a proper feed," Musso said, dismissing his escort after checking that both men had cell phone coverage.

Caitlin wore the uniform of the day: a winter-weight battle dress outfit designed for the forests of Cold War Europe. It was infused with enough starch that she imagined it could deflect bullets and knife strikes at the right angle. In many respects, Echelon's undercover operative blended in with the Texas Defense Force personnel, who retained the same BDUs as the U.S. Armed Forces. Only the blue embroidery of her name tag and collar rank marked her as an outsider. She would have preferred to have worn the lighter summer-weight battle dress uniforms she sometimes donned for fieldwork, but they were too ripped and faded for use here. There would be no explaining how Colonel Murdoch had gotten them so scruffy-looking, sitting behind a desk in the United Kingdom.

Musso seemed to have deliberately dressed down, opting for a pair of hard-wearing boots, jeans, an old polo shirt, and a jacket that looked like an insulated rain slicker. She wondered if he was drawing from James Kipper's style guide. Sending his own message.

"All righty, then," McCutcheon declared, clapping his hands together as though hangovers weren't something he had to worry about. "Let's go see the big bad wolf."

40

FORT HOOD, KILLEEN, TEXAS, ADMINISTRATIVE DIVISION

Low clouds heavy with the threat of freezing rain had turned the wasteland between Temple and Killeen darker than one of the lowest, most benighted levels of Hades. But that suited Sofia Pieraro's purposes just fine. She was used to moving through the night quietly, unseen. The unpleasant conditions would keep Blackstone's troopers inside their guardhouses, nursing cups of cocoa possibly fortified with a shot or two of something stronger. Or they would gather around oil drums and small bonfires, stamping their feet against the cold, their night vision wrecked by the flames. More than once on the long trek from Texas to Kansas City, they had encountered bandits who had made the same mistakes again and again. Many of them had died for it, some at Sofia's own hand. For now, however, she glided on.

All the local radio stations, which she had monitored so diligently, trumpeted the recent lifting of roadblocks between the state and federal settlements as a reassuring sign of improved relations between the Kipper and Blackstone administrations. Sofia hoped not. She would hate to think that what little faith her father had invested in the president had been completely misplaced. But for her, right now, the loosening of security was a godsend. The road ahead of her began to climb up a gentle hill, and she stood on the pedals of the salvaged mountain bike to bring more of her strength to bear. The *shoooosh* of the bicycle's tires and her own steady breathing were the only sounds she could hear beyond the call of an occasional night bird.

She strained in the dark to pick up anything that might warn her of danger nearby. Voices. Vehicle noises. The clink of bottles or cutlery. Anything that might indicate the presence nearby of TDF troopers or indeed of anybody who might attempt to interfere with her plans.

But there was nothing. Not this far out from Killeen and Fort Hood. She calculated that she was well within the territory of the state government now. The fields on either side of the road were sown with winter crops tended by indentured workers from the south. They would be locked up in their barracks now, and the attention of the guards focused in on them, not out toward the night.

Approaching the crest of the small hill, she slowed, stopped, and dismounted. The figure of the young teenage girl, diminutive in the vastness of the empty land, remained so still and quiet for so long that she disappeared into the background. While Sofia waited and allowed her senses to flow outward, searching for any sign of threat, a long-eared jackrabbit hopped onto the road not ten yards away from her. With its filthy, matted fur it was difficult to see at first, even with her dark-adapted eyes. But she caught the movement in her peripheral vision as it hopped across the tarmac. Were she on the trail, as she had been so long ago in another life, she might have shot the rabbit or used a hunting bow if stealth was in order to secure her meal for the day. But she had eaten well before leaving Temple and had no need of sustenance.

What she needed was to pass through Blackstone's defenses and into the heart of his lair.

After a few minutes, satisfied that she remained alone on the road, she pushed off, soon cresting the gentle rise and coasting down the slope on the far side. The moderate elevation provided her with a view of Fort Hood for the first time. It seemed to blaze in the night like a fierce jewel, but she knew that was an illusion. So used was she to traveling through the haunted ruins of America that even a few hundred houses lit up and a few streetlights strung between them were enough to create the impression of bountiful life and energy in the middle of an almost infinite wilderness.

She slipped down toward her destination, applying the hand brakes occasionally lest she accelerate to a speed at which she could not stop in a controlled fashion whenever she wanted. Sofia tried to relate the small, sparkling jewelry box of the city ahead of her to the maps she had memorized and carried in her backpack. It was not easy. Not cloaked as she was in obsidian darkness. But again, she did not allow any sense of uncertainty to undermine her determination. She already had chosen the place in which she would lie up and wait for an opportunity to present itself. She had a rough working idea of how she might use the city's terrain to her advantage.

And if that idea proved to be ill founded, she would adapt.

She had learned that from her father and her friends. To survive, to get what you needed, you had to adapt.

The road leveled out, and she began to pedal again.

41

FORT HOOD, KILLEEN, TEXAS, ADMINISTRATIVE DIVISION

Polished floors, fresh paint on the walls, and crystal-clear windows filled the Territorial Capitol Building of Texas, formerly U.S. Army III Corps headquarters, with an unnaturally pure level of sunlight. Caitlin's saluting arm got a workout on the approach to the building, greeting one Texas Defense Force soldier or officer after another. She essayed a casual salute, not sloppy but not parade-ground-perfect either. Good enough to do the job. Those she encountered seemed respectful. Then again, she was dressed in almost the exact same uniform as the TDF troopers. By the time the soldiers figured out she was a fed, it was too late to retract the salute or try any disrespectful behavior.

Once she was indoors, the saluting stopped, for which Caitlin was grateful. Like all formality, it grew to be a tiresome exercise.

"Kate," Musso said. He pointed at her standard-issue BDU hat.

"Oh, sorry. Thanks," she said, removing her cover.

Small, stupid mistakes like that would be her undoing. She killed soldiers, but she didn't live around them, her husband being the sole exception, and Bret was long past caring to maintain a soldierly disposition. She stowed her hat before the overly hungover Ty McCutcheon could notice the gaffe.

As soon as they were inside, she began taking sight pictures of the building's layout. She had blueprints of the original design, including the security net, courtesy of Echelon field services, but there had been some structural and quite a bit of cosmetic work done since the Blackstone administration had moved in. She noted as best she could where the fundamental layout had been changed and where the obvious surveillance devices—CCTV, infrared traps, motion sensors, and so on— were to be found. The building was secured, but no more than she would have expected of a civilian government facility, which was what the Territorial Capital Building was in spite of the military trappings. The main defenses seemed to be the two civilian guards at the concierge station.

As they traveled deeper into the HQ, she found civilians intermingled with soldiers in about equal numbers, all wearing the same combination of business casual. It was wrapped a little more tightly than in Seattle. Many suits, but not all with ties. There were far fewer nose rings and statement T-shirts, but again, the vibe was no different from that of the Federal Center in Temple. Musso fit right in, at least in appearance. Caitlin was the odd one out as they arrived in a large wood-paneled anteroom.

A civilian secretary, an African-American woman, stood up and smiled in greeting. "Good morning. The governor will see you. Ma'am, may I take your coat?"

Caitlin processed her surroundings while taking off her field jacket. "Yes, ma'am, thank you." She tagged a slightly more sophisticated motion sensor in a corner of the ceiling, alarms tied in to the windows, and an inert magic eye guarding the entrance to Blackstone's inner office. Again, nothing special.

After handing over their coats, they made their way into a large, comfortable space recently hacked out of the old building layout. It smelled of fresh paint and high-quality coffee roasting on a sideboard next to a silver tray piled high with fresh rolls, smoked salmon, and pastries. There was no filing system to be seen. No computer on his desk. No signs of a wall safe.

"Oh, the governor has just stepped out," his secretary said. "I'm sure he'll be back momentarily. Please make yourselves comfortable. Can I pour you some coffee?"

"No, we'll be fine, thank you," Musso replied.

The secretary left them.

An array of framed photographs, plaques, awards, and certificates hung along a wall of what appeared to be highly polished cherry. In one image, a backdrop of burning oil wells bracketed a young group of officers standing on top of a blackened Iraqi tank. In another photo, a smiling Colonel Blackstone shook hands with Bill Clinton without a hint of the reserve evident in the officers around him. A third photo, a faded color image, showed a pair of oldsters pinning a set of lieutenant's bars on a very young man.

At the center of the wall was a shadow box filled with a substantial collection of ribbons, qualification badges, and division patches. Musso didn't waste a second glance at the wall, perhaps because he had seen it all before. Caitlin took the opportunity to inspect the whole display more closely, as it afforded her an opportunity to walk around the office and scope it out.

Ty McCutcheon sidled up next to her and removed his sunglasses. "Impressive career. Enlisted at eighteen for Nam and ended up as a ranger. You'll have to forgive him for that."

"Not a fan of the 75th Ranger Regiment?" she asked.

"I was air force once upon a time, like you, Colonel," McCutcheon replied, as if that explained it. "Drove me a Warthog. The general, though, he's the real deal. Rose from the ranks the old-fashioned way. By killing those in need of it. Did his time and got a slot at Officer Candidate School. First in his family to go to college, you know."

She did know but said nothing.

"Did well there," McCutcheon continued. "Third in class. Picked up his commission, and then they sent him off to college." The governor's aide pointed up at the framed bachelor of arts in political science diploma from NYU.

A toilet flushed at the far end of the office, followed by the sound of running water.

"And the rest is a very boring story for the most part," a new voice called out. "Don't let Ty blow too much smoke up your ass on my account. It feels nice, but the surgeon general says it's bad for you."

Caitlin turned, expecting to find George C. Scott or Jack Nicholson growling lines of handcrafted dialogue at her. The only other general she'd had recent experience of aside from Musso was a newly retired General Stephen F. Murphy, who had taken up a deputy director's chair with Echelon in Vancouver. Murphy did indeed growl, never smiled, and looked like he would genuinely enjoy crushing testicles with his bare hands. This man, the bogeyman who exercised the fears and anxieties of half the country, approached them from his private washroom, looking like he should have been tending a garden somewhere. A bit too gray, a bit too round, a bit too soft at the edges, with a rather grand Roman nose and a twinkle in his eye. A friendly twinkle. The beard, less old navy than Santa Claus, only served to enhance the disarming warmth of his smile.

"Jackson Blackstone," he announced, extending his hand. "Welcome to Fort Hood, Colonel Murdoch."

Caitlin took his hand, a firm, somewhat callused grip. "Thank you, Governor."

"My, that's quite a grip you've got there, Colonel. You wouldn't be an old chopper pilot, would you?"

"No, sir. Tennis."

"Ah, my wife is a fan. I'm afraid I'm not. Fishing is my personal obsession. One I don't get to enjoy nearly as much I had planned to after hanging up my uniform."

Blackstone spared a sideways glance for Tusk Musso, much the way a frustrated academic might look at a particularly dim student. "Musso," he said, "always a pleasure."

The president's unofficial ambassador nodded. "Blackstone."

The governor suddenly clapped his hands together, producing a sound like a rifle crack. "Does anyone have any interest in breakfast? I know it's late, but I haven't eaten yet. Between my morning exercise and the blizzard of paperwork that follows me everywhere, I often don't. But I saved myself a fine river trout. Caught yesterday, but not by me, I'm afraid to say. I'd been intending to save it for lunch. But it would make an excellent breakfast with some toast and avocado and a cup of fine Costa Rican robusta."

Caitlin shook her head. "Negative, sir. We ate before we came on post."

"Colonel, please. Relax." Blackstone smiled. "You can step down from DEFCON 1. I'm not the ogre everyone makes me out to be. I haven't had anybody dragged behind a gun carriage since I retired."

McCutcheon was the only one who smiled. Caitlin maintained a studied neutrality, and Musso gave the governor his stone face.

"Damn, you know, this will be a very long morning if we have to stare each other down like this." Blackstone sighed. "How about a cup of coffee and a doughnut? Breakfast of champions. Would that suffice as a peace offering, Colonel? Initially? I'm afraid I gave up smoking some years ago, so a peace pipe is out of the question."

Caitlin had to admit she could murder for another cup of coffee. She decided to give a bit. "Earl Gray all day does get tiresome. A cup of coffee would be agreeable, sir."

"Please, Colonel, 'Jack' will do. I'm not in uniform anymore. And we're behind closed doors. Ty . . ." Blackstone regarded his aide with the same judgmental expression he'd laid on Musso, tempered in this case by familiarity and a regretful shake of the head. "You look like you need a cup yourself. Got a little carried away making new friends last night, I'll wager. Your penance is to fetch a fresh pot."

The office was divided into two parts. The first was a sitting area softened with leather couches and armchairs arranged around a polished cherrywood coffee table. Bookshelves ran the length of one wall, only half filled. A small kitchenette with a glass-front fridge and a coffeepot completed the sitting area. The other half was a simple, featureless table of oak with a neat stack of files on the left-hand side.

Caitlin chose a seat facing Blackstone, who settled himself on the couch across from her. Musso took up a flanking position, and McCutcheon came around with fresh mugs of coffee. She savored the aroma of premium beans. The powdered shit back in Temple was undrinkable.

"We've managed to stabilize the neighboring states near the Canal Zone," Blackstone explained. "Reopening links to Costa Rica is one of the fringe benefits of those stability operations."

She took a sip and nodded. "Very good, sir. Was it worth deploying a third of the Texas Defense Force to Panama for a cup of joe, though?"

He grinned like Saint Nick on Christmas morning. "Well, it's *pretty good* coffee, but I didn't order the deployment for that alone. The canal is vital to maintaining communications with Puerto Rico and America's eastern seaboard. And it doesn't hurt to engage the Federation as far forward as possible. Morales would love to control that piece of real estate. He used to regularly send his envoys here to jump up and down and demand we 'return' it."

He made a quotation mark gesture with his free hand.

"As entertaining as it was to poke the dancing monkeys with a stick, I sent them on to Kipper. It's really his lookout. Roberto's so-called diplomats don't bother coming here anymore. My only regret is that we have less contact now and an even poorer picture of their capabilities and intent. Hopefully, you can help with that, Colonel."

She'd accepted the coffee. Why not throw him a bone? "'Kate' will be fine. What is your assessment of the threat, sir? It's not exactly looming large with the national command authority. And you've had longer to ponder it than I have. I've spent the last three years assisting in the transfer of military matériel to the United Kingdom."

Blackstone's features darkened momentarily, driving back the softness, hardening around the edges. Caitlin thought she caught a glimpse of his temper in that brief interlude.

"History's idea of a joke," Blackstone said. "We bailed the Brits out in 1941 with Lend-Lease; now they step in to return the favor. And don't they love to remind us of the reversal in fortunes."

"Blackstone . . ." Musso sat forward.

"Easy there, Marine," the governor said, holding up his hand. "I will put my rancor away. But I can't promise it won't flare. Unlike Mr. Kipper, I'm not much impressed by the helping hand our so-called nearest and dearest allies have been lending. I feel the need to check my wallet every time they reach out for us. Kate, the fact is the South American Federation has the makings of a blue-water navy, one that can outclass our own. They're not there yet, but the trend lines are not good. We are on the way down. They are on the way up. Musso here has had first-hand experience of what we might face down at Gitmo before he threw in the towel . . ."

The general made a Herculean effort to count the ceiling tiles above his head.

"Sir?" Caitlin held up her hand. "May I be frank with you? I am not a politician. I might report to one in Mr. Culver for the moment, but I'm an air force officer. I care about the mission. I am not at all interested in writing history as it transpires or interpreting the politics of that history. It would be helpful to my mission and your own interests if you simply gave me your opinion without providing a critique of the president and his policies."

Jackson Blackstone sized her up and smiled again. It was warm, paternal, the sort of expression he might offer his daughter or grand-daughter after she'd surprised and impressed him.

"Fair enough, Kate," he said, leaning back with his coffee. "I'm just glad that Machiavellian motherfucker Jed Culver saw fit to send you down here on the quiet. Trust a devil like him to recognize one in Roberto. So. Let's talk unpleasant realities. The Federation Navy poses a significant potential risk to the U.S. Navy and the Texas Coast Guard in the local theater of operations."

Caitlin held the reins of her skepticism tightly. Last time she checked, there was no war with Roberto under way and no theater of operations within which it was being fought. Blackstone carried on regardless.

"They have maintained an extensive fleet of Type 209 submarines taken from the navies of constituent states, or former states, I suppose, and it is our belief that these subs are being used right now to infiltrate agents into North and Central America. In our sphere of influence—by which I mean America's, lest you mistake me. My coast guard intelligence folks tell me the 209s are providing material support to the pirate groups that operate out of Mexican and Cuban ports. Their air power is a frequent concern of mine. They possess sufficient capacity to attack the Panama Canal Zone. Half of the TDF Air Guard is tied down in Panama serving as a deterrent against that very threat. Unfortunately, half of the guard often sits on the ground for want of spare parts. I can't get Seattle to free up my requests for spares or support from the U.S. Navy and Air Force. Perhaps your own assessment will help break open that logjam, Kate."

"I'll make no promises," Caitlin replied, "other than to assess the intelligence without bias. I'll report to Mr. Culver. What he puts in front of the president is up to him."

"Fair is fair," Blackstone said, reaching for the coffeepot. "Musso, you up for a fresh cup? You look like you're drifting off, old man."

In fact, he looked like he was lost in some old memory. "No, I'm fine. Thank you," Tusk said once he'd rejoined them.

"Kate?"

She demurred. "We have all of the data you've cited so far, sir," she said. "None of it implies a need for urgent policy or resource action. Not given the way our forces are already overstretched. Is there some other reason you're concerned about the Federation?"

Special Agent Monroe had little interest in his answer. But she had her role to play, and Colonel Murdoch would not have been impressed with Blackstone's case thus far. The governor and his aide exchanged a glance. McCutcheon excused himself and left the office.

"You read much history, Kate?" Blackstone asked.

"Some, sir. In college. Mostly course-related."

"Of course. But you would be familiar with the big picture between the wars last century. The rise of the absolute tyrants and the super-states. Hitler's Germany. The Soviet Union. And the little Hitlers here and there. Saddam. The interchangeable ayatollahs."

She indicated some familiarity with the twentieth century.

"That's good," Blackstone said. "Because I think we're living through something similar. The 1920s and '30s, Kate. They were a his-torical discontinuity, by which I mean the orderly progression of his-tory was shattered. By the slaughter of the Great War. It destroyed empires, refashioned the world, swept away an old order, and for three decades, and arguably for more, there was no sense of continuity. You change a few decisions here or there, you change what comes after-ward forever. There was no reason we had to win in 1945. No reason why it had to be the Soviets who lost in 1989, either. It seems inevitable looking back, what the commies used to call the correlation of forces, but it was really just one day after another, one decision here, an action taken or not taken there. FDR dying of polio. The Depression running much deeper for longer. Nixon not getting caught and poisoning the well forever after."

The governor looked as though he was enjoying himself with his free-ranging lecture, right up to the point where Musso interrupted him.

"Are we going somewhere today, Professor?"

A hint of annoyance crossed his face, but he composed himself. "Ever the literalist, eh, Musso?" he sighed. "A common failing of the jarhead. A lack of imagination and a refusal to learn from history. My service commenced all the way back in Vietnam, and you know what I learned there, Kate?"

"No, sir."

"The United States Marine Corps was the finest implement ever crafted for getting young American lads killed for no good reason at all."

She felt Musso radiate waves of hostility and sensed the tension that suddenly strained at every muscle in his body. Blackstone, meanwhile, seemed to be enjoying himself again, grinning like a cat in front of a big bowl of cream.

"I learned lessons in Vietnam, Kate. But I learned even more later, including the most important, which was to never stop learning, to never stop questioning your basic assumptions. Colin Powell, God rest his soul wherever it may have been taken, used to be fond of lecturing us about the lessons of Vietnam and the limits of power. But he never questioned himself about whether those limits had changed in the years between our ignoble defeat in Vietnam—for that is what it was, and the revisionists be damned—and the moment of half-achieved victory he engineered in the first Gulf War. If he had asked himself that question, I don't believe we would have been sitting in the desert in 2003, waiting to finish the job, when the Wave swept everything away."

"I don't recall you being in the desert in '03, Governor," said Musso, as though he were actually racking his memory. "Weren't you in . . . Fort Lewis? Yes, that's right. I seem to recall something about a military junta you were trying to impose there."

None of the anger she had seen flash in his eyes was evident in Blackstone's reaction to the taunt. He laughed.

"Indeed, I was not in the desert, Tusk. Nor you, as I recall."

Caitlin was certain this was a cue to revisit the subject of Musso's surrender of Guantánamo to the Venezuelans and prepared to intercede before the meeting descended into a shambles. But the governor waved off Musso's diversionary attack.

"I suppose we should cherish the memory of Powell for not finishing the job the first time around. It meant we were lucky enough to have so many of our forces outside the Wave in March '03. But what I really wanted to say, Kate, is that I believe we are living through a time of shattered, discontinuous history, and I have come to the conclusion that it will fall to us, as it fell to our grandfathers, to resist a tyranny, to prevent it establishing itself in our world."

"You see yourself as Winston Churchill, then, Governor?" Musso deadpanned.

"No, but I see us facing the same question Churchill faced in the years when he alone stood before the truth of what was coming."

McCutcheon returned with a steel briefcase before his boss could build up another head of steam. He placed it on the table around which they sat, careful not to scratch the surface. After entering separate combinations for both locks, he snapped open the lid and took out two folders, which he handed to Caitlin and Musso. Inside hers, Caitlin found transcripts of interviews and photographs of four men.

"What you have here," said Ty McCutcheon, "is a record of the interrogation of the surviving members of a Federation special forces squad captured by long-range TDF patrols in central Florida—"

"Wait a minute," Musso protested. "Florida?"

"Hey, I said long range," McCutcheon replied.

"You're not supposed to be in Florida."

"Neither are they."

Caitlin could see the exchange getting off topic. This incident was obviously why Blackstone had sought to mend his fences with Seattle. This was why he thought he needed help. A point of weakness.

"Gentlemen," she said in Katherine Murdoch's best warning voice. "Perhaps you could give us the *Reader's Digest* version, Mr. McCutcheon?"

Blackstone's aide checked with his boss, who nodded.

"These four men were captured in the St. Teresa area, an hour south of Tallahassee. They were part of a six-man squad, but two of their number were killed during the encounter with our lurps."

Long-range recon patrols, Caitlin reminded herself. An old Vietnam term. Nowhere in her briefing papers had it mentioned the TDF pushing lurps all the way into the Florida panhandle. That was still pirate-controlled territory.

"Long story short, Roberto knows it will be a good ten or fifteen years before he's consolidated his power and built up his military forces to the point where he can go head to head with us," said McCutcheon. There was no trace of the drunken frat boy who had entertained everybody in the bar last night. Not much trace of a hangover, either. "Our residual power is considerable, for now. Meanwhile, he's trying to weld together a transnational force from the bits and pieces he cherry-picked from the carcasses of the South American states he took over."

Caitlin glanced across at Musso, who had lost interest in butting heads with Blackstone and was immersed in the documentation.

"But Morales understands that we are completely overstretched in the three areas we do control: the Pacific Northwest, the New York–New England enclave, and Texas. From the debriefing of his special forces guys, we've ascertained that he is interested in seeding colony settlements well outside our area of influence and direct control. That's what these guys were doing. Forward recon. The idea is they grab up the turf, establish squatters' rights, and dare us to do something about it when we eventually discover them."

Caitlin didn't bother reading the transcripts. As Colonel Murdoch, she was willing to take McCutcheon's word for the gist of the document.

"That didn't work for Baumer and Ozal in New York," she said, curious to see whether either man would react to the two names. They didn't, for which she had to credit them. "Surely New York disabused Morales of the idea he could just wander in here and plant his flag?"

Blackstone seemed pleased to have been asked that one. "That's where Morales has proven himself to be smarter than Powell," he replied. "Predictably enough for a former gang leader. You would expect him to understand turf wars. What he learned from New York was modesty. When you sit down and read the transcripts, and I don't expect you to do so now, you'll see the Federation takes away from New York a realization not to challenge us openly, head on. There's no military component to what they were planning in Florida apart from the special forces doing advance reconnaissance. They intend to set up small, discrete civilian colonies, to grow them quietly, until the point where the colonies would declare themselves for the South American Federation rather than us. At that point, it would actually benefit Morales if we responded in the way we did in New York. They could then sweep in and portray themselves as the protector. Any civilian casualties would count against us. The settlements would beg for protection from the imperialist gringos. Roberto could move some of his better assets up here to shield them, and unless Seattle is willing to spill a lot of supposedly innocent blood, he gets to hold on to his gains. He gets a continental foothold on the edge of a very empty continent. Or that was the plan, anyway. Until we caught his special operators."

"They weren't that special, as it turned out." McCutcheon grinned.

"We'll need to debrief the prisoners ourselves," said Musso, who appeared to be trying to keep an open mind.

"Not a problem," the aide shot back. "Well, sorry . . . there *is* a problem with one of them. He didn't survive the initial debrief. But the other three are just raring to go, Tusk."

Musso sent a withering look his way, although Caitlin could see that the former marine had been thrown by the unexpected development. As much by Fort Hood's activities in Florida as by Roberto Morales, she imagined. She purposely closed the folder and returned it to the table.

"This is interesting, gentlemen," she said. "And I mean that. The chief of staff and, I imagine, the president will be both interested and grateful to see this. It will go into my report." She glanced over at General Musso. "But given that we've caught this so early, do you really think it's necessary to reassign scarce military resources when we could achieve the same result, scaring him off, with a quiet diplomatic word?"

"Ty? Would you?" Blackstone asked, nodding toward the pastry tray.

"Sure," said his aide, standing up to retrieve a Danish.

"I suppose we could do that, Kate," Blackstone said. "Me, I'm an old-fashioned guy. I'd just nuke the son of a bitch. You take this information back to Seattle, you might even find that James Ritchie agrees with me for once. After all, he tossed off a couple at Chávez on Musso's behalf."

The federal officer shrugged off yet another dig at his Guantánamo record. "This does need to be dealt with," he began, holding up one of the interrogation transcripts. "But Colonel Murdoch is correct. You caught this early. It's a little problem, needing little effort to address. Especially since we have the prisoners. There's no explaining them away."

At that, Blackstone mulled so long that Caitlin started to wonder whether he intended simply to ignore Musso's words. He did reply eventually.

"One way or another, we have to address this. Not so much the immediate question, I agree. Morales won't be setting up any wildcat colonies now that we've tumbled to his scheme. But everything I said before about reaching a discontinuous moment in history, Kate, I stand by," Blackstone said, returning his attention to her quite pointedly. He accepted a pastry from his aide but didn't eat it right away. "There was a time when no power on earth would have dared contemplate a claim on this continent. Now, there are days I wonder which of them wouldn't. You know, Governor Palin can see Russia from her front porch, and she tells me they seem to be getting closer every day."

Caitlin put down her coffee cup and uncrossed her legs, making as if to stand up.

"Gentlemen," she said again. "You will understand that before saying anything else I would like to examine these documents in detail. I'm happy to go with Mr. McCutcheon to do so, if you don't want to release them into our custody."

Blackstone looked like he was about to answer, when his fixer spoke up. "We had these copies made up for you. But if you'd like some time to study them, I'm happy for you to use my office, Colonel Murdoch." McCutcheon raised an eyebrow at Blackstone. "Perhaps an hour's break, Governor?"

"An hour sounds about right. If you'd like to take charge of our guests, Ty?"

"Be a pleasure, sir."

Caitlin stood up, hoping her impetus would draw Musso along behind her. She had what she wanted. McCutcheon's documents were interesting, but what she really needed was access to his office. That was where they obviously kept the administration's sensitive files.

42

DARWIN, NORTHERN TERRITORY

It was an unsettling experience, shopping while being stalked by your would-be murderer. The experience was made worse by Nick Pappas's recommendation yesterday of a rather depressing-looking department store in the center of the old town as the place where Julianne might get herself suitably attired for her second cameo as a junior with Downing, Street and Kemp.

This part of Darwin did not look as deeply changed by the enormous volumes of money that had flowed into the city over the last few years. Two new high-rise towers were emerging from holes in the ground that covered entire blocks, but most of the old streetscape remained unaffected. The city had been rebuilt in the late 1970s after Cyclone Tracy, and the aesthetically worthless architecture of that period was everywhere. It rather did Jules's head in, seeing the many global-brand boutiques, all sparkling and shining like exquisite jewelry boxes, trading within the tatty shells of these buildings. Although some outlets, one being the department store toward which she was walking now, were obvious diehards from an earlier era, the long un-broken stretches of high-street retail, expensive cafés, bistros, and bars all evidenced a rapid shift away from a utilitarian central business district toward something more akin to a playground for superrich out-casts. She didn't recognize many of the fashion names and could only assume they were the local franchises of start-ups from Chinese city-states.

It would be lovely, she thought, to have been the mistress of some obscenely wealthy mining magnate who was around to bother you only one week out of every two or three months. In that case, she'd probably have spent a few days swanning around this strange, isolated mini-Monaco, melting her sugar daddy's plastic with some gold-medal-standard shopping.

But not getting sniped at from a rooftop or run over while crossing the street was a reality she could live with, too.

Julianne did her best to try to pick out Shah's men from the crowded footpath and thought maybe she caught a glimpse of somebody who looked like a Gurkha across the road. But then, in Darwin, one could quickly amass examples of people from all over the world. Her best estimate was that maybe a third of those teeming through this part of town had grown up here. The rest were new arrivals and, specifically, members of the city's new, arriviste class. Wealthy, displaced, and not a little anxious to embed themselves as deeply as possible in their new home. For all the fuck-off money and ostentatious display of signifi-cance in this place, as a child of one of the oldest surviving aristocratic lines in the world (even if, or perhaps because, her own family's posi-tion in that line had come a cropper), Jules was aware of a low-grade, subaural hum vibrating just under the surface of things. Status anxiety. The gnawing fear that having survived one cataclysmic breakup of the established order, one might find oneself at the pointy end of any sub-sequent reordering, no matter how much smaller in scale.

She began to understand why Shah and his neighbors felt their posi-tions were so tenuous. Nothing was settled here in spite of the clean streets and the gleaming newness of everything. It was all still in furious motion. Convulsed. Deranged. And dangerous with it. As if to emphasize the point, she saw an armored vehicle roll through an intersection farther up the street.

Jules hurried into the store, out of the heat, and sighed with relief after pushing through another superchilled air curtain. She'd noticed the same effect at the Sirocco Café. It felt something like walking through a gentle waterfall, but it was a piece of technology she had not encountered before then. Perhaps the design had been stolen from some Wave-washed laboratory in the United States where researchers were still puddled wherever they happened to have been standing. The market for Disappeared intellectual property had run white-hot for a while in 2004 and 2005, until Seattle regained some semblance of control over its borders. She'd even considered getting into the game herself, except that the Rhino had been such a complete bloody boy scout over the issue.

He still thought of himself as one of the good guys at heart, even with all the people smuggling, the stealing, and the murder on the high seas. Thoughts of her friend and former business partner brought with them a confusion of emotions: fond recall, concern for his well-being, and a rekindled anxiety about whoever might be trying to fuck with her own well-being. Jules reached around and lightly touched the SIG Sauer holstered in the small of her back. She could always feel the pistol there, digging into her spine, but the gesture gave her some comfort, anyway.

The department store was doing its best, but it still looked shabby and somewhat down at heel compared with its newer, smaller rivals. There seemed to be more old-time locals shopping in here, though, she noticed. Sticking with the tried and true out of pure stubbornness, no doubt. It was the work of only a few minutes to find the women's wear department, where a question to a sales assistant—an Aboriginal girl—soon had her fingering through a carousel of off-the-rack business suits. She chose a conservative lightweight navy-blue suit with matching pants before wasting another hundred and fifty bucks on a pair of cheap medium heels.

God, it was like being back at college again: scrimping, saving, making do. How dreadfully fucking depressing this could get . . .

As she was paying for the purchases and holding back a creeping sense of ennui at having to wear them, the Nokia buzzed in her pocket. A text message from Pappas: the Rhino had been transferred to the Coonawarra Base Hospital, where she could find him in intensive care. Downing had contacted the hospital and told them that one of his juniors would be in to look after Mr. Ross's arrangements.

At last she could look in on him. Jules was comforted also by the knowledge that so many people were putting themselves out on her behalf. She doubted she'd have been as helpful as Nick and Piers if a complete stranger had bowled up to her in need of succor and protection. But of course she had Mr. Shah to thank for that. She undoubtedly had Pappas to thank for the final piece of information, however:

A phone number in America—for Miguel!

She was so surprised and so grateful, she almost forgot to collect her change from the salesgirl. Then she nearly left the two bags of shopping behind on the counter.

After thanking the young woman, Jules hurried out of the store and flagged down a pedicab. She'd have preferred an air-conditioned taxi, but a quick check up and down the street confirmed there were none to be had. The pedicab driver, a thin wiry foreigner of indeterminate race, asked her where she wanted to go before quoting a price of ten dollars. Unsure whether one was supposed to haggle, she agreed, keen to return to the motel and make contact with her dear old friends.

Again she checked for evidence of Shah's men following her, of anybody following her, but saw nothing. The pedicab was shaded but open to the elements, allowing the speed of their passage to create a breeze that offered scant relief from the heat of the afternoon. She wondered how her driver endured it.

She played with the phone, a model she'd never seen before. It had no keypad, an obvious omission that had thrown her for a second while she tried to open the text. Apparently, the screen itself was the keyboard. Gadgets and widgets had never much interested this daughter of the English nobility, and mobile phones in particular set her teeth on edge. She assumed the government probably could track you via your SIM card or the phone's chip or whatever, which meant she rarely carried a mobile. On those rare occasions, she'd use a throw-down, a cheap prepaid or stolen handset, and always kept the thing switched off until the very moment it was needed, after which she'd toss it immediately.

There were three numbers saved in the phone Pappas had given her: one for the burly SAS veteran, one for Shah, and the last for their lawyer friend. A little more fiddling around brought up an electronic map of the city, with the location of the Coonawarra Base Hospital highlighted by a ridiculous cartoon paper clip that jumped up and down while pointing at the relevant location.

"Right, right, I fucking get it, okay?" she muttered at the annoying screen icon. "Jesus, how do you turn the stupid thing off . . ."

Before she could work it out, the pedicab had pulled up in front of the Banyan View Lodge. Jules thanked the driver, who was slick with sweat but breathing normally. She paid him with a plastic ten-dollar banknote and checked to see whether they'd been followed before hurrying inside.

As she had expected, the room was stifling. She flicked on the primitive air-con, which rumbled into life without much promise of relief. For a few seconds, it felt as though the temperature actually increased before blessed cool air started to fall from the ceiling vents.

Jules unclipped the holster and began undressing. When she was down to her underwear, she stopped, bleeding off heat as the climate control system labored heroically to dump a little arctic goodness into her room. She had no idea what time it was in the American Midwest but found herself pondering something else about Pappas's text. He'd located Miguel in Kansas City . . . Now, that was odd. The way Julianne understood it, Miguel had taken Mariela, Sofia, little Maya, Grandma Ana and all the others to the United States after qualifying for the resettlement scheme, or homestead thingy, or whatever the hell the Yanks called it. So why would he be in Kansas City now and not out on a farm somewhere in Texas?

She remembered Kansas City vaguely, having stopped there with Rhino early in the year to arrange transport to New York City. They'd never made it into the city itself, staying instead at a moldy hostel a block away from the airport. A joyous time spent trying to sleep through the sound of planes, trains, and Rhino's titanic snoring before getting the hell out for points east.

Jules set her mind back to the task of working out what time it was over there. Early afternoon in Darwin now, so that would make it . . . what, sometime late at night, yesterday evening, where he was? The phone had a Web browser, and she thought about doing a quick MSN search, but impatience forced her to just call the number. Given her limited experience with mobile phones and especially with the keypad-less variety like this Nokia, it took her awhile to work out that she only had to touch the number Nick had entered in its long form.

An annoying ear worm of a jazz tune about Kansas City began to run on a loop in her mind. She frowned it away.

Jules heard a faint buzzing as the connection went through. A phone was ringing somewhere. She worried that she might be waking Miguel or the kids but smiled at the prospect of Mariela waking up beside her husband and demanding to know the identity of this strange *mujer* he was talking to so late at night.

After standing there nearly naked under the air-conditioner for al-most a minute, she began to suspect that no one was home. Jules was surprised at just how disappointed she felt. She had no good news for Miguel, just a warning to watch out for Henry Cesky's goons. But she'd been looking forward to the conversation. Now she was left hanging on the line in this shitty motel room, wondering whether maybe she'd ended up dialing the wrong number or something. When the call cut out, she tried again without any great hope and eventually with the same nonresult. She bit down on her frustration. Not even an answering machine.

"Bugger."

She accepted defeat for now. Delving into the larger of the two shopping bags, Julianne pulled out the business suit and started getting dressed once more, hating the feel of the anonymous office clothes. There was nothing to be done about it, though. She wanted so much to see the Rhino, and if she wanted to see Rhino, she had to play along.

43

Fingerprint lock.

McCutcheon's office was protected by the same array of security measures as those guarding Blackstone's, but with an additional tweak. Caitlin and Musso stood behind him as he laid his thumb onto the glass plate of a Krupp Systems Dynalock TRS-5 fingerprint scanner. Reputed to be the best in the world. Released into the wild by Krupp only three months earlier. Beat that and you would gain access to the office within, where you could then trip the pressure pad just behind the door, the passive IR sensors mounted in the corner of the room, or the proximity alarm sitting atop his desk next to a laptop that was disconnected from the building's intranet.

"If you wouldn't mind averting your eyes for a second, folks."

"Of course, Ty," said the always cooperative, always security-conscious Colonel Katherine Murdoch.

"Oh, so we *are* friends . . . Kate?" he said, teasing her gently. "That's how it works? I show you my nasties"—he held up the secured briefcase with the dossiers inside—"and you suddenly want to be friends again with old Tyrone McCutcheon?"

Caitlin smiled, conceding his point. "Perhaps just friendly colleagues," she volleyed back.

She then looked away so he could enter the PIN to deactivate two of the three security systems within the room. The pressure pad and the infrared sensors. The proximity alarm, which sat on his desk looking like a stainless steel egg, he deactivated with an RFID tag on his key ring. She caught Musso's concerned expression as they stood there with their backs turned. He obviously was thinking ahead, assuming she would want to gain entry to this office without the permission of its occupant. With McCutcheon standing a couple of feet away, Caitlin could hardly reassure Seattle's main man in Texas that it wasn't going to be a problem, so she let it slide.

"All righty, we're good to go," McCutcheon announced. "Secret trapdoor to the piranha pool has been closed. Laser-beam chain saws deactivated. Hoo and aah!"

She had a momentary vision of Bret saying the same thing the last morning they had spent together.

This office was nearly as large as Blackstone's but with none of the triumphalist personal touches. A single framed photograph of an older woman who bore an unmistakable family resemblance to McCutcheon sat on his desk next to a signed baseball. A large Ansel Adams print of winter in Yellowstone Park hung from one wall in front of a nest of lounge chairs. Otherwise nothing. Not even a view. Ty McCutcheon's office had no windows. It was cut off from the outside world. Caitlin felt . . . not so much the thrill of vindication, rather, the cold comfort of a wager with herself that had just paid off. There may well have been other treasure troves in which she could dig for the secrets of Jackson Blackstone, but she'd almost certainly find buried treasure right here.

She took in every detail of the space as she followed the two men over to the lounge area, which reminded her of a display setting in a furniture store. As if it was meant to be admired rather than used. Unlike his boss's desk, which looked like it might have come off one of Lord Nelson's warships, McCutcheon worked on a glass-top table to which there was nothing beyond the thick sandwich of opaque green glass and two Z-form metal trusses serving as legs. No networking cables ran to the laptop, not even a power cord. The computer was a stand-alone system save for the ugly steel chain that secured it to one of the table legs.

There were no filing cabinets in the room, no bureau within which documents might be stored. The files they were about to read must have come from a repository elsewhere in the building, probably from TDF's intelligence division. That was fine. What she wanted was access to the drive on that laptop.

What she got, for the moment, was an offer of more coffee and cake. McCutcheon confessed a weakness for cake in the morning, a legacy, he said, of a German grandmother. Caitlin turned down both offers, but Musso surprised her by volunteering for a second breakfast.

"Well, I like cake," he said in response to her quizzical look.

"I wouldn't trust a man who didn't, Tusk," said McCutcheon, who was making himself very comfortable again with everyone's first name. "So I'll let you read up on the doings and the goings-on over in Florida. And then we can talk through any questions you might have. I imagine you'll also want to expedite the rendition of the prisoners to Seattle so that NIA and defense intelligence can have a piece of them."

"I imagine you're correct," Musso replied.

For a second she thought McCutcheon might be about to leave them alone in his office while he tended to cake and coffee orders. Not that she would have been so foolish as to attempt to crack open his lappy and take a peek while he was doing that. McCutcheon didn't make such a rookie error or attempt such an obvious entrapment. Instead he simply used the phone to order the refreshments.

"Bathroom's through there if and when you need it," he told them both, jerking his thumb over toward the far side of the room, where a door opened up onto a small kitchenette and beyond that into a washroom.

"I think I might, if you don't mind," said Musso, heading in that direction. "Too much damn coffee."

Blackstone's aide waited until the general had left before speaking again.

"I'm sorry things haven't worked out so well between us and Seattle,

Kate," he said while working through the same elaborate procedure as before for unlocking the briefcase. "The old man, you know, was fairly cut up about what happened back there after the Wave. Particularly Kipper's role. He thought they'd worked together pretty well to pull that city through, so it was a bit of a shock to turn around and find he'd been stabbed in the back like that. You can understand the man would have difficulties working with the president again."

Caitlin's care factor was zero. Her one brief encounter with James Kipper, a difficult satellite call from the back of a C-130 just before she parachuted into New York, hadn't made her a fan. But then Kipper had not been found to have an undeclared arrangement with Ahmet Ozal, one of Baumer's closest allies, the man who had freed Baumer from prison in Guadeloupe before joining him in New York as one of his senior lieutenants.

"Ty," she replied, deliberately using his first name, "as I said before, the politics are of no interest to me. Even if I hadn't spent the last couple of years exiled in England, they still wouldn't interest me. I can appreciate their importance to you, but *this* is what's important to me. I can promise you I will take a fair appraisal of what I find in here back to Jed Culver. You convince him, you've convinced the president." She held up the file he had just handed her.

"Fair enough," McCutcheon said. "I'm just hoping this visit might be a chance for us to start over again. The old man, too. Sincerely. I don't mind telling you, he's freaked by Morales. He really sees him as a little Hitler. Like Saddam could've been if the Israelis hadn't taken care of business. The way Roberto's pulled things together down there after the total collapse . . . you have to admit, he seems to know what he's doing."

Caitlin couldn't help thinking about the half-assed theater of the absurd she'd encountered in Uruguay. As vicious a little prick as Morales undoubtedly was, he had a long way to go before graduating from puffed-up gang lord to genuine threat. That didn't mean everybody shared her perception, however. And if Blackstone was shifting his animus away from Kipper and onto Roberto, who was she to discourage him?

"We're all trying to do our best for the country, Ty," she said. "It would be unusual, and probably unhealthy, if we didn't differ about what we thought was best. But you're right about this development in Florida. The president does not care for foreign powers meddling within our borders. He didn't care for it in New York. He didn't care for it in Alaska. I can assure you he won't care for it in Florida. This will be answered."

Musso returned at that moment, just as the coffee and cake arrived.

"Outstanding," McCutcheon declared.

The file review took an hour and a half. Caitlin found it professionally interesting and asked all the questions expected of her, but she allowed Tusk Musso to make most of the running. She could see that he'd been blindsided by the intelligence out of Florida and was having to recalibrate his threat detectors in regard to the Federation, but the former marine lawyer remained skeptical, and he would not let go of his displeasure with Texas for pushing into areas of the country that were none of its concern. He didn't climb aboard Blackstone's bandwagon, but he proved himself willing to change his mind about whether a problem existed in the first place.

Caitlin excused herself after an hour to use the bathroom. While in there, she checked her equipment. Two of the three miniature microphones embedded in her uniform had failed, but the third had picked up the subtly changing tones of the PIN code McCutcheon had entered into the antique keypad controlling the infrared and pressure pad systems in his room. The scanner embedded deep within the guts of her Siemens phone had intercepted and stored his RFID tag as soon as he'd sent it to the proximity sensor designed to create an exclusion zone around his laptop.

An anxious moment passed while the Echelon agent checked that she had captured the data, but this was not something she could leave until they'd returned to the safety of Temple. If all three of her microphone pickups had failed, she would have needed to manufacture another reason to return to McCutcheon's office with him later in the day to make another attempt at collecting his PIN.

No problemo, she told herself, letting go of a breath she hadn't even realized she was holding.

Back in the office, the two former military officers had sidetracked into a discussion of power projection capabilities. Musso remained underwhelmed. McCutcheon tried to sell him a story about Morales seeking out a number of surviving former Argentine military types with experience of the failed Falklands invasion.

"Why would he even be doing that, Tusk? Who cares what those old losers think? Unless he's trying to avoid making the same mistakes they did, right?"

"I can see that he has sought them out," the other man conceded, waving a piece of paper that must have confirmed the fact. "But you have to remember that he's trying to build, or rebuild, a military force, a Frankenstein's force in many ways. Stitched together from the body parts of half a dozen militaries that were dismembered during the collapse. Those Argentine officers are the only men anywhere on the continent with actual command-level combat experience of state-on-state conflict. Why wouldn't he seek them out?"

"So what, we just ignore it?"

"No, I'm not saying that, but it doesn't mean we rush to conclusions, either."

McCutcheon didn't look like he was getting angry, but he was deeply invested in his theory and wasn't about to abandon it to undergraduate skepticism. For Caitlin, and Colonel Murdoch for that matter, it was irrelevant.

"Gentlemen," she said, riding in over the top of them, "you are both confusing data with meaning. It is an occupational hazard of intelligence analysis."

She took the piece of paper from Musso and scanned it quickly.

"What we have here is data. President Morales summoned a cadre of retired officers from the former Argentine military to his palace in Santiago. Five of the six officers stayed on in the capital. They have since been observed working at the Federation's directorate of naval intelligence."

She put the paper down and looked from one man to the other.

"That is *information,* gentlemen. Verified. And nice work, by the way," she added, nodding to McCutcheon. "The NIA will be thrilled to discover that Texas has its own foreign intelligence service and that they've been scooped."

"Whatever. We don't like to brag, Colonel." The aide gave a shrug.

"Uh-huh. Moving right along . . . But the *meaning* of this information is not yet established. I could suggest any number of interpretations of the data. You have suggested one. General Musso has suggested another. I'm going to recommend that this matter be put into the channel. You said before that you hoped our current visit might provide an opportunity for a new start between the two administrations. If you mean that, a team of federal marshals could be here tomorrow morning to take custody of the prisoners, and you could nominate some of your people who had charge of Florida and your surveillance operation in Santiago to return to Seattle, and maybe on to Vancouver, to debrief Defense, NIA, and Echelon."

Both of them looked surprised, but it was McCutcheon who spoke first.

"I don't know that the governor would be very happy about involving a lot of foreigners in this, Kate."

"It's not my call to make," Caitlin said. "We have responsibility for this region under the Vancouver agreement, and that will necessarily involve Echelon. Sooner rather than later."

"But still . . ."

"Still nothing," she countered. "If you want to make Morales a priority, and particularly if you want to get to the bottom of what he's doing raking over the coals of the Falklands with the Argentinians, then Echelon will have a stake. It may have nothing to do with us, Ty. Did it ever occur to you, to either of you, that the meaning of this information is what it is? That Morales is looking to grab the Falklands and their offshore deposits? If that were so, there would be no avoiding Echelon's involvement. Because the Brits would need to know."

McCutcheon shook his head, but not in denial. It was more a gesture of surprise, as though the idea had never occurred to him.

"Data and meaning," repeated Caitlin. "It's all about frame of reference. General Musso?"

The de facto ambassador shook his head. He did not look happy.

"Mr. McCutcheon, this is disturbing on so many levels," he began. "On the face of it, I agree with you that what you have uncovered should be of some concern. However, I am also disturbed by the way in which it was uncovered. You've spoken a number of times this morning of the need to repair relations between Seattle and Fort Hood. Now, one of the reasons that relations have come to the present sorry state is because of Governor Blackstone's insistence on running a virtual shadow state down here. Duplicating our capabilities, usurping the federal government's prerogatives, abrogating agreements signed in good faith, and bending us over for an ass fucking with malice—for no reason other than the governor's unseemly enjoyment of fucking the president in the ass whenever the mood should take him."

Righteous indignation was turning to genuine anger.

"Did it ever occur to you or Governor Blackstone that by running your own foreign intelligence service, you could potentially be crossing over with legitimate operations of the National Intelligence Agency, or any of the service intelligence agencies, or Echelon or allied agencies, with which, I both hope and presume, you would have no formal or informal liaison arrangements?"

If he meant to unsettle or intimidate McCutcheon, he failed. Blackstone's aide waved off the attack.

"We took our concerns to Seattle, and they blew us off," McCutcheon replied. "I can understand that. The president has a lot more to worry about than half a dozen wrinkled old fascists coming out of retirement to dance the Macarena for Roberto. But we are a lot closer to what we perceive as a growing problem down here and, granted, we don't have national responsibilities to divert us. Governor Blackstone is a big believer in self-sufficiency. This is a problem. We decided in the first instance to look into it ourselves. We decided it's bigger and more complicated than even we imagined, so we're kicking it upstairs to the big boys. We figured you'd be happy about that. It's a growth experience for us. We're learning to let go and trust you."

"Oh, spare me . . ."

"Gentlemen, please. I don't know how many times I have to say the politics are irrelevant. At least for the moment. Can we at least agree that we'll deal with this as quickly as possible?"

"So you're on board for the big win?" McCutcheon asked, sounding hopeful.

"I will prepare a threat assessment for Mr. Culver," she promised.

"And I'll make sure it gets to him with priority, but that will require some give on your part. As much as the domestic politics are irrelevant, they're also inevitable. You're just going to have to accept that, Ty. The NIA, in particular, is going to be pissed."

"Oh, those weenies are always pissed. It's their natural state of being."

"Well, for once they'll have reason to be," Caitlin stated firmly. "Nobody's saying you can't gather intelligence. Or that you shouldn't. But if you're going to do it, would it kill you to let us know?"

McCutcheon was gracious enough to look abashed. "I suppose not. As long as we know we'll be taken seriously."

"That I can guarantee," she said. "I've only been working for the chief of staff for a short time, but he impressed me as a man who takes threats seriously. Now, if we can finish reviewing these files, we should talk to the governor again before heading back to Temple and reporting in. Then, if you have no objections, I would like to set up an office over here." She framed the statement as a question and left it hanging.

"Colonel Murdoch, are you sure about that?" Musso asked.

"I'm sure I need to be here, sir, but whether or not they will have me is another matter."

She smiled at McCutcheon, suffusing more warmth into the gesture than she'd allowed herself to display all morning. He still seemed a little nonplussed by the suggestion, but as she suspected, Tyrone was a sucker for a pretty girl.

"Well, I'm sure we'd love to have you for a sleepover, Kate, if General Musso can bear to let you out of his sight."

"Good," said Caitlin. "I'd like to wrap this up as quickly as possible."

44

DARWIN, NORTHERN TERRITORY

Julianne had called a taxi for the trip from Doctors Gully out to Coonawarra Base Hospital before adding the number to the phone's contact list, growing ever more adept at negotiating the Nokia's wealth of functions. Her new jacket was just long enough to conceal the SIG Sauer holstered in the small of her back, but she'd have to be careful about bending over or raising her arms. Not a good look for a young lawyer on the rise, letting everybody know you're armed, even in freeport-era Darwin. However, she'd been able to augment her disguise after coming across a pair of suitably bookish-looking spectacles in a bedside drawer that obviously had been left behind by the previous occupant.

She shouldn't have been surprised when Shah's man Granger turned up to drive her to the hospital. But she was, just a little. She'd become so used to the idea of her invisible security blanket that there were times when she wondered whether they were there at all.

"Nah, you're stuck with us now, mate," Granger told her.

"But how did you even know to come and get me? I just called the switchboard."

"Magic!" he said in a stage whisper. "So your mate's over at the Coonawarra, is he? Fuckin' swish. It's where I'd want to be if I got my arse blown up."

Granger put the car into drive and pulled out, heading back toward the city center.

Jules, still holding the phone in her hand, was surprised to see the screen light up, displaying a Microsoft Where 2.0 map. A blue dot moved slowly along the representation of the street they were driving down. The stupid-looking paper clip with the big cartoon eyes was back, though, jumping up and down and pointing at the dot. A speech bubble appeared next to it. I SEE YOU ARE TRAVELING TO YOUR DESTINATION, it read. WOULD YOU LIKE DIRECTIONS?

"What the fuck . . ."

Granger looked over and down at the handset in her lap. "Oh, not fucking Clippy," he grunted. "Do you mind?"

She passed the phone over to him. A series of quick, bewildering thumb gestures later and the Australian handed it back without the animated paper clip.

"Fucking Microsoft," he said. "If only the Wave had been just a little bit bigger. Used to be an Apple man myself. Fucking sad, eh?"

For the next few minutes they drove north as if heading out to Shah's compound. Granger explained that the hospital, like so much of the city, was new. It had been built over the bones of an old naval base eccentrically located some distance inland. Like the army, Australia's senior service had been persuaded to give up a piece of valuable real estate by the promise of a massive new facility, including the docks currently being built to homeport the Combined Fleet not far from her motel.

"Had to happen," Granger added, as they slipped past the turnoff near the airport that would have taken them on to Shah's. "There were so many new people in town, the place was bursting at the seams. They needed to build new everything: roads, houses, bloody hospitals. There was plenty of land, but not everybody wants to live next to a military base. They're noisy. Things go boom all the time."

Darwin International Airport looked even busier than the last time she'd driven past. A couple of jet fighters screamed down the main runway, moving so quickly that it was difficult to make out the markings on their tails, but she thought she recognized the Singaporean flag. A massive construction zone glided by on the right, looking for all the world like an open-cut mine. A small patch of bare waste ground separated the cyclone fencing on the eastern edge of the building site from a multilevel car park belonging to the new hospital.

"Used to be a detention facility, a jail for illegal migrants," Granger said, indicating the massive structure. "Course, they had to move that as well once they started getting hundreds of boatloads of reffos turning up every week. Got a huge place out in the desert now. Fucking Sandline got the contract for that. They can have it for all I care."

Jules could see no evidence of the site's former use. To her, the campus of the Coonawarra Base Hospital looked like a modern business park, with gleaming white and blue glass offices separated by verdant walking paths that must have been watered constantly to keep them such a lustrous green. Young saplings stood at short, regular intervals and eventually would shade most of the grounds.

"So the development authority built this, too?"

"With a bit of federal money, yes, but mostly it was the FPDA."

She took that in without comment. The money and power politics reminded her of some of the Asian Tiger capitals back in the early 1990s, before their economies imploded. She didn't imagine that would happen here. Darwin seemed to be thriving as the terminal point for insane volumes of money seeking shelter from the torments of the post-Wave world. *Pete would've loved this,* she thought.

Yes, poor Pete Holder, her former doofus in crime on board the old *Diamantina,* would have seen a dollar to be made at every turn, especially somewhere like New Town. Jules could only begin to imagine the trouble he'd have landed in there.

"Fuck, forgot to put the meter on," Granger said as they pulled up at the main entrance to the hospital. "Guess we'll call it a freebie."

"I don't know how long I'll be here, Mr. Granger, or even whether

I'll get to see Rhino," she told him, preparing to step out into the blistering heat. "Will you be around?"

"We're always around, love," he replied. "Just call for a taxi using that same phone. Me or one of the other boys will turn up."

"And the other boys, they would be . . . ?"

"Around."

"I'm afraid that won't be possible."

"But I was sent out here specifically to talk with him," said Julianne, trying her best to match the officious tone of the matron. She'd dealt with this type before—punishing old dykes of a kind often found in large institutions populated by women: boarding schools, hospitals, and female prisons.

"I'm sure I could not care less about what you were sent out here to do, young lady. Mr. Ross is under deep sedation. An induced coma, indeed. He has been very badly injured, and I have very specific instructions from his surgeon and, I might add, from the police, that he is not to be disturbed. I don't know what you hope to achieve, anyway. Do you understand what a coma is?"

Jules drew on all her reserves of patience. She'd at least made it past reception and into the office of this terrible battle-ax. The room seemed to have been decorated by the same designer with a disregard for budget as the police station at Bagot Road. The chair in which the matron's ample behind was parked, for instance, looked like about three thousand dollars' worth of ass-planting technology.

"Look," Jules said, softening her tone. "I'm sorry if we got off on the wrong foot. But I'm new in this job, I'm just finding my way through, and quite frankly my boss is a rather scary South African man and, I suspect, eats puppies for breakfast. If I have to return to the office and tell him I didn't even get past the front door, let alone see our client, I fear for my safety. And for the puppies."

She had found in the past that playing helpless and needy often worked with these old buzzards. You had to appeal to their sense of importance. This one was no different. Jules could actually feel the older woman weakening at the pathetic plight of this blue-suited pretty young thing, out of her depth, far from home, in desperate need of indulgence by a firm-handed matronly type.

"I accept it will be impossible to talk to him if he's unconscious," Julianne went on, adjusting her square-rimmed glasses for maximum effect. "But it would mean a lot if I could just lay eyes on him, Matron. Make sure he's all in one piece." She hesitated. "He is all in one piece, isn't he?"

Such heartfelt concern for a client seemed to strike a nerve.

"He hasn't lost any limbs or organs," the woman replied, gradually losing her battle-ax demeanor. "But he does have some bad burns and quite a few stitches—" She held up a meaty hand suddenly to ward off Julianne's distress. "He's in good hands, though. Royal Darwin Hospital is a world center of excellence for the treatment of burns and explosive trauma, and some of their best people are consulting surgeons here. Mr. Ross is under their care."

"But still, if I could just see him?"

She wasn't going to relent, and the head nurse could see that.

"Oh, I suppose I could let you put your head in the ward for one minute. But you must stay well within the infection control zone. Under no circumstances must you approach him or attempt to communicate with him. Do you understand?"

"I do. Thank you."

She had thought the matron might summon an underling to escort her up there, but apparently she didn't trust this eager young thing to behave herself. Almost expecting to be hauled along by the ear like a naughty child, Jules followed along in her wake. She passed through a number of infection barriers to end up masked and gowned in an observation room, where she was able to see the Rhino through a large window. She had to remind herself to stay in character as her throat clenched and tears threatened to well up.

Two nurses in biohazard suits were changing his dressings, allowing her a glimpse of incinerated flesh. She forced herself to remain composed lest she be overwhelmed with pity and rage. If Cesky had walked into the room, she would have pulled out her pistol and shot him in the face, the consequences be damned.

Cesky wasn't here, yet he was a specter, hovering over all of them.

Would this particular outrage be enough for him? Or would he send his people back to finish the job? She resolved to shut the bastard down before he got another chance.

"Thank you, Matron," she said quietly.

"It's very upsetting," the older woman replied. "Even when you don't know them personally."

"Yes," Jules agreed. "It is."

She bade a silent farewell to her old shipmate before following the matron out of the observation room and retracing their steps back to her office. Julianne thanked the woman again as she left. She was just about to call up Granger but instead found herself hurrying into the nearest bathroom, first to splash cold water on her face and then to stagger into a cubicle and vomit up her breakfast.

She emerged, shaky and light-headed, after a few minutes. The driver answered on the second ring when she eventually made the call and pulled up outside the hospital entrance just two minutes later.

"Jeez, you look like death warmed up," he said as she half climbed, half fell into the seat beside him. "A bit rough, was it?"

"It could've been better," she muttered.

"Okay, sorry to hear that. Where to now?"

She wanted to talk to Shah, but they had agreed to keep their distance while she trailed her coat about town, looking to draw out Cesky's hitter.

"I think I'd like to go down to the marina at Gonzales Road," she said. "See if I can find anybody down there who saw anything that might help. You know, suspicious-looking coves planting bombs and suchlike. I suppose there'd be surveillance cameras everywhere, but Old Bill has probably laid hands on those already."

"Without a fucking doubt," Granger agreed.

He pointed the car west for the drive to the waterfront. The driver seemed to appreciate that his passenger was not in much of a mood for any conversation.

Julianne closed her eyes and concentrated on not seeing visions of the Rhino lying comatose, crippled, and burned in a hospital bed. She found she had no choice, though. She couldn't stop thinking about the Rhino. So she forced herself to remember him in some of his better moments. Lecturing her about boutique beer in New York, for instance. Smoking Greg Norman's cigars with Miguel on board the yacht. Flirting outrageously with Fifi while grilling out on deck . . .

Good times. Amazingly good, considering how they'd come about.

Jules was almost smiling when the other car hit them.

45

The timer beeped on the ballistic gel mold. She gave it another thirty seconds, just to be safe, before opening the little unit and removing the yellow thumb-sized gel disk. The rubbery blob was about the size of a slightly elongated dime. Caitlin held it up to the light to check the impression.

Perfect.

She now had Ty McCutcheon's thumbprint, lifted from his bourbon glass in the bar the previous evening. Securing the print had been a matter of little concern. Musso had arranged the staff roster and spoken to their waitress before she'd come on duty. The woman, an army comm specialist in her day job, had kept Caitlin's glass topped up with iced tea instead of Highland Park and had whipped away McCutcheon's smooth-sided tumbler, securing it in a Ziploc bag as soon as he'd finished his first Maker's Mark.

Caitlin stowed the thumbprint in a small plastic container that she snap closed and zipped into the pocket of her leather jacket. Low clouds scudded across the sky outside the window of the empty room on the top floor of the Kyle Hotel. She had a good view across downtown from here, a vantage point that let her appreciate how much the tiny federal settlement resembled a village carved from a deep forest. Just a block or two back from the cleared streets, Temple was reverting to nature. Head-high razor grass grew thick and wild, and small stands of trees obscured the roof lines of low-set buildings that had not burned or collapsed. A thick, dark cloud, a flock of birds, lifted off from the forest canopy a few streets away, startled by something on the ground, perhaps. A feral cat? A dog pack? She'd heard plenty of both the previous night.

The higher floors of the Kyle Hotel were unoccupied. A short jog up the fire escape put her well beyond the reach of the bugs in her room. Her cell phone, a late-model Siemens, confirmed that. It was thicker and heavier than it should have been, tightly packed with augmented technologies, including the RFID interceptor she'd used in McCutcheon's office. The handset's scan function continuously sought out anomalous electronic signatures within a ten-meter radius but had found nothing here. This room was clean.

She flipped open the cell and keyed in her code to access the Echelon network. It took a little longer than usual to acquire the satellite, but less than a minute later she had a secure channel to Vancouver. The overwatch desk put her through to Larrison immediately.

"Hey, Wales, it's me, your favorite."

"Hello," he said. "I've been waiting to hear from you. I have a message from Jed Culver to forward to Colonel Murdoch from a Special Agent Dan Colvin in KC."

"What's Colvin say?"

The deputy director's reply came back squashed and a little delayed by the encryption software.

"He says he got the phone data you were after. From that hit-and-run you thought was more hit than run. The Mexican farmer and his girlfriend. One of the cells was a burner, completely untraceable. But Colvin got lucky, or the other guy got lazy, with the second phone. It's a high-end satellite unit. Explains why he was using it in KC, I guess, because of the shitty local network."

"Yeah," said Caitlin. "Colvin told me that if you don't have access to the federal system, your phone's basically bricked. So what did he get?"

"Sat phone was registered to a ghost, which isn't surprising. But it was being used right at the moment your man Pieraro was run down. And then the call terminated."

"Our spotter?"

"Almost certainly. Satellite logs traced the phone out to the spot where the KC cops found the burned-out vehicle."

She paced the empty room, ending up near the window, where she was able to gaze out over the streets of Temple again. A bus pulled up at the Federal Center, unloading what looked like a party of homesteaders on their way to the mandate. They stretched their legs as they took a break on the lawn in front of the old city building.

"So no ID on either the spotter or the driver?"

"No, but they found the driver. Or somebody they're pretty sure was the driver."

"Deader than Elvis, I'll bet."

"And then some. The body was burned. The hands cut off, and for bonus points somebody ran over the head a couple of times."

"Huh. Thorough."

"Not so much. Because whoever this spotter is, he's still using the satellite phone."

Her laugh was short and humorless. "Stupid. Mother. Fucker."

Caitlin shook her head as she watched a group of children playing tag in front of the Federal Center. She was pretty sure she recognized Sergeant Milosz down there, in uniform, watching over them while enjoying a cigarette. Occasionally he would dart into the pack of children, grabbing one who was proving difficult for the others to catch and holding the struggling, laughing child upside down by the ankles.

"So what do we have on them?" she asked.

The time delay caused Wales's earlier reply to run over the question.

"Yes," he said. "Natural selection at work."

There was a moment of confusion while he disentangled her question from his reply before he continued. "Here's the thing, Caitlin. The sat phone was picked up by DSD on a programmed sweep by Darwin Station."

"Defense Signals Directorate? He's Down Under?"

"In Darwin. The Deadwood of the new millennium. Been there just over two days. Allowing for flight duration, must've lit out from KC directly. I asked our local franchise to follow up on it. The connections are starting to go fractal, but I think they're worth following. The Aussies are happy enough to look into it. They don't want a freelance hitter on their turf, especially not in Darwin with all the Chinese and Indian players they have going through there. There's even a trade mission from the Federation in town this week. Probably nothing to do with our hitter, but you can imagine how the Echelon station in Sydney was all over it once we told them. Put one of their best guys on it. He's already got some good intel."

"Anything for me?" asked Caitlin, who hadn't expected any joy from Special Agent Colvin and now found herself more confused by the meaning of Pieraro's killing, if indeed it had any meaning.

"Doesn't look like it," Wales told her. "Random crossover."

She concentrated hard, trying to recall the case notes she'd studied in Kansas City. It wasn't easy. There had been so much data to take in. She thought she remembered that the Pieraros had spent time in the refugee camps in Australia before being accepted into a homesteading program in the Federal Mandate. But whether that was significant, she couldn't say.

There was nothing for it but to press on with the things she could control.

"Okay, thanks for that, Wales," she said. "If anything else turns up, especially from Darwin, I'd like to know. And if someone could pass Colonel Murdoch's thanks on to Colvin, that'd be good. He put himself out for us. I have no idea what it all means, but Darwin's a hell of a long way from Fort Hood. Even farther from Kansas City. And I'm going to need your help here in the next couple of hours."

"Just give me a second," he said. "I'll get my paper and pencil and get started on the laundry list."

"You're sure about this?"

Concern furrowed the brow of General Tusk Musso, USMC (retired). His office was much less grand than that of his opposite number
over in the Hood. Unlike in Blackstone's lair, there was no sign he had
ever served in the military. Just pictures of his family on the desk, a
woman and two boys Caitlin knew had Disappeared.

"The sooner I do it, the sooner I can get out of this graveyard and go
home, General."

Musso sat back and regarded her with a contemplative air. "So your
home isn't here anymore? America, I mean—not Temple, of course."

"It's where the heart is, sir," she said, being careful not to stare at the
pictures of his dead family, even though, as the only adornment in the
spartan office, those images drew the eye. She wondered if a day went
by when he didn't think of them. The same way she didn't think of
Bret or Monique.

Probably not. Musso seemed like a good man, and he probably had
been a much better father than she was a mother.

"Can't argue with that," he agreed, apparently speaking to her private thoughts. "Are they letting you stay in camp over at the Hood?"

"As if I'd want to," she replied. "They might have some surveillance
rigs over there actually worth the money they spent on them."

Her Siemens handset lay on Musso's desk, the screen lit up, displaying an image of one of the bugs in her room. It sat squatting between
them like a poisonous metal spider. The director of the Federal Center
couldn't stop his gaze from drifting back toward it. Even though Caitlin had used the cell phone to scan his office and declared it clean, she
could tell that the former marine had been rocked by the revelation of
a traitor somewhere within his command. He was being very circum-
spect now, as if he thought Mad Jack Blackstone himself was listening
to every word. Caitlin, however, had more faith in her equipment and
in TDF security's general lameness.

"I'll have more freedom of action if I'm not right under their noses,"
she said. "There's plenty of accommodation in Killeen. I've asked them
to find me a room over there."

"They'll be all over you like a cheap Chinese suit," he said, frowning
at the cell phone.

"Just a day at the office, sir, and hopefully it won't even be necessary, except as cover. If I can get in and out tonight, Colonel Murdoch will be on a scheduled flight three days from now, with McCutcheon and Blackstone waving her off at the airport."

"And if that doesn't pan out?"

Caitlin paused just long enough to feel her heart beat once.

"I'll get out, with the data."

Musso leaned back in his chair, looking tired. "In a way, I hope you fail," he said.

She looked at him, tilting her head in an unspoken query.

"I think Blackstone is genuinely seeking rapprochement," he explained, eyeing the file that filled his in-tray.

In there was everything McCutcheon had on the South American Federation's op in Florida, or at least everything he said he had. There might have been intelligence he'd held back to avoid exposing any further TDF ops outside Texas. Nonetheless, Blackstone had agreed to hand over the captured infiltrators to a team of federal marshals who were scrambling to fly down from Kansas City by the end of the day.

"I can't say I'm happy about this other bullshit," Musso said, nodding at her cell phone. "But I can understand it. Mad Jack seems genuine in his paranoia about Morales. He's going to want any kind of leverage he can get with Seattle's man, or woman. You being Echelon, I'm sure you'd understand."

Caitlin smiled. "My first field assignment was bugging the French and EU trade ministers at a GATT meeting. Long time ago. In a galaxy far, far away."

"Yeah," Musso grunted. He pointed at the Siemens. "I'm still going to have to deal with this. Bring in the FBI, I suppose. But I'll leave it until you're gone."

"That'd be a big help, sir. And if you could organize my stunt double, too?"

"No problem. We can use Amy, the waitress from the other night. She did good with McCutcheon, and I trust her. She fought in New York. Reenlisted right after, when the TDF recruiters were really trawling for custom. Sign-on bonuses, free houses, transfer of benefits, everything. But she's a believer."

"You don't have to sell me," she said. "Before I used her on Mc-

Cutcheon, I had Vancouver run her through the filter. She's clean, as far as they could tell."

At this, one of Musso's eyebrows climbed toward to the ceiling. "I see. And did you run me through your filters as well?"

"You bet. I'd run everyone if I had the time and resources. But I don't. And so this shit happens." Her turn to nod toward the augmented phone she'd used to sniff out the bugs in her quarters when she'd first arrived.

Musso appeared to take no lasting offense at having been vetted by Echelon. Caitlin found him an easy man to work with. A lot of military people held her profession in low regard, but Tusk didn't seem to be the sort to judge.

"I'm going to have to revise your final report," he said. "Colonel Murdoch's, that is. I don't think Blackstone is right about Morales being an immediate threat. But I think maybe we do have to take him a little more seriously. That Federation special forces team in Florida wasn't an invading horde, but it's a factor we need to plug in. I'm afraid the president needs to know about that and that Governor Blackstone has his own SF teams wandering around the countryside, too."

"If you tell him now, you blow my cover," she said, suddenly worried that Musso's Boy Scout gene was going to bring them all undone.

"No, not necessarily. After all, it's my job to act as liaison to Fort Hood. This is exactly the sort of information I'm supposed to pass back. It would draw more attention if I didn't and Mad Jack decided to get on the phone and yell at the president for ignoring him again."

"So you're going to lie?"

"I'm going to tell the truth but not the whole truth. In my experience, the president cares little for briefings by military officers. He can hardly keep their ranks in his head, let alone their names. He just wants the job done. I'm sure I can shade Colonel Murdoch into insignificance for now. But I can't make this Florida thing go away. Not with it sending the governor bugshit."

Musso shook his head and looked as though he was disgusted with himself.

"The great game, Caitlin. It never ends, does it? We have our own people sniffing around the Federation all the time, I'm sure."

She maintained a studied neutrality at that.

"Who knows," he continued, "even if it's paranoid bullshit, it might be enough for Mad Jack and Kipper to put aside their differences. The enemy of my enemy might just make us friends. Something like that. I've already sent a preliminary briefing note through to Jed Culver, and he's on my case for more detail. And your report."

A headache began to form behind Caitlin's eyes.

"That could be tricky. Seeing as how I'm not really a USAF colonel."

"The tangled webs we weave, Agent Monroe."

She breathed out heavily. Once this mission was done with, she planned to cut her entanglements, but it would be interesting to see what happened to Culver if she couldn't give him Blackstone's head on a plate. The Colonel Murdoch jacket wasn't meant to be worn in earnest. It was thin cover for a quick and dirty job. And there was always Wales, too, of course. Her former controller would go down with Jed Culver, and *that* she did care about.

Musso was still talking, however, and she had to set aside those thoughts.

"In many ways, Caitlin, if your mission is successful, you'll set this country back on its heels for a decade. Or longer. Conceivably, you could even cause a complete break between Seattle and Texas. You could turn differences of opinion into a casus belli."

Caitlin picked up her phone and stowed it away in a deep jacket pocket. She felt none of the bleakness of spirit that seemed to have taken hold of Musso.

"But think about those differences, sir. They're not cosmetic. It's not just politics or a personal feud. Culver and Wales briefed you before I came down. You know why I'm here. For New York. For what this asshole did to us in New York." *And for myself,* she didn't add.

"I do," he said, sounding very tired now. "I do. Some things you neither forgive nor forget."

He stood up and reached his hand out to shake hers.

"Good luck, Agent Monroe. Good luck to us all."

46

DARWIN, NORTHERN TERRITORY

She experienced a point of paralyzing clarity just before the impact. Sensing Granger's sudden tension, Jules felt herself pressed back into the seat as he accelerated. Something large and dark and moving much too quickly loomed in her peripheral vision on the driver's side of the car. That part of her mind—trained as it had been by years at sea to judge the lines of force conspiring to undo her while sailing small boats through the huge, angry seas—passed from slumber to full sentience in the space between instants. She registered the inevitability of a collision in the stuttering hundredths of a second before the hollow thunder of impact. The whole world, and them within it, lurched sideways as it broke apart in a bright, shattered mandala of atomized glass and shrieking, collapsing metal.

A blur of color. A violent Catherine wheel of optics, stretching and encircling them at cyclonic velocity as the car spun around, tires exploding like gunshots.

A small, almost abstracted part of her rational mind waited for the cab to flip over and over, for the roof to collapse and crush them. But after an eternity of splintered fractions and fragments of time, they came to rest with a slight jerk as inertia tugged back at the momentum of impact.

She heard Granger cursing weakly and became aware of blood everywhere, but whether hers or his, she could not be sure. After the savage, caterwauling din of the crash, the silence that followed seemed to roar in her ears like a force nine gale. But not so loudly that she couldn't hear the tinkling of glass and the tortured creak of metal as the weight of the wreckage resettled itself.

The crunch of boots on gravel. Running. Men shouting.

Gunshots cracked and popped somewhere nearby, but muted, perhaps by distance, perhaps because her ears were full of blood. Granger cursed again, but he trailed off into a groan as he struggled to release himself or to retrieve something from beneath his seat.

Jules could not put one thought after another in any sort of coherent fashion. She was annoyed at ruining the clothes she'd bought just hours ago even though she hated them and would have thrown them away. She felt cool despite the heat of the day pouring in through the damaged windscreen, which looked as though a giant had put his fist through it.

And still the gunfire popped and crackled. Until, without preamble, a single shot roared with the concussive power of a small bomb going off beside her head. Someone screamed—it was her; she was screaming—at a blast wave of mutilation. Blood, bone, skin, gore. And Granger yelling and roaring and trying to push her head down between her knees as he fired out of his window with the cut-down shotgun.

Two bangs sounded next to her ear, followed by metallic crunching, and then her door was open and she caught a glimpse of a blade. She tried to cry out, to warn Granger of the threat. But he was snarling and shouting as he fired off round after round from the pump-action shotgun.

Julianne tried to sit up, but this man was too strong. But then the blade was gone, and her seat belt had been cut, and she was being dragged out of the vehicle and away. Away from the burning oil, the iron blood, the tangy aftertaste of gunfire. She fought to free herself until she recognized Birendra's voice.

"It is fine. It is good. You are safe, Ms. Julianne. You are safe. Just come with us; we have to go. Now."

The world was a red mask of death and chaos. Her eyes were tacky with blood. What little she could see and understand gave her to believe that they had been rammed at an intersection and two more cars had blocked them in. Both of the blocking cars were burning, riddled with bullet holes. She and Granger had been ambushed and would have died save for three carloads of Shah's men who had materialized from the traffic flow.

Some of the attackers lay on the ground. One man in a pair of Levi's cutoffs lay across the hood of the cab, still twitching from the last sparks of his neurons as they faded away.

The gunfire had ceased, she realized. It had stopped some unknown time ago. Her internal clock seemed to have been damaged in the crash. Had she been here for hours?

"Come on," said Birendra. "We have to get you to a hospital. The others can chase them down."

Although hardly able to stand, she shook herself free of the Gurkha and the second man hurrying her toward their waiting SUV. Other vehicles in the Shah Security group pulled off down the road at high speed in hot pursuit.

"They're getting away?" she croaked. "No. We have to go now. I'm coming now."

She reached around and flapped her hand at the small of her back. The SIG Sauer was still there, and for the first time she became aware of a burning pain at the base of her spine, as though she'd been punched there by a stone fist.

"Come on, then," said an exasperated Birendra. "We have to move quickly. There is no time."

He hurried her gently but firmly over to the last SUV, a black Volvo XC90. The endorphin rush her body had released immediately after the crash was wearing off, and she was walking into a world of pain. A radio crackled with reports of the chase.

"In pursuit. Speed approaching a hundred and ten kilometers per hour. Taking intermittent small arms fire."

"Hop in, Ms. Julianne," came a familiar voice. She blinked away the thin crust of dried blood and found Shah patting the seat next to him in the rear of the vehicle. He didn't seem to care that she was about to bleed all over his soft cream-colored leather. Brass casings had burned small holes into the upholstery and carpet. She thanked him as he handed her an antiseptic wet wipe.

"We must go now if we are to catch them," he told her, smiling.

A PKM very much like Fifi's old machine gun rested on the wound-down car window. Shah pulled it inside and handed it to one of his men in the back in return for a more reasonable, G36 carbine. Birendra helped Jules up before climbing into the front passenger seat. The driver reversed, slamming into another vehicle before snapping it into gear, jerking them around with almost the same amount of force as that created by the crash. Once they were straight and true, he stomped on the gas before the last door was closed, launching them into the disrupted traffic stream.

Birendra grabbed the radio's microphone. "Status?"

"Speed now a hundred and twenty kilometers per hour. We're eighty meters behind and closing. Still taking small arms fire."

"Return fire at your discretion. We're coming up on your six now," Birendra said.

She heard a siren and searched fruitlessly for any sign of the police until she realized the warbling Klaxon was coming from somewhere just outside. The driver had fired up his own siren. Seeing her confusion, Shah smiled. He appeared serene in the middle of the chaos.

"Do you forget, Ms. Julianne, that I am an FPDA-approved security contractor? Licensed and bonded to the development authority and subcontracted to the city to maintain order during emergencies. I think there has been enough gunfire and bloodshed this morning to consti-tute an emergency. And two vehicles are currently fleeing the scene of that gunfire at high speed, endangering law-abiding motorists and pe-destrians and threatening the dignity and repose of the city at large. It is our duty to pursue them. And so we shall. You are still armed?"

She shifted in her seat and retrieved the SIG Sauer. Her neck muscles and most of those in her upper back seized up as she did so; she ignored the discomfort. The weapon felt heavy in her hand. It felt like something that could open up all sorts of possibilities.

"How is Granger?" she asked.

Shah turned off his smile while he answered. "Mr. Cooley acquitted himself admirably," he said. "He detected the ambush as the attacking vehicle sped through the red light, and he accelerated his own vehicle early enough to avoid being rammed amidships, so to speak. The impact was still significant, but it spun you around rather than smashing and flipping your vehicle into the deep ditch by the side of the road, as was intended, I believe."

The driver, a man Jules did not recognize, whipped the steering wheel back and forth as he weaved through the traffic at more than a hundred klicks an hour. They passed a pair of police cruisers going in the opposite direction. The cops showed no signs of providing backup today.

"But is Granger okay, Shah? He looked terrible after the crash."

The old Gurkha nodded. "He has sustained injury. But he shall live and probably recuperate. Mr. Cooley is one of my best men. Even shocked and disoriented by the collision, he managed to hold off your attackers while our support vehicles closed in. He killed one of them, in fact, as the man was leaning into the car to shoot you both." This seemed to amuse Shah greatly, and his face lit up again, smiling with Taoist contentment.

"Oh . . . I guess I didn't notice," said Jules, not really believing the words as they came out of her mouth.

Had Granger blown some bugger's head off right next to her? She shook her own head in wonder, aggravating the strained muscles in her neck again.

"How many of them are there?" she asked.

Birendra drew out his seat belt so that he could turn around to answer. "There were about thirty of them, Miss Julianne. Many more than we expected."

"I am certain we will find that Mr. Cesky's agents have secured support from one of my rivals," said Shah. "I recognized two of the men back at the intersection. Freelancers. And not in the way Mr. Pappas is a freelancer. These men are scavengers. Not skilled or reliable enough to secure permanent employment with any reputable contractor, they sell their services on the gray market, doing work like this, one or two steps away from the agency holding the original commission."

The driver swung hard left, taking them off the main drag past the airport and away from the thickening chaos of the traffic banked up there. Jules was not familiar enough with the city's layout to know where they were headed, but down in her gut she suspected the destination was New Town. Shah leaned forward to mutter instructions to the driver, who sped up to the point where every course correction, every small turn of the wheel to whip them around a slower car, threw the Volvo's occupants back and forth across the cabin.

Ahead of them, Julianne could just make out the rear of two late-model cars. Streamlined and low to the ground, they wove through the stop-and-start traffic like barracudas streaking through schools of slow-moving guppies. Flickers of flash suppressors could be seen as tracer rounds zipped toward them. One of the shooters emptied a clip into a passing civilian vehicle, causing it to slam into oncoming traffic.

"*Evasive,*" the radio crackled.

"Oh, shit," said Jules.

The driver cranked the wheel, taking their car across two lanes. He ran up the shoulder until he was clear of the collision site before whipping back into the proper lane. The scenery outside changed in brief strobes of blurred imagery. The Volvo screamed through the wide, dusty streets of a factory and warehouse district before bursting out onto a wide four-lane arterial road that swept alongside the upper reaches of the harbor.

"*Speed increasing,*" the radio said. The pursuit vehicles were zeroing in on the fleeing hit squad. "*Closing. Fifty meters. I'm going to try and ram him . . .*"

A black pepper cloud suddenly enveloped one of Shah's Land Cruisers, shredding the passenger compartment into disassociated bits of glass, flesh, metal, and bone. Bursts of flame brewed up around the undercarriage as the vehicle turned over on its side. The other pursuit SUV whipped around their fallen comrades before ramming the offending vehicle off the road.

"Stay with that one," Birendra ordered. "We'll take the last one."

"Grenade launcher," Shah remarked as they passed the burning ruins of his men. "This is most unfortunate."

There, up ahead on the left, Jules could see the marina where the Rhino had moored his boat. Police tape still fluttered across the entrance near the manager's hut. She then caught a sunburst flaring off the tinted rear windows of the car in front as it screeched through a hard right turn and disappeared into the diabolical labyrinth of the city's red-light district.

"Oh, God, we'll lose them," she said, despair in her voice.

"They cannot move at speed now," Shah assured her.

Yeah, Shah, but neither can we, she thought to herself.

Within moments they had reached the corner where their quarry had just entered New Town. The driver yanked the wheel once more and took them into the congested chaos, blowing through a pile of garbage as he did so. The stench of rotten eggs, meat, and vegetable matter saturated the inside of the Volvo. Jules resisted the urge to gag.

She craned around awkwardly to see how much backup Shah had. She could see one other SUV, an older Toyota of some sort. Red and blue flashers turned inside its grille work, adding their own urgency to the bubble the driver had placed on the roof. She might have shaken her head had it not been so painful to move. The longer she was in this city, the less she understood it.

"Where are the police?" she asked.

"They will be back at the crash site," said Shah. "But Northern Territory and city law prohibits them from exceeding the speed limit by more than twenty kilometers an hour even while in hot pursuit. There have been incidents. Pedestrian fatalities."

As if to underscore that point, they passed a trio of bodies lying face-down in the bone-dry dust, their blood spilling into the earth. Crowds had gathered but kept their distance, as if the corpses somehow might transmit the violence of their ending through simple proximity.

"But we—"

"We do not answer to the city or territory," he explained patiently. "We are licensed by the development authority."

Birendra spoke up again from the front seat, where he was loading shells into a military-style shotgun. "They would not follow us into New Town, anyway, Miss Julianne."

"Turning right," their driver said, giving another brutal hoist on the steering wheel. The Volvo scraped past a pair of pedestrians, the vortex of the vehicle's passing yanking their hats off into the rubbish.

They roared past the Freaks tattoo and body-piercing shop, where a cluster of preteens fitted with enough metal to build a small bicycle stood in the street, gawking at the chase. A bald man with a white goatee came out waving a cricket bat, shouting curses at them as the front of the car knocked over a fifty-five-gallon drum of rancid fryer oil from some nearby greasy spoon. The driver didn't waste much time using the horn. He simply nudged, shoved, and rammed vehicles out of the way with the crunch of plastic, metal, and glass. Birendra was ready at the window, the muzzle of his shottie in prominent view.

The Volvo's windows were tinted, allowing Jules to lean forward and search for Cesky's men without having to squint into the fierce antipodean light. At this time of day, the sun burned with the intensity of an unshielded furnace, a nuclear fire rendering everything outside the car into flat, monochromatic severity. It was the wet season, but the monsoons had failed for three years running, and the urgency of their pursuit had thrown up thick clouds of dust and trash.

Vehicles blared their horns, and drivers leaned out to abuse them until they saw Birendra with his shotgun. Once they clocked that, they wasted little time in moving to clear the way. Slower vehicles found themselves shoved into stalls, crushing products and proprietors alike. The rubberneck brigade materialized at each individual tragedy to gawk and enjoy the spectacle without providing anything in the way of assistance.

As Julianne watched their target negotiate a left-hand turn at high speed to take them even deeper into the district, her eyes went wide at the sight of a pedicab suddenly launched into the air a hundred meters ahead of them. The bright orange rickshaw, its driver and passenger separated as they headed into orbit, perversely reminded her of that old footage of the space shuttle coming apart after launch.

They followed the turn into a tighter alleyway, pushing past a cluster of what looked like military tents on the left, with a high climbing wall of shipping containers to the right laced together with metal mesh walkways. The passage of Cesky's team snapped free lines of laundry, adding to the confusion. The still airborne bits of tighty whities, naughty nothings, and bed linen drifted down onto the windshield of the Volvo. A rain of rubbish, beer cans, and bottles fell down on them from directly above, thrown by enraged locals. The wipers came on when a particularly nasty bit of brown fluid hit the windshield, showing the exact contents of somebody's poorly digested dinner from the night before.

The last vehicle took another turn, this time to the right, crashing through a chain-link fence.

"Brace, brace, brace!" the driver shouted.

He took the turn at high speed onto what appeared to be some sort of makeshift basketball court. A basketball bounced off the back of the Volvo as a mixed group of players stood in the vehicle's wake, popping off rounds, which shattered the back windshield. "Suppress," Shah ordered.

A quick burst from the PKM in the rear brought the gangland protest to a stop.

Jules heard the metallic snap and lock of Shah ramming home a magazine into his G36. He was careful to make sure that the safety was still on, leading her to check her own weapon. It suddenly felt inadequate.

The surface was rough, testing the XC90's suspension, but at least it was sealed after a fashion. As the driver wrenched them around into the side street down which the car ahead had sped, she felt and heard the loss of traction once the wheels hit a section of dirt road. It was probably bare earth from when this place was . . . what, a garbage dump? Five or six years ago? She couldn't remember the details as she'd been told them.

The congestion was much worse in here than it had been out on the wider main avenue. Granger had told her something about most of the cross-streets in New Town being unsurveyed, as though the back routes and minor alleys were contingent spaces, pathways through the crush left over by accident rather than design. She could see that here. The streetscape was bedlam, a derangement of building styles that couldn't agree even on a common footpath. The covered verandas of two bars—she assumed they were bars because of all the drunks spilling out to gawk at the chase—pushed out a good meter or two deeper into the roadway, creating a dead space where traffic could not flow. Some cars and motorcycles and even one horse were parked in there, or tied up in the case of the horse.

On the opposite side of the street, another building appeared to have burned down recently, and the vacant lot had been occupied by street vendors offering not just games of chance, stolen electronics, and salvaged goods from America but an open-air distillery and even a butcher. She was amazed to see gutted hogs hanging from poles, covered in flies, while scabrous half-feral dogs fought over piles of entrails beneath their carcasses.

In here, there was no chance of forcing a passage by brute speed, and the way ahead was quickly blocked. Stalled traffic, meandering pedestrians, animals, sightseers, they all conspired to bring the pursuit to a halt.

"And we're done," the driver announced as he braked and cut the engine.

Birendra was out of the door and racking a round into his shotgun before Jules could get her seat belt undone. She flinched as the weapon roared twice, then three times.

"What the fuck?" she said.

But Shah was already gone, taking the machine pistol and the spare clips with him. Both he and the driver charged ahead into the space created by Birendra when he'd fired his warning shots into the air. Their second car skidded to a halt a few inches from the Volvo's rear bumper, and three more men, all heavily armed, emerged at a run. A nearby club pumped out Nelly's "Hot in Herre" loudly enough for Jules to make out all the words. Nelly wanted his bitch to take off all her clothes.

"Better get a move on if you want to be in for the kill," the new driver told her, grinning. He obviously was staying to guard the vehicles. He was armed with a long black shotgun just like Birendra's, but he also took out a taser and fired it up experimentally.

Jules didn't fancy his lot, having to protect two expensive cars filled to the gills with the sorts of goodies this crowd of cutthroats and ne'er-do-wells would love to have gotten their hands on. As she set off after the others, she heard him tell the crowd, "First bloke who tries it on gets a couple of thousand volts up the arse. Anybody wants to have a go after that, I'll blow your fuckin' head off as per the operational guidelines of the Free Port Development Authority, section 56, paragraph B, regulations pertaining to the use of force by contracted fuckin' security consultants."

Jules was sorely tempted to see how that turned out, but she had to run to keep up with Shah and his men. She heard no gunfire from behind, so perhaps the unlucky soul on guard duty would be all right. She didn't doubt that he would stick that nasty-looking taser up somebody's bottom. He seemed just the type for it. Then again, so was she.

Ahead of her, however, she could hear the first crackle of gunfire from somewhere beyond a green-fronted payday loan shop. The gunfire expedited the emptying of the street life into the relative safety of the Lone Star Bar and Doug's Tattoos and Smoking Accessories. She felt a thousand eyes on her as she ran through the rapidly vacated streets with her SIG Sauer pistol in hand, ignoring the stitch in her side, dodging and jumping over potholes and ditches filled with raw sewage. Piles of rubbish and debris reached as high as the second story of many of the shops, where children picked through the bits to see if there was anything to eat or sell.

Although the sun was almost directly overhead, she was soon running in shade as the side street narrowed dramatically, becoming little more than a crooked shaft bored deep into a squalid mass of tumble-down shacks, hovels, and filthy open-fronted bars wrought from shipping containers in a fashion not unlike that of the office complex at Shah's business premises. Unlike him, however, the owners of these bottom-feeding operations had not a care for good order or cleanliness.

In one place, which seemed to service a purely Chinese market, blood was pooling under the bar stools of its patrons, who all turned on their perches to watch her run past. She had no idea where the blood was coming from or whether it was human. Impassable to road traffic, the undrained passageway doglegged around to the right between two saloons that appeared to loom over the alleyway—this was due to the verandas on their upper floors cantilevering out to such an extent that only a few inches separated them, creating the effect of a tunnel. As narrow as the path was through here, at least it was clear.

She could see why now, even in the gloom. Brass shell cases gleamed in the mud, picking up the reflection of neon lights and red candlelit lanterns from what she assumed was the door of a Chinese brothel. A man lay dead, facedown in the filth. Dark arterial blood leaked from five or more bullet holes punched into his torso. The wound that had killed him, however, was almost certainly a shotgun blast that had carried away the better part of his head, spraying it over the fibrous cement panels of the saloon in front of which he'd died.

One of Shah's men was waiting for her a short distance ahead, nodding when he saw her and gesturing for her to hurry up. He waited next to a solid steel door that opened onto a gloomy staircase. A short Chinese woman ranted at him in a language neither of them understood, undeterred by the presence of the man's weapons. "They fucked off in here," he said.

Jules heard the cough and bark of back-and-forth gunfire from somewhere inside. She also could hear what sounded like the roar of a crowd. "What the hell is this place?" she asked as she flicked off the safety on her pistol.

"Fight club," he said without further explanation. "Come on."

They plunged into the darkness, past a drunk lying in his own vomit and shit. The stench of the man was sick-making.

Shah's man took the stairs, leading upward, two or three steps at a time. Julianne's body was seizing up, her muscles clenching and stiffening painfully after the shock of the crash. She had trouble even raising her head to follow his progress. Nonetheless, she charged after him without hesitation. For the first time in months she felt like she was finally ahead of the play. If they could just lay hands on these fuckers . . .

An automatic weapon coughed in the dark, and her escort lifted off his feet before crashing into the wall and sliding to the floor, leaving a dark organic smear behind. Another man stepped out of a doorway and jumped when he saw her.

Jules dived for cover, pumping rounds down the hallway while ducking through a door into a red-lit room full of candles.

The man roared in pain. "Bitch! I'm gonna fuck you up!"

American, she thought. Jules heard his footsteps. Scrambling back to the inside corner of the room, she waited for the asshole to step inside.

The muzzle of his weapon came through first as he charged in without sweeping the area. Jules took her time to line up the front of her SIG Sauer with the side of the bastard's head and squeezed off a double tap that dropped him like a sack of shit.

She flinched and shuddered as blowback splattered her with skull chips and small gobs of gray matter. Biting down on her revulsion, she scrambled out past the body and checked on the man Shah had left behind to look after her, but his sightless eyes could see her no more. She swore once and picked up his G36 to supplement her handgun.

The confidence she had felt rushing in behind him had evaporated entirely. She'd expected that they would sweep in behind a trail of dead men left by Shah and Birendra and their comrades. Where had the guy she'd just killed come from? He was a white male, American, and that was all she knew. He could have been one of Cesky's men, a hitter who'd hidden himself to ambush stragglers like her before doubling back to take Shah from behind. Or he could have been some unfortunate punter or an employee of this "fight club" who simply was defending his place of business from a pack of murderous buggers who had just invaded it.

Oh, bloody hell, she thought. *Nothing's ever simple, is it?*

The more deeply she pushed into the building, the louder the crowd noise from downstairs grew. She stepped over two more bodies as she worked her way around a corner and another one on a stairway leading down to what she assumed was the second floor. This building really seemed to have no coherence or logic to its internal design. Corridors branched off to nowhere. Sometimes doors stood open or closed down the dead ends. Sometimes the hallways literally led nowhere, for no reason.

More gunfire.

More cheering and shouting and rumbling from beneath her.

She followed the gunfire as best she could through the poorly lit space.

The gunfire and the trail of dead.

Another two left turns and she found Birendra propped up against a wall, nursing a leg wound. He was sweating and struggling to maintain his composure as he applied a pressure dressing. He started to reach for his gun, stopping himself when he recognized her. Relief flickered over his otherwise impassive features.

"Ms. Julianne," he said. "Mr. Shah has him, one floor down. He wishes you to go on ahead. My wound is not serious. I can tend to it myself."

Jules answered that with a very dubious look. "Jesus Christ, Birendra, at least let me patch you up. You can keep an eye on the corridor behind me. I'm afraid the chap you left to look after me won't be joining us. Some little bastard did for him down on the first floor. Popped out of a room at the top of the stairs and shot him."

"A stay-behind," Birendra grunted, as she tied off the tourniquet he had fashioned for himself.

"I wouldn't have a clue. But I killed him, anyway. It seemed the decent thing to do."

"Yes," he said through gritted teeth. "Now you must go. We must finish this quickly before any others come . . . Down the hallway, first left, and take the stairs down. You will find Mr. Shah through the second door on the right. Ignore the bodies."

"Thanks," she said, giving his shoulder what she hoped was a reassuring squeeze. He hefted his shotgun to point it down the hallway up which she had just come.

Somewhere below her, it sounded like hundreds of men were chanting along in an animalistic ritual. The floorboards, possibly the framework of the entire building, was thumping in time to it, as though hundreds of feet were stamping out a beat together. The tempo picked up, building to a crescendo, before erupting into what sounded like applause and shouts of encouragement.

She hurried on, following Birendra's directions. Another of Shah's men stood guarding the access to the next floor via the stairwell. He watched over three corpses that seemed to have been piled neatly on top of one another. She vaguely recognized him from her visit to the compound the other day. He nodded brusquely and jerked his head in the direction of the doorway a little farther down the hall. Julianne safed her weapon, raising an eyebrow in question.

He nodded. It was safe.

"It's me, Shah," she called out softly as she tapped on the door, fearing to walk in unannounced.

"Come in, Ms. Julianne," Shah replied. "There's somebody I would like you to meet."

47

It was a strange assignment, not difficult but nerve-racking in its own way. Corporal Summers had taken a couple of semesters of high school drama, many years ago it felt like, in the lost time before the Wave. She had no illusions about her acting ability, but then General Musso and Colonel Murdoch had assured her she wasn't going after an Oscar.

Like they still gave them out.

And like Colonel Murdoch was a real air force colonel.

In Amy Summers's experience, USAF colonels were either full-time fliers or full-time paper pushers, especially nowadays when there were many fewer USAF colonels to go around. She'd been happy, even intrigued, by the Kim Possible mission they'd given her on Sunday evening, keeping Colonel Murdoch sober and bagging a set of fingerprints off that asshole from Fort Hood. That had been fun enough, but this was just weird, even a little scary.

"You'll be fine," General Musso told her just before giving her a hand-drawn diagram detailing the location of the listening devices in Colonel Murdoch's room. "It's all audio, no cameras. We just need you to go in, put yourself to bed, and go to sleep."

And to tell nobody, she thought. That was the real deal. Nobody could know she was pretending to be Murdoch. And Murdoch was . . . well, who the hell knew?

Certainly not Corporal Amy Summers.

Master Sergeant Milosz pulled over in the civilian jeep at their rendezvous point, the corner of East Avenue A and North 20th Street in the ashen wasteland of Temple's western reaches. This part of town had burned some time after the Wave, and the landscape was an eerie wilderness of ruins and scrubby regrowth. Caitlin could hear animals moving through the thickets as she waited in the burned-out remains of a brick bungalow. She had her pistol to hand, the Kimber Warrior, and Milosz had told her to think nothing of shooting at anything with teeth that got too close.

"This is for what I am supposed to be doing tonight," he'd said. "Hunting vermin and dog packs. People will expect gunfire, and in this part of the town, everything east of 14th Street, is off-limits."

It made for a decent enough pickup point. According to Caitlin's watch, Corporal Summers would be climbing under her blankets right about now.

As Milosz cranked on the hand brake, Caitlin emerged from the shadows of the ruined dwelling. She holstered her weapon and slung a small backpack over one shoulder, throwing up black puffs of dust and ash as she picked a way through the front garden out to her ride.

"So, Colonel Murdoch, I see you are PFC Murdoch now, yes?"

"I'm still the same girl inside, Sergeant," she replied as she climbed in.

"So probably not Colonel Murdoch, then."

"Probably not, Sergeant Milosz, formerly of GROM. I'm sure you know the drill."

"Like the fat Sergeant Schultz of Stalag 13, I know nothing," he said with a grin. His teeth gleamed white in the darkness of the cabin.

"Mr. Musso, he asks Milosz to undertake special mission for him. Milosz is happy to comply. Anything to escape tedious discussion of football which is not football back at hotel."

The Ranger was in BDUs, as was she, although her uniform was slightly different, being that of a private first class in the Texas Defense Force—her battered winter-weight camouflage with the proper tags sewn on. Tusk Musso had seen to that personally. Her shoulder patch marked her as a combat veteran of the now-defunct 1st Armored Division. The triangular patch was similar to the one on her other shoulder, representing the 49th Armored Division, now of the TDF. She knew enough from a potted history of both to breeze by anyone who might stop her briefly.

"For purposes of propriety, ma'am, what should I be calling you?" the Polish noncom asked as they pulled away from the curb.

The roads in this part of Temple had been cleared a few years ago but neglected ever since. They were not impassable, but Milosz was not able to drive at speed. He had to maneuver the jeep carefully back to Adams Avenue, which was cleared regularly.

"Kate will do," she said. "So, Sergeant, you ready to drive me back into the lion's den?"

"Of course, Miss Kate. I have chosen route that will avoid usual patrols of TDF knuckle draggers. Is long and winding road, like song by English Beatles, but it will put you within easy walk of lion's den. I shall wait for you for extraction."

"I may not get back to a rendezvous," she cautioned.

Milosz shrugged. "I fought in Iraq and New York. Nothing in life is certain, Miss Kate. Not for you, not for Milosz, not for anyone. But I shall wait. I have foraged some literature and some mandarins, which I found in Killeen this morning. Mandarins," he repeated with evident satisfaction, "they are much more convenient than oranges."

He handed her a brown paper bag filled with three examples of the convenient fruit and a copy of *The Great Gatsby*. The affable Pole kept a stash of mandarins in a separate bag for himself, she noted.

"This book I read in New York during the battle," he continued. "It survived with me, and so now I think it charmed. Irrational, stupid, but I cannot let it go. It is listed as a great American novel, which I suppose it is, although I still do not understand this Gatsby man. Perhaps, if you take this book, it might be of luck to you, too. And you might be able to explain this Gatsby to me when next we meet."

Caitlin took the paper bag, finding herself unexpectedly touched by the soldier's gesture. "Why, thank you, Sergeant," she said. "I promise I'll read this book again. It's been a long time. Not tonight, of course, but I will read it."

Milosz's face lit up as they pulled onto Adams and began to speed up.

"So you are familiar with this Gatsby character? Who is he, do you think, Miss Kate? He appears to be a little shady to me. Perhaps one thing, perhaps another."

The jeep began to eat up the tarmac as they headed for the Dodgen Loop. The break in the clouds sealed itself up again, plunging the ruined landscape outside the car back into darkness.

"Well, let's see," Caitlin replied. "As I recall, Gatsby is us, Sergeant Milosz. All of us. As you say, perhaps one thing, perhaps another. Not really to be trusted."

Milosz nodded sagely. "I see. I thought he was filthy rum Johnny who made free with other men's women. Good thing for him to be shot in pool at end of book, no? It is what makes America great to be weeding out his sort."

"Who's to know, Sergeant?" Caitlin said as they rounded the corner and sped up, heading for Fort Hood. "Who's to know?"

48

DEARBORN HOUSE, SEATTLE, WASHINGTON

James Kipper was still uncomfortable hearing his own voice on the radio. He couldn't help thinking of Kermit the Frog addressing issues of national importance.

"Oh, just get over yourself," Barbara told him. "You have a nice, deep presidential voice. You're just not used to hearing it like everybody else."

"She's right," Culver said, as he swirled a small measure of brandy in a crystal snifter. He was leaning an elbow on the mantelpiece over the drawing room's fireplace. "You sound fine, Mr. President."

It wasn't unusual for the chief of staff to be working through the middle of the evening, but it wasn't every night he joined the First Family in their private quarters, either. He was here tonight at Kip's insistence. Jed was one of the few people he could trust not to let due deference to the office get in the way of calling "Bullshit!" when the call had to be made.

A brief fanfare of trumpets on the radio announced the start of his weekly fireside chat, which this Monday night they really were huddled around a crackling fire to hear, as were most people in Seattle and beyond, with wood- or coal-fired heaters. Now into the third week of December, one could smell the smoke in the air at night.

The trumpets still irked Kip. Every couple of weeks he tried to sell the producers on the idea of introducing his weekly pep talk with one of his favorite tracks: "Takin' Care of Business" by Bachman-Turner Overdrive. "But it's *appropriate*," he'd protest when everybody said no. As always, the supreme executive power of the president of the United States of America turned out to be not so supreme after all. He'd eaten plenty of pizzas with way more supreme than anything he could ever call on. So trumpets it was.

"*Hi everybody,*" said Kipper on the radio while Kipper in real life finished off the last two bites of his toasted ham and cheese sandwich. The president started the broadcast, as always, with a discussion of the events of the last week. It wasn't just political catch-up. Kipper liked to chew over "the goings-on" all around the country and overseas if necessary. He liked to think that listeners might pay attention to him while he was talking about the budget or some legislative vote after they'd heard him discuss that week's sports results, unusual weather, and any WTF items in the news. Jed Culver was strangely indulgent about this, generally letting him have his way on the basis of "connecting with the average asshole." Not how the former city engineer would have put it, but then, Jed's phrasing rarely was.

"*I hope you've all been keeping safe and warm during the weather we've been having,*" he told his listeners. "*And looking after each other, too. Whether you're in the city or out on the frontier, if you have a neighbor or a family member or friend you think might need help, don't sit around wondering. Reach out and find out.*"

In the drawing room at Dearborn House, Kipper took a sip from his beer to cover another wince of discomfort. He did mean what he said on the radio, but he always felt awkward putting it into words and even more awkward when reading the lines that Jed had added to his notes for the show. Fucking "reach out and find out"; who spoke like that? His chief of staff seemed able to read his mind and shook his head as if dismissing any concerns before Kip had even voiced them.

Finding that he'd finished his beer and seeing that his wife needed a top-up on her wine, Kip excused himself and hurried through to the kitchen. He didn't need to hear himself mouthing platitudes about "reaching out and finding out," but he did want to get back in time to listen to that week's correspondence. It was his habit each week, again encouraged by Jed, to read three or four of the many letters written to him by his listeners, or as Jed insisted on calling them, voters. Although, since many of the letters came from children, that wasn't entirely accurate. He grabbed a fresh Redhook Ale from the fridge and the ass end of a bottle of some French Chardonnay that Barb had been working through before hurrying back. He returned just as his radio self was finishing reading a letter from a small boy in Kansas City, an Indian migrant who wanted to know why people at school were so unkind.

"Well, Ravi, a lot of the time, when people are teasing you or being mean to you, it's not about you at all. It's about them not feeling very good about themselves. And thinking, maybe, that if they can make somebody else feel bad, it might make them feel better."

KILLEEN, TEXAS, ADMINISTRATIVE DIVISION

Why did she bother listening to this rubbish? Sofia was tempted to pull the tiny earphones out and throw them away in disgust. She often felt that way when listening to President Kipper's radio talks. He was one of those men who were always trying to see the best in people even when there was nothing good to be seen.

She pulled the blanket tighter around herself, huddling deeper into the armchair that looked out on the empty street. Her fourth, and she suspected her last, hideout. At least in Temple or Killeen. If she got out alive, she supposed that the rest of her life would be spent in hideouts.

"If I could speak to those boys who are bullying you, Ravi," the president said, *"I would ask them just how tough they really are. Do you think they're as tough as one of our cavalry troopers chasing pirates out of the West Coast cities? Or one of our railroad men, like your dad, working right out in the wilderness, way past the frontier? Are they even as tough as old Mrs. Cooper, the lady who wrote the last letter I read out, who gets up before the*

*sun every morning to attend to her chickens so she can take fresh eggs down
to the militia post for all the men and women there who've been up through
the night keeping her safe from bandits? What do you think, Ravi? Do you
think those guys at school are that tough? I don't. But I'll bet you are."*

Madre de dios, she thought, rolling her eyes in the darkness. No wonder Papa had despaired of the federales ever doing anything about the
murder of their family. Or about any of the attacks down in Texas.

Sofia shook her head, causing the blanket to rustle loudly in her ears.
One of the earplugs for her little transistor radio came out, but rather
than pulling out the other one and giving up on the broadcast, she
hunted around inside the folds of the blanket until she'd found it and
pressed it back in.

It was a terrible thing to lose faith in someone. Not the worst thing
in the world, of course, and Sofia Pieraro was well acquainted with the
worst things in the world. But she keenly felt her disappointment with
President Kipper. She had written him a letter once, just after they'd
arrived in Kansas City. She'd told him exactly what had happened
when the road agents attacked their farm and of the atrocities she witnessed on the trail. And of how it had to be true that Jackson Blackstone was responsible for it all. But James Kipper had not read that
letter on the radio. He hadn't answered her questions about what he
was going to do. He certainly hadn't sent any tough cavalry troopers
down into the mandate to chase the road agents away. Or even to catch
them and hang them by their necks, as her father and the Mormons
had done.

She ate a handful of old tinned fruitcake, washed down with a cup
of metallic-tasting water. She was deep inside Blackstone's territory
and could not afford the luxury of hot food or a camp light. Hunkered
down in an empty house near the edge of Fort Hood, she had to be very
careful about attracting attention to herself. It was possible, she had
discovered, to move about the town during the day, but it was best to
maintain the appearance of a dutiful servant running an errand. Having spent just enough time walking the streets of Killeen to build up a
mental map of the place that she could relate to the actual maps she
carried with her, Sofia preferred to remain in hiding. And this small
suburban bungalow, just one in a street that had been reclaimed from

the Disappeared, was an excellent hiding place. The Texas settlement authorities were more organized than Seattle's, and the entire street and half of the subdivision in the streets around it stood ready to accept the next wave of arrivals and settlers in Blackstone's kingdom. There was no electricity yet, not that she would have used it. But water ran freely from the faucet, and praise be to God, it ran hot thanks to the solar panels up on the roof. Even in winter they produced deliciously hot water at the turn of a tap. The first thing she'd done after breaking in and securing her new campsite was to run a deep, steaming bath.

"And I'd like the rest of you to think about that, too," Kipper continued. *"We have better things to be doing than fighting among each other."*

Here it comes, Sofia thought. The weekly sermon about everybody just getting on together. She could take no more of it. She was tired from the effort of sneaking herself out of Temple and into Killeen. If only she'd been able to take Cindy's advice and catch the shuttle bus that ran between the two settlements, but little Mexican girls toting survival packs and their own artillery support were better off making their transport arrangements privately.

Camped now on the western edge of town, she couldn't see the military base, but she knew it was only ten minutes past the empty school over the road and the golf course behind it. The golf links had grown wild in the years since the Wave and were surrounded by a high chain-link fence from which signs hung promising that the course would reopen by the end of 2010. That was years away yet, and Sofia was grateful for the lack of progress toward the goal. The wild grass and thick stands of trees would provide her with ample cover when she needed to approach the fort.

She turned off the radio and returned the little unit to her main backpack. It was late now, and she had rested through part of today already, but she knew from having stood the midnight watch so many times on the trail that it was best to take whatever rest one could when the chance came along.

After readying the smaller backpack and checking her weapons, Sofia retired to the main bedroom, where she already had drawn the heavy curtains. There was no linen for the bed, but she had her sleeping bag and the blanket she'd salvaged from the motel back in Temple.

Crawling into the bag and tenting the blanket above her head, she used a small torch to take a few minutes to study her map of the town and the army base yet again. Once confident of the route, she flicked off the torch and laid her head down, saying a prayer for the souls of her family and all the friends she had lost.

"So I'm just asking Governor Blackstone to put aside any personal ill feeling he might have toward me and to ask himself whether he thinks that constantly butting heads is what's best for the country. We have our differences. Very serious differences. But I hope that in the end we can put them aside. There's just too much work to do."

Kipper turned off the radio with the remote. His appealing glance toward Barbara and Jed brought forth very different responses. His wife smiled almost apologetically; the White House chief of staff struggled to rein in his frustration.

"Too soft, Jed?"

Culver placed his empty brandy snifter on the mantelpiece. He folded his arms, chewed his lip, and invested a few moments in staring at the rug in front of the hearth.

"Well, you know my view, sir. We should be muscling up to Mad Jack, knocking him off balance. Not giving him a chance to set his defenses."

"Spoken like an old college wrestler," said Barb, smiling a little.

"Maybe so," he conceded. "But you know, Mr. President, that we have to do something about this guy, and sometime soon. Do you really want to be cozying up to a guy you're about to punch in the back of the head?"

Kip smiled. "That'd have to be the best place to be, wouldn't it, Jed? Nice and close so I can hit him even harder."

Culver ignored the rhetoric fend and paced over to the drinks cabinet with exaggerated care to fix himself a bourbon. He was drinking a little heavily of late, Kip thought. Even during the worst days of the fighting in New York, Jed had restricted himself to two drinks an evening, and only after clocking out. Not that any of them ever really went off duty.

"You're surely not going to fall for this bait and switch with Morales, are you?" Culver asked.

Kipper stole a glance at his wife. The First Lady had been vetted for her own security clearance, but she knew nothing yet about the Federation's special forces personnel they'd caught down in St. Teresa, Florida or, rather, that Blackstone had caught. As for Kip, he didn't know which of those recent revelations from Tusk Musso angered him more: Roberto Morales's pissant little colonization scam or the fact that yet again Blackstone had let his imperial ego get the better of him, this time by pushing his forces into parts of the country where they had absolutely no right to be.

Barbara tilted her head, inquisitively. "Is this one of those conversations where I should discreetly leave the room?"

Jed answered for his boss. "Nah, Barb. You're going to be hearing all about it soon enough, anyway." He threw down the bourbon in one hit and topped up the glass once more.

The president could see the gears in the other man's mind clanking and grinding as he forced himself to walk away from the drinks bar. Kip worried about him. His weight was getting out of hand, and he was normally much better than this at handling pressure. Since taking on the jihadi prisoners last week as a special project, however, his chief of staff seemed moodier and more irascible than ever. He even disappeared at times, absenting himself from the routine of Dearborn House for a whole day just recently without an explanation beyond muttering "Fucking Vancouver" when asked. Kip wondered if he was leaning on him too much.

"Mad Jack had some long-range patrols scouting around in northern Florida," he explained to his wife.

"That's a long way from Texas," she replied, cocking one eyebrow.

"Oh, yeah," said Culver.

Kipper frowned at him before continuing. "Well, that's par for the course with the governor. He's got his fingers stuck into cookie jars he shouldn't all over the place. This is just the latest. But for once I'm not much fussed about it, because it might turn out to be helpful. TDF grabbed up a small squad of Federation special ops guys who were looking to become a giant pain in the ass somewhere down the line.

Forewarned is forearmed, as Grandma used to say, and I think for once we might actually owe Blackstone a thank you. It's still early enough in the story for us to respond without having to start throwing around aircraft carriers and army groups. Neither of which, you might've noticed, we can spare."

Jed left his bourbon on the mantelpiece untouched and dropped himself into an armchair with an audible grunt.

"So you're not going to be giving him what he wants, then? We're not gearing up for a war down there?"

"I'm going to pay him the courtesy of taking his paranoia seriously," Kipper said, "because at least in this instance, it's paid off for us. But no, I don't see that we need to be pulling very limited resources out of the Pacific or the Atlantic or even out of the heartland, for that matter. I agree with Tusk and this air force colonel—what's her name, the one he's got down there with him. We let Roberto know that we're awake to him and that if we catch them doing it again, we'll send a cruise missile through his bedroom window one night. A gangster like him, he'll understand that. Respect it, too."

Jed Culver appeared to be discomfited by the conversation, which Kip thought unusual. After all, he was actually agreeing with his chief of staff. Most days of the week, Jed had to be restrained from throwing cruise missiles through people's bedroom windows. Maybe it was the drink. He hadn't volunteered the name of Musso's USAF analyst when Kipper couldn't recall it, and it was taking care of those little details that the former attorney prided himself on. The man was a super-computer in a three-piece suit. It was how he'd caught the link between Blackstone and the Turkish businessman Ozal, and from there to Baumer.

"Better knock off the drinks, buddy. It's slowing you down," Kip said, trying for a light tone.

"Yeah, you're right . . . I'm sorry, Kip. I don't like to admit it, but sometimes it just all piles up on top of me."

It was Barbara who stood up and fetched him his bourbon from the mantelpiece.

"Oh, Jed," she said. "Finish your drink, get yourself home to Marilyn, and have a proper rest. You can start all over again tomorrow.

Even Machiavelli took a break every now and then. I think Kip forgets sometimes how much you do for him." She leveled a severely disapproving look at her husband. "I think he forgets just how much work you put into protecting him from Jack Blackstone, for one thing."

Kipper was about to protest, but Culver beat him to it.

"Don't be too hard on him, Barb," he replied. "He's got me to protect him from Blackstone but nobody to protect him from me."

And with that, he threw down his drink, mumbled good night, and took himself off to find a car and driver.

"Jed really needs a day off," Kip said once they were alone. "D'you think he'd like to come and do a bit of trail walking with me?"

Barbara Kipper didn't need to answer. The look on her face told him exactly how stupid a question that had been.

49

DARWIN, NORTHERN TERRITORY

She had never seen the man before. He wasn't even vaguely familiar, and he was the sort of chap one would have noticed. All elbows, knees, and awkward angularity, this man looked like he'd stand about six and a half feet. Had he been standing.

When Jules first saw him, he was slumped in a chair, his hands secured behind his back and his feet fastened to the legs with plastic zip ties. One of Shah's young Gurkhas—Baran, if she remembered correctly—stood behind him with a drawn kukri dagger. The shining silver blade remained free of blood so far, but she knew that Baran would not return it to his scabbard without a few drops to taste. She wondered if the man in the chair knew that.

"Miss Julianne, I would like you to meet Norman Parmenter," said Shah, handing her the captive's wallet.

She ignored the man's murderous glare. The wallet was thick with plastic and paper, some of it quite old and faded. Dockets, receipts, a few handwritten notes, all of it the sort of thing one found in any man's wallet when he didn't clean it out very often. It lent credence to the notion that this might well be Norman Parmenter. Whoever the fuck he was.

Of course, that source of credence could have been very carefully constructed. But she thought not. Commando Barbie back in New York was the sort of person you might expect to lob herself into your life with an artfully constructed false identity. Even Nick Pappas, she thought, might have a passing acquaintance with such things. But there was something about Parmenter's old, battered wallet, with a couple of faded photographs of him posing with some woman at the seaside, that suggested authenticity.

Downstairs, the rock concert, dogfight, mixed martial arts tournament, or whatever was rolling along at high volume, the punters seemingly unconcerned with a brief outbreak of gunplay on the upper floors. The room in which they were enjoying a chat with Parmenter appeared to be an unused office. An old metal desk, some plastic chairs, and the 2007 Pirelli calendar—the first one published after a three-year hiatus—constituted the sum of its furnishings.

Jules hobbled over to sit on the desk next to Shah, feeling her bruises and strained muscles every inch of the way. Her neck was so stiff and sore, she had to turn her whole body rather than just moving her head. She needed a long hot bath, a cold G&T, and some answers. She needed to know that the Rhino was going to pull through and that Cesky was going to leave off. She didn't need him brought to justice or anything so fucking infantile. She just wanted to be left alone. Perhaps, with one of his hirelings now in her possession, they could come to an understanding: he could give up his vengeance kick, and she could keep her mouth shut about it. She was about to speak, to ask their prisoner why he was trying to kill her and her friends, when somebody rapped gently on the office door.

Shah bade whoever it was to enter, and Nick Pappas appeared. He smiled at Jules and said somewhat cryptically, "We've got fifteen minutes."

Shah seemed to understand what he meant.

"This the last of the Mohicans, is it?" Pappas said, pointing at Parmenter, who still hadn't spoken.

The Australian was holding a phone identical to the one he'd given her at the café yesterday morning. Unlike Julianne, Pappas knew exactly what he was doing. The screen lit up as his fingers danced over it, and after a few seconds he held up the mobile to compare their prisoner with an image that had appeared on the screen.

"What do you reckon?" he asked, passing the phone to Shah. The old soldier took it and spent a few moments considering the likeness. He nodded at the young Gurkha, fluttering his fingers under his chin. Grabbing a handful of Parmenter's lanky gray hair, Baran pulled his head back with brute force so that they could all get a look at his face.

"Fuck you," he growled in a recognizably American accent. He sounded as though he hailed from the Northeast, like the Rhino. Jules wondered how he'd gotten into this line of work. Ex-military? Mafia? He didn't look the type. Creepy rather than hard.

Shah passed the phone to Julianne. She couldn't immediately make out what she was looking at, but the meaning of the image soon resolved itself. It was a still, taken from security footage at the Gonzales Road Marina. A man was walking away from the Rhino's mooring. A long-billed baseball cap hid his face, but there was no mistaking the unusually tall frame or the stiff, inelegant gait of a man who was all knees and elbows.

"Well, it wouldn't stand up in court," said Jules, "but you can say fuckity bye-bye to any legal recourse, Norman. You're well out of luck. So unless you're interested in finding out what it feels like to have a kukri dagger inside your windpipe, I'd suggest you entertain us with a little story."

Shah inclined his head almost imperceptibly at the young man carrying the cruel blade. Baran was still holding Parmenter's head back by his hair, but the blade flashed up now and described a short transition across the man's brow. The fighting knife had been sharpened to such a fine edge that there was probably no pain. At first. Just a cold burning sensation followed by shock. Blood began pouring from a long gash, blinding the captive, who squealed at the unexpected violation.

"Jeez, mate," said Pappas. "You'd better watch out with that thing. It's sharp. You'll end up scalping the bloke."

Parmenter began to gobble for air as though he were drowning. Panic took over. Shah came off the desk in one fluid movement and drove a spear-hand strike into his solar plexus. It would have knocked the American onto his back had Baran not braced himself for the impact. Instead, it drove all the air from Parmenter's body without doubling him up. The restraints kept him secured.

"Mr. Parmenter will require a minute to compose himself," Shah declared.

Julianne took the chance to squeeze Pappas's arm in greeting. She'd been so surprised when he walked in, yet his appearance was not really unexpected. Not when she thought about it. Shah obviously relied on him as a conduit to the local power structure and the shadow state that was the real power in the city.

"Do we have time for this? I mean, here?" she asked waving her hand around the room.

"We've got about ten minutes," Nick replied. "Then we'll have to move him." He didn't explain any further, but neither did he give the impression that further explanation was necessary.

"Deep breaths, Mr. Parmenter," Shah said. "That's right. You'll feel better in no time, as soon as you've told us everything we need to know. I'm sure you understand the alternative. It would be overly dramatic to go into details."

Parmenter struggled to fill his lungs and blink away the blood that was blinding him.

Julianne turned back to him. "Who's paying you?" she demanded to know. "I don't care how much. I just want to know who sent you and who else is on your list."

Baran pulled Parmenter's head back again, slowly this time, lest he actually remove the man's scalp. Jules blanched at the sight of bone inside the gaping, lipless maw the kukri dagger had opened up. The Gurkha laid the edge of the knife hard up against Parmenter's nose. It had a salutary effect.

"Rubin," the prisoner rasped, as if fearful that he might not get the information out quickly enough. "His name is Sam Rubin."

She had been so sure he would say Henry Cesky's name that she was momentarily knocked sideways. And then she laughed. A short, joyless sound.

"What a wanker," she said. "Rubin was the cutout Cesky used to get the Rhino and me to Manhattan. He was the guy we were supposed to get the papers for, the deeds to the Sonoma gas field."

A smile broke out over her face like the first dawn of spring. Pappas was still frowning, but Shah understood. His head bobbed up and down as he folded his arms.

"The useless bastard has been using the same cover, the same cutout, to organize his contractors," Jules continued. "It was probably a good idea at the time. He's probably using some dead guy as a patsy. Nick, I'm sure if you look into this Samuel Rubin of the California bar or whatever, you'll find he ceased to exist shortly after morning teatime on March 14, 2003. He's a black box. Cesky can use him to hide all his bloody villainy, or at least this villainy. There's probably other stuff he's done that he's hidden elsewhere. But Rubin is the contact point for this fucking teddy bear's picnic. He was our contact for New York, and he was this loser's contact when New York didn't work out. It's a dead certainty that if we'd been able to shake down the other hitters, they'd have given us the same information: they were working for Samuel Rubin. The name that ties Henry Cesky to our friend Norman, here by way of the idiots he sent after us in Manhattan."

Shah remembered now. "Mr. Cesky sends his regards," he quoted. He was nodding like Pappas. But he wasn't finished.

A raised eyebrow was all it took for the knife to dig into the side of Parmenter's nose. Blood flowed immediately, and the erstwhile contract killer made a desperate gurgling sound as he tried to push himself away from the blade. Shah's man held him fast.

"I'm afraid we're not done yet, Mr. Parmenter," said the older Gurkha. "Am I right to assume you were in charge of this operation locally?"

Parmenter replied with a guttural grunting noise that sounded like assent.

"And you were supplied with a line of credit and introductions so that you might raise whatever support you would need here in Darwin. Is that correct?"

Again the prisoner did his best to agree without moving his head in any way that would cause his nose to end up on the floor. Shah waved his fingers, and the knife was withdrawn. Parmenter wheezed out a ragged sigh.

"The men you hired for today's operation," said Shah. "Where did you find them? Who gave you their names?"

The fear was back in Parmenter's eyes, and he shook his head in short, jerky motions, spraying droplets of bright red blood in a fan in front of him.

"Come along now, Mr. Parmenter. I can understand your being nervous. The men you dealt with were undoubtedly dangerous and unpleasant. But you are here with us now."

He paused a beat.

"And we can also be very dangerous and most unpleasant. And in contrast with your hirelings, who are all now dead, our competence is not in question. So, Mr. Parmenter, I ask you again, in this quiet room, where nobody in the world knows you to be, and immediately outside of which the bodies of your accomplices are stacked like cordwood, whom did you go to for your hired help?"

"Whom?" Pappas asked, in a jolly tone. "Are you sure it's not 'who'?"

"No," said Jules, playing along. "Definitely 'whom.'"

Parmenter's face was a mask of blood below the line cut into his forehead. It made it difficult for Julianne to be certain, but she thought he might have lost much of his coloring.

"You must have heard my friend say we are on rather a tight schedule here this morning," Shah went on, his tone conversational. "It would be of no moment for us to add one more body to those we have piled up outside. And in a minute, I am afraid, we may have to. Unless you are able to satisfy my curiosity. Who, Mr. Parmenter, put you in touch with your subcontractors? You must have had references. You have not long been in Australia. So who is your local contact?"

"Oh, come on! I thought we'd settled on 'whom,'" Pappas joked.

Parmenter began to shake. The slightest of tremors at first but building quickly to such an intensity that the chair began to rattle against the floor. Shah held out his hand for the kukri dagger.

"Sandline, it was Sandline," said Parmenter, as though coughing up a fur ball. "I got in three days ago and went straight to Sandline. Rubin made the introductions."

The name dropped like a cannonball at their feet. Cesky somehow had linked up with one of the biggest private military companies and security contractors working in the Northern Territory.

"Well, that could be tricky," Pappas said. "What do you want to do about that?"

Shah smiled. "For now, I will do nothing. If one stands by the bank of the river long enough, the severed heads of one's enemies will float by. So for now, I will stand by the river."

Pappas checked his watch. "Well, time to hit the frog and toad, my friends," he said. "What do you want to do with this criminal mastermind?"

Parmenter fixed him with an expression of woebegone helplessness. "You have to let me go," he pleaded, directing his words at Jules. "It's nothing personal, ma'am. Weren't nothing personal when you killed my guys today. Same thing for me. I just took a job, and believe me, I'm happy to walk away from it. Your friend, Ross, the big guy, I'm sorry about that. I—"

She took one step forward and swung the base of her pistol grip into his face with as much force as she could, connecting with his cheekbone and shattering it. The dull, wet crack sounded like a tree branch breaking, and Parmenter went over with the inevitability of a rotten oak falling to a woodsman's ax. As he crashed to the ground, Jules drove a kick into his face, smashing his nose flat. None of the other men moved to stop her.

"Who else?" she shouted. "Was there anyone else besides the Rhino and me? Did you have any other contracts from Rubin?"

She didn't see much point in asking him about Cesky. It would only confuse him.

"Julianne?" said Pappas, but she ignored him.

The SIG Sauer was still warm from the rounds she had fired downstairs. It was in her hand, pointing at the man on the floor before even she knew what she was doing. Jules fired one shot, and Parmenter's kneecap exploded in red ruin. He screamed, and she stamped down on the joint she had just destroyed.

"Who else, you manky little cunt? Who else have you killed?"

"Just the Lebanese guy," he wailed. "Zood. His stupid fucking name was Zood."

She *almost* relaxed at that. Her body, which had tightened itself into a giant fist, *almost* unclenched.

"And a Mexican," Parmenter hurried to add in case she thought he was trying to hide something from her. "Just a Mexican. After I did Zood, they said I did good," he blabbed, snorkeling air in through a thick soup of mucus and blood. "So they sent me to Kansas City. It was just a few days ago, and . . ."

Julianne felt her blood running cold down to the core. Her entire universe narrowed in on this bloody-nosed, half-scalped bag of pus.

Baran ducked left. It was his only option.

The gun fired three times in quick succession. Every shot went into Norman Parmenter's guts before she pumped a fourth into his sternum. Before she could regret it. And before the others could stop her. Each time the SIG Sauer kicked in her hand, she pulled the trigger again, the report drowning out her shrieks of rage. Each spent brass casing sailed over her head, tracing a trail of smoke in a lazy arc through the air.

Miguel. Oh, Miguel . . .

Cesky had killed her friend. And maybe his family. And Cesky had been able to send this worthless shitbag to do that because she'd been so wrapped up in her own problems; she hadn't made an effort to warn him after Galveston, after Sydney.

A dark fog descended on the disused office, as though the blood pouring from Parmenter's wounds had blinded her, too. Hot gusts of fury blew through her mind, and she became lost, detached from the world. She was distantly aware of insensate anger exploding from deep within her soul, emerging into the world in the form of a terrible violence. No one made a move for her until she'd emptied the entire clip into the mashed ruin of the killer's shattered skull. Only after the third click did anyone attempt to restrain her.

She was kicking a corpse. No longer feeling even the slightest discomfort from her injuries. Just kicking and kicking the dead weight, feeling bones crack and skin tear. Until she was wailing like a little girl lost. Enfolded in Shah's massive arms. Pouring oceans of tears into his shirtfront. Falling and turning and reaching for something to hold on to.

But finding nothing.

50

FORT HOOD, KILLEEN, TEXAS, ADMINISTRATIVE DIVISION

Midnight in Blackstone's Texas.

Once onto 27th Street, she did her best to look like she belonged. Although there was not a great deal of pedestrian traffic so late at night, it wasn't uncommon to see troopers in uniform and civvies moving about the post. Vehicles passed her without slowing down. She had a moment of anxiety when a Fort Hood police cruiser stopped at the intersection of 27th and 761st Tank Battalion Avenue, but after a short delay, they rolled on down the road.

Probably checking that they got the right doughnuts, she thought.

In uniform, Caitlin was just scenery, part of the Fort Hood landscape. She wondered whether Milosz had finished his mandarins yet. He wasn't far away, laid up in one of the hundreds of empty tract houses that lay between Robert Gray Airfield and the fort, waiting to meet up with her again when she was done. She had no concerns on his behalf. As with Corporal Summers, she'd run Milosz through the Echelon data core, a process that also plugged into the FBI and NIA main-frames. Because he was a foreign national who'd been cleared to join the U.S. Army as a special operator, the return on the query was exten-sive. Service in Iraq and New York, as he had said, but decorated twice in the latter theater, which he hadn't mentioned. She was confident that the kung fu of Master Sergeant Fryderyk Milosz, formerly of GROM, was more than a match for the TDF.

She just wondered whether she was.

Checking her Siemens phone, she calculated that she was too far away to walk to III Corps. Milosz had dropped her as close as he dared, but that was not very close. She would need wheels. The free buses weren't running, although she did see a cab pass through every so often, usually loaded with a squad of drunks trying to get back to the barracks. Proceeding west down 761st, she looked around for a vehicle.

She gave a beat-up-looking Honda Civic some thought—easiest car in automotive history to boost—before catching sight of a Hummer parked in front of an office building girded with scaffolding. Chalk blocks behind the tires and its windows being all zipped up told her the vehicle was parked for the night or until someone needed it.

The bumper number meant nothing to her. She couldn't fit it into her understanding of the TDF's order of battle. In the pre-Wave days, she would have snapped a digital shot and sent it to Echelon for in-quiry. She was a completist like that. Her husband probably could have read its meaning, but he wasn't there. And if he had been, Bret would have just boosted it. "Static," he would tell her. "Just so much static. Take the thing and be done with it."

Caitlin looked up and down the street, checking that it was clear, before she opened the plastic-canvas door and scoped the padlocked cable holding the steering wheel in place. A few minutes of effort with her pick set, and she'd popped the lock. After removing the chalk blocks, she flipped the starter switch, waiting for the warm-up light to fade out before cranking the beast. Soon she was cruising down 761st Tank Battalion Avenue with enough gas to carry her to San Antonio if she wanted. Keeping an eye out for MPs, civilian police, and TDF se-curity, she watched the barracks, field houses, and shops of Fort Hood pass behind her as she drove through the night.

Caitlin ditched the vehicle at the old headquarters building for the

U.S. Army's 1st Cavalry Division. It was a good place to leave a stolen Hummer. When the cav had come back from the Middle East, they'd ended up crammed into Fort Hood along with a lot of other assets awaiting reassignment or demobilization. There were over a hundred of the same squat, blocky vehicles parked in a lot, still awaiting new homes within the U.S. military or export to any foreign power willing to pay the asking price. Her briefing notes had made it clear that the Hood did a roaring trade in surplus weapons and equipment despite Blackstone's protests regarding Seattle's military surplus sales.

Working her way across 761st from the northwest, she approached III Corps headquarters on foot. Although it was brightly lit, there were no guard towers, no spotlights, no razor wire or ravenous dogs. It could have been any business park in the pre-Disappearance United States. It was just an office complex, really, not the Death Star.

She opened a link back to Echelon Prime and sent an encrypted data burst from her cell. Just under three thousand kilometers away, a systems operator in the technical services directorate received the message he'd been waiting for.

A single keystroke was all that was required to unleash the malware that had been reformatted to attack a specific server in the IT section at Fort Hood. Triple-masked infiltrators buried within standard data-matching protocols were now insinuating themselves into the control schemata for the relevant sectors. A microsecond of static and white noise would mark the instant at which local control failed and a remote authority took over. With that, the first layer of defense had fallen. Eight monitors, taking feeds from a random cycle of CCTV cameras around the Territorial Capital Building of Texas, would now have begun playing cached data looped from their own hard storage. The two security guards working the graveyard shift, who wouldn't have noticed the split second of flickering disturbance on their monitors in the reception hall, no doubt were continuing their discussion of the best pre-Wave titty bars in Houston without breaking stride.

Back in the field, the operative's cell phone vibrated silently to confirm the subversion as she approached Blackstone's headquarters. Pulling out her lock-picking equipment from a breast pocket—a nine-piece set, strictly old school—Caitlin went to work on a door at the rear of the complex. There was nothing special about the lock on the fire escape she had chosen, and the two sets of pins separated after a few minutes' painstaking work. Then came the moment she always dreaded when relying on off-site intervention and backup. If technical services hadn't subverted the building's layered defenses, she would trip an alarm in the next two seconds.

Caitlin carefully pushed open the door . . .

She couldn't hear any alarms, but that didn't mean that red lights weren't flashing and buzzers sounding somewhere else. She doubted the local security chimps would have the wit to tackle her quietly. They'd arrive with lights twirling and sirens blaring in the night. But having them arrive at all would still constitute an epic fuck-up.

She closed the door behind her.

Almost no natural light penetrated beyond a few steps into the internal corridors. A pair of night vision goggles set to low-light amplification took care of that detail. Besides allowing her to navigate with confidence, the LLAMPS headset would let her pick out the telltale filigree of laser-based trip wire systems. She hadn't seen any when she'd passed through here during the day, but that wasn't to say there were none on site.

Caitlin moved as quickly as she could, wary of raising the alarm via a clumsy footfall that would echo around such an empty building. She had plotted out a course that would avoid the front desk, where she knew the two night watchmen were now on duty. But naturally, there was no guarantee the guards weren't stalking the halls at the same time she was. If they were any good at their job, they'd be doing so at random intervals.

Pushing her senses out ahead of her, reaching for the finely balanced mental state that her teachers in Japan had explained to her as mind, no-mind, Special Agent Caitlin Monroe moved deeper into the heart of Blackstone's keep.

At one point she halted. The arrhythmic footfall of a man with a slight limp was moving toward her. A moment later, a flashlight beam stabbed out and played over a fire extinguisher at the T junction just ahead of her. She did not reach for her weapon, since it was unlikely that the man was aware of her presence. More likely, he was just ticking off a spot check. The flashlight seemed to cut out before she heard the faint click of the guard switching it off. His footsteps shuffled away.

Her heart rate slightly elevated, she waited until she could be certain he was gone before resuming her intrusion.

A simple laser trap guarded the next intersection, but she cleared the single line of light with a leap that mirrored a basic crescent kick with a midair twist. Again, she landed silently.

Flitting past the door to Blackstone's office, Caitlin cataloged the security fixtures. She had no intention of entering, but her training called forth the Pavlovian reaction.

A few heartbeats later, she stood outside McCutcheon's office. A small green LED confirmed Vancouver had subverted the PIN lock. Taking the gel-form thumbprint, she pressed it against her own digit and laid both on the receiving plate.

Nothing.

She tried again.

Nothing. Not even a red light to indicate a failed match.

Frowning, she stared at the device as if to bid it to do her bidding through sheer force of personality. Then a more rational response kicked in. She licked the gel, feeling the ridge lines of McCutcheon's thumbprint at the tip of her tongue.

This time she was rewarded with a second green light. The thick metallic *chunk* of steel bolts disengaging sounded as loud as church bells. As she pushed open the door, she pointed her phone at the proximity sensor on his desk and zapped it with the RFID tag. The infrared sensor flickered a red warning light, but nowhere in Texas. Over in Vancouver, a systems operator would be dunking his cheese cruller in a mocha latte, raising his coffee in salute to the unknown agent who'd just crossed the last threshold.

Even though Caitlin knew the pressure pad just inside the door had been deactivated, she still maneuvered around it, taking an exaggerated step to the right to avoid tripping the device. She closed the door behind her with one foot, looking for all the world like a ballerina as she did so. Or possibly a ninja who dabbled in ballet as a hobby.

With the door closed and the last of the sensors disabled, she moved quickly. Before turning on the laptop, she plugged in the unusually heavy Siemens phone and activated the software package she'd pulled down from the satellite before leaving Temple. Agent Monroe had attended a number of technical services training seminars over the years at which a number of excellent teachers had attempted to instruct her at a basic level in aggressive ELINT incursion programming. She had failed every course. Caitlin had no more idea of what was happening between the phone and the powered-down laptop than a garden-variety couch potato had of the magic that delivered his favorite cable shows. But she recalled enough of the general principles to know that somewhere inside her very smart phone, a malign assortment of software sprites were arranging themselves into a formation designed to penetrate the in-depth defenses of Tyrone McCutcheon's ruggedized Toshiba.

Complex multilevel passwords, dual-factor authentication, full disk encryption, and file protection were subjects she had never really understood. But she did understand that when the progress bar on the phone showed "100%," she was to turn on the laptop. Free-roaming software spiders poured out of the Siemens cell and into the target computer. As it woke up, the Toshiba's operating system was decapitated and the disk began to boot from her phone. The digital swarm flowed over the machine's primary defenses, shutting them down before they could send out an alert to warn of unauthorized access. Utterly formidable digital ramparts crumbled as the Echelon malware interceded between the hardware's microprocessors and the operating system's memory management unit, decoupling them and eroding the fluid architecture before it had a chance to realize it was collapsing.

Another person might have been tempted to go rooting around in the laptop's directory to hunt for particular documents. Caitlin stood well away from the keyboard and resisted any such urges, however. She'd once turned off Bret's Xbox while it was doing something not entirely dissimilar to the actions of the Siemens phone, dumping its system software and updating from a remote server. Or something.

In the end, it was all about one machine butt raping another. And she had learned from the unfortunate Xbox episode, if not from her instructors at tech services, to keep her fucking hands to herself while the machines got their awesome on.

After seven and a half excruciating minutes, the phone vibrated again. The data had been extracted and uploaded to the satellite. It was already unpacking itself into a dedicated directory on a dark server in Vancouver, where the same systems operator would be scanning it to check for exactly the sort of malevolent digital magic he had just wielded to extract the files. It was safe to disconnect.

Caitlin unhooked her cell and waited until the suicide agents left behind by the phone had shut down McCutcheon's computer after obliterating all trace of their passage through its silicon hallways. The Toshiba winked off shortly afterward.

The room seemed preternaturally still and quiet.

And then the door opened.

51

The drive to Madison Park was too far even with a government car and driver. Jed called Marilyn and told her he'd be staying in the town house for the night. She had a couple of friends over and was already three sheets to the wind, so at least he wasn't in trouble there. Their kids, Melanie and Roger, could not tear themselves away from their game consoles to say good night. Jed didn't much care by that point. He just wanted a shower, something to eat, and sleep. If he could sleep.

It was a calculated gamble, turning somebody like Caitlin Monroe loose on Blackstone. He had no doubt that within a couple of days the impasse would be ancient history. But whether Monroe would deliver to him the information he needed to remove the governor of Texas quietly or whether they were hours away from some violent, nightmarish blood swarm, he couldn't say. And not having control was killing him.

He couldn't control the fact that Blackstone had sent special operators to Florida and stumbled across an apparent piece of villainy by Roberto down there. Just as he couldn't control the fact that a certain Colonel Murdoch had loomed in the president's consideration.

Kip had no idea who Murdoch was, of course. For James Kipper, one more military officer writing one more report was a matter of supreme indifference. For Jed, however, the president's sudden inconvenient awareness of the existence of Murdoch was a source of diabolical uncertainty. It was so frustrating having to wait on other people to finish something he had set in train. Especially since the end result could see him remembered as a national hero or sent to jail.

His indigestion felt like a fist squeezing tightly just below his rib cage. Pizza was the worst thing in the world for it, but pizza was what he felt like. And for the moment at least, it was about the only thing in his life he could control. Plus, he knew that for half an hour or so the food would be a blessed relief as it sopped up his stomach acids. After closing the door of the apartment behind him and silently thanking Marilyn's forgetfulness—she hadn't turned off the heating system when she'd left for home—Jed dialed up for a four-cheese pizza from the place on the corner and poured himself a double measure of Mylanta as an aperitif.

He channel surfed the news stations for a few minutes, but that did nothing to settle his stomach or his nerves. Fox News, as usual at this time of night, was taking its feed directly from Sky in the United Kingdom. The Greens' leader, Sandra Harvey, was on MSNBC, causing him to surf rapidly away from that channel, and the local news station was still obsessing about the weather. In the end, he left it on a movie channel where John Wayne was trying to remake his image in *The Searchers*. He had just enough time for a shower and one glass of Bulleit bourbon before his pizza arrived.

Jed knew he shouldn't have been inhaling so many tons of cheese and starchy carbs that late at night. Marilyn was already on his case about the extra weight he was carrying, and she had a point.

"Soon as I put this asshole away," he promised himself aloud as he levered out the first slice. "I will bury Mad Jack Blackstone, and then I'll get myself back into shape. Maybe even go back to wrestling. But there's not much fucking point pretending it's going to happen before then, is there, Duke?"

He saluted the TV with his drink.

He probably should have had a glass of wine with the pizza, but he was on a roll with the bourbon and didn't want to change drinks. It would just make for a worse hangover in the morning.

After sluicing down the last piece with another slug of antacid, Jed washed his hands and took a legal pad and pencil to bed with him. There he began to sketch the outlines of the problems he was dealing with and what, if any, solutions he might apply.

"Blackstone, for now, I can't do anything about," he said aloud. But he wrote down the name "Murdoch," circled it, and penned a question mark.

Of course, he had never intended for Kipper to find out about Agent Monroe's mission in Texas. Since the president had expressly forbidden any such mission, there was a fair chance he would be unhappy to learn of it, especially if he found out before Monroe was able to effect a result. Jed imagined she would do so quickly, but he would have to build a firewall around her to prevent Kip from having any contact with the fictional air force colonel. At least until she was done.

"Distraction."

He wrote the word underneath the first entry and followed it up with another question mark.

"Prisoners."

Jed had done some preliminary work on the question of what to do with the prisoners they still held from the fighting in New York. It was an issue the president wanted to deal with and move past. It was also an issue that spoke to the better angels of Kipper's nature, unlike his own, and that made it ripe for exploitation.

The next hour passed quickly as Culver mapped out a plan for dealing with the prisoners in a way he knew would appeal to Kip. As a bonus, it also would meet with the approval of Secretary Humboldt, meaning that he should be able to whip up a small shit storm of enthusiasm for it in the short term. Like tomorrow. Kipper's natural inclination would be to let Tusk Musso make the running on any initial response to this bullshit in Florida. For once, Jed had reason to be grateful for Kip's natural skepticism about national security issues. Give him the choice between dealing with a security issue and an engineering challenge and with a question of development or resettlement, and you would do your dough cold betting on the former.

When he finally looked up from the legal pad, which he had filled with pages of scrawled notes and diagrams, it was after midnight. He wondered what might be happening in Texas, if anything, and resisted the urge to call Wales Larrison in Vancouver.

He could talk to him first thing in the morning. No point waking the man up to deal with something over which he had no control. For the moment at least, the president remained unaware that Monroe was operating within the boundaries of the United States, in direct contravention of his wishes. Perhaps they could keep it that way.

52

"Well, this is awkward."

"You could put the gun down, Ty. Might help."

"I don't think so," he said, smiling disingenuously. "And if you could keep your hands where I can see them and stay out of striking range, which I presume to be considerable in your case, we'll be cool."

He took a step back into the corridor, allowing her a better view of the two security guards flanking him, both with their handguns drawn and pointed none too steadily at her head. One of them moved toward her, reaching for a set of handcuffs.

"Whoa. I really wouldn't do that if I was you, Sam," McCutcheon said. "You don't want to get too close to her."

Damn.

The governor's main man grinned as though he'd just laid down the winning card. "Gee, this is a surprise, isn't it? The international superspy gets her ass handed to her by a bunch of hicks. Embarrassing much?"

"A bit. But how?" she asked. "Surely not the clowns you had monitoring my room back in Temple."

She had her hands up and the night vision goggles pushed back on her head. One of only two advantages she held at that moment. Another second and she would have put on the NVGs, blinding herself when McCutcheon had thrown open the door and flooded the room with light.

He laughed. "No. Rest assured, your surveillance shift is still listening to whoever you put in your room. I checked in with them earlier. She snores, which you don't. Those boys are probably jerkin' their gherkins right now while they tell each other exactly how many ways they'd fuck you from Sunday."

"Nice to know I still got it," said Caitlin.

"Oh, you got it, baby. And I want it. Now hand it over."

He pointed his gun at her phone.

"Just lay it on the floor and step away."

"You didn't tell me how you blew my cover, Ty. You know, in the movies the supervillain has the decency to explain that sort of thing."

She crouched down and laid the cell at her feet before backing away. McCutcheon sent one of the security guards through to collect it while keeping his gun aimed at the center of her face.

"I'm more of a senior henchman than your actual supervillain," he replied. "But for what it's worth, you can blame your husband. Well, if you ever get to see him again."

"Bret?"

"Oh, don't be too hard on old Melly. He meant well. He loves you, and he's very proud of you. That's why he sent a wedding photo to an old army buddy of mine, a ranger, too, who forwarded it to their regimental association, who then published it in their newsletter. Their *electronic* newsletter."

She closed her eyes.

"Yes, you remember now? Hatches, matches, and dispatches. That newsletter covers them all. And of course, Bret was quite the fifteen-minute celebrity for a while there. *Army Times* correspondent, one of

what, half a dozen who survived the Wave? He wrote some great dispatches out of Iraq. Pulitzer Prize–winning stuff, if there'd still been a
Pulitzer Prize. So yeah, when an old boy of the 75th Ranger Regiment
makes good like that and marries himself a pretty girl, it's a feel-good
story. The sort of thing that gets a good run in the old boys' newsletter.
You know, to lift the spirits. People have been so darn gloomy since the
end of the world."

She said nothing.

"It was the old man who remembered you. Well, not you but your
husband. The governor doesn't wear the uniform anymore, of course.
Wouldn't be right. But he keeps up with the regimental news, makes
sure to get along to the annual reunion. It's good politics, if nothing
else. We have a lot of rangers down here. Soon as he met you, bells
started ringing. You are a good-looking woman, *Caitlin,* the sort a man
would remember. He had me scouring back issues of the newsletter,
convinced he'd seen a story on you there. And he had. But not about
Colonel Murdoch. No, the story he'd seen had been about the wedding
of old boy made good Bret Melton to a USAID staffer, Caitlin Monroe.
And there you were, pretty as a picture. But really, Caitlin, a white
dress? In your case, I think not."

Still she gave him nothing. It wasn't Bret's fault. He'd sent a photo
to an old army buddy, a guy who hadn't been able to make it to the
wedding. The way old buddies do.

"I can see you calculating the odds and the angles, Caitlin," he said.
"So if you want to unburden yourself of that awfully heavy handgun
you're carrying and any USB sticks or data disks you might've used to
copy my files, you'd make me feel a lot less like shooting you in the
face."

As she reached slowly for the weapon, all three men adjusted their
stances. She slowly placed the pistol on the ground and kicked it over
to them.

"The phone is the data disk," she replied. "I'm sure you'll want to
pat me down. But it's all in there," she lied. "Encrypted, I'm afraid."

"I'd love to pat you down, but I could do without the broken arm,"
McCutcheon said. "It's a pity, really. I was wondering last night at
drinks whether your devotion to duty and country might let me score

a free blow job from Colonel Murdoch. Now we'll never know. And don't sweat the phone. I'm sure we can find some redneck genius somewhere to figure out how your cell works. Don't be too hard on yourself, by the way. Some of it was just bad luck. It's a small world these days.

"We didn't clue in to who you were right away. The boss just had a feeling that he knew of you from somewhere, and not as an air force wing nut. Me, I'd never heard of a Colonel Murdoch. And the USAF, especially these days, it's a small town, let me tell you. It was when you said you'd been exiled in the UK for a couple of years that the penny dropped. The governor remembered the wedding story. Just one of those things. If you hadn't mentioned it, you might not have jogged his memory about good old Bret and the newly minted Mrs. Melton. That's some tough shit, eh?"

McCutcheon did love the sound of his own voice. She didn't bother feeding his ego with a reply. The way he was grinning now, it didn't look like he needed it.

"Come on, Caitlin. We better go see the old man and figure out exactly how much damage you've done."

SEATTLE, WASHINGTON

He thought at first that it was his bedside alarm. Jed Culver groaned until he realized the ring tone was wrong. He had a phone call.

He wasn't ruinously drunk or hungover, but the brandy and bourbon lay heavy on his brow as he struggled out of a fitful slumber. His indigestion came roaring back, too, courtesy of the four-cheese pizza. For a second, he couldn't understand why Marilyn wasn't in bed; then he remembered she was back home and he was crashed out in the town house. The entirety of the evening came rushing back in on him: the unpleasant surprise of discovering that Kipper knew of Colonel Murdoch and her mission in Fort Hood, thanks to Blackstone and the Federation's special operators, who'd turned out to be anything but special.

Jed's voice was so croaky and thickened with alcohol and sleep that he couldn't even get the words out at first. He coughed to clear his throat.

"Culver," he said. "What's up?"

As soon as he heard Echelon's deputy director of special clearances on the line, all his grogginess sluiced away on an adrenaline surge.

"It's Wales Larrison, Mr. Culver. We have a problem. In fact, we have two of them."

"That trick you guys pulled breaking into our system, looping the security footage back over itself, that was fucking brilliant," McCutcheon raved.

He sat next to her in the back of a Humvee, both of them being driven across the base to Blackstone's home residence. Caitlin's hands were cuffed behind her back, and the former air force man kept his gun trained on her midsection while maintaining as much separation between them as he could. The driver's head bobbed in time to the bass beat of a song he was listening to through earphones plugged into his Zune.

Lil fucking Wayne again. There was no escaping the guy.

"A bit *too* brilliant, though," her captor went on. "We probably wouldn't have noticed anything, except I was standing at the security desk with my boys when I saw myself walking down a corridor on the other side of the building. Whoops!"

Caitlin maintained the stillness and silence within, which she had cocooned herself ever since she'd handed over the cell phone and her Kimber pistol.

"You're like a Bond villain, you know that?" said McCutcheon. "All of you spooks are the same. All so intent on getting your ninja merit badge, throwing your little smoke bombs, doing your Spiderman thing up on the ceiling, that you forget it would be simpler to just walk in through the front door! You probably could've hidden in a broom closet and not been caught."

She ignored him and concentrated on her breathing. He seemed relaxed, which wasn't surprising given that she was wearing the handcuffs and he was pointing a gun at her liver. But he shouldn't have been relaxed. He should have been freaking. Because Caitlin hadn't stored the data from his laptop on her augmented cell phone. Everything had been uploaded and transmitted back to Vancouver. Either he didn't know that or there was nothing on the laptop worth worrying about. She doubted the latter. Not with the lengths to which they'd gone to secure the thing from interference.

Unless, of course, that, too, had merely been a charade to entrap her.

Echelon's senior field agent did not have enough information to reach a conclusion, and so she did not bother. What mattered now was waiting for an opportunity to reverse the flow of this encounter.

Culver pressed the phone so hard to his ear, it was starting to hurt his head.

"How many dead?" he asked.

"Two here that we are aware of. Down there, I couldn't say."

"Jesus Christ, Larrison, how long does it take to do a simple body count?"

"There's nothing simple about this, Mr. Culver. We have confirmation from Australia that Henry Cesky hired Parmenter to kill Pieraro and Zood here and Ms. Balwyn and Mr. Ross in Darwin. And that was after hiring other contractors who failed in the same goals. Parmenter also appears to have killed his accomplice in Kansas City, but we have no idea who that was yet."

Jed rubbed his temples, which were pounding with a headache. He felt ill and desperately wanted to hang up, vomit, and crawl back under the sheets.

"And you're telling me this is connected, but it's not connected to what Agent Monroe is doing at Fort Hood?"

"Only tangentially, sir. Our information is that Pieraro and his family were on the boat commandeered by Ms. Balwyn. Pieraro attacked and humiliated Cesky in Acapulco while Balwyn was interviewing him for a place on board the yacht. Pieraro turned up on the margins of Agent Monroe's mission because his was one of the four cases regarding attacks on homesteaders you'd flagged for her interest while she was in Kansas City. That's the only connection."

For one brief, shining moment Jed had entertained the idea of possibly fitting up Blackstone for the Pieraro killing. Unfortunately, Lar-

rison, like James Kipper, was not the sort of man to countenance villainy of that ilk.

A damn shame, Jed thought. *If only I wasn't surrounded by Boy Scouts.*

He washed down a couple of painkillers with the cup of water he kept by the bed. When you were this deep in the briar patch, there was only one thing to do: start hacking your way out.

"Okay," he sighed. "Thank you for informing me about Cesky. As soon as we're finished here, call the FBI and have him picked up. The first time the president will hear about it will be when he turns on his radio in the morning. We can't have any suggestion of him knowing or doing anything about a case involving his biggest supporter."

"No, sir, we can't," Larrison agreed. "And Agent Monroe?"

"Yes, what are we to do with you, Miss Monroe?"

Jackson Blackstone stood before her in a plaid dressing gown, nursing a glass of warm milk. With floor-to-ceiling bookshelves behind him and a golden retriever curled up on a leather couch, he looked like a greeting card granddad. His demeanor was disappointed, deeply disappointed, rather than enraged. She wasn't sure whether that was a good sign.

Caitlin stood in front of him, dressed as one of his troopers, with her hands still cuffed behind her. McCutcheon was the only other person in the room. But two squads of TDF soldiers waited outside the governor's humble residence, leaning up against the Humvees, smoking and laughing quietly.

Still she said nothing.

"Been like this all night," McCutcheon chimed in. "Worst case of sour grapes I've ever seen."

"I'm curious about what you hoped to achieve," Blackstone said. "Does the president imagine I would submit to the indignity of being hauled up for impeachment on the basis of a couple of files illegally removed from my assistant's office? Nothing you have on that device of yours is admissible in anything even resembling a court. What did you hope to achieve?"

On her phone. Blackstone thought the data were still on her phone.

"Just the truth," she replied.

"Hell's bells, we can stop looking for the cat, Governor," McCutcheon quipped. "It doesn't have her tongue, after all."

"The truth is negotiable, Miss Monroe, easily molded, pliable. Like the ballistics gel you used to defeat our fingerprint scanner. The truth can be shaped to take whatever form we need it to take."

"Did that little peckerhead send you down here because he's still got his panties bunched up about the homesteaders?" Blackstone asked. He took a sip of his warm milk. It left a noticeable mustache behind in the hairs of his beard. He sucked at them, a disconcerting sight.

"I am sure the president would want to know why his homesteaders were being attacked, Governor, when yours weren't. And why only some of the mandate settlements were targeted by road agents."

The aide answered that one. "Well, duh, because we don't want a lot of sand niggers and wetbacks and crazy fucking worshippers of the six-armed elephant god moving in here and fucking everything up for us. Didn't we make that obvious?"

Blackstone lowered himself into an armchair. "Goddammit, Ty, I thought we made it obvious to everyone," he said with a grunt. "Don't get me wrong, Agent Monroe. I'm not one of these cranks who thinks the Disappearance was the vengeance of God laid upon us for our wicked, wicked ways. I have no idea what it was. Could've been a bunch of alien space bats throwing a big butterfly net over us to scoop up our souls and blend them into a really tasty breakfast shake. Who would know?"

Caitlin shifted slowly from foot to foot, working through an imperceptible series of isometric exercises to keep herself warmed up and ready to explode if and when she had the chance.

"But I am a crank about some things," Blackstone continued. "About culture, for one thing. Not race, as everyone imagines. You all assume I'm some sort of racist, when I'm not. Allow me to make myself crystal clear, young lady. Race is a myth. It does not exist. Black, white, red, yellow, slant-eyed, nappy-haired, hook-nosed, or whatever, we are all brothers under the skin. I really believe that."

She allowed herself to look bored and frustrated. It gave her an excuse to take in her surroundings. They were gathered in Blackstone's

living room. The library and lounge where he was sitting was a modest but comfortable space. It led to a dining room in one direction and to an alcove overlooking the garden in the other. With three flutes and a piccolo resting on an occasional table and a piano sitting against one wall, this small space appeared to be a music room opening onto the lawn through French doors. They were closed against the chill of the night, but through them she could still hear the soldiers.

The house was not what she had expected. Unlike his office, his private living space was quite restrained. He didn't hide himself away within a compound, nor was his residence the finest property available within Fort Hood. A simple two-story home, it stood on the edge of a golf course on the eastern end of the small city.

"I'm sorry, Ms. Monroe, am I boring you?"

She turned her attention back to the old man in the dressing gown. "Yes."

He smiled. "That's too bad. You are a captive audience, after all. And it's important you understand this, Agent Monroe. I think it's important that we all understand it. Especially well-intentioned liberals like your President Kipper."

"He was your president, too, last time I checked."

"Touché. You are correct. We respect the office if not the man. Would you answer a question for me, Caitlin? I hope you don't mind me calling you that. I feel that after a rocky start, we've come to know each other so much better this evening."

It was her turn to shrug.

"If I do not care about race—and truly, I don't—what is it you think separates my politics, my beliefs, from the president's? No, don't answer—it's a rhetorical question. Allow me to answer. It's *culture*. Like President Kipper, like most thinking people, I do believe all men are born equal. But they do not end their lives that way, do they? And the difference, Ms. Monroe, is culture."

He seemed to spot something of interest on the bookshelf.

"Could you get me that copy of Ambrose, please, Ty? On the third shelf, next to Davis Hanson."

McCutcheon was careful to keep his gun trained on Caitlin and to stay well away from her while he retrieved the book, which he passed to Blackstone. The old man searched for the passage he wanted. It didn't take very long. The copy was well thumbed and dog-eared.

She had endured many forms of torture over the years but had never been read to by a pompous blowhard while being held prisoner. For a moment, Caitlin thought she was about to log another unique personal experience in her long and varied career, until Blackstone merely smiled and closed the book again. As though he had needed to remind himself of something.

"This is an excellent book," he said. "Have you read it? *Band of Brothers.*"

"No, but I think we have the video somewhere at home."

"Of course you do. The thing I like about Ambrose is the facility he has with both the big things and the little. Nowadays, I imagine we would say something like 'the macro and micro.' Which is part of our problem. *Brothers* is a particularly fine piece of work because of the effort Ambrose took to follow those men from their first moments as soldiers through to the end of the war. It's at the end of the war that he tells us a profound truth."

Caitlin watched McCutcheon in her peripheral vision as he circled around to stand over by the French doors. She couldn't keep an eye on him while Blackstone expected to have her full attention.

"These men from Easy Company, 506th Parachute Infantry Regiment of the 101st Airborne Division, had jumped into Normandy, toughed out the siege of Bastogne, and muscled their way into Adolf Hitler's Eagle's Nest. They had been tested. They had been scourged. They had reason to respect the Germans' fighting abilities but no reason to admire them as a people. They had suffered too much for admiration. And yet, when they found themselves in Germany at last, they also found themselves admiring the spirit and tenacity of the German *Volk.*"

The governor was warming to his topic now, reminding her of an eccentric professor rather than an ego-driven homicidal maniac. Caitlin had the impression that this was a lecture he had delivered many times before. She would have liked to have checked whether McCutcheon's eyes were glazing over.

"Their army defeated," continued Blackstone, really beginning to sound as though he was quoting himself, "their Reich in ruins, their most treasured myth of the Aryan superman torn apart by a mongrel alliance, the Germans nevertheless wasted no time in applying themselves to the mission of rebuilding and recovery. It was in such stark contrast to the French civilians the paratroopers had encountered earlier in the war that in some ways, the men of Easy Company found the Germans to be more like them than the people they were fighting for."

"So you'd like to be a good German?" she asked.

"No, I'd settle for being a good American. I'd settle for us all being good Americans. And I do believe that anyone can be a good American as long as they commit to it. A commitment that asks more of us than simply memorizing a cheat sheet for a citizenship test and learning how to fill in a welfare form."

"Look, I can see this is important to you, but it's not to me."

"WELL, IT SHOULD BE!"

A few droplets of milk from the bottom of the glass splashed on his dressing gown as he roared at her. He brushed them off as he recomposed himself and the dog fled from the room.

She'd actually flinched a little bit when Blackstone exploded. But Caitlin used the opportunity to steal another glance at McCutcheon . . . Still standing by the windows. Still training his pistol on her.

"I apologize," said Blackstone. "But it's that sort of attitude which came so very close to laying us low before the Disappearance. The Germans, and for that matter the Japanese, whom we once considered to be an inferior race, did not create the miracle of their postwar reconstruction because of some genetic superiority. They did it because of cultural superiority. Some cultures, Miss Monroe, are meant to succeed. And some are meant to fail. Some cultures—and take a deep breath now, because I'm going to be controversial—are *better.* And that is where I part company with President Kipper. He will not acknowledge this basic truth. I do not believe he can even see it. And his policies are leading us into perdition because of that. I cannot control what happens in Seattle or anywhere Seattle holds sway. Not yet. But by God, I can control what happens down here. And I will not allow this country to go down the toilet because of the weakness and self-indulgence of a man who cannot recognize a simple truth. Some cultures are strong. And some cultures are weak. And he is rebuilding this country from the wretched, cast-off failures of some of the most benighted cultures on the face of this planet. He will bring us to ruin."

"I really wish you'd mentioned that this morning," said Caitlin, "when I had my Spy Girl outfit on. That was quite a rant. It'd go viral on MSN."

"Do we have any idea where she is?" Culver asked, wondering if there might be a chance to avoid a second civil war. His head was completely clear. He felt absolutely wretched and sick, but his mind, at least, was moving.

"If she's with her personal data unit," said Larrison, "I'm afraid she appears to be at Governor Blackstone's residence."

Okay, Jed thought. *We probably just crapped out on avoiding that whole second civil war thing.*

"Any way of confirming that, Mr. Director?"

"Not unless we can get eyes on the target. And right now we have none. Agent Monroe does have an extraction plan. Overwatch is attempting to open a secure comm channel to an effector, a ranger noncom by the name of Milosz."

"Why can't you get him now?" Jed asked. "Surely he's got a cell or something."

"I said we were trying to open a *secure* channel, Mr. Culver. There's no point telling Milosz to attempt a hostile extraction if they know he's coming."

Hostile extraction? Oh, sweet Jesus.

Jed tried to think it through, to calm the black panic gnawing at him. The situation wasn't entirely bleak. Caitlin Monroe, it seemed, had done an extraordinary job. She had somehow obtained the entire contents of a computer used by Blackstone's principal aide and delivered them safely to Echelon. Larrison's people were going to be days unraveling the treasure trove of data and documents, but already there were indications that they had enough to charge Blackstone with everything from violation of federal occupational health and safety laws up to and including treason.

In that sense, it was all hookers and blow from here. Even the most mossback conservatives could not support Mad Jack when they had a look at the New York files.

But it still left Culver exposed. He'd sought the dispatch of an Echelon agent on a mission for which the legal standing was questionable at best. More important, it was a mission the president had expressly forbidden. There was no parsing the language to obscure the fact that the chief of staff had disobeyed a direct order from James Kipper and in doing so probably had broken enough laws to see him jailed until sometime after the heat death of the universe.

That wasn't great. But even worse was the fact that with Monroe compromised, Blackstone was aware, at least to some extent, that he, too, was exposed. If he knew that Echelon had his files, he was entirely capable, in Jed's opinion, of seceding from the Union. If he wasn't aware of what they had on him, he might try to cover it up by simply disposing of the woman and turning her presence in Texas back on Seattle. This was what a guy like Wales Larrison called blowback. The deputy director sounded calm, even sanguine, on the line from Vancouver. Jed supposed he was used to these things blowing up in his face. After all, he'd seen most of his network in France rolled up back in 2003. Caitlin Monroe was the sole survivor of that betrayal.

Although the best outcome to the immediate crisis would be for Monroe to disappear while leaving Jed with enough documentation of Blackstone's villainy to destroy him at his leisure, the White House chief of staff knew he had to act quickly to maintain some semblance of control.

"The Federal Center down in Temple," he said. "Talk me through what kind of assets we have down there, Mr. Director."

"Really. This is fascinating and not at all creepy," Caitlin continued. "But really off topic. You asked what I hoped to achieve. I want to know what the fuck went wrong in New York."

Blackstone shifted uncomfortably in his chair and shot a glance over at McCutcheon before trying to cover up his loss of self-control with bombast.

"What happened in New York, young lady," he said in a lecturing tone, "is that President Kipper learned a harsh lesson in the realities of life. He had been running down the defenses of this country, selling off some of our finest assets in the worst sort of dime-store auctions, and in New York the chickens came home to roost."

Caitlin stared at him for two seconds. Long enough for him to squirm.

"Sweet suffering disco Jesus," she said. "Could you be any more patronizing or have you run out of metaphors to mix up?"

Blackstone bristled but had no chance to reply before she spoke again.

"Your administration signed a salvage contract with a Turkish shipping company controlled by a man called Ahmet Ozal. Save the bluster. If I didn't already know that, we wouldn't be here. The contract wasn't notarized in America. But I did obtain a copy in Europe. Ozal provided ships to transport jihadi fighters across the Atlantic and into New York. He was also responsible for springing Bilal Baumer from a French prison cell in Guadeloupe, where he'd been rotting away quite nicely, thank you very much."

"Stuff and nonsense," Blackstone protested.

"No, it's history, *Jack*," she said. "And so are you unless there's a good reason you took it upon yourself to commit treason."

She was ready for him this time when he exploded.

"IT WAS *NOT* TREASON!"

"Governor . . ." McCutcheon warned.

"The hell with her," Blackstone snapped, his cheeks turning bright red. "I will not be traduced in my own house. I will not have my patriotism questioned by the likes of this mercenary whore."

"Good for you, big guy," she said. "So the jihadi nutjobs you paid twenty-five million dollars to invade America and kill a couple of thousand of your fellow citizens while, incidentally, making one hell of a mess of midtown Manhattan—what was up with that again?"

"I am sure the governor will tell you it was all a horrible mistake. It wasn't meant to turn out that way. And he would be right in that . . ."

Caitlin's face distorted into a rictus of animalistic rage as she spun around to confront a new presence in the room.

He stood there dressed casually in jeans and a pink polo top. His accent was German, but he had worked on it assiduously and could have passed for a New Jersey native. His Ottoman heritage betrayed him only insofar as his olive skin stood out in a roomful of Anglo-Saxons who had endured a long winter.

Bilal Baumer positively beamed at her.

"Caitlin," he said. "It's been too long."

53

SEATTLE, WASHINGTON

"Tusk Musso has a bunch of special ops-capable rangers down there," said Wales Larrison. "Most of them with experience in village fighting in the Middle East and a tour of Manhattan."

"That sounds excellent," Jed said. "Wake Tusk up and tell him we have an agent needing extraction. Hostile extraction."

Larrison hesitated long enough for Jed to know there was a "but" coming.

"The reason most of them are down in Temple, Mr. Culver, is to recover from Manhattan. I know most of the civilians down there consider it a hardship posting because of the relationship with Fort Hood, but for those troopers, thirteen months of escorting survey teams around the countryside is akin to a vacation."

"Vacation's over, Mr. Director," Jed snapped. "Get Musso out of bed and get their asses on the road. Now!"

"With all due respect, sir, we don't even know if Agent Monroe is under duress."

"When people say 'with all due respect,' Mr. Larrison, in my experience they mean anything but. So I'm not going to bother. You tell me she went in undercover. She cracked their system, uploaded the data, and now she's gone off-line, but you can track her, or at least her handset, to Blackstone's residence. I know you intelligence types hate to make assumptions, but I think we can safely jump to the conclusion that the brown stuff has well and truly hit the fan and we have a limited amount of time to clean this shit up before we're all covered in it."

To Larrison's credit, he didn't back down. "If that is so, Mr. Culver, sending a stick of rangers in to kick down the governor's door isn't going to help. But it will surely escalate the problem. I would suggest that if we must intervene, we maintain the minimum possible profile. Sergeant Milosz is awaiting a signal to extract Monroe. We do not have a secure channel to him, but we can still contact him by telling him to find a safe channel and briefing him. It will take time we may not have, but I guarantee it's a better idea than starting a civil war."

A worsening headache added to Jed's misery, a steady, growing pain that felt like somebody boring a knuckle into his temple. His hands shook, and six slices of four-cheese pizza sat heavy in his gut, leaving him feeling clammy and nauseous.

"Right," he said, exhaling sharply. "I'm not going to tell you how to do that. Just get it done. And you're right, of course. I'm sorry. Kicking in the fucking door and killing every motherfucker inside probably isn't going to help. No matter how satisfying it might be to contemplate. My apologies, Larrison. I just . . ." He fought back the urge to vomit and a painful surge of indigestion. "It's just that we're so close to nailing this, I don't want it to fall apart at the last moment. So let's get on it."

Culver hung up the phone without saying good-bye. Dizziness almost knocked him back to the mattress when he tried to stand, forcing him to lean against the wall and suck in a couple of long drafts of air. When the dark blurs at the edge of his vision receded, he pushed into the small ensuite bathroom and ran a hot shower. He needed to clear his head and think. And maybe throw up properly.

Fucking pizza, he thought. I've got fucking food poisoning from that four-cheese son of a bitch. He leaned against the sink and struggled to draw in a lungful of air. His reflection in the mirror looked wretched. He was positively green, and dark black pouches stood out under his eyes. He shook off his own problems, however. He had more important things to deal with.

Incomplete information. That was the problem.

Monroe had done her job. She had punched through Blackstone's defenses, and although Jed had not seen the data, Larrison assured him it was enough to bring down the governor for good. So there was that. It wouldn't be a matter of just dropping the file on his desk and telling Mad Jack that he was going down. It would have to be handled with some finesse. It might even mean giving the bastard a way to escape honorably. As much as Jed seethed with a hunger to revenge himself on this cocksucker for all the trouble he'd caused, he also recognized that larger issues were in play. There was no point taking Blackstone down if he pulled down the temple around him.

And there was still Monroe to consider. They had no idea why Monroe, or at least the locator chip tracking her handset, had suddenly crossed Fort Hood and come to rest in Blackstone's residence.

A terrible thought occurred to Jed. Terrible yet heavy with possibility. It brought his acid reflux surging up painfully, all but unbearably.

If Monroe had proved to herself that Blackstone's link to Baumer was not just incidental, might she have decided to settle any perceived personal debt with Mad Jack in spite of his direct order to the contrary?

He actually laughed at that as he stepped into the shower and let the hot water play over his head, an unkind, braying bark that did as little to improve his mood as the shower did to make him feel any better physically. He was really suffering. It was starting to worry him. But not as much as Agent Monroe.

Had she done to him what he'd done to Kip? Namely, act with a semblance of obedience for the sole purpose of arranging events to suit herself.

He scrubbed at his scalp as the stinging hot water battered away at the edges of his hangover and his illness. He was having trouble swallowing and wondered whether he might be coming down with the flu. There was a monster flu bug going around Seattle right now, like something out of Stephen King. Be just his fucking luck to get it when he could least afford to. He leaned both hands against the wall and let the hot water massage the back of his neck. His belly hung huge and low over his thighs.

He was going to have to get back into shape when this was done. He'd been promising Marilyn for months that he would do something about his weight and his fitness, but there was always some reason, some excellent excuse for not taking that first step. Another meeting, another crisis, another fire to put out. How the hell was he supposed to look after himself when he spent every waking hour and then some looking after the country? And if a guy couldn't reward himself at the end of the day with a decent drink and a lousy fucking pizza . . . well, fuck. What was the point?

His stomach rolled over again. He gritted his teeth and promised himself he would do something as soon as he could. Marilyn was right. He'd really let himself go.

First, however, first he had to finish Blackstone and deal with whatever Monroe had set in train down there. Maybe Kipper had been right about her. Maybe she was the wrong tool. A tactical nuke when a stiletto was more appropriate.

She'd done something similar in the Federation, he recalled, after breaking Lupérico out of that detention center. Caitlin Monroe had taken what she needed for her mission in that instance and then taken a man's life of her own accord.

How would she play this one? he wondered.

54

She launched herself at him.

Even with her hands cuffed behind her, Caitlin flew at Baumer in a blur, as straight and swift as an arrow. An armchair stood in the way, a deep club chair clad in dark brown leather and studded with burnished brass buttons. She mounted it as though running up a set of steps, kicking off as she pivoted on one foot and lashed out with the other, aiming a flying side kick at his throat. She meant to crush his larynx with the blade of her foot.

Baumer was ready for her and had begun to dodge the impact even as she mounted the chair. He slipped sideways, executing a creditable sidestep that she noted as having all the hallmarks of karate training. Caitlin turned the pile driver of her flying *yoko geri* into a vicious roundhouse snap aimed at his head. Baumer, already raising his hands to deflect the attack, switched to a stopping block but didn't focus the technique in time. Caitlin's *mawashi geri* crashed through his defense. He cried out in pain as she shattered his forearm, snapping the ulna like a dry twig.

Even so, the broken bone absorbed enough of the blow to ward off the worst of the impact on his skull. She felt a glancing, dissatisfying impression of her steel-capped boot cracking his cheekbone, but before the energy could transfer itself into his brainpan, he had spun to the floor. Baumer, she knew, had some hand-to-hand skills: basic attack and defense methodology stolen, ironically enough, from the Israeli-developed Krav Maga combat system and polished to a pretty high sheen. But his training was straightforward and practical. Good enough for somewhere like New York. Hers had been obsessive and refined. And all but pointless in the circumstances she now found herself in.

Pain, a bright white neutron star of pain, exploded in her chest as McCutcheon kicked her away from the man she intended to kill. He appeared within her peripheral vision just as she thudded down on a thick Persian rug after executing the attempted kick to Baumer's skull. Caitlin landed on her side, exhaling, dropping as much hip and shoulder as she could into the fall, but she remained at a disadvantage to a man on his feet with the length of a whole room to line up his attack. McCutcheon drove a snap kick into her center body mass, and she flew into the bookshelf, grunting, as it forced the last of the air from her lungs.

"Enough!" he barked, quickly backing away, holding a gun on her.

"I probably wouldn't have done that in your position, Miss Monroe," said Blackstone. "After all, you'll be leaving with young Billy Bob in a few minutes. And now you've simply exacerbated the bad blood between you."

"What the fuck . . ." spat Caitlin.

Blackstone shook his head. "Please, harsh language isn't necessary. Ty, could you attend to Mr. Baumer? I suspect he's going to need a medic. If you pass me your gun, I'm sure I can persuade Miss Monroe to behave herself."

The appearance of six TDF troopers at the French doors drew Caitlin's attention away from her longtime nemesis.

The men looked anxious, uncertain as to whether to come barging in or wait outside when they saw Blackstone holding the pistol and obviously still in control.

"Might be an idea if we had the fellows wait in here for a few minutes," said the governor. "Miss Monroe has a reputation as a difficult woman. I can see it's well deserved."

His aide nodded before limping over to the doors to let them in. He'd hurt himself kicking her. But he'd hurt Caitlin even worse. She could feel a couple of cracked ribs grinding against each other as she found her feet.

Baumer looked ashen, his previous confidence entirely gone. He fixed her with a glare, suffused with murderous intent.

"Gonna pay for that, whore."

"Now, then, where were we?" Blackstone said. "Oh, yes, you were traducing my honor, my patriotism, and my judgment."

He shot her in the leg.

Caitlin registered the roar of the handgun before the shock of the bullet tearing into her thigh. She screamed an obscenity as she went down, the leg snatched away from beneath her as if by a giant hook. She had been shot before, but it never got any easier. The pain and trauma and sense of violation were new every time. Still, her training ran deep, and she controlled her collapse toward the floor, screaming to empty the air from her lungs and tucking both arms around her wounded ribs and pushing her chin into her chest to save herself from a concussion should her head hit the floor. The impact wasn't so bad. The bullet had stunned her nervous system, and she was still numb. It would be a few seconds before she felt the real pain.

Echelon's senior field operative found herself down at the same level as Baumer, who was still struggling to recover from the kick to his face. His good arm seemed weak and rubbery as Ty McCutcheon, having returned from opening the doors, bent down to support him and haul him back to his feet. If Caitlin could have dragged herself over to put out his eyes and choke the life from his body, she would have. But she knew that Mad Jack would put a bullet in her head before she got close. The debilitating rage of being so close to the man who had sent killers after her husband and child, of being within killing distance herself but unable to act, was nearly as crippling as her wound.

Then the shock of the bullet gave way to floods of pain coursing through her body. She sucked in a mouthful of air, tasting blood and bile as she propped herself up against a dark leather couch, the companion piece to the single-seater she'd used as a platform to fly at Baumer. The lounge was covered in lush, ornate splatters of her blood, shining in the light of a low-hanging chandelier, smelling of earth and copper and corruption.

She was the only thing moving in the room. The TDF squad had entered and now stood gawking at the scene. Baumer leaned unsteadily against the bookshelf, waves of loathing coming off him like heat. Blackstone sat like a fat, aged monarch in his dressing gown, holding McCutcheon's pistol on her. Nine men watched the sole woman in the room without comment as, grinding her teeth against the agony, she contorted her lower body to slip her good leg and then her injured limb through the handcuffs. Her head swam, and dark red spots filled her vision as she did so. She moved slowly, and nobody tried to stop her. A childhood memory arose of a small dog, its back legs and half its spine crushed by a car on the road in front her house on another military base. Edwards AFB, where her father was stationed when she was six. The neighborhood kids all stood there silently, watching the dog as it struggled to drag itself off the tarmac, unable in the end to escape the anchor of its crushed innards holding it in place. Surrounded by armed and hostile men, she felt like that poor animal.

Twenty-five years ago, Caitlin Monroe had walked through the ranks of mute, staring children and crushed the head of that little dog with one fierce stomp. She was crying as she did so, distraught that such a hard mercy should fall to her when larger, older children stood by, doing nothing.

She would be damned if she'd die crippled and immobilized. If Blackstone wanted her to stop, let him finish it with a bullet. Once she had her hands in front of her again, she tore one of the sleeves from her uniform to fashion a bandage.

The gunshot had torn a chunk of flesh from her thigh about the size of half a tennis ball. She could see bone lying white in a crater of shredded muscle and meat. Dark swirling whirlpools tugged at her consciousness, trying to drag her under, but Caitlin swore under her breath and poured all of her will into not passing out as she tended to the wound. She was intimate with pain and fear in a way that most human beings were not. She held the moment close to her, controlled it. She was pain. She would become death. This was life in the raw. Existence itself. Unyielding, unforgiving, and inescapable. She knew that endurance was a matter of degrees, of inches, of pushing herself for a few more breaths or heartbeats. All would pass.

"Outstanding!" Blackstone cried, clapping loudly in approval. "By God, that's the spirit! Honestly, Caitlin, if only we had more Americans like you."

"There'd be less Americans like you," she said through clenched teeth, continuing to bind her wound, stanching the blood flow.

His laughter was rich and generous.

"Maybe so, maybe so. But that's not how this is going to be. You'll leave in a few minutes with our other guest. Frankly, I'll be glad to see the back of you both. Mr. Baumer has had me at a significant disadvantage since he and Ozal duped us into supporting what I thought was a perfectly reasonable chance to inconvenience Kipper in New York. As far as I knew, Ozal was an honest pirate. He promised to tie up Kipper while we consolidated during a difficult interlude down here. I'm afraid I am as much a victim of Mr. Baumer as you."

"So why don't you just shoot him and do us all a favor?" Caitlin seethed. She was shivering and sweating as she tightened the bandage on her wounded leg. "Or even better, give me the gun and I'll do it. Promise."

She leveled a glare at Baumer that was loaded with almost as much violence as the kick that had shattered his cheekbone. His face was swelling, one eye socket disappearing behind a mound of bruised flesh. He looked a little concussed. Like her, however, he was regrouping and found it within himself to sneer back. She could tell from the way his eyes twitched that the gesture hurt him.

Blackstone chuckled indulgently. "I'm sure you would. And don't believe that part of me wouldn't enjoy watching you. Right before you turned the gun on me. But I need Mr. Baumer alive. Unlike you, he has proven himself to be competent. Not so much at running a holy war but certainly at covering his ass afterward. I'm afraid he has a small mountain of incriminating documents, unlike you, and they are pro-

tected by a dead-man switch. If he should expire, the documents would be released into the wild. And we couldn't have that. It would prove fatally embarrassing."

Inwardly, Caitlin was recalculating her chances. This loser obviously had no idea she'd successfully sent the data to Wales. She might well be better off leaving with Baumer. She had his measure.

"So you've been protecting him since New York?" she said, stringing out the encounter as she turned over all the options, working the possible angles and combinations like a Rubik's Cube.

She and Baumer exchanged another look of mutual loathing.

"He has not been protecting me," the jihadist said. His voice was muffled by the injury and swelling. "He has been protecting himself."

"And what, you're going to give up your hold on Blackstone for passage out of here with me?"

Baumer carefully constructed a grin from the remains of his face. It was a tenuous thing, held together by force of will. "Not just out of here but out of America. With you, Caitlin. And with Mr. McCutcheon, who will take possession of the New York documents and recordings when I am safe."

"Road trip." McCutcheon's motor mouth was back. "Gonna be fun."

"You gotta be fucking kidding me," Caitlin said. "You got suckered by this whackjob in New York and now you're trusting him *again*? Fuck me."

"Maybe later," Ty replied. "Clocks a tickin' right now, though. Governor?"

"We're not trusting him, Agent Monroe," Blackstone said, ignoring his aide for the moment. "But yes, we are dealing with him. And he with us. Sometimes in war you have to make alliances, however temporary, with one enemy while you face another."

For a second or two she was blank. She had no idea what he was talking about. And then . . .

"Oh, for fuck's sake . . . Morales? You're still obsessing about that bean-eating fuckwit?"

"Not obsessing, Agent Monroe. Preparing."

She shook her head, convinced now beyond doubt that she was talking to a madman.

Blackstone started to respond, but he didn't get a chance. His next

words were cut off by the deafening trip hammer of a machine gun fired from just outside.

Training and instinct took over as Caitlin rolled for cover behind a large leather couch. She heard glass shattering. Wood splintered. Men screamed and died in a storm of automatic fire. Ignoring the shrieking agony in her wounded leg, she crawled away from the sound of the gun, scuttling after Baumer, who had dropped, as she had, at the first report. He was heading for the door of the library, toward the hallway. She moved slowly, constrained by the handcuffs and her leg wound. The grating of her cracked ribs added to the pain and difficulty.

Confusion and riot were all around. Caitlin no longer could place anyone in the room. Baumer. McCutcheon. Blackstone. Or any of the TDF troopers who had been standing by the French doors. In her memory she saw a stuttering replay of at least three soldiers dancing a disjointed bloody jig as dozens of rounds chewed through them. The staccato uproar of an AK-47 unloading an entire magazine on automatic drowned out the screaming.

At the end of the lounge she stopped. McCutcheon was crouched behind another chair on the far side of the room. She locked eyes with him for half a second before he moved, launching himself toward the exit through which Baumer had just disappeared.

The gun roared. She saw McCutcheon's head fly apart in a kaleidoscope of blood and horror. A handgun fired unsteadily, coughing back weakly at the snarl of the Kalashnikov. Blackstone firing uncontrolled, emptying his clip, but to no effect. Caitlin could not see him directly without exposing herself to the shooter, but she could make out the governor's reflection in a window on the far side of the room. He had been hit, like her, in the leg. But the round that had taken him had been larger and was traveling much faster. He groaned pitiably as he tried to lever himself up out of his chair.

Then the firing stopped, and the whole world changed in just seconds.

Caitlin heard the metallic chunking sound of somebody swapping out a magazine. She risked a furtive peak over the furniture. The arms of the lounge chair were split and torn. Stuffing spilled from them like yellow fairy floss. As she pushed herself up, the gun fired again and an

evil wind swept over Blackstone, shredding his dressing gown, punching huge gobbets of meat and gore out of his body, and throwing him backward into his bookshelf.

The girl.

Caitlin found herself struck dumb and paralyzed by the shock of recognition.

She knew this girl. Knew of her, anyway.

The Mexican refugee. From the murdered settler family. In the madness of death and violence, Caitlin couldn't remember the name of the girl's father. The man who'd been run down in Kansas City. But she thought she recalled the daughter's name.

"Sophie. Sophie, don't shoot!"

The teenager turned the muzzle of the gun on her, and Caitlin recognized the fugue state of close-quarter battle in her eyes. She was gone, lost in the killing.

"Sophie. I came for your father," Caitlin shouted. "For . . . for Manuel."

The gun stopped tracking in her direction. The girl looked confused and then upset.

"Miguel," she said in a small voice. "My father was Miguel Pieraro. He was a good man. And this . . . this . . . Blackstone killed him."

The hard lines and planes of the teenager's face collapsed. It was like watching a burning tower go down. She was a pyre of vengeance and lone justice, and then it all fell in on itself, and Sofia Pieraro was a little girl in a room full of dead men and shredded bodies.

She gasped and dropped to the floor.

SEATTLE, WASHINGTON

Jed grunted as his face struck the wet tiles of the bathroom. His arm was on fire, burning as though held in a furnace. A great crushing weight bore down on his chest as he gagged and struggled to draw air into his lungs. With his good hand, he raked at his breastbone as though he might be able to tear through and wrench out his own heart, fling it from his body before it betrayed him completely.

It was killing him just when he needed to be at his strongest.

Another pile driver slammed into his chest, and he moaned as bubbles of spit foamed on his blue lips. The phone was close. He could see it as though through a long tunnel. But in his rational mind, as clouded as it was by a descending premonition of doom, he knew, he absolutely knew, that it was within reach. If he could just get to it. Dial emergency. But he couldn't move. Giant rubber clown hands had seized the base of his spine and started to squeeze. The grotesque sensation felt like a python running up his back, accelerating as it raced for the base of his neck. He felt the spasms close up his throat as though he were being strangled. Jed worked his jaws as if to protest, but no sound came out save for a gurgling moan.

Even in this extremity, his reptilian cunning did not desert him. As dark wings folded over Jed Culver, he wondered, should he survive, whether having suffered a massive heart attack might count in his favor, win him a few sympathy points, when Kipper was deciding just how high to hang him.

Caitlin held up her cuffed hands where Sofia Pieraro could see them. She advanced slowly, cautiously, even though every nerve in her body compelled her to turn and chase after Baumer.

"It's okay, honey. He's gone. They're all gone. You did well. You just need to put the gun away. Or give it to me. There's another man here we need to get. Somebody working with Blackstone."

The carnage and destruction were hellish. The girl had unloaded the better part of two clips into her targets at close range. The fresh barnyard stench of slaughter, so familiar to Caitlin, was still so dense and surprising that it caused her to gag. Blood, chunks of flesh, bone shards, and viscera were all mixed in promiscuously and sprayed around the room as if thrown from buckets.

"You're done here. You have to come with me now," said the Echelon agent, injecting as much authority into her voice as she dared. This girl could flip either way, dropping into catatonia or turning the last of her ammunition on Caitlin and then herself.

She limped past the corpse of Jackson Blackstone. His dressing gown had come open, spilling the contents over his gore-soaked pajamas.

"Can you give me the gun, Sofia?" Caitlin asked softly. She listened for the howls of approaching sirens. It wouldn't be long. Holding both hands, still cuffed, out to the Mexican girl, she said, "I can get us out of here, Sofia. But we need to go now."

The teenager seemed to reach a decision. She snatched the AK-47 close to herself.

"No," she said, firmly. "This is mine. I keep the gun."

"Fair enough, then. But we have to get going. Follow me."

"Okay," the Pieraro girl said, seeming not to care what happened now as long as she had the gun. Before she moved toward Caitlin, however, the young woman took something from her pocket—three Polaroids, it looked like—and dropped it on Blackstone's corpse.

Caitlin didn't bother to limp over and find out what sort of calling card she'd left. This chick was fucking crazy, anyway.

She did almost stop to pick up the handgun Blackstone had used to wound her until she remembered him firing without result at Pieraro. She checked to see if the girl was wounded, but she appeared to have escaped without a scratch. Caitlin wasn't surprised. It had been a long time since the governor had seen combat, and he had been firing wildly.

"Why don't we just go this way?"

Pieraro had stopped following her and had turned back toward the French doors and the darkness outside.

"There is another man here," Caitlin replied. "We have to get him. He was a road agent," she added, improvising from her sketchy recall of the Pieraro file. The mere mention of the words "road agent" galvanized a response from the teenager. Her face hardened, and she strode up beside Caitlin, taking her by the arm and supporting her as the American hobbled along, trying to keep up.

"Be careful," Caitlin warned as Sofia led the way out of the library and into a hallway in the center of the house. It was well lit, making good targets of both of them.

A blood trail led toward the front door, which stood open.

"Oh, no. You. Fucking. Don't."

Caitlin set her course for the exit and accelerated as best she could. Every step drove white-hot spikes of pain through her leg, arcing up her spine and into her head. To her surprise, Sofia ran ahead of her and loosed a short burst of fire out of the open doorway just before she ran through.

Nice moves, kid, thought the veteran field operator.

"You! Stop now."

Another short, rattling bark from the AK-47 lit up the night outside as Caitlin hurried after the younger woman. She feared that after running from light into dark her night vision would be ruined, but she needn't have worried. Sofia Pieraro stood on the front deck, leveling the assault rifle at Bilal Baumer, who had both hands in the air and was staring at her as if pursued by an apparition from the seventh level of hell. He was injured. Porch lights bathed him in a soft yellow glow. One of his eyes was swollen shut, and that side of his face looked grossly misshapen. When he saw Caitlin emerge from the house, he started to move again slowly, stopping only when the gun roared and plowed up the earth around his feet.

Caitlin pushed past the civilian and charged at Baumer, advancing on him in great lopsided strides. He smiled.

She caught a glimpse of porch light on the blade that appeared in his right hand.

"I will shoot him," Sofia cried.

"No! Don't!"

Caitlin put herself between them deliberately. Turning slightly side on to Baumer, she faced him with her injured leg to the fore, placing most of her weight on the rear foot. Her hands came up in a guard position, using the chain link of her handcuffs to ward off the knife, which came flashing in at her as Baumer cried out, *"Allahu Akbar!"*

She was ready for his feint and did not commit her block until he had switched the arc of his attack at the last moment, turning a backhanded slash into an overhead stab aimed at the base of her neck. She pivoted on her good leg, keeping the turning circle as small as possible, parrying the stroke, and whipping her elbow back into his broken cheekbone.

Crack!

He cried out in shock and pain. Caitlin reversed the flow of her defensive sweep, channeling her *ki* through her forearms and into a looping shield that landed concussive hammer fists on his face, shredding his lips and breaking his nose.

Holding her body close to his, jamming his knife between them so that he had no chance to use it, she raked the handcuffs down the length of his arm until she had proper control of the weapon hand.

After keeping most of her weight off the injured leg until the last possible moment, she gritted her teeth and stepped through, absorbing the pain as she dragged his hand across the front of her body and down toward his hip. Reversing the direction of her attack as she brought the captive limb up, Caitlin fed Baumer's arm into a figure-four entanglement. A downward sword-slashing move broke his arm in three places.

As he screamed, she pistoned up on her good leg, groaned as she transitioned briefly to the other, then leaped high, pulling him backward with the handcuffs as she swept them over his head and around his throat. Pivoting again on her good leg, she dropped into a half-hip throw, taking him over fast and hard. His spine snapped a fraction of a second before she twisted, screamed with pain one last time, and shattered the vertebrae in his neck. She came down on top of his limp, twitching body.

She was crying. Crying with pain, and rage, and relief, and horror, when the young woman appeared by their entwined bodies.

"I know you," Caitlin said, expecting to die. "I knew of your father. A good man. I know what they did to your family."

She waved a hand weakly back in the direction of Blackstone and his men. It was all she had.

Sofia Pieraro was shaking. She tried to smile, but her face was twitching and rubbery, and the effect was perverse.

Caitlin awkwardly disentangled herself from Baumer's body. "If you want to help me, you can give me a hand up," she said. "We still need to get out of here."

She could hear sirens coming closer. Boots pounding up a gravel path.

"Miss Kate. Miss Kate. Are you in there?"

A familiar voice. A Polish accent.

"It is Milosz. Of GROM."

"Come with me," Caitlin said. "Come quickly if you want to live."

TWO MONTHS LATER

"The big bastard? The Rhino? He's about ten, maybe fifteen minutes up the track that way," said the park ranger.

"You know him?" Jules asked.

He grinned. "Everyone knows the Rhino. Up that way." He pointed along the track that crawled uphill, skirting the edge of the Noosa National Park.

It was crowded with tourists and locals. The latter were easy to pick out in their bare feet and board shorts, most of them carrying short boards around the headland to a surf break that was far enough off the tourist trail to discourage day-trippers. The tourists were just as easy to spot: pink-skinned English backpackers, Chinese tour groups, small pods of fair-haired Swedes and Germans. And Americans, of course. There was no missing them: the loudest, most colorful diaspora in the world.

Those who'd washed up here on the Sunshine Coast tended to be the wealthier, luckier ones. There was nothing like the big American ghettos of western Sydney or New Town anywhere near this strip of Queensland coastal heaven. Shah had even told her that the odious St.

John siblings, Phoebe and Jason, had bought themselves a family compound up in the nearby Glass House Mountains. She hadn't seen those wankers since they'd left the *Aussie Rules* in Sydney and very much hoped that wouldn't change while she was in town to visit the Rhino.

The park ranger had gone back to pointing out a koala high in a gum tree to twenty or thirty squealing primary school children, so she didn't bother thanking him for the directions. Jules craned her head back but couldn't make out the animal within the clutter of the subtropical rain forest canopy. She didn't think koalas lived in rain forests, even the dry subtropical kind, but there were plenty of gum trees salted in among the screw pine and rain trees and bracken fern.

She took a swig from a water bottle and resumed the trek up the headland. "Not a bad day for it," she mumbled to herself.

The coastline curved away in a series of scalloped bays, most of them home to easily surfed point breaks. Those closer to the seaside village of Noosa were crowded with holiday makers. The farther up the trail she climbed through thick forests of beach lily and passion vine, the more challenging the surf conditions down below seemed to become, thinning out the crowds. Julianne was glad of the shade from the forest, even though the humidity beneath the canopy seemed much worse than it had back on the beach. After five minutes of climbing, her T-shirt was stained with dark sweat patches and she had finished most of her bottle of water.

Joggers ran past her in both directions, drenched with perspiration. Neither the heat not the climb seemed to bother the surfers, at least those heading out for a ride. They ran nearly as quickly as the joggers.

Jules was in no rush. As far as she knew, there was only one track in and out, so she wouldn't miss him. She did her best to enjoy the walk. An easterly breeze pushed tentatively into the fringes of the forest, dappling the path with sunlight as the foliage hissed and swayed. Breaks in the vegetation afforded a view to the north, where the coast curved gently around to form what seemed to be a massive open bay. The main tourist beach was crowded with thousands of bathers playing in the gentle surf break. A couple of yachts and some smaller cabin cruisers, one of them hers, rode at anchor farther out.

She found him standing on a sunny platform, watching the surf crashing into the base of the rocky headland hundreds of feet below. There was no mistaking Rhino A. Ross. Even after a couple of months of enforced rest and wrapped in bandages, he looked like a powerful, if wounded, pachyderm. Leaned up against a safety rail entwined with orchids and Guinea flowers, his chin resting on his hands, he presented a lonesome, melancholy aspect.

"Hello, Rhino," she said.

He stood and turned, and the woebegone air that had hung around him was banished by a smile and a roar.

"Miss Jules!"

He wore an eye patch—always would now—and she could tell that half of one bandaged hand was missing, but it didn't stop him from wrapping her in a fierce hug and clapping her on the back with strength enough to wind her.

"How are you, Rhino? I called in at Shah's villa looking for you, but the guy at the front desk said you'd gone for your morning walk."

"Same time every morning," he said. "The best way to get your health back is just to get out of bed every morning and chase it. Although I'm not as fleet on the hoof as I used to be."

One of his knees was still wrapped in a compression dressing.

"And was that your fine vessel I saw at anchor in the bay this morning, Miss Jules?"

"No, it's Shah's. I'm taking it down to Sydney for him. As a favor, you know."

The Rhino smiled. During the last month or two, the favors had been a one-way street. The old Gurkha had looked after both of them very well.

"Come sit yourself down in the shade, Miss Julianne," he offered. "Be a shame to ruin that peaches-and-cream complexion of yours."

The Rhino retrieved a dark wooden walking stick from where he'd leaned it against the fence, waving her off when she tried to lend him a hand.

"Prefer to haul my own fat ass around, if you don't mind, Miss Jules. No offense. Bad habit for a Rhino to get into, letting others do the heavy lifting for him."

"Of course," she replied, taking a seat on a bench shaded by a small stand of mock olive trees wrapped in a dark creeper heavy with electric orange flowers.

The water below them was an opalescent green, fading to a deep blue farther out. She wondered how many hours a day he spent up here gazing off toward the horizon. America was out there somewhere beyond the edge of the world, what was left of it, anyway.

He lowered himself carefully onto the perch. Jules winced involuntarily, imagining the discomfort of his burns and all that fresh scar tissue.

"Did you see the news this morning?" she asked. "Henry made the news. The real news, I mean, not just the blogs."

"Don't have much time for the news these days," he said. "Just the weather and the fishing reports, and I can get those by sticking my head out the window or hobbling down to the coffee shop."

She took a piece of folded newsprint from the pocket of her shorts. It was damp and frayed but still legible. Both of his hands were bandaged, and one of them was missing three fingers. Jules unfolded the clipping and held it out for him to read.

"Presidential confidant Cesky to face consecutive life terms," he quoted from the headline. A smile formed at the edge of his mouth but died there. "That's good news, I suppose," he said. "If they convict him. If I had my way, though, he'd a-been thrown to the sharks. Worthless motherfucker."

He read the rest of the report while she held the piece of paper as steadily as she could in the breeze. She was done crying. She'd emptied herself of tears back in Darwin.

"Still no sign of his daughter, then? Little Sofia," he said quietly after finishing the story.

Julianne didn't reply. Miguel's daughter had disappeared soon after his murder. The police and the FBI had listed her as a missing person, but she doubted they were doing much to find her. America was full of missing people.

"Do you think Cesky got her?" Jules asked.

"I hope not," the Rhino said. "For Miguel's sake, I would hope not. That poor family; they were good people. They deserved none of it."

"This life." Jules sighed. "Deserve's got nothing to do with it."

They sat in silence for a few minutes. Surfers, joggers, and bush walkers passed by them in both directions.

"Good of Shah to let you have his place down here," she said after a while, for want of anything better to fill the space between them.

"Another good man," said the Rhino.

"You think you'll go back to Darwin when you're better? Shah says there's a job for you anytime you want."

The Rhino leaned forward and rested his chin on the handle of his walking stick. "Yeah, I know. Piloting an armed cruiser for him off Bougainville. The big copper mine up there has had some problems with pirates and gun runners. It wouldn't be a million miles away from the work I used to do for the coast guard."

She closed her eyes and let the sun play over her face. "You wouldn't be working for yourself, though, would you, Rhino?" she asked, reading his mind. "Wasn't that always the plan?"

"That's the thing about plans, Miss Jules. They almost never survive contact with the enemy." He plucked a flower and sniffed it before tossing the bright orange bloom into the undergrowth behind them. "And what about you?" he asked. "I don't see you working as a delivery girl in the long term."

She opened her eyes again and smiled. "No, neither do I. I had thought I might try my luck back in the States, you know, after they got hold of me to testify against Cesky. Bloody video link put paid to that idea, didn't it?"

The Rhino nodded. He'd given his initial deposition from a hospital bed in Darwin. Like her, he'd been raped by Cesky's lawyers.

"Come on," he grunted, pushing himself up off the bench, "walk back with me. We'll have an early lunch."

They started back down the trail. Jules was forced to fall in behind him every time they passed somebody heading up toward the headland.

"You didn't answer my question," he said over his shoulder. "What now for Lady Julianne Balwyn? Back to the ancestral estate, perhaps? I hear the new feudalism is all the rage in old England. Or is it the cruel sea for you again, m'lady? High adventure? Fortune and glory?"

She laughed. Not loudly and not for long, but she did laugh.

"No, Rhino," she said. "An early lunch is what now for Lady Julianne. And maybe a nap in the afternoon."

ONE YEAR LATER

The inauguration was a simple ceremony, at Kipper's insistence. He knew Jed had wanted something a little grander, something more significant, as a way of reassuring people that not everything was lost. And there were times when Kip almost gave in to it, but in the end he went with his gut. The country was best served by a return to basics. After being sworn in for a second time, President James Kipper gave a brief speech in the drawing room at Dearborn House before hosting a reception for two hundred guests, all of whom he had chosen personally.

There were no invites for any of his supporters from the Machine, as Jed used to call the political movement that had evolved out of the resistance to Jackson Blackstone—a strictly ironic turn of phrase. Jed Culver had not thought much of the Machine even though it had delivered two presidential elections.

His supporters were all hitting it hard at a warehouse party on the other side of Seattle. He'd send a video message later, but he had made it clear that as a working parent he wouldn't be turning up to tie one on. Instead, he circulated among the guests at Dearborn with a beer in hand and an ear for their stories. From the veterans of New York. Militiamen and women from the frontier forts. Workers from the railway projects and power plants. Teachers. Farmers. Two hundred Americans, young and old, whose lives, every day of them, were devoted to rebuilding the republic. His only real concession to politics in this—and something that Jed would have approved of—was making sure that at least half of the guests came from Texas, including the new Governor, an altogether easier to deal with retired general by the name of Murphy, newly returned from a short stint in Vancouver.

Well, the Texas delegates weren't his only concession to politics, he had to admit. There were three guests at the reception whose presence was purely political, a statement from James Kipper that he stood by the legacy of his chief of staff.

"Thank you, Kip," said a quiet and restrained Marilyn Culver. "Jed would've loved this." She gestured around the room with her champagne glass. She'd hardly touched a drop in over an hour.

"No, Marilyn, he wouldn't," Kipper replied. He, too, scanned the roomful of ordinary people, none of them donors or players or significant for any reason beyond their humble contribution to the life of the nation. "He would have wanted to know what these assholes could possibly do for us."

He finished by leaning toward her and speaking quietly in a passable imitation of Culver's Louisiana drawl. A few people standing close by, trying not to be obvious about eavesdropping, turned toward him. But people, especially in Seattle, were well used to the president's informal manners. Marilyn squeezed his forearm in thanks.

"It's still nice for the kids to be here," she said. "They had a very hard time of it after their father died. Some of the things people were saying about him. The most terrible lies, Kip. You know how kids can be, how they take these things to heart."

Kipper fixed Culver's widow with his sternest, most presidential look.

"Marilyn," he told her, "you are to pay no heed to any of that bullshit. Jed had enemies because he sought them out. He was a guy who knew right from wrong, and he wasn't afraid to act on that knowledge. A guy like that, he gets people upset. But he does it for the right reasons. A lot of the things Jed did for this country, people will never know about. You and the kids will never know, either. That's just the way it has to be. But what people can know is that I thought Jed Culver was a good man, and he did the right thing."

He had to hug Marilyn then, because she teared up and all but fell into his arms.

"Oh, God, Kip. I miss the Jedi Master," she said, her voice muffled by tears and the lapel of his suit where she'd buried her face.

Kipper caught his wife's eye across the drawing room. Barb sent him an unspoken query, asking if he was all right. Did he need her to come and rescue him? The president of the United States shook his head and patted down Marilyn Culver's hair.

"It's okay, buddy," he said. "You let it all out."

He had to fend off his protocol chief with a fierce glare at one point, but most people were cool enough to give them some space even in a very crowded reception room. These were all good people, thought Kip. Real people. The country could do no better than to entrust its future to them.

He felt ashamed about having to lie to them about what had happened in Texas and the role his main fixer had played down there. But as he stood comforting Jed's wife and thinking about how badly things could have gone, James Kipper reconciled himself to the necessity of doing wrong for the greater good.

Jed Culver would have been proud of him.

TWO YEARS LATER

"This is the first and final boarding call for all passengers traveling on Japan Airlines flight 16, Sydney to Tokyo, code shared with our Oneworld partners British Airways and Qantas."

"At last," Sofia said as she gathered up her magazine and water bottle from the coffee table in the Qantas lounge, stuffing them into the small backpack she would take with her on the plane.

"What, you're that keen to be shot of us, are you, mate?"

"Oh, piss off," she replied, but without malice. She had grown used to the Australian sense of humor. "You just can't wait to get rid of me so you can get down to the pub early."

Her Echelon mentor repaid the quick comeback with a smile. "You know me too well, Mariela," he said, using her cover name. "Come on, I'll walk you down to the gate. Reckon you've been just about my worst student ever. Wouldn't surprise me if you got lost between here and the plane. Fuck knows what's gonna happen when you get to Tokyo."

"Ha. I'll be unpacking truly epic amounts of awesome and win, that's what. Probably so much that they'll just give me my black belt as soon as I turn up at the dojo."

"More like they're gonna hand your arse to you on a sushi platter," he said.

"They're gonna try." She laughed. "Caitlin told me all about it."

Nick Pappas, Echelon's station chief in Sydney, nodded at that. "You'd do well to listen to her advice."

They walked out of the club lounge and joined the flow of foot traffic through Sydney's international terminal toward the departure gate. Neither of them spoke for a minute. After eighteen months of training at Echelon's remote Snowy Mountains campus, Sofia Pieraro was entirely comfortable with the exchange of secrets that could be loaded into an unspoken conversation. She was also more familiar with the woman who had saved her from certain capture and execution in Texas. The woman she had possibly saved when she stormed into Blackstone's residence, intending to die if it meant a chance to settle the blood debt he owed her.

Caitlin Monroe had been generous about that. Sofia knew her now as both a friend and, somewhat problematically, an Echelon legend. Almost a figure of mythology. Her own controllers, her trainers, and even Pappas—her last mentor and probably her first overwatch controller when she returned from Japan and began to earn her place in the organization—had all scoffed at the idea that she'd rescued the infamous Caitlin Monroe. "Just got in her fucking way, more likely," as Nick had put it. "Probably stopped her killing everyone five minutes earlier."

Sofia had bristled at first. She had been a proud if profoundly damaged young woman when they spirited her away from America, disappearing her as effectively as the Wave had taken hundreds of millions of souls five years earlier. She had done something as a mere girl that the mighty Echelon had dispatched and nearly lost its champion to achieve. She had laid a hard vengeance upon Jackson Blackstone for his crimes in Texas and New York.

Although at the time she hadn't given a shit about anything but the blood on his hands from the murder of her family and, she'd presumed, her father. Nick Pappas had set her straight on that. She knew it was a purely calculated move by Echelon, assigning him to mentor her through reception and early training. He had witnessed the death of the man who actually had taken Papa's life and put poor Maive Aronson into a coma, where she still lay.

Sofia had needed many months to get past the idea that Blackstone had had nothing to do with her father's murder, that it had been this Cesky creature whom Papa had beaten down for causing trouble with Miss Julianne all those years before in Acapulco. She still remembered very fondly the kind and pretty English lady from the yacht on which they'd all escaped from *el colapso*. For a long time she had wanted to grow up to be just like her. And she still marveled at the idea that Miss Julianne had killed this Parmenter, shot him and kicked him to death right in front of Pappas, before bringing down the man who had sent him and an unknown number of other assassins out into the world to exact his petty revenge on those he thought had slighted him.

The idea that a friend of Papa's, indeed the original savior of the Pieraro clan, had exacted their revenge for her finally reconciled Sofia to letting go.

She would do now what Miguel Pieraro had always wanted. She would live, and eventually the family would grow again through her. But first she had a debt to pay off. Having been delivered from evil that night in Fort Hood, Sofia had been given to understand, and she accepted it without demur, that a responsibility had been laid upon her by that salvation. The premise sat easily with a Catholic. She would devote this first part of her new life to the fight against evil, raking for it where it had always lain, in the hearts of men.

But not men like her father or Nick Pappas, who guided her now through the crush of the terminal with a paternal hand on her shoulder. They had grown very close. The last time she had spoken with Caitlin, when her savior had visited the campus in the Snowy Mountains, she'd told Sofia that would happen. Echelon was a family, said Agent Monroe, and in Pappas, of whom she knew and approved, Sofia could be assured that she had somebody she could trust as if he were her own father.

Nick would never replace her papa, of course, but Caitlin had been right. As a mentor, he had taken on many of the responsibilities she now understood Miguel Pieraro had carried on his own from the day their family had been taken from them in Madison County. To keep her safe. To protect her from evil. And to prepare her to go out into the world and fight the good fight.

Sofia was ready.

"I'll see you in a year," Pappas said, when they reached the gate. He put out his hand rather formally and uncomfortably, as though forcing restraint on himself.

"Not if I see you first," she replied, grinning and standing on tiptoe to kiss him good-bye quickly on the cheek.

FOUR YEARS LATER

The last refugee family departed from Melton Farm a week before Monique's fifth birthday. Caitlin and Bret had planned to celebrate the occasion with a small party, but as so often happened with working parents, time got away from them. The animals, as always, needed tending. The Ministry of Resources chose that week to send through a survey team to inspect the progress of their latest GM oat crop. Monique was about to start her prep year of primary school. Her little brother, Harry, was acting out his separation anxieties during his first week at kindergarten. And Caitlin had no idea when she'd volunteered to sit on the village's royal wedding committee that the meetings would prove as frustrating and nearly as murderous as the long search for Bilal Baumer had been. So in the end they marked the departure of their last American refugees with a glass of wine on the front porch at the end of a long summer's day.

"We've still got Monique's birthday party next week," Bret said. "Half the village will be along for that, anyway. We could do something then."

"I suppose so," Caitlin replied without any great enthusiasm.

She was underwhelmed by the idea of hand-to-hand battle at home with the vicar and Mrs. Dingley about fucking Will and Kate's wedding. The sleep-deprived mother of two was just contemplating a second glass of wine when Bret pointed out the vehicle, a white Peugeot by the look of it, coming over the rise and down the long unsealed road to the farmhouse.

"Government car," he said with confidence.

"I think so," Caitlin agreed, suddenly aware of the pistol in the holster at the small of her back. She still carried it everywhere. The Kimber Warrior was so much a part of her that mostly she forgot it was there. It had now been, what, nearly four years since she'd last pulled the trigger on a man.

"Maybe you should get the kids inside and run the bath, honey," she suggested. "It might be for me."

Her husband gave her a measured look before staring long and hard at the approaching car again. "Those days are over," he said before disappearing inside. "Monique! Harry! Bath time. Let's go!"

She heard the squeals and thunder of children running to attend to their father's command. Outside the farmhouse, training imprinted at the molecular level caused her to scan her surroundings for any obvious threats and then for any nonobvious ones.

Nothing.

The car bore HM Government license plates. As it turned off the approach road and onto the driveway, which wound in through a stand of apple trees before looping around a small broken fountain in front of the farmhouse, she recognized the occupants. And smiled.

"Dalby and . . . Oh, my God, Wales!" She beamed. "This must be bad news."

Her two favorite former overwatch controllers returned the friendly greeting, crunching over the gravel to say hello, to shake hands, and in Wales's case to wrap her in a bear hug, a maneuver made difficult by the presents he was carrying for the children.

"I'm sorry I didn't call ahead, Caitlin," the American said. "But Dalby and I were on our way back early from something at Salisbury Plain, and I just couldn't forgive myself if I didn't take the opportunity to call in and say hello. It's been too long."

She aimed a skeptical frown at the gifts he was carrying.

"I didn't know that London Cage had opened up a Toys 'R' Us franchise," she said, dryly. "Just picked those up on the way, did you?"

Wales had the good grace to look a little embarrassed. "Well, I was always going to be dropping by," he replied. "So it seemed a good idea to have them with me. An American Girl doll for Monique. They're making them again, you know. And LEGO Star Wars for young Harry."

Her skepticism grew even more pronounced. "So you've been talking to Bret, then, I see."

"Perhaps just a little," Francis Dalby admitted. "That wine looks damned inviting. I notice your five years in this country have not softened your manners any, young lady. Perhaps you would like to invite your old friends and employers in."

"Or perhaps not," she mocked, turning around and walking back into the house, waving them along behind her. She could hear the bath running upstairs and the children laughing as they splashed about in it.

"Bret," she called up, "it's Dalby and Wales. Are you going to come down for a drink when you're finished up there?"

"Sorry. I knew they were coming," he called back. "They said they'd torture me if I let on."

"Sounds about right," Caitlin muttered as she led her guests through to the kitchen. A pot of osso bucco in the oven was about twenty minutes away from being ready, and the places were already set for dinner. Four plates at the big table and two at the smaller children's table, where Monique and Harry ate most of their meals. Bret had used the royal wedding plates he'd insisted on buying last week. His idea of irony.

"Your field craft is getting rusty down here," Dalby said.

"It's sharp enough for dealing with country vicars and village alderman," she replied. "Sit down. I'll open a new bottle. We had half of this last night, and it's oxidized. Life in the boonies. What can I say?"

"Well, you could say how happy you are to see us," said Wales, teasing her.

"I am, Wales. As long as you're not here to try to talk me back into the office. I'm retired now. A lady of leisure."

She uncorked a bottle of Côtes du Rhone and poured a generous measure into two clean glasses.

"You're not completely retired, Caitlin," Wales pointed out. "Dalby here tells me you're kicking ass as a guest lecturer down at the college in London. And you're not averse to doing a bit of consultancy here and there."

She smiled. "Paperwork, Wales. I read papers and I write them. That's all I do these days. When I'm not looking after the children. Or riding shotgun on the preparation for the crucial contribution of our little village to the wedding of the fucking century. Which is all the time."

"Wales and Dalby!" boomed her husband, who had reappeared at the kitchen door with a glass in hand and a guilty look about him.

"You could've at least given me enough warning to let me get changed out of my shitkickers," she scolded him.

Bret looked sheepish but basically unapologetic. "LEGO Star Wars buys a lot of silence."

They finished the bottle of red wine before serving dinner and drank another one with it. The children took themselves off to bed with dire warnings that their new toys would disappear if they weren't asleep within ten minutes while the men finished off all the osso buco, which Caitlin had hoped would last for a couple of days. She returned from tucking in Harry and Monique to find the three of them gathered around a newly opened bottle of Highland Park, courtesy of Dalby, discussing the prospects for the United States with Kipper's second term drawing to an end and Sandra Harvey and Sarah Palin looking like the front-runners to punch it out in the big vote.

By the time they'd accounted for most of the whiskey, sitting by the fireplace in the lounge room after dinner, Caitlin had decreed that the visitors would have to stay the night.

"Be just like you two to survive a lifetime of fucking villainy only to do yourselves in driving pissed at night. You'd probably get lost and end up back on one of the live firing ranges on the plain."

It was well after midnight before Bret and Dalby crashed, leaving Caitlin curled up in a lounge chair in front of the hearth, talking to Wales.

"We would have you back in a New York minute, you know," he told her. "I wouldn't want you to die wondering about that."

"Wales, I was in New York for a minute or two in April '07, you might recall," she said. "I don't feel the need to go back. I'm out of it, Wales. I push a shopping cart around the local supermarket now, and my idea of adventure is when Harry wets himself in that cart and he's not wearing a diaper." She shook her head at that unpleasant memory.

Wales Larrison, these days the global director of Echelon, didn't smile. He sized her up as though she were a challenging puzzle.

"Do you remember the young girl you brought to us just before you left and came home, here?" he asked, waving a hand to take in the lounge room and the farm beyond it.

"Sofia," Caitlin said. "Of course I do. How'd she work out? She'd have been in the field for a few years by now."

Larrison took his time again.

"As always," he said eventually, "you've done well for us, Caitlin. She was a good find. We haven't had an asset as good as her since . . . well, since you left, to be truthful."

"That's very flattering, Wales. But I left. And I'm not coming back."

The scar tissue just under her hairline where they'd opened her up to remove the tumor back in 2003, was throbbing. It did that at times.

"She wasn't just good for us, for the office," Wales continued, swirling his whiskey before holding the tumbler up to the firelight. The flames threw long, snaking shadows across the room. "I still believe, Caitlin, that there was a chance your last mission in Texas could have ended very differently. There was a good chance that if Blackstone had lived and if Kipper moved against him with the information you took, I think there was a very good chance he would have tried to take Texas out of the Union. It could have meant civil war. Sofia Pieraro averted that outcome when she put him down. Those three IDs she left at the scene, the road agents, they helped us sell the story of Blackstone's death as a bandit raid."

Caitlin took a sip of her drink. Unlike the others, she had switched to mineral water hours earlier.

"Funny thing about those guys," she said. "They belonged to Blackstone. They were in McCutcheon's files. That never came out, did it?"

"It didn't need to," Wales replied. "Sofia gave us more than enough to start spinning the myth that Jackson Blackstone was a murdered patriot. And you gave us her."

"Yeah. A patriot. Nicely fucking done, Wales."

Larrison finished his drink and put it aside. "Yes," he said. "And she's done very well for us ever since."

"How did Sofia take to that? The idea that Blackstone gets to go down in history as a martyred hero."

The smile on Wales's long, deeply lined faced was wintry. "Like you, Caitlin, she's a realist these days. Or she would be . . ."

"I sense there's a 'but' coming."

"But." Larrison nodded. "Now she has disappeared for real."

Caitlin said nothing, but Wales seemed disinclined to add anything to his statement.

"That's too bad," she eventually replied. "But what does that have to do with me?"

"You spent a lot of time with Sofia, lying low after Fort Hood," Larrison said. "You got to know her at a very vulnerable time. You probably know her as well as anybody in the agency, including her mentor. On all of her profiles and evaluations, she identified you as a significant figure in her salvation."

"It's late, Wales. Really late."

"I'd like you to come back, Caitlin. I need you to find Sofia Pieraro. She's somewhere in the South American Federation. She was working deep inside Roberto's regime for us. And then she went dark. The same way you went dark after Fort Hood. We need you back, Caitlin. We need to know what's happened down there. What might be about to happen."

Larrison held up one hand before she could reply. "I don't want you to answer me now, because I know what your answer will be, now. Will you promise me you will sleep on it, though, and talk to Bret in the morning? And then talk to me. Morales is a problem we've never encountered before. Not since the Disappearance, anyway. A madman in charge of an emerging superstate. He's already rattling the saber over the Falklands. You know what that means, Caitlin. You know how far the consequences can run."

He didn't do anything so gauche as let his gaze drift upstairs where her children were sleeping. He didn't have to. He knew her too well.

Caitlin was quiet for a long time. Finally she pushed herself up out of her chair.

"I'm going to bed, Wales. I'll see you in the morning."

Acknowledgments

So, the end of a story. Time to look back and say thank you not just to everyone who contributed to this book but also to those who helped with the other two that came before it. Some have been with me all the way. Betsy Mitchell, Cate Paterson, and Joel Naoum at Random House and Pan Macmillan. Russ Galen, my agent. You don't know them, but without them you would not be holding this book in your hands.

Others popped in and out during the long journey, editing here, publishing there, sprinkling fairy dust on the marketing and publicity machine. Yes, that black engine. They all need to be given a hearty slap on the back and bought a drink as well, because the Disappearance series was mostly published in the darkest days of the Great Recession, and the tireless efforts of the sales and marketing teams from both houses need a particularly loud "Huzzah!" Most of you, I never even met. But you have my deep thanks for what is largely a thankless job.

And hell, while we're on it, how about a shout out to the frontline troops. The guys and gals in bookstores, actual real-world bookstores, with shelves and everything, who've sold so many copies of these babies for me. Some of you I do know personally. Most I don't. Again, thank you.

On a personal note, as ever, props to my blog buddies. They know who they are and how much they contribute to the creation of each book. One of the really lovely things about the modern world is the way that authors don't have to hide themselves in the garret all the time now. If you want to reach out and spend time with your readers, even make some of them your friends, you can do so. My readers and friends hang out at my blog, Cheeseburger Gothic.

Many more hang out at the digital cocktail party known as Twitter. Hugely distracting but enormous fun, this social not-working service has become a very important part of my work. The cloud is the greatest instant feedback service ever cobbled together from electrons and rubber bands. I can't possibly even begin to name everyone who's helped me out with a research question here or a bit of encouragement there. They know who they are.

And last but most important: Jane, Anna, and Thomas. The rest of you get the best of me. My public face. All shiny and smiley and scrubbed till my belly button shines.

They get the real me. The deadline me. The scruffy, smelly, grumpy where's-my-goddamned-cup-of-coffee me. Feel for them.

I do.

ABOUT THE AUTHOR

JOHN BIRMINGHAM is the author of the cult classic *He Died with a Felafel in His Hand*, the award-winning history *Leviathan*, and the trilogy comprising *Weapons of Choice, Designated Targets*, and *Final Impact*. *Without Warning* was published in 2008.

Between writing books he contributes to a wide range of newspapers and magazines on topics as diverse as the future of media and national security. Before becoming a writer he began his working life as a research officer with the Defense Department's Office of Special Clearances and Records.

John Birmingham refuses to build a website, but you can find him online at his blog, http://cheeseburgergothic.com, and on Twitter @ johnbirmingham.

ABOUT THE TYPE

This book was set in Granjon, a modern recutting of a typeface produced under the direction of George W. Jones, who based Granjon's
design upon the letter forms of Claude Garamond (1480–1561). The
name was given to the typeface as a tribute to the typographic designer
Robert Granjon.